EVERYMAN'S LIBRARY

EVERYMAN,
I WILL GO WITH THEE,
AND BE THY GUIDE,
IN THY MOST NEED
TO GO BY THY SIDE

LORRIE MOORE

COLLECTED STORIES

WITH AN INTRODUCTION
BY LAUREN GROFF

EVERYMAN'S LIBRARY
Alfred A. Knopf New York London Toronto
393

THIS IS A BORZOI BOOK
PUBLISHED BY ALFRED A. KNOPF

www.randomhouse/everymans
www.everymanslibrary.co.uk

ISBN 978-0-375-71238-8 ((US)
978-1-84159-393-7 (UK)

A CIP catalogue reference for this book is available from the
British Library

Typography by Peter B. Willberg

Book design by Barbara de Wilde and Carol Devine Carson

Typeset in the UK by Input Data Services, Isle Abbotts, Somerset

Printed and bound in Germany by GGP Media GmbH, Pössneck

LORRIE MOORE

CONTENTS

INTRODUCTION

Literature, when I was young, was dead, white, and mostly male. It was unusual for even the nerdiest kids of my generation to know otherwise; in school, we'd been given Steinbeck, Shakespeare, Huxley, Hemingway, Thoreau, Stephen Crane, T. S. Eliot, Edgar Allan Poe, et cetera, with a few dips beyond the pale into Sylvia Plath or the Brontës, who – albeit also dead and white – shocked us all by daring to be female. Those of us who received on our birthdays a dutiful fistful of gift certificates to mall bookstores used them to stock up on the foundational texts, the Whitmans, Flauberts, and Henry Jameses of the world, until we felt more or less comfortable swimming in the shallows of the canon. My second semester in college, I decided to take an introductory fiction-writing class in what I see now was a furious attempt to set off a bomb in the galleries of literature, where the white marble busts of dead male authors glared down at me from plinths in their endless rows. The day I picked up my course packet from the printers, I began to read it on my walk home, and though the afternoon was windy and cold and slippery with ice, I dawdled, slower and slower, until I had come to a full and frozen stop in the middle of the sidewalk. At last I gave up on dinner and studying, went to my room, and did not stop reading until I finished the whole packet in the middle of the night. When I looked up, I found that the doors of my mind had been blown wide open. Suddenly, here was the work of contemporary women: brilliant, inventive, wild, diverse, astonishingly alive. Here was Grace Paley, snappish and political, Toni Cade Bambara, whose stories made me breathless, Louise Erdrich, Mavis Gallant, Alice Munro. Most of all, here was Lorrie Moore.

It is impossible to overstate how deeply it can move you to discover, in a literary world that you love all the way to the bedrock but find mostly barren of any trace of yourself, a voice that could be your own, if only refined into art. Moore's short stories were a series of small explosions: smart, perceptive, despairing, so modern they thrummed with the urgency of my own young person's anxieties and obsessions, so mordantly funny that I laughed out of sheer, astonished, often gleeful pain. My gateway Lorrie Moore was "How to Become a Writer," from her first collection *Self-Help*, which, in an unofficial survey of most of my writer friends was their first hit of her, too. Irony is sometimes difficult for the young and naive, and in the second-person apostrophizing of the story, I found actual directives about how to be a writer that I swallowed whole and believed with my entire being. When I read, "First, try to be something, anything, else," I thought, Yes! because I had tried pre-med for precisely one day, until I understood that being a pediatrician meant an endless parade of sick kids; when later in the story I read, "The only happiness you have is writing something new, in the middle of the night, armpits damp, heart pounding, something no one has yet seen. You have only those brief, fragile, untested moments of exhilaration when you know: you are a genius," I thought, All right, if Lorrie Moore says this is what will happen, I'll try it. So I did. Soon, those ecstatic hours in the deep of night became my most secret, most beloved, most lasting of joys. Writers are solitary beasts, but not one of us has ever entered a life of writing alone, and most of us can identify the voice that guided us through the blind and treacherous tunnels that we must enter when we go from being a reader to being a writer. Lorrie Moore was this for me.

In an essay in her collection *See What Can Be Done*, she writes that, "A book by a woman, a book that began up close, on the heart's porch, was a treat, an exhilaration, and finally, I think, that is why women who became writers did so: to create more books in the world by women, to give themselves something more to read." In those heady early days of writing fiction, love-drunk with contemporary short stories, I went one step further: I not only wanted to create more books so that I could give myself something to read; I wanted to create more books in the very particular voice of Lorrie Moore. That this was a fool's errand would become painfully clear in a few years; Lorrie Moore's voice is, of course, singular and irreproducible.

Those of us who worked hard to understand what a literary voice even *is* can observe, with awe, how the sharpness, clarity, and wit of Moore's voice was evident from the very beginning of her writing life. She was nineteen and on a scholarship at St.

Lawrence, a small liberal arts college in New York State, when she won *Seventeen* Magazine's fiction contest. She'd grown up a dreamy, bookish child in Glens Falls, New York to parents who were involved in amateur theater and who, perhaps in only apparent paradox, read passages from the Bible at dinner every night. After college, she became a paralegal in New York City, wrote one of the stories that would appear in 1985 in *Self-Help*, and after two years of midtown Manhattan office work, went on to Cornell to earn an M.F.A. After graduation, she stayed on at Cornell as a lecturer, then she moved to Madison, Wisconsin to begin a professorship there. A year after *Self-Help*, Moore published *Anagrams*, a novel with a brilliant and experimental structure: it's a variation on themes, the characters restarting over and over into new, slightly different stories, which work together to prime the reader for emotional devastation in the longest, final version. The collection *Like Life*, which came out in 1990, contains the widely anthologized story "You're Ugly, Too," which was also Moore's first story of many to appear in *The New Yorker.* In 1994, she published *Who Will Run the Frog Hospital?*, a slender and nearly perfect book about longing and love in a friendship between teenaged girls in a small town near the border of New York State and Canada. Four years later, in 1998, the story collection *Birds of America* was published, which finally brought Moore an international reputation for being a literary genius of the highest order. *Birds of America* contains many of my favorite Lorrie Moore stories, including the one that I have actual holy feelings about, the harrowing and famous "People Like That Are the Only People Here: Canonical Babbling in Peed Onk." This is a story written from the deepest part of the soul; it sings with rage and despair, cuts you with its violent maternal love, and wears its wit like the pitch-black bravado of a man facing a firing squad. Moore's third novel, *A Gate at the Stairs*, a rich work about race, class, loss, and the Midwest after 9/11, was published in 2009; it's a book so dark and deeply-felt and harrowing that I still carry it around inside my heart like one of my own personal ghosts. In 2013, Moore left the University of Wisconsin to teach at Vanderbilt in Nashville, where she published her most recent story collection, the bold and wide-ranging *Bark*.

When critics speak of Lorrie Moore's voice, they tend to focus on her humor; it is such a dazzling gift that it can blind even a good reader to the endless other modes and varieties of mastery in her work. Moore's jokes, puns, wordplay, and gimlet eye do build to create a comedic surface tension that's unequaled in its range and sophistication. Her characters put their humor to a wide variety of uses: to try to smooth over awkwardness, to defang their terror, to stave off despair, to endear themselves to lovers they sense are drawing away, to armor themselves against the aggressions of others, to put up a brave front when it seems that everything around them is caving in, to gesture helplessly at the absurdity of the world. In the story "Real Estate," the "Ha!" repeated beyond the point of absurdity with which the character Ruth responds to her husband's "parade of flings" pushes into a sense of panic, and then almost hysterical pain. It replicates the way that our thoughts of betrayal can metastasize and overwhelm us and breed ever more (often imaginary) betrayals. Each time I read this story, I sit in discomfort with these pages, reading each "Ha!" as another fling that Ruth has tormented herself with, another memory of a night in which her husband had said he'd be working late, another woman friend she now holds in suspicion.

While the effect of the humor is important, a deeper level of complication becomes apparent when one begins to consider the infinitely tangled emotions that give rise to the humor. In the story "Debarking," when middle-aged divorcé Ira is weirded out by his new girlfriend Zora's near-sexual dependency on her surly adolescent son and humiliated over and over again by the boy, he doesn't ever respond the way he wants to but instead bites back in the comfort of his mind by thinking up new verses to add to the jokey collection he's writing, a "little volume of doggerel, its tentative title *Women from Venus, Men from Penis.*" In this case and in so many more, the humor in Moore's stories erupts when a clear-sighted character has a devastating observation so urgent that it rises up out of their depths, but – because they are inherently kind and don't want to cause pain – the observation gets warped or twisted just before it reaches consciousness. When it is at last released, it has crumpled under its own weight and has become humor. Jokes, puns, and wit become survival techniques of people who would never be as cruel in life as their internal critics are. Lorrie Moore once wrote in an essay on the television series *True Detective* that "simultaneously embracing laughter and the object of that laughter is only irony and Keatsian intelligence, not assassination," and her specialty is a laugh that's at the same time a blow to the heart because her sympathy and generosity are always with her characters. She excels in showing the way that people are often at their funniest when they're least intending to be funny, as when, in the story "What You Want To Do Fine," the character Mack says, in trying to mend his relationship with his wife Annie, "There's something that with time grows between people . . . Something that grows whether you like it or not," and Annie cries out, "Gunk! . . . Gunk grows between people!" We laugh out of surprise and because the word "gunk" is inherently funny, but also because in the word's harshness and bluntness, Annie's despair and her frustration with the hapless Mack become palpable. Though she is a minor character, in this single word she blazes off the page and into reality. We have all been Annie at least once in our lives.

But voice is a far broader idea than simply that of wit or humor, and counterbalancing the black magic of Moore's humor are her equally witchy gifts in music and metaphor. Lorrie Moore was born to a musical family, her in-person speaking voice is a melodious alto, and there is so much music in her stories that nearly every one comes with its own soundtrack of *La Bohème* and Muzak and Dionne Warwick, "Oklahoma!," "Sexual Healing," or "Alfie," movie themes, "The Star-Spangled Banner," "country songs with the words *devil woman*," and so on. What makes her prose so deceptively easy to read, despite its complexity and sophistication, is its attentiveness to underlying prose rhythm and the musical shapes that her words make in the ear. She writes of this musical underpinning in an early essay, saying that in her childhood, "I was obsessed with songs . . . and I often think that that is what I tried to find later in literature: the feeling of a song; the friendly, confiding voice of a letter but the cadence and feeling of a song. When a piece of prose hit rhythms older, more familiar and enduring than itself, it seemed then briefly to belong to nature, or at least to the world of music, and that's when it seemed to me 'artistic' and good." The story "Beautiful

Grade" ends with a paragraph so fine that it sings in the reader's depths like a nightmarish incantation:

> . . . deep in his private January boyhood, he knew, there were colors that were true: the late-afternoon light was bluish and dark, the bruised tundra of the snowbanks scary and silver and cold. Stepping slowly at first, the hulking monster-man, the demon-man, red and giant, with a single wing growing out of its back, would begin to chase Bill. It chased him faster and faster, up and down every tiny hill to home, casting long shadows that would occasionally, briefly, fall upon them both like a net. While the church bells chimed their four o'clock hymn, the monster-man would fly in a loping, wonky way, lunging and leaping and skittering across the ice toward Bill's heels. Bill rounded a corner. The demon leaped over a bin of road salt. Bill cut across a path. The demon followed. And the terror of it all – as Bill flung himself onto his own front porch and into the unlocked and darkened house, slamming the door, sinking back against it, sliding down onto the doormat, safe at last among the clutter of boots and shoes but still gasping the wide lucky gasps of his great and narrow escape – was thrilling to him in a world that had already, and with such indifferent skill, forsaken all its charms.

This internal music of Moore's was apparent from her beginning as a writer: the irony in the how-to stories of her first book *Self-Help* relies deeply upon an underlying driving rhythm like the urgent boom-chicka-boom of the guitar in a country and western song.

Likewise, her astonishing facility with metaphor was early apparent. In "What Is Seized," a story written when she was twenty-four and also collected in *Self-Help*, she writes, "Forgiveness lives alone and far off down the road, but bitterness and art are close, gossipy neighbors, sharing the same clothesline, hanging out their things, getting their laundry confused." Abstract ideas are most elegantly transplanted into a reader's mind when they're likened to images shared in common; this particular metaphor feels dead-on because it is so precise, surprising, and complex. "People Like That Are The Only People Here" is a story overbrimming with devastating metaphor, metaphor grasped at as though it were the only thing that could keep the drowning mother afloat. This story contains the most perfect definition of fiction that I've ever read, in the three consecutively expanding metaphors that the husband of the writer-narrator uses to try to convince her to write about their baby's illness for money. Fiction, he says, is "the unlivable life, the strange room tacked onto the house, the extra moon that is circling the earth unbeknownst to science." Our sense of being in on the metafictional joke – we are even at this moment reading a short story about a baby's illness – is compounded and replicated on a smaller scale when we learn that the husband was only quoting his wife back to her. Fiction isn't life; fiction is only *like* life. Fiction is life's metaphor.

In recent years, Moore's work has seemed to become more overtly political with its references to wars in the Middle East, 9/11, and Abu Ghraib, but critics often overlook how political her fiction always has been. When you live in a patriarchy, it is inherently political to insist that the internal life of women is of great interest and deserving of exploration, that their love lives merit the crisp attention of literary art, that the domestic sphere is a battleground equal in importance to more masculine spaces. Moore's writing has always been subversive, sometimes so much so that its subversions are invisible to its intended targets. She is fond of structural subversion, as seen in the stories that rewrite a well-known story of a previous master ("Signs and Symbols" by Nabokov in "Referential," *The Wings of the Dove* by Henry James in "Wings"), or that dip into the fantastical ("The Juniper Tree," "Two Boys,"), or spin variations on themes, as in the stories that make up *Anagrams*. There are also the destabilizations that so often happen with the humor of women. A joke can decentralize power structures because it is transactional in nature: when a person laughs at a joke, that person has let something in, and the joker has created an opening into which she can slip her subversions without offending the forces-that-be. A funny writer is a writer to whom the reader gives a great deal of power, and gladly.

It was perhaps this wild subversiveness, this confident and almost offhand seizing of power, that I responded to so deeply in Lorrie Moore's work, why I bought *Birds of America* the day it was released, why I read my copies of her books to tatters. In the three years after I graduated from college, I ground out my daytime hours as a bartender in Philadelphia and an office toady in

California so that I could spend all my energy and thought in my nighttime writing. At last, after having written three apprentice novels, I'd had enough of floundering alone and applied to M.F.A. programs. The day I got into the one at the University of Wisconsin-Madison, I wept for hours, because that was the program where Lorrie Moore taught. In the months between my acceptance and the first class in Lorrie's workshop, I wrote like a woman possessed, mostly because I wanted to honor my debt to her; I wanted to make Lorrie Moore proud. But when Lorrie swept in that first night of class, I barely had the courage to look up; I am shy, but also looking at the person who had written so many stories that I venerated and dissected and put back together was a little like looking at the sun. And maybe, too, I was afraid that perhaps, in herself, Lorrie Moore would not be like her work, that there would be a gap between the mind that created the work and the person who carried that mind around. This fear was laid to rest as soon as she sat down and sighed and looked at us with a wry and trailing, *Well* . . . that seemed to mean that although we didn't look all that promising, she was willing to be pleasantly surprised.

I was relieved to discover that Lorrie Moore is exactly like her fiction: brilliant, warm, hilarious, clear-sighted, wise. When it was my turn to be workshopped, I felt ill at the thought of handing Lorrie Moore an ersatz and far worse version of her own stories, and swiftly began to write in a different mode that, after some pain, became my own. Yet Lorrie was never unkind, and in class when she did not like something, her opinion came abundantly clear in the length of her hesitation to pronounce upon it aloud. When she loved a piece of writing, she would begin to speak of it in a low and careful voice, but soon her innate shyness would burn off and she would become carried away, her voice would go faster and become more emphatic, she would point out ever deeper complexities and layers in the work, her eyes would flash in delight; and when at last she finished speaking and fell silent, we would all slowly let out the breath we hadn't known we'd been holding, sure that this is what a bird feels in the downdraft of a rocket. These bursts of passion in class were as thrilling to me as her stories were on the page. She was as generous in life as she was in her fiction, too: the best night in graduate school was when she came out to sing with us at karaoke, and it surprised no one at all to discover that Lorrie Moore has a beautiful voice and knows esoteric musical theater numbers to an intimidating degree. She celebrated our triumphs and our theses with champagne and cheese platters; she celebrated our flawed and ridiculous and often unloveable selves. We have come nearly fifteen years and many thousands of miles away from that first class in Madison where I sat in a prickly anguish of anticipation waiting to meet my hero, but Lorrie's is still the voice I hear when I'm considering whether a piece is finished or not; her moral rigor when it comes to the right words in the right order has been my steady friend; her healthy skepticism has murmured to me often enough that it has kept me from too much embarrassment.

Yet Lorrie Moore's voice has always been clearest in her many brilliant works of fiction, which, no matter how often you read them, are an endlessly rich and renewing source of pleasure and inspiration. Ordering the stories in this collection alphabetically, instead of chronologically, is a stroke of genius, because it frees the reader of any collection's implicit obligation to read the work consecutively. You can dip into and out of this story collection, savor or glut yourself, flit or hover, see connections in new juxtapositions, return over and over to the story you need the most in the fraught or dark or stuck moments in your own life; you can, in short, treat the *Collected Stories* of Lorrie Moore like the psalmbook it so stealthily resembles. How lucky we are that we have Lorrie Moore's voice to reflect this lunatic world back to us and show us how to see it in all its devastating hilarity. How lucky we are to be able to hold such beauty in our hands and let it sing inside us.

Lauren Groff

LAUREN GROFF is the author of five books, including the National Book Award Finalists, *Fates and Furies*, a novel, and *Florida*, a story collection.

CHRONOLOGY

DATE	AUTHOR'S LIFE	LITERARY CONTEXT
1957	Born 13 January in Glens Falls, New York.	Bradbury: *Dandelion Wine*. Cheever: *The Wapshot Chronicle*. Kerouac: *On the Road*. Nabokov: *Pnin*. Rand: *Atlas Shrugged*. West: *The Fountain Overflows*.
1960		Lee: *To Kill a Mockingbird*. O'Brien: *The Country Girls*. Updike: *Rabbit* tetralogy (to 1981).
1961		Heller: *Catch-22*. McCullers: *Clock Without Hands*. Salinger: *Franny and Zooey*. Yates: *Revolutionary Road*.
1962		Lessing: *The Golden Notebook*. Nabokov: *Pale Fire*. Spark: *The Prime of Miss Jean Brodie*. Yates: *Eleven Kinds of Loneliness*.
1963		Friedan: *The Feminine Mystique*. M. McCarthy: *The Group*. Plath: *The Bell Jar*.
1964	Visits New York World's Fair. Sees Michelangelo's *Pietà*.	Bellow: *Herzog*. Porter: *Collected Stories*.
1965		Baldwin: *Going to Meet the Man*. Drabble: *The Millstone*. Mailer: *An American Dream*. Plath: *Ariel*.
1966		Rhys: *Wide Sargasso Sea*. Sexton: *Live or Die*.
1967		Márquez: *One Hundred Years of Solitude*.
1968		Barthelme: *Unspeakable Practices, Unnatural Acts*. Didion: *Slouching Towards Bethlehem*.

HISTORICAL EVENTS

Civil Rights Commission established to safeguard voting rights in US. Viet Cong guerrillas attack South Vietnam. EEC founded (Treaty of Rome). USSR launches world's first artificial satellites, Sputnik 1 and 2. First commercial nuclear reactor opens, Pennsylvania. First Frisbees marketed. Ultrasound scanning pioneered in Scotland.

J. F. Kennedy elected US President.

Attempted US invasion of Cuba, Bay of Pigs. Berlin Wall erected. Yuri Gagarin first man in space.

Cuban Missile Crisis. First cassette tapes.

Kennedy assassinated; Lyndon Johnson becomes President. Equal Pay Act in US.

Civil Rights Act outlaws racial discrimination in US. Martin Luther King receives Nobel Peace Prize. The Beatles' first American tour. Leonid Brezhnev ousts Nikita Khrushchev in USSR.

US bombs North Vietnam. Large-scale anti-Vietnam War demonstrations begin. Malcolm X assassinated. Selma to Montgomery march against black voter suppression. Voting Rights Act.

Black Panthers founded, Oakland, California. Mao Zedong launches Cultural Revolution in China.

Racial violence in many US cities; Johnson appoints commission to investigate causes. "Summer of Love," Haight-Ashbury, California. Six-Day War between Israel and Arab states. Che Guevara shot dead, Bolivia.

Students protest in US and throughout Europe. Martin Luther King assassinated. Richard Nixon elected US President. Soviet invasion of Czechoslovakia.

DATE	AUTHOR'S LIFE	LITERARY CONTEXT
1969		Bradbury: *I Sing the Body Electric.* Oates: *Them.* Sexton: *Love Poems.*
1971		Du Maurier: *Don't Look Now.* M. McCarthy: *Birds of America.* Munro: *Lives of Girls and Women.* O'Connor: *The Complete Stories.*
1973		Pynchon: *Gravity's Rainbow.*
1974	Graduates from Glens Falls High School and on various scholarships goes to St. Lawrence University in Canton, New York.	Heller: *Something Happened.* Jong: *Fear of Flying.* Paley: *Enormous Changes at the Last Minute.*
1975		Alther: *Kinflicks.* Bellow: *Humboldt's Gift.*
1976	Wins first place in *Seventeen* magazine fiction contest.	Carver: *Will You Please Be Quiet, Please?* Kingston: *The Woman Warrior.*
1977		Atwood: *Dancing Girls.* Morrison: *Song of Solomon.*
1978	Graduates *summa cum laude* from St. Lawrence. Misses overlap with Viggo Mortensen by one year.	Cheever: *Collected Stories.* French: *The Women's Room.* Lessing: *Collected Stories.* McEwan: *In Between the Sheets.*
1979		Calvino: *If on a winter's night a traveler.* Carter: *The Bloody Chamber and Other Stories.* Phillips: *Black Tickets.* Sorrentino: *Mulligan Stew.* Updike: *Too Far to Go.*
1980		Bowen: *Collected Stories.* Robinson: *Housekeeping.* Welty: *Collected Stories.*
1981		Carver: *What We Talk About When We Talk About Love.*
1982	Awarded MFA from Cornell University.	Márquez: *Chronicle of a Death Foretold.* Tyler: *Dinner in the Homesick Restaurant.* Walker: *The Color Purple.*

HISTORICAL EVENTS

Neil Armstrong first man on moon. US troops begin withdrawal from Vietnam. Woodstock rock festival attended by 400,000 in New York State.

US voting age lowered to eighteen. India and Pakistan border disputes erupt into full-scale war. Disney World theme park opens in Florida. Greenpeace founded.

Military coup in Chile: General Pinochet comes to power. Yom Kippur War; oil crisis. Supreme Court in US rules that abortion is legal. Mobile phones first marketed.

Nixon resigns after Watergate scandal; Gerald Ford becomes US President. Bangladesh famine.

Vietnam War ends. Bill Gates and Paul Allen found Microsoft.

Jimmy Carter becomes US President. Chairman Mao dies. First Apple computer.

Elvis Presley dies. *Star Wars*, *Saturday Night Fever*, *Annie Hall* première.

Camp David Agreement signed by Carter, President Sadat of Egypt and Israeli prime minister Menachem Begin. First "test-tube baby," Louise Brown, born in Oldham, England.

Soviet troops occupy Afghanistan. Carter and Brezhnev sign SALT II. Shah of Iran forced into exile; Ayatollah Khomeini establishes an Islamic state; American embassy siege in Tehran. Margaret Thatcher becomes the UK's first female prime minister.

Ronald Reagan elected US President. Iran–Iraq War begins (to 1988). Lech Walesa, shipyard worker, leads strikes in Poland.

Sandra Day O'Connor first woman to serve on the US Supreme Court. Maiden voyage of Space Shuttle. IBM Personal Computer launched. Beginning of 1980s stock market boom in US. War between UK and Argentina over Falkland Islands.

DATE	AUTHOR'S LIFE	LITERARY CONTEXT
1983		Carver: *Cathedral.* Mason: *Shiloh and Other Stories.*
1984	Begins teaching at the University of Wisconsin-Madison.	Oates: *Last Days: Stories.* Phillips: *Machine Dreams.* Updike: *The Witches of Eastwick.*
1985	First collection of stories, *Self-Help*, published.	Delillo: *White Noise.* Mason: *For In Country.* Paley: *Later the Same Day.* Tyler: *The Accidental Tourist.*
1986	First novel, *Anagrams*, published.	Atwood: *The Handmaid's Tale.* Davis: *Break It Down.* Ford: *The Sportswriter.* Lively: *Pack of Cards.* Munro: *The Progress of Love.*
1987		Morrison: *Beloved.* Wolfe: *The Bonfire of the Vanities.*
1988		Atwood: *Cat's Eye.* Tyler: *Breathing Lessons.*
1989		Smiley: *Ordinary Love and Good Will.* Tan: *The Joy Luck Club.*
1990	Second collection of stories, *Like Life*, published.	Byatt: *Possession.* Pritchett: *Complete Short Stories.*
1991		Alvarez: *How the García Girls Lost their Accents.* Cisneros: *Woman Hollering Creek and Other Stories.* Smiley: *A Thousand Acres.*
1992	Prix de Rome, American Academy of Arts and Letters.	C. McCarthy: *All the Pretty Horses.* Tartt: *The Secret History.* Trevor: *Collected Stories.*
1993		Ng: *Bone.* Proulx: *The Shipping News.* Shields: *The Stone Diaries.*
1994	Second novel, *Who Will Run the Frog Hospital?*, published.	Danticat: *Breath, Eyes, Memory.* Heller: *Closing Time.* Oates: *What I Lived For.*
1995		Ford: *Independence Day.* Nabokov: *Collected Stories.* Smiley: *Moo.*
1996		Atwood: *Alias Grace.* Danticat: *Krik? Krak!*

HISTORICAL EVENTS

US troops invade Grenada after government overthrown. Reagan announces "Star Wars." CDs launched.

Reagan re-elected in landslide. Indian prime minister Indira Gandhi assassinated. Famine in Ethiopia.

Reform begins in USSR under new General Secretary of the Communist Party, Mikhail Gorbachev.

US bombs Libya. Gorbachev–Reagan summit. Nuclear explosion in Chernobyl, USSR. Space Shuttle Challenger explodes.

Reagan makes Berlin Wall speech. World population reaches 5 billion.

George Bush elected US President. Soviet troops withdrawn in large numbers from Afghanistan.

Berlin Wall dismantled, Communism collapses in Eastern Europe. USSR holds first democratic elections. Tiananmen Square massacre in China. US troops invade Panama. Tim Berners Lee invents the World Wide Web.

Nelson Mandela released in South Africa. Boris Yeltsin elected first leader of Russian Federation after end of Communist rule.

Gulf War begins. War breaks out in former Yugoslavia. Apartheid ends in South Africa. Bush and Gorbachev sign START arms reduction treaty.

Bill Clinton elected US President. Riots in Los Angeles.

Palestinian leader Yasser Arafat signs peace agreement with Israeli prime minister Yitzhak Rabin. Janet Reno first female Attorney General of the US.

Mandela's ANC takes power after South African elections. Civil war in Rwanda. Russia takes military action in Chechen Republic.

Rabin assassinated in Israel. Oklahoma City bombing. Launch of Ebay.

Clinton re-elected US President. Dolly the sheep successfully cloned in Scotland.

DATE	AUTHOR'S LIFE	LITERARY CONTEXT
1996 *cont.*		Dubus: *Dancing After Hours.* Gallant: *Collected Stories.* Jen: *Mona in the Promised Land.*
1997		Bellow: *The Actual.* Bolaño: *Last Evenings on Earth.* Kennedy: *Original Bliss.* Roth: *American Pastoral.*
1998	First Prize, O. Henry Award. Third collection of stories, *Birds of America*, published.	DeLillo: *Underworld.* Morrison: *Paradise.* Munro: *The Love of a Good Woman.* Roth: *I Married a Communist.*
1999	*Birds of America* finalist for the National Book Critics Circle Award.	Lahiri: *Interpreter of Maladies.* Proulx: *Close Range: Wyoming Stories.* Sontag: *In America.*
2000	*The Irish Times* International Fiction Prize.	Atwood: *The Blind Assassin.* Kingsolver: *Prodigal Summer.* Oates: *Blonde.* Rhodes: *Anthropology: And a Hundred Other Stories.* Smiley: *Horse Heaven.*
2001	Inducted into American Academy of Arts and Sciences.	Franzen: *The Corrections.* Russo: *Empire Falls.*
2002		Eugenides: *Middlesex.* Shields: *Unless.*
2003		Morrison: *Love.*
2004	Rea Award for Short Fiction.	Danticat: *The Dew Breaker.* Robinson: *Gilead.* Tyler: *The Amateur Marriage.*
2005	PEN/Malamud Award for Short Fiction.	Didion: *The Year of Magical Thinking.*
2006	Inducted into American Academy of Arts and Letters.	Eisenberg: *Twilight of the Superheroes.* Horn: *The World to Come.* MacLaverty: *Matters of Life and Death.*
2007		Danticat: *Brother, I'm Dying.* Russo: *Bridge of Sighs.* Smiley: *Ten Days in the Hills.*
2008	Canvasses for Barack Obama presidential campaign in Indiana and Wisconsin.	Hustvedt: *The Sorrows of an American.* Lahiri: *Unaccustomed Earth.* Proulx: *Just the Way It Is.* Robinson: *Home.* A. Smith: *The First Person.*

CHRONOLOGY

HISTORICAL EVENTS

Hong Kong sovereignty given back to China by Britain. Economic crisis: stock markets around the world crash, Dow Jones Industrial Average plummets. Madeleine Albright first female Secretary of State in US. Death of Princess Diana in Paris. Wi-Fi invented.

Clinton impeached over sex scandal (acquitted 1999).

Ethnic Albanians attacked by Serbs in Kosovo; US leads NATO in bombing of Belgrade.

George W. Bush elected US President. Vladimir Putin succeeds Yeltsin as Russian President. Slobodan Milosevic's regime collapses in former Yugoslavia.

Al-Qaeda attacks New York's World Trade Center; US and allies take action against Taliban in Afghanistan. Wikipedia launched.

Bush declares "War on Terror." Moscow theater hostage crisis.

US and British troops invade Iraq; Saddam Hussein captured.

Bush re-elected US President. Terrorist bombings in Madrid. Tsunami in Indian Ocean. Facebook launched.

Hurricane Katrina floods New Orleans. Terrorist bombings in London.

Iran joins "nuclear club"; North Korea tests nuclear weapon.

Virginia Tech shooting. Bush reduces US forces in Iraq. Al Gore and UN climate scientists win Nobel Peace Prize. iPhone introduced. Kindle marketed.

Barack Obama, Democratic Senator from Illinois, becomes first black presidential nominee in US. Collapse of Lehman Brothers triggers world financial crisis. Viggo Mortensen nominated for an Academy Award.

DATE	AUTHOR'S LIFE	LITERARY CONTEXT
2009	Third novel, *A Gate at the Stairs*, published.	Davis: *Collected Stories.* Kingsolver: *The Lacuna.* Munro: *Too Much Happiness.*
2010	Finalist for the Orange Prize and for the PEN/Faulkner Award.	Franzen: *Freedom.* Samson: *Perfect Lives.* Tóibín: *The Empty Family.*
2011		Bradbury: *Collected Stories* (to 2014). Ferrante: *My Brilliant Friend.* Oates: *The Corn Maiden and Other Nightmares.*
2012		McGregor: *This Isn't the Sort of Thing That Happens to Someone Like You.* Munro: *Dear Life.* Taylor: *Complete Short Stories.* Tyler: *The Beginner's Goodbye.*
2013	Relocates to Vanderbilt University in Nashville.	Adichie: *Americanah.* Lahiri: *The Lowland.* Messud: *The Woman Upstairs.* Russell: *Vampires in the Lemon Grove.* Saunders: *Tenth of December: Stories.* Tartt: *The Goldfinch.*
2014	Fourth collection of stories, *Bark*, published. Shortlisted for the Frank O'Connor International Short Story Award.	Atwood: *Stone Mattress.* Hall: *Mrs Fox.* Kennedy: *All the Rage.* Melnik: *Snow in May.* Smiley: *The Last Hundred Years Trilogy* (to 2015).
2015		Lispector: *The Complete Stories.* Morrison: *God Help the Child.* Simpson: *Cockfosters.* Tyler: *A Spool of Blue Thread.*
2016		Oyeyemi: *What Is Not Yours Is Not Yours.*
2017	Awarded Cullman fellowship at New York Public Library.	Lively: *The Purple Swamp Hen and Other Stories.*
2018	Publishes *See What Can Be Done*, a miscellany of non-fiction. Mary McCarthy Award, Bard College.	Johnson: *The Largesse of the Sea Maiden.*
2019		

HISTORICAL EVENTS

Ongoing world financial crisis. H1N1 ("swine flu") global pandemic.

Healthcare Reform Bill passed by President Obama. Deepwater Horizon (BP rig) oil spill in Gulf of Mexico. US combat mission ends in Iraq. iPad introduced.

"Arab Spring": protests and rebellions against repressive regimes across Middle East. Syrian Civil War begins. Osama Bin Laden killed by US Navy Seals.

Obama re-elected US President. Mars Science Laboratory ("Curiosity Rover") lands on Mars. Hurricane Sandy.

Edward Snowden leaks classified documents revealing mass surveillance by the US National Security Agency. Boston Marathon bombing.

Russia annexes Crimea. ISIS declares Islamic Caliphate.

Black Lives Matter protests begin in US. Supreme Court rules that all states have to recognize same-sex marriage. Islamic terror attacks in Paris. Refugee crisis in Europe.

UK referendum on EU membership results in "Leave" vote. Donald Trump wins US presidential election.

Trump takes up office of President, promising to "make America great again" and fueling rise of populism worldwide. North Korean crisis (to 2018). Viggo Mortensen nominated for an Academy Award.

US leaves Iran nuclear deal. #MeToo movement goes global.

Viggo Mortensen nominated for an Academy Award.

AUTHOR'S NOTE

I realize that alphabetizing disrupts the hypothetical coherence of any individual collection and is inconvenient to the poor soul who would like to trace or discover the ostensible artistic development of a writer. Attempting to glimpse the growth of an author through chronological arrangement is, in my opinion, often a fool's errand and even if possible and successful is somewhat embarrassing to the young author who remains alive within the older one. If one wants to line everything up timewise the original collections are still in print for that purpose. But I didn't want this volume to be one that simply glued all my previous books together in the obvious, sequential order. I hoped instead to let the magical alphabet set individual stories side by side in an otherwise unexpected way so that friction or frost might occur: they could jostle and rap and spark or repel. Rub their cold shoulders. Get cozy or surreal in the manner that chance juxtapositions sometimes produce. There could be unexpected chiming or clanging. It might all be like a playlist set to *shuffle*. I have a bit of librarian in me, but I also advise any reader to browse and proceed however they would like. When I listen to my own music library I sometime listen to all the *M*s where there are many haunting songs with the words *midnight* or *moon* in the title. Here, alas, I have no titles beginning with M and offer my apologies.

LM

THE COLLECTED STORIES OF LORRIE MOORE

AGNES OF IOWA

HER MOTHER HAD given her the name Agnes, believing that a good-looking woman was even more striking when her name was a homely one. Her mother was named Cyrena, and was beautiful to match, but had always imagined her life would have been more interesting, that she herself would have had a more dramatic, arresting effect on the world and not ended up in Cassell, Iowa, if she had been named Enid or Hagar or Maude. And so she named her first daughter Agnes, and when Agnes turned out not to be attractive at all, but puffy and prone to a rash between her eyebrows, her hair a flat and bilious hue, her mother backpedaled and named her second daughter Linnea Elise (who turned out to be a lovely, sleepy child with excellent bones, a sweet, full mouth, and a rubbery mole above her lip that later in life could be removed without difficulty, everyone was sure).

Agnes herself had always been a bit at odds with her name. There was a brief period in her life, in her mid-twenties, when she had tried to pass it off as French – she had put in the accent grave and encouraged people to call her "On-yez." This was when she was living in New York City, and often getting together with her cousin, a painter who took her to parties in TriBeCa lofts or at beach houses or at mansions on lakes upstate. She would meet a lot of not very bright rich people who found the pronunciation of her name intriguing. It was the rest of her they were unclear on. "On-yez, where are you from, dear?" asked a black-slacked, frosted-haired woman whose skin was papery and melanomic with suntan. "Originally." She eyed Agnes's outfit as if it might be what in fact it was: a couple of blue things purchased in a department store in Cedar Rapids.

"Where am I from?" Agnes said it softly. "Iowa." She had a tendency not to speak up.

"Where?" The woman scowled, bewildered.

"Iowa," Agnes repeated loudly.

The woman in black touched Agnes's wrist and leaned in confidentially. She moved her mouth in a concerned and exaggerated way, like a facial exercise. "No, dear," she said. "*Here* we say *O-hi-o*."

That had been in Agnes's mishmash decade, after college. She had lived improvisationally then, getting this job or that, in restaurants or offices, taking a class or two, not thinking too far ahead, negotiating the precariousness and subway flus and scrimping for an occasional manicure or a play. Such a life required much exaggerated self-esteem. It engaged gross quantities of hope and despair and set them wildly side by side, like a Third World country of the heart. Her days grew messy with contradictions. When she went for walks, for her health, cinders would spot her cheeks and soot would settle in the furled leaf of each ear. Her shoes became unspeakable. Her blouses darkened in a breeze, and a blast of bus exhaust might linger in her hair for hours. Finally, her old asthma returned and, with a hacking, incessant cough, she gave up. "I feel like I've got five years to live," she told people, "so I'm moving back to Iowa so that it'll feel like fifty."

When she packed up to leave, she knew she was saying good-bye to something important, which was not that bad, in a way, because it meant that at least you had said hello to it to begin with, which most people in Cassell, Iowa, she felt, could not claim to have done.

A year and a half later, she married a boyish man twelve years her senior, a Cassell realtor named Joe, and together they bought a house on a little street called Birch Court. She taught a night class at the Arts Hall and did volunteer work on the Transportation Commission in town. It was life like a glass of water: half-empty, half-full. Half-full. Half-full. Oops: half-empty. Over the years, she and Joe tried to have a baby, but one night at dinner, looking at each other in a lonely way over the meat loaf, they realized with shock that they probably never would. Nonetheless, after six years, they still tried, vandalizing what romance was left in their marriage.

"Honey," she would whisper at night when he was reading under the reading lamp and she had already put her book away and curled toward him, wanting to place the red scarf over the lamp shade but knowing it would annoy him and so not doing it. "Do you want to make love? It would be a good time of month."

And Joe would groan. Or he would yawn. Or he would already be asleep. Once, after a long, hard day, he said, "I'm sorry, Agnes. I guess I'm just not in the mood."

She grew exasperated. "You think *I'm* in the mood?" she said. "I don't want to do this any more than you do," and he looked at her in a disgusted way, and it was two weeks after that that they had the sad dawning over the meat loaf.

At the Arts Hall, formerly the Grange Hall, Agnes taught the Great Books class, but taught it loosely, with cookies. She let her students turn in poems and plays and stories that they themselves had written; she let them use the class as their own little time to be creative. Someone once even brought in a sculpture: an electric one with blinking lights.

After class, she sometimes met with students individually. She recommended things for them to write about or read or consider in their next project. She smiled and asked if things were going well in their lives. She took an interest.

"You should be stricter," said Willard Stauffbacher, the head of the Instruction Department; he was a short, balding musician who liked to tape on his door pictures of famous people he thought he looked like. Every third Monday, he conducted the monthly departmental meeting – aptly named, Agnes liked to joke, since she did indeed depart mental. "Just because it's a night course doesn't mean you shouldn't impart standards," Stauffbacher said in a scolding way. "If it's piffle, use the word *piffle*. If it's meaningless, write *meaningless* across the top of every page." He had once taught at an elementary school and once at a prison. "I feel like I do all the real work around here," he added. He had posted near his office a sign that read RULES FOR THE MUSIC ROOM:

I will stay in my seat unless [sic] permission to move.
I will sit up straight.
I will listen to directions.
I will not bother my neighbor.
I will not talk when Mr. Stauffbacher is talking.
I will be polite to others.
I will sing as well as I can.

Agnes stayed after one night with Christa, the only black student in her class. She liked Christa a lot – Christa was smart and funny, and Agnes sometimes liked to stay after with her to chat. Tonight, Agnes had decided to talk Christa out of writing about vampires all the time.

"Why don't you write about that thing you told me about that time?" Agnes suggested.

Christa looked at her skeptically. "What thing?"

"The time in your childhood, during the Chicago riots, walking with your mother through the police barricades."

"Man, I lived that. Why should I want to write about it?"

Agnes sighed. Maybe Christa had a point. "It's just that I'm no help to you with this vampire stuff," Agnes said. "It's formulaic, genre fiction."

"You would be of more help to me with *my childhood*?"

"Well, with more serious stories, yes."

Christa stood up, perturbed. She grabbed back her vampire story. "You with all your Alice Walker and Zora Hurston. I'm just not interested in that anymore. I've done that already. I read those books years ago."

"Christa, please don't be annoyed." *Please do not talk when Mr. Stauffbacher is talking.*

"You've got this agenda for me."

"Really, I don't at all," said Agnes. "It's just that – you know what it is? It's that I'm just sick of these vampires. They're so roaming and repeating."

"If you were black, what you're saying might have a different spin. But the fact is, you're not," Christa said, and picked up her coat and strode out – though ten seconds later, she gamely stuck her head back in and said, "See you next week."

* * *

"We need a visiting writer who's black," Agnes said in the next depart mental meeting. "We've never had one." They were looking at their budget, and the readings this year were pitted against Dance Instruction, a program headed up by a redhead named Evergreen.

"The Joffrey is just so much central casting," said Evergreen, apropos of nothing. As a vacuum cleaner can start to pull up the actual thread of a carpet, her brains had been sucked dry by too much yoga. No one paid much attention to her.

"Perhaps we can get Harold Raferson in Chicago," Agnes suggested.

"We've already got somebody for the visiting writer slot," said Stauffbacher coyly. "An Afrikaner from Johannesburg."

"What?" said Agnes. Was he serious? Even Evergreen barked out a laugh.

"W. S. Beyerbach. The university's bringing him in. We pay our five hundred dollars and we get him out here for a day and a half."

"Who?" asked Evergreen.

"This has already been decided?" asked Agnes.

"Yup." Stauffbacher looked accusingly at Agnes. "I've done a lot of work to arrange for this. *I've* done all the work!"

"Do less," said Evergreen.

When Agnes first met Joe, they'd fallen madly upon each other. They'd kissed in restaurants; they'd groped, under coats, at the movies. At his little house, they'd made love on the porch, or the landing of the staircase, against the wall in the hall by the door to the attic, filled with too much desire to make their way to a real room.

Now they struggled self-consciously for atmosphere, something they'd never needed before. She prepared the bedroom carefully. She played quiet music and concentrated. She lit candles – as if she were in church, praying for the deceased. She donned a filmy gown. She took hot baths and entered the bedroom in nothing but a towel, a wild fishlike creature of moist, perfumed heat. In the nightstand drawer she still kept the charts a doctor once told her to keep, still placed an *X* on any date she and Joe actually had sex. But she could never show these to her doctor; not now. It pained Agnes to see them. She and Joe looked like worse than bad shots. She and Joe looked like idiots. She and Joe looked dead.

Frantic candlelight flickered on the ceiling like a puppet show. While she waited for Joe to come out of the bathroom, Agnes lay back on the bed and thought about her week, the bloody politics of it, how she was not very good at politics. Once, before he was elected, she had gone to a rally for Bill Clinton, but when he was late and had kept the crowd waiting for over an hour, and when the sun got hot and bees began landing on people's heads, when everyone's feet hurt and tiny children began to cry and a state assemblyman stepped forward to announce that Clinton had stopped at a Dairy Queen in Des Moines and that was why he was late – Dairy Queen! – she had grown angry and resentful and apolitical in her own sweet-starved thirst and she'd joined in with some other people who had started to chant, "Do us a favor, tell us the flavor."

Through college she had been a feminist – basically: she shaved her legs, *but just not often enough*, she liked to say. She signed day-care petitions, and petitions for Planned Parenthood. And although she had never been very aggressive with men, she felt strongly that she knew the difference between feminism and Sadie Hawkins Day – which some people, she believed, did not.

"Agnes, are we out of toothpaste or is this it – oh, okay, I see."

And once, in New York, she had quixotically organized the ladies' room line at the Brooks Atkinson Theatre. Because the play was going to start any minute and the line was still twenty women long, she had gotten six women to walk across the lobby with her to the men's room. "Everybody out of there?" she'd called in timidly, allowing the men to finish up first, which took awhile, especially with other men coming up impatiently and cutting ahead in line. Later, at intermission, she saw how it should have been done. Two elderly black women, with greater expertise in civil rights, stepped very confidently into the men's room and called out, "Don't mind us, boys. We're coming on in. Don't mind us."

"Are you okay?" asked Joe, smiling. He was already beside her. He smelled sweet, of soap and minty teeth, like a child.

"I think so," she said, and turned toward him in the bordello light of their room. He had never acquired the look of maturity anchored in sorrow that burnished so many men's faces. His own sadness in life – a childhood of beatings, a dying mother – was like quicksand, and he had to stay away from it entirely. He permitted no unhappy memories spoken aloud. He stuck with the same mild cheerfulness he'd honed successfully as a boy, and it made him seem fatuous – even, she knew, to himself. Probably it hurt his business a little.

"Your mind's wandering," he said, letting his own eyes close.

"I know." She yawned, moved her legs onto his for warmth, and in this way, with the candles burning into their tins, she and Joe fell asleep.

The spring arrived cool and humid. Bulbs cracked and sprouted, shot up their green periscopes, and on April first, the Arts Hall offered a joke lecture by T. S. Eliot, visiting scholar. "The Cruelest Month," it was called. "You don't find that funny?" asked Stauffbacher.

April fourth was the reception for W. S. Beyerbach. There was to be a dinner afterward, and then Beyerbach was to visit Agnes's Great Books class. She had assigned his second collection of sonnets, spare and elegant things with sighing and diaphanous politics. The next afternoon there was to be a reading.

Agnes had not been invited to the dinner, and when she asked about this, in a mildly forlorn way, Stauffbacher shrugged, as if it were totally out of his hands. I'm a *published poet*, Agnes wanted to say. She *had* published a poem once – in *The Gizzard Review*, but still!

"It was Edie Canterton's list," Stauffbacher said. "I had nothing to do with it."

She went to the reception anyway, annoyed, and when she planted herself like a splayed and storm-torn tree near the cheese, she could actually feel the crackers she was eating forming a bad paste in her mouth and she became afraid to smile. When she finally introduced herself to W. S. Beyerbach, she stumbled on her own name and actually pronounced it "On-yez."

"On-yez," repeated Beyerbach in a quiet Englishy voice. Condescending, she thought. His hair was blond and white, like a palomino, and his eyes were blue and scornful as mints. She could see he was a withheld man; although some might say *shy*, she decided it was *withheld*: a lack of generosity. Passive-aggressive. It was causing the people around him to squirm and blurt things nervously. He would simply nod, the smile on his face faint and vaguely pharmaceutical. Everything about him was tight and coiled as a door spring. From living in *that country*, thought Agnes. How could he live in that country?

Stauffbacher was trying to talk heartily about the mayor. Something about his old progressive ideas, and the forthcoming convention center. Agnes thought of her own meetings on the Transportation Commission, of the mayor's leash law for cats, of his new squadron of meter maids and bicycle police, of a councilman the mayor once slugged in a bar. "Now, of course, the mayor's become a fascist," said Agnes in a voice that sounded strangely loud, bright with anger.

Silence fell all around. Edie Canterton stopped stirring the punch. Agnes looked about her. "Oh," she said. "Are we not supposed to use *that word* in this room?" Beyerbach's expression went blank. Agnes's face burned in confusion.

Stauffbacher appeared pained, then stricken. "More cheese, anyone?" he asked, holding up the silver tray.

* * *

After everyone left for dinner, she went by herself to the Dunk 'N Dine across the street. She ordered the California BLT and a cup of coffee, and looked over Beyerbach's work again: dozens of images of broken, rotten bodies, of the body's mutinies and betrayals, of the body's strange housekeeping and illicit pets. At the front of the book was a dedication – *To DFB (1970–1989)*. Who could that be? A political activist, maybe. Perhaps it was the young woman referred to often in his poems, "a woman who had thrown aside the unseasonal dress of hope," only to look for it again "in the blood-blooming shrubs." Perhaps if Agnes got a chance, she would ask him. Why not? A book was a public thing, and its dedication was part of it. If it was too personal a question for him, *tough*. She would find the right time, she decided. She paid the check, put on her jacket, and crossed the street to the Arts Hall, to meet Beyerbach by the front door. She would wait for the moment, then seize it.

He was already at the front door when she arrived. He greeted her with a stiff smile and a soft "Hello, Onyez," an accent that made her own voice ring coarse and country-western.

She smiled and then blurted, "I have a question to ask you." To her own ears, she sounded like Johnny Cash.

Beyerbach said nothing, only held the door open for her and then followed her into the building.

She continued as they stepped slowly up the stairs. "May I ask to whom your book is dedicated?"

At the top of the stairs, they turned left down the long corridor. She could feel his steely reserve, his lip-biting, his shyness no doubt garbed and rationalized with snobbery, but so much snobbery to handle all that shyness, he could not possibly be a meaningful critic of his country. She was angry with him. *How can you live in that country?* she again wanted to say, although she remembered when someone had once said that to her – a Danish man on Agnes's senior trip abroad to Copenhagen. It had been during the Vietnam War and the man had stared meanly, righteously. "The United States – how can you live in that country?" the man had asked. Agnes had shrugged. "A lot of my stuff is there," she'd said, and it was then that she first felt all the dark love and shame that came from the pure accident of home, the deep and arbitrary place that happened to be yours.

"It's dedicated to my son," Beyerbach said finally.

He would not look at her, but stared straight ahead along the corridor floor. Now Agnes's shoes sounded very loud.

"You lost a son," she said.

"Yes," he said. He looked away, at the passing wall, past Stauffbacher's bulletin board, past the men's room, the women's room, some sternness in him broken, and when he turned back, she could see his eyes filling with water, his face a plethora, reddened with unbearable pressure.

"I'm so sorry," Agnes said.

Side by side now, their footsteps echoed down the corridor toward her classroom; all the anxieties she felt with this mournfully quiet man now mimicked the anxieties of love. What should she say? It must be the most unendurable thing to lose a child. Shouldn't he say something of this? It was his turn to say something.

But he would not. And when they finally reached her classroom, she turned to him in the doorway and, taking a package from her purse, said simply, in a reassuring way, "We always have cookies in class."

Now he beamed at her with such relief that she knew she had for once said the right thing. It filled her with affection for him. Perhaps, she thought, that was where affection began: in an unlikely phrase, in a moment of someone's having unexpectedly but at last said the right thing. *We always have cookies in class.*

She introduced him with a bit of flourish and biography. Positions held, universities attended. The students raised their hands and asked him about apartheid, about shantytowns and homelands, and he answered succinctly, after long sniffs and pauses, only once referring to a question as "unanswerably fey," causing the student to squirm and fish around in her purse for something, nothing, Kleenex perhaps. Beyerbach did not seem to notice. He went on, spoke of censorship, how a person must work hard not to internalize a government's program of censorship, since that is what a government would like best, for *you* to do it *yourself*, and how he was not sure he had not succumbed. Afterward, a few students stayed and shook his hand, formally, awkwardly, then left. Christa was the last. She, too, shook his hand and then started chatting amiably. They knew someone in common – Harold Raferson in Chicago! – and as Agnes quickly wiped the seminar table to clear it of cookie crumbs, she tried to listen, but couldn't really hear. She made a small pile of crumbs and swept them into one hand.

"Good night" sang out Christa when she left.

"Good night, Christa," said Agnes, brushing the crumbs into the wastebasket.

Now she stood with Beyerbach in the empty classroom. "Thank you so much," she said in a hushed way. "I'm sure they all got quite a lot out of that. I'm very sure they did."

He said nothing, but smiled at her gently.

She shifted her weight from one leg to the other. "Would you like to go somewhere and get a drink?" she asked. She was standing close to him, looking up into his face. He was tall, she saw now. His shoulders weren't broad, but he had a youthful straightness to his carriage. She briefly touched his sleeve. His suitcoat was corduroy and bore the faint odor of clove. This was the first time in her life that she had ever asked a man out for a drink.

He made no move to step away from her, but actually seemed to lean toward her a bit. She could feel his dry breath, see up close the variously hued spokes of his irises, the grays and yellows in the blue. There was a sprinkling of small freckles near his hairline. He smiled, then looked at the clock on the wall. "I would love to, really, but I have to get back to the hotel to make a phone call at ten-fifteen." He looked a little disappointed – not a lot, thought Agnes, but certainly a little.

"Oh, well," she said. She flicked off the lights and in the dark he carefully helped her on with her jacket. They stepped out of the room and walked together in silence, back down the corridor to the front entrance of the hall. Outside on the steps, the night was balmy and scented with rain. "Will you be all right walking back to your hotel?" she asked. "Or—"

"Oh, yes, thank you. It's just around the corner."

"Right. That's right. Well, my car's parked way over there. So I guess I'll see you tomorrow afternoon at your reading."

"Yes," he said. "I shall look forward to that."

"Yes," she said. "So shall I."

The reading was in the large meeting room at the Arts Hall and was from the sonnet book she had already read, but it was nice to hear the poems again, in his hushed, pained tenor. She sat in the back row, her green raincoat sprawled beneath her on the seat like a leaf. She leaned forward, onto the seat ahead of her, her back an angled stem, her chin on double fists, and she listened like that for some time. At one point, she closed her eyes, but the image of him before her, standing straight as a compass needle, remained caught there beneath her lids, like a burn or a speck or a message from the mind.

Afterward, moving away from the lectern, Beyerbach spotted her and waved, but Stauffbacher, like a tugboat with a task, took his arm and steered him elsewhere, over toward the side table with the little plastic cups of warm Pepsi. We are both men, the gesture seemed to say. We both have *bach* in our names. Agnes put on her green coat. She went over toward the Pepsi table and stood. She drank a warm Pepsi, then placed the empty cup back on the table. Beyerbach finally turned toward her and smiled familiarly. She thrust out her hand. "It was a wonderful reading," she said. "I'm very glad I got the chance to meet you." She gripped his long, slender palm and locked thumbs. She could feel the bones in him.

"Thank you," he said. He looked at her coat in a worried way. "You're leaving?"

She looked down at her coat. "I'm afraid I have to get going home." She wasn't sure whether she really had to or not. But she'd put on the coat, and it now seemed an awkward thing to take off.

"Oh," he murmured, gazing at her intently. "Well, all best wishes to you, Onyez."

"Excuse me?" There was some clattering near the lectern.

"All best to you," he said, something retreating in his expression.

Stauffbacher suddenly appeared at her side, scowling at her green coat, as if it were incomprehensible.

"Yes," said Agnes, stepping backward, then forward again to shake Beyerbach's hand once more; it was a beautiful hand, like an old and expensive piece of wood. "Same to you," she said. Then she turned and fled.

For several nights, she did not sleep well. She placed her face directly into her pillow, then turned it some for air, then flipped over to her back and opened her eyes, staring at the far end of the room through the stark angle of the door frame toward the tiny light from the bathroom which illumined the hallway, faintly, as if someone had just been there.

For several days, she thought perhaps he might have left her a note with the secretary, or that he might send her one from an airport somewhere. She thought that the inadequacy of their good-bye would haunt him, too, and that he might send her a postcard as elaboration.

But he did not. Briefly, she thought about writing him a letter, on Arts Hall stationery, which for money reasons was no longer the stationery, but photocopies of the stationery. She knew he had flown to the West Coast, then off to Tokyo, then Sydney, then back to Johannesburg, and if she posted it now, perhaps he would receive it when he arrived. She could tell him once more how interesting it had been to meet him. She could enclose her poem from *The Gizzard Review.* She had read in the newspaper an article about bereavement – and if she were her own mother, she could send him that, too.

Thank God, thank God, she was not her mother.

* * *

Spring settled firmly in Cassell with a spate of thundershowers. The perennials – the myrtle and grape hyacinths – blossomed around town in a kind of civic blue, and the warming air brought forth an occasional mosquito or fly. The Transportation Commission meetings were dreary and long, too often held over the dinner hour, and when Agnes got home, she would replay them for Joe, sometimes bursting into tears over the parts about the photoradar or the widening interstate.

When her mother called, Agnes got off the phone fast. When her sister called about her mother, Agnes got off the phone even faster. Joe rubbed her shoulders and spoke to her of carports, of curb appeal, of asbestos-wrapped pipes.

At the Arts Hall, she taught and fretted and continued to receive the usual memos from the secretary, written on the usual scrap paper – except that the scrap paper this time, for a while, consisted of the extra posters for the Beyerbach reading. She would get a long disquisition on policies and procedures concerning summer registration, and she would turn it over and there would be his face – sad and pompous in the photograph. She would get a simple phone message – "Your husband called. Please phone him at the office" – and on the back would be the ripped center of Beyerbach's nose, one minty eye, an elbowish chin. Eventually, there were no more, and the scrap paper moved on to old contest announcements, grant deadlines, Easter concert notices.

At night, she and Joe did yoga to a yoga show on TV. It was part of their effort not to become their parents, though marriage, they knew, held that hazard. The functional disenchantment, the sweet habit of each other had begun to put lines around her mouth, lines that looked like quotation marks – as if everything she said had already been said before. Sometimes their old cat, Madeline, a fat and pampered calico reaping the benefits of life with a childless couple during their childbearing years, came and plopped herself down with them, between them. She was accustomed to much nestling and appreciation and drips from the faucet, though sometimes she would vanish outside, and they would not see her for days, only to spy her later, in the yard, dirty and matted, chomping a vole or eating old snow.

For Memorial Day weekend, Agnes flew with Joe to New York, to show him the city for the first time. "A place," she said, "where if you're not white and not born there, you're not automatically a story." She had grown annoyed with Iowa, the pathetic thirdhand manner in which the large issues and conversations of the world were encountered, the oblique and tired way history situated itself there – if ever. She longed to be a citizen of the globe!

They roller-skated in Central Park. They looked in the Lord & Taylor windows. They went to the Joffrey. They went to a hair salon on Fifty-seventh Street and there she had her hair dyed red. They sat in the window booths of coffee shops and got coffee refills and ate pie.

"So much seems the same," she said to Joe. "When I lived here, everyone was hustling for money. The rich were. The poor were. But everyone tried hard to be funny. Everywhere you went – a store, a manicure place – someone was telling a joke. A *good* one." She remembered it had made any given day seem bearable, that impulse toward a joke. It had been a determined sort of humor, an intensity mirroring the intensity of the city, and it seemed to embrace and alleviate the hard sadness of people having used one another and marred the earth the way they had. "It was like brains having sex. It was like every brain was a sex maniac." She looked down at her pie. "People really worked at it, the laughing," she said. "People need to laugh."

"They do," said Joe. He took a swig of coffee, his lips out over the cup in a fleshy flower. He was afraid she might cry – she was getting that look again – and if she did, he would feel guilty and lost and sorry for her that her life was not here anymore, but in a far and boring place now with him. He set the cup down and tried to smile. "They sure do," he said. And he looked out the window at the rickety taxis, the oystery garbage and tubercular air, seven pounds of chicken giblets dumped on the curb in front of the restaurant where they were. He turned back to her and made the face of a clown.

"What are you doing?" she asked.

"It's a clown face."

"What do you mean, 'a clown face'?" Someone behind her was singing "I Love New York," and for the first time she noticed the strange irresolution of the tune.

"A regular clown face is what I mean."

"It didn't look like that."

"No? What did it look like?"

"You want me to do the face?"

"Yeah, do the face."

She looked at Joe. Every arrangement in life carried with it the sadness, the sentimental shadow, of its not being something else, but only itself: she attempted the face – a look of such monstrous emptiness and stupidity that Joe burst out in a howling sort of laughter, like a dog, and then so did she, air exploding through her nose in a snort, her head thrown forward, then back, then forward again, setting loose a fit of coughing.

"Are you okay?" asked Joe, and she nodded. Out of politeness, he looked away, outside, where it had suddenly started to rain. Across the street, two people had planted themselves under the window ledge of a Gap store, trying to stay dry, waiting out the downpour, their figures dark and scarecrow-ish against the lit window display. When he turned back to his wife – his sad young wife – to point this out to her, to show her what was funny to a man firmly in the grip of middle age, she was still bent sideways in her seat, so that her face fell below the line of the table, and he could only see the curve of her heaving back, the fuzzy penumbra of her thin spring sweater, and the garish top of her bright, new, and terrible hair.

1993

AMAHL AND THE NIGHT VISITORS: A GUIDE TO THE TENOR OF LOVE

11/30. UNDERSTAND THAT YOUR cat is a whore and can't help you. She takes on love with the whiskery adjustments of a gold-digger. She is a gorgeous nomad, an unfriend. Recall how just last month when you got her from Bob downstairs, after Bob had become suddenly allergic, she leaped into your lap and purred, guttural as a German chanteuse, familiar and furry as a mold. And Bob, visibly heartbroken, still in the room, sneezing and giving instructions, hoping for one last cat nuzzle, descended to his hands and knees and jiggled his fingers in the shag. The cat only blinked. For you, however, she smiled, gave a fish-breath peep, and settled.

"Oh, well," said Bob, getting up off the floor. "Now I'm just a thing of her kittenish past."

That's the way with Bob. He'll say to the cat, "You be a good girl now, honey," and then just shrug, go back downstairs to his apartment, play jagged, creepy jazz, drink wine, stare out at the wintry scalp of the mountain.

12/1. Moss Watson, the man you truly love like no other, is singing December 23 in the Owonta Opera production of *Amahl and the Night Visitors*. He's playing Kaspar, the partially deaf Wise Man. Wisdom, says Moss, arrives in all forms. And you think, Yes, sometimes as a king and sometimes as a hesitant phone call that says the king'll be late at rehearsal don't wait up, and then when you call back to tell him to be careful not to let the cat out when he comes home, you discover there's been no rehearsal there at all.

At three o'clock in the morning you hear his car in the driveway, the thud of the front door. When he comes into the bedroom, you see his huge height framed for a minute in the doorway, his hair lit bright as curry. When he stoops to take off his shoes, it is as if some small piece of his back has given way, allowing him this one slow bend. He is quiet. When he gets into bed he kisses one of your shoulders, then pulls the covers up to his chin. He knows you're awake. "I'm tired," he announces softly, to ward you off when you roll toward him. Say: "You didn't let the cat out, did you?"

He says no, but he probably should have. "You're turning into a cat mom. Cats, Trudy, are the worst sort of surrogates."

Tell him you've always wanted to run off and join the surrogates.

Tell him you love him.

Tell him you know he didn't have rehearsal tonight.

"We decided to hold rehearsal at the Montessori school, what are you now, *my* mother?"

In the dark, discern the fine hook of his nose. Smooth the hair off his forehead. Say: "I love you Moss are you having an affair with a sheep?" You saw a movie once where a man was having an affair with a sheep, and acted, with his girlfriend, the way Moss now acts with you: exhausted.

Moss's eyes close. "I'm a king, not a shepherd, remember? You're acting like my ex-wife."

His ex-wife is now an anchorwoman in Missouri.

"Are you having a regular affair? Like with a person?"

"Trudy," he sighs, turns away from you, taking more than his share of blanket. "You've got to stop this." Know you are being silly. Any second now he will turn and press against you, reassure you with kisses, tell you oh how much he loves you. "How on earth, Trudy," is what he finally says, "would I ever have the time for an affair?"

12/2. Your cat is growing, eats huge and sloppy as a racehorse. Bob named her Stardust Sweetheart, a bit much even for Bob, so you and Moss think up other names for her: Pudge, Pudgemuffin, Pooch, Poopster, Secretariat, Stephanie, Emily. Call her all of them. "She has to learn how to deal with confusion," says Moss. "And we've gotta start letting her outside."

Say: "No. She's still too little. Something could happen." Pick her up and away from Moss. Bring her into the bathroom with you. Hold her up to the mirror. Say: "Whossat? Whossat pretty kitty?" Wonder if you could turn into Bob.

12/3. Sometimes Moss has to rehearse in the living room. King Kaspar has a large black jewelry box about which he must sing to the young, enthralled Amahl. He must open drawers and haul out beads, licorice, magic stones. The drawers, however, keep jamming when they're not supposed to. Moss finally tears off his fake beard and screams, "I can't do this shit! I can't sing about money and gewgaws. I'm the tenor of love!" Last year they'd done *La Bohème* and Moss had been Rodolfo.

This is the sort of thing he needs you for: to help him with his box. Kneel down beside him. Show him how one of the drawers is off its runner. Show him how to pull it out just so far. He smiles and thanks you in his berserk King Kaspar voice: "Oh, thank you, thank you, thank you!" He begins his aria again: " 'This is my box. This is my box. I never travel without my box.' "

All singing is, says Moss, is sculpted howling.

Say, "Bye." Wheel the TV into the kitchen. Watch MacNeil-Lehrer. Worry about Congress.

Listen to the goose-call of trains, all night, trundling by your house.

12/4. Sometimes the phone rings, but then the caller hangs up.

12/5. Your cat now sticks her paws right in the water dish while she drinks, then steps out from her short wade and licks them, washes her face with them, repeatedly, over the ears and down, like an itch. Take to observing her. On her feet the gray and pink configurations of pads and fur look like tiny baboon faces. She sees you watching, freezes, blinks at you, then busies herself again, her face in her belly, one leg up at a time, an intent ballerina in a hairy body stocking. And yet she's growing so quickly, she's clumsy. She'll walk along and suddenly her hip will fly out of whack and she'll stop and look at it, not comprehending. Or her feet will stumble, or it's difficult for her to move her new bulk along the edges of furniture, her body pushing itself out into the world before she's really ready. It puts a dent in her confidence. She looks at you inquiringly: *What is happening to me?* She rubs against your ankles and bleats. You pick her up, tuck her under your chin, your teeth clenched in love, your voice cooey, gooey with maternity, you say things like, "How's my little dirt-nose, my little fuzz-face, my little honey-head?"

"Jesus, Trudy," Moss yells from the next room. "Listen to how you talk to that cat."

12/6. Though the Christmas shopping season is under way, the store you work at downtown, Owonta Flair, is not doing well. "The malls," groans Morgan, your boss. "Every Christmas the malls! We're doomed. These candy cane slippers. What am I gonna do with these?"

Tell her to put one slipper from each pair in the window along with a mammoth sign that says, MATES INSIDE. "People only see the sign. Thom McAn did it once. They got hordes."

"You're depressed," says Morgan.

12/7. You and Moss invite the principals, except Amahl, over to dinner one night before a rehearsal. You also invite Bob. Three kings, Amahl's unwed mother, you, and Bob: this way four people can tell cranky anecdotes about the production, and two people can listen.

"This really is a trashy opera," says Sonia, who plays Amahl's mother. "Sentimental as all get-out." Sonia is everything you've always wanted to be: smart, Jewish, friendly, full-haired as Easter basket grass. She speaks with a mouthful of your spinach pie. She says she likes it. When she has swallowed, a piece of spinach remains behind, wrapped like a gap around one of her front teeth. Other than that she is very beautiful. Nobody says anything about the spinach on her tooth.

Two rooms away the cat is playing with a marble in the empty bathtub. This is one of her favorite games. She bats the marble and it speeds around the porcelain like a stock car. The noise is rattley, continuous.

"What is that weird noise?" asks Sonia.

"It's the beast," says Moss. "We should put her outside, Trudy." He pours Sonia more wine, and she murmurs, "Thanks."

Jump up. Say: "I'll go take the marble away."

Behind you you can hear Bob: "She used to be mine. Her name is Stardust Sweetheart. I got allergic."

Melchior shouts after you: "Aw, leave the cat alone, Trudy. Let her have some fun." But you go into the bathroom and take the marble away anyhow. Your cat looks up at you from the tub, her head cocked to one side, sweet and puzzled as a child movie star. Then she turns and bats drips from the faucet. Scratch the scruff of her neck. Close the door when you leave. Put the marble in your pocket.

You can hear Balthazar making jokes about the opera. He calls it *Amyl and the Nitrates.*

"I've always found Menotti insipid," Melchior is saying when you return to the dining room.

"Written for NBC, what can you expect," Sonia says. Soon she is off raving about *La Bohème* and other operas. She uses words like *verismo*, *messa di voce*, Montserrat Caballe. She smiles. "An opera should be like contraception: about *sex*, *not* children."

Start clearing the plates. Tell people to keep their forks for dessert. Tell them that no matter what anyone says, you think *Amahl* is a beautiful opera and that the ending, when the mother sends her son off with the kings, always makes you cry. Moss gives you a wink. Get brave. Give your head a toss. Add: "Papage*no*, Papage*na* – to me, *La Bohème*'s just a lot of scarves."

There is some gulping of wine.

Only Bob looks at you and smiles. "Here. I'll help you with the plates," he says.

Moss stands and makes a diversionary announcement: "Sonia, you've got a piece of spinach on your tooth."

"Christ," she says, and her tongue tunnels beneath her lip like an elegant gopher.

12/8. Sometimes still Moss likes to take candlelight showers with you. You usually have ten minutes before the hot water runs out. Soap his back, the wide moguls of his shoulders registering in you like a hunger. Press yourself against him. Whisper: "I really do like *La Bohème*, you know."

"It's okay," Moss says, all forgiveness. He turns and grabs your buttocks.

"It's just that your friends make me nervous. Maybe it's work, Morgan that forty-watt hysteric making me crazy." Actually you like Morgan.

Begin to hum a Dionne Warwick song, then grow self-conscious and stop. Moss doesn't like to sing in the shower. He has his operas, his church jobs, his weddings and bar mitzvahs – in the shower he is strictly off-duty. Say: "I mean, it *could* be Morgan."

Moss raises his head up under the spray, beatific, absent. His hair slicks back, like a baby's or a gangster's, dark with water, shiny as a record album. "Does Bob make you nervous?" he asks.

"Bob? Bob suffers from terminal sweetness. I like Bob."

"So do I. He's a real gem."

Say: "Yeah, he's a real chum."

"I said *gem*," says Moss. "Not *chum*." Things fall quiet. Lately you've been mishearing each other. Last night in bed you said, "Moss, I usually don't like discussing sex, but—" And he said, "I don't like disgusting sex either." And then he fell asleep, his snores scratching in the dark like zombies.

Take turns rinsing. Don't tell him he's hogging the water. Ask finally, "Do you think Bob's gay?"

"Of course he's gay."

"How do you know?"

"Oh, I don't know. He hangs out at Sammy's in the mall."

"Is that a gay bar?"

"Bit of everything." Moss shrugs.

Think: Bit of everything. Just like a mall. "Have you ever been there?" Scrub vigorously between your breasts.

"A few times," says Moss, the water growing cooler.

Say: "Oh." Then turn off the faucet, step out onto the bath mat. Hand Moss a towel. "I guess because I work trying to revive our poor struggling downtown I don't get out to these places much."

"I guess not," says Moss, candle shadows wobbling on the shower curtain.

12/9. Two years ago when Moss first moved in, there was something exciting about getting up in the morning. You would rise, dress, and, knowing your lover was asleep in your bed, drive out into the early morning office and factory traffic, feeling that you possessed all things, Your Man, like a Patsy Cline song, at home beneath your covers, pumping blood through your day like a heart.

Now you have a morbid fascination with news shows. You get up, dress, flick on the TV, sit in front of it with a bowl of cereal in your lap, quietly curse all governments everywhere, get into your car, drive to work, wonder how the sun has the nerve to show its face, wonder why the world seems to be picking up speed, even old ladies pass you on the highway, why you don't have a single erotic fantasy that Moss isn't in, whether there really are such things as vitamins, and how would you rather die cancer or a car accident, the man you love, at home, asleep, like a heavy, heavy heart through your day.

"Goddamn slippers," says Morgan at work.

* * *

12/10. The cat now likes to climb into the bathtub and stand under the dripping faucet in order to clean herself. She lets the water bead up on her face, then wipes herself, neatly dislodging the gunk from her eyes.

"Isn't she wonderful?" you ask Moss.

"Yeah. Come here you little scumbucket," he says, slapping the cat on the haunches, as if she were a dog.

"She's not a dog, Moss. She's a cat."

"That's right. She's a cat. Remember that, Trudy."

12/11. The phone again. The ringing and hanging up.

12/12. Moss is still getting in very late. He goes about the business of fondling you, like someone very tired at night having to put out the trash and bolt-lock the door.

He sleeps with his arms folded behind his head, elbows protruding, treacherous as daggers, like the enemy chariot in *Ben-Hur*.

12/13. Buy a Christmas tree, decorations, a stand, and lug them home to assemble for Moss. Show him your surprise.

"Why are the lights all in a clump in the back?" he asks, closing the front door behind him.

Say: "I know. Aren't they great? Wait till you see me do the tinsel." Place handfuls of silver icicles, matted together like alfalfa sprouts, at the end of all the branches.

"Very cute," says Moss, kissing you, then letting go. Follow him into the bathroom. Ask how rehearsal went. He points to the kitty litter and sings: "'This is my box. I never travel without my box.'"

Say: "You are not a well man, Moss." Play with his belt loops.

12/14. The white fur around the cat's neck is growing and looks like a stiff Jacobean collar. "A rabato," says Moss, who suddenly seems to know these things. "When are we going to let her go outside?"

"Someday when she's older." The cat has lately taken to the front window the way a hypochondriac takes to a bed. When she's there she's more interested in the cars, the burled fingers of the trees, the occasional squirrel, the train tracks like long fallen ladders, than she is in you. Call her: "Here pootchy-kootchy-honey." Ply her, bribe her with food.

12/15. There are movies in town: one about Brazil, and one about sexual abandonment in upstate New York. "What do you say, Moss. Wanna go to the movies this weekend?"

"I can't," says Moss. "You know how busy I am."

12/16. The evening news is full of death: young marines, young mothers, young children. By comparison you have already lived forever. In a kind of heaven.

12/17. Give your cat a potato and let her dribble it about soccer-style. She's getting more coordinated, conducts little dramas with the potato, pretends to have conquered it, strolls over it, then somersaults back after it again. She's not bombing around, crashing into the sideboards anymore. She's learning moves. She watches the potato by the dresser leg, stalks it, then pounces. When she gets bored she climbs up onto the sill and looks out, tail switching. Other cats have spotted her now, have started coming around at night. Though she will want to go, do not let her out the front door.

12/18. The phone rings. You say hello, and the caller hangs up. Two minutes later it rings again, only this time Moss answers it in the next room, speaks softly, cryptically, not the hearty phone voice of the Moss of yesteryear. When he hangs up, wander in and say, blasé as paste, "So, who was that?"

"Stop," says Moss. "Just stop."

Ask him what's the big deal, it was Sonia wasn't it.

"Stop," says Moss. "You're being my wife. Things are repeating themselves."

Say that nothing repeats itself. Nothing, nothing, nothing. "Sonia, right?"

"Trudy, you've got to stop this. You've been listening to too much *Tosca*. I'm going out to get a hamburger. Do you want anything?"

Say: "I'm the only person in the whole world who knows you, Moss. And I don't know you at all anymore."

"That's a different opera," he says. "I'm going out to get a hamburger. Do you want anything?"

Do not cry. Stick to monosyllables. Say: "No. Fine. Go."

Say: "Please don't let the cat out."

Say: "You should wear a hat it's cold."

12/19. Actually what you've been listening to is Dionne Warwick's Golden Hits – musical open heart surgery enough for you. Sometimes you pick up the cat and waltz her around, her purr staticky and intermittent as a walkie-talkie.

On "Do You Know the Way to San Jose," you put her down, do an unfortunate charleston, while she attacks your stockinged feet, thinking them large rodents.

Sometimes you knock into the Christmas tree.

Sometimes you collapse into a chair and convince yourself that things are still okay.

When Robert MacNeil talks about mounting inflation, you imagine him checking into a motel room with a life-size, blow-up doll. This is, once in a while, how you amuse yourself.

When Moss gets in at four in the morning, whisper: "There are lots of people in this world, Moss, but you can't be in love with them all."

"I'm not," he says, "in love with the mall."

* * *

12/20. The mall stores stay open late this last week before Christmas. Moss is supposed to be there, "in the gazebo next to the Santa gazebo," for an *Amahl and the Night Visitors* promotional. Decide to drive up there. Perhaps you can look around in the men's shops for a sweater for Moss, perhaps even one for Bob as well. Last year was a bad Christmas: you and Moss returned each other's gifts for cash. You want to do better this year. You want to buy: sweaters.

The mall parking lot, even at 7 p.m., is, as Moss would say, packed as a bag, though you do manage to find a space.

Inside the mall entranceway it smells of stale popcorn, dry heat, and three-day-old hobo urine. A drunk, slumped by the door, smiles and toasts you with nothing.

Say: "Cheers."

To make your journey down to the gazebos at the other end of the mall, first duck into all the single-item shops along the way. Compare prices with the prices at Owonta Flair: things are a little cheaper here. Buy stuff, mostly for Moss and the cat.

In the pet food store the cashier hands you your bagged purchase, smiles, and says, "Merry Christmas."

Say: "You, too."

In the men's sweater shop the cashier hands you your bagged purchase, smiles, and says, "Merry Christmas."

Say: "You, too."

In the belt shop the cashier hands you your bagged purchase, smiles, and says, "Come again."

Say: "You, too." Grow warm. Narrow your eyes to seeds.

In the gazebo next to the Santa gazebo there is only an older man in gray coveralls stacking some folding chairs.

Say: "Excuse me, wasn't *Amahl and the Night Visitors* supposed to be here?"

The man stops for a moment. "There's visitors," he says, pointing out and around, past the gazebo to all the shoppers. Shoppers in parkas. Shoppers moving slow as winter. Shoppers who haven't seen a crosswalk or a window in hours.

"I mean the opera promotional."

"The singers?" He looks at his watch. "They packed it in a while ago."

Say thank you, and wander over to Cinema 1-2-3 to read the movie posters. It's when you turn to go that you see Moss and Bob coming out together from the bar by the theater. They look tired.

Adjust your packages. Walk over. Say: "Hi. I guess I missed the promo, so I was thinking of going to a movie."

"We ended it early," says Moss. "Sonia wasn't feeling well. Bob and I just went into Sammy's for a drink."

Look and see the sign that, of course, reads SAMMY'S.

Bob smiles and says, "Hello, Trudy." Because Bob says *hello* and never *hi*, he always manages to sound a little like Mister Rogers.

You can see some of Moss's makeup and glue lines. His fake beard is sticking out from his coat pocket. Smile. Say: "Well, Moss. Here all along I thought it was Sonia, and it's really Bob." Chuck him under the chin. Keep your smile steady. You are the only one smiling. Not even Bob. You have clearly said the wrong thing.

"Fuck off, Trudy," Moss says finally, palming his hair back off his forehead.

Bob squirms in his coat. "I believe I forgot something," he says. "I'll see you both later." And he touches Moss's arm, turns, disappears back inside Sammy's.

"Jesus Christ, Trudy." Moss's voice suddenly booms through the mall. You can see a few stores closing up, men coming out to lower the metal night gates. Santa Claus has gotten down from the gazebo and is eating an egg roll.

Moss turns from you, charges toward the exit, an angry giant with a beard sticking out of his coat pocket. Run after him and grab his sleeve, make him stop. Say: "I'm sorry, Moss. What am I doing? Tell me. What am I doing wrong?" You look up at his face, with the orange and brown lines and the glue patches, and realize: He doesn't understand you've planned your lives together. That you have even planned your deaths together, not really deaths at all but more like a *pas de deux*. Like Gene Kelly and Leslie Caron in *An American in Paris*, only older.

"You just won't let people be," says Moss, each consonant spit like a fish bone.

Say: "People be? I don't understand. Moss, what is happening to us?" You want to help him, rescue him, build houses and magnificent lawns around him.

"To *us*?"

Moss's voice is loud. He puts on his gloves. He tells you you are a child. He needs to get away. For him you have managed to reduce love, like weather, to a map and a girl, and he needs to get away from you, live someplace else for a while, and think.

The bag with the cat food slips and falls. "The opera's in three days, Moss. Where are you going to go?"

"Right now," he says, "I'm going to get a hamburger." And he storms toward the mall doors, pushes against all of them until he finds the one that's open.

Stare and mumble at the theater candy concession. "Good and Plenty. There's no Good and Plenty." Your bangs droop into your vision. You keep hearing "Jingle Bells," over and over.

In the downtown theaters of your childhood, everything was made of carved wood, and in the ladies' rooms there were framed photographs of Elizabeth Taylor and Ava Gardner. The theaters had names: The Rialto, The Paramount. There were ushers and Good and Plenty. Ushers with flashlights and bow ties. That's the difference now. No ushers. Now you have to do everything by yourself.

"Trudy," says a voice behind you. "Would you like to be accompanied to the movies?" The passive voice. It's Bob's. Turn to look at him, but as with the Good and Plenty, you don't really see, everything around you vague and blurry as glop in your eye.

Say: "Sure. Why not."

In Cinema 3, sit in seats close to the aisle. Listen to the Muzak. The air smells like airplane air.

"It's a strange thing about Moss," Bob is saying, looking

straight ahead. "He's so busy with the opera, it pushes him up against certain things. He ends up feeling restless and smothered. But, Trudy, Moss is a good man. He really is."

Don't say anything, and then say, finally, "Moss who?"

Stare at the curtain with the rose-tinted lights on it. Try to concentrate on more important matters, things like acid rain.

Bob taps his fingers on the metal arm of the seat. Say: "Look, Bob. I'm no idiot. I was born in New York City. I lived there until I was four. Come on. Tell me: Who's Moss sleeping with?"

"As far as I know," says Bob, sure and serious as a tested hypothesis, "Moss isn't sleeping with anyone."

Continue staring at the rose lights. Then say in a loud contralto: "He's sleeping with *me*, Bob. That's who he's sleeping with."

When the lights dim and the curtains part, there arrive little cigarette lighters on the screen telling you not to smoke. Then there are coming attractions. Bob leans toward you, says, "These previews are horrible."

Say: "Yeah. Nothing Coming Soon."

There are so many previews you forget what movie you've come to see. When the feature presentation comes on, it takes you by surprise. The images melt together like a headache. The movie seems to be about a woman whose lover, losing interest in her, has begun to do inexplicable things like yell about the cat, and throw scenes in shopping malls.

"What is this movie about?"

"Brazil," whispers Bob.

The audience has begun to laugh at something someone is doing; you are tense with comic exile. Whisper: "Bob, I'm gonna go. Wanna go?"

"Yes, in fact, I do," says Bob.

It's ten-thirty and cold. The mall stores are finally closed. In the parking lot, cars are leaving. Say to Bob: "God, look how many people shop here." The whole world suddenly seems to you like a downtown dying slow.

Spot your car and begin to head toward it. Bob catches

your sleeve. "My car's the other way. Listen. Trudy. About Moss: No matter what's going on with him, no matter what he decides he has to do, the man loves you. I know he does."

Gently pull your sleeve away. Take a step sideways toward your car. Headlights, everywhere headlights and tires crunching. Say: "Bob, you're a sweet person. But you're sentimental as all get-out." Turn on the nail of your boot and walk.

At home the cat refuses to dance to Dionne Warwick with you. She sits on the sill of the window, rumbling in her throat, her tail a pendulum of fluff. Outside, undoubtedly, there are suitors, begging her not to be so cold-hearted. "Ya got friends out there?" When you turn off the stereo, she jumps down from the sill and snakes lovingly about your ankles. Say something you never thought you'd say. Say: "Wanna go out?" She looks at you, all hope and supplication, and follows you to the door, carefully watching your hand as it moves for the knob: she wants you to let her go, to let her go and be. Begin slowly, turn, pull. The suction of door and frame gives way, and the cold night insinuates itself like a kind of future. She doesn't leave immediately. But her whole body is electrified, surveying the yard for eyes and rustles, and just to the left of the streetlight she suddenly spots them – four, five, phosphorescent glints – and, without a nudge, without ever looking back, she scurries out, off the porch, down after, into some sweet unknown, some somehow known unknown, some yet very old religion.

12/21. Every adoration is seasonal as Christmas.

Moss stops by to get some things. He's staying with Balthazar for a few days, then after the opera and Christmas and all, he'll look for an efficiency somewhere.

Nod. "Efficiency. Great. That's what hell is: efficient." You want to ask him if this is all some silly opera where he's leaving in order to spare you his tragic, bluish death by consumption.

He says, "It's just something I've got to do." He opens

cupboards in the kitchen, closets in the hallway, pulls down boxes, cups, boots. He is slow about it, doesn't do it in a mean way, you are grateful for that.

"What have you been doing tonight?" he asks, not looking, but his voice is urgent as a touch.

"I watched two hours of MacNeil-Lehrer. You can get it on channel seven and then later on channel four."

"Right," says Moss. "I know."

Pause. Then say: "Last night I let the cat out. Finally."

Moss looks at you and smiles.

Smile back and shrug, as if all the world were a comedy you were only just now appreciating. Moss begins to put a hand to your shoulder but then takes it back. "Congratulations, Trudy," he murmurs.

"But she hasn't come back yet. I haven't seen her since last night."

"She'll come back," says Moss. "It's only been a day."

"But it's been a whole day. Maybe I should put in ads."

"It's only been one day. She'll come back. You'll see."

Step away from him. Outside, in front of the streetlight, something like snow is falling. Think back again to MacNeil-Lehrer. Say in a level tone: "You know, there are people who know more about it than we do, who say that there is no circumnavigating a nuclear war, we will certainly have one, it's just a matter of time. And when it happens, it's going to dissolve all our communications systems, melt silicon chips—"

"Trudy, please." He wants you to stop. He knows this edge in your voice, this MacNeil-Lehrer edge. All of the world knotted and failing on your tongue.

"And then if you're off living someplace else, in some efficiency, how will I be able to get in touch with you? There I'll be, Moss, all alone in my pink pom-pom slippers, the entire planet exploding all around, and I won't be able to talk to you, to say—" In fifth grade you learned the first words ever spoken on the telephone: *Mr. Watson, come here, I want you.* And suddenly, as you look at him, at the potatoey fists of his cheeks, at his broom-blonde hair, it hits you as it would a child: Someday, like everybody, this man you truly love like no other is going to die. No matter how much you love him, you cannot save him. No matter how much you love: nothing, no one, lasts.

"Moss, we're not safe."

And though there's no flutter of walls, or heave of the floor, above the frayed-as-panic rug, shoes move, and Moss seems to come unstuck, to float toward you, his features beginning to slide in downward diagonals, some chip in his back dissolving, allowing him to bend. His arms reach out to bring you close to his chest. The buttons of his shirt poke against you, and his chin hooks, locks around your neck. When he is gone, the world will grow dull as Mars.

"It's okay," he whispers, his lips moving against your hair. Things grow fuzzy around the edge like a less than brilliant lie. "It's okay," says Moss.

1984

BEAUTIFUL GRADE

IT'S A CHILLY NIGHT, bitter inside and out. After a grisly month-long court proceeding, Bill's good friend Albert has become single again – and characteristically curatorial: Albert has invited his friends over to his sublet to celebrate New Year's Eve and watch his nuptial and postnuptial videos, which Albert has hauled down from the bookcase and proffered with ironic wonder and glee. At each of his three weddings, Albert's elderly mother had videotaped the ceremony, and at the crucial moment in the vows, each time, Albert's face turns impishly from his bride, looks straight into his mother's camera, and says, "I do. I swear I do." The divorce proceedings, by contrast, are mute, herky-jerky, and badly lit ("A clerk," says Albert): there are wan smiles, business suits, the waving of a pen.

At the end, Albert's guests clap. Bill puts his fingers in his mouth and whistles shrilly (not every man can do this; Bill himself didn't learn until college, though already that was thirty years ago; three decades of ear-piercing whistling – youth shall not be wasted on the young). Albert nods, snaps the tapes back into their plastic cases, turns on the lights, and sighs.

"No more weddings," Albert announces. "No more divorces. No more wasting time. From here on in, I'm just going to go out there, find a woman I really don't like very much, and give her a house."

Bill, divorced only once, is here tonight with Debbie, a woman who is too young for him: at least that is what he knows is said, though the next time it is said to his face, Bill will shout, "I beg your pardon!" Maybe not shout. Maybe squeak. Squeak with a dash of begging. Then he'll just hurl himself to the ground and plead for a quick stoning. For now, this second, however, he will pretend to a braver, more evolved heart, explaining to anyone who might ask how much easier it would be to venture out still with his ex-wife, someone his own age, but no, not Bill, not big brave Bill: Bill has entered something complex, spiritually biracial, politically tricky, and, truth be told, physically demanding. Youth will not be wasted on the young.

Who the hell is that?

She looks fourteen!

You can't be serious!

Bill has had to drink more than usual. He has had to admit to himself that on his own, without any wine, he doesn't have a shred of the courage necessary for this romance.

("Not to pry, Bill, or ply you with feminist considerations, but, excuse me – you're dating a twenty-five-year-old?"

"Twenty-four," he says. "But you were close!")

His women friends have yelled at him – or sort of yelled. It's really been more of a cross between sighing and giggling. "Don't be cruel," Bill has had to say.

Albert has been kinder, more delicate, in tone if not in substance. "*Some* people might consider your involvement with this girl a misuse of your charm," he said slowly.

"But I've worked hard for this charm," said Bill. "Believe me, I started from scratch. Can't I do with it what I want?"

Albert sized up Bill's weight loss and slight tan, the sprinkle of freckles like berry seeds across Bill's arms, the summer whites worn way past Labor Day in the law school's cavernous, crowded lecture halls, and he said, "Well then, *some* people might think it a mishandling of your position." He paused, put his arm around Bill. "But hey, I think it has made you look very – tennisy."

Bill shoved his hands in his pockets. "You mean the whole kindness of strangers thing?"

Albert took his arm back. "What are you talking about?" he asked, and then his face fell in a kind of melting, concerned way. "Oh, you poor thing," he said. "You poor, poor thing."

Bill has protested, obfuscated, gone into hiding. But he is too tired to keep Debbie in the closet anymore. The body has only so many weeks of stage fright in it before it simply gives up and just goes out onstage. Moreover, this semester Debbie is no longer taking either of his Constitutional Law classes. She is no longer, between weekly lectures, at home in his bed, with a rented movie, saying things that are supposed to make him laugh, things like "Open up, doll. Is that drool?" and "Don't you dare think I'm doing this for a good grade. I'm doing this for a *beautiful* grade." Debbie no longer performs her remarks at him, which he misses a little, all that effort and desire. "If I'm just a passing fancy, then I want to pass fancy," she once said. Also, "Law school: It's the film school of the nineties."

Debbie is no longer a student of his in any way, so at last their appearance together is only unattractive and self-conscious-making but not illegal. Bill can show up with her for dinner. He can live in the present, his newly favorite tense.

But he must remember who is here at this party, people for whom history, acquired knowledge, the accumulation of days and years is everything – or is this simply the convenient shorthand of his own paranoia? There is Albert, with his videos; Albert's old friend Brigitte, a Berlin-born political scientist; Stanley Mix, off every other semester to fly to Japan and study the zoological effects of radiation at Hiroshima and Nagasaki; Stanley's wife, Roberta, a travel agent and obsessive tabulator of Stanley's frequent flyer miles (Bill has often admired her posters: STEP BACK IN TIME, COME TO ARGENTINA says the one on her door); Lina, a pretty visiting Serb teaching in Slavic Studies; and Lina's doctor husband, Jack, a Texan who five years ago in Yugoslavia put Dallas dirt under the laboring Lina's hospital bed so that his son could be "born on Texan soil." ("But the boy is a total *sairb*," Lina says of her son, rolling her lovely *r*'s. "Just don't tell Jack.")

Lina.

Lina, Lina.

Bill is a little taken with Lina.

"You are with Debbie because somewhere in your pahst ease some pretty leetle girl who went away from you," Lina said to him once on the phone.

"Or, how about because everyone else I know is married."

"Ha!" she said. "You only believe they are married."

Which sounded, to Bill, like the late-night, adult version

of *Peter Pan* – no Mary Martin, no songs, just a lot of wishing and thinking lovely thoughts; then afterward all the participants throw themselves out the window.

And never, never land?

Marriage, Bill thinks: *it*'s the film school of the nineties.

Truth be told, Bill is a little afraid of suicide. Taking one's life, he thinks, has too many glitzy things to offer: a real edge on the narrative (albeit retrospectively), a disproportionate philosophical advantage (though again, retrospectively), the last word, the final cut, the parting shot. Most importantly, it gets you the hell out of there, wherever it is you are, and he can see how such a thing might happen in a weak but brilliant moment, one you might just regret later while looking down from the depthless sky or up through two sandy anthills and some weeds.

Still, Lina is the one he finds himself thinking about, and carefully dressing for in the morning – removing all dry-cleaning tags and matching his socks.

Albert leads them all into the dining room and everyone drifts around the large teak table, studying the busily constructed salads at each place setting – salads, which, with their knobs of cheese, jutting chives, and little folios of frisée, resemble small Easter hats.

"Do we wear these or eat them?" asks Jack. In his mouth is a piece of gray chewing gum like a rat's brain.

"I admire gay people," Bill's voice booms. "To have the courage to love whom you want to love in the face of all bigotry."

"Relax," Debbie murmurs, nudging him. "It's only salad."

Albert indicates in a general way where they should sit, alternating male, female, like the names of hurricanes, though such seating leaves all the couples split and far apart, on New Year's Eve no less, as Bill suspects Albert wants it.

"Don't sit next to him – he bites," says Bill to Lina as she takes a place next to Albert.

"Six degrees of separation," says Debbie. "Do you believe

that thing about how everyone is separated by only six people?"

"Oh, *we*'re separated by at least six, aren't we, darling?" says Lina to her husband.

"At least."

"No, I mean by *only* six," says Debbie. "I mean strangers." But no one is listening to her.

"This is a political New Year's Eve," says Albert. "We're here to protest the new year, protest the old; generally get a petition going to Father Time. But also eat: in China it's the Year of the Pig."

"Ah, one of those years of the Pig," says Stanley. "I love those."

Bill puts salt on his salad, then looks up apologetically. "I salt everything," he says, "so it can't get away."

Albert brings out salmon steaks and distributes them with Brigitte's help. Ever since Albert was denied promotion to full-professor rank, his articles on Flannery O'Connor ("A Good Man Really *Is* Hard to Find," "Everything That Rises *Must Indeed* Converge," and "The Totemic South: The Violent *Actually Do* Bear It Away!") failing to meet with collegial acclaim, he has become determined to serve others, passing out the notices and memoranda, arranging the punch and cookies at various receptions. He has not yet become very good at it, however, but the effort touches and endears. Now everyone sits with their hands in their laps, leaning back when plates are set before them. When Albert sits down, they begin to eat.

"You know, in Yugoslavia," says Jack, chewing, "a person goes to school for four years to become a waiter. Four years of waiter school."

"Typical Yugoslavians," adds Lina. "They have to go to school for four years to learn how to serve someone."

"I'll bet they do it well," Bill says stupidly. Everyone ignores him, for which he is grateful. His fish smells fishier than the others – he is sure of it. Perhaps he has been poisoned.

"Did you hear about that poor Japanese foreign student who stopped to ask directions and was shot because he was thought to be an intruder?" This is Debbie, dear Debbie. How did she land on this?

"Oh, God, I know. Wasn't that terrible?" says Brigitte.

"A shooting like that really makes a lot of sense, too," says Bill, "when you think about how the Japanese are particularly known for their street crime." Lina chortles and Bill pokes at his fish a little.

"I guess the man thought the student was going to come in and reprogram his computer," says Jack, and everyone laughs.

"Now is that racist?" asks Bill.

"Is it?"

"Maybe."

"I don't think so."

"Not in any real way."

"It's just us."

"What's that supposed to mean?"

"Would anyone like more food?"

"So Stanley," says Lina. "How is the research going?"

Is this absent querying or pointed interrogation? Bill can't tell. The last time they were all together, they got into a terrible discussion about World War II. World War II is not necessarily a good topic of conversation generally, and among the eight of them, it became a total hash. Stanley yelled, Lina threatened to leave, and Brigitte broke down over dessert: "I was a little girl; I was there," Brigitte said of Berlin.

Lina, whose three uncles, she'd once told Bill, had been bayoneted by Nazis, sighed and looked off at the wallpaper – wide pale stripes like pajamas. It was impossible to eat.

Brigitte looked accusingly at everyone, her face swelling like a baked apple. Tears leaked out of her eyes. "They did not have to bomb like that. Not like that. They did not have to bomb so much," and then she began to sob, then choke back sobs, and then just choke.

It had been a shock to Bill. For years, Brigitte had been the subject of his skeptical, private jokes with Albert. They would make up fake titles for her books on European history: *That*

Kooky Führer and *Hitler: What a Nutroll!* But that evening, Brigitte's tears were so bitter and full, after so many years, that it haunted and startled him. What did it mean to cry like that – *at dinner?* He had never known a war in that way or ever, really. He had never even known a dinner in that way.

"Fine," says Stanley to Lina. "Great, really. I'm going back next month. The small-head-size data is the most interesting and conclusive thus far." He chews his fish. "If I got paid by the word, I'd be a rich man." He has the supple, overconfident voice of a panelist from the Texaco Opera Quiz.

"Jack here gets paid by the word," says Bill, "and that word is *Next?*" Perhaps Bill could adroitly switch the subject away from nuclear devastation and steer it toward national health plans. Would that be an improvement? He remembers once asking Lina what kind of medicine Jack practiced. "Oh, he's a gynecological surgeon," she said dismissively. "Something to do with things dropping into the vagina." She gave a shudder. "I don't like to think about it."

Things dropping into the vagina. The word *things* had for some reason made Bill think of tables and chairs, or, even more glamorously, pianos and chandeliers, and he has now come to see Jack as a kind of professional mover: the Allied Van Lines of the OB-GYN set.

"After all this time, Bill is still skeptical about doctors," Jack now says.

"I can see that," says Stanley.

"I once had the wrong tonsil removed," says Bill.

"Are you finding a difference between Hiroshima and Nagasaki?" persists Lina.

Stanley turns and looks at her. "That's interesting that you should ask that. You know, Hiroshima was a uranium bomb and Nagasaki a plutonium. And the fact is, we're finding more damaging results from the uranium."

Lina gasps and puts down her fork. She turns and looks in an alarmed way at Stanley, studying, it seems, the condition of his face, the green-brown shrapnel of his dried acne cysts, like lentils buried in the skin.

"They used two different kinds of bombs?" she says.

"That's right," says Stanley.

"You mean, all along, right from the start, this was just an experiment? They designed it explicitly right from the beginning, as *something to study*?" Blood has rushed to her face.

Stanley grows a little defensive. He is, after all, one of the studiers. He shifts in his chair. "There are some very good books written on the subject. If you don't understand what happened regarding Japan during World War Two, you would be well advised to read a couple of them."

"Oh, I see. Then we could have a better conversation," says Lina. She turns away from Stanley and looks at Albert.

"Children, children," murmurs Albert.

"World War Two," says Debbie. "Wasn't that the war to end all wars?"

"No, that was World War One," says Bill. "By World War Two, they weren't making any promises."

Stanley will not relent. He turns to Lina again. "I have to say, I'm surprised to see a Serbian, in a matter of foreign policy, attempting to take the moral high ground," he says.

"Stanley, I used to like you," says Lina. "Remember when you were a nice guy? I do."

"I do, too," says Bill. "There was that whole smiling, handing-out-money thing he used to do."

Bill feels inclined to rescue Lina. This year, she has been through a lot. Just last spring, the local radio station put her on a talk show and made her answer questions about Bosnia. In attempting to explain what was going on in the former Yugoslavia, she said, "You have to think about what it might mean for Europe to have a nationalist, Islamic state," and "Those fascist Croats," and "It's all very complicated." The next day, students boycotted her classes and picketed her office with signs that read GENOCIDE IS NOT 'COMPLICATED' and REPENT, IMPERIALIST. Lina had phoned Bill at his office. "You're a lawyer. They're hounding me. Aren't these students breaking a law? Surely, Bill, they are breaking a law."

"Not really," said Bill. "And believe me, you wouldn't want to live in a country where they were."

"Can't I get a motion to strike? What is that? I like the way it sounds."

"That's used in pleadings or in court. That's not what you want."

"No, I guess not. From them, I just want no more motion. Plus, I want to strike them. There's nothing you can do?"

"They have their rights."

"They understand nothing," she said.

"Are you okay?"

"No. I banged up the fender parking my car, I was so upset. The headlight fell out, and even though I took it into the car place, they couldn't salvage it."

"You've gotta keep those things packed in ice, I think."

"These *cheeldren*, good God, have no conception of the world. I am well known as a pacifist and resister; I was the one last year in Belgrade, buying gasoline out of Coke bottles, hiding a boy from the draft, helping to organize the protests and the radio broadcasts and the rock concerts. Not them. I was the one standing there with the crowd, clapping and chanting beneath Milosevic's window: 'Don't count on us.'" Here Lina's voice fell into a deep Slavic singsong. "Don't count on us. Don't count on us." She paused dramatically. "We had T-shirts and posters. That was no small thing."

"'Don't count on us?'" said Bill. "I don't mean to sound skeptical, but as a political slogan, it seems, I don't know, a little . . ." Lame. It lacked even the pouty energy and determination of "Hell no, we won't go." Perhaps some obscenity would have helped. "Don't fucking count on us, motherfucker." That would have been better. Certainly a better T-shirt.

"It was all very successful," said Lina indignantly.

"But how exactly do you measure success?" asked Bill. "I mean, it took time, but, you'll forgive me, we *stopped* the war in Vietnam."

"Oh, you are all so obsessed with your Vietnam," said Lina.

The next time Bill saw her, it was on her birthday, and she'd had three and a half whiskeys. She exclaimed loudly about the beauty of the cake, and then, taking a deep breath, she dropped her head too close to the candles and set her hair spectacularly on fire.

What does time measure but itself? What can it assess but the mere deposit and registration of itself within a thing?

A large bowl of peas and onions is passed around the table.

They've already dispensed with the O. J. Simpson jokes – the knock-knock one and the one about the sunglasses. They've banned all the others, though Bill is now asked his opinion regarding search and seizure. Ever since he began living in the present tense, Bill sees the Constitution as a blessedly changing thing. He does not feel current behavior should be made necessarily to conform to old law. He feels personally, for instance, that he'd throw away a few First Amendment privileges – abortion protest, say, and all telemarketing, perhaps some pornography (though not Miss April 1965 – never!) – in exchange for gutting the Second Amendment. The Founding Fathers were revolutionaries, after all. They would be with him on this, he feels. They would be for making the whole thing up as you go along, reacting to things as they happened, like a great, wild performance piece. "There's nothing sacred about the Constitution; it's just another figmentary contract: it's a palimpsest you can write and write and write on. But then whatever is there when you get pulled over are the rules for then. For now." Bill believes in free speech. He believes in expensive speech. He doesn't believe in shouting "Fire" in a crowded movie theater, but he does believe in shouting "Fie!" and has done it twice himself – both times at *Forrest Gump*. "I'm a big believer in the Rules for Now. Also, Promises for Now, Things to Do for Now, and the ever-handy This Will Do for Now."

Brigitte glares at him. "Such moral excellence," she says.

"Yes," agrees Roberta, who has been quiet all evening, probably figuring out airfare upgrades for Stanley. "How attractive."

"I'm talking theoretical," says Bill. "I believe in common sense. In theory. Theoretical common sense." He feels suddenly cornered and misunderstood. He wishes he weren't constantly asked to pronounce on real-life legal matters. He has never even tried an actual case except once, when he was just out of law school. He'd had a small practice then in the basement of an old sandstone schoolhouse in St. Paul, and the sign inside the building directory said WILLIAM D. BELMONT, ATTORNEY-AT-LAW: ONE LEVEL DOWN. It always broke his heart a little, that *one level down.* The only case he ever took to trial was an armed robbery and concealed weapon case, and he had panicked. He dressed in the exact same beiges and browns as the bailiffs – a subliminal strategy he felt would give him an edge, make him seem at least as much a part of the court "family" as the prosecutor. But by the close of the afternoon, his nerves were shot. He looked too desperately at the jury (who, once in the deliberation room, and in the time it took to order the pizza and wolf it down, voted unanimously to convict). He'd looked imploringly at all their little faces and said, "Ladies and gentlemen, if my client's not innocent, I'll eat my shorts."

At the end of his practice, he had taken to showing up at other people's office parties – not a good sign in life.

Now, equipped with a more advanced degree, like the other people here, Bill has a field of scholarly, hypothetical expertise, plus a small working knowledge of budgets and parking and E-mail. He doesn't mind the E-mail, has more or less gotten used to it, its vaguely smutty Etch-A-Sketch, though once he found himself lost in the Internet and before he knew it had written his name across some bulletin board on which the only other name was "Stud Boy." Mostly, however, his professional life has been safe and uneventful. Although he is bothered by faculty meetings and by the word *text* – every time he hears it, he feels he should just give up, go off and wear a powdered wig somewhere – it intrigues Bill to belong to academe, with its international hodgepodge and asexual attire, a place where to think and speak *as if* one has lived is always preferable to the alternatives. Such a value cuts down on regrets. And Bill is cutting down. He is determined to cut down. Once, he was called in by the head of the law school and admonished for skipping so many faculty meetings. "It's costing you about a thousand dollars in raises every year," said the dean.

"Really?" replied Bill, "Well, if that's all, it's worth every dime."

"Eat, eat," says Albert. He is bringing in the baked potatoes and dessert cheeses. Things are a little out of whack. *Is a dinner party a paradigm of society or a vicious pantomime of the family?* It is already 10:30. Brigitte has gotten up again to help him. They return with sour cream, chives, grappa and cognac. Debbie looks across the table at Bill and smiles warmly. Bill smiles back. At least he thinks he does.

This taboo regarding age is to make us believe that life is long and actually improves us, that we are wiser, better, more knowledgeable later on than early. It is a myth concocted to keep the young from learning what we really are and despising and murdering us. We keep them sweet-breathed, unequipped, suggesting to them that there is something more than regret and decrepitude up ahead.

Bill is still writing an essay in his head, one of theoretical common sense, though perhaps he is just drinking too much and it is not an essay at all but the simple metabolism of sugar. But this is what he knows right now, with dinner winding up and midnight looming like a death gong: life's embrace is quick and busy, and everywhere in it people are equally lacking and well-meaning and nuts. *Why not admit history's powers to divide and destroy? Why attach ourselves to the age-old stories in the belief that they are truer than the new ones? By living in the past, you always know what comes next, and that robs you of surprises. It exhausts and warps the mind. We are lucky simply to be alive together; why get differentiating and judgmental about who is here among us? Thank God there is anyone at all.*

"I believe in the present tense," Bill says now, to no one in particular. "I believe in amnesty." He stops. People are looking but not speaking. "Or is that just fancy rhetoric?"

"It's not that fancy," says Jack.

"It's fancy," Albert says kindly, ever the host, "without being schmancy." He brings out more grappa. Everyone drinks it from the amber, green, and blue of Albert's Depression glass glasses.

"I mean—" Bill begins, but then he stops, says nothing. Chilean folk music is playing on the stereo, wistful and melancholy: "Bring me all your old lovers, so I can love you, too," a woman sings in Spanish.

"What does that mean?" Bill asks, but at this point he may not actually be speaking out loud. He cannot really tell. He sits back and listens to the song, translating the sad Spanish. Every songwriter in their smallest song seems to possess some monumental grief clarified and dignified by melody, Bill thinks. His own sadnesses, on the other hand, slosh about in his life in a low-key way, formless and self-consuming. *Modest* is how he sometimes likes to see it. No one is modest anymore. Everyone exalts their disappointments. They do ceremonious battle with everything; they demand receipts and take their presents back – all the unhappy things that life awkwardly, stupidly, without thinking, without bothering even to get to know them a little or to ask around! has given them. They bring it all back for an exchange.

As has he, hasn't he?

The young were sent to earth to amuse the old. Why not be amused?

Debbie comes over and sits next to him. "You're looking very rumpled and miffed," she says quietly. Bill only nods. What can he say? She adds, "Rumpled and miffed – doesn't that sound like a law firm?"

Bill nods again. "One in a Hans Christian Andersen story," he says. "Perhaps the one the Ugly Duckling hired to sue his parents."

"Or the one that the Little Mermaid retained to stick it to the Prince," says Debbie, a bit pointedly, Bill thinks – who can tell? Her girlish voice, out of sheer terror, perhaps, has lately adorned itself with dreamy and snippy mannerisms.

Probably Bill has single-handedly aged her beyond her years.

Jack has stood and is heading for the foyer. Lina follows.

"Lina, you're leaving?" asks Bill with too much feeling in his voice. He sees that Debbie, casting her eyes downward, has noted it.

"Yes, we have a little tradition at home, so we can't stay for midnight." Lina shrugs a bit nonchalantly, then picks up her red wool scarf and lassoes her neck with it, a loose noose. Jack holds her coat up behind her, and she slides her arms into the satin lining.

It's sex, Bill thinks. They make love at the stroke of midnight.

"A tradition?" asks Stanley.

"Uh, yes," Lina says dismissively. "Just a little contemplation of the upcoming year is all. I hope you all have a happy rest of the New Year Eve."

Lina always leaves the apostrophe *s* out of New Year's Eve, Bill notes, oddly enchanted. And why *should* New Year's Eve have an apostrophe *s*? It shouldn't. Christmas Eve doesn't. Logically—

"They have sex at the stroke of midnight," says Albert after they leave.

"I knew it!" shouts Bill.

"Sex at the stroke of midnight?" asks Roberta.

"I myself usually save that for Lincoln's Birthday," says Bill.

"It's a local New Year's tradition apparently," says Albert.

"I've lived here twenty years and I've never heard of it," says Stanley.

"Neither have I," says Roberta.

"Nor I," says Brigitte.

"Me, neither," says Bill.

"Well, we'll all have to do something equally compelling," says Debbie.

Bill's head spins to look at her. The bodice of her black velvet dress is snowy with napkin lint. Her face is flushed from drink. What does she mean? She means nothing at all.

"Black-eyed peas!" cries Albert. And he dashes into the

kitchen and brings out an iron pot of warm, pasty, black-dotted beans and six spoons.

"Now this is a tradition I know," says Stanley, and he takes one of the spoons and digs in.

Albert moves around the room with his pot. "You can't eat until the stroke of midnight. The peas have to be the first thing you consume in the New Year and then you'll have good luck all year long."

Brigitte takes a spoon and looks at her watch. "We've got five minutes."

"What'll we do?" asks Stanley. He is holding his spoonful of peas like a lollipop, and they are starting to slide.

"We'll contemplate our fruitful work and great accomplishments." Albert sighs. "Though, of course, when you think about Gandhi, or Pasteur, or someone like Martin Luther King, Jr., dead at thirty-nine, it sure makes you wonder what you've done with your life."

"We've done some things," says Bill.

"Yes? Like what?" asks Albert.

"We've . . ." And here Bill stops for a moment. "We've . . . had some excellent meals. We've . . . bought some nice shirts. We've gotten a good trade-in or two on our cars – I think I'm going to go kill myself now."

"I'll join you," says Albert. "Knives are in the drawer by the sink."

"How about the vacuum cleaner?"

"Vacuum cleaner in the back closet."

"Vacuum cleaner?" hoots Roberta. But no one explains or goes anywhere. Everyone just sits.

"Peas poised!" Stanley suddenly shouts. They all get up and stand in a horseshoe around the hearth with its new birch logs and bright but smoky fire. They lift their mounded spoons and eye the mantel clock with its ancient minute hand jerking toward midnight.

"Happy New Year," says Albert finally, after some silence, and lifts his spoon in salute.

"Amen," says Stanley.

"Amen," says Roberta.

"Amen," say Debbie and Brigitte.

"Ditto," says Bill, his mouth full, but indicating with his spoon.

Then they all hug quickly – "Gotcha!" says Bill with each hug – and begin looking for their coats.

"You always seem more interested in other women than in me," Debbie says when they are back at his house after a silent ride home, Debbie driving. "Last month it was Lina. And the month before that it was . . . it was Lina again." She stops for a minute. "I'm sorry to be so selfish and pathetic." She begins to cry, and as she does, something cracks open in her and Bill sees straight through to her heart. It is a good heart. It has had nice parents and good friends, lived only during peacetime, and been kind to animals. She looks up at him. "I mean, I'm romantic and passionate. I believe if you're in love, that's enough. I believe love conquers all."

Bill nods sympathetically, from a great distance.

"But I don't want to get into one of these feeble, one-sided, patched-together relationships – no matter how much I care for you."

"Whatever happened to love conquers all, just four seconds ago?"

Debbie pauses. "I'm older now," she says.

"You kids. You grow up so fast."

Then there is a long silence between them, the second in this new New Year. Finally, Debbie says, "Don't you know that Lina's having an affair with Albert? Can't you see they're in love?"

Something in Bill drops, squares off, makes a neat little knot. "No, I didn't see." He feels the sickened sensation he has sometimes felt after killing a housefly and finding blood in it.

"You yourself had suggested they might be lovers."

"I did? Not seriously. Really? I did?"

"But Bill, hadn't you heard? I mean, it's all over campus."

Actually, he had heard some rumors; he had even said,

"Hope so" and once "May God bless their joyous union." But he hadn't meant or believed any of it. Such rumors seemed ham-handed, literal, unlikely. And yet wasn't reality always cheesy and unreliable just like that; wasn't fate literal in exactly that way? He thinks of the severed, crossed fingers found perfectly survived in the wreckage of a local plane crash last year. Such fate was contrary and dense, like a dumb secretary, failing to understand the overall gestalt and desire of the wish. He prefers a deeper, cleverer, even tardy fate, like that of a girl he knew once in law school who, years before, had been raped, shot, and left for dead but then had crawled ten hours out of the woods to the highway with a .22 bullet in her head and flagged a car. That's when you knew that life was making something up to you, that the narrative was apologizing. That's when you knew God had glanced up from his knitting, perhaps even risen from his freaking wicker rocker, and staggered at last to the window to look.

Debbie studies Bill, worried and sympathetic. "You're just not happy in this relationship, are you?" she says.

These terms! This talk! Bill is not good at this; she is better at it than he; she is probably better at everything than he: at least she has not used the word *text*.

"Just don't use the word *text*," he warns.

Debbie is quiet. "You're just not happy with your life," she says.

"I suppose I'm not." *Don't count on us. Don't count on us, motherfucker.*

"A small bit of happiness is not so hard, you know. You could manage it. It's pretty much open-book. It's basically a take-home."

Suddenly, sadness is devouring him. The black-eyed peas! Why aren't they working? Debbie's face flickers and tenses. All her eye makeup has washed away, her eyes bare and round as lightbulbs. "You were always a tough grader," she says. "Whatever happened to grading on a curve?"

"I don't know," he says. "Whatever happened to that?"

Her eyelids lower and she falls soundlessly across his lap,

her hair in a golden pinwheel about her head. He can feel the firm watery press of her breasts against his thigh.

How can he assess his life so harshly and ungratefully, when he is here with her, when she is so deeply kind, and a whole new year is upon them like a long, cheap buffet? How could he be so strict and mean?

"I've changed my mind," he says. "I'm happy. I'm bursting."

"You are not," she says, but she turns her face upward and smiles hopefully, like something brief and floral and in need of heat.

"I am," he insists, but looks away, to think, to think of anything else at all, to think of his ex-wife – *Bring me all your old lovers, so I can love you, too* – still living in St. Paul with his daughter, who in five years will be Debbie's age. He believes that he was happy once then, for a long time, for a while. "We are this far from a divorce," his wife had said bitterly at the end. And if she had spread her arms wide, they might have been able to find a way back, the blinking, intermittent wit of her like a lighthouse to him, but no: she had held her index finger and her thumb up close to her face in a mean pinch of salt. Still, before he left, their marriage a spluttering but modest ruin, only two affairs and a dozen sharp words between them, they'd come home from the small humiliations they would endure at work, separately and alone, and they'd turn them somehow into desire. At the very end, they'd taken walks together in the cool wintry light that sometimes claimed those last days of August – the air chill, leaves already dropping in wind and scuttling along the sidewalk, the neighborhood planted with ocher mums, even the toughest weeds in bridal flower, the hydrangea blooms gone green and drunk with their own juice. Who would not try to be happy?

And just as he had then on those walks, he remembers now how, as a boy in Duluth, he'd once imagined a monster, a demon, chasing him home from school. It was one particular winter: Christmas was past, the snow was dirty and crusted, his father was overseas, and his young sister, Lily, home from the hospital's iron lung, lay dying of polio in her bed upstairs at home. His parents had always – discreetly, they probably felt, though also recklessly and maybe guiltily, too – enjoyed their daughter more than their serious older boy. Perhaps it was a surprise even to themselves. But Bill, in studying their looks and words, had discerned it, though in response he had never known what to do. How could he make himself more enjoyable? With his father away, he wrote long boring letters with everything spelled correctly. "Dear Dad, How are you? I am fine." But he didn't mail them. He saved them up, tied them in a string, and when his father came home, he gave him the packet. His father said "Thank you," tucked the letters in his coat, and never mentioned them again. Instead, every day for a year, his father went upstairs and wept for Lily.

Once, when she'd still been pretty and well, Bill went through an entire day repeating everything Lily said, until she cried in torment and his mother slapped him hard against the eye.

Lily had been enjoyed. They enjoyed her. Who could blame them? Enjoyable girl! Enjoyable joy! But Bill could not attain such a thing, either side of it, for himself. He glimpsed it all from behind some atmosphere, from across some green and scalloped sea – "Dear Dad, How are you? I am fine" – as if it were a planet that sometimes sparkled into view, or a tropical island painted in hot, picture-book shades of orange.

But deep in his private January boyhood, he knew, there were colors that were true: the late-afternoon light was bluish and dark, the bruised tundra of the snowbanks scary and silver and cold. Stepping slowly at first, the hulking monster-man, the demon-man, red and giant, with a single wing growing out of its back, would begin to chase Bill. It chased him faster and faster, up and down every tiny hill to home, casting long shadows that would occasionally, briefly, fall upon them both like a net. While the church bells chimed their four o'clock hymn, the monster-man would fly in a loping, wonky way, lunging and leaping and skittering across the ice toward Bill's heels. Bill rounded a corner. The demon leapt over a bin of road salt. Bill cut across a path. The demon followed. And the terror of it all – as Bill flung himself onto his own front porch and into the unlocked and darkened house, slamming the door, sinking back against it, sliding down onto the doormat, safe at last among the clutter of boots and shoes but still gasping the wide lucky gasps of his great and narrow escape – was thrilling to him in a world that had already, and with such indifferent skill, forsaken all its charms.

1995

CHARADES

IT'S FITTING THAT Christmas should degenerate to this, its barest bones. The family has begun to seem to Therese like a pack of thespians anyway; everyone arrives, performs for one another, catches early flights out, to Logan or O'Hare. Probably it's appropriate that a party game should literally appear and insert itself in the guise of a holiday tradition (which it isn't). Usually, no one in Therese's family expresses much genuine feeling anyway; everyone aims instead – though gamely! – for enactments.

Each year now, the stage is a new one – their aging parents, in their restless old age, buying and selling town houses, moving steadily southward from Maine. The real estate is Therese's mother's idea. Since he's retired, Therese's father has focused more on bird feeders; he is learning how to build them. "Who knows what he'll do next?" Her mother sighs. "He'll probably start carving designs into the side of the house."

This year, they are in Bethesda, Maryland, near where Andrew, Therese's brother, lives. Andrew works as an electrical engineer and is married to a sweet, pretty, part-time private detective named Pam. Pam is pixie-haired and smiley. Who would ever suspect her of discreetly gathering confidences and facts for one's adversaries? She freezes hams. She makes Jell-O salad days in advance. She and Andrew are the parents of a one-and-a-half-year-old named Winnie, who already reads.

Reads the reading videos on TV, but reads.

Everyone has divided into teams, four and four, and written the names of famous people, songs, films, plays, books on scraps of wrapping paper torn off the gifts hours earlier. It is another few hours until Therese and her husband Ray's flight, at 4:30, from National Airport. "Yes," says Therese, "I guess we'll have to forgo the 'Averell Harriman: Statesman for All Seasons' exhibit."

"I don't know why you couldn't catch a later flight," says Therese's sister, Ann. She is scowling. Ann is the youngest, and ten years younger than Therese, who is the oldest, but lately Ann's voice has taken up a prissy and matronly scolding that startles Therese. "Four-thirty," says Ann, pursing her lips and propping her feet up on the chair next to her. "That's a little ridiculous. You're missing dinner." Her shoes are pointy and Victorian-looking. They are green suede – a cross between a courtesan's and Peter Pan's.

The teams are divided in such a way that Therese and Ray and her parents are on one team, Andrew and Pam, Ann and Tad, Ann's fiancé, on the other. Tad is slender and red-haired, a marketing rep for Neutrogena. He and Ann have just become engaged. After nearly a decade of casting about in love and work, Ann is now going to law school and planning her summer wedding. Since Therese worked for years as a public defender and is currently, through a fluky political appointment, a county circuit court judge, she has assumed that Ann's decision to be a lawyer is a kind of sororal affirmation, that it will somehow mean the two of them will have new things in common, that Ann will have questions for her, observations, forensic things to say. But this seems not to be so. Ann appears instead to be preoccupied with trying to hire bands and caterers, and to rent a large room in a restaurant. "Ugh," said Therese sympathetically. "Doesn't it make you want to elope?" Therese and Ray were married at the courthouse, with the file clerks as witnesses.

Ann shrugged. "I'm trying to figure out how to get everybody from the church to the restaurant in a way that won't wrinkle their outfits and spoil the pictures."

"Really?" asked Therese. "You are?"

The titles are put in two big salad bowls, each team receiving the other's bowl of titles. Therese's father goes first. "All right! Everyone ready!" He has always been witty, competitive, tense; games have usually brought out the best and worst in him. These days, however, he seems anxious and elderly. There is a pain in his eyes, something sad and unfocused that sometimes stabs at them – the fear of a misspent life, or an uncertainty as to where he's left the keys. He signals that his assigned name is a famous person. No one could remember how to signal that and so the family has invented one: a quick pompous posture, hands on hips, chin in air. Mustering up a sense of drama, Therese's father does this well.

"Famous person!" Everyone shouts it, though of course there is someone who shouts "Idiot" to be witty. This time, it is Therese's mother.

"Idiot!" she shouts. "Village idiot!"

But Therese's father has continued signaling the syllables, ignoring his wife, slapping the fingers of his right hand hard on his left sleeve. The famous person has three names. He is doing the first name, first syllable. He takes out a dollar bill and points to it.

"George Washington," shouts Ray.

"George Washington Carver!" shouts Therese. Therese's father shakes his head angrily, turning the dollar around and pointing at it violently. It bothers him not to be able to control the discourse.

"Dollar bill," says Therese's mother.

"Bill!" says Therese. At this, her father begins nodding and pointing at her psychotically. *Yes, yes, yes.* Now he makes stretching motions with his hands. "Bill, Billy, William," says Therese, and her father points wildly at her again. "William," she says. "William Kennedy Smith."

"Yes!" shouts her father, clapping his hands and throwing his head back as if to praise the ceiling.

"William Kennedy Smith?" Ann is scowling again. "How did you get that from just William?"

"He's been in the news." Therese shrugs. She does not know how to explain Ann's sourness. Perhaps it has something to do with Ann's struggles in law school, or with Therese's being a circuit court judge, or with the diamond on Ann's finger, which is so huge that it seems, to Therese, unkind to wear it around their mother's, which is, when one gets right down to it, a chip. Earlier this morning, Ann told Therese that she is going to take Tad's name, as well. "You're going to call yourself Tad?" Therese asked, but Ann was not amused.

Ann's sense of humor was never that flexible, though she used to like a good sight gag.

Ann officiously explained the name change: "Because I believe a family is like a team, and everyone on the team should have the same name, like a color. I believe a spouse should be a team player."

Therese no longer has any idea who Ann is. She liked her better when Ann was eight, with her blue pencil case, and a strange, loping run that came from having one leg a quarter of an inch longer than the other. Ann was more attractive as a child. She was awkward and inquiring. She was cute. Or so she seemed to Therese, who was mostly in high school and college, slightly depressed and studying too much, destroying her already-bad eyes, so that now she wore glasses so thick her eyes swam in a cloudy way behind them. This morning, when she'd stood listening to Ann talk about team players, Therese had smiled and nodded, but she felt preached at, as if she were a messy, wayward hippie. She wanted to grab her sister, throw herself upon her, embrace her, shut her up. She tried to understand Ann's dark and worried nuptial words, but instead she found herself recalling the pratfalls she used to perform for Ann – Therese could take a fall straight on the face – in order to make Ann laugh.

Ann's voice was going on now. "When you sit too long, the bodices bunch up. . . ."

Therese mentally measured the length of her body in front of her and wondered if she could do it. Of course she could. Of course. But *would* she? And then suddenly, she knew she would. She let her hip twist and fell straight forward, her arm at an angle, her mouth in a whoop. She had learned to do this in drama club when she was fifteen. She hadn't been pretty, and it was a means of getting the boys' attention. She landed with a thud.

"You still do that?" asked Ann with incredulity and disgust. "You're a judge and you still *do* that?"

"Sort of," said Therese from the floor. She felt around for her glasses.

Now it is the team player herself standing up to give clues

to her team. She looks at the name on her scrap of paper and makes a slight face. "I need a consultation," she says in a vaguely repelled way that perhaps she imagines is sophisticated. She takes the scrap of wrapping paper over to Therese's team. "What is this?" Ann asks. There in Ray's handwriting is a misspelled *Arachnophobia*.

"It's a movie," says Ray apologetically. "Did I spell it wrong?"

"I think you did, honey," says Therese, leaning in to look at it. "You got some of the *o*'s and *a*'s mixed up." Ray is dyslexic. When the roofing business slows in the winter months, instead of staying in with a book, or going to psychotherapy, he drives to cheap matinees of bad movies – "flicks," he calls them, or "cliffs" when he's making fun of himself. Ray misspells everything. Is it *input* or *imput*? Is it *averse, adverse,* or *adversed*? *Stock* or *stalk*? *Carrot* or *karate*? His roofing business has a reputation for being reasonable, but a bit slipshod and second-rate. Nonetheless, Therese thinks he is great. He is never condescending. He cooks infinite dishes with chicken. He is ardent and capable and claims almost every night in his husbandly way to find Therese the sexiest woman he's ever known. Therese likes that. She is also having an affair with a young assistant DA in the prosecutor's office, but it is a limited thing – like taking her gloves off, clapping her hands, and putting the gloves back on again. It is quiet and undiscoverable. It is nothing, except that it is sex with a man who is not dyslexic, and once in a while, Jesus Christ, she needs that.

Ann is acting out *Arachnophobia*, the whole concept, rather than working syllable by syllable. She stares into her fiancé's eyes, wiggling her fingers about and then jumping away in a fright, but Tad doesn't get it, though he does look a little alarmed. Ann waves her Christmas-manicured nails at him more furiously. One of the nails has a little Santa Claus painted on it. Ann's black hair is cut severely in sharp, expensive lines, and her long, drapey clothes hang from her shoulders, as if still on a hanger. She looks starved and rich and enraged. Everything seems struggled toward and forced, a little cartoonish, like the green shoes, which may be why her fiancé suddenly shouts out, "Little Miss Muffett!" Ann turns now instead to Andrew, motioning at him encouragingly, as if to punish Tad. The awkward lope of her childhood has taken on a chiropracticed slink. Therese turns back toward her own team, toward her father, who is still muttering something about William Kennedy Smith. "A woman shouldn't be in a bar at three o'clock in the morning, that's all there is to it."

"Dad, that's ludicrous," whispers Therese, not wanting to interrupt the game. "Bars are open to everyone. Public Accommodations Law."

"I'm not talking about the cold legalities," he says chastisingly. He has never liked lawyers, and is baffled by his daughters. "I'm talking about a long-understood *moral code.*" Her father is of that Victorian sensibility that deep down respects prostitutes more than it does women in general.

"'Long-understood moral code'?" Therese looks at him gently. "Dad, you're seventy-five years old. Things change."

"*Arachnophobia!*" Andrew shouts, and he and Ann rush together and do high fives.

Therese's father makes a quick little spitting sound, then crosses his legs and looks the other way. Therese looks over at her mother and her mother is smiling at her conspiratorially, behind Therese's father's back, making little donkey ears with her fingers, her sign for when she thinks he's being a jackass.

"All right, forget the William Kennedy Smith. Doll, your turn," says Therese's father to her mother. Therese's mother gets up slowly but bends gleefully to pick up the scrap of paper. She looks at it, walks to the center of the room, and shoves the paper scrap in her pocket. She faces the other team and makes the sign for a famous person.

"Wrong team, Mom," says Therese, and her mother says "Oops," and turns around. She repeats the famous person stance.

"Famous person," says Ray encouragingly. Therese's mother nods. She pauses for a bit to think. Then she spins around, throws her arms up into the air, collapses forward onto the floor, then backward, hitting her head on the stereo.

"Marjorie, what are you doing?" asks Therese's father. Her mother is lying there on the floor, laughing.

"Are you okay?" Therese asks. Her mother nods, still laughing quietly.

"Fall," says Ray. "Dizziness. Dizzy Gillespie."

Therese's mother shakes her head.

"Epilepsy," says Therese.

"Explode," says her father, and her mother nods. "Explosion. Bomb. Robert Oppenheimer!"

"That's it." Her mother sighs. She has a little trouble getting back up. She is seventy and her knees are jammed with arthritis.

"You need help, Mom?" Therese asks.

"Yeah, Mom, you need help?" asks Ann, who has risen and walked toward the center of the room, to take charge.

"I'm okay." Therese's mother sighs, with a quiet, slightly faked giggle, and walks stiffly back to her seat.

"That was great, Ma," says Therese.

Her mother smiles proudly. "Well, thank you!"

After that, there are many rounds, and every time Therese's mother gets anything like Dom De Luise or Tom Jones, she does her bomb imitation again, whipping herself into a spastic frenzy and falling, then rising stiffly again to great applause. Pam brings Winnie in from her nap and everyone oohs and aahs at the child's sweet sleep-streaked face. "There she is," coos Aunt Therese. "You want to come see Grandma be a bomb?"

"It's your turn," says Andrew impatiently.

"Mine?" asks Therese.

"I think that's right," says her father.

She gets up, digs into the bowl, unfolds the scrap of wrapping paper. It says "Jekylls Street." "I need a consultation here. Andrew, I think this is your writing."

"Okay," he says, rising, and together they step into the foyer.

"Is this a TV show?" whispers Therese. "I don't watch much TV."

"No," says Andrew with a vague smile.

"What is it?"

He shifts his weight, reluctant to tell her. Perhaps it is because he is married to a detective. Or, more likely, it is because he himself works with Top Secret documents from the Defense Department; he was recently promoted from the just plain Secret ones. As an engineer, he consults, reviews, approves. His eyes are suppressed, annoyed. "It's the name of a street two blocks from here." There's a surly and defensive curve to his mouth.

"But that's not the title of anything famous."

"It's a place. I thought we could do names of places."

"It's not a famous place."

"So?"

"I mean, we all could write down the names of streets in our neighborhoods, near where we work, a road we walked down once on the way to a store—"

"You're the one who said we could do places."

"I did? Well, all right, then, what did I say was the sign for a place? We don't have a sign for places."

"I don't know. You figure it out," he says. A saucy rage is all over him now. Is this from childhood? Is this from hair loss? Once, she and Andrew were close. But now, as with Ann, she has no idea who he is anymore. She has only a theory: an electrical engineer worked over years ago by high school guidance counselors paid by the Pentagon to recruit, train, and militarize all the boys with high math SAT scores. "From M.I.T. to MIA," Andrew once put it himself. "A military-industrial asshole." But she can't find that satirical place in him anymore. Last year, at least, they had joked about their upbringing. "I scarcely remember Dad reading to us," she'd said.

"Sure he read to us," said Andrew. "You don't remember him reading to us? You don't remember him reading to us silently from the *Wall Street Journal*?"

Now she scans his hardening face for a joke, a glimmer, a bit of love. Andrew and Ann have seemed close, and Therese feels a bit wistful, wondering when and how that happened.

She is a little jealous. The only expression she can get from Andrew is a derisive one. He is a traffic cop. She is the speeding flower child.

Don't you know I'm a *judge*? she wants to ask. A judge via a fluke political appointment, sure. A judge with a reputation around the courthouse for light sentencing, true. A judge who is having an affair that mildly tarnishes her character – okay. A softy; an easy touch: but a judge nonetheless.

Instead, she says, "Do you mind if I just pick another one?"

"Fine by me," he says, and strides brusquely back into the living room.

Oh, well, Therese thinks. It is her new mantra. It usually calms her better than *ohm*, which she also tries. *Ohm* is where the heart is. *Ohm* is not here. *Oh, well. Oh, well.* When she was first practicing law, to combat her courtroom stage fright, she would chant to herself, *Everybody loves me. Everybody loves me*, and when that didn't work, she'd switch to *Kill! Kill! Kill!*

"We're doing another one," announces Andrew, and Therese picks another one.

A book and a movie. She opens her palms, prayerlike for a book. She cranks one hand in the air for a movie. She pulls on her ear and points at a lamp. "Sounds like *light*," Ray says. His expression is open and helpful. "Bite, kite, dite, fight, night—"

Therese signals yes, that's it.

"Night," repeats Ray.

"Tender Is the Night," says her mother.

"Yes!" says Therese, and bends to kiss her mother on the cheek. Her mother smiles exuberantly, her face in a kind of burst; she loves affection, is hungry and grateful for it. When she was younger, she was a frustrated, mean mother, and so she is pleased when her children act as if they don't remember.

It is Andrew's turn. He stands before his own team, staring at the red scrap in his hand. He ponders it, shakes his head, then looks back toward Therese. "This must be yours," he says with a smirk that maybe is a good-natured smirk. Is there such a thing? Therese hopes.

"You need a consultation?" She gets up to look at the

writing; it reads, "The Surrey with the Fringe on Top." "Yup, that's mine," she says.

"Come here," he says, and the two of them go back down the corridor toward the foyer again. This time, Therese notices the photographs her parents have hung there. Photographs of their children, of weddings and Winnie, though all the ones of Therese seem to her to be aggressively unflattering, advertising an asymmetry in her expression, or the magnified haziness of her eyes, her hair in a dry, peppery frizz. Vanity surges in her: surely there must have been better pictures! The ones of Andrew, of Ann, of Tad, of Pam and Winnie are sunlit, posed, wholesome, pretty. But the ones of Therese seem slightly disturbed, as if her parents were convinced she is insane.

"We'll stand here by the demented-looking pictures of me," says Therese.

"Ann sent her those," says Andrew.

"Really?" says Therese.

He studies her hair. "Didn't your hair used to be a different color? I don't remember it ever being quite that color. What *is* that color?"

"Why, whatever do you mean?"

"Look," he says, getting back to the game. "I've never heard of this," and he waves the scrap of paper as if it were a gum wrapper.

"You haven't? It's a song: 'Geese and chicks and ducks better scurry, when I take you out in the surrey . . .' "

"No."

"No?" She keeps going. She looks up at him romantically, yearningly. " 'When I take you out in my surrey, when I take you out in my surrey with the fringe on—' "

"No," Andrew interrupts emphatically.

"Hmm. Well, don't worry. Everyone on your team will know it."

The righteous indignation is returning to his face. "If *I* don't know it, what makes you think *they'll* know it?" Perhaps this is because of his work, the technosecrecy of it. *He* knows; *they* don't.

"They'll know it," Therese says. "I guarantee." She turns to leave.

"Whoa, whoa, whoa," says Andrew. The gray-pink of rage is back in his skin. What has he become? She hasn't a clue. He is successfully top secret. He is classified information. "I'm not doing this," he says. "I refuse."

Therese stares at him. This is the assertiveness he can't exercise on the job. Perhaps here, where he is no longer a cog-though-a-prized cog, he can insist on certain things. The Cold War is over, she wants to say. But what has replaced it is this: children who have turned on one another, now that the gods – or were they only guards? – have fled. "Okay, fine," she says. "I'll make up another."

"We're doing another one," announces Andrew triumphantly as they go back into the living room. He waves the paper scrap. "Have any of you ever even heard of a song called 'The Surrey with the Fringe on Top'?"

"Sure," says Pam, looking at him in a puzzled way. No doubt he seems different to her around the holidays.

"You have?" He seems a bit flummoxed. He looks at Ann. "Have you?"

Ann looks reluctant to break ranks with him but says, quietly, "Yeah."

"Tad, how about you?" he asks.

Tad has been napping off and on, his head thrown back against the sofa, but now he jerks awake. "Uh, yeah," he says.

"Tad's not feeling that well," says Ann.

In desperation, Andrew turns toward the other team. "And you all know it, too?"

"I don't know it," says Ray. He is the only one. He doesn't know a show tune from a chauffeur. In a way, that's what Therese likes about him.

Andrew sits back down, refusing to admit defeat. "Ray didn't know it," he says.

Therese can't think of a song, so she writes "Clarence Thomas" and hands the slip back to Andrew. As he ponders his options, Therese's mother gets up and comes back holding Dixie cups and a bottle of cranberry drink. "Who would like some cranberry juice?" she says, and starts pouring. She hands the cups out carefully to everyone. "We don't have the wineglasses unpacked, so we'll have to make do."

"We'll have to make do" is one of their mother's favorite expressions, acquired during the Depression and made indelible during the war. When they were little, Therese and Andrew used to look at each other and say, "We'll have to make do-do," but when Therese glances over at Andrew now, nothing registers. He has forgotten. He is thinking only of the charade.

Ray sips his a little sloppily, and a drop spills on the chair. Therese hands him a napkin and he dabs at the upholstery with it, but it is Ann who is swiftly up, out to the kitchen, and back with a cold, wet cloth, wiping at Ray's chair in a kind of rebuke.

"Oh, don't worry," her mother is saying.

"I think I've got it," says Ann solemnly.

"I'm doing my clues now," says Andrew impatiently. Therese looks over at Winnie, who, calm and observant in her mother's arms, a pink incontinent Buddha who knows all her letters, seems like the sanest person in the room.

Andrew is making a sweeping gesture with his arm, something meant to include everyone in the room.

"People," says Tad.

"Family," says Pam.

Ann has come back from the kitchen and sits down on the sofa. "Us," she says.

Andrew smiles and nods.

"Us. Thom-us," says Ann. "Clarence Thomas."

"Yes," says Andrew with a clap. "What was the time on that?"

"Thirty seconds," says Tad.

"Well, I guess he's on the tip of everyone's tongue," says Therese's mother.

"I guess so," says Therese.

"It was interesting to see all those black people from Yale," says Therese's mother. "All sitting there in the Senate caucus room. I'll bet their parents were proud."

Ann did not get in to Yale. "What I don't like," she says, "is all these black people who don't like whites. They're so hostile. I see it all the time in law school. Most white people are more than willing to sit down, be friendly and integrated. But it's the blacks who are too angry."

"Imagine that," says Ray.

"Yes. Imagine," says Therese. "Why would they be angry? You know what else I don't like? I don't like all these gay men who have gotten just a little too somber and butch. You know what I mean? They're so funereal and upset these days! Where is the mincing and *high-spiritedness* of yesteryear? Where is the *gayness* in *gay*? It's all so confusing and inconvenient! You can't tell who's who without a goddamn *Playbill*!" She stands up and looks at Ray. It is time to go. She has lost her judicial temperament hours ago. She fears she is going to do another pratfall, only this time she will break something. Already she sees herself carted out on a stretcher, taken toward the airport, and toward home, saying the final words she has to say to her family, has always had to say to her family. Sounds like *could cry*.

"Good-bye!"

"Good-bye!"

"Good-bye!"

"Good-bye!"

"Good-bye!"

"Good-bye!"

"Good-bye!"

But first Ray must do his charade, which is Confucius. "Okay. I'm ready," he says, and begins to wander around the living room in a wild-eyed daze, looking as confused as possible, groping at the bookcases, placing his palm to his brow. And in that moment, Therese thinks how good-looking he is and how kind and strong and how she loves nobody else in the world even half as much.

1992

CHILDCARE

THE COLD CAME late that fall, and the songbirds were caught off guard. By the time the snow and wind began in earnest, too many had been suckered into staying, and instead of flying south, instead of already having flown south, they were huddled in people's yards, their feathers puffed for some modicum of warmth. I was looking for a babysitting job. I was a student and needed money, so I would walk from interview to interview in these attractive but wintry neighborhoods, past the eerie multitudes of robins pecking at the frozen ground, dun gray and stricken – though what bird in the best of circumstances does not look a little stricken – until at last, late in my search, at the end of a week, startlingly, the birds had disappeared. I did not want to think about what had happened to them. Or, rather, that is an expression – of politeness, a false promise of delicacy – for in fact I wondered about them all the time: imagining them dead, in stunning heaps in some killing cornfield outside of town, or dropped from the sky in twos and threes for miles down along the Illinois state line.

I was looking in December for work that would begin in January, at the start of the spring term. I'd finished my exams and was answering ads from the student job board, ones for "childcare provider." I liked children – I did! – or, rather, I liked them O.K. They were sometimes interesting. I admired their stamina and candor. And I was good with them, in that I could make funny faces at the babies and teach the older children card tricks while speaking in the theatrically sarcastic tones that disarmed and enthralled them. But I was not especially skilled at minding children for long spells; I grew bored, perhaps like my own mother. After I'd spent too much time playing their games, my mind grew peckish and longed to lose itself in some book I had in my backpack. I was ever hopeful of early bedtimes and long naps.

I had come from Dellacrosse Central, from a small farm on

the old Perryville Road, to this university town of Troy, "the Athens of the Midwest," as if from a cave – like the priest-child of a Colombian tribe I'd read about in Anthropology 203, a boy made mystical by being kept in the dark for the bulk of his childhood and allowed only stories – no experience – of the outside world. Once brought out into light, he was in a perpetual, holy condition of bedazzlement and wonder; no story could ever equal the thing itself. And so it was with me. Nothing had really prepared me. Not the college piggy bank in the dining room, the savings bonds from my grandparents, or the used set of World Book encyclopedias, with their beautiful color charts of international wheat production and photographs of Presidential birthplaces. The flat, green world of my parents' hogless, horseless farm – its dullness, its flies, its quiet ripped open daily by the fumes and whining of machinery – twisted away and left me with a brilliant city life of books and films and witty friends. Someone had turned on the lights. Someone had led me out of the cave of Perryville Road. My brain was on fire with Chaucer, Sylvia Plath, Simone de Beauvoir. Twice a week, a young professor named Thad, dressed in jeans and a tie, stood before a lecture hall of stunned farm kids like me and spoke thrillingly of Henry James's masturbation of the comma. I was riveted. I had never before seen a man wear jeans with a tie. The Colombian cave, of course, had produced a mystic; my childhood, however, had produced only me. In the corridors, students argued over Bach, Beck, Balkanization, bacterial warfare. Out-of-state kids said things to me like "You're from the country. Is it true that if you eat a bear's liver you'll die?" They asked, "Ever know someone who did you-know-what with a cow?" Or "Is it an actual fact that pigs won't eat bananas?" What I did know was that a goat would not really eat a tin can: it just liked to lick the paste on the label. But no one ever asked me about that.

Before coming to Troy, I had never had Chinese food. But now, two blocks from my apartment, next to a shoe-repair shop, was a place called the Peking Café, where I went as often as I could for the Buddha's Delight. These odd Chinese vegetables – fungal and gnomic in their brown sauce – had for me the power of an adventure or a rite, a statement to be savored. Back in Dellacrosse, the dining was divided into "casual," which meant that you ate it standing up or took it away, and the high end, which was called "sit-down dining." At the Wie Haus Family Restaurant, where we went for sit-down, the seats were red leatherette and the walls were gemütlich and paneled, decorated with framed deep kitsch – wide-eyed shepherdesses and jesters. The breakfast menus said "Guten Morgen." Sauces were called "gravy." And the dinner menu featured cheese-curd meat loaf and steak "cooked to your likeness." On Fridays, there were fish fries or boils, at which they served "lawyers" (burbot or eelpout), so called because their hearts were in their butts. On Sundays, there was not only marshmallow-and-maraschino-cherry salad and something called Grandma Jell-O but "prime rib with *au jus*," a precise knowledge of French – or English or even food coloring – not being the restaurant's strong suit. "À la carte" meant soup or salad; "dinner" meant soup and salad. The Roquefort on the salad was called by the waitstaff "Rockford dressing." The house wines – red, white, or pink – bore the requisite bouquets of rose, soap, and graphite, a whiff of hay, a hint of Hooterville, though the menu remained mute about all this, sticking to straightforward declarations of hue. Light ale and dunkel were served. For dessert, there was usually a *Glückschmerz* pie, with the fluffy look and heft of a small snowbank. After any meal, sleepiness ensued.

Now, however, away and on my own, seduced and salted by brown sauce, I felt myself thinning and alive. The owners of the Peking Café let me linger over my books and stay as long as I wanted to: "Take your tie! No lush!" they said kindly as they sprayed the neighboring tables with disinfectant. I ate mango and papaya, nudging the stringy parts out of my teeth with a cinnamon toothpick. I had a handleless cup of hot, stale tea, poured and reheated from a pail stored in the restaurant's walkin refrigerator, and one elegantly folded fortune cookie – a short paper nerve baked in an ear. I would tug the paper slip from the stiff clutches of the cookie and save it as a bookmark. All my books had fortunes protruding like tiny tails from their pages: *You are the crispy noodle in the salad of life. You are the master of your own destiny.* My roommate, Murph – a nose-pierced, hinky-toothed blonde from Dubuque, who used black soap and black dental floss and whose quick opinions were impressively harsh (she pronounced Dubuque "Du-ba-cue") – always added the phrase "in bed" to any fortune-cookie fortune, so in my mind I read them that way, too: *You are the master of your own destiny. In bed.* Well, that was true. *Debt is a seductive liar. In bed.* Or, the less well translated, *Your fate will blossom like a bloom.* Or the sly, wise guy: *A refreshing change is in your future.* Sometimes, as a better joke, I added, *though not in bed. You will soon make money.* Or: *Wealth is a wise woman's man. Though not in bed.*

I looked daily at the employment listings. Childcare was in demand: I turned in my final papers and answered the ads. One fortyish pregnant woman after another hung up my coat, sat me in her living room, then waddled out to the kitchen, got my tea, and waddled back in, clutching her back, slopping tea onto the saucer, and asking me questions. "What would you do if our little baby started crying and wouldn't stop?" "Are you available evenings?" "What do you think of as a useful educational activity for a small child?" I had no idea. I had never seen so many pregnant women in such a short period of time – five in all. It alarmed me. They did not look radiant. They looked reddened with high blood pressure and frightened. I gave them my references and a written summary of my experience. My experience was not all that much – just the Pitskys and the Schultzes back home. I had once, as part of a class project on human reproduction, carried around for an entire week a sack of flour the exact weight and feel of an infant. I'd swaddled it and cuddled it and placed it in safe, cushioned places for naps. But once, when no one was looking, I stuffed it into my backpack with a lot of sharp pens, and it got stabbed. My books, powdery white the rest of the term, became a joke in the class. I left this off my résumé. But the rest I'd typed up. To gild the lily-livered, as my dad sometimes said, I wore to my interviews what the department stores called "a career jacket," and perhaps the women liked the professionalism of that. They were professionals themselves. Two were lawyers, one was a journalist, one was a doctor, one a high-school teacher. Where were the husbands? "Oh, at work," the women said vaguely. All except the journalist, who said, "Good question!"

The last house I went to was a gray stucco prairie house with a chimney cloaked in dead ivy. Some desiccated mums were still in pots on the porch. Ice frosted the crisp heads of the flowers. Leaning against the house were a shovel and a rake, and tucked into a corner of the porch were two phone books still in shrink-wrap. The woman of the house opened the door. She was pale and compact, no sags or pouches, linen skin tight across the bone. The hollows of her cheeks were powdered darkly, as if with the pollen of a tiger lily. Her hair was cropped short and dyed the fashionable bright auburn of a ladybug. Her earrings were buttons of deepest orange, her leggings mahogany, her sweater rust-colored, and her lips a maroonish brown. She looked like a highly controlled oxidation experiment. "Come in," she said, and I entered, mutely at first and then, as always, apologetically, as if I were late, though I wasn't.

The woman closed the heavy oak door behind me, and I stamped my feet on the braided rug I was standing on, to shake off the snow. I started to take off my shoes. "Oh, you don't have to take off your shoes," she said. "There's too much of that prissy Japanese stuff going on in this town. Bring in the mud." She smiled – big, theatrical, a little crazy. I had forgotten her name and was hoping she'd say it soon; if she didn't, she might not say it at all.

"I'm Tassie Keltjin," I said, thrusting out my hand. She took it and then studied my face. "Yes," she said absently, unnervingly scrutinizing each of my eyes. Her gaze made a slow, observing circle around my nose and mouth. "I'm Sarah Brink," she said finally. I was not used to being looked at close up, not used to the thing I was looking at looking back. Certainly my own mother had never done such looking, and in general my face had the kind of smooth, round stupidity that did not prompt the world's study. I had always felt as hidden as the hull in a berry, as secret and fetal as the curled fortune in a cookie, and such hiddenness was not without its advantages, its egotisms, its grief-fed grandiosities. "Here, let me take your coat," Sarah Brink said finally, and only then, as she lifted it off me and headed across the foyer to hang it on a hat rack, did I notice that she was as thin as a pin, not pregnant at all.

She led me into the living room, stopping at the large back window first. I followed her, tried to do what she did. In the yard, most of a sizable oak tree split by lightning had been hacked and stacked by the garage for winter firewood. Near its old stump, another tree – tenuous, young, with the look of a swizzle stick – had been planted, trussed, and braced. But Sarah wasn't studying the trees. "Oh, for the love of God, look at those poor dogs," she said. We stood there, watching. The dogs next door were being kept in their yard by an invisible electric fence. One of them, a German shepherd, understood the fence, but the other one, a little terrier, did not. The German shepherd would get a game of chase going around the yard and lead the terrier right to the electrified border and then stop short, leaving the terrier to barrel on ahead into the electricity. The stunned terrier would then come racing back, shrieking with pain. "This has been going on for weeks," Sarah said.

"Reminds me of dating," I said, and Sarah spun her head around, to size me up again. Heat flew to my face. Dating? What did I know of it? My roommate, Murph, had done all the dating and had essentially abandoned me so that she could now sleep every night with this new guy she'd met. She had bequeathed me her vibrator, a strange swirling, buzzing thing that when switched to "High" gyrated in the air like someone's bored thick finger going whoop-de-do. Whose penis could this possibly resemble? Someone who had worked in a circus, perhaps. Maybe Burt Lancaster's in "Trapeze." I kept the thing on the kitchen counter, where Murph had left it for me, and occasionally I used it to stir my chocolate milk.

Sarah turned back to the window. "The neighbors just put in that invisible fence," she said. "In November. I'm sure it causes M.S. or something."

Then she got down to business. "Have a seat. Here's the deal." She motioned with an arm tossed suddenly out in a spasm. "Childcare," she began, but then stopped, as if that were sufficient.

I sat down on a chair that was upholstered in a kind of pillow ticking. "Childcare," like "healthcare," had become one word. I was about to become a dispenser of it. I opened my backpack and began fumbling through it, looking for a copy of my résumé. Sarah sat across from me on a pale-gray sofa, the very brightness of her looking as if it might stain the cushions. She twisted her legs up and around each other in such a way that the lower half of one gave the illusion of jutting out of the upper half of the other, as if she had the backward knees of a crane. She began clearing her throat, so I stopped fumbling and set the backpack aside. "Already the winter air is getting to me," she said. She turned and coughed again loudly, in that parched fashion that doctors call "unproductive." She patted her flat stomach. "Here's the deal," she said again. "We are adopting."

"Adopting?"

"A baby. We are adopting a baby. That's why we're advertising for a sitter. We'd like to line someone up ahead of time for some regular hours."

I didn't know anything about adoption. I'd known only one adopted girl when I was growing up, Becky Sussluch, who at sixteen was spoiled and beautiful and having an affair with a mussed and handsome student teacher whom I myself had a crush on. In general, I thought of adoption much as I thought of most things in life: uneasily. Adoption seemed both a cruel joke and a lovely daydream – a nice way of avoiding the blood and pain of giving birth, or, from a child's perspective, a realized fantasy of your parents not really being your parents. Your genes could thrust one arm in the air and pump up and down. Yes! You were not actually related to *them*!

"Congratulations," I murmured now to Sarah. Was that what one said?

Sarah's face lit up gratefully, as if no one had yet said an encouraging word to her on the matter. "Why, thank you! I have so much work at the restaurant that everyone I mention this to acts peculiar and quiet, so meanly worried for me. They say, 'Really!' and then all this tension springs to their mouths. They think I'm too old."

I accidentally nodded. I had no idea, conversationally, where we were. I searched, as I too often found myself having to do, to find a language, or even an octave, in which to speak. I wondered how old she was.

"I own Petit Moulin," Sarah Brink added.

Petit Moulin. I knew of it. It was one of those expensive restaurants downtown, every entrée freshly hairy with dill, every soup and dessert dripped upon as preciously as a Pollock, fillets and cutlets sprinkled with lavender dust once owned by pixies – restaurants to which students never went, unless newly pinned to a fraternity boy or dating an assistant dean or hosting a visit from concerned suburban parents. I knew that Petit Moulin served things that sounded like instruments – timbales, quenelles. God only knew what they were. I had once tried to study the menu in its lit case near the entrance, and as I stared at the words the sting of my own exile had moistened my eyes. The lowest price for an entrée was twenty-two dollars, the highest, forty-five. Forty-five! You could get a Taiwanese oil-and-water bra for that price!

I fumbled in my bag again for my résumé, and found it folded and bent but handed it to Sarah anyway. I spoke. "My father supplied a few of the restaurants around here. A few years back it was, I think."

Sarah Brink looked at my résumé. "Are you related to Bo Keltjin – Keltjin potatoes?"

It startled me to hear my father's potatoes – Kennebecs, Norlands, Pontiacs, Yukon golds, some the size of marbles, some grapefruits, depending on drought and digging times and what the beetles were up to – summed up and referred to that way right here in her living room. "That's my dad," I said.

"Why, I remember your father very well. His Klamath pearls were famous. Also the yellow fingerlings. And his purple Peruvians and Rose Finns were the first to be sold in those little netted berry pints, like jewels. I'd rush out to the farmers' market at six a.m. to get them. Come April, I should put those back on the menu." She was getting dreamy. Still, it was nice to hear my father spoken well of. He was not really respected as a farmer back home: he was a hobbyist, a truck farmer, with no real acreage, just some ducks (that every fall raped one another in a brutal fashion we never got used to), a dog, a tractor, a Web site (a Web site, for Christ's sake!), and two decorative, brockle-headed cows of dubious dairiness. We had also once had an ebullient pig named Helen, who would come when you called her name and smiled like a dolphin when you spoke to her. And then we didn't see her for a few days, and one morning over bacon and eggs my brother said, "Is this Helen?" and I dropped my fork and said, "This is Helen? Is this Helen?!" The next pig we got we never met, and its name was No. WK3746.

"Yeah, his potatoes have a rep – at least in certain places," I hastened to add. "Even my mother admires them, and she's hard to please. She used to call them *pommes de terre de l'air.*"

"That's funny," Sarah said.

I feared that Sarah was one of those women who, instead of laughing, said, "That's funny," or, instead of smiling, said, "That's interesting," or instead of saying, "You are a stupid blithering idiot," said, "Well, I think it's a little more complicated than that." I never knew what to do around such people, especially the ones who, after you spoke, liked to say, enigmatically, "I see." Usually I just went mute.

"Potatoes are grown from the eyes of other potatoes," I said, apropos of God knows what.

"Yes." Sarah looked at me searchingly. "Your father seemed like a nice man. How old is he now?"

"Forty-five."

"Forty-five! Why, I'm forty-five. That means I'm old

enough to be your . . ." She took a breath, still processing her own amazement.

"To be my dad?" I said.

Sarah Brink laughed, a quasi-laugh, a socially constructed laugh – a collection of predetermined notes, like the chimes of a doorbell.

"So here's the job description," she said when the laugh was through.

Walking home, I tried to remember everything that Sarah Brink had said to me. It was a mile back to my apartment, so I replayed long snippets of her voice, though the cold air was the sort that bullied a walker into mental muteness. *This is an incredibly important position for us, even if we are hiring at the last minute. If we hire you, we would like you to be there with us for everything, from the very first day. We would like you to feel like part of our family, since, of course, you* will *be part of it.*

I tried to think who Sarah Brink reminded me of, though I was sure it wasn't anyone I'd actually met. Probably she reminded me of a character from a television show I'd watched years before. But not the star. Definitely not the star. More like the star's neatnik roommate or the star's kooky cousin from Cleveland. I knew that, even once she had a baby, she would never be able to shake the Auntie Mame quality from her mothering. There were worse things, I supposed.

My apartment was in one of those old frame houses close to campus, in the student ghetto that abutted the university stadium. Across the street, the gray concrete stadium wall rose three times higher than any building around, and overshadowed the neighborhood in a bleak and brutal way. In spring and fall, convening marching bands, with their vibrating tubas and snares, routinely rattled our windowpanes. On Sunday mornings, after the game, the sidewalk was littered with cardboard signs that read, "I Need Tickets."

In the hallway of my apartment, the phone-machine light was blinking and I pressed Play, turned up the volume, then went on into my bedroom, where I flopped down on my bed, in the Icelandic afternoon dusk, door open, to listen. A long, uncertain silence preceded the message. "Yes, hello, this is Sarah Brink phoning for Tassie Keltjin." There was another long, uncertain silence. I sat straight up to hear if there was anything else. "Could she phone me back sometime this evening? Thank you very much."

I got up and rewound the machine and played the message from Sarah Brink again. What was I frightened of? I wasn't sure. But I decided to wait until the morning to phone her back. I got into my nightgown, made a grilled-cheese sandwich and some mint tea, then took them back into my room, where I consumed them in bed. Ringed by crumbs and grease, newspapers and a book, I fell asleep.

I woke up in a blaze of white sun. I had neglected to pull down the shades and it had snowed during the night; the morning rays reflected off the snow on the sills and on the low adjacent roof, setting the room on fire with daylight. I tried not to think about my life. I did not have any good, solid plans for it long term – no bad plans, either, no plans at all – and the lostness of that, compared with the clear ambitions of my friends (marriage, children, law school), sometimes shamed me. Other times, in my mind I defended such a condition as morally and intellectually superior – my life was open and ready and free – but that did not make it any less lonely. I got up, trudged barefoot across the cold floor, and made a cup of coffee, with a brown plastic Melitta filter and a paper towel, dripping it into a single ceramic mug that said "Moose Timber Lodge." Murph had gone there once, for a weekend, with her new B.F.

The phone rang again before I'd had time to let the coffee kick in and give me words to say; nonetheless, I picked up the receiver.

"Hi, is this Tassie?" the newly familiar voice said.

"Yes, it is." I frantically gulped at my coffee. What time was it? Too soon for calls.

"This is Sarah Brink. Did I wake you? I'm sorry. I'm calling too early, aren't I?"

"Oh, no," I said, lest she think I was a shiftless bum. Better a lying sack of shit. "I didn't know whether I'd left a message on the correct machine or not. And I wanted to get back to you as soon as possible before you accepted an offer from someone else." Little did she know – none of the five other women had even called. "I've talked it over with my husband, and we'd like to offer you the job."

Could she even have checked the references I'd listed? Had there been enough time?

"Oh, thank you," I said.

"We'll start you at ten dollars an hour, with the possibility of raises down the line. The problem is this: the job starts today."

"Today?" I sipped again.

"Yes, I'm sorry. We're going to Kronenkee to meet the birth mother, and we'd like you to come with us."

"Yes, well, I think that would be O.K."

"So you accept the position?"

"Yes, I guess I do."

"You do? You can't know how happy you've made me."

"Really?" I asked, all the while wondering, Where's the new employee's first-day orientation meeting? Where is the "You've Picked a Great Place to Work" PowerPoint presentation? The coffee was kicking in, but not helpfully.

"Oh, yes, really," she said. "Can you be here by noon?"

The appointment with the birth mother was for two p.m. at the Perkins restaurant in Kronenkee, a town an hour away with a part-German, part-Indian name that I'd always assumed meant "wampum." The social worker who ran the adoption agency was supposed to meet us there with the birth mother, so that we could all cheerfully assess one another. I had walked the half hour to Sarah Brink's house and then waited twenty minutes while she scrambled around doing things, making quick phone calls to her restaurant – "Meeska, the Concord coulis has got to be more than grape jam!" – or searching madly for her sunglasses ("I hate that snow glare on those two-lane roads"), all the while apologizing to me from the next room. In the car, on our way up, I sat next to her in the front seat, since her husband, Edward, whom, strangely, I still hadn't met, couldn't get out of some meeting or other and had apparently told Sarah to go ahead without him. "Marriage," Sarah said, sighing. As if I had any idea what that meant.

I looked sideways at Sarah, who was hatless, with a long cranberry scarf coiled twice about her neck. The sun caught the shiny artifice of her hair as well as the stray tufts of white lint on her peacoat. Still, especially with the sunglasses in winter – something I had seldom seen before – she looked glamorous. I was not used to speaking to adults, so I felt comfortable just being quiet with her, and soon she turned on the classical-music station and we listened to Mussorgsky's "Pictures at an Exhibition" and "Night on Bald Mountain" for the entire ride. "They've told me the birth mother is very beautiful," Sarah said, at one point. And I said nothing, not knowing what to say.

We waited in the second booth at Perkins, Sarah and I sitting on the same side, to leave the opposite seat open for the two people we were waiting for. Sarah ordered Perkins's Bottomless Pot of Coffee for the entire table, and the waitress went away to get it. "Oh, look, here they are," Sarah murmured, and I looked up to see a heavily made-up middle-aged woman in a deep-pink parka holding the arm of a girl probably my age, maybe younger, who was very pregnant, very pretty, and who, as I could see, even from that distance, when she smiled at us, had scarcely a tooth in her head. We stood and moved toward them. The girl wore an electronic bracelet on her wrist, but was clearly unembarrassed by this because she energetically thrust her hand out of her sleeve in greeting. I shook it. "Hi," she said to me. I wondered what she had done, and why the bracelet was not around her ankle instead. Perhaps she had been very, very bad and had two.

"Hi," I replied, trying to smile companionably and not stare at her stomach.

"This is the mother, here," the woman in the pink parka told the pregnant girl, indicating Sarah. "Sarah Brink? Amber Bowers."

"Hi – it's so wonderful to meet you." Sarah grasped Amber's hand warmly and shook it for too long. Amber kept turning back hopefully toward me, as if she were as baffled as

I was to be in the company of these mysterious middle-aged women.

"I'm Tassie Keltjin," I said quickly, shaking Amber's penalized hand again. The delicate knobs of her wrists and her elegant fingers were a strange contrast to her toothlessness and the hard plastic parole band. "I'm going to work for Sarah, as a childcare provider."

"And I'm Letitia Gherlich," the adoption-agency woman said, shaking my hand, though not letting go of Amber's coat sleeve, as if she might escape. Amber did have the face, if not currently the body, of someone who perhaps more than once had made a run for it.

"Hey, Letitia," Sarah said, and threw her arms around her as if they were old friends, though Letitia stiffened a little.

After that, things moved with swiftness and awkwardness both, like something simultaneously strong and broken. We hung up coats, we ordered, we ate, we made chitchat about the food and the snow. "Oh, there's my probation officer," Amber said, giggling; her face brightened, as if she had a little crush on him. "I think he sees us. He's sitting right over there by the window." We looked up to see the probation officer, his blue jacket still on, his bottomless Diet Coke stacked with ice. A going-to-seed hunk in a windbreaker: the world seemed full of them. We all just stared to buy ourselves time, I suppose, and to avoid the actual question of Amber's crimes.

Letitia began to speak to Sarah, on Amber's behalf. "Amber is happy to meet Tassie as well as you, Sarah." Here Amber looked across at me and rolled her eyes, as if we were two girls out with our embarrassing mothers. I had been noticing Amber's face, which was as lovely as advertised but sassy, with a strange electricity animating it; with the missing teeth she seemed like a slightly sophisticated hillbilly or an infant freak. Her hair was a gingery blond, shoulder length, as straight and coarse as a horse's tail.

Letitia, perhaps nervous about the sticky parts of a deal, went on cheerily, "The birth father is white. I did mention that to you, didn't I?"

Sarah said nothing, her face momentarily inscrutable.

Letitia continued. "Tall and good-looking, like Amber."

Amber smiled happily. "We broke up," she said, shrugging.

"Do you have a picture of him, though? To show Sarah?" Letitia was selling the idea of the handsome white-boy dad.

"I don't think I ever had a damn picture of him," Amber said, shaking her head. Now she looked at me, grinning. "Except in my mind. My mind's a regular exhibition." The phrase was oddly reminiscent of the Mussorgsky we'd listened to in the car. And her mouth, with its few and crooked teeth, bits of shell awash on a reef of gum, seemed a curious home for her voice, which was slowly surprising, with its intelligence and humor. There was a lull now. Amber suddenly leaned back, physically uncomfortable.

"So, where's your husband?" she asked Sarah.

I examined Sarah's face for the stiffened look of the accused.

"He's, oh, he's at a meeting his lab is having with the university. I run my own restaurant in town, so I can make up my own schedule as far as meetings go. But, well, he's at the beck and call of others – at least today he is."

"Do you think you really have time for a baby, owning a restaurant and all?" Amber was not shy. If she had been shy, not one of us would be at Perkins right now.

Sarah refused to be flustered. She'd clearly heard remarks of this sort a dozen times. But before she could speak Letitia spoke for her.

"That's why Tassie is here. Tassie's the backup. But Sarah will always be around. She'll be the mom. And she can do a lot of her work right out of the house – isn't that right, Sarah?"

What work could Sarah do from the house? Yell at Meeska about the coulis?

"Absolutely," Sarah said. "Oh, I forgot. I brought you a present, Amber." She took a CD from her purse. "It's a mixed CD of my favorite classical music."

Amber took it and stashed it in her bag with the most fleeting of glances. Perhaps she'd had a slew of these lunches as a means of collecting goodies, which she would later sell on eBay. "And I have a present for you, too," she said, and handed Sarah a foil-wrapped pat of butter she plucked from the bowl on the table.

"Mine's wrapped!" Amber said, smiling wickedly. The CD hadn't been. A scalding boldness gripped Amber's face, then a kind of guilt, then drifty blankness, like songs off a jukebox list, flipped through unchosen.

"Thanks!" Sarah said gamely. You had to hand it to her. She opened up the butter and applied it to her mouth like lip gloss. "Prevents chapped lips."

"You're welcome," Amber said.

When we all walked out to the parking lot, the probation officer followed. An American flag was flapping noisily next to the Perkins sign; the air was picking up wind and snow. The probation officer walked to his car and got in but did not start it. Amber's face was completely lit up. I saw that she was fantastically in love with him. She was not concentrating on any of us, and something about this provoked Sarah.

"Well," she said, studying Amber with an artificial smile.

"Yes, well," Amber said.

"All right, then," Letitia said.

"Can I give you some advice, Amber?" Sarah asked, standing there, as Letitia clutched Amber even tighter. The windbreakered parole officer gave a wave and drove off.

"What?" Amber said to Sarah, but to me she smiled and said, "He was definitely following me."

"When I was your age, I had some rebellious ideas," Sarah continued her unsolicited advice to Amber. "I got in trouble now and again, here and there, but I realized it was because I was doing things I wasn't any good at. Look at this." She tapped Amber's electronic bracelet with a gloved index finger. "You're eighteen. Don't sell drugs. You're no good at it. Do something you're good at."

Sarah meant this tough-love speech compassionately, I could see, but Amber's face flushed with insult, then hardened. "That's what I'm trying to do," she said indignantly, and tore herself from Letitia's grip, walked over to what was apparently Letitia's car, and got in on the passenger side.

Baby, it's scold outside, Murph would have said if she had been there.

"We'll talk later," Letitia called to Sarah, waving goodbye and hurrying off to Amber.

"Well," Sarah said as we both got into her car. "That was, for all intents and purposes, a complete disaster." She started up the engine. "You know?" she continued. "I always do the wrong thing. I do the wrong thing so much that the times I actually do the right thing stand out so brightly in my memory that I forget I always do the wrong thing."

We rode home mostly in silence, Sarah offering me gum, then cough drops, both of which I took, thanking her. When I glanced over at her, driving without her sunglasses, her scarf wrapped now around her head like a babushka, she seemed watery, far away, lost in thought, and I wondered how a nice, attractive girl – for I thought I had glimpsed on the way up the girl she once was, her face still and thoughtful, her hair in the sun ablaze with light – how a girl like that became a lonely woman with a yarny schmatte on her head, became this, whatever it was. After a childhood of hungering to be an adult, I no longer felt much hunger. Unexpected fates had begun to catch my notice. These middle-aged women seemed very tired to me, as if hope had been wrung out of them and replaced with a deathly, walking sort of sleep.

Sarah's cell phone played the beginning of "Eine Kleine Nachtmusik," its vigorous twang not unlike a harpsichord, and so not completely offensive to the spirit of Mozart, who perhaps did not have to roll about in his grave as much as so many of his colleagues did, since the advent of electronic things.

Sarah pulled the phone from her bag, slowing the car slightly as she did. "Excuse me," she said to me. "Yeah?" she said into the phone. All this despite the bumper sticker on her car that read, "Perhaps You Would Drive Better with That Cell Phone Shoved up Your Ass." She also had one that said, "If God Speaks Through Burning Bushes, Let's Burn Bush and Listen to What God Says." It was interesting to me that such a woman, one with such rhetorical violence affixed to her car, had got past the adoption agency's screening procedures, whatever they were.

"Sarah, hi, it's Letitia," I heard.

I don't know why I could hear so clearly – perhaps Sarah was a little deaf and had the volume turned up high.

"Hi, Letitia." I believed I wasn't supposed to listen, so I looked out the window at the bleak snowy landscape; the sun was low and feeble, dissolving whitely like a lemon drop. Each town we passed through had a Dairy Queen, with customers lined up, even in winter. When I looked back at Sarah I saw her powdered, thinning skin like a crêpe, with the same light freckles as a crêpe, her gnarly-knuckled hand, arthritic from chopping herbs, going through her spiky russet hair, knocking back her scarf.

Education had not entirely elevated my concerns in life. It had probably not even assisted my analyses of these concerns. I was too fresh from childhood. Subconsciously, my deepest brain still a cupboard of fairy tales, I suppose I believed that if a pretty woman was no longer pretty she had done something bad to deserve it. I had a young girl's belief that this kind of negative aging would never happen to me. Death would happen to me – I knew this from reading British poetry. But the drying, hunching, blanching, hobbling, fading, fattening, thinning, slowing? I would just not let those things happen to *moi*.

Sarah switched ears, making it harder for me to hear, but then switched back and slowed to let a convoy of trucks pass. I could hear Letitia: "If this doesn't work out with Amber, there are babies on the international market. We've had a lot of luck with South America. Paraguay has opened up again, and other countries, too. And they're not all brown there, either. There's been a lot of German influence, and some of these kids are beautiful, very blond, or blue-eyed, or both."

"Well, thanks for the info," Sarah said brusquely. "Get back to me on Amber." Letitia then said something I couldn't make out, and Sarah said quickly, "Gotta run – there's an ice patch ahead," and snapped the phone shut.

"The babies of Nazis," Sarah said, shaking her head.

"They're hawking Nazi babies. Racially superior. Unbelievable." She raked her fingers yet again through the bright desert grass of her hair. "Blue eyes!" she cried. "The human race has really come a long way!" She shook her head again, this time with a horsey, nasal exhalation of disgust.

"Yeah," I said dopily.

"You may be too young to know this yet, but eventually you will look around and notice: Nazis always have the last laugh."

Then we were wordless through the towns of Terre Noire and Fond du Marais, places named both whimsically and fearfully by French fur traders, before the subsequent flattened pronunciations by Scandinavian farmers made the names even more absurd: "Turn Ore" and "Fondu Morass."

"You'll find I say about eighty-nine per cent of what's on my mind," Sarah said. "For the other eleven per cent? I use a sauna."

She put a CD in the car player. "Bach's first French suite. Do you know it?" After some clicking and static, it began, stately and sad. "I think so," I said, not sure at all. My friends had already begun to lie, to bluff a sophistication that they felt they would authentically possess by the end of the ten-second bluff. I was not only less inclined this way but less skilled. "Maybe not, though," I added. Then, "Wait, it's ringing a bell."

"Oh, it's the most beautiful thing," she said. "Especially with this pianist." It was someone humming along with the light dirge of the Bach. Later, I would own every loopy Glenn Gould recording available, but there in the car with Sarah was the first time I'd ever heard him play. The piece was like an elegant interrogation made of tangled yarn, a query from a well-dressed man in a casket, not yet dead. It proceeded slowly, like a careful equation, and then not: if *x* equals *y*, if major equals minor, if death equals part of life and life part of death, then what is the sum of the infinite notes of this one phrase? It asked, answered, re-asked, its moody asking a refinement of reluctance or dislike. I had never heard a melody quite like it.

Outside my house, Sarah put the car in park. She patted me on the shoulder, then let her hand run down my coat sleeve. "Thanks," she said. "Phone me when you get back into town after Christmas." Her face looked fantastically sad.

"O.K.," I said. "Sounds good." *Sounds good.* It was the Midwestern girl's reply to everything. It appeared to clinch a deal, was somewhat the same as the more soldierly *Good to go*, except that it was promiseless – mere affirmative description. It got you away, out the door.

2009

COMMUNITY LIFE

WHEN OLENA WAS a little girl, she had called them lie-berries – a fibbing fruit, a story store – and now she had a job in one. She had originally wanted to teach English literature, but when she failed to warm to the graduate study of it, its french-fried theories – a vocabulary of arson! – she'd transferred to library school, where everyone was taught to take care of books, tenderly, as if they were dishes or dolls.

She had learned to read at an early age. Her parents, newly settled in Vermont from Tirgu Mures in Transylvania, were anxious that their daughter learn to speak English, to blend in with the community in a way they felt they probably never would, and so every Saturday they took her to the children's section of the Rutland library and let her spend time with the librarian, who chose books for her and sometimes even read a page or two out loud, though there was a sign that said PLEASE BE QUIET BOYS AND GIRLS. No comma.

Which made it seem to Olena that only the boys had to be quiet. She and the librarian could do whatever they wanted.

She had loved the librarian.

And when Olena's Romanian began to recede altogether, and in its stead bloomed a slow, rich English-speaking voice, not unlike the librarian's, too womanly for a little girl, the other children on her street became even more afraid of her. *"Dracula!"* they shouted. *"Transylvaniess!"* they shrieked, and ran.

"You'll have a new name now," her father told her the first day of first grade. He had already changed their last name from Todorescu to Resnick. His shop was called "Resnick's Furs." "From here on in, you will no longer be Olena. You will have a nice American name: Nell."

"You make to say ze name," her mother said. "When ze teacher tell you *Olena*, you say, '*No, Nell.*' Say *Nell.*"

"Nell," said Olena. But when she got to school, the teacher, sensing something dreamy and outcast in her, clasped her hand and exclaimed, "Olena! What a beautiful name!" Olena's heart filled with gratitude and surprise, and she fell in close to the teacher's hip, adoring and mute.

From there on in, only her parents, in their throaty Romanian accents, ever called her Nell, her secret, jaunty American self existing only for them.

"Nell, how are ze ozer children at ze school?"

"Nell, please to tell us what you do."

Years later, when they were killed in a car crash on the Farm to Market Road, and the Nell-that-never-lived died with them, Olena, numbly rearranging the letters of her own name on the envelopes of the sympathy cards she received, discovered what the letters spelled: *Olena*; *Alone*. It was a body walled in the cellar of her, a whiff and forecast of doom like an early, rotten spring – and she longed for the Nell-that-never-lived's return. She wished to start over again, to be someone living coltishly in the world, not someone hidden away, behind books, with a carefully learned voice and a sad past.

She missed her mother the most.

The library Olena worked in was one of the most prestigious university libraries in the Midwest. It housed a large collection of rare and foreign books, and she had driven across several states to get there, squinting through the splattered tempera of insects on the windshield, watching for the dark tail of a possible tornado, and getting sick, painfully, in Indiana, in the rest rooms of the dead-Hoosier service plazas along I-80. The ladies' rooms there had had electric eyes for the toilets, the sinks, the hand dryers, and she'd set them all off by staggering in and out of the stalls or leaning into the sinks. "You the only one in here?" asked a cleaning woman. "You the only one in here making this racket?" Olena had smiled, a dog's smile; in the yellowish light, everything seemed tragic and ridiculous and unable to stop. The flatness of the terrain gave her vertigo, she decided, that was it. The land was windswept; there were no smells. In Vermont, she had felt cradled by mountains. Now, here, she would have to be brave.

But she had no memory of how to be brave. Here, it seemed, she had no memories at all. Nothing triggered them. And once in a while, when she gave voice to the fleeting edge of one, it seemed like something she was making up.

She first met Nick at the library in May. She was temporarily positioned at the reference desk, hauled out from her ordinary task as supervisor of foreign cataloging, to replace someone who was ill. Nick was researching statistics on municipal campaign spending in the state. "Haven't stepped into a library since I was eighteen," he said. He looked at least forty.

She showed him where he might look. "Try looking here," she said, writing down the names of indexes to state records, but he kept looking at *her.* "Or here."

"I'm managing a county board seat campaign," he said. "The election's not until the fall, but I'm trying to get a jump on things." His hair was a coppery brown, threaded through with silver. There was something animated in his eyes, like pond life. "I just wanted to get some comparison figures. Will you have a cup of coffee with me?"

"I don't think so," she said.

But he came back the next day and asked her again.

The coffee shop near campus was hot and noisy, crowded with students, and Nick loudly ordered espresso for them both. She usually didn't like espresso, its gritty, cigarish taste. But there was in the air that kind of distortion that bent you a little; it caused your usual self to grow slippery, to wander off and shop, to get blurry, bleed, bevel with possibility. She drank the espresso fast, with determination and a sense of adventure. "I guess I'll have a second," she said, and wiped her mouth with a napkin.

"I'll get it," said Nick, and when he came back, he told her some more about the campaign he was running. "It's important to get the endorsements of the neighborhood associations," he said. He ran a bratwurst and frozen yogurt stand called Please Squeeze and Bratwursts. He had gotten to know a lot of people that way. "I feel alive and relevant, living my life like this," he said. "I don't feel like I've sold out."

"Sold out to what?" she asked.

He smiled. "I can tell you're not from around here," he said. He raked his hand through the various metals of his hair. "*Selling out.* Like doing something you really never wanted to do, and getting paid too much for it."

"Oh," she said.

"When I was a kid, my father said to me, 'Sometimes in life, son, you're going to find you have to do things you don't want to do,' and I looked him right in the eye and said, 'No fucking way.'" Olena laughed. "I mean, you probably always wanted to be a librarian, right?"

She looked at all the crooked diagonals of his face and couldn't tell whether he was serious. "Me?" she said. "I first went to graduate school to be an English professor." She sighed, switched elbows, sinking her chin into her other hand. "I did try," she said. "I read Derrida. I read Lacan. I read *Reading Lacan.* I read 'Reading *Reading Lacan*' – and that's when I applied to library school."

"I don't know who Lacan is," he said.

"He's, well – you see? That's why I like libraries: No whos or whys. Just 'where is it?'"

"And *where* are you from?" he asked, his face briefly animated by his own clever change of subject. "Originally." There was, it seemed, a way of spotting those not native to the town. It was a college town, attractive and dull, and it hurried the transients along – the students, gypsies, visiting scholars and comics – with a motion not unlike peristalsis.

"Vermont," she said.

"Vermont!" Nick exclaimed, as if this were exotic, which made her glad she hadn't said something like Transylvania. He leaned toward her, confidentially. "I have to tell you: I own one chair from Ethan Allen Furniture."

"You do?" She smiled. "I won't tell anyone."

"Before that, however, I was in prison, and didn't own a stick."

"Really?" she asked. She sat back. Was he telling the truth? As a girl, she'd been very gullible, but she had always learned more that way.

"I went to school here," he said. "In the sixties. I bombed a warehouse where the military was storing research supplies. I got twelve years." He paused, searching her eyes to see how she was doing with this, how *he* was doing with it. Then he fetched back his gaze, like a piece of jewelry he'd merely wanted to show her, quick. "There wasn't supposed to be anyone there; we'd checked it all out in advance. But this poor asshole named Lawrence Sperry – Larry Sperry! Christ, can you imagine having a name like that?"

"Sure," said Olena.

Nick looked at her suspiciously. "He was in there, working late. He lost a leg and an eye in the explosion. I got the federal pen in Winford. Attempted murder."

The thick coffee coated his lips. He had been looking steadily at her, but now he looked away.

"Would you like a bun?" asked Olena. "I'm going to go get a bun." She stood, but he turned and gazed up at her with such disbelief that she sat back down again, sloppily, sidesaddle. She twisted forward, leaned into the table. "I'm sorry. Is that all true, what you just said? Did that really happen to you?"

"What?" His mouth fell open. "You think I'd make that up?"

"It's just that, well, I work around a lot of literature," she said.

" 'Literature,' " he repeated.

She touched his hand. She didn't know what else to do. "Can I cook dinner for you some night? Tonight?"

There was a blaze in his eye, a concentrated seeing. He seemed for a moment able to look right into her, know her in a way that was uncluttered by actually knowing her. He seemed to have no information or misinformation, only a kind of photography, factless but true.

"Yes," he said, "you can."

Which was how he came to spend the evening beneath

the cheap stained-glass lamp of her dining room, its barroom red, its Schlitz-Tiffany light, and then to spend the night, and not leave.

Olena had never lived with a man before. "Except my father," she said, and Nick studied her eyes, the streak of blankness in them, when she said it. Though she had dated two different boys in college, they were the kind who liked to leave early, to eat breakfast without her at smoky greasy spoons, to sit at the counter with the large men in the blue windbreakers, read the paper, get their cups refilled.

She had never been with anyone who stayed. Anyone who'd moved in his box of tapes, his Ethan Allen chair.

Anyone who'd had lease problems at his old place.

"I'm trying to bring this thing together," he said, holding her in the middle of the afternoon. "My life, the campaign, my thing with you: I'm trying to get all my birds to land in the same yard." Out the window, there was an afternoon moon, like a golf ball, pocked and stuck. She looked at the calcified egg of it, its coin face, its blue neighborhood of nothing. Then she looked at him. There was the pond life again in his eyes, and in the rest of his face a hesitant, warm stillness.

"Do you like making love to me?" she asked, at night, during a thunderstorm.

"Of course. Why do you ask?"

"Are you satisfied with me?"

He turned toward her, kissed her. "Yes," he said. "I don't need a show."

She was quiet for a long time. "People are giving shows?"

The rain and wind rushed down the gutters, snapped the branches of the weak trees in the side yard.

He had her inexperience and self-esteem in mind. At the movies, at the beginning, he whispered, "Twentieth Century-Fox. Baby, that's you." During a slapstick part, in a library where card catalogs were upended and scattered wildly through the air, she broke into a pale, cold sweat, and he moved toward her, hid her head in his chest, saying, "Don't look, don't look." At the end, they would sit through the long credits – gaffer, best boy, key grip. "That's what *we* need to get," he said. "A grip."

"Yes," she said. "Also a *negative cutter.*"

Other times, he encouraged her to walk around the house naked. "If you got it, do it." He smiled, paused, feigned confusion. "If you do it, have it. If you flaunt it, do it."

"If you have it, got it," she added.

"If you say it, mean it." And he pulled her toward him like a dancing partner with soft shoes and the smiling mouth of love.

But too often she lay awake, wondering. There was something missing. Something wasn't happening to her, or was it to him? All through the summer, the thunderstorms set the sky on fire while she lay there, listening for the train sound of a tornado, which never came – though the lightning ripped open the night and lit the trees like things too suddenly remembered, then left them indecipherable again in the dark.

"You're not feeling anything, are you?" he finally said. "What is wrong?"

"I'm not sure," she said cryptically. "The rainstorms are so loud in this part of the world." The wind from a storm blew through the screens and sometimes caused the door to the bedroom to slam shut. "I don't like a door to slam," she whispered. "It makes me think someone is mad."

At the library, there were Romanian books coming in – Olena was to skim them, read them just enough to proffer a brief description for the catalog listing. It dismayed her that her Romanian was so weak, that it had seemed almost to vanish, a mere handkerchief in a stairwell, and that now, daily, another book arrived to reprimand her.

She missed her mother the most.

On her lunch break, she went to Nick's stand for a frozen yogurt. He looked tired, bedraggled, his hair like sprockets. "You want the Sperry Cherry or the Lemon Bomber?" he asked. These were his joke names, the ones he threatened really to use someday.

"How about apple?" she said.

He cut up an apple and arranged it in a paper dish. He squeezed yogurt from a chrome machine. "There's a fund-raiser tonight for the Teetlebaum campaign."

"Oh," she said. She had been to these fund-raisers before. At first she had liked them, glimpsing corners of the city she would never have seen otherwise, Nick leading her out into them, Nick knowing everyone, so that it seemed her life filled with possibility, with homefulness. But finally, she felt, such events were too full of dreary, glad-handing people speaking incessantly of their camping trips out west. They never really spoke *to* you. They spoke toward you. They spoke at you. They spoke near you, on you. They believed themselves crucial to the welfare of the community. But they seldom went to libraries. They didn't read books. "At least they're *contributers to the community*," said Nick. "At least they're not sucking the blood of it."

"Lapping," she said.

"What?"

"Gnashing and lapping. Not sucking."

He looked at her in a doubtful, worried way. "I looked it up once," she said.

"Whatever." He scowled. "At least they care. At least they're trying to give something back."

"I'd rather live in Russia," she said.

"I'll be back around ten or so," he said.

"You don't want me to come?" Truth was she disliked Ken Teetlebaum. Perhaps Nick had figured this out. Though he had the support of the local leftover Left, there was something fatuous and vain about Ken. He tended to do little isometric leg exercises while you were talking to him. Often he took out a Woolworth photo of himself and showed it to people. "Look at this," he'd say. "This was back when I had long hair, can you believe it?" And people would look and see a handsome teenaged boy who bore only a slight resemblance to the puffy Ken Teetlebaum of today. "Don't I look like Eric Clapton?"

"Eric Clapton would never have sat in a Woolworth photo booth like some high school girl," Olena had said once, in the caustic blurt that sometimes afflicts the shy. Ken had looked at her in a laughing, hurt sort of way, and after that he stopped showing the photo around when she was present.

"You can come, if you want to." Nick reached up, smoothed his hair, and looked handsome again. "Meet me there."

The fund-raiser was in the upstairs room of a local restaurant called Dutch's. She paid ten dollars, went in, and ate a lot of raw cauliflower and hummus before she saw Nick back in a far corner, talking to a woman in jeans and a brown blazer. She was the sort of woman that Nick might twist around to look at in restaurants: fiery auburn hair cut bluntly in a pageboy. She had a pretty face, but the hair was too severe, too separate and tended to. Olena herself had long, disorganized hair, and she wore it pulled back messily in a clip. When she reached up to wave to Nick, and he looked away without acknowledging her, back toward the auburn pageboy, Olena kept her hand up and moved it back, to fuss with the clip. She would never fit in here, she thought. Not among these jolly, activist-clerk types. She preferred the quiet poet-clerks of the library. They were delicate and territorial, intellectual, and physically unwell. They sat around at work, thinking up Tom Swifties: *I have to go to the hardware store, he said wrenchingly.*

Would you like a soda? he asked spritely.

They spent weekends at the Mayo Clinic. "An amusement park for hypochondriacs," said a cataloger named Sarah. "A cross between Lourdes and *The New Price Is Right*," said someone else named George. These were the people she liked: the kind you couldn't really live with.

She turned to head toward the ladies' room and bumped into Ken. He gave her a hug hello, and then whispered in her ear, "You live with Nick. Help us think of an issue. I need another issue."

"I'll get you one at the issue store," she said, and pulled away as someone approached him with a heartily extended hand and a false, booming "Here's the man of the hour." In the bathroom, she stared at her own reflection: in an attempt at extroversion, she had worn a tunic with large slices of watermelon depicted on the front. What had she been thinking of?

She went into the stall and slid the bolt shut. She read the graffiti on the back of the door. *Anita loves David S.* Or: *Christ + Diane W.* It was good to see that even in a town like this, people could love one another.

"Who were you talking to?" she asked him later at home.

"Who? What do you mean?"

"The one with the plasticine hair."

"Oh, Erin? She does look like she does something to her hair. It looks like she hennas it."

"It looks like she tacks it against the wall and stands underneath it."

"She's head of the Bayre Corners Neighborhood Association. Come September, we're really going to need her endorsement."

Olena sighed, looked away.

"It's the democratic process," said Nick.

"I'd rather have a king and queen," she said.

The following Friday, the night of the Fish Fry Fund-raiser at the Labor Temple, was the night Nick slept with Erin of the Bayre Corners Neighborhood Association. He arrived back home at seven in the morning and confessed to Olena, who, when Nick hadn't come home, had downed half a packet of Dramamine to get to sleep.

"I'm sorry," he said, his head in his hands. "It's a sixties thing."

"A sixties thing?" She was fuzzy, zonked from the Dramamine.

"You get all involved in a political event, and you find yourself sleeping together. She's from that era, too. It's also that, I don't know, she just seems to really care about her community. She's got this reaching, expressive side to her. I got caught up in that." He was sitting down, leaning forward on his knees, talking to his shoes. The electric fan was blowing on him, moving his hair gently, like weeds in water.

"A sixties thing?" Olena repeated. "A sixties thing, what is that – like 'Easy to Be Hard'?" It was the song she remembered best. But now something switched off in her. The bones in her chest hurt. Even the room seemed changed – brighter and awful. Everything had fled, run away to become something else. She started to perspire under her arms and her face grew hot. "You're a murderer," she said. "That's finally what you are. That's finally what you'll always be." She began to weep so loudly that Nick got up, closed the windows. Then he sat down and held her – who else was there to hold her? – and she held him back.

He bought her a large garnet ring, a cough drop set in brass. He did the dishes ten straight days in a row. She had a tendency to go to bed right after supper and sleep, heavily, needing the escape. She had become afraid of going out – restaurants, stores, the tension in her shoulders, the fear gripping her face when she was there, as if people knew she was a foreigner and a fool – and for fifteen additional days he did the cooking and shopping. His car was always parked on the outside of the driveway, and hers was always in first, close, blocked in, as if to indicate who most belonged to the community, to the world, and who most belonged tucked in away from it, in a house. Perhaps in bed. Perhaps asleep.

"You need more life around you," said Nick, cradling her, though she'd gone stiff and still. His face was plaintive and suntanned, the notes and varnish of a violin. "You need a greater sense of life around you." Outside, there was the old rot smell of rain coming.

"How have you managed to get a suntan when there's been so much rain?" she asked.

"It's summer," he said. "I work outside, remember?"

"There are no sleeve marks," she said. "Where are you going?"

She had become afraid of the community. It was her enemy. Other people, other women.

She had, without realizing it at the time, learned to follow Nick's gaze, learned to learn his lust, and when she did go out, to work at least, his desires remained memorized within her. She looked at the attractive women he would look at. She turned to inspect the face of every pageboy haircut she saw from behind and passed in her car. She looked at them furtively or squarely – it didn't matter. She appraised their eyes and mouths and wondered about their bodies. She had become him: she longed for these women. But she was also herself, and so she despised them. She lusted after them, but she also wanted to beat them up.

A rapist.

She had become a rapist, driving to work in a car.

But for a while, it was the only way she could be.

She began to wear his clothes – a shirt, a pair of socks – to keep him next to her, to try to understand why he had done what he'd done. And in this new empathy, in this pants role, like an opera, she thought she understood what it was to make love to a woman, to open the hidden underside of her, like secret food, to thrust yourself up in her, her arch and thrash, like a puppet, to watch her later when she got up and walked around without you, oblivious to the injury you'd surely done her. How could you not love her, gratefully, marveling? She was so mysterious, so recovered, an unshared thought enlivening her eyes; you wanted to follow her forever.

A man in love. That was a man in love. So different from a woman.

A woman cleaned up the kitchen. A woman gave and hid, gave and hid, like someone with a May basket.

She made an appointment with a doctor. Her insurance covered her only if she went to the university hospital, and so she made an appointment there.

"I've made a doctor's appointment," she said to Nick, but he had the water running in the tub and didn't hear her. "To find out if there's anything wrong with me."

When he got out, he approached her, nothing on but a towel, pulled her close to his chest, and lowered her to the floor, right there in the hall by the bathroom door. Something was swooping, back and forth in an arc above her. May Day, May Day. She froze.

"What was that?" She pushed him away.

"What?" He rolled over on his back and looked. Something was flying around in the stairwell – a bird. "A bat," he said.

"Oh my God," cried Olena.

"The heat can bring them out in these old rental houses," he said, stood, rewrapped his towel. "Do you have a tennis racket?"

She showed him where it was. "I've only played tennis once," she said. "Do you want to play tennis sometime?" But he proceeded to stalk the bat in the dark stairwell.

"Now don't get hysterical," he said.

"I'm already hysterical."

"Don't get— There!" he shouted, and she heard the *thwack* of the racket against the wall, and the soft drop of the bat to the landing.

She suddenly felt sick. "Did you have to kill it?" she said.

"What did you want me to do?"

"I don't know. Capture it. Rough it up a little." She felt guilty, as if her own loathing had brought about its death. "What kind of bat is it?" She tiptoed up to look, to try to glimpse its monkey face, its cat teeth, its pterodactyl wings veined like beet leaves. "What kind? Is it a fruit bat?"

"Looks pretty straight to me," said Nick. With his fist, he tapped Olena's arm lightly, teasingly.

"Will you stop?"

"Though it *was* doing this whole astrology thing – I don't know. Maybe it's a zodiac bat."

"Maybe it's a brown bat. It's not a vampire bat, is it?"

"I think you have to go to South America for those," he said. "Take your platform shoes!"

She sank down on the steps, pulled her robe tighter. She felt for the light switch and flicked it on. The bat, she could now see, was small and light-colored, its wings folded in like a packed tent, a mouse with backpacking equipment. It had a sweet face, like a deer, though blood drizzled from its head. It reminded her of a cat she'd seen once as a child, shot with a BB in the eye.

"I can't look anymore," she said, and went back upstairs.

Nick appeared a half hour later, standing in the doorway. She was in bed, a book propped in her lap – a biography of a French feminist, which she was reading for the hairdo information.

"I had lunch with Erin today," he said.

She stared at the page. Snoods. Turbans and snoods. You could go for days in a snood. "Why?"

"A lot of different reasons. For Ken, mostly. She's still head of the neighborhood association, and he needs her endorsement. I just wanted to let you know. Listen, you've gotta cut me some slack."

She grew hot in the face again. "I've cut you some slack," she said. "I've cut you a whole forest of slack. The whole global slack forest has been cut for you." She closed the book. "I don't know why you cavort with these people. They're nothing but a bunch of clerks."

He'd been trying to look pleasant, but now he winced a little. "Oh, I see," he said. "Miss High-Minded. You whose father made his living off furs. Furs!" He took two steps toward her, then turned and paced back again. "I can't believe I'm living with someone who grew up on the proceeds of tortured animals!"

She was quiet. This lunge at moral fastidiousness was something she'd noticed a lot in the people around here. They were not good people. They were not kind. They played around and lied to their spouses. But they recycled their newspapers!

"Don't drag my father into this."

"Look, I've spent years of my life working for peace and

free expression. I've been in prison already. I've lived in a cage! I don't need to live in another one."

"You and your free expression! You who can't listen to me for two minutes!"

"Listen to you what?"

"Listen to me when I" – and here she bit her lip a little – "when I tell you that these people you care about, this hateful Erin what's-her-name, they're just small, awful, nothing people."

"So they don't *read enough books*," he said slowly. "Who the fuck cares."

The next day he was off to a meeting with Ken at the Senior Citizens Association. The host from *Jeopardy!* was going to be there, and Ken wanted to shake a few hands, sign up volunteers. The host from *Jeopardy!* was going to give a talk.

"I don't get it," Olena said.

"I know." He sighed, the pond life treading water in his eyes. "But, well – it's the American way." He grabbed up his keys, and the look that quickly passed over his face told her this: she wasn't pretty enough.

"I hate America," she said.

Nonetheless, he called her at the library during a break. She'd been sitting in the back with Sarah, thinking up Tom Swifties, her brain ready to bleed from the ears, when the phone rang. "You should see this," he said. "Some old geezer raises his hand, I call on him, and he stands up, and the first thing he says is, 'I had my hand raised for ten whole minutes and you kept passing over me. I don't like to be passed over. You can't just pass over a guy like me, not at my age.'"

She laughed, as he wanted her to.

This hot dog's awful, she said frankly.

"To appeal to the doctors, Ken's got all these signs up that say 'Teetlebaum for tort reform.'"

"Sounds like a Wallace Stevens poem," she said.

"I don't know what I expected. But the swirl of this whole event has not felt right."

She's a real dog, he said cattily.

She was quiet, deciding to let him do the work of this call.

"Do you realize that Ken's entire softball team just wrote a letter to *The Star*, calling him a loudmouth and a cheat?"

"Well," she said, "what can you expect from a bunch of grown men who pitch underhand?"

There was some silence. "I care about us," he said finally. "I just want you to know that."

"Okay," she said.

"I know I'm just a pain in the ass to you," he said. "But you're an inspiration to me, you are."

I like a good sled dog, she said huskily.

"Thank you for just – for saying that," she said.

"I just sometimes wish you'd get involved in the community, help out with the campaign. Give of yourself. Connect a little with something."

At the hospital, she got up on the table and pulled the paper gown tightly around her, her feet in the stirrups. The doctor took a plastic speculum out of a drawer. "Anything particular seem to be the problem today?" asked the doctor.

"I just want you to look and tell me if there's anything wrong," said Olena.

The doctor studied her carefully. "There's a class of medical students outside. Do you mind if they come in?"

"Excuse me?"

"You know this is a teaching hospital," she said. "We hope that our patients won't mind contributing to the education of our medical students by allowing them in during an examination. It's a way of contributing to the larger medical community, if you will. But it's totally up to you. You can say no."

Olena clutched at her paper gown. *There's never been an accident, she said recklessly.* "How many of them are there?"

The doctor smiled quickly. "Seven," she said. "Like dwarfs."

"They'll come in and do what?"

The doctor was growing impatient and looked at her watch. "They'll participate in the examination. It's a learning visit."

Olena sank back down on the table. She didn't feel that she could offer herself up this way. *You're only average, he said meanly.*

"All right," she said. "Okay."

Take a bow, he said sternly.

The doctor opened up the doorway and called a short way down the corridor. "Class?"

They were young, more than half of them men, and they gathered around the examination table in a horseshoe shape, looking slightly ashamed, sorry for her, no doubt, the way art students sometimes felt sorry for the shivering model they were about to draw. The doctor pulled up a stool between Olena's feet and inserted the plastic speculum, the stiff, widening arms of it uncomfortable, embarrassing. "Today we will be doing a routine pelvic examination," she announced loudly, and then she got up again, went to a drawer, and passed out rubber gloves to everyone.

Olena went a little blind. A white light, starting at the center, spread to the black edges of her sight. One by one, the hands of the students entered her, or pressed on her abdomen, felt hungrily, innocently, for something to learn from her, in her.

She missed her mother the most.

"Next," the doctor was saying. And then again. "All right. Next?"

Olena missed her mother the most.

But it was her father's face that suddenly loomed before her now, his face at night in the doorway of her bedroom, coming to check on her before he went to bed, his bewildered face, horrified to find her lying there beneath the covers, touching herself and gasping, his whispered "Nell? Are you okay?" and then his vanishing, closing the door loudly, to leave her there, finally forever; to die and leave her there feeling only her own sorrow and disgrace, which she would live in like a coat.

There were rubber fingers in her, moving, wriggling

around, but not like the others. She sat up abruptly and the young student withdrew his hand, moved away. "He didn't do it right," she said to the doctor. She pointed at the student. "He didn't do it correctly!"

"All right, then," said the doctor, looking at Olena with concern and alarm. "All right. You may all leave," she said to the students.

The doctor herself found nothing. "You are perfectly normal," she said. But she suggested that Olena take vitamin B and listen quietly to music in the evening.

Olena staggered out through the hospital parking lot, not finding her car at first. When she found it, she strapped herself in tightly, as if she were something wild – an animal or a star.

She drove back to the library and sat at her desk. Everyone had gone home already. In the margins of her notepad she wrote, "Alone as a book, alone as a desk, alone as a library, alone as a pencil, alone as a catalog, alone as a number, alone as a notepad." Then she, too, left, went home, made herself tea. She felt separate from her body, felt herself dragging it up the stairs like a big handbag, its leathery hollowness something you could cut up and give away or stick things in. She lay between the sheets of her bed, sweating, perhaps from the tea. The world felt over to her, used up, off to one side. There were no more names to live by.

One should live closer. She had lost her place, as in a book.

One should live closer to where one's parents were buried.

Waiting for Nick's return, she felt herself grow dizzy, float up toward the ceiling, look down on the handbag. Tomorrow, she would get an organ donor's card, an eye donor's card, as many cards as she could get. She would show them all to Nick. "Nick! Look at my cards!"

And when he didn't come home, she remained awake through the long night, through the muffled thud of a bird hurling itself against the window, through the thunder leaving and approaching like a voice, through the Frankenstein light of the storm. Over her house, in lieu of stars, she felt the bright heads of her mother and father, searching for her, their eyes beaming down from the sky.

Oh, there you are, they said. *Oh, there you are.*

But then they went away again, and she lay waiting, fist in her spine, for the grace and fatigue that would come, surely it must come, of having given so much to the world.

1991

DANCE IN AMERICA

I TELL THEM dance begins when a moment of hurt combines with a moment of boredom. I tell them it's the body's reaching, bringing air to itself. I tell them that it's the heart's triumph, the victory speech of the feet, the refinement of animal lunge and flight, the purest metaphor of tribe and self. It's life flipping death the bird.

I make this stuff up. But then I feel the stray voltage of my rented charisma, hear the jerry-rigged authority in my voice, and I, too, believe. I'm convinced. The troupe dismantled, the choreography commissions dwindling, my body harder to make limber, to make go, I have come here for two weeks – to Pennsylvania Dutch country, as a "Dancer in the Schools." I visit classes, at colleges and elementary schools, spreading Dance's holy word. My head fills with my own yack. What interior life has accrued in me is depleted fast, emptied out my mouth, as I stand before audiences, answering their fearful, forbidding *German* questions about art and my "whorish dances" (the thrusted hip, the sudden bump and grind before an *attitude*). They ask why everything I make seems so "feministic."

"I think the word is *feministical*," I say. I've grown tired. I burned down my life for a few good pieces, and now this.

With only one night left, I've fled the Quality Inn. (CREAMED CHICKEN ON WAFFLE $3.95 reads the sign out front. How could I leave?) The karaoke in the cocktail lounge has kept me up, all those tipsy and bellowing voices just back from the men's room and urged to the front of the lounge to sing "Sexual Healing" or "Alfie." I've accepted an invitation to stay with my old friend Cal, who teaches anthropology at Burkwell, one of the myriad local colleges. He and his wife own a former frat house they've never bothered to renovate. "It was the only way we could live in a house this big," he says. "Besides, we're perversely fascinated by the wreckage." It is Fastnacht, the lip of Lent, the night when the locals make hot fried dough and eat it in honor of Christ. We are outside, before dinner, walking Cal's dog, Chappers, in the cold.

"The house *is* amazing to look at," I say. "It's beat-up in such an intricate way. Like a Rauschenberg. Like one of those beautiful wind-tattered billboards one sees in the California desert." I'm determined to be agreeable; the house, truth be told, is a shock. Maple seedlings have sprouted up through the dining room floorboards, from where a tree outside has pushed into the foundation. Squirrels the size of collies scrabble in the walls. Paint is chipping everywhere, in scales and blisters and flaps; in the cracked plaster beneath are written the names of women who, in 1972, 1973, and 1974, spent the night during Spring Rush weekend. The kitchen ceiling reads "Sigma power!" and "Wank me with a spoon."

But I haven't seen Cal in twelve years, not since he left for Belgium on a Fulbright, so I must be nice. He seems different to me: shorter, older, cleaner, despite the house. In a burst of candor, he has already confessed that those long years ago, out of friendship for me, he'd been exaggerating his interest in dance. "I didn't get it," he admitted. "I kept trying to figure out the *story*. I'd look at the purple guy who hadn't moved in awhile, and I'd think, So what's the issue with *him*?"

Now Chappers tugs at his leash. "Yeah, the house." Cal sighs. "We did once have a painter give us an estimate, but we were put off by the names of the paints: Myth, Vesper, Snickerdoodle. I didn't want anything called Snickerdoodle in my house."

"What *is* a Snickerdoodle?"

"I think they're hunted in Madagascar."

I leap to join him, to play. "Or eaten in Vienna," I say.

"Or worshiped in L.A." I laugh again for him, and then we watch as Chappers sniffs at the roots of an oak.

"But a myth or a vesper – they're always good," I add.

"Crucial," he says. "But we didn't need paint for that."

Cal's son, Eugene, is seven and has cystic fibrosis. Eugene's whole life is a race with medical research. "It's not that I'm not for the arts," says Cal. "*You're* here; money for the arts brought you here. That's wonderful. It's wonderful to see you after all these years. It's wonderful to fund the arts. *It's* wonderful; you're wonderful. The arts are so nice and wonderful. But really: I say, let's give all the money, every last fucking dime, to science."

Something chokes up in him. There can be optimism in the increments, the bits, the chapters; but I haven't seen him in twelve years and he has had to tell me the whole story, straight from the beginning, and it's the whole story that's just so sad.

"We both carried the gene but never knew," he says. "That's the way it works. The odds are one in twenty, times one in twenty, and then after that, still only one in four. One in sixteen hundred, total. Bingo! We should move to Vegas."

When I first knew Cal, we were in New York, just out of graduate school; he was single, and anxious, and struck me as someone who would never actually marry and have a family, or if he did, would marry someone decorative, someone slight. But now, twelve years later, his silver-haired wife, Simone, is nothing like that: she is big and fierce and original, joined with him in grief and courage. She storms out of PTA meetings. She glues little sequins to her shoes. English is her third language; she was once a French diplomat to Belgium and to Japan. "I miss the caviar" is all she'll say of it. "I miss the caviar so much." Now, in Pennsylvania Dutchland, she paints satirical oils of long-armed handless people. "The locals," she explains in her French accent, giggling. "But I can't paint hands." She and Eugene have made a studio from one of the wrecked rooms upstairs.

"How is Simone through all this?" I ask.

"She's better than I am," he says. "She had a sister who died young. She expects unhappiness."

"But isn't there hope?" I ask, stuck for words.

Already, Cal says, Eugene has degenerated, grown worse, too much liquid in his lungs. "Stickiness," he calls it. "If he were three, instead of seven, there'd be *more* hope. The researchers are making some strides; they really are."

"He's a great kid," I say. Across the street, there are old Colonial houses with candles lit in each window; it is a

Pennsylvania Dutch custom, or left over from Desert Storm, depending on whom you ask.

Cal stops and turns toward me, and the dog comes up and nuzzles him. "It's not just that Eugene's great," he says. "It's not just the precocity or that he's the only child I'll ever have. It's also that he's such a good person. He accepts things. He's very good at understanding everything."

I cannot imagine anything in my life that contains such sorrow as this, such anticipation of missing someone. Cal falls silent, the dog trots before us, and I place my hand lightly in the middle of Cal's back as we walk like that through the cold, empty streets. Up in the sky, Venus and the thinnest paring of sickle moon, like a cup and saucer, like a nose and mouth, have made the Turkish flag in the sky. "Look at that," I say to Cal as we traipse after the dog, the leash taut as a stick.

"Wow," Cal says. "The Turkish flag."

"You're back, you're back!" Eugene shouts from inside, dashing toward the front door as we step up onto the front porch with Chappers. Eugene is in his pajamas already, his body skinny and hunched. His glasses are thick, magnifying, and his eyes, puffed and swimming, seem not to miss a thing. He slides into the front entryway, in his stocking feet, and lands on the floor. He smiles up at me, all charm, like a kid with a crush. He has painted his face with Merthiolate and hopes we'll find that funny.

"Eugene, you look beautiful!" I say.

"No I don't!" he says. "I look *witty*."

"Where's your mother?" asks Cal, unleashing the dog.

"In the kitchen. Dad, Mom says you have to go up to the attic and bring down one of the pans for dinner." He gets up and chases after Chappers, to tackle him and bring him back.

"We have a couple pots up there to catch leaks," Cal explains, taking off his coat. "But then we end up needing the pots for cooking, so we fetch them back."

"Do you need some help?" I don't know whether I should

be with Simone in the kitchen, Cal in the attic, or Eugene on the floor.

"Oh, no. You stay here with Eugene," he says.

"Yeah. Stay here with me." Eugene races back from the dog and grabs my leg. The dog barks excitedly.

"You can show Eugene your video," Cal suggests as he leaves the room.

"Show me your dance video," he says to me in a singsong. "Show me, show me."

"Do we have time?"

"We have fifteen minutes," he says with great authority. I go upstairs and dig it out of my bag, then come back down. We plug it into the VCR and nestle on the couch together. He huddles close, cold in the drafty house, and I extend my long sweater around him like a shawl. I try to explain a few things, in a grown-up way, how this dance came to be, how movement, repeated, breaks through all resistance into a kind of stratosphere: from recalcitrance to ecstasy; from shoe to bird. The tape is one made earlier in the week. It is a demonstration with fourth graders. They each had to invent a character, then design a mask. They came up with various creatures: Miss Ninja Peacock. Mr. Bicycle Spoke Head. Evil Snowman. Saber-toothed Mom: "Half-girl-half-man-half-cat." Then I arranged the kids in a phalanx and led them, with their masks on, in an improvised dance to Kenny Loggins's "This Is It."

He watches, rapt. His brown hair hangs in strings in his face, and he chews on it. "There's Tommy Crowell," he says. He knows the fourth graders as if they were royalty. When it is over, he looks up at me, smiling, but businesslike. His gaze behind his glasses is brilliant and direct. "That was really a wonderful dance," he says. He sounds like an agent.

"Do you really think so?"

"Absolutely," he says. "It's colorful and has lots of fun, interesting steps."

"Will you be my agent?" I ask.

He scowls, unsure. "I don't know. Is the agent the person who drives the car?"

"Dinner's ready!" Simone calls from two rooms away, the "Wank me with a spoon" room.

"Coming!" shouts Eugene, and he leaps off the couch and slides into the dining room, falling sideways into his chair. "*Whoo*," he says, out of breath. "I almost didn't make it."

"Here," says Cal. He places a goblet of pills at Eugene's place setting.

Eugene makes a face, but in the chair, he gets up on his knees, leans forward, glass of water in one hand, and begins the arduous activity of taking all the pills.

I sit in the chair opposite him and place my napkin in my lap.

Simone has made a soup with hard-boiled eggs in it (a regional recipe, she explains), as well as Peking duck, which is ropy and sweet. Cal keeps passing around the basket of bread, anxiously, talking about how modern man has only been around for 45,000 years and probably the bread hasn't changed much since then.

"Forty-five thousand years?" says Simone. "That's all? That can't be. I feel like we've been *married* for that long."

There are people who talk with their hands. Then there are people who talk with their arms. Then there are people who talk with their arms over their head. These are the ones I like best. Simone is one of those.

"Nope, that's it," says Cal, chewing. "Forty-five thousand. Though for about two hundred thousand years before that, early man was going through all kinds of anatomical changes to get where we are today. It was a *very* exciting time." He pauses, a little breathlessly. "I wish I could have been there."

"Ha!" exclaims Simone.

"Think of the parties," I say.

"Right," says Simone. "'Joe, how've you been? Your head's so *big* now, and, well, what is this crazy thing you're doing with your thumb?' A lot like the parties in Soda Springs, Idaho."

"Simone used to be married to someone in Soda Springs, Idaho," Cal says to me.

"You're kidding!" I say.

"Oh, it was very brief," she says. "He was ridiculous. I got rid of him after about six months. Supposedly, he went off and killed himself." She smiles at me impishly.

"Who killed himself?" asks Eugene. He has swallowed all the pills but one.

"Mommy's first husband," says Cal.

"Why did he kill himself?" Eugene is staring at the middle of the table, trying to think about this.

"Eugene, you've lived with your mother for seven years now, and you don't know why someone close to her would want to kill himself?" Simone and Cal look straight across at each other and laugh brightly.

Eugene smiles in an abbreviated and vague way. He understands this is his parents' joke, but he doesn't like or get it. He is bothered they have turned his serious inquiry into a casual laugh. He wants information! But now, instead, he just digs into the duck, poking and looking.

Simone asks about the school visits. What am I finding? Are people nice to me? What is my life like back home? Am I married?

"I'm not married," I say.

"But you and Patrick are still together, aren't you?" Cal says in a concerned way.

"Uh, no. We broke up."

"You broke up?" Cal puts his fork down.

"Yes," I say, sighing.

"Gee, I thought you guys would never break up!" he says in a genuinely flabbergasted tone.

"*Really*?" I find this reassuring somehow, that my relationship at least looked good from the outside, at least to someone.

"Well, not *really*," admits Cal. "Actually, I thought you guys would break up long ago."

"Oh," I say.

"So *you* could marry her?" says the amazing Eugene to his

father, and we all laugh loudly, pour more wine into glasses, and hide our faces in them.

"The thing to remember about love affairs," says Simone, "is that they are all like having raccoons in your chimney."

"Oh, not the raccoon story," groans Cal.

"Yes! The raccoons!" cries Eugene.

I'm sawing at my duck.

"We have raccoons sometimes in our chimney," explains Simone.

"Hmmm," I say, not surprised.

"And once we tried to smoke them out. We lit a fire, knowing they were there, but we hoped that the smoke would cause them to scurry out the top and never come back. Instead, they caught on fire and came crashing down into our living room, all charred and in flames and running madly around until they dropped dead." Simone swallows some wine. "Love affairs are like that," she says. "They all are like that."

I'm confused. I glance up at the light, an old brass octopus of a chandelier. All I can think of is how Patrick said, when he left, fed up with my "selfishness," that if I were worried about staying on alone at the lake house, with its squirrels and call girl–style lamps, I should just rent the place out – perhaps to a nice lesbian couple like myself.

But Eugene, across from me, nods enthusiastically, looks pleased. He's heard the raccoon story before and likes it. Once again, it's been told right, with flames and gore.

Now there is salad, which we pick and tear at like crows. Afterward, we gaze upon the bowl of fruit at the center of the table, lazily pick a few grapes off their stems. We sip hot tea that Cal brings in from the kitchen. We sip until it's cool, and then until it's gone. Already the time is ten o'clock.

"Dance time, dance time!" says Eugene when we're through. Every night, before bed, they all go out into the living room and dance until Eugene is tired and falls asleep on the sofa. Then they carry him upstairs and tuck him in.

He comes over to my chair and takes my hand, leads me out into the living room.

"What music shall we dance to?" I ask.

"You choose," he says, and leads me to the shelf where they keep their compact discs. Perhaps there is some Stravinsky. Perhaps *Petrouchka*, with its rousing salute to Shrovetide.

"Will you come see me tomorrow when you visit the fourth graders?" he asks as I'm looking through the selection. Too much Joan Baez. Too much Mahler. "I'm in room one oh four," he says. "When you visit the fourth graders, you can just stop by my classroom and wave to me from the door. I sit between the bulletin board and the window."

"Sure!" I say, not knowing that, in a rush, I will forget, and that I'll be on the plane home already, leafing through some inane airline magazine, before I remember that I forgot to do it. "Look," I say, finding a Kenny Loggins disc. It has the song he heard earlier, the one from the video. "Let's play this."

"Goody," he says. "Mom! Dad! Come on!"

"All right, Eugenie-boy," says Cal, coming in from the dining room. Simone is behind him.

"I'm Mercury, I'm Neptune, now I'm Pluto so far away," says Eugene, dashing around the room, making up his own dance.

"They're doing the planets in school," says Simone.

"Yes," says Eugene. "We're doing the planets!"

"And which planet," I ask him, "do you think is the most interesting?" Mars, with its canals? Saturn, with its rings?

Eugene stands still, looks at me thoughtfully, solemnly. "Earth, of course," he says.

Cal laughs. "Well, that's the right answer!"

"This is it!" sings Kenny Loggins. "This is it!" We make a phalanx and march, strut, slide to the music. We crouch, move backward, then burst forward again. We're aiming to create the mildewy, resinous sweat smell of dance, the parsed, repeated movement. Cal and Simone are into it. They jiggle and link arms. "This is it!" In the middle of the song, Eugene suddenly sits down to rest on the sofa, watching the grown-ups. Like the best dancers and audiences in the world, he is determined not to cough until the end.

"Come here, honey," I say, going to him. I am thinking

not only of my own body here, that unbeguilable, broken basket, that stiff meringue. I am not, Patrick, thinking only of myself, my lost troupe, my empty bed. I am thinking of the dancing body's magnificent and ostentatious scorn. This is how we offer ourselves, enter heaven, enter speaking: we say with motion, in space, This is what life's done so far down here; this is all and what and everything it's managed – this body, these bodies, that body – so what do you think, Heaven? What do you fucking think?

"Stand next to me," I say, and Eugene does, looking up at me with his orange warrior face. We step in place: knees up, knees down. Knees up, knees down. Dip-glide-slide. Dip-glide-slide. "This is it!" "This is it!" Then we go wild and fling our limbs to the sky.

1993

DEBARKING

IRA HAD BEEN divorced six months and still couldn't get his wedding ring off. His finger had swelled doughily around it – a combination of frustrated desire, unmitigated remorse, and misdirected ambition, he said to friends. "I'm going to have to have my entire finger surgically removed." The ring (supposedly gold, though now that everything he had ever received from Marilyn had been thrown into doubt, who knew) cinched the blousy fat of his finger, which had grown around it like a fucking happy vine. "Maybe I should cut off the whole hand. And send it to her," he said on the phone to his friend Mike, with whom he worked at the State Historical Society. "She'll understand the reference." Ira had already ceremoniously set fire to his wedding tux – hanging it on a tall stick in his backyard, scarecrow-style, and igniting it with a Bic lighter. "That sucker went up really fast," he gasped apologetically to the fire marshal, after the hedge caught too, and before he was brought overnight to the local lockdown facility. "*So* fast. Maybe it was, I don't know, like the residual dry-cleaning fluid."

"You'll remove that ring when you're ready," Mike said now. Mike's job approving historical preservation projects on old houses left him time to take a lot of lenient parenting courses and to read all the lenient parenting books. "Here's what you do for your depression. I'm not going to say lose yourself in charity work. I'm not going to say get some perspective by watching our country's news each evening and by contemplating those worse off than yourself, those, say, who are about to be blown apart by bombs. I'm going to say this: Stop drinking, stop smoking. Eliminate coffee, sugar, dairy products. Do this for three days, then start everything back up again. *Bam.* I guarantee you, you will be so happy."

"I'm afraid," Ira said softly, "that the only thing that would make me happy right now is snipping the brake cables on Marilyn's car."

"Spring," Mike said helplessly, though it was still only the end of winter. "It can really hang you up the most."

"Hey. You should write songs. Just not too often." Ira looked at his hands. Actually he *had* once gotten the ring off in a hot, soapy bath, but the sight of his denuded finger, naked as a child's, had terrified him and he had shoved the ring back on.

On the other end of the phone Ira could hear Mike sighing and casting about. Cupboard doors closed loudly. The refrigerator puckered open, then *whooshed* shut. Ira knew that Mike and Kate had had their troubles – as the phrase went – but always their marriage had held. "I'd divorce Kate," Mike had once confided to Ira, "but she'd kill me." "Look," Mike said now, "why don't you come to our house Sunday for a little Lent dinner. We're having some people by and who knows?"

"Who knows?" asked Ira.

"Yes – who knows?"

"What's a Lent dinner?"

"We made it up. For Lent. We didn't really want to do Mardi Gras. Too disrespectful, given the international situation."

"So you're doing Lent. I'm unclear on Lent. I mean, I know what Lent means to those of us in the Jewish faith. But we don't usually commemorate these transactions with meals. Usually there's just a lot of sighing."

"It's like a pre-Easter Prince of Peace dinner," said Mike slowly.

There were no natural predators in this small, oblivious, and tolerant community, and so strange creatures and creations abounded. "Prince of *Peace*? Not – of *Minneapolis*?"

"You're supposed to give things up for Lent. Last year we gave up our faith and reason; this year we are giving up our democratic voice, our hope." Ira had already met most of Mike's *goyishe* friends. Mike himself was low-key, tolerant, self-deprecating to a flaw. A self-described "ethnic Catholic," he once complained dejectedly about not having been cute enough to have been molested by a priest. "They would just shake my hand very quickly," he said. Mike's friends, however, tended to be tense, intellectually earnest Protestants who drove new, metallic-hued cars and who within five minutes of light conversation could be counted on at least twice to use the phrase "strictly within the framework of." "Kate has a divorcée friend she's inviting," Mike said. "I'm not trying to fix you up. I really hate that stuff. I'm just saying come. Eat some food. It's the start of Eastertime and, well, hey: we could use a Jew over here." Mike laughed heartily.

"Yeah, I'll reenact the whole thing for you," said Ira. He looked at his swollen ring finger again. "Yessirree. I'll come over and show you all how it's done."

Ira's new house, though it was in what his realtor referred to as "a lovely, pedestrian neighborhood," abutting the streets named after presidents, boasting, instead, streets named after fishing flies (Caddis, Hendrickson, Gold-Ribbed Hare's Ear Road), was full of slow drains, leaky burners, stopped-up pipes, and excellent dust for scrawling curse words. *Marilyn blows sailors*. The draftiest windows he duct-taped up with sheets of plastic on the inside, as instructed by Homeland Security; cold air billowed the plastic inward like sails on a boat. On a windy day it was quite something. "Your whole house could fly away," said Mike, looking around.

"Not really," said Ira. "But it *is* spinning. It's very interesting, actually."

The yard had already grown muddy with March and the flower beds were greening with the tiniest sprigs of stinkweed and quack grass. By June the chemical weapons of terrorism aimed at the heartland might prove effective in weeding the garden. "This may be the sort of war I could really use!" Ira said out loud to a neighbor. Mike and Kate's house, on the other hand, with its perfect lines and friendly fussiness, reeking, he supposed, of historical preservation tax credits, seemed an impossible dream to him, something plucked from a magazine article about childhood memories conjured on a deathbed. Something seen through the window by the Little Match Girl. Outside, the soffits were perfectly squared. The crocuses were like bells and the Siberian violets like grape candies scattered in the grass. Inside, the smell of warm food almost made him weep, and with his coat still on he rushed past Kate to throw his arms around Mike, kissing him on both cheeks. "All the beautiful men must be kissed!" Ira exclaimed.

After he got his coat off, and had wandered into the dining room, he toasted with the champagne he himself had brought. There were eight guests there, most of whom he knew to *some* degree, but really that was enough. That was enough for everyone. Still, they raised their glasses with him. "To Lent!" Ira cried. "To the final days!" And in case that was too grim, he added, "And to the coming Resurrection! May it happen a little closer to home this time! Jesus Christ!" Soon he wandered back into the kitchen and, as he felt was required of him, shrieked at the pork. Then he began milling around again, apologizing for the Crucifixion: "We really didn't intend it," he murmured, "not really, not the killing part? We just kind of got carried away? You know how spring can get a little crazy, but believe me, we're all really, really sorry." Kate's divorced friend was named Zora, and was a pediatrician. Although no one else did, she howled with laughter, and when her face wasn't blasted apart with it or her jaw snapping mutely open and shut like a scissors (in what Ira recognized was postdivorce hysteria; "How long have you been divorced?" he later asked her. "Eleven years," she replied), Ira could see she was very beautiful: short black hair; eyes a clear, reddish hazel, like orange pekoe tea; a strong aquiline nose, probably a snorer; thick lashes that spiked out wrought and black as the tines of a fireplace fork. Her body was a mix of thin and plump, her skin lined and unlined, in that rounding-the-corner-to-fifty way. *Age and youth,* he chanted silently, *youth and age, sing their songs on the very same stage.* Ira was working on a modest little volume of doggerel, its tentative title *Women from Venus; Men from Penis.* Either that, or *Soccer Dad: The Musical.*

Like everyone he knew, he could discern the hollowness in people's charm only when it was directed at someone other than himself. When it was directed at him, the person just seemed so totally *nice.* And so Zora's laughter, in conjunction with her beauty, doomed him a little, made him grateful beyond reason.

Immediately, he sent her a postcard, one of newlyweds dragging empty Spam cans from the bumper of their car. He wrote: *Dear Zora, Had such fun meeting you at Mike's.* And then he wrote his phone number. He kept it simple. In courtship he had a history of mistakes, beginning at sixteen with his first girlfriend, for whom he had bought at the local head shop the coolest thing he had then ever seen in his life: a beautifully carved wooden hand with its middle finger sticking up. He himself had coveted it tremulously for a year. How could she not love it? Her contempt for it, and then for him, had left him feeling baffled and betrayed. With Marilyn he had taken the other approach and played hard to get, which had turned their relationship into a never-ending Sadie Hawkins Day, with subsequent marriage to Sadie an inevitably doomed thing – a humiliating and interminable Dutch date.

But this, the Spam postcard and the note, he felt contained the correct mix of offhandedness and intent. This elusive mix – the geometric halfway point between stalker and Rip van Winkle – was important to get right in the world of middle-aged dating, he suspected, though what did he really know of this world? It had been so long, the whole thing seemed a kind of distant civilization, a planet of the apings! – graying, human flotsam with scorched internal landscapes mimicking the young, picking up where they had left off decades ago, if only they could recall where the hell that was. Ira had been a married man for fifteen years, a father for eight (poor little Bekka, now rudely transported between houses in a speedy, ritualistic manner resembling a hostage drop-off), only to find himself punished for an idle little nothing, nothing, nothing flirtation with a colleague, punished with his wife's *actual* affair and false business trips (Montessori conventions that never existed), and finally a petition for divorce mailed from a motel. Observing others go through them, he used to admire midlife crises, the courage and shamelessness and existential daring of them, but after he'd watched his own wife, a respectable nursery school teacher, produce and star in a full-blown one of her own, he found the sufferers of such crises not only self-indulgent but greedy and demented, and he wished them all weird unnatural deaths with various contraptions easily found in garages.

He received a postcard from Zora in return. It was of Van Gogh's room in Arles. Beneath the clockface of the local postmark her handwriting was big but careful, some curlicuing in the *g*'s and *f*'s. It read, *Had such fun meeting you at Mike's.* Wasn't that precisely, word for word, what he had written to her? There was no *too*, no emphasized *you*, just the exact same words thrown back at him like in some lunatic postal Ping-Pong. Either she was stupid or crazy or he was already being too hard on her. Not being hard on people – "You *bark* at them," Marilyn used to say – was something he was trying to work on. When he pictured Zora's lovely face, it helped his tenuous affections. She had written her phone number and signed off with a swashbuckling Z – as in *Zorro.* That was cute, he supposed. He guessed. Who knew. He had to lie down.

He had Bekka for the weekend. She sat in the living room, tuned to Cartoon Network. She liked Road Runner and *Justice League.* Ira would sometimes watch her mesmerized face, the cartoons flashing on the creamy screen of her skin, her eyes still and wide, bright with reflected shapes caught there like holograms in marbles. He felt inadequate as her father, but in general attempted his best: affection, wisdom, reliability, plus not ordering pizza every night, though tonight he had again caved in. Last week Bekka had said to him, "When you and Mommy were married we always had mashed potatoes for supper. Now you're divorced and we always have spaghetti."

"Which do you like better?" he had asked.

"Neither!" she had shouted, summing up her distaste for everything. "I hate them both."

Tonight he had ordered the pizza half plain cheese, and half with banana peppers and jalapeños. The two of them sat together in front of *Justice League*, with TV trays, eating slices from their respective sides. Chesty, narrow-waisted heroes in bright colors battled their enemies with righteous confidence and, of course, laser guns. Bekka finally turned to him. "Mommy says that if her boyfriend Daniel moves in I can have a dog. A dog and a bunny."

"*And* a bunny?" Ira said. When the family was still together, unbroken, the four-year-old Bekka, new to numbers and the passage of time, used to exclaim triumphantly to her friends, "Mommy and Daddy say I can have a dog! When I turn eighteen!" There'd been no talk of bunnies. But perhaps the imminence of Easter had brought this on. He knew Bekka loved animals. She had once, in a bathtime reverie, named her five favorite people, four of whom were dogs. The fifth was her own blue bike.

"A dog *and* a bunny," Bekka repeated, and Ira had to repress images of the dog with the rabbit's bloody head in its mouth.

"So, what do you think about that?" he asked cautiously, wanting to get her opinion on the whole Daniel thing.

Bekka shrugged and chewed. "Whatever," she said, her new word for "You're welcome," "Hello," "Good-bye," and "I'm only eight." "I really just don't want all his stuff there. Already his car blocks our car in the driveway."

"Bummer," said Ira, his new word for "I must remain as neutral as possible" and "Your mother's a whore."

"I don't want a stepfather," Bekka said.

"Maybe he could just live on the steps," Ira said, and Bekka smirked, her mouth full of mozzarella.

"Besides," she said. "I like Larry better. He's stronger."

"Who's Larry?" Ira said, instead of "Bummer."

"He's this other dude," Bekka said. She sometimes referred to her mother as a "dudette." "She's a dudette, all right," Ira would say.

"Bummer," said Ira now. "Big, big bummer."

* * *

He phoned Zora four days later, so as not to seem discouragingly eager. He summoned up his most confident acting. "Hi, Zora? This is Ira," and then waited – narcissistically perhaps, but what else was there to say? – for her response.

"Ira?"

"Yes. Ira Milkins."

"I'm sorry," she said. "I don't know who you are."

Ira gripped the phone and looked down at himself, suddenly finding nothing there. He seemed to have vanished from the neck down. "We met last Sunday at Mike and Kate's?" His voice quavered. If he ever actually succeeded in going out with her, he was going to have to take one of those date-rape drugs and just pass out on her couch.

"Ira? Ohhhhhhhhh – Ira. Yeah. The Jewish guy."

"Yeah, the Jew. That was me." Should he hang up now? He did not feel he could go on. But he must go on. *There* was a man of theater for you.

"That was a nice dinner," she said.

"Yes, it was."

"I usually skip Lent completely."

"Me, too," said Ira. "It's just simpler. Who needs the fuss?"

"But sometimes I forget how reassuring and conjoining a meal with friends can be, especially at a time like this."

Ira had to think about the way she'd used *conjoining*. It sounded New Agey and Amish, both.

"But Mike and Kate run that kind of house. It's all warmth and good-heartedness."

Ira thought about this. What other kind of home was there to run, if you were going to bother? Hard, cold, and mean: that had been his own home with Marilyn, at the end. It was like those experimental monkeys with the wire-monkey moms. What did the baby monkeys know? The wire mother was all they had, all they knew in their hearts, and so they clung to it, as had he, even if it was only a coat hanger. *Mom*. So much easier to carve the word into your arm. You were used to pain. You'd been imprinted. As a child, for a fifth-grade science project, in the basement of his house, he'd once tried to reproduce Konrad Lorenz's experiment with baby ducks. But he had screwed up with the incubation lights and had cooked the ducks right in their eggs, stinking up the basement so much that his mother had screamed at him for days. Which was a science lesson of some sort – the emotional limits of the *Homo sapiens* working Jewish mom – but it was soft science, so less impressive.

"What kind of home do *you* run?" he asked.

"Home? Oh, I mean to get to one of those. Right now, actually, I'm talking to you from a pup tent."

Oh, she was a funny one. Perhaps they would laugh and laugh their way into the sunset. "I *love* pup tents," he said. What was a pup tent exactly? He'd forgotten.

"Actually, I have a teenage son, so I have no idea what kind of home I have anymore. Once you have a teenager, everything changes."

Now there was silence. He couldn't imagine Bekka as a teenager. Or rather, he could, sort of, since she often acted like one already, full of rage at the incompetent waitstaff that life had hired to take and bring her order.

"Well, would you like to meet for a drink?" Zora asked finally, as if she had asked it many times before, her tone a mingling of both weariness and the cheery, pseudoprofessionalism of someone in the dully familiar and official position of being single and dating.

"Yes," said Ira. "That's exactly why I called."

"You can't imagine the daily dreariness of routine pediatrics," said Zora, not touching her wine. "Ear infection, ear infection, ear infection. Whoa. Here's an exciting one: juvenile onset diabetes. Day after day you just have to look into the parents' eyes and repeat the same exciting thing: 'There are a lot of viruses going around.' I had thought about going into pediatric oncology, because when I asked other doctors why they'd gone into such a seemingly depressing thing, they said, 'Because the *kids* don't get depressed.' That seemed interesting to me. And hopeful. But then when I asked doctors in the same field why they were retiring early, they said they were sick of seeing kids die. The kids don't get depressed, they just die! These were my choices in med school. As an undergraduate I took a lot of art classes and did sculpture, which I still do a little, to keep those creative juices flowing! But what I would really like to do now is write children's books. I look at some of those books out in the waiting room and I want to throw them in the fish tank. I think, *I could do better than that.* I started one about a hedgehog."

"Now what's a hedgehog exactly?" Ira was eyeing her full glass and his own empty one. "I get them mixed up with groundhogs and gophers."

"They're— Well, what does it matter if they are all wearing little polka-dotted clothes, vests and hats and things," she said irritably.

"I suppose," he said, now a little frightened. What was wrong with her? He did not like stressful moments in restaurants. They caused his mind to wander strangely to random thoughts like *Why are these things called* napkins *rather than* lapkins? or *I'll bet God really loves butter.* He tried to focus on the visuals, what she was wearing, which was a silk, pumpkin-colored blouse he hesitated complimenting her on lest she think he was gay. Marilyn had once threatened to call off their wedding because he had strenuously complimented the fabric of her gown and then had shopped too long and discontentedly for his own tuxedo, failing to find just the right shade of "mourning dove," a color he had read of in a wedding magazine. "Are you homosexual?" she had asked. "You must tell me now. I won't make the same mistake my sister did."

Perhaps Zora's irritability was only creative frustration. Ira understood. Though his position was with the Historical Society's Human Resources Office, he liked to help with the society's exhibitions, doing posters and dioramas and once even making a puppet for a little show the society had put on about the first governor. Thank God for meaningful work! He understood those small, diaphanous artistic ambitions that overtook people and could look like nervous breakdowns.

"What happens in your hedgehog tale?" Ira asked, then

settled in to finish up his dinner, eggplant parmesan that he wished now he hadn't ordered. He was coveting Zora's wodge of steak. Perhaps he had an iron deficiency. Or perhaps it was just a desire for the taste of metal and blood in his mouth. Zora, he knew, was committed to meat. While everyone else's cars were busy protesting the prospect of war or supporting the summoned troops, Zora's Honda had a bumper sticker that said, RED MEAT IS NOT BAD FOR YOU. FUZZY, GREENISH BLUE MEAT IS BAD FOR YOU.

"The hedgehog tale? Well," Zora began. "The hedgehog goes for a walk, because he is feeling sad – it's based on a story I used to tell my son. The hedgehog goes for a walk and comes upon this strange yellow house that has a sign on it that says, WELCOME, HEDGEHOG: THIS COULD BE YOUR NEW HOME, and because he's been feeling sad, the thought of a new home appeals. So he goes in and inside is a family of alligators – Well, I'll spare you the rest, but you can get the general flavor of it from that."

"I don't know about that family of alligators."

She was quiet for a minute, chewing her beautiful ruby steak. "Every family is a family of alligators," she said.

"Well – that's certainly one way of looking at it." Ira glanced at his watch.

"Yeah. To get back to the book. It gives me an outlet. I mean, my job's not terrible. Some of the kids are cute. But some are impossible, of course, some are disturbed, some are just spoiled and ill-behaved. It's hard to know what to do. We're not allowed to hit them."

"You're 'not allowed to hit them'?" He could see she had now made some progress with her wine.

"I'm from Kentucky," she said.

"Ah." He drank from his water glass, stalling.

She chewed thoughtfully. Merlot was beginning to etch a ragged, scabby line in the dead skin of her bottom lip. "It's like Ireland but with more horses and guns."

"Not a lot of Jews down there." He had no idea why he said half the things he said. Perhaps this time it was because he had once been a community-based historian, digging in archives for the genealogies and iconographies of various ethnic groups, not realizing that other historians generally thought this a sentimental form of history, shedding light on nothing; and though shedding light on nothing seemed not a bad idea to him, when it became available, he had taken the human resources job.

"Not too many," she said. "I did know an Armenian family growing up. At least I *think* they were Armenian."

When the check came, she ignored it, as if it were some fly that had landed and would soon be taking off again. So much for feminism. Ira pulled out his state-workers credit card and the waitress came by and whisked it away. There were, he was once told, four seven-word sentences that generally signaled the end of a relationship. The first was "I think we should see other people." (Which always meant another seven-word sentence: "I am already sleeping with someone else.") The second seven-word sentence was, reputedly, "Maybe you could just leave the tip." The third was "How could you again forget your wallet?" And the fourth, the killer of all killers, was "Oh, look, I've forgotten my wallet, too!"

He did not imagine they would ever see each other again. But when he dropped her off at her house, walking her to her door, Zora suddenly grabbed his face with both hands, and her mouth became its own wet creature exploring his. She opened up his jacket, pushing her body inside it, against his, the pumpkin-colored silk of her blouse slid upon his shirt. Her lips came away in a slurp. "I'm going to call you," she said, smiling. Her eyes were wild, as if with gin, though she had only been drinking wine.

"OK," he mumbled, walking backward down her steps, in the dark, his car still running, its headlights bright along her street.

He was in her living room the following week. It was beige and white with cranberry accents. On the walls were black-framed photos of her son, Bruno, from all ages, including now. There were pictures of Bruno lying prone on the ground. There were pictures of Bruno and Zora together, he hidden in the folds of her skirt, and she hanging her then-long hair down into his face, covering him completely. There he was again, leaning in between her knees, naked as a cello. There were pictures of him in the bath, though in some he was clearly already at the start of puberty. In the corner stood perhaps a dozen wooden sculptures of naked boys she had carved herself. "One of my hobbies, which I was telling you about," she said. They were astounding little things. She had drilled holes in their penises with a brace and bit to allow for water in case she could someday sell them as garden fountains. "These are winged boys. The beautiful adolescent boy who flies away. It's from mythology. I forget what they're called. I just love their little rumps." He nodded, studying the tight, sculpted buttocks, the spouted, mushroomy phalluses, the long backs and limbs. So: this was the sort of woman he'd been missing out on not being single all these years. What had he been thinking of staying married for so long?

He sat down and asked for wine. "You know, I'm just a little gun-shy romantically," he said apologetically. "I don't have the confidence I used to. I don't think I can even take my clothes off in front of another person. Not even at the gym, frankly. I've been changing in the toilet stalls. After divorce and all."

"Oh, divorce will do that to you totally," she said reassuringly. She poured him some wine. "It's like a trick. It's like someone puts a rug over a trapdoor and says, 'Stand there.' And so you do. Then boom." She took out a hashish pipe, lit it, sucking, then gave it to him.

"I've never seen a pediatrician smoke hashish before."

"Really?" she said, with some difficulty, her breath still sucked in.

The nipples of her breasts were long, cylindrical, and stiff, so that her chest looked somewhat as if two small sink plungers had flown across the room and suctioned themselves there. His mouth opened hungrily to kiss them.

"Perhaps you would like to take off your shoes," she whispered.

"Oh, not really," he said.

There was sex where you were looked in the eye and beautiful things were said to you, and then there was what Ira used to think of as yoo-hoo sex: where the other person seemed spirited away, not quite there, their pleasure mysterious and crazy and only accidentally involving you. "Yoo-hoo?" was what his grandmother always called before entering a house where she knew someone but not well enough to know whether they were actually home.

"Where *are* you?" Ira said in the dark. He decided in a case such as this he could feel a chaste and sanctifying distance. It wasn't he who was having sex. The condom was having sex and he was just trying to stop it. Zora's candles on the nightstand were heated to clear pools in their tins. They flickered smokily. He would try not to think about how before she had even lit them and pulled back the bedcovers he had noticed the candles were already melted down to the size of buttons, their wicks blackened to a crisp. It was not good to think about the previous burning of the bedroom candles of a woman who had just unzipped your pants. Besides, he was too grateful for the fact of those candles – especially with all those little wonder boys in the living room. Perhaps his whitening chest hair would not look so white. This was what candles were made for: the sad, sexually shy, out-of-shape, middle-aged him. How had he not understood this in marriage? Zora herself looked ageless, like a nymph with her short hair, although once she got Ira's glasses off, she became a blur of dim and shifting shapes and might as well have been Dick Cheney or Lon Chaney or Lee Marvin or the Blob, except that she smelled good and but for the occasional rough patch had the satiny skin of a girl.

She let out a long, spent sigh.

"Where did you go?" he asked again anxiously.

"I've been right here, silly," she said and pinched his hip. She lifted one of her long legs up and down outside the covers. "Did you get off?"

"I beg your pardon?"

"Did you get off?"

"'Get off'?" Someone else had once asked him the same question, when he'd stopped in the jetway to tie his shoe after debarking from a plane.

"Have an orgasm? With some men it's not always clear."

"Yes, thank you, I mean, it was – to me – very clear."

"You're still wearing your wedding ring," she said.

"It's stuck, I don't know why—"

"Let me get at that thing," she said and pulled hard on his finger, but the loose skin around his knuckle bunched up and blocked it.

"Ow," he finally said. His skin was abraded.

"Perhaps later with soap," she said. She lay back and swung her legs up in the air again.

"Do you like to dance?" he asked.

"Sometimes," she said.

"I'll bet you're a wonderful dancer," said Ira.

"Not really," she said. "But I can always think of things to do."

"That's a nice trait."

"You think so?" she asked, and she leaned in and began tickling him.

"I don't think I'm that ticklish," he said.

"Oh." She stopped.

"I mean, I'm probably a *little*," he added, "just not a lot."

"I would like you to meet my son," she said.

"Is he here?"

"He's under the bed. Bruny?" Oh, these funny ones were funny.

"What is his name?"

"Bruno. I call him Bruny. He's with his dad this week."

The extended families of divorce. Ira tried not to feel jealous. It was quite possible he was not mature enough to date a divorced woman. "Tell me about his dad."

"His dad? His dad is another pediatrician, but he was really into English country dancing. Where eventually he met a lass. Alas."

Ira would write that down in his book. *Alas, a lass.* "I don't think anyone should dance in a way that's not just regular dancing," said Ira. "It's not normal. That's just my opinion."

"Well, he left a long time ago. He said he'd made a terrible mistake getting married. He said that he just wasn't capable of intimacy. I know that's true for some people, but I had never actually heard anyone say that out loud about themselves."

"I know!" said Ira. "Even Hitler never said that! I mean, I don't mean to compare your ex to Hitler *as a leader.* Only as a man."

Zora stroked his arm. "Do you feel ready to meet Bruno? I mean, he didn't care for my last boyfriend at all. That's why we broke up."

"Really?" This silenced Ira for a moment. "If I left those matters to my daughter, I'd be dating a beagle."

"I believe children come first." Her voice now had a steely edge.

"Oh, yes, yes, so do I," he said quickly. He felt suddenly paralyzed and cold.

She reached into the nightstand drawer, took out a vial, and bit into a pill. "Here, take half," she said. "Otherwise we won't get any sleep at all. Sometimes I snore. Probably you do, too."

"This is so cute," Ira said warmly. "Our taking these pills together."

He staggered through his days, tired and unsure. At the office he misplaced files. Sometimes he knocked things over by accident – a glass of water or the benefits manual. News of the coming war, too, was taking its toll. He lay in bed at night, the moments before sleep a kind of stark acquaintance with death. What had happened to the world? March still did not look completely like spring, especially with the plastic sheeting duct-taped to his windows. When he tried to look out, the trees seemed to be pasted onto the waxy dinge of a wintry-looking sky. He wished this month had a less military verb for a name. Why March? How about a month named Skip? That could work.

He got two cats from the pound so that Bekka could have some live pet action at his house, too. He and Bekka went to the store and stocked up on litter and cat food.

"Provisions!" exclaimed Ira.

"In case the war comes here, we can eat the cat food," suggested Bekka.

"Cat food, heck. We can eat the cats," said Ira.

"That's disgusting, Dad."

Ira shrugged.

"You see, that's one of the things Mom didn't like about you!" she added.

"Really? She said that?"

"Sort of."

"Mom likes me. She's just very busy."

"Whatever."

He got back to the cats. "What should we name them?" One should always name food.

"I don't know." Bekka studied the cats.

Ira hated the precious literary names people gave pets – characters from opera and Proust. When he'd first met Marilyn, she had a cat named Portia, but Ira had insisted on calling it Fang.

"I think we should name them Snowball and Snowflake," said Bekka, looking glassy-eyed at the two golden tabbies.

"They don't look like a snowball or a snowflake," said Ira, trying not to let his disappointment show. Sometimes Bekka seemed completely banal to him. She had spells of inexplicable and vapid conventionality. He had always wanted to name a cat Bowser. "How about Bowser?" In the pound someone with name tag duty had named them "Jake" and "Fake Jake," but the quotation marks around their names seemed an invitation to change them.

"Fireball and Fireflake," Bekka tried again.

Ira looked at her, he hoped, beseechingly and persuasively. "*Really?* Fireball and Fireflake don't really sound like cats that would belong to you."

Bekka's face clenched tearily. "You don't know me! I live with you only part-time! The other part of the time I live with Mom, and she doesn't know me either! The only person who knows me is me!"

"OK, OK," said Ira. The cats were eyeing him warily. In time of war never argue with a fireball or a fireflake. Never argue with the food. "Fireball and Fireflake." What were those? Two lonely middle-aged people on a date.

"Why don't you come to dinner?" Zora phoned one afternoon. "I'm making spring spaghetti, Bruny's favorite, and you can come over and meet him. Unless you have Bekka tonight."

"No, I don't," Ira said mournfully. "What is spring spaghetti?"

"Oh, it's the same as regular spaghetti, you just serve it kind of lukewarm. Room temperature. With a little fresh basil."

"What should I bring?"

"Oh, perhaps you could just bring a small appetizer and some dessert," she said. "And maybe a salad, some bread if you're close to a bakery, and a bottle of wine. Also an extra chair, if you have one. We'll need an extra chair."

"OK," he said.

He was a litttle loaded down at the door. She stepped outside, he thought to help him, but she simply put her arms around him and kissed him. "I have to kiss you now here outdoors. Bruny doesn't like to see that sort of thing." She kissed Ira in a sweet, rubbery way on the mouth. Then she stepped back in, smiling, holding the door open for him. Oh, the beautiful smiles of the insane. Soon, he was sure, there would be a study that showed that the mentally ill were actually more attractive than other people. Dating proved it! The aluminum foil over his salad was sliding off and the brownies he had made for dessert were still warm and underneath the salad bowl were probably heating and wilting the lettuce. He attempted a familiar and proprietary stride through her living room, though he felt neither, then dumped everything on her kitchen table.

"Oh, thank you," she said and placed her hand on the small of his back. He was deeply attracted to her. There was nothing he could do about that.

"It smells good," he said. "You smell good." Some mix of garlic and citrus and baby powder overlaid with nutmeg. Her hand wandered down and stroked his behind. "I've got to run out to the car and get the appetizer and the chair," he said and made a quick dash. When he came back in, handed her the appetizer – a dish of herbed olives (he knew nothing about food; someone at work had told him you could never go wrong with herbed olives: "Spell it out – h-e-r b-e-d. Get it?") – and then set the chair up at Zora's little dining table for two (he'd never seen one not set up for at least four), Zora looked brightly at him and whispered, "Are you ready to meet Bruny?"

Ready. He did not know precisely what she meant by that. It seemed she had reversed everything, that she should be asking Bruno, or Bruny, or Brune, if he was ready to meet *him*. "Ready," he said.

There was wavery flute music from behind a closed door down the hallway. "Bruny?" Zora called. The music stopped. Suddenly a barking, howling voice called *"What?"*

"Come out and meet Ira, please."

There was silence. There was nothing. Nobody moved at all for a very long time. Ira smiled politely. "Oh, let him play," he said.

"I'll be right back," said Zora, and she headed down the hall to Bruno's room, knocked on the door, then went in, closing it behind her. Ira stood there for a while, then he picked up the Screwpull, opened the bottle of wine, and began to drink. After several minutes Zora returned to the kitchen, sighing. "Bruny's in a bit of a mood." Suddenly a door slammed and loud, trudging footsteps brought Bruno, the boy himself, into the kitchen. He was barefoot and in a T-shirt and gym shorts, his legs already darkening with hair. His eyebrows sprouted in a manly black V over the bridge of his nose. He was not tall, but he was muscular already, broad-shouldered and thick-limbed, and he folded his arms across his chest and leaned against the wall in weary belligerence.

"Bruny, this is Ira," said Zora. Ira put his wineglass down and thrust out his hand to introduce himself. Bruno unfolded his arms but did not shake hands. Instead, he thrust out his chin and scowled. Ira picked up his wineglass again.

"So, good to meet you. Your mother has said a lot of wonderful things about you." He tried to remember one.

Bruno looked at the appetizer bowl. "What's this grassy gunk all over the olives." It was not really a question, so no one answered it. Bruno turned back to his mother. "May I go back to my room now?"

"Yes, dear," said Zora. She looked at Ira. "He's practicing for the woodwind competition next Saturday. He's very serious."

When Bruno had tramped back down to his room, Ira leaned in to kiss Zora, but she pulled away. "Bruny might hear us," she whispered.

"Let's go to a restaurant. Just you and me. My salad's no good."

"Oh, we couldn't leave Bruno here alone. He's only sixteen."

"I was working in a steel factory when I was sixteen!" Ira decided not to say. Instead he said, "Doesn't he have friends?"

"He's between social groups right now," Zora said defensively. "It's difficult for him to find other kids who are as intellectually serious as he is."

"We'll rent him a movie," said Ira. "Excuse me, a *film*. A foreign film, since he's serious. A documentary. We'll rent him a foreign documentary!"

"We don't have a VCR."

"You don't have a VCR?" At this point Ira found the silverware and helped set the table. When they sat down to eat and poured more wine in their glasses, Bruno suddenly came out and joined them, with no beckoning. The spring spaghetti was tossed in a large glass bowl with grated cheese. "Just how you like it, Brune," said Zora.

"So, Bruno. What grade are you in?"

Bruno rolled his eyes. "Tenth," he said.

"So college is a ways off," said Ira, accidentally thinking out loud.

"I guess," said Bruno, who then tucked into the spring spaghetti.

"So – what classes are you taking in school, besides music?" asked Ira, after a long awkward spell.

"I don't take music," he said with his mouth full. "I'm in All-State Woodwinds."

"All-State Woodwinds! Interesting! Do you take any courses in like, say, American history?"

"They're studying the Amazon rain forest yet again," said Zora. "They've been studying it since preschool."

Ira slurped with morose heartiness at his wine – he had spent too much of his life wandering about in the desert of his own drool, oh, the mealtime assaults he had made on his own fragile consciousness – and some dribbled on his shirt. "For Pete's sake, look at this." He dabbed at the wine spot with his napkin and looked up at Bruno, with an ingratiating grin. "Someday this could happen to you," Ira said, twinkling in Bruno's direction.

"That would never happen to me," muttered Bruno.

Ira continued dabbing at his shirt. He began thinking of his book. *Though I be your mother's beau, no rival I, no foe, faux foe.* He loved rhymes. *Fum! Thumb! Dumb!* They were harmonious and joyous in the face of total crap.

Bruno began gently kicking his mother under the table. Zora began playfully to nudge him back, and soon they were both kicking away, their energetic footsie causing them to slip in their chairs a little, while Ira pretended not to notice, cutting his salad with the edge of his fork, too frightened to look up very much. After a few minutes – when the footsie had stopped and Ira had exclaimed, "Great dinner, Zora!" – they all stood and cleared their places, taking the dishes into the kitchen, putting them in a messy pile in the sink. Ira started halfheartedly to run warm water over them, and Zora and Bruno, some distance behind him, began to jostle up against each other, ramming lightly into each other's sides. Ira glanced over his shoulder and saw Zora now step back and assume a wrestler's starting stance, as Bruno leaped toward her, heaving her over his shoulder, then running her into the living room, where, Ira could see, Bruno dumped her, laughing, on the couch.

Should Ira join in? Should he leave?

"I can still pin you, Brune, when we're on the bed," Zora said.

"Yeah, right," said Bruno.

Perhaps it was time to go. Next time Ira would bring over a VCR for Bruno and just take Zora out to eat. "Well, look at the time! Good to meet you, Bruno," he said, shaking the kid's large, limp hand. Zora stood breathlessly. She walked Ira out to his car, helping to carry his chair and salad bowl. "It was a lovely dinner," said Ira. "And you are a lovely woman. And your son seems so bright and the two of you are adorable together."

Zora beamed, seemingly mute with happiness. If only Ira had known how to speak such fanciful baubles during his marriage, surely Marilyn would never have left him.

He gave Zora a quick kiss on the cheek – the heat of her wrestling had heightened her beautiful nutmeg smell – then kissed her again on the neck, near her ear. Alone in the car on the way home he thought of all the deeply wrong erotic attachments made in wartime, all the crazy romances cooked up quickly by the species to offset death. He turned the radio on: the news of the Mideast was so surreal and bleak that when he heard the tonnage of the bombs planned for Baghdad, he could feel his jaw fall slack in astonishment. He pulled the car over, turned on the interior light, and gazed in the rearview mirror just to see what his face looked like in this particular state. He had felt his face drop in this manner once before – when he got the divorce papers from Marilyn, now *there* was shock and awe for you; there was *decapitation* – but he had never actually seen what he looked like this way. So. Now he knew. Not good: stunned, pale, and not all that bright. It wasn't the same as self-knowledge, but life was long and not that edifying, and one sometimes had to make do with randomly seized tidbits.

He started up again, slowly; outside it had begun to rain, and at a brightly lit intersection of two gas stations, one QuikTrip, and a KFC, half a dozen young people in hooded yellow slickers were holding up signs that read HONK FOR PEACE. Ira fell upon his horn, first bouncing his hand there, then just leaning his whole arm into it. Other cars began to do the same, and soon no one was going anywhere, a congregation of mourning doves! but honking like geese in a wild chorus of futility, windshield wipers clearing their fan-shaped spaces on the drizzled night glass. No car went anywhere for the change of two lights. For all its stupidity and solipsism and scenic civic grief, it was something like a gorgeous moment.

Despite her reading difficulties, despite the witless naming of the cats, Ira knew Bekka was highly intelligent. He knew from the time she spent lying around the house, bored and sighing, saying, "Dad? When will childhood be over?" This was a sign of genius! As were other things. Her complete imperviousness to the adult male voice, for instance. Her scrutiny of all food. With interest and hesitancy, she studied the antiwar lawn signs that bestrewed the neighborhood. WAR IS NOT THE PATH TO PEACE, she read slowly aloud. Then added, "Well duh."

WAR IS NOT THE ANSWER, she read on another. "Well that doesn't make sense," she said to Ira. "War *is* the answer," she said. "It's the answer to the question What's George Bush going to do real soon?"

The times Bekka stayed at Ira's house, she woke up in the morning and told him her dreams. "I had a dream last night that I was walking with two of my friends and we met a wolf. But I made a deal with the wolf. I said, 'Don't eat me. These other two have more meat on them.' And the wolf said, 'OK,' and we shook on it and I got away."

Or "I had a strange dream last night that I was a bad little fairy."

She was in contact with her turmoil and with her ability to survive. How could that be anything less than emotional brilliance?

One morning she said, "I had a really scary dream. There was this tornado with a face inside? And I married it." Ira smiled. "It may sound funny to you, Dad, but it was really scary."

He stole a look at her school writing journal once and found this poem:

Time moving.
Time standing still.
What is the difference?
Time standing still is the difference.

He had no idea what it meant, but he knew it was awesome. He had given her the middle name Clio, after the muse of History, so of course she would know very well that time standing still *was* the difference – whatever that meant. He himself felt he was watching history from the dimmest of backwaters, a land of beer and golf, the horizon peacefully fish-gray, the sky a suicide silver, the windows duct-taped with plastic sheeting so that he felt he was observing life from a plastic container, like a leftover, peering into the tallow fog of the world. *Time moving. Time standing still.*

The major bombing started on the first day of spring. "It's happening," Ira said into Mike's answering machine. "The whole thing is starting now."

Zora called and asked him to the movies. "Sure," Ira said. "I'd love to."

"Well, we were thinking of this Arnold Schwarzenegger movie, but Bruno would also be willing to see the Mel Gibson one." *We.* He was dating a tenth grader now. Even in tenth grade he'd never done that. Well, now he'd see what he'd been missing.

They picked him up at six-forty, and, as Bruno made no

move to cede the front seat, Ira sat in the back of Zora's Honda, his long legs wedged together at a diagonal like a lady riding sidesaddle. Zora drove carefully, not like a mad hellcat at all, which for some reason he'd thought she would. As a result they were late for the Mel Gibson movie and had to make do with the Arnold Schwarzenegger one. Ira thrust money at the ticket taker saying, "Three please," and they all wordlessly went in, their computerized stubs in hand. "So you like Arnold Schwarzenegger?" Ira said to Bruno as they headed down one of the red-carpeted corridors.

"Not really," muttered Bruno. Bruno sat between Zora and Ira, and together they all passed a small container of popcorn back and forth. Ira jumped up twice to refill it back out in the lobby, a kind of relief for him from Arnold, whose line readings were less brutish than they used to be, but not less brutish enough. Afterward, heading out into the parking lot, Bruno and Zora reenacted body-bouncing scenes from the film, throwing themselves against each other's backs and shoulders with great, giggling force. When they reached the car, Ira was again relegated to the backseat.

"Shall we go to dinner?" he called up to the front.

Both Zora and Bruno were silent.

"Shall we?" he tried again cheerfully.

"Would you like to, Bruno?" asked Zora. "Are you hungry?"

"I don't know," Bruno said, peering gloomily out the window.

"Did you like the movie?" asked Ira.

Bruno shrugged. "I dunno."

They went to a barbecue place and got ribs and chicken. "Let me pay for this," said Ira, though Zora had never offered. He would spare them the awkwardness.

"Oh, OK," she said.

Afterward, Zora dropped Ira at the curb, where Ira stood for a minute, waving, in front of his house. Bruno flung the back of his hand toward him, not actually looking. Zora waved vigorously through the open window over the top of the car. He watched them roll down the end of the block and disappear around the corner. He went inside and made himself a drink with cranberry juice and rum. He turned on the TV news and watched the bombing. Night bombing, so you could not really see.

A few mornings later was the first of a new month, his birthday month. The illusion of time flying, he knew, was to make people think life could have more in it than it actually could. Actually, time flying could make human lives seem victorious over time itself. Time flew so fast that in ways it failed to make an impact. People's lives fell between its stabbing powers like insects between raindrops. "We cheat the power of time with our very brevity!" he said aloud to Bekka, feeling confident she would understand, but she only just kept petting the cats. The house had already begun to fill with the acrid-honey smell of cat pee, though neither he nor Bekka seemed to mind. Spring! One more month and it would be May, his least favorite. Why not a month named Can? Or Must! Well, maybe not Must. Zora phoned him early, with a dour tone. "I don't know. I think we should break up," she said.

"You do?"

"Yes, I don't see that this is going anywhere. Things aren't really moving forward in any way I can understand. And I don't think we should waste each other's time."

"Really?" Desperation washed through him.

"It may be fine for some, but dinner, movie, then sex is not my idea of a relationship."

"Maybe we could eliminate the movie?"

"We're adults—"

"True. I mean, we are?"

"—and what is the point, if there are clear obstacles or any unclear idea of where this is headed, of continuing? It becomes difficult to maintain faith. We've hardly begun seeing each other, I realize, but already I just don't envision us as a couple."

"I'm sorry to hear you say that." He was now sitting down in his kitchen. He could feel himself trying not to cry.

"Let's just move on," she said with gentle firmness.

"Really? Is that honestly what you think? I feel terrible."

"April Fools'!" she cried out into the phone.

His heart rose to his throat, then sank to his colon, then bobbed back up close to the surface of his rib cage, where his right hand was clutching at it. Were there paddles somewhere close by that could be applied to his chest?

"I beg your pardon?" he asked faintly.

"April Fools'," she said again, laughing. "It's April Fools' Day."

"I guess," he said, gasping a little, "I guess that's the kind of joke that gets better the longer you think about it."

He had never been involved with the mentally ill before, but he now felt more than ever that there should be strong international laws against them being too good-looking.

"How are you liking Zora?" asked Mike over a beer, after work, after they'd mulled over the war and Dick Cheney's tax return, which had just been reprinted in the paper. Why wasn't there a revolution? Was everyone too distracted with tennis and sex and iris bulbs? Marxism in the spring lacked oomph. Ira had just hired someone to paint his house, so that now in his front lawn he had two signs: WAR IS NOT THE ANSWER in blue and on the other side, in black and yellow, JENKINS PAINTING IS THE ANSWER.

"Oh, Zora's great." Ira paused. "Great. Just great. In fact, do you perhaps know any other single women?"

"Really?"

"Well, it's just that she might not be all that mentally *well*." Ira thought about the moment, just last night, at dinner, when she'd said, "I love your mouth most when it does that odd grimace in the middle of sex," and then she contorted her face so hideously, Ira felt he had been struck. Later in the evening she had said, "Watch this," and she took her collapsible umbrella, placed its handle on the crotch of her trousers, then pressed the button that sent it rocketing out, unfurled, like a cartoon erection. Ira did not know who or what she was, though he wanted to cut her slack, give her a break, bestow upon her the benefit of the doubt – all those paradoxical clichés of supposed generosity, most of which he had denied his wife. He tried not to think that the only happiness he might have been fated for had already occurred, had been with Bekka and Marilyn, when the three of them were together. A hike, a bike ride – he tried not to think that his crazy dream of family had shown its sweet face only long enough to torment him for the rest of his life though scarcely long enough to sustain him through a meal. To torture oneself with this idea of family happiness while not actually having a family, he decided, might be a fairly new circumstance in social history. People were probably not like this a hundred years ago. He imagined an exhibit at the society. He imagined the puppets.

"Sanity's conjectural," said Mike. His brow furrowed thoughtfully. "Zora's very attractive, don't you think?"

Ira thought of her beautiful, slippery skin, the dark, sweet hair, the lithe sylph's body, the mad, hysterical laugh. She had once, though only briefly, insisted that Man Ray and Ray Charles were brothers. "She is attractive," Ira said. "But you say that like it's a good thing."

"Right now," said Mike, "I feel like anything that isn't about killing people is a good thing."

"This may be about that," said Ira.

"Oh, I see. Now we're entering the callow, glib part of spring."

"She's wack, as the kids say."

Mike looked confused. "Is that like wacko?"

"It's like wacko, but not like *Waco* – at least I don't think so. At least not yet. I would stop seeing her, but I don't seem to be able to. Especially now with all that's happening in the world, I can't live without some intimacy, companionship, whatever you want to call it, to face down this global craziness."

"You shouldn't use people as human shields." Mike paused. "Or – I don't know – maybe you should."

"I can't let go of hope, of the illusion of something coming out of this romance, I'm sorry. Divorce is a trauma, believe me, I know. Its pain is a national secret! But that's not it. I can't let go of love. I can't live without love in my life. Hold my hand," said Ira. His eyes were starting to water. Once when he was a small child he had gotten lost, and when his mother had finally found him, four blocks from home, she had asked him if he had been scared. "Not really," he had said, sniffling pridefully. "But then my eyes just suddenly started to water."

"I beg your pardon?" asked Mike.

"I can't believe I just asked you to hold my hand," said Ira, but Mike had already taken it.

The hashish was good. The sleeping pills were good. He was walking slowly around the halls at work in what was a combination of serene energy and a nap. With his birthday coming up, he went to the doctor for his triennial annual physical and, mentioning a short list of nebulous symptoms, he was given dismissive diagnoses of "benign vertigo," "pseudo gout," and perhaps "migraine aura," the names, no doubt, of rock bands. "You've got the pulse of a boy, and the mind of a boy, too," said his doctor, an old golfing friend.

Health, Ira decided, was notional. Palm Sunday – all these *goyim* festivals were preprinted on his calendar – was his birthday, and when Zora called he blurted out that information. "It is?" she said. "You old man! Are you feeling undernookied? I'll come over Sunday and read your palm. If you know what I mean." Wasn't she cute? Dammit, she was cute. She arrived with Bruno and a chocolate cake in tow. "Happy birthday," she said. "Bruno helped me make the frosting."

"Did you now," Ira said to Bruno, patting him on the back in a brotherly embrace that the boy attempted to duck and slide out from under.

They ordered Chinese food and talked about high school, Advanced Placement courses, homeroom teachers, and James Galway (soulful mick or soulless dork, who could decide?). Zora brought out the cake. There were no candles so Ira lit a match, stuck it upright in the frosting, and blew it out. His wish had been a vague and general one of good health for Bekka. No one but her. He had put nobody else in his damn wish. Not the Iraqi people; not the GIs; not Mike, who had held his hand; not Zora. This kind of focused intensity was bad for the planet.

"Shall we sit on Bruno?" Zora was laughing and backing her sweet tush into Bruno, who was now sprawled out on Ira's sofa, resting. "Come on!" she called to Ira. "Let's sit on Bruno." She was now sitting on the boy's hip while Bruno protested in a laughing, grunting manner.

At this point Ira was making his way toward the liquor cabinet. He believed there was some bourbon there. He would not need ice. "Would you care for some bourbon?" he called over to Zora, who was now wrestling with Bruno and looked up at Ira and said nothing. Bruno, too, looked at him and said nothing.

Ira continued to pour. Zora straightened up and walked over to him. He was both drinking bourbon and eating cake. He had a pancreas like a rock. "We should probably go," said Zora. "It's a school night."

"Oh, OK," said Ira, swallowing. "I mean, I wish you didn't have to."

"School. What can you do? I'm going to take the rest of the cake home for Bruny's lunch tomorrow. It's his favorite."

Heat and sorrow filled Ira. The cake had been her only present to him. He closed his eyes and nuzzled his face into hers. "Not now," she whispered. "He gets upset."

"Oh," Ira said. "Well, then I'll walk you out to the car." And there he gave her a quick hug. She walked around the car and got in on the driver's side. He stepped back up on the curb and knocked on the window of the passenger's side to say good-bye to Bruno. But the boy would not turn. He flipped his hand up, showing Ira the back of it.

"Bye! Thank you for sharing my birthday with me!" Ira called out. Where affection fell on its ass, politeness could step up. But then there was the heat and sorrow again just filling his face. Zora's Honda lights went on, then the engine, then the whole vehicle flew down the street.

* * *

At Bekka's coo-coo private school, to which Marilyn had years ago insisted on sending her, the students and teachers were assiduously avoiding talk of the war. In Bekka's class they were doing finger-knitting while simultaneously discussing their hypothetical stock market investments. The class was doing best with preferred stock in Kraft, GE, and GM; watching their investments move slightly every morning on the Dow Jones was also helping their little knitted scarves. It was a right-brain, left-brain thing. For this, Ira forked over nine thousand dollars a year. Not that he really cared. As long as she was in a place safe from war – the alerts were moving from orange to red to orange; no information, just duct tape and bright, mind-wrecking colors – turning Bekka into a knitting stockbroker was OK with him. *Exploit the system, man!* he himself used to say, in college. He could, however, no longer watch TV. He packed it up, along with the VCR, and brought the whole thing over to Zora's. "Here," he said. "This is for Bruno."

"You are so nice," she said, and kissed him near his ear and then on his ear. Possibly he was madly in love with her.

"The TV's broken," said Ira, when Bekka came that weekend and asked about it. "It's in the shop."

"Whatever," Bekka said, pulling her scarf yarn along the floor so the cats could play.

When next he picked Zora up to go out, she said, "Come on in. Bruno's watching a movie on your VCR."

"Does he like it? Should I say hello to him?"

Zora shrugged. "If you want."

He stepped into the house, but the TV was not in the living room. It was in Zora's bedroom, where, spread out half-naked on Zora's bedspread, as he himself had been just a few evenings before, lay Bruno. He was watching Bergman's *The Magic Flute*.

"Hi, Brune," he said. The boy said nothing, transfixed, perhaps not hearing him. Zora came in and pressed a cold glass of water against the back of Bruno's thigh.

"Yow!" cried Bruno.

"Here's your water," said Zora, walking her fingers up one of his legs.

Bruno took the glass and placed it on the floor. The singing on the same television screen that had so recently brought Ira the fiery bombing of Baghdad seemed athletic and absurd, perhaps a kind of joke. But Bruno remained riveted. "Well, enjoy the show," said Ira, who didn't really expect to be thanked for the TV, though now actually knowing he wouldn't be made him feel a little crestfallen.

On the way back out Ira again noticed the sculptures in the corner of the living room. Zora had added two new ones. They were more abstract, made entirely out of old recorders and other woodwinds, but were recognizably boys, priapic with piccolos. "A flute would have been too big," explained Zora, shortly after Ira had said, "So . . . you've been doing some new work!"

At the restaurant the sound system was playing Nancy Wilson singing "For All We Know." The walls, like love, were *trompe l'oeil* – walls painted as viewful windows, though only a fool wouldn't know they were walls. The menu, like love, was full of delicate, gruesome things – cheeks, tongues, thymus glands. The candle, like love, flickered – in the brass tops of the sugar bowl and salt and pepper shakers. He tried to capture Zora's gaze, which seemed to be darting around the room. "It's so nice to be here with you," he said. She turned and fixed him with a smile, repaired him with it. She was a gentle, lovely woman. Something in him kept coming stubbornly back to that. Here they were two lonely adults in a crazy world lucky to have found each other even if it was just for the time being. But now tears were drizzling down her face. Her mouth, collecting them in its corners, was retreating into a pinch.

"Oh, no, what's the matter?" He reached for her hand, but she pulled it away to hide her eyes behind it.

"I just miss Bruny," she said.

He could feel his heart go cold, despite himself. Oh, well. Tomorrow was Easter. All would rise from the dead.

"Don't you think he's fine?"

"It's just – I don't know. It's probably just me coming off my antidepressants."

"You've been on antidepressants?" he asked sympathetically.

"Yes, I was."

"You were on them when I first met you?" Maybe he had wandered into a whole *Flowers for Algernon* thing.

"Yes, indeedy. I went on them two years ago, after my so-called 'nervous breakdown.'" And here she put two fingers in the air, to do quotation marks, but all of her fingers inadvertently sprang up and her hands clawed the air.

He didn't know what he should say. "Would you like me to take you home?"

"No, no, no. Oh, maybe you should. I'm sorry. It's just I feel I have so little time with him now. He's growing up so fast. I just wish I could go back in time." She blew her nose.

"I know what you mean."

"You know, once I was listening to some friends talk about traveling in the Pacific. They left Australia early one morning and arrived in California the evening of the day before. And I thought, I'd like to do that – keep crossing the international date line and get all the way back to when Bruno was a little boy again."

"Yeah," said Ira. "I'd like to get back to that moment where I signed my divorce agreement. I have a few changes I'd like to make."

"You'd have to bring a pen," she said strangely.

He studied her, to memorize her face. "I would never time-travel without a pen," he said.

She paused. "You look worried," she said. "You shouldn't do that with your forehead. It makes you look old." Then she began to sob.

He found her coat and took her home and walked her to the door. Above the house the hammered nickel of the moon gave off its murky shine. "It's a hard time in the world right now," Ira said. "It's hard on everybody. Go in and make yourself a good stiff drink. People don't drink the way they used to. That's what started this whole Iraq thing to begin with: it's a war of teetotalers. People have got to get off their wagons and their high horses and—" He kissed her forehead. "I'll call you tomorrow," he said, though he wouldn't. She squeezed his arm and said, "Sleep well." As he backed out of her driveway, he could see through her front bedroom window, where the TV was firing its colorful fire and Bruno was laid out in a shirtless stupor. Ira could see Zora come in, sit down, cuddle close to Bruno, put her arm around him, and rest her head on his shoulder.

Ira brusquely swung the car away, down the street. Was this *his* problem? Was he too old-fashioned? He had always thought he was a modern man. He knew, for instance, how to stop and ask for directions! And he did it a lot! Of course, afterward, he would sometimes stare at the guy and say, "Who the hell told you that bullshit?"

He had his limitations.

He had not gone to a single seder this week, for which he was glad. It seemed a bad time to attend a ceremony that gave thanks in any way for the slaughter of Middle Eastern boys. He had done that last year. He headed instead to the nearest bar, a dank, noisy dive called Sparky's, where he used to go just after Marilyn left him. When he was married he never drank, but after he was divorced, he used to come in even in the mornings for beer, toast, and fried side meat. All his tin-penny miseries and chickenshit joys would lead him once again to Sparky's. Those half-dozen times he had run into Marilyn at a store – this small town! – he had felt like a dog seeing its owner. Here was the person he knew best in life, squeezing an avocado and acting like she didn't see him. *Oh, here I am, oh, here I am!* But in Sparky's, he knew, he was safe from such unexpected encounters, and after any such unexpected encounters he had often come here. He could sit alone and moan to Sparky. Some people consulted Marcus Aurelius for philosophy about the pain of existence. Ira consulted Sparky. Sparky himself didn't actually have that much to say about the pain of existence. He mostly leaned across the bar, drying a smudgy glass with a dingy towel, and said, "Choose life!" then guffawed.

"Bourbon straight up," said Ira, picking the bar stool closest to the TV so that war news would be hardest to watch from there. Or so he hoped. He let the sharp, buttery elixir of the bourbon warm his mouth, then swallowed its neat, sweet heat. He did this over and over, ordering drink after drink, until he was lit to the gills. At which point he looked up and saw there were other people gathered at the bar, each alone on a chrome-and-vinyl stool, doing the same. "Happy Easter," Ira said to them, lifting his glass with his left hand, the one with the wedding ring still jammed on. "The dead shall rise! The dead are risen! The damages will be mitigated! The Messiah is back among us squeezing the flesh – that nap went by quickly, eh? May all the dead arise! No one has really been killed at all – OK, God looked away for a second to watch some *I Love Lucy* reruns, but he is back now. Nothing has been lost. All is restored. He watching over Israel, slumbers not nor sleeps!"

"Somebody slap that guy," said the man in the blue shirt at the end.

2003

ESCAPE FROM THE INVASION OF THE LOVE-KILLERS

GERARD MAINES LIVED across the hall from a woman named Benna, who four minutes into any conversation always managed to say the word *penis*. He was not a prude, but, nonetheless, it made him wince. He worked with children all day, taught a kind of aerobics to pre-schoolers, and the most extreme language he was likely to hear seemed to him to be in code, in acronyms, or maybe even in German – *boo-boo, finky, peenick* – words that were difficult to figure out even in context, and words, therefore, from which he felt quite safe. He suspected it was not unlike people he knew who hated operas in translation. "Believe me," they would explain, "you just don't want to know what they're saying."

Today they were talking about families.

"Fathers and sons," she said, "they're like governments: always having sword fights with their penises."

"Really," said Gerard, sitting at her kitchen table, gulping at near-beer for breakfast. He palmed his beard like a man trying to decide.

"But what do I know." She smiled and shrugged. "I grew up in a trailer. It's not like a real family with a house." This was her excuse for everything, her own self-deprecating refrain; she'd grown up in a trailer in upstate New York and was therefore unqualified to pronounce on any of the subjects she continued to pronounce on.

Gerard had his own line of self-excuse: "I was a retard in my father's play."

"A retard in your father's play?"

"Yes," he said, realizing that faced with the large questions of life and not finding large answers, one must then settle for makeshift, little answers, just as on any given day a person must at least eat *something*, even if it was not marvelous and huge. "He wrote plays in our town. Then he did the casting and directing. It was harder to venture out through the rest of life after that."

"How awful for you," said Benna, pouring more near-beer into both their glasses.

"Yes," he said. He loved her very much.

Benna was a nightclub singer. Four nights a week she put on a black mini-dress and what she wearily called her Joan-Crawford-catch-me-have-me shoes, and went off to sing at the various cocktail lounges around Fitchville. Sometimes Gerard would go see her and drink too much. In the spotlight up front she seemed to him hopelessly beautiful, a star, her glass jewelry launching quasars into the audience, her laughter rumbling into the mike. He'd watch other men fall in love with her; he knew the fatuous gaze, the free drinks sent over between songs – he'd done that himself. Sometimes he would stay for all three sets and buy her a hamburger afterward or just give her a ride home. Other times, when it was crowded, he would leave her to her fans – the businessmen with loosened neckties, the local teenage girls who idolized her, the very musicians she hired to play with her – and would go home and sit in his bathroom, in his bone-dry tub, with his clothes on, waiting. The way their apartments were laid out, their bathrooms shared a wall, and Gerard could sit in his own tub and await her two-in-the-morning return, hear her enter her bathroom, hear her pee, hear the ruckle of the toilet-paper roll, the metal-sprung flush, the sliding shower door, the squirt, spray, hiss of the water. Sometimes he would call to her through the tiles. She would turn off the shower and yell, "Gerard, are you talking to me?"

"Yes, I'm talking to you. No. I'm talking to Zero Mostel."

"Listen, I'm tired. I'm going to bed."

Once she came home at three in the morning, completely drunk, and knocked on his door. When he opened it, she was slumped against the frame, eyes closed, shoes in hand. "Gerard," she drawled, thrusting her shoes at him, "will you make love to me?" and then she sank to the floor and passed out.

Every morning she downed a whole six-pack of near-beer. "You know, I'm a widow," she said, and then told him quickly about a husband, a lawyer who had been killed in a car crash.

"You're so young," murmured Gerard. "It must have been devastating."

"Nah," she exhaled, and then, peeling an orange, sang "O what a beautiful mourning," just that line. "I don't know," she said, and shrugged.

Near their apartment building was a large baseball field, rarely used. From Gerard's living-room window he could see the field's old rotting scoreboard, weathered as driftwood, its paint peeling but still boasting the neat and discernible lettering: HOME and VISITOR. When he'd first moved into the apartment, the words seemed to mock him – scoring, underscoring, his own displacement and aloneness – so much that he would close the blinds so as not to have to look at them.

Occasionally now, however, late at night, he would venture out onto the diamond and, if it was summer and warm, would sprawl out on the ground at a place just to the left of the pitcher's mound and stare up at the sky. It was important to dizzy yourself with stars, he thought. Too often you forgot they were even there. He could stare at one star, one brilliant and fidgety star, so long that his whole insides seemed suddenly to rush out into the sky to meet it. It was like the feeling he'd had as a boy playing baseball, focusing on the pitched ball with such concentration that the bat itself seemed at the crucial moment to leap from him with a loud smack and greet the ball mid-air.

As an adult he rarely had those moments of connection, though what ones he'd had recently seemed mostly to be with the children he taught. He'd be showing them how to do reaches and bends – like trees, he would tell them – and when he put on music and finally had them do it, their eyes would cry "Look at me! I'm doing it!" the sudden bonds between them and him magical as home runs. More and more he was becoming convinced that it was only through children that one could connect with anything anymore, that in this life it was only through children that one came home, became a home, that one was no longer a visitor.

"Boy, are you sentimental," Benna told him. "I feel like I'm talking to a Shirley Temple movie." Benna was a woman who knew when she was ovulating by the dreams she'd have of running through corridors to catch trains; she was also a woman who said she had no desire to have children. "I watched my friend Eleanor give birth," she said. "Once you've seen a child born you realize a baby's not much more than a reconstituted ham and cheese sandwich. Just a little anagram of you and what you've been eating for nine months."

"But look at the stars," he wanted to say to her. "How does one get there?" But then he thought of her singing in the Ramada Inn cocktail lounge, her rhinestones flashing out into the dark of the place, and thought that maybe in a certain way she was already there. "Tell me why you don't want to have children," Gerard asked her. He had for a solid week recently allowed himself the fantasy of someday having a family with her, although she had shown no real interest in him after that one night in his doorway, and usually went out with other men anyway. He would sometimes hear them clunk up and down the stairs.

"You know me," she said. "I grew up in a trailer. Your own father made you a retard. You tell me why you want to have kids."

Gerard thought about the little deaf boy in his class, a boy named Barney, how just today Barney had said loudly in his garbled and unconsonanted speech, "Please, Mr. Maines, when you stand behind, can you stomp your feet louder?" The only way Barney could hear the music and the beat was through the vibrations in the floor. Gerard had smiled, kind and hearty, and said "Certainly, young man," and something raced and idled in his heart.

"Sometimes I think that without children we remain beasts or dust. That we are like something lost at sea."

Benna looked at him and blinked, her eyes almost swelling, as if with allergy. She took a long glug of near-beer, swallowed, then shrugged. "Do you?" she said. "I think maybe I'm just too exhausted from work."

"Yes, well," said Gerard, attempting something lighthearted, "I guess that's why they call it *work*. I guess that's why they don't call it *table tennis*."

"What are you watching?" Gerard had knocked on her door and sauntered in. Benna was curled under a blanket on the sofa, watching television. Gerard tried to smile, had even been practicing it, feeling the air on his teeth, his cheeks puff up into his vision, the slight rise of his ears up the sides of his head.

"Some science-fiction thing," she said. "Escape from something. Or maybe it's invasion of something. I forget."

"Who are those figures rimmed in neon?" he asked, sitting beside her.

"Those are the love-killers. They love you and then they kill you. They're from another planet. Supposedly."

He looked at her face. It was pale, without make-up, and the narrow planes of her cheeks seemed exquisite as bone. Her hair, pulled off her face into a rubber band, shone auburn in the lamplight. Just as she was, huddled in a blanket that had telltale signs of dog hair and coffee, Gerard wanted more than anything else to hold her in his arms. And so, in a kind of rush out of himself, he leaned over and kissed Benna on the mouth.

"Gerard," she said, pulling away slightly. "I like you very much, but I'm just not feeling sexual these days."

He could feel the dry chap of her lips against his, still there, like a ten-second ghost. "You go out with men," he insisted, quickly hating the tone of his own voice. "I hear them."

"Look. I'm going through life alone now," she said. "I can't think of men or penises or marriage or children. I work too hard. I don't even masturbate."

Gerard sank into the back of the sofa, feeling himself about to speak something bitter, something that tomorrow he would apologize for. What he said was, "What, do you need an audience for *everything*?" And without waiting for a reply, he got up to return to his own apartment where VISITOR and HOME, like a rigged and age-old game, would taunt him even through the blinds. He stood and went back across the hall, where he lived.

1985

FOES

BAKE McKURTY WAS NO stranger to the parasitic mixings of art and commerce, literature and the rich. "Hedge funds and haiku!" he'd exclaimed to his wife, Suzy – and yet such mixings seemed never to lose their swift, stark capacity to appall. The hustle for money met the hustle for virtue and everyone washed their hands in one another. It was a common enough thing, though was there ever enough soap to cut the grease? "That's what your lemon is for," Suzy would say, pointing at the twist in the martini he was not supposed to drink. Still, now and again, looking up between the crabmeat cocktail and the palate-cleansing sorbet sprinkled with fennel pollen dust, he felt shocked by the whole thing.

"It's symbiosis," said Suzy as they were getting dressed to go. "Think of it being like the krill that grooms and sees for the rock shrimp. Or that bird who picks out the bugs from the rhino hide."

"So we're the Seeing Eye krill," he said.

"Yes!"

"We're the oxpeckers."

"Well, I wasn't going to say that," she said.

"A lot in this world has to do with bugs," said Bake.

"Food," she said. "A lot has to do with grooming and food. Are you wearing that?"

"What's wrong with it?"

"Lose the— What are those?"

"Suspenders."

"They're red."

"OK, OK. But you know, I never do that to you."

"I'm the sighted krill," she said. She smoothed his hair, which had recently become a weird pom-pom of silver and maize.

"And I'm the blind boy?"

"Well, I wasn't going to say that either."

"You look good. Whatever it is you're wearing. See? I say nice things to *you*!"

"It's a sarong." She tugged it up a little.

He ripped off the suspenders. "Well, here. You may need these."

They were staying at a Georgetown B and B to save a little money, a town house where the owner-couple left warm cookies at everyone's door at night to compensate for their loud toddler, who by 6:00 a.m. was barking orders and pointing at her mother to fetch this toy or that. After a day of sightseeing – all those museums prepaid with income taxes; it was like being philanthropists come to investigate the look of their own money – Suzy and Bake were already tired. They hailed a cab and recited the address of the event to the cabbie, who nodded and said ominously, "Oh, yes."

Never mind good taste, here at this gala even the usual diaphanous veneer of seemliness had been tossed to the trade winds: the fund-raiser for *Lunar Lines Literary Journal – 3LJ* as it was known to its readers and contributors; "the magazine" as it was known to its staff, as if there were no others – was being held in a bank. Or at least a former bank, one which had recently gone under, and which now sold squid-ink orecchiette beneath its vaulted ceilings, and martinis and grenache from its former teller stations. Wood and marble were preserved and buffed, glass barriers removed. In the evening light the place was golden. It was cute! So what if subtle boundaries of occasion and transaction had been given up on? So what if this were a mausoleum of greed now danced in by all? He and Suzy had been invited. The passive voice could always be used to obscure blame.

The invitation, however, to this D.C. fund-raiser seemed to Bake a bit of a fluke, since *Man on a Quarter, Man on a Horse*, Bake's ill-selling biography of George Washington (in a year when everyone was obsessed with Lincoln, even the efficiently conflated Presidents' Day had failed to help his book sales), would appear to fit him to neither category of guest.

But *Lunar Lines*, whose offices were in Washington, had excerpted a portion of it, as if in celebration of their town. And so Bake was sent two free dinner tickets. He would have to rub elbows and charm the other guests – the rich, the magazine's donors, who would be paying five hundred dollars a plate. Could he manage that? Could he be the court jester, the town clown, the token writer at the table? "Absolutely," he lied.

Why had he come? Though it was named after the man he had devoted years of affectionate thought and research to, he had never liked this city. An ostentatious company town built on a marsh – a mammoth, pompous chit-ridden motor vehicle department run by gladiators. High-level clerks on the take, their heads full of unsound sound bites and falsified recall. "Yes! How are you? It's been a while." Not even "It's been a long time," because who knew? Perhaps it hadn't been. Better just to say, neutrally, "It's been a while," and no one could argue.

He clung to Suzy. "At least the wine is good," she said. They weren't really mingling. They were doing something that was more like a stiff list, a drift and sway. The acoustics made it impossible to speak normally, and so they found themselves shouting inanities, then just falling mute. The noise of the place was deafening as a sea, and the booming heartiness of others seemed to drown all possibility of happiness for themselves.

"Soon we'll have to find our table," he shouted, glancing out at the vast room filled with a hundred white-clothed circles, flickering with candlelight. Small vases of heather sprigs that could easily catch fire had been placed in the centers as well. So were little chrome cardholders declaring the table numbers. "What number are we?"

Suzy pulled the tag from what he facetiously called her "darling little bag," then shoved it back in. "Seventy-nine," she said. "I hope that's near the restroom."

"I hope it's near the exit."

"Let's make a dash for it now!"

"Let's scream 'fire!' "

"Let's fake heart attacks!"

"Do you have any pot?"

"We flew here – remember? I wouldn't bring pot on an airplane."

"We're losing our sense of adventure. In all things."

"This is an adventure!"

"You see, that's what I mean."

At the ringing of a small bell everyone was to sit – not just the ones already in wheelchairs. Bake let Suzy lead as they wended their way, drinks in hand, between the dozens of tables that were between them and number 79. They were the first ones there, and when he looked at the place cards and saw that someone had placed Suzy far away from him, he quickly switched the seating arrangements and placed her next to him, on his left. "I didn't come this far not to sit next to you," he said, and she smiled wanly, squeezing his hand. These kinds of gestures were necessary, since they had not had sex in six months. "I'm sixty and I'm on antidepressants," Bake had said when Suzy had once (why only once?) complained. "I'm lucky my penis hasn't dropped off."

They remained standing by their seats, waiting for their table to fill up: Soon a young investor couple from Wall Street who had not yet lost their jobs. Then a sculptor and her son. Then an editorial assistant from *3LJ.* Then last, to claim the seat to his right, a brisk young Asian woman in tapping heels. She thrust her hand out to greet him. Her nails were long and painted white – perhaps they were fake: Suzy would know, though Suzy was now sitting down and talking to the sculptor next to her.

"I'm Linda Santo," the woman to his right said, smiling. Her hair was black and shiny and long enough so that with a toss of the head she could swing it back behind her shoulder and short enough that it would fall quickly forward again. She was wearing a navy blue satin dress and a string of pearls. The red shawl she had wrapped over her shoulders she now placed on the back of her seat. He felt a small stirring in him. He had always been attracted to Asian women, though he knew he mustn't ever mention this to Suzy, or to anyone really.

"I'm Baker McKurty," he said, shaking her hand.

"*Baker*?" she repeated.

"I usually go by Bake." He accidentally gave her a wink. One had to be very stable to wink at a person and not frighten them.

"*Bake*?" She looked a little horrified – if one could be horrified only a little. She was somehow aghast – and so he pulled out her chair to show her that he was harmless. No sooner were they all seated than appetizers zoomed in. Tomatoes stuffed with avocados and avocados with tomatoes. It was a witticism – with a Christmasy look though Christmas was a long way away.

"So where are all the writers?" Linda Santo asked him while looking over both her shoulders. The shiny hair flew. "I was told there would be writers here."

"You're not a writer?"

"No, I'm an evil lobbyist," she said, grinning slightly. "Are you a writer?"

"In a manner of speaking, I suppose," he said.

"You are?" She brightened. "What might you have written?"

"What might I have written? Or, what did I actually write?"

"Either one."

He cleared his throat. "I've written several biographies. Boy George. King George. And now George Washington. That's my most recent. A biography of George Washington. A captivating man, really, with a tremendous knack for real estate. And a peevishness about being overlooked for promotion when he served in the British army. The things that will start a war! And I'm not like his other biographers. I don't rule out his being gay."

"You're a biographer of Georges," she said, nodding and unmoved. Clearly she'd been hoping for Don DeLillo.

This provoked him. He veered off into a demented heat. "Actually, I've won the Nobel Prize."

"Really?"

"Yes! But, well, I won it during a year when the media

weren't paying a lot of attention. So it kind of got lost in the shuffle. I won – right after 9/11. In the shadow of 9/11. Actually, I won right as the second tower was being hit."

She scowled. "The Nobel Prize for Literature?"

"Oh, for literature? No, no, no – not for literature." His penis now sat soft as a shrinking peach in his pants.

Suzy leaned in on his left and spoke across Bake's plate to Linda. "Is he bothering you? If he bothers you, just let me know. I'm Suzy." She pulled her hand out of her lap, and the two women shook hands over his avocado. He could see Linda's nails were fake. Or, if not fake, something. They resembled talons.

"This is Linda," said Bake. "She's an evil lobbyist."

"Really!" Suzy said good-naturedly, but soon the sculptor was tapping her on the arm and she had to turn back and be introduced to the sculptor's son.

"Is it hard being a lobbyist?"

"It's interesting," she said. "It's hard work but interesting."

"That's the best kind."

"Where are you from?"

"Chicago."

"Oh, really," she said, as if he had announced his close connection to Al Capone. Anyone he ever mentioned Chicago to always brought up Capone. Either Capone or the Cubs.

"So you know the presidential candidate for the Democrats?"

"Brocko? Love him! He's the great new thing. He's a writer himself. I wonder if he's here." Now Baker, as if in mimicry, turned and looked over both of *his* shoulders.

"He's probably out with his terrorist friends," Linda said.

"He has terrorist friends?" Bake himself had a terrorist friend. Midwesterners loved their terrorist friends, who were usually fine and boring citizens still mythically dining out on the sins of long-ago youth. They never actually killed anyone – at least not intentionally. They aged and fattened in the ordinary fashion. They were rehabilitated. They served their time. And, well, if they didn't, because of *infuriating class privilege that allowed them to just go on as if nothing had ever happened,* well, they raised each other's children and got advanced degrees and gave back to society in other ways. He supposed. He didn't really know much about Chicago. He was actually from Michigan, but when going anywhere he always flew out of O'Hare.

"Uh, yeah. That bomber who tried to blow up federal buildings right here in this town."

"When Brocko was a kid? That sixties guy? But Brocko doesn't even like the sixties. He thinks they're so . . . sixties. The sixties took his mother on some wild ride away from him."

"The sixties *made* him, my friend."

Bake looked at her more closely. Now he could see she wasn't Asian. She had simply had some kind of plastic surgery: skin was stretched and draped strangely around her eyes. A botched eye job. A bad face-lift. An acid peel. Whatever it was: Suzy would know exactly.

"Well, he was a young child."

"So he says."

"Is there some dispute about his age?"

"Where is his birth certificate?"

"I have no idea," said Bake. "I have no idea where my own is."

"Here is my real problem: this country was founded by and continues to be held together by people who have worked very hard to get where they are."

Bake shrugged and wagged his head around. Now would not be the time to speak of timing. It would be unlucky to speak of luck. Could he speak of people having things they didn't deserve, in a roomful of such people? She continued. "And if you don't understand *that*, my friend, then we cannot continue this conversation."

The sudden way in which the whole possibility of communication was now on the line startled him. "I see you've researched the founding of this country." He would look for common ground.

"I watched *John Adams* on HBO. Every single episode."

"Wasn't the guy who played George Washington uncanny?

I did think Jefferson looked distractingly like Martin Amis. I wonder if Martin is here?" He looked over his shoulders again. He needed Martin Amis to get over here right now and *help* him.

Linda looked at him fiercely. "It was a great miniseries and a great reminder of the founding principles of our nation."

"Did you know George Washington was afraid of being buried alive?"

"I didn't know about that."

"The guy scarcely had a fear except for that one. You knew he freed his slaves?"

"Hmmmm."

She was eating; he was not. This would not work to his advantage. Nonetheless he went on. "Talk about people who've toiled hard in this country – and yet, not to argue with your thesis too much, those slaves didn't all get ahead."

"Your man Barama, my friend, would not even be in the running if he wasn't black."

Now all appetite left him entirely. The food on his plate, whatever it was, splotches of taupe, dollops of orange, went abstract like a painting. His blood pressure flew up; he could feel the pulsing twitch in his temple. "You know, I never thought about it before but you're right! Being black really *is* the fastest, easiest way to get to the White House!"

She said nothing, and so he added, "Unless you're going by cab, and then, well, it can slow you down a little."

Chewing, Linda looked at him, a flash in her eyes. She swallowed. "Well, supposedly we've already had a black president."

"We have?"

"Yes! A Nobel Prize–winning author said so!"

"Hey. Take it firsthand from me: don't believe everything that a Nobel Prize winner tells you. I don't think a black president ever gets to become president when his nightclub-singer mistress is holding press conferences during the campaign. That would be – that would be a *white* president. Please pass the salt."

The shaker appeared before him. He shook some salt around on his plate and stared at it.

Linda made a stern, effortful smile, struggling to cut something with her knife. Was it meat? Was it poultry? It was consoling to think that, for a change, the rich had had to pay a pretty penny for their chicken while his was free. But it was not consoling *enough*. "If you don't think I as a woman know a thing or two about prejudice, you would be sadly mistaken," Linda said.

"Hey, it's not that easy being a man, either," said Bake. "There's all that cash you have to spend on porn, and believe me, that's money you never get back."

He then retreated, turned toward his left, toward Suzy, and leaned in. "Help me," he whispered in her ear.

"Are you charming the patrons?"

"I fear some object may be thrown."

"You're supposed to charm the patrons."

"I know, I know, I was trying to. I swear. But she's one of those who keeps referring to Brocko as Barama." He had violated most of Suzy's dinner talk rules already: no politics, no religion, no portfolio tips. *And unless you see the head crowning, never look at a woman's stomach and ask if she's pregnant.* He had learned all these the hard way.

But in a year like this one, there was no staying away from certain topics.

"Get back there," Suzy said. The sculptor was tapping Suzy on the arm again.

He tried once more with Linda Santo the evil lobbyist. "Here's the way I see it – and this I think you'll appreciate. It would be great at long last to have a president in the White House whose last name ends with a vowel."

"We've never had a president whose last name ended with a vowel?"

"Well, I don't count Coolidge."

"You're from what part of Chicago?"

"Well, just outside Chicago."

"Where outside?"

"Michigan."

"Isn't Michigan a long way from Chicago?"

"It is!" He could feel the cold air on the skin between his socks and his pant cuffs. When he looked at her hands they seemed frozen into claws.

"People talk about the rock-solid sweetness of the heartland, but I have to say: Chicago seems like a city that has taken too much pride in its own criminal activity." She smiled grimly.

"I don't think that's true." Or was it? He was trying to give her a chance. What if she was right? "Perhaps we have an unfulfilled streak of mythic hankering. Or perhaps we don't live as fearfully as people do elsewhere," he said. Now he was just guessing.

"You wait, my friend, there are some diabolical people eyeing that Sears Tower as we speak."

Now he was silent.

"And if you're in it when it happens, which I hope you're not, but if you are, if you are, if you are, if you're eating lunch at the top or having a meeting down below or whatever it is you may be doing, you will be changed. Because I've been there. I know what it's like to be bombed by terrorists – I was in the Pentagon when they crashed that plane right down into it and I'll tell you: I was burned alive but not dead. I was burned *alive*. It lit me inside. Because of that I know more than ever what this country is about, my friend."

He saw now that her fingernails really were plastic, that the hand really was a dry frozen claw, that the face that had seemed intriguingly exotic had actually been scarred by fire and only partially repaired. He saw how she was cloaked in a courageous and intense hideosity. The hair was beautiful, but now he imagined it was probably a wig. Pity poured through him: he'd never before felt so sorry for someone. How could someone have suffered so much? How could someone have come so close to death, so unfairly, so painfully and heroically, and how could he still want to strangle them?

"You were a lobbyist for the Pentagon?" was all he managed to say.

* * *

"Any faux pas?" asked Suzy in the cab on the way back to the B and B, where warm cookies would await them by their door, and snore strips on their nightstand.

"Beaucoup faux," said Bake. He pronounced it *foze*. "Beaucoup verboten foze. Uttering my very name was like standing on the table and peeing in a wineglass."

"What? Oh, please."

"I'm afraid I spoke about politics. I couldn't control myself."

"Brocko is going to win. His daughters will like it here. All will be well. Rest assured," she said, as the cab sped along toward Georgetown, the street curbs rusted and rouged with the first fallen leaves.

"Promise?"

"Promise."

He was afraid to say more.

He did not know how much time he and Suzy might even have left together, and an endgame of geriatric speed dating – everyone deaf and looking identical: "What? I can't hear you? What? You again? Didn't I just see you?" – all taking place midst bankruptcy and war, might be the real circle of hell he was destined for.

"Don't ever leave me," he said.

"Why on earth would I do that?"

He paused. "I'm putting in a request not just for *on earth*, but for even after that."

"OK," she said, and squeezed his meaty thigh. At least he had once liked to think of it as meaty.

"I fear you will soon discover some completely obvious way to find me less than adequate."

"You're adequate," she said.

"I'm adequate enough."

She kept her hand there on his leg, and on top of hers he placed his, the one with the wedding ring she had given him, identical to her own. He willed all his love into the very ends of his fingertips, and as his hand clasped hers he watched the firm, deliberate hydraulics of its knuckles and joints. But she had already turned her head away and was looking out the window, steadily, the rest of the ride back, showing him only her beautiful hair, which was gold and flashing in the passing streetlamps, as if it were something not attached to her at all.

2008

FOUR CALLING BIRDS, THREE FRENCH HENS

WHEN THE CAT DIED on Veterans Day, his ashes then packed into a cheesy pink-posied tin and placed high upon the mantel, the house seemed lonely and Aileen began to drink. She had lost all her ties to the animal world. She existed now in a solely man-made place: the couch was furless, the carpet dry and unmauled, the kitchen corner where the food dish had been no longer scabby with Mackerel Platter and hazardous for walking.

Oh, Bert!

He had been a beautiful cat.

Her friends interpreted the duration and intensity of her sorrow as a sign of displaced mourning: her grief was for something larger, more appropriate – it was the impending death of her parents; it was the son she and Jack had never had (though wasn't three-year-old Sofie cute as a zipper?); it was this whole Bosnia, Cambodia, Somalia, Dinkins, Giuliani, NAFTA thing.

No, really, it was just Bert, Aileen insisted. It was just her sweet, handsome cat, her buddy of ten years. She had been with him longer than she had with either Jack or Sofie or half her friends, and he was such a smart, funny guy – big and loyal and verbal as a dog.

"What do you mean, *verbal as a dog*?" Jack scowled.

"I swear it," she said.

"Get a grip," said Jack, eyeing her glass of blended malt. Puccini's "Humming Chorus," the Brahms "Alto Rhapsody," and Samuel Barber's Adagio for Strings all murmured in succession from the stereo. He flicked it off. "You've got a daughter. There are holidays ahead. That damn cat wouldn't have shed one tear over you."

"I really don't think that's true," she said a little wildly, perhaps with too much fire and malt in her voice. She now spoke that way sometimes, insisted on things, ventured out on a limb, lived dangerously. She had already – carefully, obediently – stepped through all the stages of bereavement: anger, denial, bargaining, Häagen-Dazs, rage. Anger to rage – who said she wasn't making progress? She made a fist but hid it. She got headaches, mostly prickly ones, but sometimes the zigzag of a migraine made its way into her skull and sat like a cheap, crazy tie in her eye.

"I'm sorry," said Jack. "Maybe he would have. Fundraisers. Cards and letters. Who can say? You two were close, I know."

She ignored him. "Here," she said, pointing at her drink. "Have a little festive lift!" She sipped at the amber liquor, and it stung her chapped lips.

"Dewar's," said Jack, looking with chagrin at the bottle.

"Well," she said defensively, sitting up straight and buttoning her sweater. "I suppose you're out of sympathy with Dewar's. I suppose you're more of a *Do-ee*."

"That's right," said Jack disgustedly. "That's right! And tomorrow I'm going to wake up and find I've been edged out by Truman!" He headed angrily up the stairs, while she listened for the final clomp of his steps and the cracking slam of the door.

Poor Jack: perhaps she had put him through too much. Just last spring, there had been her bunion situation – the limping, the crutch, and the big blue shoe. Then in September, there had been Mimi Andersen's dinner party, where Jack, the only non-smoker, was made to go out on the porch while everyone else stayed inside and lit up. And *then*, there had been Aileen's one-woman performance of "the housework version of *Lysistrata*." "No Sweepie, No Kissie," Jack had called it. But it had worked. Sort of. For about two weeks. There was, finally, only so much one woman on the vast and wicked stage could do.

"I'm worried about you," said Jack in bed. "I'm being earnest here. And not in the Hemingway sense, either." He screwed up his face. "You see how I'm talking? Things are wacko around here." Their bookcase headboard was so stacked with novels and sad memoirs, it now resembled a library carrel more than a conjugal bed.

"You're fine. I'm fine. Everybody's fine," said Aileen. She tried to find his hand under the covers, then just gave up.

"You're someplace else," he said. "Where are you?"

The birds had become emboldened, slowly reclaiming the yard, filling up the branches, cheeping hungrily in the mornings from the sills and eaves. "What is that *shrieking*?" Aileen asked. The leaves had fallen, but now jays, ravens, and house finches darkened the trees – some of them flying south, some of them staying on, pecking the hardening ground for seeds. Squirrels moved in poking through the old apples that had dropped from the flowering crab. A possum made a home for himself under the porch, thumping and chewing. Raccoons had discovered Sofie's little gym set, and one morning Aileen looked out and saw two of them swinging on the swings. She'd wanted animal life? Here was animal life!

"Not this," she said. "None of this would be happening if Bert were still here." Bert had patrolled the place. Bert had kept things in line.

"Are you talking to me?" asked Jack.

"I guess not," she said.

"What?"

"I think we need to douse this place in repellent."

"You mean, like, bug spray?"

"Bug spray, Bugs Bunny," chanted Sofie. "Bug spray, Bugs Bunny."

"I don't know what I mean," said Aileen.

At her feminist film-critique group, they were still discussing *Cat Man*, a movie done entirely in flashback from the moment a man jumps off the ledge of an apartment building. Instead of being divided into acts or chapters, the movie was divided into floor numbers, in descending order. At the end of the movie, the handsome remembering man lands on his feet.

Oh, Bert!

One of the women in Aileen's group – Lila Conch – was angry at the movie. "I just hated the way anytime a woman character said anything of substance, she also happened to be half-naked."

Aileen sighed. "Actually, I found those parts the most true to life," she said. "They were the parts I liked best."

The group glared at her. "Aileen," said Lila, recrossing her legs. "Go to the kitchen for us, dear, and set up the brownies and tea."

"Seriously?" asked Aileen.

"Uh – yes," said Lila.

Thanksgiving came and went in a mechanical way. Aileen and Jack, with Sofie, went out to a restaurant and ordered different things, as if the three of them were strangers asserting their ornery tastes. Then they drove home. Only Sofie, who had ordered the child's Stuffed Squash, was somehow pleased, sitting in the car seat in back and singing a Thanksgiving song she'd learned at day care. "'Oh, a turkey's not a pig, you doink / He doesn't say *oink* / He says *gobble, gobble, gobble.*'" Their last truly good holiday had been Halloween, when Bert was still alive and they had dressed him up as Jack. They'd then dressed Jack as Bert, Aileen as Sofie, and Sofie as Aileen. "Now, I'm you, Mommy," Sofie had said when Aileen had tied one of her kitchen aprons around her and pressed lipstick onto her mouth. Jack came up and rubbed his Magic Marker whiskers against Aileen, who giggled in her large pink footie pajamas. The only one who wasn't having that much fun was Bert himself, sporting one of Jack's ties, and pawing at it to get it off. When he didn't succeed, he gamely dragged the tie around for a while, trying to ignore it. Then, cross and humiliated, he waddled over to the corner near the piano and lay there, annoyed. Remembering this, a week later – when Bert was dying in an oxygen tent at the vet's, heart failing, fluid around his lungs (though his ears still pricked up when Aileen came to visit him; she wore her usual perfume so he would know her smell, and hand-fed him cat snacks when no one else could get him to eat) – Aileen had felt overwhelmed with sorrow and regret.

"I think you should see someone," said Jack.

"Are we talking a psychiatrist or an affair?"

"An affair, of course." Jack scowled. "An *affair*?"

"I don't know." Aileen shrugged. The whiskey she'd been drinking lately had caused her joints to swell, so that now when she lifted her shoulders, they just kind of stayed like that, stiffly, up around her ears.

Jack rubbed her upper arm, as if he either loved her or was wiping something off on her sleeve. Which could it be? "Life is a long journey across a wide country," he said. "Sometimes the weather's good. Sometimes it's bad. Sometimes it's so bad, your car goes off the road."

"Really."

"Just go talk to someone," he said. "Our health plan will cover part."

"Okay," she said. "Okay. Just – no more metaphors."

She got recommendations, made lists and appointments, conducted interviews.

"I have a death-of-a-pet situation," she said. "How long does it take for you to do those?"

"I beg your pardon?"

"How long will it take you to get me over the death of my cat, and how much do you charge for it?"

Each of the psychiatrists, in turn, with their slightly different outfits, and slightly different potted plants, looked shocked.

"Look," Aileen said. "Forget Prozac. Forget Freud's abandonment of the seduction theory. Forget Jeffrey Masson – or is it *Jackie* Mason? The only thing that's going to revolutionize *this* profession is Bidding the Job!"

"I'm afraid we don't work that way," she was told again and again – until finally, at last, she found someone who did.

"I specialize in Christmas," said the psychotherapist, a man named Sidney Poe, who wore an argyle sweater vest, a crisp bow tie, shiny black oxfords, and no socks. "Christmas specials. You feel better by Christmas, or your last session's free."

"I like the sound of that," said Aileen. It was already December first. "I like the sound of that a lot."

"Good," he said, giving her a smile that, she had to admit, looked crooked and unsound. "Now, what are we dealing with here, a cat or a dog?"

"A cat," she said.

"Whoa-boy." He wrote something down, muttered, looked dismayed.

"Can I ask you a question first?" asked Aileen.

"Certainly," he said.

"Do you offer Christmas specials because of the high suicide rates around Christmas?"

"'The high suicide rates around Christmas,'" he repeated in an amused and condescending way. "It's a myth, the high suicide rates around Christmas. It's the *homicide* rate that's high. Holiday homicide. All that time the family suddenly gets to spend together, and then *bam*, that *egg*nog."

She went to Sidney Poe on Thursdays – "Advent Thursdays," she called them. She sat before him with a box of designer Kleenex on her lap, recalling Bert's finer qualities and golden moments, his great sense of humor and witty high jinks. "He used to try to talk on the phone, when *I* was on the phone. And once, when I was looking for my keys, I said aloud, 'Where're my keys?' and he came running into the room, thinking I'd said, Where's my *kitty*?"

Only once did she actually have to slap Sidney awake – lightly. Mostly, she could just clap her hands once and call his name – *Sid!* – and he would jerk upright in his psychiatrist's chair, staring wide.

"In the intensive care unit at the animal hospital," Aileen continued, "I saw a cat who'd been shot in the spine with a BB. I saw dogs recovering from jaw surgery. I saw a retriever who'd had a hip replacement come out into the lobby dragging a little cart behind him. He was so happy to see his owner. He dragged himself toward her and she knelt down and spread her arms wide to greet him. She sang out to him and cried. It was the animal version of *Porgy and Bess*." She paused for a minute. "It made me wonder what was going on in this country. It made me think we should ask ourselves, What in hell's going on?"

"I'm afraid we're over our time," said Sidney.

The next week, she went to the mall first. She wandered in and out of the stores with their thick tinsel and treacly Muzak Christmas carols. Everywhere she went, there were little cat Christmas books, cat Christmas cards, cat Christmas wrapping paper. She hated these cats. There were boring, dopey, caricatured, interchangeable – not a patch on Bert.

"I had great hopes for Bert," she said later to Sidney. "They gave him all the procedures, all the medications – but the drugs knocked his kidneys out. When the doctor suggested putting him to sleep, I said, 'Isn't there anything else we can do?' and you know what the doctor said? He said, 'Yes. An autopsy.' A thousand dollars later and he says, 'Yes. An autopsy.'"

"Eeeeyew," said Sid.

"A cashectomy," said Aileen. "They gave poor Bert a cashectomy!" And here she began to cry, thinking of the sweet, dire look on Bert's face in the oxygen tent, the bandaged tube in his paw, the wet fog in his eyes. It was not an animal's way to die like that, but she had subjected him to the full medical treatment, signed him up for all that metallic and fluorescent voodoo, not knowing what else to do.

"Tell me about Sofie."

Aileen sighed. Sofie was adorable. Sofie was terrific. "She's fine. She's great." Except Sofie was getting little notes sent home with her from day care. "Today, Sofie gave the teacher the finger – except it was her index finger." Or "Today, Sofie drew a mustache on her face." Or "Today, Sofie demanded to be called 'Walter.'"

"Really."

"Our last really good holiday was Halloween. I took her trick-or-treating around the neighborhood, and she was so cute. It was only by the end of the night that she began to catch on to the whole concept of it. Most of the time, she was so excited, she'd ring the bell, and when someone came to the door, she'd thrust out her bag and say, 'Look! I've got treats for you!'"

Aileen had stood waiting, down off the porches, on the sidewalk, in her big pink footie pajamas. She'd let Sofie do the talking. "I'm my mommy and my mommy's me," Sofie explained.

"I see," said the neighbors. And then they'd call and wave from the doorway. "Hello, Aileen! How are you doing?"

"We've got to focus on Christmas here," said Sidney.

"Yes," said Aileen despairingly. "We've only got one more week."

On the Thursday before Christmas, she felt flooded with memories: the field mice, the day trips, the long naps together. "He had limited notes to communicate his needs," she said. "He had his 'food' mew, and I'd follow him to his dish. He had his 'out' mew, and I'd follow him to the door. He had his 'brush' mew, and I'd go with him to the cupboard where his brush was kept. And then he had his existential mew, where I'd follow him vaguely around the house as he wandered in and out of rooms, not knowing exactly what or why."

Sidney's eyes began to well. "I can see why you miss him," he said.

"You can?"

"Of course! But that's all I can leave you with."

"The Christmas special's up?"

"I'm afraid so," he said, standing. He reached to shake her hand. "Call me after the holiday and let me know how you feel."

"All right," she said sadly. "I will."

She went home, poured herself a drink, stood by the mantel. She picked up the pink-posied tin and shook it, afraid she might hear the muffled banging of bones, but she heard nothing. "Are you sure it's even him?" Jack asked. "With animals, they probably do mass incinerations. One scoop for cats, two for dogs."

"*Please*," she said. At least she had not buried Bert in the local pet cemetery, with its intricate gravestones and maudlin inscriptions – *Beloved Rexie: I'll be joining you soon.* Or, *In memory of Muffin, who taught me to love.*

"I got the very last Christmas tree," said Jack. "It was leaning against the shed wall, with a broken high heel, and a cigarette dangling from its mouth. I thought I'd bring it home and feed it soup."

At least she had sought something more tasteful than the cemetery, sought the appropriate occasion to return him to earth and sky, get him down off the fireplace and out of the house in a meaningful way, though she'd yet to find the right day. She had let him stay on the mantel and had mourned him deeply – it was only proper. You couldn't pretend you had lost nothing. A good cat had died – you had to begin there, not let your blood freeze over. If your heart turned away at this, it would turn away at something greater, then more and more until your heart stayed averted, immobile, your imagination redistributed away from the world and back only toward the bad maps of yourself, the sour pools of your own pulse, your own tiny, mean, and pointless wants. Stop here! Begin here! Begin with Bert!

Here's to Bert!

Early Christmas morning, she woke Sofie and dressed her warmly in her snowsuit. There was a light snow on the ground and a wind blew powdery gusts around the yard. "We're going to say good-bye to Bert," said Aileen.

"Oh, Bert!" said Sofie, and she began to cry.

"No, it'll be happy!" said Aileen, feeling the pink-posied tin in her jacket pocket. "He wants to go out. Do you remember how he used to want to go out? How he would mee-ow at the door and then we would let him go?"

"Mee-ow, mee-ow," said Sofie.

"Right," said Aileen. "So that's what we're going to do now."

"Will he be with Santa Claus?"

"Yes! He'll be with Santa Claus!"

They stepped outside, down off the porch steps. Aileen

pried open the tin. Inside, there was a small plastic bag and she tore that open. Inside was Bert: a pebbly ash like the sand and ground shells of a beach. Summer in December! What was Christmas if not a giant mixed metaphor? What was it about if not the mystery of interspecies love – God's for man! Love had sought a chasm to leap across and landed itself right here: the Holy Ghost among the barn animals, the teacher's pet sent to be adored and then to die. Aileen and Sofie each seized a fistful of Bert and ran around the yard, letting wind take the ash and scatter it. Chickadees flew from the trees. Frightened squirrels headed for the yard next door. In freeing Bert, perhaps they would become him a little: banish the interlopers, police the borders, then go back inside and play with the decorations, claw at the gift wrap, eat the big headless bird.

"Merry Christmas to Bert!" Sofie shouted. The tin was now empty.

"Yes, Merry Christmas to Bert!" said Aileen. She shoved the tin back into her pocket. Then she and Sofie raced back into the house, to get warm.

Jack was in the kitchen, standing by the stove, still in his pajamas. He was pouring orange juice and heating buns.

"Daddy, Merry Christmas to Bert!" Sofie popped open the snaps of her snowsuit.

"Yes," said Jack, turning. "Merry Christmas to Bert!" He handed Sofie some juice, then Aileen. But before she drank hers, Aileen waited for him to say something else. He cleared his throat and stepped forward. He raised his glass. His large quizzical smile said, This is a very weird family. But instead, he exclaimed, "Merry Christmas to everyone in the whole wide world!" and let it go at that.

1993

GO LIKE THIS

If an elephant missteps and dies in an open place,
the herd will not leave him there . . .
—LEWIS THOMAS *The Lives of a Cell*

I HAVE WRITTEN BEFORE. Three children's books: *William, William Takes a Trip, More William*. Perhaps you've heard of them. In the first, William gets a duck, builds it a house with a doorbell. In the second, William goes to Wildwood and has a good time. In the third, William finds a wildebeest in his closet. It messes up his room. Life is tough all around.

I was planning a fourth book, but I didn't know finally what William should do. So instead, I am writing of rational suicide – no oxymoron there. I eschew all contradictions, inconsistencies, all stripes with plaids. I write as a purist, a lover of skim milk, a woman who knows which pieces of furniture look right together in the living room. A month ago I was told I have cancer. It was not the clean, confined sort I might have hoped for, suspended neatly in my breast with its slippery little convolutions turned tortuously inward on itself, hardened, wizened to a small extractable walnut. Or even two. It had spread through my body like a clumsy uninvited guest who is obese and eats too much, still finding, filling rooms. I tried therapy for three weeks, wearing scarves, hiding hairbrushes. I turned up the stereo when rushing into the bathroom to be sick. Blaine heard my retching above the Mozart only twice. Mommyouallright? Her voice had a way of drifting through the door, a small, misplaced melody that had lost its way, ending up in a room full of plumbing and decaying flesh, cavorting innocently with the false lilac aerosol and the mean stench of bile and undigested foods. Okay, honey, I'm okay. Hell, I'm okay.

Dr. Torbein said that many women go like this for months and improve. Live many years after. Go Christmas shopping, have birthday cakes, all those simple pleasures, now you certainly would like that wouldn't you, Elizabeth?

I am not a skinny child with charge cards, I said. You can't honestly expect me to like this. And please: don't call me Elizabeth.

He was taken aback, vaguely annoyed. Ad lib unpleasantries, my, my. He did not have lines for this. He took off his glasses, no, perhaps you'd call them spectacles, and stared at me over his clipboard, the glare one gives a fractious child who is not going to get ice cream. This is not going to be easy, he informed me. (No maple walnut.) But women have survived much greater damage than you have suffered, much worse odds, worse pain than this.

Well, waddaya know, I cheered heartily. Bully for them.

Now Elizabeth, he scolded. He started to raise a finger, then changed his mind. Go like this, he said instead, demonstrating that I should lift my arm as high as possible over my head so he could examine tissue, feel for further lumps or something. He began to whistle "Clementine."

Ouch! I shrieked. He stopped whistling.

Dreadful sorry, he murmured, trying to probe more gently.

I try not to look at my chest. It is ravaged, paved over, mowed down by the train tracks and parking lots of the Surgical Way. I know there are absences, as if the hollows were the surreptitious marks of a child's spoon in tomorrow night's dessert. The place where I thought my soul was located when I was five is no longer there.

I haven't worn falsies since junior high, I smiled and told the doctor, my future spreading before me, a van Ruisdael cemetery. Thank god I don't have to take gym like y'know wadda mean, doc?

Joanie, Joanie, my friend with the webbed toes, why do I make Dr. Torbein so uncomfortable, don't you think he'd be used to this by now, he must get it all the time, even if he doesn't get it *all* all the time, you know what I mean? (Joanie smiles and looks at her feet a lot.) I mean, he's got his glasses so far down here, see, that he has to tuck two of his chins back into the recesses of his throat in order to read The Clipboard, which seems to grow out of his gut like some visceral suburbia, and unless we are speaking of the ferrous content of blood, he is utterly ill at ease with irony and gets twitches, like this, see? (Horrid, feeble humor.)

Joanie groans and rolls her eyeballs like Howdy Doody. Jesusmaryandjoseph, Liz, she sighs. (Only Catholics can say that.) You're really getting silly.

Even wit deteriorates, I say, my eye running fast out of twinkles.

I have decided on Bastille Day. It is a choice of symbol and expedience. Elliott will have time enough before he begins teaching again in the fall. Blaine will not go to camp this year and can spend some time with Elliott's folks upstate. As it will be unbearably hot, I'm sure, I will tell everyone to wear light clothes. No black, no ties, no hats, no coats. The dead are cruel to inflict that misery in July. Open-toed shoes and parasols de rigueur, I will tell everyone. (Ditto: pastels, seersucker, flasks and vials of Scotch, cocaine.) They should require little prompting. They're enlightened. They've seen others go like this before. They read the papers, see the movies, watch the television broadcasts. They know how it's done. They know what for. It's existential. It's Hemingway. It's familiar. They know what to do.

When I told Elliott of my suicide we were in the kitchen bitching at each other about the grease in the oven. Funny, I had planned on telling him a little differently than No one has fucking cleaned this shithole in weeks Elliott I have something to tell you. It wasn't exactly Edna Millay.

I have lain. In bed. So many nights. Thinking of how it would be when I told him. And plotting, ruminating, remembering the ways our bodies used to love each other, touch, waltz. Now my body stands in the corner of the gym by the foul lines and extra crepe paper and doesn't get asked to dance at all. Blighted, beaten, defeated friend. I rock it, hold it like a sick child; alone, my body and I, we weep for the missing parts. I never question Elliott's reluctance to have sex with me. It is not the same body to him, with his simple, boyish perceptions of the physical. It's okay, I say, but I look at the curve of his bones, the freckled skin of his back, something wildly magical still, something precious. I always think he's the first one to drop off to sleep at night, but I have often awoken in the morning to find the hand lotion bottle on the floor by his side of the bed, so I know it's not always so. It's like some rude poem of my stupidity, of this space grown between us. (Oh, Elliott, I am so sorry.) I return the lotion to the bathroom sometimes only to discover it by the bed again the next morning. I never hear him. (Elliott, is there nothing I can do? Is there nothing?)

He looked a little white, standing there by the oven. He took my hand, kissed it, held it between his, patted it. Let's think about it for a day or two or whatever. Then we'll discuss it further.

Then we'll discuss it further, I repeated.

Yes, he said.

Yes, I said.

But we didn't. Not really. Oh, it drifted piecemeal into subsequent dialogues like a body tossed out to sea and washed days later back into shore, a shoe there, a finger here, a breastbone in weed tide-bumping against the sand. But we never truly discussed it, never truly. Instead, allusions, suggestions, clues, silent but palpable, crawled out of the night ocean, as in a science fiction movie: black and slow they moved in and arranged themselves around the apartment like precocious, breathing houseplants, like scavengers.

I heard Elliott last night. He thought I was asleep, but I could see his motions under the covers and the tense drop of his jaw. I thought of Ivan Ilych who, dying, left his overweight wife in the master bedroom (with the knickknacks?) to sleep alone in a small room next to the study.

Darkness. The late spring sky has strangely emptied. The moon rummages down in the alleyway like somebody's forgotten aunt.

I have invited our closest friends over tonight, seated them around the living room, and told them that I wanted to die, that I had calculated how much Seconal was required. They are a cool intellectual lot. They do not gasp and murmur among themselves. I say I have chosen suicide as the most rational and humane alternative to my cancer, an act not so much of self-sacrifice as of beauty, of sparing. I wanted their support.

You have obviously thought this out, says Myrna, the poet whom I have loved since childhood for the burlap, asthma-rasp of her voice, making decisions of a lifetime with the speed of deli orders. She can dismiss lovers, choose upholstery, sign on dotted lines, and fly to Olbia faster than anyone I know. She is finality with a hard obsidian edge. We are dealing, she continues, with a mind, as Williams put it, like a bed all made up. You have our love and our support, Liz.

I look around and try to smile gratefully as Myrna seems to speak for everyone, even without conferring. A miracle, that woman. There appears to be no dissent.

I say, Well now, and sip my Scotch and think of my bed in the next room strangled in the twists of sheets and blankets, edges dragging on the floor. I am not afraid of death, I decide to add. I am afraid of what going on like this will do to me and to my daughter and to my husband.

Elliott, arranged next to me on the sofa, looks at his fingers, which tip to tip form a sort of steeple between his knees.

I am getting into the swing of it. I tell them the cancer is poisoning at least three lives and that I refuse to be its accomplice. This is not a deranged act, I explain. Most of them have known for quite a while my belief that intelligent suicide is almost always preferable to the stupid lingering of a graceless death.

There is silence, grand as Versailles. It seems respectful.

Shennan, Algonquin princess with black braids and sad eyes, stands and says in the oratory deadpan of sixth-grade book reports: I think I can speak for Liz when I say that suicide can be, often is, the most definitive statement one can make about one's life, to say that it's yours and that you are not going to let it wither away like something decaying in a refrigerator drawer. As it is Liz's life to do with as she pleases, so it is her death. As long as Liz and I have known one another, I think we have both realized that she would probably be a suicide. It is no inchoate fancy. It is Liz's long-held vision, a way of meeting one's death squarely, maturely. It is an assertion of life, of self.

(Ah, Shennan dear, yes, but didn't I always say that seventy-one would be better than forty-two, in love as I am with prime numbers, those curious virginal devils, and they could always say, ah, yes, she died in her prime – even at seventy-one – good god I'm really getting awful, Joanie, what did I tell you, babe?)

Shennan finishes by saying it is the culmination of a life philosophy, the triumph of the artist over the mortal, physical world.

It will possibly be the most creative act Liz has ever accomplished, adds my husband. I mean, it could be viewed that way.

He swallows with some difficulty, his wonderful Adam's apple gliding up and down his throat, a tiny flesh elevator. I think of the warm beers, unfinished books, the buttonless sweaters, and the miscarriages upstairs. I wonder if he could be right.

I think it is beautiful she is doing this for me, Elliott adds as a further announcement. He squeezes my shoulder. I look for tears in his eyes and think I spot the shiny edge of one, like a contact lens.

Well now, I say.

Now we all get up and cry and eat brie and wheat thins. Joanie steps toward me with her husband, William. Until now no one has mentioned God.

I fear for you, Liz. She is crying. I hold her. Why didn't you tell me this before? she murmurs. Oh, Liz, I fear hell for you. What are you doing?

William doesn't bullshit: It's crap, Liz. There's no such thing as an aesthetic suicide. You're not going to be able to stand back afterward and say by jove what a damn good job I did of it. You'll make the *Post*, Liz, not the Whitney. This all smacks of some perverse crypto-Catholic martyrdom of yours. It's deluded. It's a power play.

(I can clear my throat louder than anyone I know.)

I appreciate your candor, William.

You know, he continues, a roomful of people, it sounds beautiful, but it's fishy. Something's not right underneath.

Joanie the star of catechism class: We love you, Liz. God loves you, please—

I understand, I interrupt, if you cannot help me do it.

Help you *do* it? they chorus, horrified. They leave early, forgetting their umbrellas. The room is reeling.

Frank Scherman Franck pulls at his cowlick, sips Cherry Heering. His cowlick bounces back up again, something vaguely lewd. You are a marvel, Liz, he coos. It's a brave and awesome thing you are doing. I never thought you'd actually go through with it, but here you are . . .

(Cherry Heering, Hairy Cherring.) Do you believe in God, Frank Scherman Franck? I ask.

Well, long story, he begins. We have a kind of mutual agreement: I won't believe in him and he won't believe in me. That way no one gets hurt.

Sometimes I still believe in God, Frank Scherman Franck, I say, but then that belief flies away from me like a child on a swing, back and forth, back and forth, and I do not really say this. (Cow lick, lick cow.) I notice William has returned for his umbrella. He stops Elliott in the foyer, says something urgent, something red. I can hear Elliott's reply: If I saw or felt any ambivalence I would, William, but there's no ambivalence. She's sure. She's strong. She knows what she's doing. I have to believe in her.

Excuse me, I say to Frank as I run off to hide temporarily in the bathroom. I lock the door behind me and bury my face in Elliott's bathrobe hanging on the inside hook like a sheepish animal. Hug. Clutch. Press. Cry. I could get lost in it, this vast white country of terrycloth, the terrain of it against my face, Elliott's familiar soapy smells inextricable, filling, spinning my head. I turn around and sink back against the door, against the robe. I do not look in the mirror. This place is a mausoleum of pills and ceramic and fluorescent lights blinking on and off so quickly you think they're on all the time, those clever devils. But we know better don't we. This is where the dead belong, with the dying belonging to the dead belonging to no one. This is not supposed to go like this. I am getting drunk. I think we were supposed to sit around rather politely, perhaps even woodenly, and discuss this thing, cool as iced tea, a parlor of painters and poets like the Paris salons, like television, and we would all agree (my reasoning flawless) that my life ultimately meant my death as well and that it was a right both civil and humane to take whatever actions my free will so determined yadada yadada, and they would pronounce me a genius and not steal the best lines and they would weep just the right amount that anyone should weep for Bastille Day and no one would fucking mention God or hell and when I stepped out of the bathroom I would not see Shennan eyeing Elliott's ass as the two of them stand alone in the kitchen, one slicing cheese, the other arranging crackers, nor would I have to suffer the aphasic stupidity of the articulate (therefore unforgivable) who when offered the topaz necklace of a dying woman do not know what to say (and Myrna, this is not Myrna, Myrna is a poet who flies to Olbia, dismisses lovers, sculpts in words, her poems like the finest diamonds in the finest Fabergés of the finest Czar, not faltering, defeated by topaz). I do not like to watch Myrna grope; she doesn't do it well.

I am something putrid. I wonder if I smell, decaying from the inside out like fruit, yet able to walk among them like the dead among the living, like Christ, for a while, only for a while, until things begin to show, until things become uncomfortable. I return to the living room, grin weakly, stand among my friends. I am something incorrect: a hair in the cottage cheese. Something uncouth: a fart in the elevator.

Go like this; my husband pushes my head between my knees.

Ugh, what a night, I say, huh.

Ssshhhh. Be quiet. This increases the oxygen to the cortex. You know you're not supposed to drink like that.

I inhale four times with the drama of the first amphibian. How am I doing so far?

The sun is up, depressing me like the mindless smile of a cheerleader. My face is the big bluish-white of white elephants.

The phone rings.

It is Olga, her quiet Slavic cheekbones pale and calming even through the wires, her voice a learned English breathiness affected in the style of too much late night Joan Fontaine. She is sorry, she says, for not having spoken much to me last night. She felt a little bewildered both by my announcement and by the reaction of the others. It was, she says, as if they had already known before and had nothing but clinically prepared affirmations for me, convinced as always of Liz's sound-mindedness.

Well, the dissent left early, I say, and forgot its umbrella.

I, too, am dissenting, she says slowly, like Jane Eyre. Don't the others know what you still have to offer, in terms of your writing, in terms of your daughter?

Olga, I despise people propping my pillows.

Olga is getting cheeky: Perhaps the time has come for you to learn to need people, Liz. And to be patient. You haven't earned your death yet. You want the orgasm without the foreplay.

Look, Olga, at this point I'd take what I could get. Don't

get too sexual on me, okay, sweetie? (I can feel myself starting to get mean, my tone invidious.)

Please, Liz. I'm trying to tell you what your sister might have told you. I mean, I couldn't let last night just sit there like that, Shennan standing there like an Indian priestess celebrating death in this fraudulent guise of a philosophy, and Myrna – well, Myrna will be Myrna.

(And sometimes not, I think. God, I'm not in the mood for this. Olga, dear, go back to the moors.)

I care so much for you, Liz, she continues. (Oh, Rochester, take her the fuck away.) It's just that . . . it's like you and your death, you're facing each other like loners from a singles bar who have scarcely spoken. You haven't really kissed or touched and yet are about to plunge into bed together.

(Sex again. Jane Eyre, indeed.)

Honestly, Olga. All this erotica on a Sunday. Has Richard returned for free piano lessons or something? (I am cruel; a schoolmaster with a switch and a stool.) I really must see what Blaine is shouting about; she's downstairs and has been calling to me for a while now. It may be one of her turtles or something.

Liz, look. I don't want to go like this. Let's have lunch soon.

(We make plans to make plans.)

I think about what William should do.

Elliott and I have weekly philharmonic seats. I am in bed this Friday, not feeling up to it.

Go ahead, I say. Take Blaine. Take Shennan.

Liz, he drawls, a mild reprimand. He sits at the bed's edge, zooted, smelling of Danish soap, and I think of Ivan Ilych's wife, off to the theater while her husband's kidneys floated in his eyes like cataracts, his legs propped up on the footboard by the manservant – ah, where are the manservants?

Elliott, look at how I'm feeling today. I can't go like this. Please, go ahead without me.

You feel pretty bad, huh, he says, looking at his watch

at the same time. He gives me the old honey I'll bring you home a treat, like I'm a fucking retard or something whose nights can be relieved of their hellish sameness with gifts of Colorforms and Sky Bars.

Enjoy, enjoy, you asshole, I do not chirp.

It is already July. The fireflies will soon be out. My death flashes across my afternoon like a nun in white, hurrying, evanescing, apparitional as the rise of heat off boulevards, the parched white of sails across cement, around the corner, fleeing the sun. I have not yet seen the face, it is hooded, perhaps wrapped, but I know the flow, the cloth of her, moving always in diagonals, in waves toward me, then footlessly away again.

We told Blaine tonight. We had decided to do it together. We were in the living room.

You're going to die, she said, aren't you? before I had a chance to say, Now you're young and probably don't understand. She has developed a habit of tucking her hair nervously behind her ears when she does not want to cry. She is prophetic. Tuck, tuck.

Yes. And we told her why. And I got a chance, after all, to say you're young and probably don't understand, and she got a chance to look at me with that scrambled gaze of contempt and hurt that only fourth-graders know, and then to close her eyes like an angel and fall into my arms, sobbing, and I sobbed too into that hair tucked behind those ears and I cursed God for this day and Blaine of course wanted to know who would take her to clarinet class.

Tuck, tuck. She lay her head in my lap like a leaky egg. We stayed like that for an hour. I whispered little things to her, smoothing back her hair, about how much I loved her, how patient she would have to be, how strong. At nine-thirty she went silently to her room and lay in bed, swollen-eyed, facing the wall like a spurned and dying lover.

I realize now what it is that William should do. When the badass wildebeest comes out of the closet and messes up his room, William should blow a trumpet and make the wildebeest cease and desist. He should put his foot down and say, Enough of this darned nonsense, silly wildebeest: Let's get this room picked up! I am practically certain that wildebeests listen to trumpets.

I would tell this to Elliott, but the wildebeest was in the third book. And I finished that long ago.

No, I must think of something else.

Oh God, it's not supposed to go like this. There I was like Jesus, sure as a blazing rooster, on Palm Sunday riding tall, dauntless as Barbra Streisand, now suddenly on Thursday shoved up against the softer edges of my skin and even Jesus, look, he's crying and whimpering and heaving so, Christ, he pees in his pants, please god, I mean God, don't let me go like this but let me stay right in this garden next to the plastic flamingoes and let me croon the blues till I am crazy with them.

Elliott has a way of walking in just before dinner and kissing me as if for a publicity shot.

Who do we have out there waiting in the wings, Elliott, fucking Happy Rockefeller? Channel 6 News? Hey, baby, I'm not dead yet; I'm writing, I'm hungry: let's make love, baby, let's do it on the terrace, high and cool, sugar, hey how about the terrace Elliott babydoll, waddaya say?

And if he does not stride angrily from the room, he stays, fumbles insincerely, makes me weep. He has no taste for necrophilia, and I sigh and crave the white of his shoulders under my chin, his breath on my neck, the plum smoothness of him in my hands. And I want it still for me here now as I lie in the blue-black of this aloneness thirsting for love more than I ever thought I could.

Even at midnight the city groans in the heat. We have had no rain for quite a while. The traffic sounds below ride the night air in waves of trigonometry, the cosine of a siren, the tangent of a sigh, a system, an axis, a logic to this chaos, yes.

Tomorrow's Bastille Day, Elliott, and I want what I've written for the fourth William book changed. So far William thinks he forgot his umbrella and wanders all over the city looking for it, misfortune following him like an odious dog, until after he is splashed by a truck and nearly hit by a cab, he goes home only to realize he never forgot his umbrella at all. I want that changed. I want him to have all kinds of wonderful, picaresque adventures so that it doesn't even matter if he has lost his umbrella or not. Can you change that for me? Can you think of some wonderful adventures for me? Maybe he meets up with cowboys and a few Indians and has a cookout with music and barbecue beans.

Or meets a pretty little Indian girl and gets married, suggests Elliott, an asshole sometimes, I swear. He doesn't even realize, I guess.

My turn: Yeah, and scalps her and wins hero-of-the-day badge. I guess I'll just have to entrust it all to you, Elliott.

Don't worry, he says, gingerly stroking my hair, which I picture now like the last pieces of thread around a spool.

I really would like to finish it myself, but tomorrow is Bastille Day.

Yes, says Elliott.

Joanie, hon, Joanie with the webbed toes, I know it's late, no, no, don't feel you have to come over, no please don't, Elliott's here, it's fine. I just wanted to say I love you and don't feel sad for me please . . . you know I feel pretty good and these pills, well, they're here in a little saucer staring at me, listen, I'm going to let you go back to bed now and well you know how I've always felt about you Joan and if there is an afterlife . . . yeah well maybe *I'm* not going to heaven, okay . . . what . . . do you think I'm silly? I mean if it wouldn't scare you, maybe I'll try to get in touch, if you wouldn't mind, yes, and please keep an eye out for Blaine for me, Joan, would you, god she's so young and I only just told her about menstruation this past spring and she seemed so interested but then only said, So does that mean all twins look alike? so I know there will be other things she will want to know, you know, and she loves you, Joan, she really does. And be good to Olga for me, I have been so unkind, and remind your husband I've immortalized him, ha! yeah . . . can you believe it, dear rigid soul, and Joanie, take care of yourself and say prayers for me and for Blaine and for Elliott who did cry this morning for the first helpless time, how I do love him, Joan, despite everything

everything I can see from the round eye of this empty saucer, faintly making out a patch of droughted trees and a string of wildebeests, one by one, like the sheep of a child's insomnia, throwing in the towel, circling, lying down in the sun silently to decompose, in spite of themselves, god, there's no music, no trumpet here, it is fast, and there's no sound at all, just this white heat of July going on and on, going on like this

1980

HOW

So all things limp together for the only possible.
—BECKETT, *Murphy*

BEGIN BY MEETING him in a class, in a bar, at a rummage sale. Maybe he teaches sixth grade. Manages a hardware store. Foreman at a carton factory. He will be a good dancer. He will have perfectly cut hair. He will laugh at your jokes.

A week, a month, a year. Feel discovered, comforted, needed, loved, and start sometimes, somehow, to feel bored. When sad or confused, walk uptown to the movies. Buy popcorn. These things come and go. A week, a month, a year.

Make attempts at a less restrictive arrangement. Watch them sputter and deflate like balloons. He will ask you to move in. Do so hesitantly, with ambivalence. Clarify: rents are high, nothing long-range, love and all that, hon, but it's footloose. Lay out the rules with much elocution. Stress openness, non-exclusivity. Make room in his closet, but don't rearrange the furniture.

And yet from time to time you will gaze at his face or his hands and want nothing but him. You will feel passing waves of dependency, devotion, and sentimentality. A week, a month, a year, and he has become your family. Let's say your real mother is a witch. Your father a warlock. Your brothers twin hunchbacks of Notre Dame. They all live in a cave together somewhere.

His name means savior. He rolls into your arms like Ozzie and Harriet, the whole Nelson genealogy. He is living rooms and turkey and mantels and Vicks, a nip at the collarbone and you do a slow syrup sink into those arms like a hearth, into those living rooms, well hello Mary Lou.

Say you work in an office but you have bigger plans. He wants to go with you. He wants to be what it is that you want to be. Say you're an aspiring architect. Playwright. Painter. He shows you his sketches. They are awful. What do you think?

Put on some jazz. Take off your clothes. Carefully. It is a craft. He will lie on the floor naked, watching, his arms crossed behind his head. Shirt: brush on snare, steady. Skirt: the desultory talk of piano keys, rocking slow, rambling. Dance together in the dark though it is only afternoon.

Go to a wedding. His relatives. Everyone will compare weight losses and gains. Maiden cousins will be said to have fattened embarrassingly. His mother will be a bookkeeper or a dental hygienist. She will introduce you as his *girl.* Try not to protest. They will have heard a lot about you. Uncles will take him aside and query, What is keeping you, boy? Uncomfortable, everywhere, women in stiff blue taffeta will eye you pitifully, then look quickly away. Everyone will polka. Someone will flash a fifty to dance with the bride and she will hike up her gown and flash back: freshly shaven legs, a wide rolled-out-barrel of a grin. Feel spared. Thought you two'd be doing this by now, you will hear again. Smile. Shrug. Shuffle back for more potato salad.

It hits you more insistently. A restlessness. A virus of discontent. When you pass other men in the street, smile and stare them straight in the eye, straight in the belt buckle.

Somehow – in a restaurant or a store – meet an actor. From Vassar or Yale. He can quote Coriolanus's mother. This will seem good. Sleep with him once and ride home at 5 a.m. crying in a taxicab. Or: don't sleep with him. Kiss him good night at Union Square and run for your life.

Back at home, days later, feel cranky and tired. Sit on the couch and tell him he's stupid. That you bet he doesn't know who Coriolanus is. That since you moved in you've noticed he rarely reads. He will give you a hurt, hungry-to-learn look, with his James Cagney eyes. He will try to kiss you. Turn your head. Feel suffocated.

When he climbs onto the covers, naked and hot for you, unleash your irritation in short staccato blasts. Show him your book. Your aspirin. Your clock on the table reading 12:45. He will flop back over to his side of the bed, exasperated. Maybe he'll say something like: Christ, what's wrong? Maybe he won't. If he spends too long in the bathroom, don't ask questions.

The touchiest point will always be this: he craves a family, a neat nest of human bowls; he wants to have your children. On the street he pats their heads. In the supermarket they gather around him by the produce. They form a tight little cluster of cheeks and smiles and hopes. They look like grapes. It will all be for you, baby; reel, sway backward into the frozen foods. An unwitting sigh will escape from your lips like gas. He will begin to talk about a movie camera and children's encyclopedias, picking up size-one shoes in department stores and marveling in one high, amazed whistle. Avoid shopping together.

He will have a nephew named Bradley Bob. Or perhaps a niece named Emily who is always dressed in pink and smells of milk and powder and dirty diapers, although she is already three. At visits she will prance and squeal. She will grab his left leg like a tree trunk and not let go. She will call him nunko. He will know tricks: pulling dimes from her nose, quarters from her ears. She will shriek with glee, flapping her hands in front of her. Leg released, he will pick her up, carry her around like a prize. He is the best nunko in town.

Think about leaving. About packing a bag and slithering off, out the door.

But it is hot out there. And dry. And he can look somehow good to you, like Robert Goulet in a bathing suit.

No, it wouldn't be in summer.

Escape into books. When he asks what you're reading, hold it up without comment. The next day look across to the brown chair and you will see him reading it too. A copy from the library that morning. He has seven days. He will look over the top and wink, saying: Beat you.

He will seem to be listening to the classical music station, glancing quickly at you for approval.

At the theater he will chomp Necco wafers loudly and complain about the head in front of him.

He will ask you what *supercilious* means.

He will ask you who Coriolanus is.

He might want to know where Sardinia is located.

What's a *croissant*?

Begin to plot your getaway. Envision possibilities for civility. These are only possibilities.

A week, a month, a year: Tell him you've changed. You no longer like the same music, eat the same food. You dress differently. The two of you are incongruous together. When he tells you that he is changing too, that he loves your records, your teas, your falafel, your shoes, tell him: See, that's the problem. Endeavor to baffle.

Pace around in the kitchen and say that you are unhappy.

But I love you, he will say in his soft, bewildered way, stirring the spaghetti sauce but not you, staring into the pan as if waiting for something, a magic fish, to rise from it and say: That is always enough, why is that not always enough?

You will forget whoever it was that said never trust a thought that doesn't come while walking. But clutch at it. Apartments can shrink inward like drying ponds. You will gasp. Say: I am going for a walk. When he follows you to the door, buzzing at your side like a fly by a bleeding woman, add: *alone*. He will look surprised and hurt and you will hate him. Slam the door, out, down, hurry, it will be colder than you thought, but not far away will be a bar, smoky and dark and sticky with spilled sours. The bartender will be named Rusty or Max and he will know you. A flashy jukebox will blare Jimmy Webb. A balding, purple-shirted man to your left will try to get your attention, mouthing, singing drunkenly. Someone to your right will sniffle to the music. Blink into your drink. Hide behind your hair. Sweet green icing will be flowing down. Flowing, baby, like the Mississippi.

Next: there are medical unpleasantries. Kidneys. He will pee blood. Say you can't believe it. When he shows you later, it will be dark, the color of meat drippings. A huge invisible fist will torpedo through your gut, your face, your pounding heart.

This is no time to leave.

There will be doctor's appointments, various opinions. There is nothing conclusive, just an endless series of tests. He will have jarred urine specimens in the refrigerator among the eggs and peanut butter. Some will be in salad dressing bottles. They will be different colors: some green, some purple, some brown. Ask which is the real salad dressing. He will point it out and smile helplessly. Smile back. He will begin to laugh and so will you. Collapse. Roll. Roar together on the floor until you cannot laugh anymore. Bury your face in the crook of his neck. There will be nothing else in the world you can do. That night lie next to each other, silent, stiff, silvery-white in bed. Lie like sewing needles.

Continue to doctor-hop. Await the reports. Look at your watch. If ever you would leave him. Look at your calendar. It wouldn't be in autumn.

There is never anything conclusive, just an endless series of tests.

Once a week you will feel in love with him again. Massage his lower back when it is aching. Lay your cheek against him, feeling, listening for his kidneys. Stay like that all night, never quite falling asleep, never quite wanting to.

The thought will occur to you that you are waiting for him to die.

You will meet another actor. Or maybe it's the same one. Begin to have an affair. Begin to lie. Have dinner with him and his Modigliani-necked mother. She will smoke cigars, play with the fondue, discuss the fallacy of feminine maternal instinct. Afterward, you will all get high.

There is never anything conclusive, just an endless series of tests.

And could you leave him tripping merrily through the snow?

You will fantasize about a funeral. At that you could cry. It would be a study in post-romantic excess, something vaguely Wagnerian. You would be comforted by his lugubrious sisters and his dental hygienist mom. The four of you in the cemetery would throw yourselves at his grave's edge, heaving and sobbing like old Israeli women. You, in particular, would shout, bare your wrists, shake them at the sky, foam at the mouth. There would be no shame, no dignity. You would fly immediately to Acapulco and lounge drunk and malodorous in the casinos until three.

After dinners with the actor: creep home. Your stomach will get fluttery, your steps smaller as you approach the door. Neighbors will be playing music you recall from your childhood – an opera about a pretty lady who was bad and cut a man's hair in his sleep. You recall, recall your grandfather playing it with a sort of wrath, his visage laminated with Old Testament righteousness, the violins warming, the scenario unfolding now as you stand outside the door. Ray pawned off my ten dresses: it cascades like a waterfall. Dolly-la, Dolly-la: it is the wail, the next to the last good solo of a doomed man.

Tiptoe. It won't matter. He will be sitting up in bed looking empty. Kiss him, cajole him. Make love to him like never before. At four in the morning you will still be awake, staring at the ceiling. You will horrify yourself.

Thoughts of leaving will move in, bivouac throughout the living room; they will have eyes like rodents and peer out at you from under the sofa, in the dark, from under the sink, luminous glass beads positioned in twos. The houseplants will appear to have chosen sides. Some will thrust stems at you like angry limbs. They will seem to caw like crows. Others will simply sag.

When you go out, leave him with a sinkful of dirty dishes. He will slowly dry them with paper towels, his skin scalded red beneath the wet, flattened hair of his forearms. You will be tempted to tell him to leave them, or to use the terrycloth in the drawer. But you won't. You will put on your coat and hurry away.

When you return, the bathroom light will be on. You will see blouses of yours that he has washed by hand. They will hang in perfect half-inches, dripping, scolding from the shower curtain rod. They will be buttoned with his Cagney eyes, faintly hooded, the twinkle sad and dulled.

Slip quietly under the covers; hold his sleeping hand.

There is never anything conclusive.

At work you will be lachrymose and distracted. You will shamble through the hall like a legume with feet. People will notice.

Nightmares have seasons like hurricanes. Be prepared. You will dream that someone with a violin case is trailing you through the city. Little children come at you with grins and grenades. You may bolt awake with a spasm, reach for him, and find he is not there, but lost in his own sleep, somnambulant, is roaming through the apartment like an old man, babbling gibberish, bumping into tables and lamps, a blanket he has torn from the bed wrapped clumsily around him, toga-style. Get up. Go to him. Touch him. At first he will look at you, wide-eyed, and not see. Put your arms around his waist. He will wake and gasp and cry into your hair. In a minute he will know where he is.

Dream about rainbows, about escapes, about wizards. Your past will fly by you, event by event, like Dorothy's tornadoed neighborhood, past the blown-out window. Airborne. One by one. Wave hello, good-bye. Practice.

Begin to call in sick. Make sure it is after he has already left for work. Sit in a rocking chair. Stare around at the apartment. It will be mid-morning and flooded in a hush of sunlight. You rarely see it like this. It will seem strangely deserted, premonitory. There will be apricots shrunk to buttons on the windowsill. A fly will bang stupidly against the panes. The bed will lie open, revealed, like something festering, the wrinkles in the sheets marking time, marking territory like the capillaries of a map. Rock. Hush. Breathe.

On the night you finally tell him, take him out to dinner. Translate the entrees for him. When you are home, lying in bed together, tell him that you are going to leave. He will look panicked, but not surprised. Perhaps he will say, Look, I don't care who else you're seeing or anything: what is your reason?

Do not attempt to bandy words. Tell him you do not love him anymore. It will make him cry, rivulets wending their way into his ears. You will start to feel sick. He will say something like: Well, you lose some, you lose some. You are supposed to laugh. Exhale. Blow your nose. Flick off the light. Have a sense of humor, he will whisper into the black. Have a heart.

Make him breakfast. He will want to know where you will go. Reply: To the actor. Or: To the hunchbacks. He will not eat your breakfast. He will glare at it, stir it around the plate with a fork, and then hurl it against the wall.

When you walk up Third Avenue toward the IRT, do it quickly. You will have a full bag. People will seem to know what you have done, where you are going. They will have his eyes, the same pair, passed along on the street from face to face, like secrets, like glasses at the opera.

This is what you are.
Rushing downstairs into the steamy burn of the subway.
Unable to look a panhandler in the pan.

You will never see him again. Or perhaps you will be sitting in Central Park one April eating your lunch and he will trundle by on roller skates. You will greet him with a wave and a mouth full of sandwich. He will nod, but he will not stop.

There will be an endless series of tests.

A week, a month, a year. The sadness will die like an old dog. You will feel nothing but indifference. The logy whine of a cowboy harmonica, plaintive, weary, it will fade into the hills slow as slow Hank Williams. One of those endings.

1980

HOW TO BE AN OTHER WOMAN

MEET IN EXPENSIVE beige raincoats, on a pea-soupy night. Like a detective movie. First, stand in front of Florsheim's Fifty-seventh Street window, press your face close to the glass, watch the fake velvet Hummels inside revolving around the wing tips; some white shoes, like your father wears, are propped up with garlands on a small mound of chemical snow. All the stores have closed. You can see your breath on the glass. Draw a peace sign. You are waiting for a bus.

He emerges from nowhere, looks like Robert Culp, the fog rolling, then parting, then sort of closing up again behind him. He asks you for a light and you jump a bit, startled, but you give him your "Lucky's Lounge – Where Leisure Is a Suit" matches. He has a nice chuckle, nice fingernails. He lights the cigarette, cupping his hands around the end, and drags deeply, like a starving man. He smiles as he exhales, returns you the matches, looks at your face, says: "Thanks."

He then stands not far from you, waiting. Perhaps for the same bus. The two of you glance furtively at each other, shifting feet. Pretend to contemplate the chemical snow. You are two spies glancing quickly at watches, necks disappearing in the hunch of your shoulders, collars upturned and slowly razoring the cab and store-lit fog like sharkfins. You begin to circle, gauging each other in primordial sniffs, eyeing, sidling, keen as Basil Rathbone.

A bus arrives. It is crowded, everyone looking laughlessly into one another's underarms. A blonde woman in barrettes steps off, holding her shoes in one hand.

You climb on together, grab adjacent chrome posts, and when the bus hisses and rumbles forward, you take out a book. A minute goes by and he asks what you're reading. It is *Madame Bovary* in a Doris Day biography jacket. Try to explain about binding warpage. He smiles, interested.

Return to your book. Emma is opening her window, thinking of Rouen.

"What weather," you hear him sigh, faintly British or uppercrust Delaware.

Glance up. Say: "It is fit for neither beast nor vegetable."

It sounds dumb. It makes no sense.

But it is how you meet.

At the movies he is tender, caressing your hand beneath the seat.

At concerts he is sweet and attentive, buying cocktails, locating the ladies' lounge when you can't find it.

At museums he is wise and loving, leading you slowly through the Etruscan cinerary urns with affectionate gestures and an art history minor from Columbia. He is kind; he laughs at your jokes.

After four movies, three concerts, and two-and-a-half museums, you sleep with him. It seems the right number of cultural events. On the stereo you play your favorite harp and oboe music. He tells you his wife's name. It is Patricia. She is an intellectual property lawyer. He tells you he likes you a lot. You lie on your stomach, naked and still too warm. When he says, "How do you feel about that?" don't say "Ridiculous" or "Get the hell out of my apartment." Prop your head up with one hand and say: "It depends. What is intellectual property law?"

He grins. "Oh, you know. Where leisure is a suit."

Give him a tight, wiry little smile.

"I just don't want you to feel uncomfortable about this," he says.

Say: "Hey. I am a very cool person. I am tough." Show him your bicep.

When you were six you thought *mistress* meant to put your shoes on the wrong feet. Now you are older and know it can mean many things, but essentially it means to put your shoes on the wrong feet.

You walk differently. In store windows you don't recognize yourself; you are another woman, some crazy interior display lady in glasses stumbling frantic and preoccupied through the mannequins. In public restrooms you sit dangerously flat against the toilet seat, a strange flesh sundae of despair and exhilaration, murmuring into your bluing thighs: "Hello, I'm Charlene. I'm a mistress."

It is like having a book out from the library.

It is like constantly having a book out from the library.

You meet frequently for dinner, after work, split whole liters of the house red, then wamble the two blocks east, twenty blocks south to your apartment and lie sprawled on the living room floor with your expensive beige raincoats still on.

He is a systems analyst – you have already exhausted this joke – but what he really wants to be, he reveals to you, is an actor.

"Well, how did you become a systems analyst?" you ask, funny you.

"The same way anyone becomes anything," he muses. "I took courses and sent out resumes." Pause. "Patricia helped me work up a great resume. Too great."

"Oh." Wonder about mistress courses, certification, resumes. Perhaps you are not really qualified.

"But I'm not good at systems work," he says, staring through and beyond, way beyond, the cracked ceiling. "Figuring out the cost-effectiveness of two hundred people shuffling five hundred pages back and forth across a new four-and-a-half-by-three-foot desk. I'm not an organized person, like Patricia, for instance. She's just incredibly organized. She makes lists for everything. It's pretty impressive."

Say flatly, dully: "What?"

"That she makes lists."

"That she makes lists? You like that?"

"Well, yes. You know, what she's going to do, what she has to buy, names of clients she has to see, et cetera."

"Lists?" you murmur hopelessly, listlessly, your expensive beige raincoat still on. There is a long, tired silence. Lists? You stand up, brush off your coat, ask him what he would like to drink, then stump off to the kitchen without waiting for the answer.

At one-thirty, he gets up noiselessly except for the soft rustle of his dressing. He leaves before you have even quite fallen asleep, but before he does, he bends over you in his expensive beige raincoat and kisses the ends of your hair. Ah, he kisses your hair.

CLIENTS TO SEE
Birthday snapshots
Scotch tape
Letters to TD and Mom

Technically, you are still a secretary for Karma-Kola, but you wear your Phi Beta Kappa key around your neck on a cheap gold chain, hoping someone will spot you for a promotion. Unfortunately, you have lost the respect of all but one of your co-workers and many of your superiors as well, who are working in order to send their daughters to universities so they won't have to be secretaries, and who, therefore, hold you in contempt for having a degree and being a failure anyway. It is like having a degree in failure. Hilda, however, likes you. You are young and remind her of her sister, the professional skater.

"But I hate to skate," you say.

And Hilda smiles, nodding. "Yup, that's exactly what my sister says sometimes and in that same way."

"What way?"

"Oh, I don't know," says Hilda. "Your bangs parted on the side or something."

Ask Hilda if she will go to lunch with you. Over Reuben sandwiches ask her if she's ever had an affair with a married man. As she attempts, mid-bite, to complete the choreography of her chomp, Russian dressing spurts out onto her hands.

"Once," she says. "That was the last lover I had. That was over two years ago."

Say: "Oh my god," as if it were horrible and tragic, then try to mitigate that rudeness by clearing your throat and saying, "Well, actually, I guess that's not so bad."

"No," she sighs good-naturedly. "His wife had Hodgkin's disease, or so everyone thought. When they came up with the correct diagnosis, something that wasn't nearly so awful, he went back to her. Does that make sense to you?"

"I suppose," say doubtfully.

"Yeah, maybe you're right." Hilda is still cleaning Reuben off the backs of her hands with a napkin. "At any rate, who are you involved with?"

"Someone who has a wife that makes lists. She has List-maker's disease."

"What are you going to do?"

"I don't know."

"Yeah," says Hilda. "That's typical."

CLIENTS TO SEE
Tomatoes, canned
Health food toothpaste
Health food deodorant

Vit. C on sale, Rexall
Check re: other shoemaker, 32nd St.

"Patricia's really had quite an interesting life," he says, smoking a cigarette.

"Oh, really?" you say, stabbing one out in the ashtray.

Make a list of all the lovers you've ever had.

Warren Lasher
Ed "Rubberhead" Catapano
Charles Deats or Keats
Alfonse

Tuck it in your pocket. Leave it lying around, conspicuously. Somehow you lose it. Make "mislaid" jokes to yourself. Make another list.

Whisper, "Don't go yet," as he glides out of your bed before sunrise and you lie there on your back cooling, naked between the sheets and smelling of musky, oniony sweat. Feel gray, like an abandoned locker room towel. Watch him as he again pulls on his pants, his sweater, his socks and shoes. Reach out and hold his thigh as he leans over and kisses you quickly, telling you not to get up, that he'll lock the door when he leaves. In the smoky darkness, you see him smile weakly, guiltily, and attempt a false, jaunty wave from the doorway. Turn on your side, toward the wall, so you don't have to watch the door close. You hear it thud nonetheless, the jangle of keys and snap of the bolt lock, the footsteps loud, then fading down the staircase, the clunk of the street door, then nothing, all his sounds blending with the city, his face passing namelessly uptown in a bus or a badly heated cab, the room, the whole building you live in, shuddering at the windows as a truck roars by toward the Queensboro Bridge.

Wonder who you are.

"Hi, this is Attila," he says in a false deep voice when you pick up your office phone.

Giggle. Like an idiot. Say: "Oh. Hi, Hun."

Hilda turns to look at you with a what's-with-you look on her face. Shrug your shoulders.

"Can you meet me for lunch?"

Say: "Meet? I'm sorry, I don't eat meat."

"Cute, you're cute," he says, not laughing, and at lunch he gives you his tomatoes.

Drink two huge glasses of wine and smile at all his office and mother-in-law stories. It makes his eyes sparkle and crinkle at the corners, his face pleased and shining. When the waitress clears the plates away, there is a silence where the two of you look down then back up again.

"You get more beautiful every day," he says to you, as you hold your wine glass over your nose, burgundy rushing down your throat. Put your glass down. Redden. Smile. Fiddle with your Phi Beta Kappa key.

When you get up to leave, take deep breaths. In front of

the restaurant, where you will stride off in different directions, don't give him a kiss in the noontime throng. Patricia's office is nearby and she likes to go to the bank right around now; his back will stiffen and his eyes dart around like a crazy person's. Instead, do a quick shuffle-ball-chain like you saw Barbra Streisand do in a movie once. Wave gigantically and say: "Till we eat again."

In your office building the elevator is slow and packed and you forget to get off at the tenth floor and have to ride all the way back down again from the nineteenth. Five minutes after you arrive dizzily back at your desk, the phone rings.

"Meet me tomorrow at seven," he says, "in front of Florsheim's and I'll carry you off to my castle. Patricia is going to a copyright convention."

Wait freezing in front of Florsheim's until seven-twenty. He finally dashes up, gasping apologies (he just now got back from the airport), his coat flying open, and he takes you in tow quickly uptown toward the art museums. He lives near art museums. Ask him what a copyright convention is.

"Where leisure is a suit *and* a suite," he drawls, long and smiling, quickening his pace and yours. He kisses your temple, brushes hair off your face.

You arrive at his building in twenty minutes.

"So, this is it?" The castle doorman's fly is undone. Smile politely. In the elevator, say: "The unexamined fly is not worth zipping."

The elevator has a peculiar rattle, for all eight floors, like someone obsessively clearing her throat.

When he finally gets the apartment door unlocked, he shows you into an L-shaped living room bursting with plants and gold-framed posters announcing exhibitions you are too late for by six years. The kitchen is off to one side – tiny, digital, spare, with a small army of chrome utensils hanging belligerent and clean as blades on the wall. Walk nervously around like a dog sniffing out the place. Peek into the bedroom: in the center, like a giant bloom, is a queen-sized bed with a Pennsylvania Dutch spread. A small photo of a woman in ski garb is propped on a nightstand. It frightens you.

Back in the living room, he mixes drinks with Scotch in them. "So, this is it," you say again with a forced grin and an odd heaving in your rib cage. Light up one of his cigarettes.

"Can I take your coat?"

Be strange and awkward. Say: "I like beige. I think it is practical."

"What's wrong with you?" he says, handing you your drink.

Try to decide what you should do:

1. rip open the front of your coat, sending the buttons torpedoing across the room in a series of pops into the asparagus fern;
2. go into the bathroom and gargle with hot tap water;
3. go downstairs and wave down a cab for home.

He puts his mouth on your neck. Put your arms timidly around him. Whisper into his ear: "There's a woman, uh, another woman in your room."

When he is fast asleep upon you, in the middle of the night, send your left arm out slowly toward the nightstand like a mechanical limb programmed for a secret intelligence mission, and bring the ski garb picture back close to your face in the dark and try to study the features over his shoulder. She seems to have a pretty smile, short hair, no eyebrows, tough flaring nostrils, body indecipherably ensconced in nylon and down and wool.

Slip carefully out, like a shoe horn, from beneath his sleeping body – he grunts groggily – and go to the closet. Open it with a minimum of squeaking and stare at her clothes. A few suits. Looks like beige blouses and a lot of brown things. Turn on the closet light. Look at the shoes. They are all lined up in neat, married pairs on the closet floor. Black pumps, blue sneakers, brown moccasins, brown T-straps. They have been to an expensive college, say, in Massachusetts. Gaze into her shoes. Her feet are much larger than yours. They are like small cruise missiles.

Inside the caves of those shoes, eyes form and open their lids, stare up at you, regard you, wink at you from the insoles. They are half-friendly, conspiratorial, amused at this reconnaissance of yours, like little smiling men from the open hatches of a fleet of military submarines. Turn off the light and shut the door quickly, before they start talking or dancing or something. Scurry back to the bed and hide your face in his armpit.

In the morning he makes you breakfast. Something with eggs and mushrooms and hot sauce.

Use his toothbrush. The red one. Gaze into the mirror at a face that looks too puffy to be yours. Imagine using her toothbrush by mistake. Imagine a wife and a mistress sharing the same toothbrush forever and ever, never knowing. Look into the medicine cabinet:

Midol
dental floss
Tylenol
Merthiolate
package of eight emory boards
razors and cartridges
two squeezed in the middle toothpaste tubes: Crest *and* Sensodyne
Band-Aids
hand lotion
rubbing alcohol
three small bars of Cashmere Bouquet stolen from a hotel

On the street, all over, you think you see her, the boring hotel-soap stealer. Every woman is her. You smell Cashmere Bouquet all over the place. That's her. Someone waiting near you for the downtown express: yup, that's her. A woman waiting behind you in a deli near Marine Midland who has smooth, hand-lotioned hands and looks like she skis: good god, what if that is her. Break out in cold sweats. Stare into every pair of flared nostrils with clinical curiosity and unbridled terror. Scrutinize feet. Glance sidelong at pumps. Then look quickly away, like a woman, some other woman, who is losing her mind.

Alone on lunch hours or after work, continue to look every female over the age of twelve straight in the nose and straight in the shoes. Feel your face aquiver and twice bolt out of Bergdorf's irrationally when you are sure it is her at the skirt sale rack choosing brown again, a Tylenol bottle peeking out from the corner of her purse. Sit on a granite wall in the GM plaza and catch your breath. Listen to an old man singing "Frosty the Snowman." Lose track of time.

"You're late," Hilda turns and whispers at you. "Carlyle's been back here twice already asking where you were and if the market survey report has been typed up yet."

Mutter: "Shit." You are only on the T's: Tennessee Karma-Kola consumption per square dollar-mile of investment market. Figures for July 1980–October 1981.

Texas – Fiscal Year 1980
Texas – Fiscal Year 1981
Utah.

It is like typing a telephone directory. Get tears in your eyes.

CLIENTS TO SEE

1. Fallen in love (?) Out of control. Who is this? Who am I? And who is this wife with the skis and the nostrils and the Tylenol and does she have orgasms?
2. Reclaim yourself. Pieces have fluttered away.
3. Everything you do is a masochistic act. Why?
4. Don't you like yourself? Don't you deserve better than all of this?
5. Need: something to lift you from your boots out into the sky, something to make you like little things again, to whirl around the curves of your ears and muss up your hair and call you every single day.

6. A drug.
7. A man.
8. A religion.
9. A good job. Revise and send out resumes.
10. Remember what Mrs. Kloosterman told the class in second grade: Just be glad you have legs.

"What are you going to do for Christmas?" he says, lying supine on your couch.

"Oh. I don't know. See my parents in New Jersey, I guess." Pause. "Wanna come? Meet my folks?"

A kind, fatherly, indulgent smile. "Charlene," he purrs, sitting up to pat your hand, your silly ridiculous little hand.

He gives you a pair of leather slippers. They were what you wanted.

You give him a book about cars.

"Ma, open the red one first. The other package goes with it."

"A coffee grinder, why thank you, dear." She kisses you wetly on the cheek, a Christmas mist in her eyes. She thinks you're wonderful. She's truly your greatest fan. She is aging and menopausal. She stubbornly thinks you're an assistant department head at Karma-Kola. She wants so badly, so earnestly, to be you.

"And this bag is some exotic Colombian bean, and this is a chocolate-flavored decaf."

Your father fidgets in the corner, looking at his watch, worrying that your mom should be checking the crown roast.

"Decaf bean," he says. "That's for me?"

Say: "Yeah, Dad. That's for you."

"Who is he?" says your mom, later, in the kitchen after you've washed the dishes.

"He's a systems analyst."

"What do they do?"

"Oh . . . they get married a lot. They're usually always married."

"Charlene, are you having an affair with a married man?"

"Ma, do you have to put it that way?"

"You are asking for big trouble," she says, slowly, and resumes polishing silver with a vehement energy.

Wonder why she always polishes the silver *after* meals.

Lean against the refrigerator and play with the magnets.

Say, softly, carefully: "I know, Mother, it's not something you would do."

She looks up at you, her mouth trembling, pieces of her brown-gray hair dangling in her salty eyes, pink silverware cream caking onto her hands, onto her wedding ring. She stops, puts a spoon down, looks away and then hopelessly back at you, like a very young girl, and, shaking her head, bursts into tears.

"I missed you," he practically shouts, ebullient and adolescent, pacing about the living room with a sort of bounce, like a child who is up way past his bedtime and wants to ask a question. "What did you do at home?" He rubs your neck.

"Oh, the usual holiday stuff with my parents. On New Year's Eve I went to a disco in Morristown with my cousin Denise, but I dressed wrong. I wore the turtleneck and plaid skirt my mother gave me, because I wanted her to feel good, and my slip kept showing."

He grins and kisses your cheek, thinking this sweet.

Continue: "There were three guys, all in purple shirts and paper hats, who kept coming over and asking me to dance. I don't think they were together or brothers or anything. But I danced, and on 'New York City Girl,' that song about how jaded and competent urban women are, I went crazy dancing and my slip dropped to the floor. I tried to pick it up, but finally just had to step out of it and jam it in my purse. At the stroke of midnight, I cried."

"I'll bet you suffered terribly," he says, clasping you around the small of your back.

Say: "Yes, I did."

"I'm thinking of telling Patricia about us."

Be skeptical. Ask: "What will you say?"

He proceeds confidently: "I'll go, 'Dear, there's something I have to tell you.' "

"And she'll look over at you from her briefcase full of memoranda and say: 'Hmmmmmm?' "

"And I'll say, 'Dear, I think I'm falling in love with another woman, and I *know* I'm having sex with her.' "

"And she'll say, 'Oh my god, what did you say?' "

"And I'll say: 'Sex.' "

"And she'll start weeping inconsolably and *then* what will you do?"

There is a silence, still as the moon. He shifts his legs, seems confused. "I'll . . . tell her I was just kidding." He squeezes your hand.

Shave your legs in the bathroom sink. Philosophize: you are a mistress, part of a great hysterical you mean historical tradition. Wives are like cockroaches. Also part of a great historical tradition. They will survive you after a nuclear attack – they are tough and hardy and travel in packs – but right now they're not having any fun. And when you look in the bathroom mirror, you spot them scurrying, up out of reach behind you.

An hour of gimlets after work, a quick browse through Barnes and Noble, and he looks at his watch, gives you a peck, and says: "Good night. I'll call you soon."

Walk out with him. Stand there, shivering, but do not pout. Say: "Call you 'later' would sound better than 'soon.' 'Soon' always means just the opposite."

He smiles feebly. "I'll phone you in a few days."

And when he is off, hurrying up Third Avenue, look down at your feet, kick at a dirty cigarette butt, and in your best juvenile mumble, say: "Fuck you, jack."

Some nights he says he'll try to make it over, but there's no guarantee. Those nights, just in case, spend two hours showering, dressing, applying makeup unrecognizably, like someone in drag, and then, as it is late, and you have to work the next day, climb onto your bed like that, wearing perfume and an embarrassing, long, flowing, lacy bathrobe that is really not a bathrobe at all, but a "hostess loungecoat." With the glassed candle by your bed lit and burning away, doze off and on, arranged with excruciating care on top of the covers, the window lamp on in the living room, the door unlocked for him in case he arrives in a passionate flurry, forgetting his key. Six blocks from Fourteenth Street: you are risking your life for him, spread out like a ridiculous cake on the bed, waiting with the door unlocked, thinking you hear him on the stairs, but no. You should have a corsage, you think to yourself. You should have a goddamned orchid pinned to the chest of your long flowing hostess coat, then you would be appropriately absurd. Think: What has happened to me? Why am I lying like this on top of my covers with too much Jontue and mascara and jewelry, pretending casually that this is how I always go to bed, while a pervert with six new steak knives is about to sneak through my unlocked door. Remember: at Blakely Falls High, Willis Holmes would have done anything to be with you. You don't have to put up with this: you were second runner-up at the Junior Prom.

A truck roars by.

Some deaf and dumb kids, probably let out from a dance at the school nearby, are gathered downstairs below your window, hooting and howling, making unearthly sounds. You guess they are laughing and having fun, but they can't hear themselves, and at night the noises are scary, animal-like.

Your clock-radio reads 1:45.

Wonder if you are getting old, desperate. Believe that you have really turned into another woman:

your maiden aunt Phyllis;

some vaporish cocktail waitress;

a glittery transvestite who has wandered, lost, up from the Village.

When seven consecutive days go by that you do not hear from him, send witty little postcards to all your friends from college. On the eighth day, when finally he calls you at the office, murmuring lascivious things in German, remain laconic. Say: *"Ja . . . nein . . . ja."*

At lunch regard your cream of cauliflower soup with a pinched mouth and ask what on earth he and his wife *do* together. Sound irritated. He shrugs and says, "Dust, eat, bicker about the shower curtain. Why do you ask?"

Say: "Gee, I don't know. What an outrageous question, huh?"

He gives you a look of sympathy that could bring a dead cat back to life. "You're upset because I didn't call you." He reaches across the table to touch your fingers. Pull your hand away. Say: "Don't flatter yourself." Look slightly off to one side. Put your hand over your eyes like you have a headache. Say: "God, I'm sorry."

"It's okay," he says.

And you think: Something is backward here. Reversed. Wrong. Like the something that is wrong in "What is wrong with this picture?" in kids' magazines in dentists' offices. Toothaches. Stomachaches. God, the soup. Excuse yourself and hurry toward the women's room. Slam the stall door shut. Lean back against it. Stare into the throat of the toilet.

Hilda is worried about you and wants to fix you up with a cousin of hers from Brooklyn.

Ask wearily: "What's his name?"

She looks at you, frowning. "Mark. He's a banker. And what the hell kind of attitude is that?"

Mark orders you a beer in a Greek coffee shop near the movie theater.

"So, you're a secretary."

Squirm and quip: "More like a sedentary," and look at him in surprise and horror when he guffaws and snorts way too loudly.

Say: "Actually, what I really should have been is a dancer. Everybody has always said that."

Mark smiles. He likes the idea of you being a dancer.

Look at him coldly. Say: "No, nobody has ever said that. I just made it up."

All through the movie you forget to read the subtitles, thinking instead about whether you should sleep with Mark the banker. Glance at him out of the corner of your eye. In the dark, his profile seems important and mysterious. Sort of. He catches you looking at him and turns and winks at you. Good god. He seems to be investing something in all of this. Bankers. Sigh. Stare straight ahead. Decide you just don't have the energy, the interest.

"I saw somebody else."

"Oh?"

"A banker. We went to a Godard movie."

"Well . . . good."

"Good?"

"I mean for you, Charlene. You should be doing things like that once in a while."

"Yeah. He's real rich."

"Did you have fun?"

"No."

"Did you sleep with him?"

"No."

He kisses you, almost gratefully, on the ear. Fidget. Twitch. Lie. Say: "I mean, yes."

He nods. Looks away. Says nothing.

Cut up an old calendar into week-long strips. Place them around your kitchen floor, a sort of bar graph on the linoleum, representing the number of weeks you have been a mistress: thirteen. Put X's through all the national holidays.

Go out for a walk in the cold. Three little girls hanging out on the stoop are laughing and calling to strange men on the street. "Hi! Hi, Mister!" Step around them. Think: They have never had orgasms.

A blonde woman in barrettes passes you in stockinged feet, holding her shoes.

There are things you have to tell him.

CLIENTS TO SEE

1. This affair is demeaning.
2. Violates decency. Am I just some scampish tart, some tartish scamp?
3. No emotional support here.
4. Why do you never say "I love you" or "Stay in my arms forever my little tadpole" or "Your eyes set me on fire my sweet nubkin"?

The next time he phones, he says: "I was having a dream about you and suddenly I woke up with a jerk and felt very uneasy."

Say: "Yeah, I hate to wake up with jerks."

He laughs, smooth, beautiful, and tenor, making you feel warm inside of your bones. And it hits you; maybe it all boils down to this: people will do anything, anything, for a really nice laugh.

Don't lose your resolve. Fumble for your list. Sputter things out as convincingly as possible.

Say: "I suffer indignities at your hands. And agonies of duh feet. I don't know why I joke. I hurt."

"That is why."

"What?"

"That is why."

"But you don't really care." Wince. It sounds pitiful.

"But I do."

For some reason this leaves you dumbfounded.

He continues: "You know my situation . . . or maybe you don't." Pause. "What can I do, Charlene? Stand on my goddamned head?"

Whisper: "Please. Stand on your goddamned head."

"It is ten o'clock," he says. "I'm coming over. We need to talk."

What he has to tell you is that Patricia is not his wife. He is separated from his wife; her name is Carrie. You think of a joke you heard once: What do you call a woman who marries a man with no arms and no legs? Carrie. Patricia is the woman he lives with.

"You mean, I'm just another one of the fucking gang?"

He looks at you, puzzled. "Charlene, what I've always admired about you, right from when I first met you, is your strength, your independence."

Say: "That line is old as boots."

Tell him not to smoke in your apartment. Tell him to get out.

At first he protests. But slowly, slowly, he leaves, pulling up the collar on his expensive beige raincoat, like an old and haggard Robert Culp.

Slam the door like Bette Davis.

Love drains from you, takes with it much of your blood sugar and water weight. You are like a house slowly losing its electricity, the fans slowing, the lights dimming and flickering; the clocks stop and go and stop.

At Karma-Kola the days are peg-legged and aimless, collapsing into one another with the comic tedium of old clowns, nowhere fast.

In April you get a raise. Celebrate by taking Hilda to lunch at the Plaza.

Write for applications to graduate schools.

Send Mark the banker a birthday card.

Take long walks at night in the cold. The blonde in barrettes scuttles timelessly by you, still carrying her shoes. She has cut her hair.

He calls you occasionally at the office to ask how you are. You doodle numbers and curlicues on the corners of the Rolodex cards. Fiddle with your Phi Beta Kappa key. Stare out the window. You always, always, say: "Fine."

1981

HOW TO BECOME A WRITER

FIRST, TRY TO BE something, anything, else. A movie star/astronaut. A movie star/missionary. A movie star/kindergarten teacher. President of the World. Fail miserably. It is best if you fail at an early age – say, fourteen. Early, critical disillusionment is necessary so that at fifteen you can write long haiku sequences about thwarted desire. It is a pond, a cherry blossom, a wind brushing against sparrow wing leaving for mountain. Count the syllables. Show it to your mom. She is tough and practical. She has a son in Vietnam and a husband who may be having an affair. She believes in wearing brown because it hides spots. She'll look briefly at your writing, then back up at you with a face blank as a donut. She'll say: "How about emptying the dishwasher?" Look away. Shove the forks in the fork drawer. Accidentally break one of the freebie gas station glasses. This is the required pain and suffering. This is only for starters.

In your high school English class, look only at Mr. Killian's face. Decide faces are important. Write a villanelle about pores. Struggle. Write a sonnet. Count the syllables: nine, ten, eleven, thirteen. Decide to experiment with fiction. Here you don't have to count syllables. Write a short story about an elderly man and woman who accidentally shoot each other in the head, the result of an inexplicable malfunction of a shotgun which appears mysteriously in their living room one night. Give it to Mr. Killian as your final project. When you get it back, he has written on it: "Some of your images are quite nice, but you have no sense of plot." When you are home, in the privacy of your own room, faintly scrawl in pencil beneath his black-inked comments: "Plots are for dead people, pore-face."

Take all the babysitting jobs you can get. You are great with kids. They love you. You tell them stories about old people who die idiot deaths. You sing them songs like "Blue

Bells of Scotland," which is their favorite. And when they are in their pajamas and have finally stopped pinching each other, when they are fast asleep, you read every sex manual in the house, and wonder how on earth anyone could ever do those things with someone they truly loved. Fall asleep in a chair reading Mr. McMurphy's *Playboy*. When the McMurphys come home, they will tap you on the shoulder, look at the magazine in your lap, and grin. You will want to die. They will ask you if Tracey took her medicine all right. Explain, yes, she did, that you promised her a story if she would take it like a big girl and that seemed to work out just fine. "Oh, marvelous," they will exclaim.

Try to smile proudly.

Apply to college as a child psychology major.

As a child psychology major, you have some electives. You've always liked birds. Sign up for something called "The Ornithological Field Trip." It meets Tuesdays and Thursdays at two. When you arrive at Room 134 on the first day of class, everyone is sitting around a seminar table talking about metaphors. You've heard of these. After a short, excruciating while, raise your hand and say diffidently, "Excuse me, isn't this Bird-watching One-oh-one?" The class stops and turns to look at you. They seem to all have one face – giant and blank as a vandalized clock. Someone with a beard booms out, "No, this is Creative Writing." Say: "Oh – right," as if perhaps you knew all along. Look down at your schedule. Wonder how the hell you ended up here. The computer, apparently, has made an error. You start to get up to leave and then don't. The lines at the registrar this week are huge. Perhaps you should stick with this mistake. Perhaps your creative writing isn't all that bad. Perhaps it is fate. Perhaps this is what your dad meant when he said, "It's the age of computers, Francie, it's the age of computers."

Decide that you like college life. In your dorm you meet many nice people. Some are smarter than you. And some, you notice, are dumber than you. You will continue, unfortunately, to view the world in exactly these terms for the rest of your life.

The assignment this week in creative writing is to narrate a violent happening. Turn in a story about driving with your Uncle Gordon and another one about two old people who are accidentally electrocuted when they go to turn on a badly wired desk lamp. The teacher will hand them back to you with comments: "Much of your writing is smooth and energetic. You have, however, a ludicrous notion of plot." Write another story about a man and a woman who, in the very first paragraph, have their lower torsos accidentally blitzed away by dynamite. In the second paragraph, with the insurance money, they buy a frozen yogurt stand together. There are six more paragraphs. You read the whole thing out loud in class. No one likes it. They say your sense of plot is outrageous and incompetent. After class someone asks you if you are crazy.

Decide that perhaps you should stick to comedies. Start dating someone who is funny, someone who has what in high school you called a "really great sense of humor" and what now your creative writing class calls "self-contempt giving rise to comic form." Write down all of his jokes, but don't tell him you are doing this. Make up anagrams of his old girlfriend's name and name all of your socially handicapped characters with them. Tell him his old girlfriend is in all of your stories and then watch how funny he can be, see what a really great sense of humor he can have.

Your child psychology advisor tells you you are neglecting courses in your major. What you spend the most time on should be what you're majoring in. Say yes, you understand.

In creative writing seminars over the next two years, everyone continues to smoke cigarettes and ask the same things: "But does it work?" "Why should we care about this character?" "Have you earned this cliché?" These seem like important questions.

On days when it is your turn, you look at the class hopefully as they scour your mimeographs for a plot. They look back up at you, drag deeply, and then smile in a sweet sort of way.

You spend too much time slouched and demoralized. Your boyfriend suggests bicycling. Your roommate suggests a new boyfriend. You are said to be self-mutilating and losing weight, but you continue writing. The only happiness you have is writing something new, in the middle of the night, armpits damp, heart pounding, something no one has yet seen. You have only those brief, fragile, untested moments of exhilaration when you know: you are a genius. Understand what you must do. Switch majors. The kids in your nursery project will be disappointed, but you have a calling, an urge, a delusion, an unfortunate habit. You have, as your mother would say, fallen in with a bad crowd.

Why write? Where does writing come from? These are questions to ask yourself. They are like: Where does dust come from? Or: Why is there war? Or: If there's a God, then why is my brother now a cripple?

These are questions that you keep in your wallet, like calling cards. These are questions, your creative writing teacher says, that are good to address in your journals but rarely in your fiction.

The writing professor this fall is stressing the Power of the Imagination. Which means he doesn't want long descriptive stories about your camping trip last July. He wants you to start in a realistic context but then to alter it. Like recombinant DNA. He wants you to let your imagination sail, to let it grow big-bellied in the wind. This is a quote from Shakespeare.

Tell your roommate your great idea, your great exercise of imaginative power: a transformation of Melville to contemporary life. It will be about monomania and the fish-eat-fish world of life insurance in Rochester, New York. The first line will be "Call me Fishmeal," and it will feature a menopausal suburban husband named Richard, who because he is so depressed all the time is called "Mopey Dick" by his witty wife Elaine. Say to your roommate: "Mopey Dick, get it?" Your roommate looks at you, her face blank as a large Kleenex. She comes up to you, like a buddy, and puts an arm around your burdened shoulders. "Listen, Francie," she says, slow as speech therapy. "Let's go out and get a big beer."

The seminar doesn't like this one either. You suspect they are beginning to feel sorry for you. They say: "You have to think about what is happening. Where is the story here?"

The next semester the writing professor is obsessed with writing from personal experience. You must write from what you know, from what has happened to you. He wants deaths, he wants camping trips. Think about what has happened to you. In three years there have been three things: you lost your virginity; your parents got divorced; and your brother came home from a forest ten miles from the Cambodian border with only half a thigh, a permanent smirk nestled into one corner of his mouth.

About the first you write: "It created a new space, which hurt and cried in a voice that wasn't mine, 'I'm not the same anymore, but I'll be okay.'"

About the second you write an elaborate story of an old married couple who stumble upon an unknown land mine in their kitchen and accidentally blow themselves up. You call it: "For Better or for Liverwurst."

About the last you write nothing. There are no words for this. Your typewriter hums. You can find no words.

At undergraduate cocktail parties, people say, "Oh, you write? What do you write about?" Your roommate, who has consumed too much wine, too little cheese, and no crackers at all, blurts: "Oh, my god, she always writes about her dumb boyfriend."

Later on in life you will learn that writers are merely open, helpless texts with no real understanding of what they have written and therefore must half-believe anything and everything that is said of them. You, however, have not yet reached this stage of literary criticism. You stiffen and say, "I do not," the same way you said it when someone in the fourth grade accused you of really liking oboe lessons and your parents really weren't just making you take them.

Insist you are not very interested in any one subject at all, that you are interested in the music of language, that you are interested in – in – syllables, because they are the atoms of poetry, the cells of the mind, the breath of the soul. Begin to feel woozy. Stare into your plastic wine cup.

"Syllables?" you will hear someone ask, voice trailing off, as they glide slowly toward the reassuring white of the dip.

Begin to wonder what you do write about. Or if you have anything to say. Or if there even is such a thing as a thing to say. Limit these thoughts to no more than ten minutes a day; like sit-ups, they can make you thin.

You will read somewhere that all writing has to do with one's genitals. Don't dwell on this. It will make you nervous.

Your mother will come visit you. She will look at the circles under your eyes and hand you a brown book with a brown briefcase on the cover. It is entitled: *How to Become a Business Executive.* She has also brought the *Names for Baby* encyclopedia you asked for; one of your characters, the aging clown–schoolteacher, needs a new name. Your mother will shake her head and say: "Francie, Francie, remember when you were going to be a child psychology major?"

Say: "Mom, I like to write."

She'll say: "Sure you like to write. Of course. Sure you like to write."

Write a story about a confused music student and title it: "Schubert Was the One with the Glasses, Right?" It's not a big hit, although your roommate likes the part where the two violinists accidentally blow themselves up in a recital room. "I went out with a violinist once," she says, snapping her gum.

Thank god you are taking other courses. You can find sanctuary in nineteenth-century ontological snags and invertebrate courting rituals. Certain globular mollusks have what is called "Sex by the Arm." The male octopus, for instance, loses the end of one arm when placing it inside the female body during intercourse. Marine biologists call it "Seven Heaven." Be glad you know these things. Be glad you are not just a writer. Apply to law school.

From here on in, many things can happen. But the main one will be this: you decide not to go to law school after all, and, instead, you spend a good, big chunk of your adult life telling people how you decided not to go to law school after all. Somehow you end up writing again. Perhaps you go to graduate school. Perhaps you work odd jobs and take writing courses at night. Perhaps you are working on a novel and writing down all the clever remarks and intimate personal confessions you hear during the day. Perhaps you are losing your pals, your acquaintances, your balance.

You have broken up with your boyfriend. You now go out with men who, instead of whispering "I love you," shout: "Do it to me, baby." This is good for your writing.

Sooner or later you have a finished manuscript more or less. People look at it in a vaguely troubled sort of way and say, "I'll bet becoming a writer was always a fantasy of yours, wasn't it?" Your lips dry to salt. Say that of all the fantasies possible in the world, you can't imagine being a writer even making the top twenty. Tell them you were going to be a child psychology major. "I bet," they always sigh, "you'd be great with kids." Scowl fiercely. Tell them you're a walking blade.

Quit classes. Quit jobs. Cash in old savings bonds. Now you have time like warts on your hands. Slowly copy all of your friends' addresses into a new address book.

Vacuum. Chew cough drops. Keep a folder full of fragments.

An eyelid darkening sideways.

World as conspiracy.

Possible plot? A woman gets on a bus.

Suppose you threw a love affair and nobody came.

At home drink a lot of coffee. At Howard Johnson's order the cole slaw. Consider how it looks like the soggy confetti of a map: where you've been, where you're going – "You Are Here," says the red star on the back of the menu.

Occasionally a date with a face blank as a sheet of paper asks you whether writers often become discouraged. Say that sometimes they do and sometimes they do. Say it's a lot like having polio.

"Interesting," smiles your date, and then he looks down at his arm hairs and starts to smooth them, all, always, in the same direction.

1982

HOW TO TALK TO YOUR MOTHER (NOTES)

1982. WITHOUT HER, for years now, murmur at the defrosting refrigerator, "What?" "Huh?" "Shush now," as it creaks, aches, groans, until the final ice block drops from the ceiling of the freezer like something vanquished.

Dream, and in your dreams babies with the personalities of dachshunds, fat as Macy balloons, float by the treetops.

The first permanent polyurethane heart is surgically implanted.

Someone upstairs is playing "You'll Never Walk Alone" on the recorder. Now it's "Oklahoma!" They must have a Rodgers and Hammerstein book.

1981. On public transportation, mothers with soft, soapy, corduroyed seraphs glance at you, their faces dominoes of compassion. Their seraphs are small and quiet or else restlessly counting bus-seat colors: "Blue-blue-blue, red-red-red, lullow-lullow-lullow." The mothers see you eyeing their children. They smile sympathetically. They believe you envy them. They believe you are childless. They believe they know why. Look quickly away, out the smudge of the window.

1980. The hum, rush, clack of things in the kitchen. These are some of the sounds that organize your life. The clink of the silverware inside the drawer, piled like bones in a mass grave. Your similes grow grim, grow tired.

Reagan is elected President, though you distributed donuts and brochures for Carter.

Date an Italian. He rubs your stomach and says, "These are marks of stretch, no? Marks of stretch?" and in your dizzy mind you think: Marks of Harpo, Ideas of Marx, Ides of

March, Beware. He plants kisses on the sloping ramp of your neck, and you fall asleep against him, your underpants peeled and rolled around one thigh like a bride's garter.

1979. Once in a while take evening trips past the old unsold house you grew up in, that haunted rural crossroads two hours from where you now live. It is like Halloween: the raked, moonlit lawn, the mammoth, tumid trees, arms and fingers raised into the starless wipe of sky like burns, cracks, map rivers. Their black shadows rock against the side of the east porch. There are dream shadows, other lives here. Turn the corner slowly but continue to stare from the car window. This house is embedded in you deep, something still here you know, you think you know, a voice at the top of those stairs, perhaps, a figure on the porch, an odd apron caught high in the twigs, in the too-warm-for-a-fall-night breeze, something not right, that turret window you can still see from here, from outside, but which can't be reached from within. (The ghostly brag of your childhood: "We have a mystery room. The window shows from the front, but you can't go in, there's no door. A doctor lived there years ago and gave secret operations, and now it's blocked off.") The window sits like a dead eye in the turret.

You see a ghost, something like a spinning statue by a shrub.

1978. Bury her in the cold south sideyard of that Halloweenish house. Your brother and his kids are there. Hug. The minister in a tweed sportscoat, the neighborless fields, the crossroads, are all like some stark Kansas. There is praying, then someone shoveling. People walk toward the cars and hug again. Get inside your car with your niece. Wait. Look up through the windshield. In the November sky a wedge of wrens moves south, the lines of their formation, the very sides and vertices mysteriously choreographed, shifting, flowing, crossing like a skater's legs. "They'll descend instinctively upon a tree somewhere," you say, "but not for miles yet." You marvel, watch, until, amoeba-slow, they are dark, faraway stitches in the horizon. You do not start the car. The quiet niece next to you finally speaks: "Aunt Ginnie, are we going to the restaurant with the others?" Look at her. Recognize her: nine in a pile parka. Smile and start the car.

1977. She ages, rocks in your rocker, noiseless as wind. The front strands of her white hair dangle yellow at her eyes from too many cigarettes. She smokes even now, her voice husky with phlegm. Sometimes at dinner in your tiny kitchen she will simply stare, rheumy-eyed, at you, then burst into a fit of coughing that racks her small old man's body like a storm.

Stop eating your baked potato. Ask if she is all right.

She will croak: "Do you remember, Ginnie, your father used to say that one day, with these cigarettes, I was going to have to 'face the mucus'?" At this she chuckles, chokes, gasps again.

Make her stand up.

Lean her against you.

Slap her lightly on the curved mound of her back.

Ask her for chrissakes to stop smoking.

She will smile and say: "For chrissakes? Is that any way to talk to your mother?"

At night go in and check on her. She lies there awake, her lips apart, open and drying. Bring her some juice. She murmurs, "Thank you, honey." Her mouth smells, swells like a grave.

1976. The Bicentennial. In the laundromat, you wait for the time on your coins to run out. Through the porthole of the dryer, you watch your bedeviled towels and sheets leap and fall. The radio station piped in from the ceiling plays slow, sad Motown; it encircles you with the desperate hopefulness of a boy at a dance, and it makes you cry. When you get back to your apartment, dump everything on your bed. Your mother is knitting crookedly: red, white, and blue. Kiss her hello. Say: "Sure was warm in that place." She will seem not to hear you.

1975. Attend poetry readings alone at the local library. Find you don't really listen well. Stare at your crossed thighs. Think about your mother. Sometimes you confuse her with the first man you ever loved, who ever loved you, who buried his head in the pills of your sweater and said magnificent things like "Oh god, oh god," who loved you unconditionally, terrifically, like a mother.

The poet loses his nerve for a second, a red flush through his neck and ears, but he regains his composure. When he is finished, people clap. There is wine and cheese.

Leave alone, walk home alone. The downtown streets are corridors of light holding you, holding you, past the church, past the community center. March, like Stella Dallas, spine straight, through the melodrama of street lamps, phone posts, toward the green house past Borealis Avenue, toward the rear apartment with the tilt and the squash on the stove.

Your horoscope says: Be kind, be brief.

You are pregnant again. Decide what you must do.

1974. She will have bouts with a mad sort of senility. She calls you at work. "There's no food here! Help me! I'm starving!" although you just bought forty dollars' worth of groceries yesterday. "Mom, there is too food there!"

When you get home the refrigerator is mostly empty. "Mom, where did you put all the milk and cheese and stuff?" Your mother stares at you from where she is sitting in front of the TV set. She has tears leaking out of her eyes. "There's no food here, Ginnie."

There is a rustling, scratching noise in the dishwasher. You open it up, and the eyes of a small rodent glint back at you. It scrambles out, off to the baseboards behind the refrigerator. Your mother, apparently, has put all the groceries inside the dishwasher. The milk is spilled, a white pool against blue, and things like cheese and bologna and apples have been nibbled at.

1973. At a party when a woman tells you where she bought some wonderful pair of shoes, say that you believe shopping for clothes is like masturbation – everyone does it, but it isn't very interesting and therefore should be done alone, in an embarrassed fashion, and never be the topic of party conversation. The woman will tighten her lips and eyebrows and say, "Oh, I suppose you have something more fascinating to talk about." Grow clumsy and uneasy. Say, "No," and head for the ginger ale. Tell the person next to you that your insides feel sort of sinking and vinyl like a Claes Oldenburg toilet. They will say, "Oh?" and point out that the print on your dress is one of paisleys impregnating paisleys. Pour yourself more ginger ale.

1972. Nixon wins by a landslide.

Sometimes your mother calls you by her sister's name. Say, "No, Mom, it's me. Virginia." Learn to repeat things. Learn that you have a way of knowing each other which somehow slips out and beyond the ways you have of not knowing each other at all.

Make apple crisp for the first time.

1971. Go for long walks to get away from her. Walk through wooded areas; there is a life there you have forgotten. The smells and sounds seem sudden, unchanged, exact, the papery crunch of the leaves, the mouldering sachet of the mud. The trees are crooked as backs, the fence posts splintered, trusting and precarious in their solid grasp of arms, the asters spindly, dry, white, havishammed (Havishammed!) by frost. Find a beautiful reddish stone and bring it home for your mother. Kiss her. Say: "This is for you." She grasps it and smiles. "You were always such a sensitive child," she says.

Say: "Yeah, I know."

1970. You are pregnant again. Try to decide what you should do.

Get your hair chopped, short as a boy's.

1969. Mankind leaps upon the moon.

Disposable diapers are first sold in supermarkets.

Have occasional affairs with absurd, silly men who tell you to grow your hair to your waist and who, when you are sad, tickle your ribs to cheer you up. Moonlight through the blinds stripes you like zebras. You laugh. You never marry.

1968. Do not resent her. Think about the situation, for instance, when you take the last trash bag from its box: you must throw out the box by putting it in that very trash bag. What was once contained, now must contain. The container, then, becomes the contained, the enveloped, the held. Find more and more that you like to muse over things like this.

1967. Your mother is sick and comes to live with you. There is no place else for her to go. You feel many different emptinesses.

The first successful heart transplant is performed in South Africa.

1966. You confuse lovers, mix up who had what scar, what car, what mother.

1965. Smoke marijuana. Try to figure out what has made your life go wrong. It is like trying to figure out what is stinking up the refrigerator. It could be anything. The lid off the mayonnaise, Uncle Ron's honey wine four years in the left corner. Broccoli yellowing, flowering fast. They are all metaphors. They are all problems. Your horoscope says: Speak gently to a loved one.

1964. Your mother calls long distance and asks whether you are coming home for Thanksgiving, your brother and the baby will be there. Make excuses.

"As a mother gets older," your mother says, "these sorts of holidays become increasingly important."

Say: "I'm sorry, Mom."

1963. Wake up one morning with a man you had thought you'd spend your life with, and realize, a rock in your gut, that you don't even like him. Spend a weepy afternoon in his bathroom, not coming out when he knocks. You can no longer trust your affections. People and places you think you love may be people and places you hate.

Kennedy is shot.

Someone invents a temporary artificial heart, for use during operations.

1962. Eat Chinese food for the first time, with a lawyer from California. He will show you how to hold the chopsticks. He will pat your leg. Attack his profession. Ask him whether he feels the law makes large spokes out of the short stakes of men.

1961. Grandma Moses dies.

You are a zoo of insecurities. You take to putting brandy in your morning coffee and to falling in love too easily. You have an abortion.

1960. There is money from your father's will and his life insurance. You buy a car and a green velvet dress you don't need. You drive two hours to meet your mother for lunch on Saturdays. She suggests things for you to write about, things she's heard on the radio: a woman with telepathic twins, a woman with no feet.

1959. At the funeral she says: "He had his problems, but he was a generous man," though you know he was tight as a scout knot, couldn't listen to anyone, the only time you remember loving him being that once when he got the punchline of one of your jokes before your mom did and looked up from his science journal and guffawed loud as a giant, the two of you, for one split moment, communing like angels in the middle of that room, in that warm, shared light of mind.

Say: "He was okay."

"You shouldn't be bitter," your mother snaps. "He financed you and your brother's college educations." She buttons her coat. "He was also the first man to isolate a particular isotope of helium, I forget the name, but he should have won the Nobel Prize." She dabs at her nose.

Say: "Yeah, Mom."

1958. At your brother's wedding, your father is taken away in an ambulance. A tiny cousin whispers loudly to her mother, "Did Uncle Will have a hard attack?" For seven straight days say things to your mother like: "I'm sure it'll be okay," and "I'll stay here, why don't you go home and get some sleep."

1957. Dance the calypso with boys from a different college. Get looped on New York State burgundy, lose your virginity, and buy one of the first portable electric typewriters.

1956. Tell your mother about all the books you are reading at college. This will please her.

1955. Do a paint-by-numbers of Elvis Presley. Tell your mother you are in love with him. She will shake her head.

1954. Shoplift a cashmere sweater.

1953. Smoke a cigarette with Hillary Swedelson. Tell each other your crushes. Become blood sisters.

1952. When your mother asks you if there are any nice boys in junior high, ask her how on earth would you ever know, having to come in at nine! every night. Her eyebrows will lift like theater curtains. "You poor, abused thing," she will say.

Say, "Don't I know it," and slam the door.

1951. Your mother tells you about menstruation. The following day you promptly menstruate, your body only waiting for permission, for a signal. You wake up in the morning and feel embarrassed.

1949. You learn how to blow gum bubbles and to add negative numbers.

1947. The Dead Sea Scrolls are discovered.

You have seen too many Hollywood musicals. You have seen too many people singing in public places and you assume you can do it, too. Practice. Your teacher asks you a question. You warble back: "The answer to number two is twelve." Most of the class laughs at you, though some stare, eyes jewel-still, fascinated. At home your mother asks you to dust your dresser. Work up a vibrato you could drive a truck through. Sing: "Why do I have to do it now?" and tap your way through the dining room. Your mother requests that you calm down and go take a nap. Shout: "You don't care about me! You don't care about me at all!"

1946. Your brother plays "Shoofly Pie" all day long on the Victrola.

Ask your mother if you can go to Ellen's for supper. She will say, "Go ask your father," and you, pulling at your fingers, walk out to the living room and whimper by his chair. He is reading. Tap his arm. "Dad? Daddy? Dad?" He continues reading his science journal. Pull harder on your fingers and run back to the kitchen to tell your mother, who storms into the living room, saying, "Why don't you ever listen to your children when they try to talk to you?" You hear them arguing. Press your face into a kitchen towel, ashamed, the hum of the refrigerator motor, the drip in the sink scaring you.

1945. Your father comes home from his war work. He gives you a piggyback ride around the broad yellow thatch of your yard, the dead window in the turret, dark as a wound, watching you. He gives you wordless pushes on the swing.

Your brother has new friends, acts older and distant, even while you wait for the school bus together.

You spend too much time alone. You tell your mother that when you grow up you will bring your babies to Australia to see the kangaroos.

Forty thousand people are killed in Nagasaki.

1944. Dress and cuddle a tiny babydoll you have named "the Sue." Bring her everywhere. Get lost in the Wilson Creek fruit market, and call softly, "Mom, where are you?" Watch other children picking grapes, but never dare yourself. Your eyes are small, dark throats, your hand clutches the Sue.

1943. Ask your mother about babies. Have her read to you only the stories about babies. Ask her if she is going to have a baby. Ask her about the baby that died. Cry into her arm.

1940. Clutch her hair in your fist. Rub it against your cheek.

1939. As through a helix, as through an ear, it is here you are nearer the dream flashes, the other lives.

There is a tent of legs, a sundering of selves, as you both gasp blindly for breath. Across the bright and cold, she knows it when you try to talk to her, though this is something you never really manage to understand.

Germany invades Poland.

The year's big song is "Three Little Fishies" and someone, somewhere, is playing it.

1982

THE JEWISH HUNTER

THIS WAS IN a faraway land. There were gyms but no irony or coffee shops. People took things literally, without drugs. Laird, who wanted to fix her up with this guy, warned her beforehand in exercise class. "Look, Odette, you're a poet. You've been in po biz for what – twenty years—"

"Only fifteen, I'm sure." She had just turned forty and scowled at him over her shoulder. She had a voice menopausal with whiskey, a voice left to lurch and ruin by cigarettes. It was without a middle range, low, with sudden cracks upward. "I hate that phrase *po biz*."

"Fifteen. All right. This guy's not at all literary. He's a farm lawyer. He gets the occasional flasher, or a Gypsy from the Serbo neighborhood in Chicago, but that's as artistic as he gets. He's dealing with farmers and farms. He wouldn't know T. S. Eliot from, say, *Pinky* Eliot. He's probably never even been to Minneapolis, let alone New York."

"Who's Pinky Eliot?" she asked. They were lying side by side, doing these things where you thrust your arms between your raised knees, to tighten the stomach muscles. There was loud music to distract you from worries that you might not know anyone in the room well enough to be doing this in front of them. "Who the heck is Pinky Eliot?"

"Someone I went to fourth grade with," said Laird, gasping. "It was said he weighed more than the teacher, and she was no zipper, let me tell you." Laird was balding, and in exercise class the blood rushed across his head, bits of hair curling above his ears like gift ribbon. He had lived in this town until he was ten, then his family had moved east to New Jersey, where she had first met him, years ago. Now he had come back, like a salmon, to raise his own kids. He and his wife had two. "Little and Moist," they called them. "Look, you're in the boonies here. You got your Pinky Eliot or you got your guy who's never heard of Pinky or any Eliot."

She had been in the boonies before. To afford her apartment

in New York, she often took these sorts of library fellowships: six weeks and four thousand dollars to live in town, write unpublishable poems, and give a reading at the library. The problem with the boonies was that nobody ever kissed you there. They stared at you, up, down, but they never kissed.

Actually, once in a while you could get them to kiss.

But then you had to leave. And in your packing and going, in tearing the seams, the hems, the haws, you felt like some bad combination of Odysseus *and* Penelope. You felt funny in the heart.

"All right," she said. "What is his name?"

Laird sighed. "Pinky Eliot," he said, thrusting his arms between his knees. "Somehow in this mangled presentation, I fear I've confused you."

Pinky Eliot had lost weight, though for sure he still weighed more than the teacher. He was about forty-five, with all his hair still dark. He was not bad-looking, elf-nosed and cat-eyed, though a little soccer ball–ish through the chin and cheeks, which together formed a white sphere with a sudden scar curling grayly around. Also, he had the kind of mustache a college roommate of hers used to say looked like it had crawled up to find a warm spot to die.

They ate dinner at the only Italian restaurant in town. She drank two glasses of wine, the cool heat of it spreading through her like wintergreen. One of these days, she knew, she would have to give up dating. She had practiced declarations in the mirror. "I don't date. I'm sorry. I just don't date."

"I always kind of liked the food here," said Pinky.

She looked at his round face and felt a little bad for him and a little bad for herself while she was at it, because, truly, the food was not good: flavorless bladders of pasta passing as tortellini; the cutlets mealy and drenched in the kind of tomato sauce that was unwittingly, defeatedly orange. Poor Pinky didn't know a garlic from a Gumby.

"Yes," she said, trying to be charming. "But do you think

it's really Italian? It feels as if it got as far as the Canary Islands, then fell into the water."

"An East Coast snob." He smiled. His voice was slow with prairie, thick with Great Lakes. "Dressed all in black and hating the Midwest. Are you Jewish?"

She bristled. A Nazi. A hillbilly Nazi gastronomical moron. "No, I'm not Jewish," she said archly, staring him down, to teach him, to teach him this: "Are *you*?"

"Yes," he said. He studied her eyes.

"Oh," she said.

"Not many of us in this part of the world, so I thought I'd ask."

"Yes." She felt an embarrassed sense of loss, as if something that should have been hers but wasn't had been taken away, legally, by the police. Her gaze dropped to her hands, which had started to move around nervously, independently, like small rodents kept as pets. Wine settled hotly in her cheeks, and when she rushed more to her mouth, the edge of the glass clinked against the tooth in front that was longer than all the others.

Pinky reached across the table and touched her hair. She had had it permed into waves like ramen noodles the week before. "A little ethnic kink is always good to see," he said. "What are you, Methodist?"

On their second date they went to a movie. It was about creatures from outer space who burrow into earthlings and force them to charge up enormous sums on their credit cards. It was an elaborate urban allegory, full of disease and despair, and Odette wanted to talk about it. "Pretty entertaining movie," said Pinky slowly. He had fidgeted in his seat through the whole thing and had twice gotten up and gone to the water fountain. "Just going to the bubbler," he'd whispered.

Now he wanted to go dancing.

"Where is there to go dancing?" said Odette. She was still thinking about the part where the two main characters had traded boom boxes and it had caused them to fall in love. She wanted either Pinky or herself to say something incisive or provocative about directorial vision, or the narrative parameters of cinematic imagery. But it looked as if neither of them was going to.

"There's a place out past the county beltline about six miles." They walked out into the parking lot, and he leaned over and kissed her cheek – intimate, premature, a leftover gesture from a recent love affair, no doubt – and she blushed. She was bad at love. There were people in the world who were good at love and people who were bad at it. She was bad. She used to think she was good at love, that it was intimacy she was bad at. But you had to have both. Love without intimacy, she knew, was an unsung tune. It was all in your head. You said, "Listen to this!" but what you found yourself singing was a tangle, a nothing, a heap. It reminded her of a dinner party she had gone to once, where dessert was served on plates printed with French songs. After dinner everyone had had to sing their plate, but hers had still had whipped cream on it, and when it came her turn, she had garbled the notes and words, frantically pushing the whipped cream around with a fork so she could see the next measure. Oh, she was bad, bad like that, at love.

Pinky drove them six miles south of the county beltline to a place called Humphrey Bogart's. It was rough and wooden, high-beamed, a former hunting lodge. On a makeshift stage at the front, a country-western band was playing "Tequila Sunrise" fifteen years too late, or perhaps too soon. Who could predict? Pinky took her hand and improvised a slow jitterbug to the bass. "What do I do now?" Odette kept calling to Pinky over the music. "What do I do now?"

"This," said Pinky. He had the former fat person's careful grace, and his hand at the small of her back felt big and light. His scar seemed to disappear in the dancelight, and his smile drove his mustache up into flattering shadow. Odette had always been thin and tense.

"We don't dance much in New York," she said.

"No? What do you do?"

"We, uh, just wait in line at cash machines."

Pinky leaned into her, took her hand tightly to his shoulder, and rocked. He put his mouth to her ear. "You've got a great personality," he said.

On Sunday afternoon Pinky took her to the Cave of the Many Mounds. "You'll like this," he said.

"Wonderful!" she said, getting into his car. There was a kind of local enthusiasm about things, which she was trying to get the hang of. It involved good posture and utterances made in a chirpy singsong. *Isn't the air just snappy?* She was wearing sunglasses and an oversize sweater. "I was thinking of asking you what a Cave of Many Mounds was, and then I said, 'Odette, do you *really* want to know?'" She fished through her pocketbook. "I mean, it sounds like a whorehouse. You don't happen to have any cigarettes, do you?"

Pinky tapped on her sunglasses. "You're not going to need these. It's dark in the cave." He started the car and pulled out.

"Well, let me know when we get there." She stared straight ahead. "I take it you don't have any cigarettes."

"No," said Pinky. "You smoke cigarettes?"

"Once in a while." They drove past two cars in a row with bleeding deer strapped on them like wreaths, like trophies, *like women*, she thought. "Damn hunters," she murmured.

"What kind of cigarettes do you smoke? Do you smoke Virginia Slims?" asked Pinky with a grin.

Odette turned and lowered her sunglasses, looked out over them at Pinky's sun-pale profile. "No, I don't smoke *Virginia Slims*."

"I'll bet you do. I'll bet you smoke Virginia Slims."

"Yeah, I smoke Virginia Slims," said Odette, shaking her head. Who was this guy?

Ten miles south, there started to be signs for Cave of the Many Mounds. CAVE OF THE MANY MOUNDS 20 MILES. CAVE OF THE MANY MOUNDS 15 MILES. At 5 MILES, Pinky pulled the car over onto the shoulder. There were only trees and in the far distance a barn and a lone cow.

"What are we doing?" asked Odette.

Pinky shifted the car into park but left the engine running. "I want to kiss you now, before we get in the cave and I lose complete control." He turned toward her, and suddenly his body, jacketed and huge, appeared suspended above her, hovering, as she sank back against the car door. He closed his eyes and kissed her, long and slow, and she left her sunglasses on so she could keep her eyes open and watch, see how his lashes closed on one another like petals, how his scar zoomed quiet and white about his cheek and chin, how his lips pushed sleepily against her own to find a nest in hers and to stay there, moving, as if in words, but then not in words at all, his hands going round her in a soft rustle, up the back of her sweater to her bare waist and spine, and spreading there, blooming large and holding her just briefly until he pulled away, gathered himself back to himself, and quietly shifted the car into drive.

Odette sat up and stared out the windshield into space. Pinky moved the car back out onto the highway and picked up speed.

"We don't do that in New York," rasped Odette. She cleared her throat.

"No?" Pinky smiled and put his hand on her thigh.

"No, it's, um, the cash machines. You just . . . you wait at them. Forever. Your whole life you're just always" – her hand sliced the air – "there."

"Please do not touch the formations," the cave tour guide kept shouting over everyone's head. Along the damp path through the cave there were lights, which allowed you to see walls marbled a golden rose, like a port cheddar; nippled projections, blind galleries, arteries all through the place, chalky and damp; stalagmites and stalactites in walrusy verticals, bursting up from the floor in yearning or hanging wicklessly in drips from the ceiling, making their way, through time, to the floor. The whole cave was in a weep, everything wet and slippery; still ocher pools of water bordered the walk, which spiraled gradually down. "Nature's Guggenheim," said Odette, and because Pinky seemed not to know what she was talking about, she said, "That's an art museum in New York." She had her sunglasses perched high on her head. She looked at Pinky gleefully, and he smiled back at her as if he thought she was cute but from outer space, like something that would soon be made into a major motion picture and then later into a toy.

". . . The way you can remember which are which," the guide was saying, "is to remember: When the mites go up, the tights come down . . ."

"Get that?" said Pinky too loudly, nudging her. "The tights come down?" People turned to look.

"What are you, hard of hearing?" asked Odette.

"A little," said Pinky. "In the right ear."

"Next we come to a stalagmite which is the only one in the cave that visitors are allowed to touch. As we pass, it will be on your right, and you may manhandle it to your heart's content."

"Hmmmph," said Pinky.

"Really," said Odette. She peered ahead at the front of the group, which had now gathered unexcitedly around the stalagmite, a short stumpy one with a head rubbed white with so much touching. It had all the appeal of a bar of soap in a gas station. "I think I want to go back and look at the cave coral again."

"Which was that?" said Pinky.

"All that stuff that looked like cement broccoli. Also the chapel room with the church organ. I mean, I thought that looked pretty much like an organ."

". . . And now," the guide was saying, "we come to that part of our tour when we let you see what the cave looks like in its own natural lighting." She moved over and flicked a switch. "You should not be able to see your hand in front of your face."

Odette widened her eyes and then squinted and still could not see her hand in front of her face. The darkness was thick and certain, not a shaded, waltzing dark but a paralyzing coffin jet. There was something fierce and eternal about it, something secret and unrelieved, like a thing not told to children.

"I'm right here," Pinky said, stepping close, "in case you need me." He gave her far shoulder a squeeze, his arm around the back of her. She could smell the soupy breath of him, the spice of his neck near her face, and leaned, blind and hungry, into his arm. She reached past the scratch of her own sweater and felt for his hand.

"We can see now how the cave looked when it was first unearthed, and how it had existed eons before, in the pitch dark, gradually growing larger, opening up in darkness, the life and the sea of it trapped and never seeing light, a small moist cavern a million years in the making, just slowly opening, opening, and opening inside. . . ."

When they slept together, she almost cried. He was a kisser, and he kissed and kissed. It seemed the kindest thing that had ever happened to her. He kissed and whispered and brought her a large glass of water when she asked for one.

"When ya going back to New York?" he asked, and because it was in less than four weeks, she said, "Oh, I forget."

Pinky got out of bed. He was naked and unselfconscious, beautiful, in a way, the long, rounded lines of him, the stark cliff of his back. He went over to the VCR, fumbled with some cassettes in the dark, holding each up to the window, where there was a rainy, moony light from the street, like a dream; he picked up cassette after cassette until he found the one he wanted.

It was a tape called *Holocaust Survivors*, and the title flashed blood red on the television screen, as if in warning that it had no place there at all. "I watch this all the time," said Pinky, very quietly. He stared straight ahead in a trance of impassivity, but when he reached back to put an arm around Odette, he knew exactly where she was, slightly behind one of his shoulders, the sheet tight across her chest. "You shouldn't hide your breasts," he said, without looking. But she stayed like that, tucked close, all along the tracks to Treblinka, the gates to Auschwitz, the film lingering on weeds and wind, so unbelieving in this historical badlands, it seemed to want, in a wave of nausea and regret, to become perhaps a nature documentary. It seemed at moments confused about what it was about, a confusion brought on by knowing exactly.

Someone was talking about the trucks. How they put people in trucks, with the exhaust pipes venting in, how they drove them around until they were blue, the people were blue, and could be shoveled out from a trapdoor. Past some barbed wire, asters were drying in a field.

When it was over, Pinky turned to her and sighed. "Heavy stuff," he said.

Heavy stuff? Her breathing stopped, then sped up, then stopped again. *Who on earth was entitled to such words?*

Who on earth? She felt, in every way it was possible to feel it, astonished that she had slept with him.

She went out with him again, but this time she greeted him at his own door, with a stiff smile and a handshake, like a woman willing to settle out of court. "So casual," he said, standing in the doorway. "I don't know. You East Coast city slickers."

"We got hard hearts," she said with an accent that wasn't really any particular accent at all. She wasn't good at accents.

When they slept together again, she tried not to make too much of it. Once more they watched *Holocaust Survivors*, a different tape, out of sequence, the camera still searching hard for something natural to gaze upon, embarrassed, like a bloodshot eye weary and afraid of people and what they do. *They set fire to the bodies and to the barracks*, said a voice. *The pyres burned for many days.*

Waves lapped. Rain beaded on a bulrush. In the bathroom she ran the tap water so he couldn't hear as she sat, ill, staring at her legs, her mother's legs. When had she gotten her mother's legs? When she crept back to his bed, he was sleeping like a boy, the way men did.

In the morning she got up early and went to the closest thing there was to a deli and returned triumphantly with bagels and lox. Outside, the town had been museum dead, but the sky was lemony with sun, and elongations of light, ovals of brightened blue, now dappled Pinky's covers. She laid the breakfast out in them, and he rolled over and kissed her, his face waxy with sleep. He pointed at the lox. "You like that sort of stuff?"

"Yup." Her mouth was already full with it, the cool, slimy pink. "Eat it all the time."

He sighed and sank back into his pillow. "After breakfast I'll teach you some Yiddish words."

"I already know some Yiddish words. I'm from New York. Here, eat some of this."

"I'll teach you *tush* and *shmuck*." Pinky yawned, then grinned. "And *shiksa*."

"All the things a nice Jewish boy practices on before he marries a nice Jewish girl. I know those."

"What's wrong with you?"

She refused to look at him. "I don't know."

"*I* know," said Pinky, and he stood up on the bed, like a child about to bounce, toweringly naked, priapic. She could barely look. Oh, for a beaded bulrush. A train disappearing into a tunnel. "You're falling in love with me!" he exclaimed, gazing merrily down. She still had her coat on, and had stopped chewing. She stared, disbelievingly, up at him. Sometimes she thought she was just trying to have fun in life, and other times she realized she must be terribly confused. She narrowed her eyes. Then she opened her mouth wide so that he could see the train wreck of chewed-up bagel and lox.

"I like that," said Pinky. "You're onto something there."

Her poems, as she stated in letters to friends in New York, were not going well; she had put them on the back burner, and they had fallen behind the stove. She had met this guy. Something had happened to the two of them in a cave, she wasn't sure what. She had to get out of here. She was giving her final reading to the library patrons and matrons in less than three weeks, and that would pretty much be it. *I hope you are not wearing those new, puffy evening dresses I see in magazines. They make everyone look like sticky buns. It is cold. Love, Odette.*

Laird was curious. He kept turning his head sideways during the sit-ups. "So you and Pinky hitting it off?"

"Who knows?" said Odette.

"Well, I mean, everyone's had their difficulties in life; his I'm only a little aware of. I thought you'd find him interesting."

"Sure, anthropologically."

"You think he's a dork."

"Laird, we're in our forties here. You can't use words like *dork* anymore." The sit-ups were getting harder. "He's not a dork. He's a doofus. Maybe. Maybe a *doink*."

"You're a hard woman," said Laird.

"Oh, I'm not," pleaded Odette, collapsing on the rubber mat. "Really I'm not."

At night he began to hold her in a way that stirred her deeply. He slept with one hand against the small of her back, the other capped against her head, as if to protect her from bad thoughts. Or, perhaps, thoughts at all. How quickly bodies came to love each other, promise themselves to each other always, without asking permission. From the mind! If only she could give up her mind, let her heart swell, inflamed, her brain stepping out for whole days, whole seasons, her work shrinking to limericks. She would open her mouth before the library fellowship people, and out would come: *There once was a woman from . . .* Someone would rush to a phone booth and call the police.

But perhaps you *could* live only from the neck down. Perhaps you *could* live with the clothes you were taking off all piled on top of your head, in front of your face, not just a sweater with a too-small neck but everything caught there – pants, shoes, and socks – a crazed tangle on your shoulders, in lieu of a head, while your body, stark naked, prepared to live the rest of its life in the sticks, the boonies, the fly-over, the rain. Perhaps you could. For when she slept against him like that, all the rest of the world collapsed into a suitcase under the bed. It was the end of desire, this having. Oh, here oh here she was. He would wrap himself around her, take her head like an infant's into his hand and breathe things to her, her throat her chest, in his beginning to sleep. *Go to sleep, go to sleep with me.*

In the morning she warmed her arms over the blue zinnias of the gas jets and heated water for coffee and eggs. Over the newspaper, she pretended she and Pinky were Beatrice and Benedick, or Nick and Nora Charles, which is what she always pretended in a love affair, at least for a few days, until the evidence overwhelmed her.

"Why are you always talking with your hands?" asked Pinky. "You think you're Jewish?"

She glared at him. "You know, that's what I hate about this part of the country," she replied. "Everyone's so repressed. If you use your body in the least way while you're talking, people think you're trying out for a Broadway show."

"Kiss me," he said, and he closed his eyes.

On a weekday Pinky would be off to his office, to work on another farm bankruptcy or a case of animal abuse. "My clients," he said wearily. "You would never want to go out to eat with them. They come into my office reeking of cowshit, they lean back in the chair, set their belly out like that, then tell you about how some Humane Society bastard gave them a summons because their goat had worms." Across his face there breathed a sigh of tragedy. "It's a sad thing not to have clients you can go out to eat with." He shook his head. "It's a sad thing, a goat with worms."

There was something nice about Pinky, but that something was not Nick Charles. Pinky was more like a grave and serious brother of Nick's, named Chuck. Chuck Charles. When you had parents who would give you a name like that, there was nothing funny anymore.

"What do you write poems about?" he asked her once in the middle of the night.

"Whores," she said.

"Whores," he repeated, nodding in the dark.

She gave him books of poetry: Wordsworth, Whitman, all the *W*'s. When she'd ask him how he liked them, he would say, "Fine. I'm on page . . ." and then he would tell her what page he was on and how many pages he'd accomplished that day. "The Wadsworth is a little too literaturey for me."

"Wordsworth," she corrected. They were in his kitchen, drinking juice.

"Wordsworth. Isn't there a poet named Wadsworth?"

"No. You're probably thinking of Longfellow. That was his middle name."

"Longfellow. Now who's he again?"

"How about *Leaves of Grass*? What did you think of the poems in there?"

"OK. I'm on page fifty," he said. Then he showed her his gun, which he kept in his kitchen in a leather case, like a trombone. He kept a rifle, he said, in the basement.

Odette frowned. "You hunt?"

"Sure. Jews aren't supposed to hunt, I know. But in this part of the country it's best to have a gun." He smiled. "*Bavarians*, you know. Here, try it out. Let me see how you look with a gun."

"I'm afraid of guns."

"Nothing to be afraid of. Just heft it and look down the top of the barrel and line up the sights."

She sighed, lifted the gun, pressed the butt hard against her right shoulder, and aimed it at the kitchen counter. "Now, see the notch in the metal sticking up in the middle of your barrel?" Pinky was saying. "You have to get the bead in the middle of the notch."

She closed her left eye. "I can feel the urge coming on to blow away that cutting board," she said.

"Gun's not loaded. Probably not till spring. Turkey season. Though I've got tags for deer."

"You hunt turkeys?" She put the gun down. It was heavy.

"You eat turkey, don't you?"

"The turkeys I eat are raised on farms. They're different. They've signed on the dotted line." She paused and sighed again. "What do you do, go into a field and fire away?"

"Kind of. You try to catch them midflight. You know, I should take you deer hunting. It's the last two days, this weekend, and I've got tags. Have you ever been?"

"*Pulease*," she said.

It was cold in the woods. She blew breath clouds, then rings of cigarette smoke, into the dead ferns. "It's nice out here. You don't suppose we could just watch nature instead of shoot it."

"Without hunting, the deer would starve," said Pinky.

"So maybe we could just cook for them." They had brought along a bottle of Jim Beam, and she twisted it open and took a swig. "Have you ever been married?"

"Once," said Pinky. "God, what, twenty years ago." He quickly shouldered his rifle, thinking he heard something, but no.

"Oh," she said. "I wasn't going to ask, but then you never said anything about it, so I thought I'd ask."

"How about you?"

"Not me," said Odette. She had a poem about marriage. It began, *Marriage is the death you want to die*, and in front of audiences she never read it with much conviction. Usually she swung her foot back and forth through the whole thing.

She looked down at her chest. "I don't think orange is anyone's most flattering color," she said. They were wearing blaze-orange hats and vests. "I think we look like things placed in the middle of the road to make the cars go around."

"Shhhh," said Pinky.

She took another swig of Jim Beam. She had worn the wrong kind of boots – gray, suede, over the knees, with three-inch heels – and now she studied them with interest. One of the heels was loose, and mud was drying on the toes. "Tell me again," she whispered to Pinky, "what makes us think a deer will cross our path?"

"There's a doe bed not far from here," whispered Pinky. "It attracts bucks."

"Bucks, doe – thank God everything boils down to money, I always say."

"During mating season the doe constructs a bed for herself, and then she urinates all around the outside of it. That's how she gets her mate."

"So *that's* it," murmured Odette. "I was always peeing *in* the bed."

Pinky's gun suddenly fired into the trees, and the noise filled the woods like a war, spilling to the ground the yellowing needles of a larch.

"Ahhhhhh!" Odette screamed. "What is going on?" Guns, she was reminded then, were not for girls. They were for boys. They were invented by boys. They were invented by boys who had never gotten over their disappointment that accompanying their own orgasm there wasn't a big *boom* sound. "What the hell are you doing?"

"Damn!" shouted Pinky. "I missed!" He stood up and went crashing through the underbrush.

"Oh, my God!" cried Odette, and she stumbled after him, snapping the same twigs underfoot, ducking the same barbed wire. "Where are we going?"

"I've only wounded the deer," Pinky called over his shoulder. "I've got to kill it."

"Do you have to?"

"Keep your voice down," said Pinky.

"Fuck you," said Odette. "I'll wait for you back where we were," but there was a sudden darting from a bush behind her, and the bleeding deer leaped out, in a mournful gallop, its hip a crimson gash. Pinky raised his gun and fired, catching the deer in the neck. The air shimmered in the echo, and the leaves fell from a horse chestnut. The deer's legs buckled, and when it tipped over, dead in some berry bushes, its eyes never blinked but stayed lidless and deep, black as outer space.

"I'll leave the entrails for the hawks," Pinky said to Odette, but she was not there.

* * *

Oh, the ladies come down from the Pepsi Hotel
Their home has no other name
than the sign that was placed
like a big cola bell: Pepsi-Cola Have a Pepsi Hotel.

Only a few of Odette's poems about whores rhymed – the ones she'd written recently – but perhaps the library crowd would like those best, the anticipation of it, knowing what the next word would be *like* though not what it would *be*; stanza after stanza, it would be a combination of comfort and surprise an audience might appreciate.

The local library association had set up a lectern near the windows of the reference room and had arranged chairs in rows for about eighty people. The room was chilly and alarmingly full. When Odette read she tried to look out past the faces, toward the atlases and the biographical dictionaries. She tugged on the cowl of her sweater and pulled it up over her chin between poems. She tried to pretend people's heads were all little ears of corn, something a dance instructor had once told her ballet class to do when she was seven and they had had to dance before the parents.

They come down to the truckers
or the truckers go up
to the rooms with the curtains pell-mell.
They truck down for the fuckers
or else they fuck up
in the Pepsi Have a Pepsi Hotel.

There was silence. A door creaked open then shut. Odette looked up and saw Pinky in the back, tiptoeing over to a chair to sit. She had not seen or spoken to him in a week. Two elderly women in the front turned around to stare.

Oh, honey, they sigh; oh, honey, they say,
there are small things to give and to sell,
and Heaven's among us
so work can be play at the . . .

There were other stanzas, too many, and she sped through them. She took a sip of water and read a poem called "Sleeping Wrong." *She slept wrong on her back last night*, it began, *and so she holds her head this way, mad with loneliness, madder still with talk.* She then read another long one, titled "Girl Gets Diphtheria, Loses Looks." She looked up and out. The audience was squinting back at her, their blood sugar levels low from early suppers, their interest redirected now and then toward her shoes, which were pointy and beige. "I'll close," she said loudly into the mike, "with a poem called 'Le Cirque in the Rain.'"

> *This is not about a french monkey circus*
> *discouraged by weather.*
> *This is about the restaurant*
> *you pull up to in a cab,*
> *your life stopping there and badly,*
> *like a dog's song,*
> *your heart put in funny.*

It told the story of a Manhattan call girl worrying a crisis of faith. *What is a halo but a handsome accident / of light and orbiting dust. What is a heart / but a . . .* She looked out at the two elderly women sitting polite and half attentive, unfazed, in the front row. One of them had gotten out some knitting. Odette looked back at her page. *Chimp in the chest*, she had written in an earlier draft, and that was what she said now.

Afterward a small reception was held out by the card catalogs. There were little cubes of pepper cheese, like dice, placed upon a table. There was a checkerboard of crackers, dark and light, a roulette of cold cuts. "It's a goddamn casino." She turned and spoke to Pinky, who had come up and put his arm around her.

"I've missed you," he said. "I've been eating venison and thinking of you."

"Yes, well, thank you for coming, anyway."

"I thought you read very well," he said. "Not all of it I understood, I have to admit. Some of your stuff is a little too literaturey for me."

"Really," said Odette.

People shook her hand. They looked at her quizzically, came at her with assumptions, presumptions, what they believed was intimate knowledge of her. She felt unarmed, by comparison; disadvantaged. She lit up a cigarette.

"Do you really feel that way about men?" asked a man with a skeptical mouth.

"Do you really feel that way about women?" asked someone else.

"Your voice," said a young student. "It's like – who's that actress?"

"Mercedes McCambridge," said her friend.

"No, not her. Oh, I forget."

Several elderly couples had put on their coats and hats, but they came up to Odette to shake her hand. "You were wonderful, dear," said one of the women, gazing into Odette's nose.

"Yes," said the other, studying her own botched knitting – a scarf with an undulating edge.

"We come to these every year," said a man standing next to her. He had been searching for something to say and had come up with this.

"Well, thank you for coming this year as well," said Odette, stupidly, and dragged on her cigarette.

Kay Stevens, the woman in charge of the fellowship readings, came up and kissed her on the cheek, the sweet vanilla wax of her lipstick sticking like candy. "A big success," she said quickly, and then frowned and hurried off.

"Can I buy you a drink somewhere?" asked Pinky. He was still standing beside her, and she turned to look at him gratefully.

"Oy," she said. "Please."

Pinky drove them out past the county line to Humphrey Bogart's. He toasted her, flicked a sparkly speck of something from her cheek, looked into her eyes, and said, "Congratulations." He grew drunk, pulled his chair close, and put his head on her shoulder. He listened to the music, chewed on his cocktail straw, tapped his feet.

"Any requests?" the bandleader rumbled into the mike.

"O, give us one of the songs of Zion," shouted Pinky.

"What was that?" The words popped and roared in the mike.

"Nothing," said Pinky.

"Maybe we should go," said Odette, reaching for Pinky's hand beneath the table.

"OK," he said. "All right."

He struck a match to a candle in the dark of his bedroom, and the fire of it lit the wall in a jittery paint. He came back to her and pressed close. "Why don't I go with you to New York?" he whispered. She was silent, and so he said, "No, I think you should stay here. I could take you cross-country skiing."

"I don't like cross-country skiing," she whispered back. "It reminds me of when you're little and you put on your father's slippers and shluff around the house like that."

"I could take you snowmobiling up by Sand Lake." There was another long silence. Pinky sighed. "No, you won't. I can see you phoning your friends back East to tell them you'd decided to stay and them shrieking, 'You did *what*?' "

"You know us East Coasters," she said desperately. "We just come into a place, rape and pillage."

"You know," said Pinky, "I think you are probably the smartest person I have ever known."

She stopped breathing. "You don't get out much, do you?"

He rolled back and stared at the shadowed ceiling, its dimples and blotches. "When I was in high school, I was a bad student. I had to take special classes in this house behind the school. It was called The House."

She rubbed his leg gently with her foot. "Are you trying to make me cry?"

He took her hand, brought it out from beneath the covers, up to his mouth, and kissed it. "Everything's a joke with you," he said.

"Nothing's a joke with me. It just all comes out like one."

* * *

They spent one last night together. At his house, late, with all the lights off, they watched another cassette of *Holocaust Survivors*. It was about a boy forced to sing for the Nazis, over and over. Because he could sing, he was the last to be shot in the head, and when they shot him they missed the center of his brain. He was found alive. "I must think of happy things," he said now, old and staring off. "It may not be what others do, but it is what I must do." *He had a beautiful voice*, said a woman, another survivor. *It was beautiful like a bird that was also a god with flutes.*

"Heavy," murmured Pinky, when it was over. He pressed the remote control and turned away in the darkness, toward the wall, in a curve of covers. Odette pulled herself close, placed her hands around to the front of him, palms over the slight mounds of his breasts, her fingers deep in the light tangle of hair.

"Are you OK?" she asked.

He twisted toward her and kissed her, and in the dark he seemed to her aged and sad. He placed one of her fingers to his face. "You never asked about this." He guided her finger along his chin and cheek, letting it dead-end, like the scar, in his mustache.

"I try not to ask too many things. Once I start I can't stop."

"You want to know?"

"All right."

"I was in high school. Some guy called me a Jew, and I went after him. But I was clumsy and fat. He broke a bottle and dragged it across my face. I went home and my grandmother nearly fainted. Funny thing was, I had no idea that I *was* Jewish. My grandmother waited until the next day to tell me."

"Really," said Odette.

"You have to understand midwestern Jews: They're afraid of being found out. They're afraid of being discovered." He breathed steadily, in and out, and the window shade flapped a little from being over the radiator. "As you probably know already, my parents were killed in the camps."

Odette did not say anything, and then she said, "Yes.

I know." And at the moment she said it, she realized she did know, somehow had known it all along, though the fact of it had stayed beneath the surface, gilled and swimming like a fish, and now had burst up, gasping, with its mouth wide.

"Are you really leaving on Friday?" he asked.

"What?"

"Friday. Are you?"

"I'm sorry, I just didn't hear what you said. There's wind outside or something."

"I asked you if you were really leaving on Friday."

"Oh," she said. She pressed her face hard into his neck. "Why don't you come with me?"

He laughed wearily. "Sure," he said. "All right," knowing better than she at that moment the strange winding line between charity and irony, between shoplifting and love.

During that last day she thought of nothing but him. She packed and cleaned out her little apartment, but she had done this so often now in her life, it didn't mean anything, not in the pit of her, not anything she might have wanted it to mean.

She should stay.

She should stay here with him, unorphan him with love's unorphaning, live wise and simple in a world monstrous enough for years of whores and death, and poems of whores and death, so monstrous how could one live in it at all? One had to build shelters. One had to make pockets and live inside them. She should live where there were trees. She should live where there were birds. No bird, no tree had ever made her unhappy.

But it would be like going to heaven and not finding any of your friends there. Her life would go all beatific and empty in the eyes. And if he came to New York, well, it would bewilder him. He had never been before, and no doubt he'd spend all his time staring up at the skyscrapers and exclaiming, "Gosh, look how tall those suckers are!" He would slosh through the vagrant urine, shoelaces untied. He would walk through the dog shit awaiting him like mines. He would read the menus in the windows of restaurants and whistle at the prices. He would stare at a sidewalk drunk, prone and spread-eagled and fumbling at the crotch, and he would say, not unkindly, "That guy's really got his act together." He would look at the women.

And her restlessness would ripple, double, a flavor of something cold. She would turn from him in bed, her hands under the pillow, the digital clock peeling back the old skins of numbers. She would sigh a little for the passage of time, the endless corridor of it, how its walls washed by you on either side – darkly, fast, and ever, ever.

"What do you do, you stay overnight on the road somewhere?" he said, standing next to her car in the cold. It was Friday morning and spitting snow. He had come over and helped her load up the car.

"I drive until dark, then I check into a motel room and read until I fall asleep. Then I get up at six and drive some more."

"So, like, what are you bringing with you to read?" he asked. He seemed unhappy.

She had a *Vogue* magazine and *The Portable Jung*. "Something by Jung," she said.

"Jung?" he asked. His face went blank.

"Yeah," she sighed, not wanting to explain. "A book he wrote called *The Portable Jung*." She added, "He's a psychologist."

Pinky looked her deeply in the eyes. "I know," he said.

"You do?" She was a little surprised.

"Yeah. You should read his autobiography. It has a very interesting title."

She smiled. "Who *are* you? His autobiography? Really?"

"Yeah," said Pinky slowly. "It's called *Jung at Heart*."

She laughed loud, to please him. Then she looked at his face, to fix him like this in her mind. He was wearing a black shirt, a black sweater, black pants. He was smiling. "You look like Zorro today," she said, strangely moved. The spidery veins at his temples seemed like things under water, tentacular and drowned. She kissed him, long and at the rim of his ear, feeling in the rolls and spaces of her brain a winding, winding line. She got into the car. Though she hadn't even started up the engine, her departure had already happened, without her, ahead of her, so that what she now felt was the taunt of being left behind, of having to repeat, to imitate, of having to do it again, and now, and again.

"All this wandering that you do," he said, leaning in the window, his face white as a cream cheese, his scar the carved zigzag of a snowmobile across a winter lake. Wind blew handsomely through his hair. "How will anyone ever get close to you?"

"I don't know," she said. She shook his hand through the window and then put on her gloves.

And she thought about this all across Indiana, beneath the Easter hat of sunset that lit the motel roof in Sandusky, through the dawn of Pennsylvania, into which she soared like a birth – like someone practicing to be born. There were things she'd forget: a nightgown stuck on a hook behind the bathroom door, earrings on the motel nightstand. And all love that had overtaken her would have to be a memory, a truck on the interstate roaring up from the left, a thing she must let pass.

She would park the car right off Delancey Street; there would be a spot across the street from the hotel with the Pepsi sign and HOTEL in lights beneath. All night, sirens would keen, and traffic would whoosh and grind its way down Houston, down Canal, toward the Holland Tunnel – a bent sign to which aimed straight at her window. She would get up in the morning and go for sundries; at the corner bodega the clerk would mispress the numbers on the register, and the toothpaste would ring up at $2,000. "Two thousand dollars!" the clerk would howl, standing back and looking at Odette. "Get a *real* toothpaste!" From a long distance, and at night, a man would phone to say, doubtfully, "I should come visit on Valentine's," history of all kinds, incongruous and mangling itself, eating its own lips.

If she had spurned gifts from fate or God or some earnest

substitute, she would never feel it in that way. She felt like someone of whom she was fond, an old and future friend of herself, still unspent and up ahead somewhere, like a light that moves.

1989

JOY

IT WAS A FALL, Jane knew, when little things were being taken away. Fish washed ashore, and no one ate a clam to save their lives. Oystermen netted in the ocean beds, and the oysters were brought up dead. Black as rot and no one knew why. People far from either coast shuddered to think, saw the seas and then the whole planet rise in an angry, inky wave of chowder the size of a bowl. It was as far as their imaginations would allow, and it was too far. Did this have to do with them? They flicked off their radios, left dishes in the sink, and went out. Or they tuned to a station with songs. It was a season for losing anything small, living trinkets you'd thought were yours – a bracelet of mother-of-pearl, a lover's gift, unhinged and slipping off into the night like something yearning and tired. The rain stopped dry. The ground crumbled to lumps, and animals maddened a little with thirst. Squirrels, smelling water on the road, gnawed through the hoses in cars and later died on the shoulders. "Like so many heads," said a radio announcer, who then played a song.

Jane's cat itself had fleas, just the barest hint, and she was going to get rid of them, take the cat to the groomer's for the bath–dip–comb-out. There were rumors about fleas. They could feast on you five or six times a day and never let go. You could wake up in a night sweat with a rash and your saliva gluey and white, in ligaments as you tried to speak. You could look out at your life and no longer recognize it.

The groomer was at a vet's on the west side of town. It was where rich people took their cats, and it made Jane feel she was giving her cat the best possible care. This was a cat who slept on the pillow next to her at night. This was a cat who came running – happy to see her! – when she drove up in front of the house.

This particular morning she had to bring her cat in before eight. The dogs came in at eight-o-five, and the vet liked the cats to get there earlier, so there would be no commotion.

Jane's cat actually liked dogs, was curious about them, didn't mind at all observing them from the safety of someone's arms. So Jane didn't worry too much about the eight o'clock rule, and if she got there late, because of traffic or a delayed start on the coffee she needed two cups of simply to get dressed in the morning, no one seemed to mind. They only commented on how well-behaved her cat was.

It usually took fifteen minutes to get to the west side, such was the sprawl of the town, and Jane played the radio loudly and sang along: "I've forgotten more than she'll ever know about you." At red lights she turned to reassure the cat, who lay chagrined and shedding in the passenger's seat. Ahead of them a station wagon moved slowly, and Jane noticed in the back of it a little girl waving and making faces out the rear window. Jane waved and made faces back, sticking out her tongue when the little girl did, pulling strands of hair into her face, and winking dramatically first on one side and then the other. After several blocks, Jane noticed, however, that the little girl was not really looking at *her* but just generally at the traffic. Jane re-collected her face, pulled in her tongue, straightened her hair. But the girl's father, at the wheel, had already spied Jane in his rearview mirror, and was staring, appalled. He slowed down to get a closer look, then picked up speed to get away.

Jane got in the other lane and switched stations on the radio, found a song she liked, something wistful but with a beat. She loved to sing. At home she had the speakers hooked up in the kitchen and would stand at the sink with a hollow-handled sponge filled with dish detergent and sing and wash, sing and rinse. She sang "If the Phone Don't Ring, I Know It's You" and "What Love Is to a Dove." She blasted her way through "Jump Start My Heart," humming on the verses she didn't know. She liked all kinds of music. When she was a teenager she had believed that what the Muzak station played on the radio was "classical music," and to this day her tastes were generous and unjudging – she just liked to get into the song. Most of the time she tried not to worry about whether people might hear her, though an embarrassing thing had happened recently when her landlord had walked into the house, thinking she wasn't home, and caught her sing-speaking in an English accent. "Excuse me," said the landlord. "I'm sorry."

"Oh," she said in reply. "I was just practicing for the—Are you here to check the fuse box?"

"Yes," said the landlord, wondering who it was these days he was renting his houses out to.

Jane had once, briefly, lived in western Oregon but had returned to the Midwest when she and her boyfriend out there had broken up. He was a German man who made rocking horses and jungle gyms and who had been, like her, new to the community. His English was at times halting and full of misheard vernacular, things like "get town" and "to each a zone." One time, when she'd gotten all dressed up to go to dinner, he told her she looked "hunky-dorky." He liked to live dangerously, always driving around town with his gas tank on E. "Pick a lane and do stay in it," he yelled at other drivers. He made the worst coffee Jane had ever tasted, muddy and burned, but she drank it, and stayed long hours in his bed on Sundays. But after a while he took to going out without her, not coming home until two a.m. She started calling him late at night, letting the phone ring, then driving around town looking for his car, which she usually found in front of a tavern somewhere. It had not been like her to do things like this, but knowing that the town was small enough for her to do it, she had found it hard to resist. Once she had gotten into the car and started it up, it was as if she had crashed through a wall, gone from one room with rules into another room with no rules. When she found his car, she would go into the tavern, and if she discovered him at the bar with his arm flung loosely around some other woman, she would tap him on the shoulder and say, "Who's the go-go girl?" Then she'd pour beer onto his legs. She was no longer herself. She had become someone else, a wild West woman, bursting into saloons, the swinging doors flipping behind her. Soon, she thought, bartenders might fear her. Soon they might shout out warnings, like sailors facing a storm: *Here she comes!* And so, after a while, she left Oregon and came back here alone. She rented a house, got a job first at Karen's Stout Shoppe, which sold dresses to overweight women, then later at the cheese store in the Marshall Field's mall.

For a short time she mourned him, believing he had anchored her, had kept her from floating off into No Man's Land, that land of midnight cries and pets with too many little toys, but now she rarely thought of him. She knew there were only small joys in life – the big ones were too complicated to be joys when you got all through – and once you realized that, it took a lot of the pressure off. You could put the pressure aside, like a child's game, its box ripped to flaps at the corners. You could stick it in some old closet and forget about it.

Jane pulled into the vet's parking lot at ten after eight. She lifted the cat up into her arms, pushed the car door shut with one hip, and went inside. Although the air of the place was slightly sour – humid with animal fear, tense with medicine, muffled howls drifting in from the back – the waiting room felt pleasant to her. Hopeful with ficus trees. There were newsmagazines on the tables, and ashtrays made from Italian glass. There were matted watercolors on the wall and a silk-screened sign in a white metal frame saying, ANIMALS MUST BE LEASHED OR HELD. Jane walked up to the large semicircular counter ahead of her and placed the cat down on it. Behind her was a man seated with a leashed and lethargic golden Labrador, and Jane's cat peered around back at it, shivering a little. On the other side of the waiting room was a large poodle with the fierce look of a Doberman. His ears were long and floppy, uncut, and his owner, a young woman in her twenties, kept saying, "Come here, Rex. Lie down, baby."

"Can I help you?" asked the woman behind the counter. She had been staring at a computer screen, tapping at a keyboard and bringing up fiery columns of numbers and dates.

"I'm here to bring my cat in for grooming," said Jane. "My last name is Konwicki."

The woman behind the counter smiled and nodded. She tapped something into the computer. "And the cat's name?" she asked.

"Fluffers," said Jane. She had once thought she would name the cat Joseph, but then she had changed her mind.

The woman rolled her chair away from the computer screen. She picked up a large silver microphone and spoke into it. "Fluffers Konwicki here to be groomed." She set the microphone back down. "The groomer will be out in a minute," she said to Jane. "You can wait over there."

Jane pulled the cat to her chest and went and sat in a fake leather director's chair opposite Rex the poodle. A woman and her two children came in through the front entrance wheeling a baby carriage. The woman held open the door and the little boy and girl pushed the carriage through, all the while peering in and squeaking concerned inquiries and affectionate names. "Gooby, are you OK?" asked the boy. "Gooby knows he's at the doctor's, Mom."

"You kids wait right here," said the mom, and she approached the counter with a weary smile. She brushed her bangs off her head, then placed her hands flat out on the countertop and stared at them momentarily, as if this had been the first opportunity all morning to observe them empty. "We're bringing a cat in for surgery," she said, looking back up. "The name is Miller."

"Miller," said the woman behind the counter. She tapped something into the computer. She shook her head, then got up and looked at a clipboard near the cash register. "Miller, Miller, Miller," she said absently. "Miller. All righty! Here we are!" She smiled at Mrs. Miller. The world was again the well-oiled machine she counted on it to be: All things could eventually be found in it. "You want to wheel the cat back around here?"

Mrs. Miller turned toward her children. "Kids? Wanna bring the kitty back around here?" The little boy and girl pushed the baby carriage forward, their steps solemn and processional. The woman behind the counter stepped out from her usual post and held the door to the back part, the examination room, open. "Wheel the cat right in there," she said. She wore white shoes. You could see that now.

They were all in there for no more than a minute before

they returned, the children dragging the empty baby carriage behind them and Mrs. Miller sighing and smiling and thanking the woman in the white shoes, who told her to call sometime after three this afternoon. The anesthesia would be worn off by then, and the doctor would know better what to tell them.

"Thanks again," said Mrs. Miller. "Kids?"

"Mom, look," said the little girl. She had wandered over to where Jane was sitting and had begun to pet Jane's cat, occasionally looking up for permission to continue. "Mom, see – this lady has a cat, too." She called to her mother, but it was her brother who came up and stood beside her. The two of them stuck their tiny, star-like hands deep into the cat's fur and squished them around there.

"You like that?" said Jane to her cat, and the cat looked up at her as if he really couldn't decide. She made Fluffers' head nod a bit, as if he were answering the question.

"What is his name?" asked the little girl. Her hand had found the scruff of the cat's neck and was kneading it. The cat stretched his throat up in enjoyment.

"Fluffers," said Jane.

The girl's voice went up an octave into cat range. "Hi, Fluffers," she half sang, half squeaked. "How are you feeling today, Fluffers?"

"Is he sick?" asked the boy.

"Oh, no," said Jane. "He just comes here for a special kind of bath."

"You getting a bath, Fluffers?" cooed the girl, looking directly into the cat's eyes.

"Our cat is having an operation," said the boy.

"That's too bad," said Jane.

The boy looked at her crossly. "No, it's not," he said. "It's a good thing. Then he'll be all better."

"Well, yes, that's true," said Jane.

"Fluffers licked my finger," said the girl.

Their mother now appeared behind them, placing a palm on each of their heads. "Time to go, kiddos," she said. "Beautiful cat," she said to Jane.

* * *

The cheese shop Jane worked at, in the new mall outside of town, was called Swedish Isle, and she had recently been promoted to assistant manager. There were always just two of them in the shop, Jane and an older woman named Heffie, who minded the register while Jane stood out in front with the cheese samples, usually spreads and dips placed in small amounts on crackers. Once the manager had come by and told her that Heffie should be doing the samples and Jane should be minding the register and doing the price sheets, but the store manager was also the assistant district manager for the chain and was too busy to come by all that often. So most of the time Jane simply continued doing the samples herself. She liked the customer contact. "Care to try our chive-dill today?" she would ask brightly. She felt like Molly Malone, only friendlier and no cockles or mussels; no real seafood for miles. This was the deep Midwest. Meat sections in the grocery stores read: BEEF, PORK, and FISH STICKS.

"Free?" people would ask and pick up a cracker or a bread square from her plastic tray.

"Sure is." She would smile and watch their faces as they chewed. If it was a man she thought was handsome, she'd say, "No. A million dollars," and then giggle in the smallest, happiest way. Sometimes the beggars – lost old hippies and mall musicians – would come in and line up, and she would feed them all, like Dorothy Day in a soup kitchen. She had read a magazine article once about Dorothy Day.

"A little late, aren't you?" said Heffie today. She was tugging at the front strap of her bra and appeared generally disgruntled. Her hair was thinning at the front, and she had it clipped to the top with barrettes she was too old for. "Had to open up the register myself. It'd be curtains if the manager'd come by. Lucky I had keys."

"I'm sorry," said Jane. "I had to take my cat into the vet's this morning, way over on the west side. Any customers?" Jane gave Heffie an anxious look. It said "Please forgive me." It also said "What is your problem?" and "*Have a nice day.*" Pleasantness was the machismo of the Midwest. There was something athletic about it. You flexed your face into a smile and let it hover there like the dare of a cat.

"No, no customers," said Heffie, "but you never can tell."

"Well, thanks for opening up," said Jane.

Heffie shrugged. "You doing the samples today?"

"Thought I would, yes," said Jane, flipping through some papers attached to a clipboard. "Unless *you* wanted to." She said this with just a hint of good-natured accusation and good-natured insincerity. Heffie wasn't that interested in doing the samples, and Jane was glad. It was just that Heffie didn't much like doing anything, and whatever Jane did apparently seemed to Heffie like more fun, and easier, so sometimes the older woman complained a little by means of a shrug or a sigh.

"Nah, that's OK," said Heffie. "I'll do them some other time." She slid open the glass door to the refrigerated deli case and grabbed a lone cheese curd, the squiggly shape and bright marigold color of it like a piece from a children's game. She popped it into her mouth. "You ever been surfing?" she asked Jane.

"Surfing?" Jane repeated incredulously. She would never figure out how Heffie came up with the questions she did.

"Yeah. Surfing. You know – some people have done it. The fiberglass board that you stand on in the water and then a wave comes along?" Heffie's face was a snowy moon of things never done.

Jane looked away. "Once a couple of summers ago I went water-skiing on a lake," she said. "In Oregon." Her lover, the daredevil toymaker, had liked to do things like that. "Khem on, Jane," he had said to her. "You only live at once." Which seemed to her all the more reason to be careful, to take it easy, to have an ordinary life. She didn't like to do things where the trick was to not die.

"Water-skiing, poohf," said Heffie. "That's nothing like surfing. There's not the waves, the *risk*." Jane looked up from her clipboard and watched as Heffie waddled away, the tops of her feet swelling out over the straps of her shoes like dough. Heffie walked over to the Swiss nut rolls, put a fist down lightly on top, and gazed off.

* * *

"Care to try some of our horseradish cheddar today?" Jane smiled and held out the tray. She had placed little teaspoonfuls of spread on some sickly-looking rice crackers, and now she held them out to people like a caterer with the hors d'oeuvres at a fancy party. *Horses' douvers*, her mother used to call them, and for years Jane had had her own idea about what a douver was. "Care to try a free sample of our horseradish cheddar spread, on special today?" At least it wasn't spraying perfume at people. Last month she had met the girl who did that next door at Marshall Field's. The girl, who was from Florida originally, said to her, "Sometimes you *aim* for the eyes. It's not always an accident." Malls, Jane knew, were full of salesgirls with stories. Broken hearts, boyfriends in jail. Once last week two ten-year-old girls, one pudgy, one thin, had come up to Jane, selling chocolate bars. They looked at her as if she were just a taller version of themselves, someone they might turn into when they grew up. "Will you buy a chocolate bar?" they asked her, staring at her samples. Jane offered them a cracker with a big clump of spread, but they politely declined.

"Well, what kind of chocolate bars are you selling?"

"Almond or crisp." The pudgy girl, wearing a purple sweatshirt and lavender corduroys, clutched a worn-out paper bag to her chest.

"Is this for the Girl Scouts?" asked Jane.

The girls looked at each other. "No, it's for my brother," said the pudgy one. Her friend slapped her on the arm.

"It's for your brother's *team*," the friend hissed.

"Yeah," said the girl, and Jane bought a crispy bar and talked them into a sample after all. Which they took with a slight grimace. "D'you got a husband that drives a truck?" asked the one in purple.

"Yeah," said the other. *"Do you?"* And when Jane shook her head, they frowned and went away.

A man in a blue sweater like one her father used to wear stopped and gently plucked a cracker from her tray. "How much?" he asked, and she was about to say, "A million dollars," when she heard someone down the mall corridor call her name.

"Jane Konwicki! How are you?" A woman about Jane's age, wearing a bright-red fall suit, strode up to her and kissed her on the cheek. The man in the blue sweater like her father's slipped away. Jane looked at the woman in the red suit and for a minute didn't know who she was. But the woman's animated features all stopped for a moment and fell into place, and Jane realized it was Bridey, a friend from over fifteen years ago, who used to sit next to her in high school chorus. It was curious how people, when they stood still and you just looked, never really changed that much. No matter how the fashions swirled about a girl, the adult she became, with different fashions swirling about her, still contained the same girl. All of Bridey's ages – the child, the old woman – were there on her face. It was like an open bird feeder where every year of her, the past and the future, had come to feed.

"Bridey, you look great. What have you been up to?" It seemed a ridiculous question to ask of someone you hadn't seen since high school, but there it was.

"Well, last year I fell madly in love," Bridey said with great pride. This clearly was on the top of her list, and her voice suggested it was a long list. "And we got married, and we moved back to town after roughing it on the South Side of Chicago since forever. It's great to be back here, I can tell you." Bridey helped herself to a cheddar sample and then another one. The cheese in her mouth stuck between her front teeth in a pasty, yellowish mortar, and when she swallowed and smiled back at Jane, well, again, there it was, like something unfortunate but necessary.

"You seem so . . . *happy*," said Jane. Heffie was shuffling around noisily in the shop behind her.

"Oh, I am. I keep running into people from school, and it's just so much fun. In fact, Jane, you should come with me this evening. You know what I'm going to do?"

"What?" Jane glanced back over her shoulder and saw Heffie testing the spreads in the deli case with her finger. She would stick her finger in deep and then lick it slowly like an ice cream.

"Oh," said Bridey in a hushed and worried tone. "Is that a customer or an employee?"

"Employee," said Jane.

"At any rate, I'm going to try out for Community Chorus," continued Bridey. "It's part of my new program. I'm learning German—"

"Learning German?" Jane interrupted.

"—taking a cooking class, and I'm going to get back into choral singing."

"You were always a good singer," said Jane. Bridey had often gotten solos.

"Ach! My voice has gone to pot, but I don't care. Why don't you come with me? We could audition together. The auditions aren't supposed to be that hard."

"Oh, I don't know," said Jane, though the thought of singing again in a chorus suddenly excited her. That huge sound flying out over an audience, like a migration of birds, like a million balloons! But the idea of an audition was terrifying. What if she didn't get in? How could she ever open her mouth again to sing, even all by herself at home? How would her own voice not mortify her on the way to work in the morning, when she listened to the radio. Everything would be ruined. Songs would stick in her throat like moths. She would listen to nothing but news, and when she got to work she would be quiet and sad.

"Listen," said Bridey, "I'm terrible. Truly."

"No, you're not. Let me hear you sing something," said Jane.

Bridey looked at her quizzically, took another horseradish cheddar sample, and chewed. "What do you mean? God, these are good."

"I mean just something little. I want to know what you mean by terrible. Cuz *I'm* terrible. Here. I'll get you started. *Row, row, row your boat, gently down the stream . . .*"

"*Merrily, merrily, merrily, merrily,*" continued Bridey rather plainly. Jane wondered whether she was holding back. "*Life is but a dream.*" Bridey looked at Jane a little unhappily. "See, I told you I was bad."

"You're much better than I am," said Jane.

"Where are you living now?" Bridey pulled at the red jacket of her suit and looked around the mall.

"Out on Neptune Avenue. Near where it runs into Oak. How about you?"

"We're out in Brickmire Apartments. They have a pool, which is what sold us on the place." Bridey pointed back toward Heffie and whispered, "Does she always go snacking through everything like that?" Bridey had lifted yet another rice cracker from Jane's tray.

"You don't want to know," said Jane.

"You're right. I don't," said Bridey, and she put the rice cracker back on Jane's tray.

After work Jane drove back to the west side to pick up her cat at the vet's. She had promised Bridey that she would meet her at the auditions, which were at seven-thirty at their old high school, but her gut buckled at the thought. She tried singing in her car – *Doe, a deer, a female deer* – but her voice sounded hollow and frightened. At a red light someone in the car next to hers saw her lips moving and shook his head.

By the time she got to the vet's, the parking lot was full of cars. In the waiting room people were collected messily around the front counter, waiting their turn. Two employees behind the counter were doing all the work, one young man at the cash register, and the woman in the white shoes at the microphone, who was saying, "Spotsy Wechsler, Spotsy Wechsler." She put the microphone down. "She'll be right up," she said to a man in a jean jacket a lot like the one Jane's brother had worn all the while they were growing up. "Next?" The woman looked out at the scatter of pet owners in front of her. "Can I help someone?" No one said anything.

"You can help me," said Jane finally, "but this man was here before me. And actually so was he." One of the men ahead of her twisted back to look, red-faced, and then turned front again and spoke very quietly to the woman in the white shoes.

"My name is Miller," said the man, sternly, secretively. He wore a suit, and his tie was loosened. "I'm here to pick up the cat my wife brought in this morning for surgery."

The woman blanched. "Yes," she said, and she didn't ask for a first name. "Gooby Miller," she said into the microphone. "Gooby Miller to the waiting room." The man had taken out his wallet, but the woman said, "No charge," and went over and tapped things into her computer for a very long minute. A young high school kid appeared from the back room, carrying a box in his arms. "The Miller cat?" he said in the doorway, and the man in the suit raised his hand. The boy brought the box over and placed it on the counter.

"I'd also like to speak with the veterinarian," said the man. The woman in the white shoes looked at him fearfully, but the boy said, "Yes, he's waiting for you. Come right this way," and led the man back into the examination room, the door to which blinked brightly open to let them in, then shut behind them like a fact. The box sat all alone on the countertop.

"Can I help you?" the woman asked Jane.

"Yes. I'm here to pick up my cat from the groomer. My name is Konwicki."

The woman reached for the microphone. "And the cat's name?"

"Fluffers," said Jane.

"Fluffers Konwicki to the waiting room." The woman put the microphone down. "The cat'll be up in a minute."

"Thanks," said Jane. She looked at the cardboard box at her elbow on the counter. The box said DOLE PINEAPPLE. She listened for scratching or movement of any kind, but there was none. "What's in the box?" she asked.

The woman made a face, guilty with comedy, exaggerated. She didn't know what sort of face to make. "Gooby Miller," she said. "A dead cat."

"Oh, dear," murmured Jane. She remembered the children she'd met earlier that day. "What happened?"

The woman shrugged. "Thyroid surgery. It just died on the table. Can I help you, sir?" Someone was now bringing out Rex the poodle, who went limping toward his owner with a cast on his front foot. It was all like a dream: Things you'd seen before, in daylight, were trotted out hours later in slightly different form.

After Rex was placed in a child's toy wagon and wheeled out of the vet's, the groomer appeared bearing Fluffers, who looked dazed and smelled of flea dip laced with lilac. "He was a very good cat," said the groomer, and Jane took Fluffers in her arms and almost peeped, "Thank God they didn't bring you out in a pineapple box." What she said instead was: "And now he's all handsome again."

"Found some fleas," said the groomer. "But not all that many."

Jane quickly paid the bill and left. Dusk was settling over the highway like a mood, and the traffic had put on lights. She carried her cat to the car and was fumbling with the door on the passenger's side when she heard squeals from the opposite end of the parking lot. "Fluffers! Fluffers!" They were a child's excited shouts. "Look, it's Fluffers!"

The boy and girl Jane had spoken to that morning suddenly leaped out of the station wagon they'd been waiting in across the lot. They slammed the back doors and dashed breathlessly over to Jane and her cat. They had on little coats and hats with earflaps. It had gotten cold.

"Oh, Fluffers, you smell so good – yum, yum, yum!" said the girl, and she pressed her face into Fluffers' perfumed haunches and kept it there, beginning to cry. Jane looked up and saw that what little light there was left in the sky was frighteningly spindly, like a horse's legs that must somehow still hold up the horse. She freed one of her hands and placed it on the girl's head. "Oh, Fluffers!" came another muffled wail; the girl refused to lift her face. Her brother stood more stoically at her side. His face was pink and swollen, but something was drying hard behind the eyes. He studied Jane as if he were reorganizing what he thought was important in life. "What is your name?" he asked.

* * *

It was a little thing, just a little thing, but Jane decided not to risk the audition after all. She phoned Bridey and apologized, said she was coming down with a bug or something, and Bridey said, "Probably got it from that Heffie, always taste-testing the way she does. At any rate, I hope you'll come over for dinner sometime this week, if possible," and Jane said that yes, she would.

And she did. She went the following Thursday and had dinner with Bridey and Bridey's husband, who was a big, gentle man who did consulting work for computer companies. He was wearing a shirt printed with seahorses, like one her ex-lover the toymaker had worn when he had come east to visit, one final weekend, for old times' sake. It had been a beautiful shirt, soft as pajamas, and he'd worn it when they had driven that Sunday, out past the pumpkin fairs, to the state line, to view the Mississippi. The river had rushed by them, beneath them, a clayey green, a deep, deep khaki. She had touched the shirt, held on to it; in this lunarscape of scrub oaks and jack pines, in this place that had once at the start of the world been entirely under water and now just had winds, it was good to have a river cutting through, breaking up the land. In the distance, past a valley dalmatianed with birches, there were larger trees, cedars and goldening tamaracks – goldening! – and Jane felt that at last here was a moment she would take with her into the rest of life, *unlosable*. There seemed nothing so true as a yellow tree.

After dinner she actually went to a Community Chorus rehearsal with Bridey and sang through some of the exercises with everyone. When the sheet music was passed out, however, there wasn't enough to go around. The director took attendance and gazed accusingly out at the sopranos, saying, "Is someone here who isn't actually supposed to be?" Jane raised her hand and explained.

"I'm afraid this is not allowed. If you want to be in the chorus you must have already auditioned."

"I'm sorry," said Jane, and she stood and gave her sheet music back to the choir director. She picked up her purse, looked down at Bridey, and shrugged unhappily.

"I'll phone you," mouthed Bridey.

But it was nearly Christmas season by the time Bridey phoned, and Jane was very busy at the store. There were lots of special holiday dips and cheese rolls, and they were trying to do gift wrap besides. In the midst of it all Heffie announced she was quitting, but the day she did she brought in a bottle of champagne, and she and Jane drank it right there on the job. They poured it into Styrofoam cups and sipped it, crouching behind the deli case, craning their necks occasionally to make sure no customers had wandered in.

"To our little lives," toasted Heffie.

"On the prairie," added Jane. The champagne fizzed against the roof of her mouth. She warmed it there, washing it around, until it flattened, gliding down her throat, a heated, sweet water.

She and Heffie opened a jar of herring in cream sauce, which had a messily torn label. They dug their fingers in and ate. They sang a couple of Christmas carols they both knew, and sang them badly.

"*Let every heart prepare him a room*," sang Heffie, her mouth full of fish. The world was lovely, really, but it was tricky, and peevish with the small things, like a god who didn't get out much.

"Surfing," said Heffie. "You gotta get away from these plains winters and go someplace with waves and a warm current." Inside the deli case, the dry moons of the cheeses and the mucky spreads wore their usual plastic tags: HELLO MY NAME IS. Jane reached in and plucked out the one that said, HELLO MY NAME IS *Swiss Almond Whip*.

"Here," she said to Heffie. "This is for you." Heffie laughed, gravelly and loud, then took the tag and stuck it in one of her barrettes, up near the front, where the hair was vanishing, and the deforested scalp shone back in surprise, pale but constant, beneath.

1988

THE JUNIPER TREE

THE NIGHT ROBIN ROSS was dying in the hospital, I was waiting for a man to come pick me up – a man she had once dated, months before I began dating him – and he was late and I was wondering whether his going to see her with me was even wise. Perhaps I should go alone. Her colleague ZJ had called that morning and said, "Things are bad. When she leaves the hospital, she's not going home."

"I'll go see her tonight," I said. I felt I was a person of my word, and by saying something I would make it so. It was less like integrity perhaps and more like magic.

"That's a good idea," ZJ said. He was chairman of the theater department and had taken charge, like a husband, since Robin had asked him to; his tearfulness about her fate had already diminished. In the eighties he had lost a boyfriend to AIDS, and now all the legal and medical decision-making these last few months, he said, seemed numbingly familiar.

But then I found myself waiting, and soon it was seven-thirty and then eight and I imagined Robin was tired and sleeping in her metal hospital bed and would have more energy in the morning. When the man I was waiting for came, I said, "You know? It's so late. Maybe I should visit Robin in the morning when she'll have more energy and be more awake. The tumor presses on the skull, poor girl, and makes her groggy."

"Whatever you think is best," said the man. When I told him what ZJ had said, that when Robin left the hospital, she wasn't going home, the man looked puzzled. "Where is she going to go?" He hadn't dated Robin very long, only a few weeks, and had never really understood her. "Her garage was a pigsty," he had once said. "I couldn't believe all the crap that was in it!" And I had nodded agreeably, feeling I had won him; my own garage wasn't that great, but whatever. I had triumphed over others by dint of some unknowable charm. Now I was coming to realize that a lot of people baffled this guy, and that I would be next to become incomprehensible and unattractive. That was how dating among straight middle-aged women seemed to go in this college town: one available man every year or so just made the rounds of us all. "I can share. I'm good at sharing," Robin used to say, laughing.

"Well I'm not," I said. "I'm not good at it in the least."

"It's late," I said again to the man, and I made two gin rickeys and lit candles.

Every woman I knew here drank – daily. In rejecting the lives of our mothers, we found ourselves looking for stray volts of mother love in the very places they could never be found: gin, men, the college, our own mothers, and one another. I was the only one of my friends – all of us academic transplants, all soldiers of art stationed on a far-off base (or, so we imagined it) – who hadn't had something terrible happen to her yet.

The next morning I dressed in cheery colors. Orange and gold. There was nothing useful to bring Robin, but I made a bouquet of cut mums nonetheless and stuck them in a plastic cup with some wet paper towels holding them in. I was headed toward the front door when the phone rang. It was ZJ. "I'm leaving now to see Robin," I said.

"Don't bother."

"Oh, no," I said. My vision left me for a second.

"She died late last night. About two in the morning."

I sank down into a chair and my plastic cup of mums fell, breaking two stems. "Oh, my God," I said.

"I know," he said.

"I was going to go see her last night, but it got late and I thought it would be better to go this morning when she was more rested." I tried not to wail.

"Don't worry about it," he said.

"I feel terrible," I cried, as if this were what mattered.

"She was not doing well. It's a blessing." From diagnosis to decline had been precipitous, I knew. She was teaching, then suddenly the new chemo was not going well and she was lying outside of the emergency room, on the concrete, afraid to lie down inside because of other people's germs. Then she was placed in the actual hospital, which was full of other people's germs. She'd been there almost a week and I hadn't gotten in to see her.

"It's all so unbelievable."

"I know."

"How are *you*?" I asked.

"I can't even go there," he said.

"Please phone me if there's something I can do," I said emptily. "Let me know when the service will be."

"Sure," he said.

I went upstairs and with all my cheery clothes on got back into bed. It still smelled a little of the man. I pulled the sheet over my head and lay there, every muscle of my body strung taut. I could not move.

But I must have fallen asleep, and for some time, because when I heard the doorbell downstairs and pulled the sheet off my face, it was already dark, though the sun set these days at four, so it was hard ever to know by just looking out the windows what time it might possibly be. I flicked on the lights as I went – bedroom, hall, stairs – making my way down toward the ringing bell. I turned on the porch light and opened the door.

There stood Isabel and Pat. "We've got the gin, we've got the rickey mix," they said, holding up bags. "Come on. We're going to go see Robin."

"I thought Robin died," I said.

Pat made a face. "Yes, well," she said.

"That hospital was such a bad scene," said Isabel. She was not wearing her prosthetic arm. Except in pieces choreographed by others, she almost never did anymore. "But she's back home now and she's expecting us."

"How can that be?"

"You know women and their houses," said Pat. "It's hard for them to part company." Pat had had a massive stroke two years before, which had wiped out her ebullient personality and her short-term memory, but periodically her wounded, recovering brain cast about desperately and landed on a switch and threw it, and she woke up in a beautiful manic frenzy, seeming like the old Pat, saying, "I feel like I've been asleep for years," and she would stay like that for days on end, insomniac and babbling and reminiscing, painting her paintings, then she'd crash again, passive and mute. She was on disability leave and had a student living with her full-time who took care of her.

"Maybe we all drink too much gin," I said.

For a moment there was just silence. "Are you referring to the accident?" said Isabel accusingly. It was a car crash that had severed her arm. A surgeon and his team of residents had sewn it back on, but the arm had bled continually through the skin grafts and was painful – the first dance afterward before an audience, a solo performed with much spinning and swinging from a rope, had flung specks of blood to the stage floor – and after a year, and a small ineffectual codeine habit, she'd gone back to the same surgeon and asked him to remove it, the whole arm, she was done, she had tried.

"No, no," I said. "I'm not referring to anything."

"So hey, come on, come on!" said Pat. The switch seemed to have been thrown in her.

"Robin's waiting."

"What do I bring?"

"Bring?" Pat and Isabel burst out laughing. "You're kidding, right?" Pat said.

"She's kidding," said Isabel. She felt the sleeve of my orange sweater, which I was still wearing. "Hey. This color looks nice on you. Where did you get this?"

"I forget."

"Yeah, so do I!" said Pat, and she and Isabel burst into fits of hilarity again.

I put on shoes, grabbed a jacket, and left with them.

Isabel drove, one-armed, to Robin's. When we arrived the house was completely dark, but the streetlights showed once more the witchy strangeness of the place. Because she wrote plays based on fairy tales, Robin had planted in the yard, rather haphazardly, the trees and shrubs that figured most prominently in the tales: apple, juniper, hazelnut, and rosebushes. Unfortunately, our latitude was not the best gardening zone for these. Even braced and trussed, they had struggled, jagged and leggy; at this time of year, when they were leafless and bent, one couldn't say for sure whether they were even alive. Spring would tell.

Why would a man focus on her garage when there was this crazed landscaping with which to judge her? Make your excuses: no jury would convict.

Though why would a man focus on anything but her?

We parked in the driveway, where Robin's own car was still parked, her garage no doubt locked – even in the dark one could see the boxes stacked against the single garage window that faced the street.

"The key's under the mat," said Isabel, though I didn't know this and wondered how she did. Pat found the key, unlocked the door, and we all went in. "Don't turn on the lights," Isabel added.

"I know," whispered Pat, though *I* didn't know.

"Why can't we turn on the lights?" I asked, also in a whisper. The door closed behind us and we stood there in the quiet, pitch-black house.

"The police," said Pat.

"No, not the police," said Isabel.

"Then what?"

"Never mind. Just give it a minute and our eyes will adjust." We stood there listening to our own breathing. We didn't move, so as not to trip over anything.

And then on the opposite side of the room a small light flicked on from somewhere at the end of the far hallway; we could not see down it, but out stepped Robin, looking pretty much the same, though she had a white cotton scarf wrapped and knotted around her neck. Against the white, her teeth had a fluorescent ocher sheen, but otherwise she looked regal and appraising, and she smiled at all of us, including me – though more tentatively, I thought, at me. Then she put her finger to her lips and shook her head, so we didn't speak. She walked toward us.

"You came" were her first hushed words, directed at me. "I missed you a little at the hospital." Her smile had become clearly tight and judging.

"I am so sorry," I said.

"That's OK, they'll tell you," she said, indicating Is and Pat. "It was a little nuts."

"It was totally nuts," said Pat.

"As a result?" whispered Robin. "No hugs. Everything's a little precarious, between the postmortem and the tubes in and out all week. This scarf's the only thing holding my head on." Though she was pale, her posture was perfect, her dark red hair restored, her long thin arms folded across her chest. She was dressed as she always dressed: in black jeans and a blue sweater. She simply, newly, had the imperial standoffishness I realized only then that I had always associated with the dead. We pulled up chairs and then each of us sat.

"Should we make some gin rickeys?" Isabel asked, motioning toward the bags of booze and lime juice blend.

"We wanted to come here and each present you with something," said Pat.

"We did?" I said. I'd brought nothing. I had asked them what to bring and they had laughed it off.

Robin looked at me. "Always a little out of the loop, eh?" She smiled stiffly.

Pat was digging around in a hemp tote bag I hadn't noticed before. "Here's a little painting I made for you," she said, handing a small unframed canvas gingerly to Robin. I couldn't see what the painting was of. Robin stared at it for a very long time and then looked back up at Pat and said, "Thank you so much." She momentarily laid the painting in her lap and I could see it was nothing but a plain white blank.

I looked longingly at the paper sack of gin.

"And I have a new dance for you!" whispered Isabel excitedly at Robin.

"You do?" I said.

Robin turned to me again. "Always the last to know, huh," she said and then winced, as if speaking hurt. She clutched Pat's painting to her stomach.

Isabel stood and moved her chair out of the way. "This piece is dedicated to Robin Ross," she announced. And then, after a moment's stillness, she began to move, saying lines of poetry as she did. "'Heap not on this mound / Roses that she loved so well; / Why bewilder her with roses / That she cannot see or smell?'" There was more, and as, reciting, she flew and turned and balanced on one leg, her single arm aloft, I thought, *What the hell kind of poem is this?* It seemed rude to speak of death to the dead, and I kept checking in with Robin's face, to see how she was taking it, but Robin remained impassive. At the end, she placed the painting back in her lap and clapped. I was about to clap as well, when car headlights from the driveway suddenly arced across the room.

"It's the cops! Get down!" said Isabel, and we all hit the floor.

"They're patrolling the house," whispered Robin, lying on her back on the rug. She was hugging Pat's painting to her chest. "I guess there have been calls from a neighbor or something. Just lie here for a minute and they'll leave." The police car idled in the driveway for a minute, perhaps taking down the license number of Isabel's car, and then pulled away.

"It's OK. We can get up now," said Robin.

"Whew. That was close," said Pat.

We all got back into our chairs and there was then a long silence, like a Quaker wedding, which I came to understand was being directed at me.

"Well, I guess it's my turn," I said. "It's been a terrible month. First the election, and now this. You." I indicated Robin, and she nodded just slightly, then grabbed at her scarf and retied the knot. "And I don't have my violin or my piano here," I said. Isabel and Pat were staring at me hopelessly. "So – I guess I'll just sing." I stood up and cleared my throat. I knew that if you took "The Star-Spangled Banner" very slowly and mournfully, it altered not just the attitude of the song but the actual punctuation, turning it into a protest and a question. I sang it slowly, not without a little twang. "O say does that star-spangled banner yet wave, o'er the land of the free and the home of the brave?" Then I sat down. The three of them applauded, Isabel slapping her thigh with one hand.

"Very nice," Robin said to me. "You never sing enough," she added, ambiguously. Her smile to me was effortful and pinched. "Now I have to go," she said, and she stood, leaving Pat's painting behind on the chair, and walked into the lit hallway, after which we heard the light switch flick off. The whole house was plunged into darkness again.

"Well, I'm glad we did that," I said on the way back home. I was sitting alone in the back, sneaking some of the gin – why bother ever again with rickey mix? – and I'd been staring out the window. Now I looked forward and noticed that Pat was driving. Pat hadn't driven in years. A pickup truck with the bumper sticker NO HILLARY NO WAY roared past us, and we stared at its message as if we were staring at a swastika. Where were we living?

"Redneck," Isabel muttered at the driver.

"It's a trap, isn't it?" I said.

"What is?" asked Pat.

"This place!" exclaimed Isabel. "Our work! Our houses! The college!"

"It's all a trap!" I repeated.

But we did not entirely believe it. Somewhere inside us we were joyful orphans: our lives were right, we were zooming along doing what we wanted, we were sometimes doing what we loved. But we were inadequate as a pit crew, for ourselves or for anyone else. "It was good to see Robin," I continued from the back. "It was really good to see her."

"That's true," said Isabel. Pat said nothing. She was coming off her manic high and driving took all she had.

"All in all it was a good night," I said.

"A good night," agreed Isabel.

"Good night," Robin had said the last time I'd seen her well, standing in her own doorway. She had invited me over and we had hung out, eating her summery stir-fry, things both lonely and warm between us, when she asked about the man I was seeing, the one she had dated briefly.

"Well, I don't know," I said, a little sad. At that point I was still sitting at her table and I found myself rubbing the grain of it with one finger. "He seems now also to be seeing this other person – Daphne Kern? Do you know her? She's one of those beautician-slash-art dealers?" All the restaurants, coffee shops, and hair salons in town seemed to have suddenly gotten into hanging, showing, and selling art. This dignified, or artified, the business of serving. Did I feel I was better, more interesting, with my piano and my violin and my singing?

"I know Daphne. I took a yoga class once from her, when she was doing that."

"You did?" I could not control myself. "So what's so compelling about her?" My voice was not successfully shy of a whine. "Is she nice?"

"She's pretty, she's nice, she's intuitive," Robin said, casually ticking off the qualities. "She's actually a talented yoga instructor. She's very physical. Even when she speaks she uses her body a lot. You know, frankly? She's probably just really good in bed."

At this my heart sickened and plummeted down my left side and into my shoe. My appetite, too, shrank to a small pebble and sat in stony reserve in the place my heart had been and to which my heart would at some point return, but not in time for dessert.

"I've made a lemon meringue pie," said Robin, getting up and clearing the dishes. She was always making pies. She would have written more plays if she had made fewer pies. "More meringue than lemon, I'm afraid."

"Oh, thank you. I'm just full," I said, looking down at my unfinished food.

"I'm sorry," Robin said, a hint of worry in her voice. "Should I not have said that thing about Daphne?"

"Oh, no," I said. "That's fine. It's nothing." But soon I felt it was time for me to go, and after a single cup of tea, I stood, clearing only a few of the dishes with her. I found my purse and headed for the door.

She stood in the doorway, holding the uneaten meringue pie. "That skirt, by the way, is great," she said in the June night. "Orange is a good color on you. Orange and gold."

"Thanks," I said.

Then, without warning, she suddenly lifted up the pie and pushed it into her own face. When she pulled off the tin, meringue clung to her skin like blown snow. The foam of it covered her lashes and brows, and with her red hair for a minute she looked like a demented Queen Elizabeth.

"What the *fuck*?" I said, shaking my head. I needed new friends. I would go to more conferences and meet more people.

"I've always wanted to do that," said Robin. The mask of meringue on her face looked eerie, not clownish at all, and her mouth speaking through the white foam seemed to be a separate creature entirely, a puppet or a fish. "I've always wanted to do that, and now I have."

"Hey," I said. "There's no business like show business." I was digging in my purse for my car keys.

Long hair flying over her head, bits of meringue dropping on the porch, she took a deep dramatic bow. "Everything," she added, from behind her mask, "everything, everything, well, almost everything about it" – she gulped a little pie that had fallen in from one corner of her mouth – "is appealing."

"Brava," I said, smiling. I had found my keys. "Now I'm out of here."

"Of course," she said, gesturing with her one pie-free hand. "Onward."

for Nietzchka Keene (1952–2004)

2004

THE KID'S GUIDE TO DIVORCE

PUT EXTRA SALT ON the popcorn because your mom'll say that she needs it because the part where Inger Berman almost dies and the camera does tricks to elongate her torso sure gets her every time.

Think: Geeze, here she goes again with the Kleenexes.

She will say thanks honey when you come slowly, slowly around the corner in your slippers and robe, into the living room with Grandma's old used-to-be-salad-bowl piled high. I made it myself, remind her, and accidentally drop a few pieces on the floor. Mittens will bat them around with his paws.

Mmmmm, good to replenish those salts, she'll munch and smile soggily.

Tell her the school nurse said after a puberty movie once that salt is bad for people's hearts.

Phooey, she'll say. It just makes it thump, that's all. Thump, thump, thump – oh look! She will talk with her mouth full of popcorn. Cary Grant is getting her out of there. Did you unplug the popper?

Pretend you don't hear her. Watch Inger Berman look elongated; wonder what it means.

You'd better check, she'll say.

Groan. Make a little *tsk* noise with your tongue on the roof of your mouth. Run as fast as you can because the next commercial's going to be the end. Unplug the popper. Bring Mittens back in with you because he is mewing by the refrigerator. He'll leave hair on your bathrobe. Dump him in your mom's lap.

Hey baby, she'll coo at the cat, scratching his ears. Cuddle close to your mom and she'll reach around and scratch one of your ears too, kissing your cheek. Then she'll suddenly lean forward, reaching toward the bowl on the coffee table, carefully so as not to disturb the cat. I always think he's going to realize faster than he does, your mom will say between munches, hand to hand to mouth. Men can be so dense and frustrating. She will wink at you.

Eye the tube suspiciously. All the bad guys will let Cary Grant take Inger Berman away in the black car. There will be a lot of old-fashioned music. Stand and pull your bathrobe up on the sides. Hang your tongue out and pretend to dance like a retarded person at a ball. Roll your eyes. Waltz across the living room with exaggerated side-to-side motions, banging into furniture. Your mother will pretend not to pay attention to you. She will finally say in a flat voice: How wonderful, gee, you really send me.

When the music is over, she will ask you what you want to watch now. She'll hand you the *TV Guide*. Look at it. Say: The Late, Late Chiller. She'll screw up one of her eyebrows at you, but say *please, please* in a soft voice and put your hands together like a prayer. She will smile back and sigh, okay.

Switch the channel and return to the sofa. Climb under the blue afghan with your mother. Tell her you like this beginning cartoon part best where the mummy comes out of the coffin and roars, *CHILLER!!* Get up on one of the arms of the sofa and do an imitation, your hands like claws, your elbows stiff, your head slumped to one side. Your mother will tell you to sit back down. Snuggle back under the blanket with her.

When she says, Which do you like better, the mummy or the werewolf, tell her the werewolf is scary because he goes out at night and does things that no one suspects because in the day he works in a bank and has no hair.

What about the mummy? she'll ask, petting Mittens.

Shrug your shoulders. Fold in your lips. Say: The mummy's just the mummy.

With the point of your tongue, loosen one of the chewed, pulpy kernels in your molars. Try to swallow it, but get it caught in your throat and begin to gasp and make horrible retching noises. It will scare the cat away.

Good god, be careful, your mother will say, thwacking you on the back. Here, drink this water.

Try groaning root beer, root beer, like a dying cowboy

you saw on a commercial once, but drink the water anyway. When you are no longer choking, your face is less red, and you can breathe again, ask for a Coke. Your mom will say: I don't think so; Dr. Atwood said your teeth were atrocious.

Tell her Dr. Atwood is for the birds.

What do you mean by that? she will exclaim.

Look straight ahead. Say: I dunno.

The mummy will be knocking down telephone poles, lifting them up, and hurling them around like Lincoln Logs.

Wow, all wrapped up and no place to go, your mother will say.

Cuddle close to her and let out a long, low, admiring *Neato*.

The police will be in the cemetery looking for a monster. They won't know whether it's the mummy or the werewolf, but someone will have been hanging out there leaving little smoking piles of bones and flesh that even the police dogs get upset and whine at.

Say something like gross-out, and close your eyes.

Are you sure you want to watch this?

Insist that you are not scared.

There's a rock concert on Channel 7, you know.

Think about it. Decide to try Channel 7, just for your mom's sake. Somebody with greasy hair who looks like Uncle Jack will be saying something boring.

Your mother will agree that he does look like Uncle Jack. A little.

A band with black eyeshadow on will begin playing their guitars. Stand and bounce up and down like you saw Julie Steinman do once.

God, why do they always play them down at their crotches? your mom will ask.

Don't answer, simply imitate them, throwing your hair back and fiddling bizarrely with the crotch of your pajama bottoms. Your mother will slap you and tell you you're being fresh.

Act hurt. Affect a slump. Pick up a magazine and pretend you're reading it. The cat will rejoin you. Look at the pictures of the food.

Your mom will try to pep you up. She'll say: Look! Pat Benatar! Let's dance.

Tell her you think Pat Benatar is stupid and cheap. Say nothing for five whole minutes.

When the B-52's come on, tell her you think *they're* okay.

Smile sheepishly. Then the two of you will get up and dance like wild maniacs around the coffee table until you are sweating, whooping to the oo-ah-oo's, jumping like pogo sticks, acting like space robots. Do razz-ma-tazz hands like your mom at either side of your head. During a commercial, ask for an orange soda.

Water or milk, she will say, slightly out of breath, sitting back down.

Say shit, and when she asks what did you say, sigh: Nothing.

Next is Rod Stewart singing on a roof somewhere. Your mom will say: He's sort of cute.

Tell her Julie Steinman saw him in a store once and said he looked really old.

Hmmmm, your mother will say.

Study Rod Stewart carefully. Wonder if you could make your legs go like that. Plan an imitation for Julie Steinman.

When the popcorn is all gone, yawn. Say: I'm going to bed now.

Your mother will look disappointed, but she'll say, okay, honey. She'll turn the TV off. By the way, she'll ask hesitantly like she always does. How did the last three days go?

Leave out the part about the lady and the part about the beer. Tell her they went all right, that he's got a new silver dartboard and that you went out to dinner and this guy named Hudson told a pretty funny story about peeing in the hamper. Ask for a 7-Up.

1981

LIKE LIFE

Everybody likes the circus.
Clowns! elephants! trained horses! peanuts!
Everybody likes the circus.
Acrobats! tight-rope walkers! camels! band music!
Suppose you had a choice of going to the circus
or painting a picture. Which would you choose?
You'd choose the circus.
Everybody likes the circus.

—V. M. HILLYER AND E. G. HUEY,
A Child's History of Art

ALL THE MOVIES that year were about people with plates in their heads: Spirits from another galaxy gather in a resort town at night, taking over the townspeople – all but the man with the plate in his head. Or: A girl with a plate in her head wanders a city beach, believing she is someone else. Evidence washes up on shore. There are sailors. Or: A woman dreams of a beautiful house in which no one lives, and one day she passes the actual house – a cupola, gables, and a porch. She walks up to it, knocks on the door, and it is opened slowly by her! a woman who is a twin of herself, grinning. She has a plate in her head.

Life seemed to have become like that. It had burst out of itself, like a bug.

In February a thaw gave the city the weepy ooze of a wound. There were many colds, people coughing in the subways. The sidewalks foamed to a cheese of spit, and the stoops, doorways, bus shelters were hedged with Rosies – that is what they were called – the jobless men, women, children with gourd lumps or fevers, imploring, hating eyes, and puffed lavender mouths, stark as paintings of mouths. The Rosies sold flowers: a prim tulip, an overflowing iris. Mostly no one bought any. Mostly it was just other Rosies, trading bloom for bloom, until one of them, a woman or a child, died in the street, the others gathering around in a wail, in the tiny, dark morning hours, which weren't morning at all but night.

That year was the first that it became illegal – for those who lived in apartments or houses – not to have a television. The government claimed that important information, information necessary for survival, might need to be broadcast automatically, might need simply to burst on, which it could do. Civilization was at stake, it was said. "Already at the stake," said others, who had come to suspect that they were being spied on, controlled, that what they had thought when they were little – that the people on the television could also see you – now was true. You were supposed to leave it plugged in at all times, the plastic antenna raised in a V – for victory or peace, no one could say.

Mamie lost sleep. She began to distrust things, even her own words; too much had moved in. Objects implanted in your body – fillings, earrings, contraceptives – like satellite dishes, could be picking up messages, substituting their words for yours, feeding you lines. You never knew. Open your mouth, it might betray you with lies, with lackadaise, with moods and speak not your own. The things you were saying might be old radio programs bounced off the foil of your molars, or taxi calls fielded by the mussely glove of your ear. What you described as real might be only a picture, something from *Life* magazine you were forced to live out, after the photography, in imitation. Whole bodies, perhaps, could be ventriloquized. Approximated. You could sit on the lap of a thing and just move your lips. You could become afraid. You could become afraid someone was making you afraid: a new fear, like a gourmet's, a paranoid's paranoia.

This was not the future. This was what was with you now in the house.

Mamie lived in a converted beauty parlor storefront – a tin ceiling, a stench of turpentine, and extra sinks. At night her husband, a struggling painter, moody and beer-breathed, lay sleeping next to her, curled against her, an indifferent whistle in his nose. She closed her eyes. *What all to love in the world,* went a prayer from her childhood. What all to love?

The lumber of his bones piled close.

The radiator racked and spitting. Heat flapping like birds up the pipes.

She remained awake. On nights when she did sleep, her dreams were about the end of life. They involved getting somewhere, getting to the place where she was supposed to die, where it was OK. She was always in a group, like a fire drill or a class trip. Can we die here? Are we there yet? Which way can it possibly be?

Or else there was the house dream. Always the house dream, like the movie of the dream of the house. She would find a house, knock on the door, and it would open slowly, a wedge of dark, and then stop, her own profile greeting her, hanging there midair like a chandelier.

Death, said her husband, Rudy. He kept a small hatchet under the mattress, in case of intruders. *Death.* Last year she had gone to a doctor, who had looked at her throat and a mole on her back, studying them like Rorschachs for whatever he might see in them. He removed the mole and put it floating in a pathologist's vial, a tiny marine animal. Peering in at her throat, he said, "Precancer" – like a secret or a zodiac sign.

"*Pre*cancer?" she had repeated quietly, for she was a quiet woman. "Isn't that . . . like *life*?" She was sitting, and he was standing. He fumbled with some alcohol and cotton balls, which he kept on the counter in kitcheny-looking jars, the flour and sugar of the medical world.

He took her wrist and briefly squeezed. "It's *like* life, but it's not *necessarily* life."

There was a wrought-iron fence all around and a locked gate, but it was the bird feeder she remarked first, the wooden arms, the open mouth of boards stuck up there on a single leg. It was nearing Valentine's Day, an angry slosh of a morning, and she was on her way to a realtor, a different one this time, not far from the Fourth and Smith stop of the F train – from where you could see the Statue of Liberty. On her way, she had come upon a house with a bird feeder. A bird feeder! And a tree in front, a towering oak, over one hundred fifty years old. A grade school teacher had brought her class to it and now stood in front of it, pointing and saying, "A hundred and fifty years ago. Can anyone tell me when that was?"

But it was the bird feeder, initially: a cross with an angle-roofed shelter at the head – a naked scarecrow bedecked with horizontals like a Frank Lloyd Wright house, or an alpine motel, its wooden ledges strewn with millet seed. In the freckled snow below lay tiny condiment cups of peanut butter, knocked to the ground. A flibberty squirrel, hopping and pausing in spasms, lifted each cup to his nose and nibbled. On the feeder itself was a pair of pigeons – lidless, thick-necked, municipal gargoyles; but there, wasn't that also a sparrow? And a grosbeak?

The house was a real house, one of the few left in New York. A falling-down Edwardian Gothic with a cupola, once painted a silvery gray and now chipping. There was a porch and latticework of carpenter's lace – a house one would go to for piano lessons, if people still took piano lessons, a house invariably seized for a funeral home. It was squeezed between two storefronts – the realtor's and a laundromat.

"You're looking for a one-bedroom?" said the realtor.

"Yes," said Mamie, though it suddenly seemed both too little and too much to ask for. The realtor had the confident hair and makeup of a woman who had lived forever in New York, a woman who knew ever so wearily how to tie a scarf. Mamie studied the realtor's scarf, guessing the exact geometry of the folds, the location of the knot. If Mamie ever had surgery, scars in a crisscross up her throat, she would have to know such things. A hat, a scarf, a dot of rouge, mints in the mouth: Everyone in New York was hiding something, eventually.

The real estate agent took out an application form. She picked up a pen. "Your name?"

"Mamie Cournand."

"*What?* Here. You fill this out."

It was pretty much the same form she'd filled out previously at other agencies. What sort of apartment are you looking for; how much do you make; how do you make it . . . ?

"What is children's historical illustrator?" deadpanned the realtor. "If you don't mind me asking."

"I, uh, work on a series of history publications, picture books actually, for chil—"

"Free lance?" She looked at Mamie with doubt, suspicion, and then with sympathy to encourage candor.

"It's for the McWilliams Company." She began to lie. "I've got an office there that I use. The address is written here." She rose slightly from her seat, to point it out.

The realtor pulled away. "I'm oriented," she said.

"Oriented?"

"You don't need to reach and point. This your home and work phone? This your age . . . ? You forgot to put in your age."

"Thirty-five."

"Thirty-five," she repeated, writing it in. "You look younger." She looked at Mamie. "What are you willing to pay?"

"Um, up to nine hundred or so."

"Good luck," she snorted, and still seated in her caster-wheeled chair, she trundled over to the file cabinet, lifted out a manila folder, flipped it open. She placed Mamie's application on top. "This isn't the eighties anymore, you know."

Mamie cleared her throat. Deep in the back she could feel the wound sticking there, unhealed. "It hasn't not been for very long. I mean, just a few years." The awkward, frightened look had leaped to her eyes again, she knew. Fear making a child of her face – she hated this in herself. As a girl, she had always listened in a slightly stricken way and never spoke unless she was asked a question. When she was in college she was the kind of student sometimes too anxious to enter the cafeteria. Often she just stayed in her room and drank warm iced tea from a mix and a Hot Pot. "You live right over here?" The realtor motioned behind her. "Why are you moving?"

"I'm leaving my husband."

The corner of her mouth curled. "*In this day and age?* Good luck." She shrugged and spun around to dig through files again. There was a long silence, the realtor shaking her head.

Mamie craned her neck. "I'd like to see what you have, at any rate."

"We've got nothing." The realtor slammed the file drawer and twisted back around. "But keep trying us. We might have something tomorrow. We're expecting some listings then."

They had been married for fourteen years, living on Brooklyn's south slope for almost ten. It was a neighborhood once so Irish that even as late as the fifties, kids had played soccer in the street and shouted in Gaelic. When she and Rudy first moved in, the area was full of Italian men who barely knew Italian and leaned out of the windows of private clubs, shouting "How aw ya?" Now Hispanic girls in bright leotards gathered on the corner after school, smoking cigarettes and *scoming* the streets. *Scoming*, said the boys. Artists had taken up residence, as well as struggling actors, junkies, desperate Rosies in the street. *Watch out*, went the joke, *for the struggling actors*.

Mamie and Rudy's former beauty parlor now had a padlocked door and boarded front windows. Inside remained the original lavender walls, the gold metallic trim. They had built a loft at one end of the place, and at the other were bookcases, easels, canvases, and a drawing table. Stacked against the wall by the door were Rudy's huge paintings of snarling dogs and Virgin Marys. He had a series of each, and hoped, before he died, *before I shoot myself in the head on my fortieth birthday*, to have a gallery. Until then he painted apartments or borrowed money from Mamie. He was responsible for only one bill – utilities – and on several occasions had had to rush out to intercept Con Ed men arriving with helmets and boots to disconnect the electricity. "Never a dull moment," Rudy would say, thrusting cash into their hands. Once he had tried to pay the bill with two small still lifes.

"You don't think about the real world, Rudy. There's a real world out there." There was in him, she felt, only a fine line between insanity and charm. "A real world about to explode."

"You don't think I worry about the world *exploding*?" His expression darkened. "You don't think I get tears in my eyes every fucking day thinking about those Rembrandts at the Met and what's going to happen to them when it does?"

"Rudy, I went to a realtor today."

Probably in their marriage she had been too dreamy and inconsistent. For love to last, you had to have illusions or have no illusions at all. But you had to stick to one or the other. It was the switching back and forth that endangered things.

"Again?" Rudy sighed, ironic but hurt. Once love had seemed like magic. Now it seemed like tricks. You had to learn the sleight-of-hand, the snarling dog, the Hail Marys and hoops of it! Through all the muck of themselves, the times they had unobligated each other, the anger, the permitted absences, the loneliness grown dangerous, she had always returned to him. He'd had faith in that – abracadabra! But eventually the deadliness set in again. Could you live in the dead excellence of a thing – the stupid mortar of a body, the stubborn husk love had crawled from? Yes, he thought.

The television flashed on automatically, one of the government ads: pretty couples testifying to their undying devotion, undying bodies. "We are the Undying," they said, and they cuddled their children, who had freckles that bled together on the cheeks, and toys with glassy button eyes. *Undying*, the commercials said. *Be undying*. "I can't bear it," Mamie said. "I can't bear the brother and sister of us. I can't bear the mother and son of us. I can't bear the Undying commercials. I can't bear washing my hair in dishwashing liquid, or doing the dishes in cheap shampoo, because we're too broke or disorganized or depressed to have both at the same time." Always, they'd made do. For toilet paper they used holiday-imprinted napkins – cocktail napkins with poinsettias on them. A big box of them, with a tray, had been sent to Rudy by mistake. For towels they used bath mats. For bath mats more poinsettia napkins. They bought discount soaps with sayings on the label like *Be gentle and you need not be strong.* "We're camping out here, Rudy. This is camping!" She tried to appeal to something he would understand. "My work. It's affecting my work. Look at this!" and she went over to a small drawing table and held up her half-finished sketch of Squanto planting corn. She'd been attempting a nuclear metaphor: white man learning to plant things in the ground, which would later burst forth; how the white man had gotten carried away with planting. "He looks like a toad."

"He looks like a catcher for the Boston Red Sox." Rudy smiled. Would she smile? He grew mock-serious: "The faculties of discernment and generosity are always at war. You must decide whether you will be muse or artist. A woman cannot be both."

"I can't believe you," she said, staring accusingly around their apartment. "This is not life. This is something else," and the whole ill-lit place stared back at her, hurt, a ditzy old beauty parlor flunking someone else's math.

"Forget this Squanto thing," he said, looking compassionate. "I've got an idea for you. I've thought about it all day: a children's book called *Too Many Lesbians.*" He began motioning with his arms. "Lesbians in bushes, lesbians in trees . . . *Find the lesbians . . .*"

"I'm going out for some air," she said, and she grabbed her coat and flew out the door. It was evening already, zinc gray and chill, the puddles freezing on the walks in a thin glaze. She hurried past the shivering Rosies at the corner, hurried six blocks in a zigzag to look at the bird feeder again. Visit a place at night, she knew, and it was yours.

When she reached it, the house was dark, holding its breath, soundless so as not to be discovered. She pressed her face against the gate, the hard cilia of its ironwork, and sighed, longing for another existence, one that belonged to a woman who lived in a house like this, the lovely brow of its mansard roof, thoughtful with rooms. She felt a distrust of her own life, like those aerospace engineers reluctant to fly in planes of their own design, fearing death by their own claptrappery.

The bird feeder stood tall as a constable. There were no birds.

"You should never leave. You just always come back," whispered Rudy. *A tourist in your own despair*, he had once said. It was the title of one of his paintings. One of a snarling dog leaping over a sofa.

She stared through the small window by their bed, a strip of sky and one dim star, an asterisk to take her away briefly to an explanation – the night bragging a footnote. He held her, kissed her. Here in bed was when he seemed to her not to be doing imitations of other people. After fifteen years, she had seen all the imitations – friends, parents, movie actors – until it was a little scary, as if he were many different people at once, people to turn to, not in distress, but like a channel on television, a mind gone crazy with cable. He was Jimmy Stewart. He was Elvis Presley. "When you were growing up, were your parents funny?" she asked him once.

"*My parents?* You've got to be kidding," he said. "I mean, once in a while they *memorized* something." He was Dylan on the harmonica. Lifelike; absolutely lifelike. He was James Cagney. He was some musical blend he called Smokey Robinson Caruso.

"Don't you think we'd have beautiful children?" Rudy now pleaded, sleepily, his hand smoothing the bangs off her brow.

"They'd be nervous and insane," she murmured.

"You're strung out about your health."

"But maybe they'd also be able to do imitations."

Rudy kissed her throat, her ears, her throat again. She had to spit daily into a jar she kept in the bathroom, and to visit the clinic regularly, bringing the jar.

"You think we don't love each other anymore," he said. He was capable of tenderness. Though sometimes he was rough, pressing himself upon her with a force that startled her, wanting to make love and kissing her meanly against the wall: *come on, come on*; though his paintings had grown more violent, feverish swirls of men in business suits sodomizing animals: *this is my statement about yuppies, OK?*; though in coffee shops he often lorded over her spells of sorrowful boredom by looking disgusted while she blinked soggily into her lunch – here without his clothes on, with her face open to him, he could be a tender husband. "You think that, but it's not true." Years ago she had come to know his little lies, harmless for the most part and born of vanity and doubts, and sometimes fueled merely by a desire to hide from things whose truth took too much effort to figure out. She knew the way he would tell the same anecdotes from his life, over and over again, each time a little differently, the exaggerations and contradictions sometimes having a particular purpose – his self-portrait as Undiscovered Genius – and sometimes not seeming to have one at all. "Six inches from the door was an empty shopping cart jammed up against the door," he told her once, and she said, "Rudy, how can it be six inches from the door but also jammed up against it?"

"It was full of newspapers and tin cans, stuff like that. I don't know."

She couldn't even say when the love between them had begun to sicken, how long it had been gasping drearily over its own grave of rage and obligation. They had spent over a third of their lives together – a third, like sleep. He was the only man who had ever, even once, claimed to find her beautiful. And he had stuck with her, loved her, even when she was twenty and in terrified thrall to sex, not daring to move, out of politeness or was it timidity. He had helped her. Later she learned to crave the drugged heart of sex, the drugs at the core of it: All the necessary kissing and fussing seemed only that – necessary – to get to the drugs. But it had all been with Rudy, always with him. "Now we are truly in cahoots," she exulted, the day they were married at the county clerk's.

"I don't look good in cahoots," he said, his arm swung loosely around. "Let's go get tattoos."

What kisses there were in disappointment; sorrow fueled

them, pushed them to a place. The city writhed, and the world shut down all around. Rudy gave pouting mouths to his Virgin Marys, popped open cans of beer, watched old movies on TV. "*You are happy until you say you are happy. Then you are no longer happy*. Bonnard. The great painter of happiness articulating itself to death."

Maybe she'd thought life would provide her with something more lasting, more flattering than sexual love, but it never had, not really. For a while, she'd felt like one of the girls on the street corner: a world of leotards and drugs – drugs you hungered for and got to fast.

"Don't you think we have a very special love?" asked Rudy. But she wasn't believing in special love. Even when everyone was being practical, she believed – like a yearning for wind in winter – in only one kind of love, the kind in art: where you die for it. She had read too many books, said Rudy, Victorian novels where the children spoke in the subjunctive. *You take too much to heart*, he wrote her once, when she was away, living in Boston with an aging aunt and a sketch pad.

"I would never die for you," she said softly.

"Sure you would," said Rudy. He sighed, lay back. "Do you want a glass of water? I'll get down and get it."

At times her marriage seemed like a saint, guillotined and still walking for miles through the city, carrying its head. She often thought of the whole apartment going up in flames. What would she take with her? What few things would she grab for her new life? The thought exhilarated her. *You take too much to heart.*

In the house dream, she walks in past the gate and the bird feeder and knocks on the door. It opens slowly and she steps in, in and around, until it is she herself who is opening it, from the other side, wondering who has knocked.

"*Death*," said Rudy again. "Death by nuclear holocaust. Everyone's having those dreams. Except for me. I'm having these completely embarrassing nightmares about bad haircuts and not knowing anyone at a party."

In the morning, sun spilled in through the window by the bed. There was more light in the apartment in winter when there was snow on their overhang and it reflected sunlight inward, making garnet of the rug and striping the bed. A stray tomcat they had befriended, taken in, and fed lounged on the sill. They called him Food Man or Bill of the Baskervilles, and occasionally Rudy was kind to him, lifting the cat up high so that it could check out the bookcases, sniff the ceiling, which it liked to do. Mamie put birdseed out in the snow to attract pigeons, who would amuse the cat through the glass when he was inside. Cat TV. Rudy, she knew, hated pigeons, their lizard feet and pea brains, their strangely bovine meanness. He admired his friend Marco, who had put metal stakes outside on his air conditioner to keep pigeons from landing there.

Ordinarily Mamie was the first one up, the one to make coffee, the one to head cautiously down the makeshift rungs hammered in the side post, the one to pad out to the kitchen area, heat up water, rinse out mugs, brew coffee, get juice, and bring it all back to bed. This was how they had breakfast, the bedclothes a calico of spills.

But today, as on the other days he feared she would leave him, Rudy wormed naked out of the covers before her, jack-knifed at the loft's edge, descended to the floor with a thump. Mamie watched his body: lanky, big-eared; his back, his arms, his hips. No one ever talked about a man's hips, the hard twin saddles of them. He put on a pair of boxer shorts. "I like these underwear," he said. "They make me feel like David Niven."

He made coffee from water they stored in a plastic garbage barrel. They had it delivered this way, weekly, like seltzer, and they paid twenty dollars for it. They washed dishes in the water that came through the faucets, and they even took quick showers in it, though they risked rashes, said the government doctors. Once Mamie hadn't heard a special radio warning and had taken a shower, scrubbing hard with an old biscuit of loofah, only to step out with burning welts on her arms and shoulders: There had been a chemical pumped into the water, she learned later, one thought to impede the growth of viruses from river-rat fleas. She had soothed her skin with mayonnaise, which was all they had, and the blisters peeled open to a pink ham flesh beneath.

Except for the pleasure of Rudy bringing her coffee – the gift of it – she hated this place. But you could live with a hate. She had. It was so powerful, it had manners; it moved to one side most of the time to let you pass. It was mere dislike that clouded and nagged and stepped in front of your spirit, like a child wanting something.

Rudy returned with the coffee. Mamie rolled to the bed's edge and took the poinsettia tray from him, as he climbed back up and over her. "It's the Coffee Man," she said, trying to sound cheerful, perhaps even to chirp. Shouldn't she try? She placed the tray between them, picked up her coffee, and sipped. It was funny: With each swallow she could recast this fetid place, resee it with a caffeinated heart's eye, make it beautiful even. But it would be the drizzle of affection felt for a hated place before you left it. And she would leave. Again. She would turn the walls and sinks and the turpentined dust to a memory, make it the scene of mild crimes, and think of it with a false, willowy love.

But then you could get to calling everything false and willowy and never know anymore what was true and from the heart.

The cat came and curled up next to her. She massaged the cool, leathery wafer of its ear and plucked dust from its whiskers. He cocked his head and closed his eyes sleepily, content. How sad, she thought, how awful, how fortunate to be an animal and mistake grooming for love.

She placed a hand on Rudy's arm. He bent his head to kiss it, but then couldn't bend that far without spilling his coffee, and so straightened up again.

"Are you ever lonely?" Mamie asked him. Every moment of a morning seemed battled for, the past and future both seeking custody. She laid her cheek against his arm.

"Mamie," he said softly, and that was all.

In the last five years almost all of their friends had died.

The Indians weren't used to the illnesses that the English brought with them to the new world. Many Indians got sick. When they got chicken pox or mumps, they sometimes died. A very proud Indian might happen to wake up one morning and look in the mirror he'd gotten from an English trader and see red spots polka-dotting his face! The proud Indian would be very upset. He might hurl himself against a tree to maim himself. Or he might throw himself over a cliff or into a fire (picture).

The agent had on a different scarf today – a turquoise jacquard, twisted into a long coil that she wore wrapped around her neck like a collar. "A room," she said quickly. "Would you settle for a room?"

"I'm not sure," said Mamie. When she spoke with someone snappy and high-powered like that, she felt depressed and under siege.

"Well, come back when you are," said the agent, in her chair, trundling toward the files.

Mamie took the train into Manhattan. She would walk around the art galleries in SoHo, after she dropped off a manuscript at the McWilliams Company. Then she would come back home via the clinic. She had her glass jar in her purse.

In the McWilliams bathroom was a secretary named Goz, whom Mamie had spoken to a few times. Goz was standing in front of the mirror, applying eye makeup. "Hey, how ya doin'?" she said, when she saw Mamie.

Mamie stood next to her, washed her face off from the subway, and dug through her purse for a hairbrush. "I'm OK. How are you?"

"All right." Goz sighed. She had two wax perfume wands, mascara, and several colors of eye shadow spread out on the mirror ledge. She scrutinized her own reflection and sucked in her cheeks. "You know, it's taken me years to get my eye makeup to look like this."

Mamie smiled sympathetically. "A lot of practice, huh."

"No – years of *eye makeup*. I let it build up."

Mamie leaned over and brushed her hair upside down.

"Hmmm," said Goz a little irritably. "What have you been doing these days?"

"Oh, a children's thing again. It's the first time I've done the pictures *and* the text." Mamie straightened and threw her head back. "I'm, um, dropping off a chapter for Seth today." Her hair fell around her face in a penumbra. She looked insane.

"Oh. Hmmm," said Goz. She was watching Mamie's hair with interest. "I like *neat* hair. I don't think a woman should look as if sex has already happened."

Mamie smiled at her. "How about you? You going out a lot, having fun?"

"Yeah," said Goz a little defensively. Everyone these days was defensive about their lives. Everyone had settled. "I'm going out. I'm going out with this *man*. And my friends are going out with these *men*. And sometimes we all go out together. The trouble is we're all about thirty years younger than these guys. We'll go to a restaurant or something and I'll look around the table and like every man at our table is thirty years older than his date."

"A father-daughter banquet," said Mamie, trying to joke. "We used to have those at our church."

Goz stared at her. "Yeah," she said, finally turning to put away all her makeup. "You still with that guy who lives in a beauty parlor?"

"Rudy. My husband."

"Whatever," said Goz, and she went into a stall and closed the door.

None of the English seemed to be getting sick. This caused much whispering in the Indian villages. "We are dying," they said. "But they are not. How come?"

And so the chief, weak and ailing, would put on English clothes and go to the Englishmen (picture).

"This is for Seth Billets," Mamie said, handing the receptionist a large manila envelope. "If he has any questions, he can just phone me. Thanks." She turned and fled the building, taking the stairs rather than the elevator. She never liked to meet with Seth. He tended to be harried and abstracted, and they worked just as well together on the phone. "Mamie? Great stuff," he liked to say. "I'm sending the manuscript back with my suggestions. But ignore them." And always the manuscript arrived three weeks later with comments in the margin, like *Oh please* and *No shit*.

She bought a paper and walked downtown toward some galleries she knew on Grand Street, stopping at a coffee shop on Lafayette. Usually she ordered a cup of coffee *and* a cup of tea, as well as a brownie, propping up her sadness with chocolate and caffeine so that it became an anxiety.

"You want something or nothing?" the waitress asked her.

"What?" Startled, Mamie ordered the Slenderella.

"Good choice," said the waitress, as if it had been a test, and then hurried to the kitchen in a palsied jog.

Mamie spread the paper out at a diagonal and read, the pages stoically full of news of the war in India and, locally, of the women's bodies dredged up weekly from the Gowanus Canal. Disappeared women, with contusions. Beaten and drowned. Secretaries, students, a Rosie or two.

The Slenderella came with egg salad, and she ate it slowly, dissolving it in her mouth, its moist, mothering yellow. On the obituary page there were different deaths, young men, as in a war, and always the ending: *He is survived by his parents.*

Leaving the paper on the table as a tip, she spent the rest of the morning wandering in and out of galleries, looking at paintings that seemed much worse to her than Rudy's. Why these and not her husband's? Painting pictures was the only thing he had ever wanted to do, but no one was helping him. Age had already grabbed him in the face: His cheeks sagged houndishly, his beard was shot with white. Bristly hairs sprouted like wheat from his ears. She used to go with him to art openings, listening to people say bewildering things like "Syntax? Don't you just love *syntax*?" or "Now you know why people are starving in India – we had to wait an hour for our biriyani!" She began to leave early – while he lingered there, dressed in a secondhand pair of black leather pants he looked terrible in, chatting up the dealers, the famous, the successful. He would offer to show them his slides. Or he would go into his rap about Theoretical Disaster Art, how if you can depict atrocities, you can prevent them. "Anticipate, and imitate," he said. "You can preclude and dispirit a holocaust by depriving it of its originality; enough books and plays and paintings, you can change history by getting there first."

One East Village dealer looked him heavily in the eye and said, "You know, in a hive, when a bee has something to communicate, it does a dance. But if the bee does not stop dancing, the others sting it to death," and the dealer then turned and started talking to someone else.

Rudy always walked home alone, slow across the bridge, his life exactly the same as it was. His heart, she knew, was full of that ghetto desire to leap from poor to rich with a single, simple act, that yearning that exhausted the poor – something the city required: an exhausted poor. He would comb the dumpsters for clothes, for artbooks, for pieces of wood to build into frames and stretchers, and in the early hours of the morning he would arrive home with some huge dried flower he had scavenged, a wobbly plant stand, or a small, beveled mirror. At noon, without an apartment to paint, he might go into the city, to the corner of Broadway and Wall, to play his harmonica for coins. Sea chanteys and Dylan. Sometimes passersby would slow down on "Shenandoah," which he played so mournfully that even what he called "some plagiarist of living," in a beige all-weather coat, "some guy who wears his asshole on his sleeve," might stop on his lunch hour to let a part of himself leap up in the hearing, in communion, in reminder of times left behind. But mostly, everyone just sailed past, tense with errands, stubbing their feet on the shoe box Rudy'd placed on the sidewalk for contributions. He did not play badly. And he could look as handsome as an actor. But mad – something there in the eyes. Madmen, in fact, were attracted to him, came bounding up to him like buddies, shouting psychotically, shaking his hand and putting their arms around him while he played.

But people with money wouldn't give it to a guy with a harmonica. A guy with a harmonica had to be a drinker. To say nothing of a guy with a harmonica wearing a T-shirt that read: *Wino Cogito: I Think Therefore I Drink.* "I forget sometimes," said Rudy, unconvincingly. "I forget and wear that shirt." People with money would spend six dollars on a cocktail for themselves, but not eighty cents toward a draft beer for a guy with a shirt like that. Rudy would return home with enough cash for one new brush, and with that new brush would paint a picture of a bunch of businessmen sodomizing farm animals. "The best thing about figure painting," he liked to say, "is deciding what everyone will wear."

On days when he and his friend Marco got apartment-painting work, they would make real money, tax free, and treat themselves to Chinese food. They called their house-painting partnership We Aim for the Wall, and as a gimmick they gave out balloons. On these occasions rich people liked them – "Hey, where's my balloon, guys?" – until they discovered liquor missing or unfamiliar long-distance calls on their phone bills. As a result, referrals were rare.

And now something was happening to him. At night, even more than before, he would push her, force her, and she was growing afraid of him. *I love you*, he would murmur. *If only you knew how much.* He'd grip her painfully at the shoulders, his mouth tight on hers, his body hurting her. In museums and galleries he quietly mocked her opinions. "You don't know anything about art," he would say, scornfully shaking his head, if she liked something by someone who wasn't Rembrandt, someone he felt competitive with, someone his own age, someone who was a woman.

She began going alone, as now, whizzing around the gallery partitions and then stopping, long, in front of a piece she liked, one that pulled her in and danced a little before letting her go. She liked scenes, something with water and a boat, but she rarely found any. Mostly there was only what she called Warning Label art: *Like Man*, said one. *Love Hates*, said another.

Or she would go to a movie. A boy with a plate in his head

falls in love with a girl who spurns him. He kidnaps her, feeds her, then kills her by opening up her skull to put a plate in there, too. He props her up in a chair and paints watercolors of her in the nude.

On the subway back, in the afternoon, every beggar seemed to her to have Rudy's face, turning, leering. They would come upon her suddenly, sit next to her and belch, take out a harmonica and play an old folk tune. Or sit far away and just look. She would glance up, and every bum in the car would have his stare, persistent as pain.

She got off at Fourth Avenue and dropped her jar off at the clinic.

"We'll telemail you the results," said a young man in a silvery suit, a technician who eyed her warily.

"All right," she said.

To console herself she went to a shop around the corner and tried on clothes. She and Rudy used to do this sometimes, two young poor people, posing in expensive outfits, just to show the other what they would look like *if only*. They would step out of the dressing rooms and curtsy and bow, exasperating the salesperson. Then they would return all the clothes to the racks, go home, make love. Once, before he left the store, Rudy pulled a formal suit off the rack and screamed, "I don't go to these places!" That same night, in the throes of a nightmare, he had groped for the hatchet beneath him and raised it above her, his mouth open, his eyes gone. "Wake up," she'd pleaded, and squeezed his arm until he lowered it, staring emptily at her, confusion smashed against recognition, a surface broken for air.

"Come here," Rudy said, when she got home. He had made a dinner of fruit and spinach salad, plus large turkey drumsticks that had been on sale – a Caveman Special. He was a little drunk. The painting he had been working on, Mamie could see now, was of a snarling dog *leaping upon* a Virgin Mary, tearing at her lederhosen – not a good sign. Next to the canvas, cockroaches were smashed on the floor like maple creams.

"I'm tired, Rudy," she said.

"Come on." The cabbagey rot of his one bad molar drifted toward her like a cloud. She moved away from him. "After dinner I want you to go for a walk with me, then. At least." He belched.

"All right." She sat down at the table and he joined her. The television was on, a rerun of *Lust for Life*, Rudy's favorite movie.

"What a madman, Van Gogh," he drawled. "Shooting himself in the stomach. Any sane person would shoot themselves in the head."

"Of course," said Mamie, staring into the spinach leaves; orange sections lay dead on the top like goldfish. She chewed on the turkey leg, which was gamy and dry. "This is delicious, Rudy." *Any sane person would shoot themselves in the head.* For dessert there was a candy bar, split in two.

They went out. It was dusk, the sun not setting as quickly as in January, when it descended fast as a window shade, but now slowing a little, a lingering, hesitant light. A black eye yellowing. They walked together down the slope toward South Brooklyn, into the streak of orange that would soon be night. They seemed somehow to be racing one another, first one of them slightly ahead, then the other. They passed the old brick row homes, the St. Thomas Aquinas Church, the station stop for the F train and the G, that train that went nowhere, it was said, because it went from Brooklyn to Queens, never to Manhattan; no one was ever on it.

They continued walking beneath the el. A train roared deafeningly above them. The streetlights grew sparse, the houses smaller, fenced and slightly collapsed, like the residents of an old folks' home, waiting to die and staring. What stores there were were closed and dark. A skinny black Labrador in front of one of them sniffed at some bags of garbage, nuzzled them as if they were dead bodies that required turning to reveal the murder weapon, the ice pick in the back. Rudy took Mamie's hand. Mamie could feel it – hard, scaly, chapped from turpentine, the nails ridged as seashells, the thumbs blackened by accidents on the job, dark blood underneath, growing out.

"Look at your hands," said Mamie, stopping and holding his hand under a streetlight. There was melted chocolate still on his palm, and he pulled it away self-consciously, wiped it on his coat. "You should use some lotion or something, Rudy. Your hands are going to fall off and land on the sidewalk with a big clank."

"So don't hold them."

The Gowanus Canal lay ahead of them. Already the cold sour smell of it, milky with chemicals, blew onto their faces. "Where are we going, anyway?" she asked. A man in a buttonless coat approached them from the bridge, then crossed and kept walking. "This is a little weird, isn't it, being out here at this hour?" They had come to the drawbridge over the canal and stopped. It was strange, this toxic little vein, strange to stand above it, looking down at night, in a dangerous neighborhood, as if they were in love and entitled to such adventures. Sometimes it seemed she and Rudy were two people attempting to tango, sweating and trying, long after the orchestra had grown tired, long after everyone else had gone home.

Rudy leaned his arms on the railing of the bridge, and another train roared over them, an F train, with its raspberry-pink square. "This is the highest elevated in the city," he said, though the train was drowning him out.

Once the train had passed, Mamie murmured, "I know." When Rudy started giving tours of Brooklyn like this, she knew something was the matter.

"Don't you bet there are bodies in this water? Ones the papers haven't notified us of yet? Don't you bet that there are mobsters, and molls, and just the bodies of women that men never learned to love?"

"Rudy, what are you saying?"

"I'll bet there are more bodies here," he said, and for a moment Mamie could see the old familiar rage in his face, though it flew off again, like a bird, and in that moment there seemed nothing on his face at all, a station between trains, until his features pitched suddenly inward, and he began to cry into the sleeves of his coat, into his hard, gravelly hands.

"Rudy, what is it?" She stood behind him and held him, put her arms around his waist, her cheek against his back. There had been times he had consoled her this way, times when he had simply rubbed her back and connected her again to something: Those times when it seemed she'd floated off and was living far away, he had been like a medium calling her from the dead. "Here we are in the Backrub Cave," he'd said, hovering above her, the quilt spread over them both in a small, warm hut, all the ages of childhood returning to her with his hands. Life was long enough so that you could keep relearning things, think and feel and realize again what you used to know.

He coughed and didn't turn around. "I want to prove to my parents I'm not a fuck-up." Once, when he was twelve, his father had offered to drive him to Andrew Wyeth's house. "You wanna be an artist, dontcha, son? Well, I found out where he lives!"

"It's a little late to be worrying about what our parents think of us," she said. Rudy tended to cling to things that were beside the point – the point was always too frightening. Another train roared by, and the water beneath them wafted up sour and sulfuric. "What is it, really, Rudy? What is it you fear?"

"The Three Stooges," he said. "Poverty, Obscurity, Masturbation. Also the three *E*'s. Ennui. Anomie. Misery. Give me one good reason why we should go on living." He was shouting.

"Sorry," she sighed. She pulled away from him, brushed something from his coat. "You've caught me on a bad day." She searched his profile for an emotion, one that had found dress but not weapons. "I mean, it's life or nothing, right? You don't have to love it, you only have to—" She couldn't think of what.

"We live in a terrible world," he said, and he turned to look at her, wistful and in pain. She could smell that acrid, animal smell hot under his arms. He could smell like that sometimes, like a crazy person. One time she mentioned it, and he went immediately to perfume himself with her bath powder, coming to bed smelling like her. Another time, mistaking the container, he sprinkled himself all over with Ajax.

"Happy Valentine's Day."

"Yes," she said, fear thick in her voice. "Can we go back now?"

He would sit among them with great dignity and courtesy. "You must pray to this god of yours that keeps you so well. You must pray to him to let us live. Or, if we are to die, let us then go live with your god so that we too may know him." There was silence among the Englishmen. "You see," added the chief, "we pray to our god, but he does not listen. We have done something to offend." Then the chief would stand, go home, remove his English clothes, and die (picture).

Goz was in the ladies' room again, and she smiled as Mamie entered. "Going to ask me about my love life?" she said, flossing her teeth in front of the mirror. "You always do."

"All right," said Mamie. "How's your love life?"

Goz sawed back and forth with the floss, then tugged it out. "I don't have a love life. I have a *like* life."

Mamie smiled. She thought how nice that might be, to be peacefully free from love – love and its desire for itself – a husband and wife like two army buddies with stories and World Series bets.

"It's pure, it's stripped, it's friendly. Coffee and dispassion. You should try it." She ducked into one of the stalls and locked it. "Nothing is safe anymore," she called out from inside.

Mamie left, went to a record store, and bought records. No one had been buying them for years now, and you could get them for seventy-five cents. She bought only albums that had a song with the word *heart* in the title: *The Vernacular Heart*, *Hectic Heart*, *A Heart Is Just a Bicycle Behind Your Ribs*. Then she had to leave. Outside the dizzying heat of the store, she clutched them to her chest and walked, down through the decaying restaurant smells of Chinatown toward the Brooklyn Bridge. The sidewalks were fetid and wet, and the day was warm, as if spring had already come. Everyone was out walking. She would stop at the clinic on the way home and drop off her jar.

She thought of a dream she had had the night before. In the dream a door in the apartment opened up and suddenly there were more rooms, rooms she hadn't known existed, a whole house beneath, which was hers. There were birds living inside, and everything was very dark but beautiful, room after room, with windows open for the birds. On the walls were needlepoint samplers that read: *Die Here*. The real estate agent with the scarf kept saying, "In this day and age" and "It's a steal." Goz was there, her blond hair tipped in red and growing dark roots. Tricolor like candy corn. "Just us girls," she kept saying. It was the end of the world, and they were supposed to live there together, as long as it took to die, until their gums felt strange and they got colds and lost their hair, the television all dots and snow. She remembered some sort of movement – bunched and panicky, through stairwells, corridors, dark tunnels hidden behind paintings – and then, in the dream, it untangled to a fluttering stasis.

When she reached the bridge, she noticed some commotion, a disturbance up ahead, halfway across. Two helicopters were circling in the sky, and there was a small crowd at the center of the pedestrian walk. A fire truck and a police car whizzed by beneath her on the right, lights flashing. She walked to the edge of the crowd. "What is it?" she asked a man.

"Look." He pointed toward another man, who had climbed out over the iron mesh and crossbeams, out to the far railing of the bridge. His wrists were banded in black, and his hands held on to the suspension cables. His back arched and his body swayed out over the water below, as if caught in a web of steel parallelograms. His head dangled like someone crucified, and the wind tore through his hair. In the obscured profile, she thought she could make out the features.

"Oh, my God," she said.

"The woman in front of us says he's the guy wanted for the Gowanus Canal murders. See the police boats circling down there?" Two red-and-white speedboats were churning up water. One of the helicopters hovered noisily above.

"Oh, my God," Mamie said again, and pushed her way through the crowd. A white heat burst in her brain. A police motorbike pulled up on the walkway behind her. A policeman with pistols got off. "It's someone I know," Mamie repeated to people, and elbowed them aside. "It's someone I know." She held her purse and bag in front of her and pushed. The policeman was following close behind, so she pressed hard. When she came to the place directly across from the man, she put down her things and lifted her knee up onto the rail, swung her leg over, and began to crawl, metal to skin, toward the outer reaches of the bridge. "Hey!" someone shouted. The policeman. "Hey!" Cars sped beneath her, and an oceany wind rushed into her mouth. She tried not to look down. "Rudy!" she called out, but it seemed feeble in the roar, her throat a half throat. "It's me!" She felt surrounded by sky, moving toward it, getting closer. Her nails broke against metal. She was getting closer, close enough, soon, to grab him, to talk to him, to take his face in her hands and say something about *let's go home.* But then suddenly, too far from her, he relinquished his grip on the cables and fell, turning, his limbs like a windmill, vanishing into the East River below.

She froze. *Rudy.* Two people screamed. There was a whirring noise from the crowd behind her, people pressed to the railings. *No, not this.* "Excuse me, m'am," shouted a voice. "Did you say you knew this man?"

She inched backward on her knees, lowered herself to the walkway. Her legs were scraped and bleeding, but she didn't feel them. Someone was touching her, clamping hands around her arms. Her purse and bag were still where she'd left them, leaning against the cement, and she jerked free, grabbed them, and began to run.

She ran the rest of the way across the bridge, down into the ammonia dank of a passageway, then up again to an old ruined park, zigzagging through the fruit streets of the Heights

– Cranberry, Pineapple – along the hexagonal cobbles of the promenade, along the water, and then up left, in a ricochet against the DON'T WALK lights. She did not stop running even when she found herself in Carroll Gardens, heading toward the Gowanus Canal. *No, not this.* She ran up the slope of South Brooklyn for twenty minutes, through traffic, through red lights and sirens, beneath the scary whoop of helicopters and a bellowing plane, until she reached the house with the bird feeder, and when she got there, scarcely able to breathe, she sank down on the concrete lip of its fence and let out a cry, solitary and strangled, into her bag of songs.

The afternoon darkened. Two Rosies shuffled by, ignoring her, but slowing down, winded. They, too, decided to sit on the low wall of the fence, but chose to do so at some distance. She had already slid into the underclass of the sick, she knew, but they didn't recognize her yet. "Are you OK?" she heard one Rosie say to the other, putting her box of flowers down on the sidewalk.

"I'm OK," said her friend.

"You look worse."

"Maybe," she sighed. "The thing is you never know why you're any particular place. You get up, you move. You keep thinking there's some other way than this."

"Look at *her*," snorted the friend, motioning toward Mamie.

"What?" said the other, and then they fell silent.

A fire truck clanged by. Sirens wailed in outrage. After some time Mamie got up, slow as an arthritic, clutching only her purse – her jar still in it – leaving the records behind. She began to walk, stumbling on a raised crack in the pavement. And she noticed something: The house with the bird feeder didn't have a cupola at all. It didn't even have a bird feeder. It simply had a sign that said RESTAURANT, and there was a pigeon on it.

She walked by the Rosies and gave them a dollar for an iris. "My," said the one handing it to her.

At the apartment, the lights were on and the padlock hung open like a hook. She stood for a moment, then kicked at the door with her foot, banging the inside knob against the wall. There was no other sound, and she hesitated there in the doorway, a form of desire, a hovering thing that cannot enter a room. But slowly she took a step, the heel of her hand pressed to the doorjamb to steady her.

He was there, hair dry, wearing different clothes. His arms were raised over his head, the stray tom like a mast in his hands on top. He was moving slowly around the place, as if in a deep Oriental exercise or a dance, the cat investigating the bookshelves.

"It's you," Mamie said, frozen by the open door.

The pumpkin stench of the bathroom wafted toward her. The uriney cold rushed in from behind, carrying with it the flap of helicopters. He turned to see her, brought the cat down to his chest. "Hi." He was chewing on a difficult bit of candy, pieces of it stuck in his teeth. He pointed to his cheek, grimacing. "Jujubes," he said. "They play with your mind."

The television burst on: people chanting together, like an anthem for cola. *We are the Undying. We are . . .*

He turned away and lifted the cat up high again, close to the golden moldings of the ceiling. "Cats love this," he said. His arms were long and tireless. In the reach, his shirt had come untucked, and the soft bare skin of his waist flashed like a smile. "Where have you been?"

There was only this world, this looted, ventriloquized earth. If one were to look for a place to die, mightn't it be here? – like some old lesson of knowing your kind and returning. She was afraid, and the afraid, she realized, sought opportunities for bravery in love. She tucked the flower in her blouse. Life or death. Something or nothing. *You want something or nothing?*

She stepped toward him with a heart she'd someday tear the terror from.

Here. But not now.

1989

PAPER LOSSES

ALTHOUGH KIT AND RAFE had met in the peace movement, marching, organizing, making no nukes signs, now they wanted to kill each other. They had become, also, a little pro-nuke. Married for two decades of precious, precious life, she and Rafe seemed currently to be partners only in anger and dislike, their old lusty love mutated to rage. It was both the shame and the demise of them that hate like love could not live on air. And so in this, their newly successful project together, they were complicitous and synergistic. They were nurturing, homeopathic, and enabling. They spawned and raised their hate together, cardiovascularly, spiritually, organically. In tandem, as a system, as a dance team of bad feeling, they had shoved their hate center stage and shown a spotlight down for it to seize. *Do your stuff, baby! Who's the best? Who's the man?*

"Pro-nuke? You are? Really?" Kit was asked by friends, to whom she continued indiscreetly to complain.

"Well, no." Kit sighed. "But in a way."

"You seem like you need someone to talk to."

Which hurt Kit's feelings, since she'd felt she was talking to *them*. "I'm just concerned about the kids," Kit said.

Rafe had changed. His smile was just a careless yawn, or was his smile just stuck carelessly on? Which was the correct lyric? She did not know. But, for sure, he had changed. In Beersboro they put things neutrally, like that. Such changes were couched. No one ever said a man was now completely screwed up. They said, *The guy has changed*. Rafe had started to make model rockets in the basement. He'd become *a little different*. He was something of *a character*. The brazen might suggest, *He's gotten into some weird shit*. The rockets were tall, plastic, penile-shaped things to which Rafe carefully shellacked authenticating military decals. What had happened to the handsome hippie she had married? He was prickly and remote, empty with fury. A blankness had entered his blue-green eyes. They stayed wide and bright but nonfunctional – like dime-store jewelry. She wondered if this was a nervous breakdown, the genuine article. But it persisted for months and she began to suspect, instead, a brain tumor. Occasionally he catcalled and wolf-whistled across his mute alienation, his pantomime of hate momentarily collapsed. "Hey, cutie," he would call to her from the stairs, after not having looked her in the eye for two months. It was like being snowbound with someone's demented uncle: Should marriage be like that? She wasn't sure.

She seldom saw him anymore when he got up in the morning and left for his office. And when he came home from work, he would disappear down the basement stairs. Nightly, in the anxious conjugal dusk that was now their only life together, after the kids went to bed, the house would fill up with fumes. When she called down to him about this he never answered. He seemed to have turned into some sort of space alien. Of course later she would understand that all this meant he was involved with another woman, but at the time, protecting her own vanity and sanity, she was working with two hypotheses only: brain tumor or space alien.

"All husbands are space aliens," said her friend Jan.

"God help me, I had no idea," said Kit. She began spreading peanut butter on a pretzel and eating quickly.

"In fact," said Jan, "my sister and I call them UFOs."

It stood for something. Kit hated to ask.

"Ungrateful fuckers," Jan said.

Kit thought for a moment. "But what about the *o*?" she asked. "You said *UFO*."

There was a short silence. "Ungrateful fuckeroos," Jan added quickly. "I know that doesn't make perfect sense."

"He's in such disconnect. His judgment is so bad."

"Not on the planet he lives on. On *his* planet he's a veritable Solomon. 'Bring the stinkin' baby to me now!' "

"Do you think people can be rehabilitated and forgiven?"

"Sure! Look at Ollie North."

"Well, he lost that Senate race. He was not sufficiently forgiven."

"But he got some votes," Jan insisted.

"Yeah, and now what is he doing?"

"Now he's back promoting a line of fire-retardant pajamas. It's a life!" Jan paused. "Do you fight about it?"

"About what?" asked Kit.

"The rockets back to his homeland."

Kit sighed. "Yes, the toxic military crafts business poisoning our living space. Do I fight? I don't fight I just, well, OK: I ask a few questions from time to time. I ask, 'What the hell are you doing?' I ask, 'Are you trying to asphyxiate your entire family?' I ask, 'Did you hear me?' Then I ask, 'Did you hear me?' again. Then I ask, 'Are you deaf?' I also ask, 'What do you think a marriage is? I'm really just curious to know,' and also, 'Is this your idea of a well-ventilated place?' A simple interview, really. I don't believe in fighting. I believe in giving peace a chance. I also believe in internal bleeding." She paused to shift the phone more comfortably against her face. "I'm also interested," Kit said, "in those forensically undetectable dissolving plastic bullets. Have you heard of those?"

"No."

"Well, maybe I'm wrong about those. I'm probably wrong. That's where the Mysterious Car Crash may have to come in." In the chrome of the refrigerator she caught the reflection of her own face, part brunette Shelley Winters, part potato, the finely etched sharps and accidentals beneath her eyes a musical interlude amidst the bloat. In every movie she had seen with Shelley Winters in it, Shelley Winters was the one who died. Peanut butter was stuck high and dry on Kit's gums. On the counter a large old watermelon had begun to sag and pull apart in the middle along the curve of seeds, like a shark's grin, and she lopped off a wedge, rubbed its cool point around the inside of her mouth. It had been a year since Rafe had kissed her. She sort of cared and sort of didn't. A woman had to choose her own particular unhappiness carefully. That was the only happiness in life: to choose the best unhappiness. An unwise move, good God, you could squander everything.

The summons took her by surprise. It came in the mail,

addressed to her, and there it was, stapled to divorce papers. She'd been properly served. The bitch had been papered. Like a person, a marriage was unrecognizable in death, even buried in an excellent suit. Atop the papers themselves was a letter from Rafe suggesting their spring wedding anniversary as the final divorce date. *Why not complete the symmetry?* he wrote, which didn't even sound like him, though its heartless efficiency was suited to this, his new life as a space alien, and in keeping generally with the principles of space alien culture. The papers referred to Kit and Rafe by their legal names, Katherine and Raphael, as if it were the more formal versions of themselves who were divorcing – their birth certificates were divorcing! – and not they themselves. Rafe was still living in the house and had not told her yet he'd bought a new one. "Honey," she said trembling, "something very interesting came in the mail today."

Rage had its medicinal purposes, but she was not wired to sustain it, and when it tumbled away, loneliness engulfed her, grief burning at the center in a cold blue heat. At two different funerals of elderly people she hardly knew she went in and wept in the back row of the church like a secret lover of the deceased. She felt woozy and ill and never wanted to see Rafe – or rather, Raphael – again, but they had promised the kids this Caribbean vacation, so what could they do. This at last was what all those high school drama classes had been for: acting. She once had played the queen in *The Winter's Tale* and once a changeling child in a play called *Love Me Right Now*, written by one of the more disturbing English teachers in her high school. In both of these she learned that time was essentially a comic thing – only constraints upon it forced it to tragedy, or at least to misery. Romeo and Juliet, Tristan and Isolde – if only they'd had more time! Marriage stopped being comic when it was suddenly halted, at which point it became divorce, which time never disrupted, and so the funniness of which was never-ending.

Still, Rafe mustered up thirty seconds of utterance in order to persuade her not to join them on this vacation. "I don't think you should go," he announced.

"I'm going," she said.

"We'll be giving the children false hope."

"Hope is never false. Or it's always false. Whatever. It's just hope," she said. "Nothing wrong with that."

"I just don't think you should go." Divorce, she could see, would be like marriage: a power grab, as in who would be the dog and who would be the owner of the dog?

What bimbo did he want to give her ticket to? (Only later would she find out. "As a feminist you mustn't blame the other woman," a neighbor told her. "As a feminist I request that you no longer speak to me," Kit replied.)

And months later, in the courtroom, where she would discover that the county owned her marriage and that the county was now taking it back like a chicken franchise she had made a muck of, forbidding her to own another franchise for six more months, with the implication that she might want to stay clear of all poultry cuisine for a much longer time than that, when she had finally to pronounce in front of the robed, robotic judge and a winking stenographer whose winking seemed designed to keep the wives from crying, she would have to declare the marriage "irretrievably broken." What second-rate poet had gotten hold of the divorce laws? She would find the words sticking in her throat, untrue in their conviction. Was not everything fixable? This age of disposables, was it not also an age of fantastic adhesives? Why "irretrievably broken" like a songbird's wing? Why not "Do you find this person you were married to, and who is now sitting next to you in the courtroom, a total asshole?" That would suffice, and be more accurate. The term "irretrievably broken" sent one off into an eternity of wondering. Whereas the other did not.

She and Rafe had not yet, however, signed the papers. And there was the matter of her wedding ring, which was studded with little junk emeralds and which she liked a lot and hoped she could continue wearing because it didn't look like a typical wedding ring. He had removed his ring – which did look like a typical wedding ring – a year earlier because he said it "bothered" him. She had thought at the time he'd meant it was rubbing. He had often just shed his clothes spontaneously – when they had first met he was something of a nudist. It was good to date a nudist: things moved right along. But it was not good trying to stay married to one. Soon she would be going on chaste geriatric dates with other people whose clothes would, like hers, remain glued to the body.

"What if I can't get my ring off," she said to him now on the plane to La Caribe, the gringo enclave Rafe had chosen. She had gained a little weight in their twenty years of marriage but really not all *that* much. She had been practically a child bride! "Send me the sawyer's bill," he said. Oh, the sparkle in his eye *was* gone!

"What is wrong with you?" she said. Of course, she blamed his parents, who had somehow, long ago, accidentally or on purpose, raised him as a space alien, with space alien values, space alien thoughts, and the hollow shifty character, concocted guilelessness, and sociopathic secrets of a space alien.

"What is wrong with *you*?" he snarled. This was his habit, his space alien habit, of merely repeating what she had just said to him. It had to do, no doubt, with his central nervous system, a silicon-chipped information processor incessantly encountering new linguistic combinations, which it then had to absorb and file. Repetition bought time and assisted the storage process.

More than the girls, who were just little, she was worried about Sam, their sensitive fourth grader, who now sat across the airplane aisle moodily staring out the window at the clouds. Soon, through the machinations of the extremely progressive divorce laws – a boy needs his dad! – she would no longer see him every day; he would become a boy who no longer saw his mother every day, and he would scuttle and float a little off and away like paper carried by wind. With time he would harden: he would eye her over his glasses, in the manner of a maître d' suspecting the arrival of riffraff. But on this, their last trip as an actual family, he did fairly well at not letting on. They all slept in the same room, in separate beds, and saw other families squalling and squabbling, so that by comparison theirs – a family about to break apart forever – didn't look so bad. She was not deceived by the equatorial sea breeze and so did not overbake herself in the colonial sun; with the resort managers she shared her moral outrage at the armed guards who kept the local children from sneaking past the fence onto this white, white beach; and she rubbed a kind of resin into her brow to freeze it there and downplay the creases – to appear younger for her departing husband, though he never once looked at her. Not that she looked that good: her suitcase had gotten lost and she was forced to wear clothes purchased from the gift shop – the words LA CARIBE emblazoned across every single thing.

On the beach people read books about Rwandan and Yugoslavian genocide. This was to add seriousness to a trip that lacked it. One was supposed not to notice the dark island boys on the other side of the guards and barbed wire, throwing rocks. When a cruise ship temporarily docked in the bay, and then departed, she joined some other tourists on the beach to shout at the boat, "Don't let the door hit you in the ass!" as if they were different and not all of them tourists, seeking to console themselves with hierarchies of tourism, to keep the stone-throwing boys from one's thoughts.

There were ways of making things temporarily vanish. One could disappear oneself in movement and repetition. Sam liked only the trampoline and nothing else. There were dolphin rides, but Sam sensed their cruelty. "They speak a language," he said. "We shouldn't ride them."

"They look happy," said Kit.

Sam looked at her with seriousness from some sweet beyond. "They look happy so you won't kill them."

"You think so?"

"If dolphins tasted good," he said, "we wouldn't even know about their language." That the intelligence in a thing could undermine your appetite for it. That yumminess obscured the mind of the yummy as well as the mind of the yummer. That deliciousness resulted in decapitation. That you could only understand something if you did not desire it. How did he know these things already? Usually girls realized this first. But not hers. Her girls, Beth and Dale, were tough beyond Kit's comprehension: practical, self-indulgent, independent five-year-old twins, a system unto themselves. They had their own secret world of Montessori code words and plastic jewelry and spells of hilarity brought on mostly by the phrase "cinnamon M&M's" repeated six times fast. They wore sparkly fairy wings wherever they went, even over cardigans, and they carried wands. "I'm a big brother now," Sam had said repeatedly to everyone and with uncertain pride the day the girls were born, and after that he spoke not another word on the matter. Sometimes, silently, Kit accidentally referred to Beth and Dale as Death and Bail, as they buried their several Barbies in sand, then lifted them out again with glee. Anyone near, on a towel, reading of holocausts, turned and smiled. In this fine, far compound on the sea, the contradictions of life were grotesque and uninventable. She went to the central office and signed up for a hot stone massage: "Would you like a man or a woman?" asked the receptionist.

"Excuse me?" asked Kit, stalling – after all these years of marriage, which *did* she want? What did she know of *men* – or *women*? "There's no such thing as *men*," her friend Jan used to say, until recently. "Every man is different. The only thing they have in common is – well – a capacity for horrifying violence."

"A man or a woman – for the massage?" Kit asked now, buying time. She thought of the slow mating of snails, an entire day, being hermaphrodites and having it all be so confusing: by the time they had it figured out who was going to be the girl and who was going to be the boy someone came along with some garlic paste and just swooped them right up.

"Oh, either one," she said, and then she knew she'd get a man. Whom she tried not to look at but could smell in all his smoky aromas – tobacco, incense, cannabis – exhaling and swirling their way around him. A wiry old American pothead gone to grim seed, he had the Dickensian name of Daniel Handler, and he did not speak. He placed hot stones along her back and left them there in a line up her spine – did she think her belotioned flesh too private and precious to be touched by the likes of him? Are you *crazy*? The mad joy pulsing in her face was held over the floor by the table headpiece and at his touch her eyes filled with bittersweet tears, which then dripped out her nose, which she realized then was positioned perfectly by God as a little drainpipe for crying. The sad massage hut carpet beneath her grew a spot. He left the hot stones on her until they went cold. As each one lost its heat she could no longer feel it even there on her back, and then its removal was like a discovery that it had been there all along: how strange to forget and feel it only then, at the end; though this wasn't the same thing as the frog in the pot whose water slowly heats and boils, still it had meaning, she felt, the way metaphors of a thermal nature tended to. Then he took all the stones off and pressed the hard edges of them deep into her back, between the bones, in a way that felt mean – perhaps in embittered rage about his own life – but that more likely had no intention at all. "That was nice," she said at the end, when she saw him putting all his stones away. He had heated them in a plastic electric Crock-Pot filled with water, she saw, and now he unplugged the thing in a tired fashion.

"Where did you get those stones?" she asked. They were smooth and dark gray – black when wet, she could see.

"They're river stones," he said. "I've been collecting them for years up in Colorado." He replaced them in a metal fishing tackle box.

"You live in Colorado?" she asked.

"Used to," he said, and that was that. Later that day they would see each other at the Farmacia de Jesus and look the other way.

Kit got dressed. "Someday you, like me, will have done sufficient lab work," Jan had said. "Soon you, like me, in your next life, like me, will want them old and rich, on their deathbed, really, and with no sudden rallyings in the hospice."

"You're a woman of steel and ice," Kit had said.

"Not at all," Jan had said. "I'm just a voice on the phone, drinking a little tea."

On their last night of vacation Kit's suitcase arrived like a joke. She didn't even open it. They put out the paper doorknob flag that said WAKE US UP FOR THE SEA TURTLES. The doorknob flag had a preprinted request to be woken at 3:00 a.m. so that they could go to the beach and see the hatching of the baby sea turtles and their quick scuttle into the ocean, under the cover of night, to avoid predators. But though Sam had hung the flag carefully and before the midnight deadline, no staffperson awoke them. And by the time they got up and went down to the beach it was ten in the morning. Strangely, the sea turtles were still there. They had hatched in the night and then hotel personnel had hung on to them, in a baskety cage, to show them off to the tourists who'd been too lazy or deaf to have gotten up in time. "Look, come see!" said a man with a Spanish accent who usually rented out the scuba gear. Sam, Beth, Dale, Kit all ran over. (Rafe stayed behind to drink coffee and read the paper.) The squirming babies were beginning to heat up in the warming sun; the goldening Venetian vellum of their wee webbed feet was already edged in desiccating brown. "I'm going to have to let them go now," said the man. "You are the last ones to see these little *bebés*." He took them over to the water's edge and let them go, hours too late, to make their own way into the sea. And one by one a frigate bird swooped in, plucked them from the silver waves, and ate them for breakfast.

Kit sank down in a large chair next to Rafe. He was tanning himself, she could see, for someone else's lust. "I think I need a drink," she said. The kids were swimming.

"Don't expect me to buy you a drink," he said.

Had she even asked? Did she now call him the bitterest name she could think of? Did she stand and turn and slap him across the face in front of several passersby? Who told you *that*?

When they left La Caribe, its crab claws of land extending into the blue bay, she was glad. Staying there she had begun to hate the world. In the airports and on the planes home, she did not even try to act natural: natural was a felony. She spoke to her children calmly, from a script, with dialogue and stage directions of utter neutrality. Back home in Beersboro she unpacked the condoms and candles, her little love sack, completely unused, and threw it all in the trash. What had she been thinking? Later, when she had learned to tell this story differently, as a story, she would construct a final lovemaking scene of sentimental vengeance that would contain the inviolable center of their love, the sweet animal safety of night after night, the still-beating tender heart of marriage. But for now she would become like her unruinable daughters, and even her son, who as he aged stoically and carried on regardless would come scarcely to recall – was it past even imagining? – that she and Rafe had ever been together at all.

2006

PARIS

WEEK ONE

IN PARIS WE eat brains every night. My husband, Daniel, likes the vaporous, fishy mousse of them. They are a kind of seafood, he thinks, locked tightly in the skull, like shelled creatures in the dark caves of the ocean, sprung suddenly free and killed by light; they've grown clammy with shelter, fortressed vulnerability, dreamy nights. Me, I'm eating for a flashback.

"The grass is always greener on the other side of the fence," says Daniel, finger raised, as if the thought had just come to him via the *cervelles*. "Remember the beast you eat. And it will remember you."

I'm hoping for something Proustian, all that forgotten childhood. I mash them against the roof of my mouth, melt them, waiting for something to be triggered in my head, in empathy or chemistry or some other rush of protein. The tempest in the teacup, the typhoon in the trout; there is wine, and we drink lots of it.

We sit beside people who show us wallet pictures of their children. *"Sont-ils si mignons!"* I say. My husband constructs remarks in his own patois. *We, us, have no little ones.* He doesn't know French. But he studied Spanish once, and now, with a sad robustness, speaks of our childlessness to the couple next to us. "But," he adds, thinking fondly of our cat, "we do have a large *gato* at home."

"*Gâteau* means cake," I whisper. "You've just told them we have a large cake at home." I don't know why he always strikes up conversations with the people next to us. But he does strike them up, thinking it friendly and polite rather than oafish and irritating, which is what I think.

Afterward, we always go to the same *chocolatier* for whiskey truffles. One feels the captured storm in these, a warm storm under the tongue.

"What aggrandizement are we in, again?" my husband asks.

"What *aggrandizement*?" I say. "I don't know, but I think we're in *one of the biggies*." My husband pronounces *tirez* as if it were Spanish, *père* as if it were "pier." The affectionate farce I make of him ignores the ways I feel his lack of love for me. But we are managing. We touch each other's sleeves. We say, "Look at that!" wanting our eyes to merge, our minds to be one. We are in Paris, with its impeccable marzipan and light, its whiffs of sewage and police state. With my sore hip and his fallen arches ("fallen archness," Daniel says), we walk the quais, stand on all the bridges in the misty rain, and look out on this pretty place, secretly imagining being married to other people – right here in River City! – and sometimes not, sometimes simply wondering, silently or aloud, what will become of the world.

WEEK TWO

There is a joke about a middle-aged woman who happens upon a frog, in the woods. "Kiss me! Kiss me," says the frog, "and I'll turn into a handsome prince!"

The woman stares, entranced, but doesn't move.

"What's the matter?" asks the frog, growing impatient. "Don't you want a handsome prince?"

"I'm sorry," says the woman, "but at this point in my life I'm actually more interested in a talking frog."

"I get it," says Daniel. "That's funny. That's good." I take his hand, lay it across my mouth, press it there. In travel, your husband's body becomes yours; you become united, fused, and you have the same arguments with it that you would with your own. Travel, at those times, becomes love, possession, the second wedding – not just an excuse an unhappy person can use to wear the same clothes every day. Which is what it could be, otherwise.

The gurgling coo of pigeons awakens us each morning. "Wake up and eat the daisies," Daniel whispers to me. We watch the pigeons leap winglessly from the ledges, as if in sailor dives, only spreading their wings at the last minute.

"Is that for aerodynamics?" I ask. "Is that to work up momentum?"

"It's laziness," says Daniel. "They're just being lazy."

Here in the Marais, we wake early in the mornings and are in bed early at night. We miss National Public Radio. We miss recycling, as silly or meagre as that sounds. Everything we use here must be thrown away, and it bothers us, robbed of our rituals of composting and reclamation, our daily treks out back to the rot heap, where we offer the earth scraps of itself, returning nature to nature!, defying time!, expediting the global Easter, when all shall rise again! Though we mean to, we've never actually used the compost: it is merely an act of apology.

While here for three weeks, we live in unapologetic sin. Touristic waste, native presumption. The Parisian meanness makes us despair, grounded in opinion as it is – unlike the meanness of Americans, which is all careless ego, selfishness, the stuff of spoiled, stupid children.

At night, Daniel is tired from the medical conference at the Institut de Génétique he is here to attend. As a researcher he is mostly, recently, interested in the Tay-Sachs gene we both carry – what Jews and French Canadians have in common. ("We'll simply tell our daughter we got her retail rather than wholesale," said Daniel, after we investigated the difficult procedures of adoption, the empty room upstairs we call the Maybe's Room still empty, our desires becoming courteous, less determined, discerning the hoops and circumstances.) Now this conference seems to him bogged down with squabbles about who should be in charge of the institute itself, research ownership, other such infighting. "All the lying and coffee it takes to get anything done at all," he says, have exhausted him. "Quick, a bonbon!" he exclaims.

"Well, you're fighting the good fight," I say.

"I'm crying the good cry." He sighs.

"You're doing fine."

I teach him a version of Honeymoon Bridge. We don't keep score, but we each try to win. When Daniel gets a bad hand, he falls forward, groaning. "This hand is a foot!," a line from some dissolute uncle of his. That – along with our Chez Stadium, *mais oui*–may we jokes, and Pépé le Pew imitations – somehow keeps us amused, a brief contentment; it is a respite from our petty quarrels and brittle looks, arguing, as tourists do, about where we're going, where we are, the questions no longer just metaphorical but literal, replete with angry pointing and some disgusted grabbing of maps, right out of the other's hands.

By Wednesday morning, Daniel decides to go to a *gymnase* club before his meeting. He's up promptly, with the throaty rumble of the pigeons, the sky-whitening sun, the garbage trucks trolling along the curbs and the Siamese cat on the roof of the neighboring building, the slight honk of baby in its cry, scratching at a window to be let in. Daniel's grown restless and irritable. "This would be a great town," he says at breakfast over *café crème*, "if only everyone spoke Spanish." His voice is full of rue. "Also, why does everyone in the whole city have to touch the bread? You go to buy bread, and the baker touches it, the cashier touches it, the assistant hands it over to you, then finally you yourself just tuck it under your armpit and go out and bump into other people with it. How can we have a medical conference in a town with such unsanitary bread?"

This is not simple, jokey Ugly Americana. This is Daniel's way. It is like at home when he complains about emptying the dishwasher: "This is not a timesaving device. Why has no one invented something that will just wash these things right in the cupboard?" It is his habit to locate all the lapses and betrayals of the modern world. Yet it is also his habit to want to believe what he reads. He heads for places with signs that say *"Ici on parle anglais."* "But *on* is never there. Have you ever noticed that?"

"You're doing fine here," I say. "Think of it this way: The French love Jerry Lewis. They probably *adore* you." The world is in italics. "Think of this as a kind of *Doctors in Paris* thing. A musical." But even the italics, it seems, are losing their italics: standing tall, passing themselves off as literal and real. Straight shooters.

He gives me a look, then turns. "I like the weather," he adds enthusiastically. "You need a jacket, but you don't have to zip it!" Then he adds darkly, "It's that deportation monument. That tells you who the Parisians really are." The Deportation Memorial, in the shadow of Notre-Dame, is something we stumbled upon two days before, and it left us dumbstruck. "And another thing – you ever notice what the supreme Parisian compliment is? 'Oh, you speak French so well, without any *accent*!'"

"It's horrible," I agree. "It's rude."

"It's more than rude," he says. "It's genocidal." And he is right, I think. He is right.

With my middling French and leather jacket – unzipped! – trying to seem residential, I go with him to the gym, to get him settled there. We pay the money, and I ask the woman at the desk if there is anything else, any rule or requirement. She smiles. She looks at Daniel. "The only requirements is that you be happy man," she says. She is tan from sunlamps and is wearing an orange leotard.

"Bye," I say to him. *"Au revoir."* I leave to make my way alone along the ankle-twisting stones of the smaller crowded streets, my leather jacket squeaking like a chair. Perhaps I should go shopping – a married person's version of dating. Perhaps I should ditch the jacket and float around in the museums like a sylph, or a balloon.

People bump into me, and I say, "Whoops" or "Wope"– not words that translate into any Parisian comprehensibility, though they're the first sounds to my lips. Almost always. With everything.

Passing cafés and restaurants, I walk through the bright glances of men in love, who, looking briefly away from their lovers in order to more perfectly form a sentence, unwittingly cast their gaze across my path like a light. And so, to have accidentally caught their desire, swimming across the current of it like that, passing through, I feel loved, in a warm and random way, wandering through it as if it were a rainbow, that old trick of light, or a place in a pool where someone has peed. There is a sweet, silent rot to it.

Otherwise, it is hard, galumphing along through a sea of French women who have exquisite shoes and haircuts, overbites unruined by orthodontia, faces unbedecked by optometry, a great, nearsighted, chomping faith in their own beauty that makes them, perhaps, seem prettier than they are. It is hard to find a place for yourself in a city like this.

The trees are like candelabras. The pastries like art.

There is a smell one begins to exude here: something old-mannish and acrid, the smell of the cabbie we had coming in, something to do with the food, the wines and chèvres. My body fights travel, sends up the weapons of a homeless person, the boundaries thinly drawn, the body with its own knowledge, disorientations, defenses: the wincy sweat, the cheesy shit. It takes me walking, then sits me down again, over and over, with its own rhythms and wants.

My hip still aches from my fall last December, the cracked bone moody and susceptible to weather, but if I need to I limp. Perhaps somewhere I'll just stand against a wall and ask for coins.

"Paris," I hear a passing tourist remark. "It's one big StairMaster."

There is an Audrey Hepburn festival at one of the revival theatres on the Left Bank, and everywhere I see posters for it: Hepburn's wide eyes and mouth. "Have you ever noticed," Daniel has said, "that she looks like Anne Frank?" Now I feel as if I'm seeing pictures of Anne Frank all over town: Anne Frank in a black turtleneck. Anne Frank in an evening gown. The essence of Paris, Daniel might say. There you go: Anne Frank in an evening gown.

The italics are losing their italics.

The flower beds are full of pansies whose triangular, black centers are like the mustache of Hitler himself.

I stop at pâtisseries and get the ones with funny names: Divorce, Religieuse, Gland. I like the Divorce ones – half coffee, half chocolate – and I sit in the Luxembourg Gardens, eating my various Divorces, watching the children throw things into the pond. Planted in large, gorgeous ovals are tulips so big they look as if they'd steal your jewelry. There are school groups here on tour, the girls giddy and tired and falling into one another's laps, playing with one another's hair. The boys stand around looking exiled and sad.

I get up and walk some more, back across the river: the views of the city up and down dazzle and console. Near the Louvre, which is being cleaned, always being cleaned, two angels and some cherubs have been removed, set in locked crates at the edge of the Tuileries, and one can walk by and look at them through the slats, see them regally sitting there, a zoo of pagan saints, their winged and caged condition like the aftermath of some palace revolt in Heaven – *Aw*, I find myself thinking. *Aw*.

I go into the Louvre, but I don't stay long. It's too different now. I've lived long enough to see great museums change: their annexes and entrances, the location and arrangement of the art. My own memory, from a trip ten years ago, is a tired, old coin. Who will house that? Who will house the Museum of Museums, in order to show us how museums once were?

I decide to get on the Métro and go visit my friend Marguerite, who is a painter and printmaker, half-French, half-American, with an apartment near the Bois de Vincennes. I phone her from Châtelet. "*Allò, oui*?" she answers, which sounds to my bad ear like *à lui*, to him, to God, some religious utterance, a curse, or something to safeguard the speaker, but she explains later, "Oh, no. It's said that way just in case the caller hasn't heard the '*allò*.' It's a French distrust of technology."

"In a country *farci* with nuclear power plants?"

"*Ah, oui*," she says. "*Les contradictions*." Marguerite is a woman I met in college, and though we were not that close, we always remained interested in each other and in touch. She is the sort of woman about whom others ask "Oh, how is she? Is she still beautiful?" – she is tall and dazzling like that. And so I bring her my crush, inappropriate but useful between adult women, who need desperately to be liked and amused, and will make great use of any silent ceremony of affection.

For the time being, Marguerite is on Parisian welfare, which, I'm told, is so civilized as to provide tickets to such French necessities as movies and restaurants, and though she is loath to admit it, she is half looking for a rich husband. In her, I excuse everything I wouldn't like in anyone else.

"I'll be the one in the pith helmet," I say before I hang up, wondering what that even means.

At her Métro stop I get off and walk the three blocks to where she lives. She is sitting on the curb outside her building, like a kid rather than the forty-year-old woman she is. She has cut her hair off, shaved her head on one side, and with big, antique earrings she manages to make all long hair seem a slatternly, inelegant bore. "*Bonjour, Mademoiselle!*" I call in greeting, and when I get close go suddenly formal; I stick my hand out, and my fingers lock and go stiff, like a fistful of knives and forks. Luckily, she leaps up and hugs me, does the one kiss on the cheek, then two, three, four. "Four is chic now," she says.

"I need Dramamine for four," I say.

"It's French love!" she says and takes my arm, steers me through the locked gates and doors.

Inside, she offers me water, shows me her work, her serigraphs, her latest culinary effort (*terrine de lapin* – bowl of bunny), and even her new makeup, expensive and Japanese. There is only one remnant from college on display here, a blue-matted "Desiderata" hung discreetly on a wall, and it seems odd to see it. *Go placidly amid the noise and haste.*

What a crock.

Nonetheless, it troubles and haunts me.

"Great," I say loudly, idiotically, to everything. "Great!" She waves the makeup brushes around, the lipsticks and bottles, shouting, "Get out of my way, French women!" Which makes me laugh, because she is so beautiful already and because I have always thought of *her* as French. She points at her short skirt. "I will not cut my fashion to fit this year's conscience."

I smile. She has good legs. "Don't," I advise.

She wants to show me the galleries in her neighborhood,

to demonstrate what, in a curatorial culture, "now constitutes the dynamic."

"Great," I say. So we leave the apartment, lock the door, tramp around the neighborhood. We visit an exhibit called, "What Else Is There But Narcissism, I Often Ask Myself" – a collection of strangely silvered mirrors. We see another that is simply an arrangement of hundreds of dead pigeons. The artist, the gallery says in its writeup, was a homeless person, and this is his revenge on the pigeons who used to steal bread from his hands. After this installation opened, the gallery brochure informs us reassuringly, the artist received a grant.

"Are you OK?" asks Marguerite, noticing my walk. "You have a tourist's blister? You have one of those *underwear* blisters?"

"It's an old injury from the winter." I begin to lie. "I slipped down the icy stairs at work."

"At the Historical Society?"

"Yes," I say. I cannot tell her the truth. Or can I?

Can I tell you the truth? I might begin. And she might say, *Bien sûr.* And I would explain that, well, after weeks of fighting and months of boisterous door-slamming straight out of an old farce, Daniel pushed me down the stairs.

Non, tu blagues! she'd say.

And I would continue. *Non, je ne blague pas!* Could I tell her? I was at a cocktail party with Daniel at Doctor's Park, where his lab used to be. It always stank at Doctor's Park – some war of septic and antiseptic – and I hated it there. He was flirting with a woman, and the woman's husband turned to me and said in a rambunctious voice, "Well, your husband's number at work is certainly a number at work!" He was drunk and winked at me in a bitter way. Then he began to sing, "Every Valley girl shall be exalted," something meant for his wife to hear. They were going to have a fight when they got home. When Daniel was finished flirting, I went up to him and said, "Let's go. I need to eat."

"Why do you need to eat?" he asked, caught in the theatre of stupid assertion that was starting to become our marriage.

"Why do I *personally* need to eat?"

"Yeah."

"Because, if I don't eat," I said angrily, "I'm going to throw up from drinking too much."

When we got home, I hurled my purse across the kitchen floor. "I think maybe I should go see Earl," I said. Earl was Earl Gray, a matrimonial lawyer whom everyone in town called Mr. Tea. I believed myself to be unafraid of rupture. My engagement to Daniel had been years long and full of breakups.

"Fine," said Daniel, and we stood there, in the fluorescent light, no doubt looking greenish and out of our minds. I got sharp-tongued and judgmental, an unfortunate but necessary combination. In the beginning was the Word, and it was a reproachful one. "I can't stand this," I said finally, "not knowing what you do, with whom, what it means. I can't live like this. It's like living with a wolf in the cellar as a pet – except he's not a pet, in fact he's not even a wolf, he's a nuclear power plant!" I was drunk. "One of those shoddily constructed ones!" I marched over and threw open the basement door in some kind of attempt at illustration, if not proof. "How many other women have there been? I want to know the truth! The truth!"

He was still and silent and sorry for me. Then he said, "I can't tell you the truth."

"What do you mean you can't tell me the truth? Why can't you tell me?"

"Because you'd be shocked," said Daniel. A look of bemused surliness came over him. "Not *surprised* – just shocked."

I lunged. I swung at him with both fists, and he threw me off with such fury and determination that I stumbled backward, into the open stairwell to the basement, my feet hitting air, my whole body falling, pitching backward toward the wolf and the nuclear power plant, the world reeling, both slow and fast, as I imagined it might if a plane you were flying in began to crash – a tiny rectangle of light with Daniel in it, and then just the dark space of the basement, the pummelling thud of the steps and my hip and head and shoes, scraping and sliding, and finally me at the cement bottom, on my side, in shock, saying, *Whoops, wope, whoops.*

Perhaps there was some bit of foreseeability in it; even bad behavior must fall within some unconscious expectation in order not to seem monstrous.

Afterward, Daniel apologized and cried, and visited me for hours every day in the hospital. Performing the sweet rituals that would keep us together, he knew I could not otherwise take him back. Once the penance is performed, at least at first, one has no choice. "Think of all those good, praying people who keep God around for the rest of us," said Daniel, on his knees by my bed. "God has no choice; he must honor the rites; if it were just the rest of us riffraff down here, he'd be long gone. But he comes through because of the good ones. He honors the covenant, the vows. Think of yourself as God. Think of me as the moral mix that is all of humanity."

"Oh, please."

"Well, then, think of me as – what? I don't know."

"You know those cream puffs called Divorce?" I say now to Marguerite.

"I've seen them."

"They're so totally great. Can we get those around here?" Once, last year in Chicago, I was at a dinner party where a newlywed woman kept interrupting her husband to say in a theatrical whine, "Honey, can we get our *divorce* now? *Now* can we get our divorce?" I was the only one there who thought she was funny. I was the only one there who laughed every time. At the end of the night, she leaned forward by the door and kissed me on the lips.

"Sure! I know of a pretty good pâtisserie not far from here."

Marguerite's walk is strong and loping, impossible to match. We stop at her pâtisserie, wildly order "two Divorces," then sit outside at the neighboring *tabac* drinking *panachés* (half *bière*, half *limonade*) to go with them. "Isn't Paris amazing?" says Marguerite. "Where else would you have something like a *tabac*, half bar, half office-supply store? The thing about France is that from romance to food to whatever, they really know what goes together. Look at all the red and purple – look at the gardens and lobbies and scarves. Not every culture knows that red and purple go so well together." She pauses. "Of course, it's also a totally sexist country."

"*C'est dommage*," I say, my mouth full of Divorce. I mention the men looking around, the libidinous, head-lit bath the French women are swimming in.

"The worst thing, though," says Marguerite, "is when a man walks by you in the street, sizes you up, and says, *'Pas mal.' Pas mal!* You feel outraged in a hundred different directions. For one, you expect a little grade inflation on the streets."

I laugh in a giddy way. I've eaten too much sugar. Marguerite orders water – *"Château Chirac"* – a Parisian joke everyone knows, apparently, because it is scarcely acknowledged as a joke. The waiter barely cracks a smile and then goes off to the kitchen. *Château Chirac* is no longer funny; it is water, it is what water is called; it is what water is. And it makes me wonder how many things have begun this way, as jokes. Love, adolescence, marriage, life, death; perhaps God is looking down saying, "Geez, y'all, lighten up. This is *funny*. You're missing the into*nation*!"

"I can't give my heart away to anyone but you," Daniel said to me in the hospital. "Not that I haven't tried, of course. It's just that when I do, the other organs start a letter-writing campaign."

"Don't be clever," I said. "Don't be like that now."

"What is your favorite painting in all of Paris?" I ask Marguerite. The litre of water has come, and we gulp it down. She looks refreshed.

"Let me think," she says. She names Géricault, van Gogh, Picasso.

"All the 'o's," I say.

"All the 'o's! Actually, there's a pastel of Madame Monet, with the ribbons of her hat all untied. That's probably my favorite. She's sitting on a bright-blue sofa – the most beautiful blue you've ever seen – and she is looking straight out of the drawing, as if to say, 'I married a painter, and I still got this sofa.' I like that one. Very French."

"Do you think the Venus de Milo looks like Nicolas Cage?"

"A little," she says, smiling. "But you've got to remember. Even with all her handicaps and shyness, she's lived in Paris; she's been gazed upon by Parisians for years, so she believes – a belief as good as gold – that she's absolutely beautiful."

"Absolutely beautiful?"

"Cute. OK. She thinks she's *cute.* She thinks she's so *goddam* cute."

"Don't you hate that? Even in a statue, I just hate that."

We wander off to other galleries, where Marguerite shows me what she likes: big, broad, energetic paintings. "Sexy ones," she says.

At a show of collages – tiny, fussy, intricate little cuttings and pastings, ink squiggles, swatches of color – I go from one to the other, slow and fascinated, but Marguerite is bored. She comes up behind me. "See, I don't really like these," she says. "They're not *sexual.*"

I turn and look at her. "See, to *me*, these are totally sexual," and then we both burst out laughing, our laughs booming in the gallery, where others are whispering as if it were church.

"They're sexual, maybe – like a foot fetish is sexual," says Marguerite.

"Exactly," I say. *"Exactement."*

Afterward, we hike up to Père Lachaise to look at Jim Morrison's grave, where there is a constant beer party, and where so many bottle caps have been mashed and pounded into the dirt that they have made what looks like a carpet of coins. Over the sound of one badly tuned guitar, strummed by a barefoot German, Marguerite tells me that what she'd really like to do is make films. She knows one film she'd like to make first – stories of Algerians in the early sixties: how they were herded outside Paris, in camps, how many of them were killed, disappeared. How even now, on the outskirts of Paris, Africans in bright ski pants work the toxic jobs, the factories and power plants, how Paris is built and running on the backs of these people, on the backs of abominable history. The Nazis – well, everyone knows about the Nazis.

There is no place to put such facts, not properly. There is only one's own mournful horror, one's worthless moral vanity – which can do nothing. The bad news of the world, like most bad news, has no place to go. You tack it to the bulletin-board part of your heart. You say, *Look.* You say, *See.* That is all.

"So if this production company comes through, that is what I'd like to do, work with some of these documentary people," says Marguerite, "and make that film."

"Marguerite," I say. "That's great." That's great. "You must."

"I've been thinking about our genes," says Daniel, when I ask him how the day's conference events went. We are in bed, and it's hard to sleep. There are car alarms, motorcycle alarms, disco noises. A woman in the street below is singing, "Eef I ken mek eat there, all mek eat onywhere, eats op too you, New York, New York."

"Yes," I say.

"I mean, maybe it's all for the best. Besides the Tay-Sachs. Look at the genes. On your side there's diabetes and bad hearts."

"And bad blood."

"That's right. Bad blood. And on my side there's, well—"

"There's arrogance and not listening," I say.

"Arrogance and not listening." He laughs in a sighing way. "Did you have a good day with Marguerite? What are you thinking about?" he asks. "Was it fun? Don't worry. I can have this whole conversation by myself. You can just watch."

"I really like Marguerite," I say.

"I know you do."

I sigh, clutch the covers up under my chin.

"That's it? That's all that's on your mind?"

"Also 'Manon Lescaut,'" I say. Last week we saw a production of it at the Bastille.

"'Manon Lescaut'?"

"I'd like to die like that," I say. "All my jewelry on, and singing about madness."

"You would?"

"With all my jewelry on? Sure." Probably, in real life, I would die in a bathrobe, the telephone cradled in my neck.

"Do I know you?" asks Daniel. "You don't even wear jewelry."

"Yes, I do."

"A watch. You wear a watch. Lots of lipstick and a watch."

"It's a nice watch."

"It's gorgeous," Daniel says, now sleepy. The air in our room is damp from the rains; it has turned my hair strumpety and full, but has made Daniel's skin moist and pale, color in his cheeks coming only in the day, outside, in the hurried pace to and from drier destinations. He seems delicate and young beside me.

I keep talking. "You know, *that's* one thing Manon wasn't wearing – a watch. You don't see a lot of watch wearing in the soprano world. Have you ever noticed that? Tosca? No watch. Madame Butterfly? Again, no watch."

He is no longer paying attention, but it doesn't stop me. We have traded places. "If you gave everyone in 'La Bohème' wristwatches, you'd have a happy ending."

"You would?"

"Sure," I say. "You wouldn't have that guy singing about his coat. He'd look at his watch and go, *Yikes!*"

"Now that's what I'd like to hear. A nice aria with the word 'yikes' in it."

Daniel has never really liked opera. "What I like is philosophy," he said to me once. "Philosophy's great. Except I don't like the whole existence thing. *Do we exist?* That really pisses me off. But I like good and evil. I like *What is Art?* But just a little of *What is Art?* If you get too much, it circles back around again to *Do we exist?* – which pisses me off."

"I'm not really looking forward to going home," I say now.

"Really?"

"I feel disconnected these days, in the house, in town. The

neighbors say, 'Hello, how are you?' and sometimes I say, 'Oh, I'm feeling a little empty today. How about you?' "

"You should get a puppy," he says sleepily.

"A puppy?"

"Yeah. It's not like the cat. A puppy you can take for walks around the neighborhood, and people will stop and smile and say, 'Oh, look! What's *wrong* with your puppy?' "

"What *is* wrong with my puppy?"

"Worms, I think. I don't know. You should have taken him in to the vet's weeks ago."

"You're so mean."

"I'm sorry I'm not what you bargained for," Daniel murmurs.

I stop and think about this. "Well, I'm not what you bargained for, either, so we're even."

"No," he says faintly, "you are. You're what I bargained for."

But then he has fallen over the cliff of sleep and is snoring, his adenoids a kind of engine in his face, a motorized unit, a security system, like a white flag going up.

WEEK THREE

You can wake from one dream only to find yourself plunged into yet another, like some endless rosary of the mind. When that happens, it is hard to glimpse what is not dream; the waking, undreamed world flies by you, in rushing flashes of light and air, in loud, quick, dangerous spaces like those between the cars of a train. There is nothing you can do. You walk in the sleep of yourself and wait. You wait for the train to pass.

Daniel believes he is working something out, wrestling with his heart, his work. He wants me to bear with him. He speaks, in a coded way, of all that is tempting and bewildering him, all issues of moral drunkenness. "It's like I'm on a ride," he says. "I go up, up, and up, and then *wheeeee.*"

"Except then the keys fall out of your pocket," I say sternly. "And then you can't get back into the house."

He tries to look bemused. “I had a dream last night – I rounded a corner and someone lifted a gun and shot me, the bullet slamming straight through my sternum.” He pauses. “Do you think that’s bad luck?” He sighs, then begins to whisper. “I’m afraid of one day turning into my father. When he was my age, he left my mother for a woman twenty years younger.”

I say nothing. I melt a whiskey truffle on my tongue. In my vision there are lines running through everything; even the fabric of the drapes and upholstery seems to be raining, like the clothes in a portrait by van Gogh.

He looks sad, draws his large, man’s hand down across his face; his voice constricts with sorrow. “My mother, of course, took it with the great good humor with which it was intended.”

“She lost her mind,” I say.

“Yes,” he says. “She lost her mind.”

Eating brains – their spongy circuitry reabsorbed – we pretend is an ecological act. But perhaps it is more like monsters in a science-fiction movie. Brains! Brains! Brains! As if we have run out of our own. So far in our marriage, we’ve fought fear with ineptitude, indifference with indifference, the world blows up here and there, and our lives feel staked out in the embers, pitched and huddled in tents. We course through the hairpin turns of denials and shouts – it’s the end, it can’t be the end. We are in the loveliest city in the world: the expensive coffees, the red, chemical sunset, the *bateaux-mouches* flashing by each sooty church, lighting it up like a stage. The gendarmes hassle the African men in the Métro; the poodles defecate with impunity on the walks. You can’t name your child anything not on a national list – and this is the most civilized city on earth! The city of spring and songs and other compositions of the heart. We feel ourselves moving so minutely against some process, some momentum, that we become inadvertently a part. We feel too small to fight. Desperation, laziness, horror – they all resemble one another in their flickering movements within us, the same thrashing shorthand. *Ma chérie, is this our stop?* We feel enslaved – is that what it is? – in some turning: of rot to dirt then to winds and stars. Time for another constellation!

My husband has that look again, the look of how difficult the world is, life is, how sometimes you just want to go back to your house with the bushes around it and stay inside.

"Home," he says. The idea of it: its lovely cheat and evasion; its capitulation to longing and rest. "Home, home, home."

Where, though I harbor secret wishes of its burning, our life in flames, the crazy, wicked freedom of it, our chipping house will still be standing, safe and whole, the previous owner's rubber bands still wrapped around the doorknobs. The animals we've sealed in, with mending and patching – the mice and larks – will wake and cry within the walls, then go still. The season will be spring, but the squirrels will have eaten and rearranged the bulbs, so that only one lone daffodil – a trumpet solo – will be shivering in the yard, the flowering quince not flowering, the ground still too muddy for grass but on a sunny day suddenly ticking with hatching flies. At the Citgo station around the corner, the sparrows will once again build their nest in the paper-towel dispenser. "Don't you feel – you must – like going home?" Daniel asks, in a voice of such ailing homesickness it makes me smile.

Everywhere life is full of heroism.

I lean warmly toward him, try to get closer, in empathy and companionship, to study his face, so moist and young in these rains, to match or approximate it. "Don't be lorn, don't be blue, it's only morn, and I'm with you." I sing this, but he stiffens, then tries not to stiffen, forces a smile, but moves too quickly away. He does this often now. Something, someone, keeps him, is kept, in some other corner of his life. I can't follow him there – where that is, a place of woundedness, we are too without each other. To meet there would be to step into the strange, dark rage of strangers. But I've accrued a kind of patience, I believe, loosely, like change. I can feel the jangle and money of it. I will wait for him, I think: let him go and sicken himself, confuse himself, dash through the bad woods of himself. *Love is perennial as the grass!* I'll wait for him, my heart in epilogue, knit and reknit, perhaps as it always has been. I'll wait until I just can't wait anymore.

As far as possible without surrender be on good terms with all persons.

1994

PEOPLE LIKE THAT ARE THE ONLY PEOPLE HERE: CANONICAL BABBLING IN PEED ONK

A BEGINNING, AN END: there seems to be neither. The whole thing is like a cloud that just lands and everywhere inside it is full of rain. A start: the Mother finds a blood clot in the Baby's diaper. What is the story? Who put this here? It is big and bright, with a broken khaki-colored vein in it. Over the weekend, the Baby had looked listless and spacey, clayey and grim. But today he looks fine – so what is this thing, startling against the white diaper, like a tiny mouse heart packed in snow? Perhaps it belongs to someone else. Perhaps it is something menstrual, something belonging to the Mother or to the Babysitter, something the Baby has found in a wastebasket and for his own demented baby reasons stowed away here. (Babies: they're crazy! What can you do?) In her mind, the Mother takes this away from his body and attaches it to someone else's. There. Doesn't that make more sense?

Still, she phones the clinic at the children's hospital. "Blood in the diaper," she says, and, sounding alarmed and perplexed, the woman on the other end says, "Come in now."

Such pleasingly instant service! Just say "blood." Just say "diaper." Look what you get!

In the examination room, pediatrician, nurse, head resident – all seem less alarmed and perplexed than simply perplexed. At first, stupidly, the Mother is calmed by this. But soon, besides peering and saying "Hmmmm," the pediatrician, nurse, and head resident are all drawing their mouths in, bluish and tight – morning glories sensing noon. They fold their arms across their white-coated chests, unfold them again and jot things down. They order an ultrasound. Bladder and kidneys. "Here's the card. Go downstairs; turn left."

* * *

In Radiology, the Baby stands anxiously on the table, naked against the Mother as she holds him still against her legs and waist, the Radiologist's cold scanning disc moving about the Baby's back. The Baby whimpers, looks up at the Mother. *Let's get out of here,* his eyes beg. *Pick me up!* The Radiologist stops, freezes one of the many swirls of oceanic gray, and clicks repeatedly, a single moment within the long, cavernous weather map that is the Baby's insides.

"Are you finding something?" asks the Mother. Last year, her uncle Larry had had a kidney removed for something that turned out to be benign. These imaging machines! They are like dogs, or metal detectors: they find everything, but don't know what they've found. That's where the surgeons come in. They're like the owners of the dogs. "Give me that," they say to the dog. "What the heck is that?"

"The surgeon will speak to you," says the Radiologist.

"Are you finding something?"

"The surgeon will speak to you," the Radiologist says again. "There seems to be something there, but the surgeon will talk to you about it."

"My uncle once had something on his kidney," says the Mother. "So they removed the kidney and it turned out the something was benign."

The Radiologist smiles a broad, ominous smile. "That's always the way it is," he says. "You don't know exactly what it is until it's in the bucket."

"'In the bucket,'" the Mother repeats.

The Radiologist's grin grows scarily wider – is that even possible? "That's doctor talk," he says.

"It's very appealing," says the Mother. "It's a very appealing way to talk." Swirls of bile and blood, mustard and maroon in a pail, the colors of an African flag or some exuberant salad bar: *in the bucket* – she imagines it all.

"The Surgeon will see you soon," he says again. He tousles the Baby's ringletty hair. "Cute kid," he says.

* * *

"Let's see now," says the Surgeon in one of his examining rooms. He has stepped in, then stepped out, then come back in again. He has crisp, frowning features, sharp bones, and a tennis-in-Bermuda tan. He crosses his blue-cottoned legs. He is wearing clogs.

The Mother knows her own face is a big white dumpling of worry. She is still wearing her long, dark parka, holding the Baby, who has pulled the hood up over her head because he always thinks it's funny to do that. Though on certain windy mornings she would like to think she could look vaguely romantic like this, like some French Lieutenant's Woman of the Prairie, in all of her saner moments she knows she doesn't. Ever. She knows she looks ridiculous – like one of those animals made out of twisted party balloons. She lowers the hood and slips one arm out of the sleeve. The Baby wants to get up and play with the light switch. He fidgets, fusses, and points.

"He's big on lights these days," explains the Mother.

"That's okay," says the Surgeon, nodding toward the light switch. "Let him play with it." The Mother goes and stands by it, and the Baby begins turning the lights off and on, off and on.

"What we have here is a Wilms' tumor," says the Surgeon, suddenly plunged into darkness. He says "tumor" as if it were the most normal thing in the world.

"Wilms'?" repeats the Mother. The room is quickly on fire again with light, then wiped dark again. Among the three of them here, there is a long silence, as if it were suddenly the middle of the night. "Is that apostrophe *s* or *s* apostrophe?" the Mother says finally. She is a writer and a teacher. Spelling can be important – perhaps even at a time like this, though she has never before been at a time like this, so there are barbarisms she could easily commit and not know.

The lights come on: the world is doused and exposed.

"*S* apostrophe," says the Surgeon. "I think." The lights go back out, but the Surgeon continues speaking in the dark. "A malignant tumor on the left kidney."

Wait a minute. Hold on here. The Baby is only a baby, fed on organic applesauce and soy milk – a little prince!

– and he was standing so close to her during the ultrasound. How could he have this terrible thing? It must have been *her* kidney. A fifties kidney. A DDT kidney. The Mother clears her throat. "Is it possible it was my kidney on the scan? I mean, I've never heard of a baby with a tumor, and, frankly, I was standing very close." She would make the blood hers, the tumor hers; it would all be some treacherous, farcical mistake.

"No, that's not possible," says the Surgeon. The light goes back on.

"It's not?" says the Mother. Wait until it's *in the bucket*, she thinks. Don't be so sure. *Do we have to wait until it's in the bucket to find out a mistake has been made?*

"We will start with a radical nephrectomy," says the Surgeon, instantly thrown into darkness again. His voice comes from nowhere and everywhere at once. "And then we'll begin with chemotherapy after that. These tumors usually respond very well to chemo."

"I've never heard of a baby having chemo," the Mother says. *Baby* and *Chemo*, she thinks: they should never even appear in the same sentence together, let alone the same life. In her other life, her life before this day, she had been a believer in alternative medicine. Chemotherapy? Unthinkable. Now, suddenly, alternative medicine seems the wacko maiden aunt to the Nice Big Daddy of Conventional Treatment. How quickly the old girl faints and gives way, leaves one just standing there. Chemo? Of course: chemo! Why by all means: chemo. Absolutely! Chemo!

The Baby flicks the switch back on, and the walls reappear, big wedges of light checkered with small framed watercolors of the local lake. The Mother has begun to cry: all of life has led her here, to this moment. After this, there is no more life. There is something else, something stumbling and unlivable, something mechanical, something for robots, but not life. Life has been taken and broken, quickly, like a stick. The room goes dark again, so that the Mother can cry more freely. How can a baby's body be stolen so fast? How much can one heaven-sent and unsuspecting child endure? Why has he not been spared this inconceivable fate?

Perhaps, she thinks, she is being punished: too many baby-sitters too early on. ("Come to Mommy! Come to Mommy-Baby-sitter!" she used to say. But it was a joke!) Her life, perhaps, bore too openly the marks and wigs of deepest drag. Her unmotherly thoughts had all been noted: the panicky hope that his nap would last longer than it did; her occasional desire to kiss him passionately on the mouth (to make out with her baby!); her ongoing complaints about the very vocabulary of motherhood, how it degraded the speaker ("Is this a poopie onesie! Yes, it's a very poopie onesie!"). She had, moreover, on three occasions used the formula bottles as flower vases. She twice let the Baby's ears get fudgy with wax. A few afternoons last month, at snacktime, she placed a bowl of Cheerios on the floor for him to eat, like a dog. She let him play with the Dust-buster. Just once, before he was born, she said, "Healthy? I just want the kid to be rich." A joke, for God's sake! After he was born she announced that her life had become a daily sequence of mind-wrecking chores, the same ones over and over again, like a novel by Mrs. Camus. Another joke! These jokes will kill you! She had told too often, and with too much enjoyment, the story of how the Baby had said "Hi" to his high chair, waved at the lake waves, shouted "Goody-goody-goody" in what seemed to be a Russian accent, pointed at his eyes and said "Ice." And all that nonsensical baby talk: wasn't it a stitch? "Canonical babbling," the language experts called it. He recounted whole stories in it – totally made up, she could tell. He embroidered; he fished; he exaggerated. What a card! To friends, she spoke of his eating habits (carrots yes, tuna no). She mentioned, too much, his sidesplitting giggle. Did she have to be so boring? Did she have no consideration for others, for the intellectual demands and courtesies of human society? Would she not even attempt to be more interesting? It was a crime against the human mind not even to try.

Now her baby, for all these reasons – lack of motherly gratitude, motherly judgment, motherly proportion – will be taken away.

The room is fluorescently ablaze again. The Mother digs

around in her parka pocket and comes up with a Kleenex. It is old and thin, like a mashed flower saved from a dance; she dabs it at her eyes and nose.

"The Baby won't suffer as much as you," says the Surgeon.

And who can contradict? Not the Baby, who in his Slavic Betty Boop voice can say only *mama, dada, cheese, ice, bye-bye, outside, boogie-boogie, goody-goody, eddy-eddy,* and *car.* (Who is Eddy? They have no idea.) This will not suffice to express his mortal suffering. Who can say what babies do with their agony and shock? Not they themselves. (Baby talk: isn't it a stitch?) They put it all no place anyone can really see. They are like a different race, a different species: they seem not to experience pain the way *we* do. Yeah, that's it: their nervous systems are not as fully formed, and *they just don't experience pain the way we do.* A tune to keep one humming through the war. "You'll get through it," the Surgeon says.

"How?" asks the Mother. "How does one get through it?"

"You just put your head down and go," says the Surgeon. He picks up his file folder. He is a skilled manual laborer. The tricky emotional stuff is not to his liking. The babies. The babies! What can be said to console the parents about the babies? "I'll go phone the oncologist on duty to let him know," he says, and leaves the room.

"Come here, sweetie," the Mother says to the Baby, who has toddled off toward a gum wrapper on the floor. "We've got to put your jacket on." She picks him up and he reaches for the light switch again. Light, dark. Peekaboo: where's baby? Where did baby go?

At home, she leaves a message – "Urgent! Call me!" – for the Husband on his voice mail. Then she takes the Baby upstairs for his nap, rocks him in the rocker. The Baby waves good-bye to his little bears, then looks toward the window and says, "Bye-bye, outside." He has, lately, the habit of waving good-bye to everything, and now it seems as if he senses an imminent departure, and it breaks her heart to hear him. *Bye-bye!* She sings low and monotonously, like a small appliance, which is how he likes it. He is drowsy, dozy, drifting off. He has grown so much in the last year, he hardly fits in her lap anymore; his limbs dangle off like a pietà. His head rolls slightly inside the crook of her arm. She can feel him falling backward into sleep, his mouth round and open like the sweetest of poppies. All the lullabies in the world, all the melodies threaded through with maternal melancholy now become for her – abandoned as a mother can be by working men and napping babies – the songs of hard, hard grief. Sitting there, bowed and bobbing, the Mother feels the entirety of her love as worry and heartbreak. A quick and irrevocable alchemy: there is no longer one unworried scrap left for happiness. "If you go," she keens low into his soapy neck, into the ranunculus coil of his ear, "we are going with you. We are nothing without you. Without you, we are a heap of rocks. We are gravel and mold. Without you, we are two stumps, with nothing any longer in our hearts. Wherever this takes you, we are following. We will be there. Don't be scared. We are going, too. That is that."

"Take Notes," says the Husband, after coming straight home from work, midafternoon, hearing the news, and saying all the words out loud – *surgery*, *metastasis*, *dialysis*, *transplant* – then collapsing in a chair in tears. "Take notes. We are going to need the money."

"Good God," cries the Mother. Everything inside her suddenly begins to cower and shrink, a thinning of bones. Perhaps this is a soldier's readiness, but it has the whiff of death and defeat. It feels like a heart attack, a failure of will and courage, a power failure: a failure of everything. Her face, when she glimpses it in a mirror, is cold and bloated with shock, her eyes scarlet and shrunk. She has already started to wear sunglasses indoors, like a celebrity widow. From where will her own strength come? From some philosophy? From some frigid little philosophy? She is neither stalwart nor realistic and has trouble with basic concepts, such as the one that says events move in one direction only and do not jump up, turn around, and take themselves back.

The Husband begins too many of his sentences with "What if." He is trying to piece everything together like a train wreck. He is trying to get the train to town.

"We'll just take all the steps, move through all the stages. We'll go where we have to go. We'll hunt; we'll find; we'll pay what we have to pay. What if we can't pay?"

"Sounds like shopping."

"I cannot believe this is happening to our little boy," he says, and starts to sob again. "Why didn't it happen to one of us? It's so unfair. Just last week, my doctor declared me in perfect health: the prostate of a twenty-year-old, the heart of a ten-year-old, the brain of an insect – or whatever it was he said. What a nightmare this is."

What words can be uttered? You turn just slightly and there it is: the death of your child. It is part symbol, part devil, and in your blind spot all along, until, if you are unlucky, it is completely upon you. Then it is a fierce little country abducting you; it holds you squarely inside itself like a cellar room – the best boundaries of you are the boundaries of it. Are there windows? Sometimes aren't there windows?

The Mother is not a shopper. She hates to shop, is generally bad at it, though she does like a good sale. She cannot stroll meaningfully through anger, denial, grief, and acceptance. She goes straight to bargaining and stays there. How much? she calls out to the ceiling, to some makeshift construction of holiness she has desperately, though not uncreatively, assembled in her mind and prayed to; a doubter, never before given to prayer, she must now reap what she has not sown; she must assemble from scratch an entire altar of worship and begging. She tries for noble abstractions, nothing too anthropomorphic, just some Higher Morality, though if this particular Highness looks something like the manager at Marshall Field's, sucking a Frango mint, so be it. Amen. Just tell me what you want, requests the Mother. And how do you want it? More charitable acts? A billion starting now. Charitable thoughts? Harder, but of course! Of course! I'll do the cooking, honey; I'll pay the rent. Just tell me. *Excuse me?* Well, if not to you, to whom do I speak? Hello? To whom do I have to speak around here? A higher-up? A superior? Wait? I can wait. I've got all day. I've got the whole damn day.

The Husband now lies next to her in bed, sighing. "Poor little guy could survive all this, only to be killed in a car crash at the age of sixteen," he says.

The wife, bargaining, considers this. "We'll take the car crash," she says.

"What?"

"Let's Make a Deal! Sixteen Is a Full Life! We'll take the car crash. We'll take the car crash, in front of which Carol Merrill is now standing."

Now the Manager of Marshall Field's reappears. "To take the surprises out is to take the life out of life," he says.

The phone rings. The Husband gets up and leaves the room.

"But I don't want these surprises," says the Mother. "Here! You take these surprises!"

"To know the narrative in advance is to turn yourself into a machine," the Manager continues. "What makes humans human is precisely that they do not know the future. That is why they do the fateful and amusing things they do: who can say how anything will turn out? Therein lies the only hope for redemption, discovery, and – let's be frank – fun, fun, fun! There might be things people will get away with. And not just motel towels. There might be great illicit loves, enduring joy, faith-shaking accidents with farm machinery. But you have to not know in order to see what stories your life's efforts bring you. The mystery is all."

The Mother, though shy, has grown confrontational. "Is this the kind of bogus, random crap they teach at merchandising school? We would like fewer surprises, fewer efforts and mysteries, thank you. K through eight; can we just get K through eight?" It now seems like the luckiest, most beautiful, most musical phrase she's ever heard: K through eight. The very lilt. The very thought.

The Manager continues, trying things out. "I mean, the whole conception of 'the story,' of cause and effect, the whole idea that people have a clue as to how the world works is just a piece of laughable metaphysical colonialism perpetrated upon the wild country of time."

Did they own a gun? The Mother begins looking through drawers.

The Husband comes back into the room and observes her. "Ha! The Great Havoc that is the Puzzle of all Life!" he says of the Marshall Field's management policy. He has just gotten off a conference call with the insurance company and the hospital. The surgery will be Friday. "It's all just some dirty capitalist's idea of a philosophy."

"Maybe it's just a fact of narrative and you really can't politicize it," says the Mother. It is now only the two of them.

"Whose side are you on?"

"I'm on the Baby's side."

"Are you taking notes for this?"

"No."

"You're not?"

"No. I can't. Not this! I write fiction. This isn't fiction."

"Then write nonfiction. Do a piece of journalism. Get two dollars a word."

"Then it has to be true and full of information. I'm not trained. I'm not that skilled. Plus, I have a convenient personal principle about artists not abandoning art. One should never turn one's back on a vivid imagination. Even the whole memoir thing annoys me."

"Well, make things up, but pretend they're real."

"I'm not that insured."

"You're making me nervous."

"Sweetie, darling, I'm not that good. I can't *do this.* I can do – what can I do? I can do quasi-amusing phone dialogue. I can do succinct descriptions of weather. I can do screwball outings with the family pet. Sometimes I can do those. Honey, I only do what I can. I do *the careful ironies of daydream.* I do *the marshy ideas upon which intimate life is built.* But this? Our baby with cancer? I'm sorry. My stop was two stations back. This is irony at its most gaudy and careless. This is a Hieronymus Bosch of facts and figures and blood and graphs. This is a nightmare of narrative slop. This cannot be designed. This cannot even be noted in preparation for a design—"

"We're going to need the money."

"To say nothing of the moral boundaries of pecuniary recompense in a situation such as this—"

"What if the other kidney goes? What if he needs a transplant? Where are the moral boundaries there? What are we going to do, have bake sales?"

"We can sell the house. I hate this house. It makes me crazy."

"And we'll live – where again?"

"The Ronald McDonald place. I hear it's nice. It's the least McDonald's can do."

"You have a keen sense of justice."

"I try. What can I say?" She pauses. "Is all this really happening? I keep thinking that soon it will be over – the life expectancy of a cloud is supposed to be only twelve hours – and then I realize something has occurred that can never ever be over."

The Husband buries his face in his hands: "Our poor baby. How did this happen to him?" He looks over and stares at the bookcase that serves as the nightstand. "And do you think even one of these baby books is any help?" He picks up the Leach, the Spock, the *What to Expect*. "Where in the pages or index of any of these does it say 'chemotherapy' or 'Hickman catheter' or 'renal sarcoma'? Where does it say 'carcinogenesis'? You know what these books are obsessed with? *Holding a fucking spoon.*" He begins hurling the books off the night table and against the far wall.

"Hey," says the Mother, trying to soothe. "Hey, hey, hey." But compared to his stormy roar, her words are those of a backup singer – a Shondell, a Pip – a doo-wop ditty. Books, and now more books, continue to fly.

* * *

Take Notes.

Is *fainthearted* one word or two? Student prose has wrecked her spelling.

It's one word. Two words – *Faint Hearted* – what would that be? The name of a drag queen.

Take Notes. In the end, you suffer alone. But at the beginning you suffer with a whole lot of others. When your child has cancer, you are instantly whisked away to another planet: one of bald-headed little boys. Pediatric Oncology. Peed Onk. You wash your hands for thirty seconds in antibacterial soap before you are allowed to enter through the swinging doors. You put paper slippers on your shoes. You keep your voice down. A whole place has been designed and decorated for your nightmare. Here is where your nightmare will occur. We've got a room all ready for you. We have cots. We have refrigerators. "The children are almost entirely boys," says one of the nurses. "No one knows why. It's been documented, but a lot of people out there still don't realize it." The little boys are all from sweet-sounding places – Janesville and Appleton – little heartland towns with giant landfills, agricultural runoff, paper factories, Joe McCarthy's grave (Alone, a site of great toxicity, thinks the Mother. The soil should be tested).

All the bald little boys look like brothers. They wheel their IVs up and down the single corridor of Peed Onk. Some of the lively ones, feeling good for a day, ride the lower bars of the IV while their large, cheerful mothers whiz them along the halls. *Wheee!*

The Mother does not feel large and cheerful. In her mind, she is scathing, acid-tongued, wraith-thin, and chain-smoking out on a fire escape somewhere. Beneath her lie the gentle undulations of the Midwest, with all its aspirations to be – to be what? To be Long Island. How it has succeeded! Strip mall upon strip mall. Lurid water, poisoned potatoes. The Mother drags deeply, blowing clouds of smoke out over the disfigured cornfields. When a baby gets cancer, it seems stupid ever to have given up smoking. When a baby gets cancer, you think, Whom are we kidding? Let's all light up. When a baby gets cancer, you think, Who came up with *this* idea? What celestial abandon gave rise to *this*? Pour me a drink, so I can refuse to toast.

The Mother does not know how to be one of these other mothers, with their blond hair and sweatpants and sneakers and determined pleasantness. She does not think that she can be anything similar. She does not feel remotely like them. She knows, for instance, too many people in Greenwich Village. She mail-orders oysters and tiramisu from a shop in SoHo. She is close friends with four actual homosexuals. Her husband is asking her to Take Notes.

Where do these women get their sweatpants? She will find out.

She will start, perhaps, with the costume and work from there.

She will live according to the bromides. Take one day at a time. Take a positive attitude. *Take a hike!* She wishes that there were more interesting things that were useful and true, but it seems now that it's only the boring things that are useful and true. *One day at a time.* And *at least we have our health.* How ordinary. How obvious. One day at a time. You need a brain for that?

While the Surgeon is fine-boned, regal, and laconic – they have correctly guessed his game to be doubles – there is a bit of the mad, overcaffeinated scientist to the Oncologist. He speaks quickly. He knows a lot of studies and numbers. He can do the math. Good! Someone should be able to do the math! "It's a fast but wimpy tumor," he explains. "It typically metastasizes to the lung." He rattles off some numbers, time frames, risk statistics. Fast but wimpy: the Mother tries to imagine this combination of traits, tries to think and think, and can only come up with Claudia Osk from the fourth grade, who blushed and almost wept when called on in class, but in gym could outrun everyone in the quarter-mile fire-door-to-fence dash. The Mother thinks now of this tumor as Claudia Osk. They are going to get Claudia Osk, make her sorry. All right! Claudia Osk must die. Though it has never been mentioned before, it now seems clear that Claudia Osk should have died long ago. Who was she anyway? So conceited: not letting anyone beat her in a race. Well, hey, hey, hey: don't look now, Claudia!

The Husband nudges her. "Are you listening?"

"The chances of this happening even just to one kidney are one in fifteen thousand. Now given all these other factors, the chances on the second kidney are about one in eight."

"One in eight," says the Husband. "Not bad. As long as it's not one in fifteen thousand."

The Mother studies the trees and fish along the ceiling's edge in the Save the Planet wallpaper border. Save the Planet. Yes! But the windows in this very building don't open and diesel fumes are leaking into the ventilating system, near which, outside, a delivery truck is parked. The air is nauseous and stale.

"Really," the Oncologist is saying, "of all the cancers he could get, this is probably the best."

"We win," says the Mother.

"*Best*, I know, hardly seems the right word. Look, you two probably need to get some rest. We'll see how the surgery and histology go. Then we'll start with chemo the week following. A little light chemo: vincristine and—"

"Vincristine?" interrupts the Mother. "Wine of Christ?"

"The names are strange, I know. The other one we use is actinomycin-D. Sometimes called 'dactinomycin.' People move the *D* around to the front."

"They move the *D* around to the front," repeats the Mother.

"Yup!" the Oncologist says. "I don't know why – they just do!"

"Christ didn't survive his wine," says the Husband.

"But of course he did," says the Oncologist, and nods toward the Baby, who has now found a cupboard full of hospital linens and bandages and is yanking them all out onto the floor. "I'll see you guys tomorrow, after the surgery." And with that, the Oncologist leaves.

"Or, rather, Christ *was* his wine," mumbles the Husband. Everything he knows about the New Testament, he has gleaned from the sound track of *Godspell*. "His blood was the wine. What a great beverage idea."

"A little light chemo. Don't you like that one?" says the Mother. "*Eine kleine* dactinomycin. I'd like to see Mozart write that one up for a big wad o' cash."

"Come here, honey," the Husband says to the Baby, who has now pulled off both his shoes.

"It's bad enough when they refer to medical science as 'an inexact science,'" says the Mother. "But when they start referring to it as 'an art,' I get extremely nervous."

"Yeah. If we wanted art, Doc, we'd go to an art museum." The Husband picks up the Baby. "You're an artist," he says to the Mother, with the taint of accusation in his voice. "They probably think you find creativity reassuring."

The Mother sighs. "I just find it inevitable. Let's go get something to eat." And so they take the elevator to the cafeteria, where there is a high chair, and where, not noticing, they all eat a lot of apples with the price tags still on them.

Because his surgery is not until tomorrow, the Baby likes the hospital. He likes the long corridors, down which he can run. He likes everything on wheels. The flower carts in the lobby! ("Please keep your boy away from the flowers," says the vendor. "We'll buy the whole display," snaps the Mother, adding, "Actual children in a children's hospital – unbelievable, isn't it?") The Baby likes the other little boys. Places to go! People to see! Rooms to wander into! There is Intensive Care. There is the Trauma Unit. The Baby smiles and waves. What a little Cancer Personality! Bandaged citizens smile and wave back. In Peed Onk, there are the bald little boys to play with. Joey, Eric, Tim, Mort, and Tod (Mort! Tod!). There is the four-year-old, Ned, holding his little deflated rubber ball, the one with the intriguing curling hose. The Baby wants to play with it. "It's mine. Leave it alone," says Ned. "Tell the Baby to leave it alone."

"Baby, you've got to share," says the Mother from a chair some feet away.

Suddenly, from down near the Tiny Tim Lounge, comes Ned's mother, large and blond and sweatpanted. "Stop that! Stop it!" she cries out, dashing toward the Baby and Ned and pushing the Baby away. "Don't touch that!" she barks at the Baby, who is only a Baby and bursts into tears because he has never been yelled at like this before.

Ned's mom glares at everyone. "This is drawing fluid from Neddy's liver!" She pats at the rubber thing and starts to cry a little.

"Oh my God," says the Mother. She comforts the Baby, who is also crying. She and Ned, the only dry-eyed people, look at each other. "I'm so sorry," she says to Ned and then to his mother. "I'm so stupid. I thought they were squabbling over a toy."

"It does look like a toy," agrees Ned. He smiles. He is an angel. All the little boys are angels. Total, sweet, bald little angels, and now God is trying to get them back for himself. Who are they, mere mortal women, in the face of this, this powerful and overwhelming and inscrutable thing, God's will? They are the mothers, that's who. You can't have him! they shout every day. You dirty old man! *Get out of here! Hands off!*

"I'm so sorry," says the Mother again. "I didn't know."

Ned's mother smiles vaguely. "Of course you didn't know," she says, and walks back to the Tiny Tim Lounge.

The Tiny Tim Lounge is a little sitting area at the end of the Peed Onk corridor. There are two small sofas, a table, a rocking chair, a television and a VCR. There are various videos: *Speed*, *Dune*, and *Star Wars*. On one of the lounge walls there is a gold plaque with the singer Tiny Tim's name on it: his son was treated once at this hospital and so, five years ago, he donated money for this lounge. It is a cramped little lounge, which, one suspects, would be larger if Tiny Tim's son had actually lived. Instead, he died here, at this hospital and now there is this tiny room which is part gratitude, part generosity, part *fuck-you*.

Sifting through the videocassettes, the Mother wonders what science fiction could begin to compete with the science fiction of cancer itself – a tumor with its differentiated muscle and bone cells, a clump of wild nothing and its mad, ambitious desire to be something: something inside you, instead of you, another organism, but with a monster's architecture, a demon's sabotage and chaos. Think of leukemia, a tumor diabolically taking liquid form, better to swim about incognito in the blood. George Lucas, direct that!

Sitting with the other parents in the Tiny Tim Lounge, the night before the surgery, having put the Baby to bed in his high steel crib two rooms down, the Mother begins to hear the stories: leukemia in kindergarten, sarcomas in Little League, neuroblastomas discovered at summer camp. "Eric slid into third base, but then the scrape didn't heal." The parents pat one another's forearms and speak of other children's hospitals as if they were resorts. "You were at St. Jude's last winter? So were we. What did you think of it? We loved the staff." Jobs have been quit, marriages hacked up, bank accounts ravaged; the parents have seemingly endured the unendurable. They speak not of the *possibility* of comas brought on by the chemo, but of the *number* of them. "He was in his first coma last July," says Ned's mother. "It was a scary time, but we pulled through."

Pulling through is what people do around here. There is a kind of bravery in their lives that isn't bravery at all. It is automatic, unflinching, a mix of man and machine, consuming and unquestionable obligation meeting illness move for move in a giant even-steven game of chess – an unending round of something that looks like shadowboxing, though between love and death, which is the shadow? "Everyone admires us for our courage," says one man. "They have no idea what they're talking about."

I could get out of here, thinks the Mother. I could just get on a bus and go, never come back. Change my name. A kind of witness relocation thing.

"Courage requires options," the man adds.

The Baby might be better off.

"There are options," says a woman with a thick suede headband. "You could give up. You could fall apart."

"No, you can't. Nobody does. I've never seen it," says the man. "Well, not *really* fall apart." Then the lounge falls quiet. Over the VCR someone has taped the fortune from a fortune cookie. "Optimism," it says, "is what allows a teakettle to sing though up to its neck in hot water." Underneath, someone else has taped a clipping from a summer horoscope. "Cancer rules!" it says. Who would tape this up? Somebody's twelve-year-old brother. One of the fathers – Joey's father – gets up and tears them both off, makes a small wad in his fist.

There is some rustling of magazine pages.

The Mother clears her throat. "Tiny Tim forgot the wet bar," she says.

Ned, who is still up, comes out of his room and down the corridor, whose lights dim at nine. Standing next to her chair, he says to the Mother, "Where are you from? What is wrong with your baby?"

In the tiny room that is theirs, she sleeps fitfully in her sweatpants, occasionally leaping up to check on the Baby. This is what the sweatpants are for: leaping. In case of fire. In case of anything. In case the difference between day and night starts to dissolve, and there is no difference at all, so why pretend? In the cot beside her, the Husband, who has taken a sleeping pill, is snoring loudly, his arms folded about his head in a kind of origami. How could either of them have stayed back at the house, with its empty high chair and empty crib? Occasionally the Baby wakes and cries out, and she bolts up, goes to him, rubs his back, rearranges the linens. The clock on the metal dresser shows that it is five after three. Then twenty to five. And then it is really morning, the beginning of this day, nephrectomy day. Will she be glad when it's over, or barely alive, or both? Each day this week has arrived huge, empty, and unknown, like a spaceship, and this one especially is lit a bright gray.

"He'll need to put this on," says John, one of the nurses, bright and early, handing the Mother a thin greenish garment with roses and teddy bears printed on it. A wave of nausea hits her; this smock, she thinks, will soon be splattered with – with what?

The Baby is awake but drowsy. She lifts off his pajamas. "Don't forget, *bubeleh*," she whispers, undressing and dressing him. "We will be with you every moment, every step. When you think you are asleep and floating off far away from everybody, Mommy will still be there." If she hasn't fled on a bus. "Mommy will take care of you. And Daddy, too." She hopes the Baby does not detect her own fear and uncertainty, which she must hide from him, like a limp. He is hungry, not having been allowed to eat, and he is no longer amused by this new place, but worried about its hardships. Oh, my baby, she thinks. And the room starts to swim a little. The Husband comes in to take over. "Take a break," he says to her. "I'll walk him around for five minutes."

She leaves but doesn't know where to go. In the hallway, she is approached by a kind of social worker, a customer-relations person, who had given them a video to watch about the anesthesia: how the parent accompanies the child into the operating room, and how gently, nicely the drugs are administered.

"Did you watch the video?"

"Yes," says the Mother.

"Wasn't it helpful?"

"I don't know," says the Mother.

"Do you have any questions?" asks the video woman. "Do you have any questions?" asked of someone who has recently landed in this fearful, alien place seems to the Mother an absurd and amazing little courtesy. The very specificity of a question would give a lie to the overwhelming strangeness of everything around her.

"Not right now," says the Mother. "Right now, I think I'm just going to go to the bathroom."

When she returns to the Baby's room, everyone is there: the surgeon, the anesthesiologist, all the nurses, the social worker. In their blue caps and scrubs, they look like a clutch of forget-me-nots, and forget them, who could? The Baby, in his little teddy-bear smock, seems cold and scared. He reaches out and the Mother lifts him from the Husband's arms, rubs his back to warm him.

"Well, it's time!" says the Surgeon, forcing a smile.

"Shall we go?" says the Anesthesiologist.

What follows is a blur of obedience and bright lights. They take an elevator down to a big concrete room, the anteroom, the greenroom, the backstage of the operating room. Lining the walls are long shelves full of blue surgical outfits. "Children often become afraid of the color blue," says one of the nurses. But of course. Of course! "Now, which one of you would like to come into the operating room for the anesthesia?"

"I will," says the Mother.

"Are you sure?" asks the Husband.

"Yup." She kisses the Baby's hair. "Mr. Curlyhead," people keep calling him here, and it seems both rude and nice. Women look admiringly at his long lashes and exclaim, "Always the boys! Always the boys!"

Two surgical nurses put a blue smock and a blue cotton cap on the Mother. The Baby finds this funny and keeps pulling at the cap. "This way," says another nurse, and the Mother follows. "Just put the Baby down on the table."

In the video, the mother holds the baby and fumes are gently waved under the baby's nose until he falls asleep. Now, out of view of camera or social worker, the Anesthesiologist is anxious to get this under way and not let too much gas leak out into the room generally. The occupational hazard of this, his chosen profession, is gas exposure and nerve damage, and it has started to worry him. No doubt he frets about it to his wife every night. Now he turns the gas on and quickly clamps the plastic mouthpiece over the baby's cheeks and lips.

The Baby is startled. The Mother is startled. The Baby

starts to scream and redden behind the plastic, but he cannot be heard. He thrashes. "Tell him it's okay," says the nurse to the Mother.

Okay? "It's okay," repeats the Mother, holding his hand, but she knows he can tell it's not okay, because he can see not only that she is still wearing that stupid paper cap but that her words are mechanical and swallowed, and she is biting her lips to keep them from trembling. Panicked, he attempts to sit. He cannot breathe; his arms reach up. *Bye-bye, outside.* And then, quite quickly, his eyes shut; he untenses and has fallen not *into* sleep but aside to sleep, an odd, kidnapping kind of sleep, his terror now hidden someplace deep inside him.

"How did it go?" asks the social worker, waiting in the concrete outer room. The Mother is hysterical. A nurse has ushered her out.

"It wasn't at all like the filmstrip!" she cries. "It wasn't like the filmstrip at all!"

"The filmstrip? You mean the video?" asks the social worker.

"It wasn't like that at all! It was brutal and unforgivable."

"Why that's terrible," she says, her role now no longer misinformational but janitorial, and she touches the Mother's arm, though the Mother shakes it off and goes to find the Husband.

She finds him in the large mulberry Surgery Lounge, where he has been taken and where there is free hot chocolate in small Styrofoam cups. Red cellophane garlands festoon the doorways. She has totally forgotten it is as close to Christmas as this. A pianist in the corner is playing "Carol of the Bells," and it sounds not only unfestive but scary, like the theme from *The Exorcist*.

There is a giant clock on the far wall. It is a kind of porthole into the operating room, a way of assessing the Baby's ordeal: forty-five minutes for the Hickman implant; two and a half hours for the nephrectomy. And then, after that, three months of chemotherapy. The magazine on her lap stays open at a ruby-hued perfume ad.

"Still not taking notes," says the Husband.

"Nope."

"You know, in a way, this is the kind of thing you've *always* written about."

"You are really something, you know that? This is life. This isn't a 'kind of thing.'"

"But this is the kind of thing that fiction is: it's the unlivable life, the strange room tacked onto the house, the extra moon that is circling the earth unbeknownst to science."

"I told you that."

"I'm quoting you."

She looks at her watch, thinking of the Baby. "How long has it been?"

"Not long. Too long. In the end, maybe those're the same things."

"What do you suppose is happening to him right this second?"

Infection? Slipping knives? "I don't know. But you know what? I've gotta go. I've gotta just walk a bit." The Husband gets up, walks around the lounge, then comes back and sits down.

The synapses between the minutes are unswimmable. An hour is thick as fudge. The Mother feels depleted; she is a string of empty tin cans attached by wire, something a goat would sniff and chew, something now and then enlivened by a jolt of electricity.

She hears their names being called over the intercom. "Yes? Yes?" She stands up quickly. Her words have flown out before her, an exhalation of birds. The piano music has stopped. The pianist is gone. She and the Husband approach the main desk, where a man looks up at them and smiles. Before him is a xeroxed list of patients' names. "That's our little boy right there," says the Mother, seeing the Baby's name on the list and pointing at it. "Is there some word? Is everything okay?"

"Yes," says the man. "Your boy is doing fine. They've

just finished with the catheter, and they are moving on to the kidney."

"But it's been two hours already! Oh my God, did something go wrong? What happened? What went wrong?"

"Did something go wrong?" The Husband tugs at his collar.

"Not really. It just took longer than they expected. I'm told everything is fine. They wanted you to know."

"Thank you," says the Husband. They turn and walk back toward where they were sitting.

"I'm not going to make it." The Mother sighs, sinking into a fake leather chair shaped somewhat like a baseball mitt. "But before I go, I'm taking half this hospital out with me."

"Do you want some coffee?" asks the Husband.

"I don't know," says the Mother. "No, I guess not. No. Do you?"

"Nah, I don't, either, I guess," he says.

"Would you like part of an orange?"

"Oh, maybe, I guess, if you're having one." She takes an orange from her purse and just sits there peeling its difficult skin, the flesh rupturing beneath her fingers, the juice trickling down her hands, stinging the hangnails. She and the Husband chew and swallow, discreetly spit the seeds into Kleenex, and read from photocopies of the latest medical research, which they begged from the intern. They read, and underline, and sigh and close their eyes, and after some time, the surgery is over. A nurse from Peed Onk comes down to tell them.

"Your little boy's in recovery right now. He's doing well. You can see him in about fifteen minutes."

How can it be described? How can any of it be described? The trip and the story of the trip are always two different things. The narrator is the one who has stayed home, but then, afterward, presses her mouth upon the traveler's mouth, in order to make the mouth work, to make the mouth say, say, say. One cannot go to a place and speak of it; one cannot both see and say, not really. One can go, and upon returning make a lot of hand motions and indications with the arms. The mouth itself, working at the speed of light, at the eye's instructions, is necessarily struck still; so fast, so much to report, it hangs open and dumb as a gutted bell. All that unsayable life! That's where the narrator comes in. The narrator comes with her kisses and mimicry and tidying up. The narrator comes and makes a slow, fake song of the mouth's eager devastation.

It is a horror and a miracle to see him. He is lying in his crib in his room, tubed up, splayed like a boy on a cross, his arms stiffened into cardboard "no-no's" so that he cannot yank out the tubes. There is the bladder catheter, the nasal-gastric tube, and the Hickman, which, beneath the skin, is plugged into his jugular, then popped out his chest wall and capped with a long plastic cap. There is a large bandage taped over his abdomen. Groggy, on a morphine drip, still he is able to look at her when, maneuvering through all the vinyl wiring, she leans to hold him, and when she does, he begins to cry, but cry silently, without motion or noise. She has never seen a baby cry without motion or noise. It is the crying of an old person: silent, beyond opinion, shattered. In someone so tiny, it is frightening and unnatural. She wants to pick up the Baby and run – out of there, out of there. She wants to whip out a gun: *No-no's, eh? This whole thing is what I call a no-no.* Don't you touch him! she wants to shout at the surgeons and the needle nurses. Not anymore! No more! No more! She would crawl up and lie beside him in the crib if she could. But instead, because of all his intricate wiring, she must lean and cuddle, sing to him, songs of peril and flight: "We gotta get out of this place, if it's the last thing we ever do. We gotta get out of this place . . . there's a better life for me and you."

Very 1967. She was eleven then and impressionable.

The Baby looks at her, pleadingly, his arms splayed out in surrender. To where? Where is there to go? Take me! Take me!

That night, postop night, the Mother and Husband lie afloat in the cot together. A fluorescent lamp near the crib is kept on in the dark. The Baby breathes evenly but thinly in his drugged sleep. The morphine in its first flooding doses apparently makes him feel as if he were falling backward – or so the Mother has been told – and it causes the Baby to jerk, to catch himself over and over, as if he were being dropped from a tree. "Is this right? Isn't there something that should be done?" The nurses come in hourly, different ones – the night shifts seem strangely short and frequent. If the Baby stirs or frets, the nurses give him more morphine through the Hickman catheter, then leave to tend to other patients. The Mother rises to check on him in the low light. There is gurgling from the clear plastic suction tube coming out of his mouth. Brownish clumps have collected in the tube. What is going on? The Mother rings for the nurse. Is it Renée or Sarah or Darcy? She's forgotten.

"What, what is it?" murmurs the Husband, waking up.

"Something is wrong," says the Mother. "It looks like blood in his N-G tube."

"What?" The Husband gets out of bed. He, too, is wearing sweatpants.

The nurse – Valerie – pushes open the heavy door to the room and enters quietly. "Everything okay?"

"There's something wrong here. The tube is sucking blood out of his stomach. It looks like it may have perforated his stomach and that now he's bleeding internally. Look!"

Valerie is a saint, but her voice is the standard hospital saint voice: an infuriating, pharmaceutical calm. It says, Everything is normal here. Death is normal. Pain is normal. Nothing is abnormal. So there is nothing to get excited about. "Well now, let's see." She holds up the plastic tube and tries to see inside it. "Hmmm," she says. "I'll call the attending physician."

Because this is a research and teaching hospital, all the regular doctors are at home sleeping in their Mission-style beds. Tonight, as is apparently the case every weekend night, the attending physician is a medical student. He looks fifteen. The authority he attempts to convey, he cannot remotely inhabit. He is not even in the same building with it. He shakes everyone's hands, then strokes his chin, a gesture no doubt gleaned from some piece of dinner theater his parents took him to once. As if there were an actual beard on that chin! As if beard growth on that chin were even possible! *Our Town*! *Kiss Me Kate*! *Barefoot in the Park*! He is attempting to convince, if not to impress.

"We're in trouble," the Mother whispers to the Husband. She is tired, tired of young people grubbing for grades. "We've got Dr. 'Kiss Me Kate,' here."

The Husband looks at her blankly, a mix of disorientation and divorce.

The medical student holds the tubing in his hands. "I don't really see anything," he says.

He flunks! "You don't?" The Mother shoves her way in, holds the clear tubing in both hands. "That," she says. "Right here and here." Just this past semester, she said to one of her own students, "If you don't see how this essay is better than that one, then I want you just to go out into the hallway and stand there until you do." Is it important to keep one's voice down? The Baby stays asleep. He is drugged and dreaming, far away.

"Hmmm," says the medical student. "Perhaps there's a little irritation in the stomach."

"A little irritation?" The Mother grows furious. "This is blood. These are clumps and clots. This stupid thing is sucking the life right out of him!" Life! She is starting to cry.

They turn off the suction and bring in antacids, which they feed into the Baby through the tube. Then they turn the suction on again. This time on low.

"What was it on before?" asks the Husband.

"High," says Valerie. "Doctor's orders, though I don't know why. I don't know why these doctors do a lot of the things they do."

"Maybe they're . . . not all that bright?" suggests the Mother. She is feeling relief and rage simultaneously: there is a feeling of prayer and litigation in the air. Yet essentially, she is grateful. Isn't she? She thinks she is. And still, and still: look at all the things you have to do to protect a child, a hospital merely an intensification of life's cruel obstacle course.

* * *

The Surgeon comes to visit on Saturday morning. He steps in and nods at the Baby, who is awake but glazed from the morphine, his eyes two dark unseeing grapes. "The boy looks fine," the Surgeon announces. He peeks under the Baby's bandage. "The stitches look good," he says. The Baby's abdomen is stitched all the way across like a baseball. "And the other kidney, when we looked at it yesterday face-to-face, looked fine. We'll try to wean him off the morphine a little, and see how he's doing on Monday." He clears his throat. "And now," he says, looking about the room at the nurses and medical students, "I would like to speak with the Mother, alone."

The Mother's heart gives a jolt. "Me?"

"Yes," he says, motioning, then turning.

She gets up and steps out into the empty hallway with him, closing the door behind her. What can this be about? She hears the Baby fretting a little in his crib. Her brain fills with pain and alarm. Her voice comes out as a hoarse whisper. "Is there something—"

"There is a particular thing I need from you," says the Surgeon, turning and standing there very seriously.

"Yes?" Her heart is pounding. She does not feel resilient enough for any more bad news.

"I need to ask a favor."

"Certainly," she says, attempting very hard to summon the strength and courage for this occasion, whatever it is; her throat has tightened to a fist.

From inside his white coat, the surgeon removes a thin paperback book and thrusts it toward her. "Will you sign my copy of your novel?"

The Mother looks down and sees that it is indeed a copy of a novel she has written, one about teenaged girls.

She looks up. A big, spirited grin is cutting across his face. "I read this last summer," he says, "and I still remember parts of it! Those girls got into such trouble!"

Of all the surreal moments of the last few days, this, she thinks, might be the most so.

"Okay," she says, and the Surgeon merrily hands her a pen.

"You can just write To Dr.— Oh, I don't need to tell you what to write."

The Mother sits down on a bench and shakes ink into the pen. A sigh of relief washes over and out of her. Oh, the pleasure of a sigh of relief, like the finest moments of love; has anyone properly sung the praises of sighs of relief? She opens the book to the title page. She breathes deeply. What is he doing reading novels about teenaged girls, anyway? And why didn't he buy the hardcover? She inscribes something grateful and true, then hands the book back to him.

"Is he going to be okay?"

"The boy? The boy is going to be fine," he says, then taps her stiffly on the shoulder. "Now you take care. It's Saturday. Drink a little wine."

Over the weekend, while the Baby sleeps, the Mother and Husband sit together in the Tiny Tim Lounge. The Husband is restless and makes cafeteria and sundry runs, running errands for everyone. In his absence, the other parents regale her further with their sagas. Pediatric cancer and chemo stories: the children's amputations, blood poisoning, teeth flaking like shale, the learning delays and disabilities caused by chemo frying the young, budding brain. But strangely optimistic codas are tacked on – endings as stiff and loopy as carpenter's lace, crisp and empty as lettuce, reticulate as a net – ah, words. "After all that business with the tutor, he's better now, and fitted with new incisors by my wife's cousin's husband, who did dental school in two and a half years, if you can believe that. We hope for the best. We take things as they come. Life is hard."

"Life's a big problem," agrees the Mother. Part of her welcomes and invites all their tales. In the few long days since this nightmare began, part of her has become addicted to disaster and war stories. She wants only to hear about the sadness and emergencies of others. They are the only situations that can join hands with her own; everything else bounces off her shiny shield of resentment and unsympathy. Nothing else can even stay in her brain. From this, no doubt, the philistine world is made, or should one say recruited? Together, the parents huddle all day in the Tiny Tim Lounge – no need to watch *Oprah*. They leave Oprah in the dust. Oprah has nothing on them. They chat matter-of-factly, then fall silent and watch *Dune* or *Star Wars*, in which there are bright and shiny robots, whom the Mother now sees not as robots at all but as human beings who have had terrible things happen to them.

Some of their friends visit with stuffed animals and soft greetings of "Looking good" for the dozing baby, though the room is way past the stuffed-animal limit. The Mother arranges, once more, a plateful of Mint Milano cookies and cups of take-out coffee for guests. All her nutso pals stop by – the two on Prozac, the one obsessed with the word *penis* in the word *happiness*, the one who recently had her hair foiled green. "Your friends put the *de* in *fin de siècle*," says the Husband. Overheard, or recorded, all marital conversation sounds as if someone must be joking, though usually no one is.

She loves her friends, especially loves them for coming, since there are times they all fight and don't speak for weeks. Is this friendship? For now and here, it must do and is, and is, she swears it is. For one, they never offer impromptu spiritual lectures about death, how it is part of life, its natural ebb and flow, how we all must accept that, or other such utterances that make her want to scratch out some eyes. Like true friends, they take no hardy or elegant stance loosely choreographed from some broad perspective. They get right in there and mutter "Jesus Christ!" and shake their heads. Plus, they are the only people who not only will laugh at her stupid jokes but offer up stupid ones of their own. *What do you get when you cross Tiny Tim with a pit bull?* A child's illness is a strain on the mind. They know how to laugh in a fluty, desperate way – unlike the people who are more her husband's friends and who seem just to deepen their sorrowful gazes, nodding their heads with Sympathy. How exiling and estranging are everybody's Sympathetic Expressions! When anyone laughs, she thinks, Okay! Hooray: a buddy. In disaster as in show business.

Nurses come and go; their chirpy voices both startle and soothe. Some of the other Peed Onk parents stick their heads in to see how the Baby is and offer encouragement.

Green Hair scratches her head. "Everyone's so friendly here. Is there someone in this place who isn't doing all this airy, scripted optimism – or are people like that the only people here?"

"It's Modern Middle Medicine meets the Modern Middle Family," says the Husband. "In the Modern Middle West."

Someone has brought in take-out lo mein, and they all eat it out in the hall by the elevators.

Parents are allowed use of the Courtesy Line.

"You've got to have a second child," says a different friend on the phone, a friend from out of town. "An heir and a spare. That's what we did. We had another child to ensure we wouldn't off ourselves if we lost our first."

"Really?"

"I'm serious."

"A formal suicide? Wouldn't you just drink yourself into a lifelong stupor and let it go at that?"

"Nope. I knew how I would do it even. For a while, until our second came along, I had it all planned."

"What did you plan?"

"I can't go into too much detail, because – Hi, honey! – the kids are here now in the room. But I'll spell out the general idea: R-O-P-E."

Sunday evening, she goes and sinks down on the sofa in the Tiny Tim Lounge next to Frank, Joey's father. He is a short, stocky man with the currentless, flatlined look behind the eyes that all the parents eventually get here. He has shaved his head bald in solidarity with his son. His little boy has been battling cancer for five years. It is now in the liver, and the rumor around the corridor is that Joey has three weeks to live. She knows that Joey's mother, Heather, left Frank years ago, two years into the cancer, and has remarried and had another child, a girl named Brittany. The Mother sees Heather here sometimes with her new life – the cute little girl and the new, young, full-haired husband who will never be so maniacally and debilitatingly obsessed with Joey's illness the way Frank, her first husband, was. Heather comes to visit Joey, to say hello and now good-bye, but she is not Joey's main man. Frank is.

Frank is full of stories – about the doctors, about the food, about the nurses, about Joey. Joey, affectless from his meds, sometimes leaves his room and comes out to watch TV in his bathrobe. He is jaundiced and bald, and though he is nine, he looks no older than six. Frank has devoted the last four and a half years to saving Joey's life. When the cancer was first diagnosed, the doctors gave Joey a 20 percent chance of living six more months. Now here it is, almost five years later, and Joey's still here. It is all due to Frank, who, early on, quit his job as vice president of a consulting firm in order to commit himself totally to his son. He is proud of everything he's given up and done, but he is tired. Part of him now really believes things are coming to a close, that this is the end. He says this without tears. There are no more tears.

"You have probably been through more than anyone else on this corridor," says the Mother.

"I could tell you stories," he says. There is a sour odor between them, and she realizes that neither of them has bathed for days.

"Tell me one. Tell me the worst one." She knows he hates his ex-wife and hates her new husband even more.

"The worst? They're all the worst. Here's one: one morning, I went out for breakfast with my buddy – it was the only time I'd left Joey alone ever; left him for two hours is all – and when I came back, his N-G tube was full of blood. They had the suction on too high, and it was sucking the guts right out of him."

"Oh my God. That just happened to us," said the Mother.

"It did?"

"Friday night."

"You're kidding. They let that happen again? I gave them such a chewing-out about that!"

"I guess our luck is not so good. We get your very worst story on the second night we're here."

"It's not a bad place, though."

"It's not?"

"Naw. I've seen worse. I've taken Joey everywhere."

"He seems very strong." Truth is, at this point, Joey seems like a zombie and frightens her.

"Joey's a fucking genius. A biological genius. They'd given him six months, remember."

The Mother nods.

"Six months is not very long," says Frank. "Six months is nothing. He was four and a half years old."

All the words are like blows. She feels flooded with affection and mourning for this man. She looks away, out the window, out past the hospital parking lot, up toward the black marbled sky and the electric eyelash of the moon. "And now he's nine," she says. "You're his hero."

"And he's mine," says Frank, though the fatigue in his voice seems to overwhelm him. "He'll be that forever. Excuse me," he says, "I've got to go check. His breathing hasn't been good. Excuse me."

"Good news and bad," says the Oncologist on Monday. He has knocked, entered the room, and now stands there. Their cots are unmade. One wastebasket is overflowing with coffee cups. "We've got the pathologist's report. The bad news is that the kidney they removed had certain lesions, called 'rests,' which are associated with a higher risk for disease in the other kidney. The good news is that the tumor is stage one, regular cell structure, and under five hundred grams, which qualifies you for a national experiment in which chemotherapy isn't done but your boy is monitored with ultrasound instead. It's not all that risky, given that the patient's watched closely, but here is the literature on it. There are forms to sign, if you decide to do that. Read all this and we can discuss it further. You have to decide within four days."

Lesions? Rests? They dry up and scatter like M&M's on the floor. All she hears is the part about no chemo. Another sigh of relief rises up in her and spills out. In a life where there is only the bearable and the unbearable, a sigh of relief is an ecstasy.

"No chemo?" says the Husband. "Do you recommend that?"

The Oncologist shrugs. What casual gestures these doctors are permitted! "I know chemo. I like chemo," says the Oncologist. "But this is for you to decide. It depends how you feel."

The Husband leans forward. "But don't you think that now that we have the upper hand with this thing, we should keep going? Shouldn't we stomp on it, beat it, smash it to death with the chemo?"

The Mother swats him angrily and hard. "Honey, you're delirious!" She whispers, but it comes out as a hiss. "This is our lucky break!" Then she adds gently, "We don't want the Baby to have chemo."

The Husband turns back to the Oncologist. "What do *you* think?"

"It could be," he says, shrugging. "It could be that this is your lucky break. But you won't know for sure for five years."

The Husband turns back to the Mother. "Okay," he says. "Okay."

The Baby grows happier and strong. He begins to move and sit and eat. Wednesday morning, they are allowed to leave, and leave without chemo. The Oncologist looks a little nervous. "Are you nervous about this?" asks the Mother.

"Of course I'm nervous." But he shrugs and doesn't look that nervous. "See you in six weeks for the ultrasound," he says, waves and then leaves, looking at his big black shoes as he does.

The Baby smiles, even toddles around a little, the sun bursting through the clouds, an angel chorus crescendoing. Nurses arrive. The Hickman is taken out of the Baby's neck and chest; antibiotic lotion is dispensed. The Mother packs up their bags. The Baby sucks on a bottle of juice and does not cry.

"No chemo?" says one of the nurses. "Not even a *little* chemo?"

"We're doing watch and wait," says the Mother.

The other parents look envious but concerned. They have never seen any child get out of there with his hair and white blood cells intact.

"Will you be okay?" asks Ned's mother.

"The worry's going to kill us," says the Husband.

"But if all we have to do is worry," chides the Mother, "every day for a hundred years, it'll be easy. It'll be nothing. I'll take all the worry in the world, if it wards off the thing itself."

"That's right," says Ned's mother. "Compared to everything else, compared to all the actual events, the worry is nothing."

The Husband shakes his head. "I'm such an amateur," he moans.

"You're both doing admirably," says the other mother. "Your baby's lucky, and I wish you all the best."

The Husband shakes her hand warmly. "Thank you," he says. "You've been wonderful."

Another mother, the mother of Eric, comes up to them. "It's all very hard," she says, her head cocked to one side. "But there's a lot of collateral beauty along the way."

Collateral beauty? Who is entitled to such a thing? A child is ill. No one is entitled to any collateral beauty!

"Thank you," says the Husband.

Joey's father, Frank, comes up and embraces them both.

"It's a journey," he says. He chucks the Baby on the chin. "Good luck, little man."

"Yes, thank you so much," says the Mother. "We hope things go well with Joey." She knows that Joey had a hard, terrible night.

Frank shrugs and steps back. "Gotta go," he says. "Good-bye!"

"Bye," she says, and then he is gone. She bites the inside of her lip, a bit tearily, then bends down to pick up the diaper bag, which is now stuffed with little animals; helium balloons are tied to its zipper. Shouldering the thing, the Mother feels she has just won a prize. All the parents have now vanished down the hall in the opposite direction. The Husband moves close. With one arm, he takes the Baby from her; with the other, he rubs her back. He can see she is starting to get weepy.

"Aren't these people nice? Don't you feel better hearing about their lives?" he asks.

Why does he do this, form clubs all the time; why does even this society of suffering soothe him? When it comes to death and dying, perhaps someone in this family ought to be more of a snob.

"All these nice people with their brave stories," he continues as they make their way toward the elevator bank, waving good-bye to the nursing staff as they go, even the Baby waving shyly. *Bye-bye! Bye-bye!* "Don't you feel consoled, knowing we're all in the same boat, that we're all in this together?"

But who on earth would want to be in this boat? the Mother thinks. This boat is a nightmare boat. Look where it goes: to a silver-and-white room, where, just before your eyesight and hearing and your ability to touch or be touched disappear entirely, you must watch your child die.

Rope! Bring on the rope.

"Let's make our own way," says the Mother, "and not in this boat."

Woman Overboard! She takes the Baby back from the Husband, cups the Baby's cheek in her hand, kisses his brow and then, quickly, his flowery mouth. The Baby's heart – she can hear it – drums with life. "For as long as I live," says the Mother, pressing the elevator button – up or down, everyone in the end has to leave this way – "I never want to see any of these people again."

There are the notes.

Now where is the money?

1996

PLACES TO LOOK FOR YOUR MIND

THE SIGN SAID "Welcome to America," in bold red letters. Underneath, in smaller blue, Millie had spelled out *John Spee.* Comma, *John Spee.* She held it up against her chest like a locket, something pressed against the heart for luck: a pledge of allegiance. She was waiting for a boy she didn't know, someone she'd never even seen a photograph of, an English acquaintance of her daughter Ariel's. Ariel was on a junior semester abroad, and the boy was the brother of one of her Warwickshire dormmates. He was an auto mechanic in Surrey, and because he'd so badly wanted to come to the States, Ariel had told him that if he needed a place, he could stay with her parents in New Jersey. She had written ahead to inform them. "I told John Spee he could stay in Michael's old room, unless you are still using it as an 'office.' In which case he can stay in mine."

Office in quotation marks. Millie had once hoped to start a business in that room, something to do with recycling and other environmental projects. She had hoped to be hired on a consultant basis, but every time she approached a business or community organization they seemed confounded as to what they would consult her for. For a time Millie had filled the room with business cards and supplies and receipts for various expenses in case she ever filed a real tax form. Her daughter and her husband had rolled their eyes and looked, embarrassed, in the other direction.

"Office." Ariel made her quotation marks as four quick slashes, not the careful sixes and nines Millie had been trained long ago to write. There was something a bit spoiled about Ariel, a quiet impudence, which troubled Millie. She had written back to her daughter, Your father and I have no real objections, and certainly it will be nice to meet your friend. But you must check with us next time *before* you volunteer *our*

home." She had stressed *our home* with a kind of sternness that lingered regretlessly. "You mustn't take things for granted." It was costing them good money to send Ariel abroad. Millie herself had never been to England. Or anywhere, when you got right down to it. Once, as a child, she had been to Florida, but she remembered so little of it. Mostly just the glare of the sky, and some vague and shuddering colors.

People filed out from the Newark customs gate, released and weary, one of them a thin, red-haired boy of about twenty. He lit a cigarette, scanned the crowd, and then, spying Millie, headed toward her. He wore an old, fraying camel hair sports jacket, sneakers of blue, man-made suede, and a baseball cap, which said *Yankees*, an ersatz inscription.

"Are you Mrs. Keegan?" he asked, pronouncing it *Kaygan*.

"Um, yes, I am," Millie said, and blushed as if surprised. She let the sign, which with its crayoned and overblown message now seemed ludicrous, drop to her side. Her other hand she thrust out in greeting. She tried to smile warmly but wondered if she looked "fakey," something Ariel sometimes accused her of. "It's like you're doing everything from a magazine article," Ariel had said. "It's like you're trying to be happy out of a book." Millie owned several books about trying to be happy.

John shifted his cigarette into his other hand and shook Millie's. "John Spee," he said. He pronounced it *Spay*. His hand was big and bony, like a chicken claw.

"Well, I hope your flight was uneventful," said Millie.

"Oh, not really," said John. "Sat next to a bloke with stories about the Vietnam War and watched two movies about it. *The Deer Hunter* and, uh, I forget the other." He seemed apprehensive yet proud of himself for having arrived where he'd arrived.

"Do you have any more luggage than that? Is that all you have?"

"'Zall I got!" he chirped, holding a small duffel bag and turning around just enough to let Millie see his U.S. Army knapsack.

"You don't want this sign, do you?" asked Millie. She

creased it, folded it in quarters like a napkin, and shoved it into her own bag. Over the PA system a woman's voice was repeating, "Mr. Boone, Mr. Daniel Boone. Please pick up the courtesy line."

"Isn't that funny," said Millie.

On the drive home to Terracebrook, John Spee took out a pack of Johnny Parliaments and chain-smoked. He told Millie about his life in Surrey, his mates at the pub there, in a suburb called Worcester Park. "Never was much of a student," he said, "so there was no chance of me going to university." He spoke of the scarcity of work and of his "flash car," which he had sold to pay for the trip. He had worked six years as an auto mechanic, a job that he had quit to come here. "I may stay in the States a long time," he said. "I'm thinking of New York City. Wish I hadn't had to sell me flash car, though." He looked out at a souped-up Chevrolet zooming by them.

"Yes, that's too bad," said Millie. What should she say? On the car radio there was news of the garbage barge, and she turned it up to hear. It had been rejected by two states and two foreign countries, and was floating, homeless, toward Texas. "I used to have a kind of business," she explained to John. "It was in garbage and trash recycling. Nothing really came of it, though." The radio announcer was quoting something now. *The wretched refuse of our teeming shores*, he was saying. *Yeah, yeah, yeah*, he was saying.

"Now I'm taking a college course through the mail," Millie said, then reddened. This had been her secret. Even Hane didn't know. "Don't tell my husband," she added quickly. "He doesn't know. He doesn't quite approve of my interest in business. He's a teacher. Religious studies at the junior college."

John gazed out at the snag of car dealerships and the fast-food shacks of Route 22. "Is he a vicar or something?" He inhaled his cigarette, holding the smoke in like a thought.

"Oh, no," said Millie. She sighed a little. Hane did go to church every Sunday. He was, she knew, a faithful man. She herself had stopped going regularly over a year ago. Now she went only once in a while, like a visit to an art museum, and it saddened Hane, but she just couldn't help it. "It's not my thing," she had said to her husband. It was a phrase she had heard Ariel use, and it seemed a good one, powerful with self-forgiveness, like Ariel herself.

"The traffic on this route is almost always heavy," said Millie. "But everyone drives very fast, so it doesn't slow you down."

John glanced sideways at her. "You look a little like Ariel," he said.

"Really?" said Millie brightly, for she had always thought her daughter too pretty to have come from Hane and her. Ariel had the bones and eyes of someone else, the daughter of royalty, or a movie star. Mitzi Gaynor's child. Or the Queen's. Ironically, it had been Michael, their eldest, who had seemed so clearly theirs.

"Oh, yes," said John. "You don't think so?"

Usually in spring Millie hurried guests immediately out into the backyard so that they could see her prize tulips – which really weren't hers at all but had belonged to the people who owned the house before them. The woman had purchased prize bulbs and planted them even into the edge of the next-door neighbor's yard. The yards were small, for sure, but the couple had been a young managerial type, and Millie had thought perhaps aggressive gardening went with such people.

Millie swung the car into the driveway and switched off the ignition. "I'll spare you the tulips for now," she said to John. "You probably would like to rest. With jet lag and all."

"Yeah," said John. He got out of the car and swung his duffel bag over his shoulder. He surveyed the identical lawns, still a pale, wintry ocher, and the small, boxy split-levels, their stingy porches fronting the entrances like goatees. He looked startled. *He thought we were going to be rich Americans*, thought Millie. "Are you tired?" she said aloud.

"Not so bad." He breathed deeply and started to perspire.

Millie went up the steps, took a key out from behind the black metal mailbox, and opened the door. "Our home is yours," she said, swinging her arms wide, showing him in.

John stepped in with a lit cigarette between his teeth, his eyes squinting from the smoke. He put his bag and knapsack down and looked about the living room. There were encyclopedias and ceramic figurines. There were some pictures of Ariel placed high on a shelf. Much of the furniture was shredded and old. There was a Bible and a *Time* magazine on the coffee table.

"Let me show you your room," said Millie, and she took him down a short corridor and opened the door on the right. "This was once my son's room," she said, "but he's – he's no longer with us." John nodded somberly. "He's not dead," Millie hastened to add, "he's just not with us." She cleared her throat – there was something in it, a scratch, a bruise of words. "He left home ten years ago, and we never heard from him again. The police said drugs." Millie shrugged. "Maybe it was drugs."

John was looking for a place to flick his ashes. Millie grabbed a potted begonia from the sill and held it out for him. "There's a desk and a filing cabinet here, which I was using for my business, so you can just ignore those." On the opposite wall there was a cot and a blond birch dresser. "Let me know if you need anything. Oh! Towels are in the bathroom, on the back of the door."

"Thanks," said John, and he looked at his watch like a man with plans.

"Leftovers is all we've got tonight!" Millie emerged from the kitchen with quilted pot-holder mittens and a large cast-iron skillet. She beamed like the presenters on the awards shows she sometimes watched; she liked to watch TV when it was full of happiness.

Hane, who had met John coming out of the bathroom and had mumbled an embarrassed how-do-you-do, now sat at the head of the dining room table, waiting to serve the food. John sat kitty-corner, Michael's old place. He regarded the salad bowl, the clover outlines of the peppers, the clock stares of the tomato slices. He had taken a shower and parted his wet hair rather violently on the left.

"You'd think we'd be able to do a little better than this on your first night in America," said Hane, poking with a serving spoon at the fried pallet of mashed potatoes, turnips, chopped broccoli, and three eggs over easy. "Millie here, as you probably know already, is devoted to recycling." His tone was of good-natured mortification, a self-deprecating singsong that was his way of reprimanding his family. He made no real distinction between himself and his family. They were he. They were his feminine, sentimental side and warranted, even required, running commentary.

"It's all very fine," said John.

"Would you like skim milk or whole?" Millie asked him.

"Whole, I think," and then, in something of a fluster, he said, "Water, I mean, please. Don't trouble yourself, Mrs. Keegan."

"In New Jersey, water's as much trouble as milk," said Millie. "Have whichever you want, dear."

"Water, please, then."

"Are you sure?"

"Milk, then, I guess, thank you."

Millie went back into the kitchen to get milk. She wondered whether John thought they were poor and milk a little too expensive for them. The neighborhood probably did look shabby. Millie herself had been disappointed when they'd first moved here from the north part of town, after Ariel had started college and Hane had not been promoted to full professor rank, as he had hoped. It had been the only time she had ever seen her husband cry, and she had started to think of themselves as poor, though she knew that was silly. At least a little silly.

Millie stared into the refrigerator, not looking hungrily for something, anything, to assuage her restlessness, as she had when she was younger, but now forgetting altogether why she was there. *Look in the refrigerator,* was her husband's old joke about where to look for something she'd misplaced. "Places to look for your mind," he'd say, and then he'd recite a list.

Once she had put a manila folder in the freezer by mistake.

"What did I want?" she said aloud, and the refrigerator motor kicked on in response to the warm air. She had held the door open too long. She closed it and went back and stood in the dining room for a moment. Seeing John's empty glass, she said, "Milk. That's right," and promptly went and got it.

"So how was the flight over?" asked Hane, handing John a plate of food. "If this is too much turnip, let me know. Just help yourself to salad." It had been years since they'd had a boy in the house, and he wondered if he knew how to talk to one. Or if he ever had. "Wait until they grow up," he had said to Millie of their own two children. "Then I'll know what to say to them." Even at student conferences he tended to ramble a bit, staring out the window, never, never into their eyes.

"By the time they've grown up it'll be too late," Millie had said.

But Hane had thought, *No, it won't.* By that time he would be president of the college, or dean of a theological school somewhere, and he would be speaking from a point of achievement that would mean something to his children. He could then tell them his life story. In the meantime, his kids hadn't seemed interested in his attempts at conversation. "Forget it, Dad," his son had always said to him. "Just forget it." No matter what Hane said, standing in a doorway or serving dinner – "How was school, son?" – Michael would always tell him just to forget it, Dad. One time, in the living room, Hane had found himself unable to bear it, and had grabbed Michael by the arm and struck him twice in the face.

"This is fine, thank you," said John, referring to his turnips. "And the flight was fine. I saw movies."

"Now, what is it you plan to do here exactly?" There was a gruffness in Hane's voice. This happened often, though Hane rarely intended it, or even heard it, clawing there in the punctuation.

John gulped at some milk and fussed with his napkin.

"Hane, let's save it for after grace," said Millie.

"Your turn," said Hane, and he nodded and bowed his head. John Spee sat upright and stared.

Millie began. "'Bless this food to our use, and us to thy service. And keep us ever needful of the minds of others.' Wopes. 'Amen.' Did you hear what I said?" She grinned, as if pleased.

"We assumed you did that on purpose, didn't we, John?" Hane looked out over his glasses and smiled conspiratorially at the boy.

"Yes," said John. He looked at the ceramic figurines on the shelf to his right. There was a ballerina and a clown.

"Well," said Millie, "maybe I just did." She placed her napkin in her lap and began eating. She enjoyed the leftovers, the warm, rising grease of them, their taste and ecology.

"It's very good food, Mrs. Keegan," said John, chewing.

"Before you leave, of course, I'll cook up a real meal. Several."

"How long you staying?" Hane asked.

Millie put her fork down. "Hane, I told you: three weeks."

"Maybe only two," said John Spee. The idea seemed to cheer him. "But then maybe I'll find a flat in the Big Apple and stay forever."

Millie nodded. People from out of town were always referring to the Big Apple, like some large forbidden fruit one conquered with mountain gear. It seemed to give them energy, to think of it that way.

"What will you *do*?" Hane studied the food on his fork, letting it hover there, between his fork and his mouth, a kind of ingestive purgatory. Hane's big fear was idleness. Particularly in boys. *What will you do?*

"Hane," cautioned Millie.

"In England none of me mates have jobs. They're all jealous 'cause I sold the car and came here to New York."

"This is New Jersey, dear," said Millie. "You'll see New York tomorrow. I'll give you a timetable for the train."

"You sold your car," repeated Hane. Hane had never once sold a car outright. He had always traded them in. "That's quite a step."

* * *

The next morning Millie made a list of things for John to do and see in New York. Hane had already left for his office. She sat at the dining room table and wrote:

Statue of Liberty
World Trade Center
Times Square
Broadway 2-fors

She stopped for a moment and thought.

Metropolitan Museum of Art
Circle Line Tour

The door of the "guest" room was still closed. Funny how it pleased her to have someone in that space, someone really using it. For too long she had just sat in there doodling on her business cards and thinking about Michael. The business cards had been made from recycled paper, but the printers had forgotten to mention that on the back. So she had inked it in herself. They had also forgotten to print Millie's middle initial – Environmental Project Adviser, Mildred *R.* Keegan – and so she had sat in there for weeks, ballpointing the *R* back in, card after card. Later Ariel had told her the cards looked stupid that way, and Millie had had to agree. She then spent days sitting at the desk, cutting the cards into gyres, triangles, curlicues, like a madness, like a business turned madness. She left them, absentmindedly, around the house, and Hane began to find them in odd places – on the kitchen counter, on the toilet tank. He turned to her one night in bed and said, "Millie, you're fifty-one. You don't have to have a career. Really, you don't," and she put her hands to her face and wept.

John Spee came out of his room. He was completely dressed, his bright hair parted neat as a crease, the white of his scalp startling as surgery.

"I've made a list of things you'll probably want to do," said Millie.

John sat down. "What's this?" He pointed to the Metropolitan Museum of Art. "I'm not that keen to go to museums. We always went to the British Museum for school. My sister likes that kind of stuff, but not me."

"These are only suggestions," said Millie. She placed a muffin and a quartered orange in front of him.

John smiled appreciatively. He picked up a piece of orange, pressed it against his teeth, and sucked it to a damp, stringy mat.

"I can drive you to the station to catch the ten-o-two train, if you want to leave in fifteen minutes," said Millie. She slid sidesaddle into a chair and began eating a second muffin. Her manner was sprinkled with youthful motions, as if her body were on occasion falling into a memory or a wish.

"That would be lovely, thanks," said John.

"Did you really not like living in England?" asked Millie, but they were both eating muffins, and it was hard to talk.

At the station she pressed a twenty into his hand and kissed him on the cheek. He stepped back away from her and got on the train. "See a play," Millie mouthed at him through the window.

At dinner it was just she and Hane. Hane was talking about Jesus again, the Historical Jesus, how everyone misunderstood Christ's prophetic powers, how Jesus himself had been mistaken.

"Jesus thought the world was going to end," said Hane, "but he was wrong. It wasn't just Jerusalem. He was predicting the end for the whole world. Eschatologically, he got it wrong. He said it outright, but he was mistaken. The world kept right on."

"Perhaps he meant it as a kind of symbol. You know, poetically, not literally." Millie had heard Hane suggest this himself. They were his words she was speaking, one side of his own self-argument.

"No, he meant it literally," Hane barked a little fiercely.

"Well, we all make mistakes," said Millie. "Isn't the world

funny that way." She always tried to listen to Hane. She knew that few students registered for his courses anymore, and those that did tended to be local fundamentalists, young ignorant people, said Hane, who had no use for history or metaphor. They might as well just chuck the Bible! In class Hane's primary aim was reconciling religion with science and history, but these young "Pentecostalists," as Hane referred to them, didn't believe in science or history. "They're mindless, some of these kids. And if you want your soul nourished – and they do, I think – you've got to have a mind."

"Cleanliness is next to godliness," said Millie.

"What are you talking about?" asked Hane. He looked depressed and impatient. There were times when he felt he had married a stupid woman, and it made him feel alone in the world.

"I've been thinking about the garbage barge," said Millie. "I guess my mind's wandering around, just like that heap of trash." She smiled. She had been listening to all the reports on the barge, had charted its course from Islip, where she had relatives, to Morehead City, where she had relatives. "Imagine," she had said to her neighbor in their backyards, near the prize tulips that belonged to neither one of them. "Relatives in both places! Garbagey relatives!"

Millie wiped her mouth with her napkin. "It has nowhere to go," she said now to her husband.

Hane served himself more leftovers. He thought of Millie and this interest of hers in ecology. It baffled and awed him, like a female thing. In the kitchen Millie kept an assortment of boxes for recycling household supplies. She had boxes marked *Aluminum*, *Plastic*, *Dry Trash*, *Wet Trash*, *Garbage*. She had twice told him the difference between garbage and trash, but the distinction never meant that much to him, and he always forgot it. Last night she had told him about swans in the park who were making their nests from old boots and plastic six-pack rings. "Laying their eggs in litter," she'd said. Then she told him to be more fatherly toward John Spee, to take a friendly interest in the boy.

"Is this the end of the leftovers?" asked Hane. At his office at the college he ate very light lunches. Often he just brought a hard-boiled egg and sprinkled it carefully with salt, shaking the egg over the wastebasket if he got too much on by mistake.

"This is it," said Millie, standing. She picked up the skillet, and taking a serving spoon, scraped and swirled up the hardened, flat-bottomed remnants. "Here," she said, holding it all in front of Hane. "Open up."

Hane scowled. "Come on, Millie."

"Just one last spoonful. Tomorrow I cook fresh."

Hane opened his mouth, and Millie fed him gently, carefully, because the spoon was large.

Afterward they both sat in the living room and Hane read aloud a passage from 2 Thessalonians. Millie stared off like a child at the figurines, the clown and the ballerina, and thought about Ariel, traveling to foreign countries and meeting people. What it must be like to be young today, with all those opportunities. Once, last semester, before she'd left for England, Ariel had said, "You know, Mom, there's a girl in my class at Rutgers with exactly your name: Mildred Keegan. Spelled the same and everything."

"Really?" exclaimed Millie. Her face had lit up. This was interesting.

But Ariel was struck with afterthought. "Yeah. Only . . . well, actually she flunked out last week." Then Ariel began to laugh, and had to get up and leave the room.

At nine o'clock, after she had peeled the labels off an assortment of tin cans, and rinsed and stacked them, Millie went to pick up John Spee at the train station.

"So what all did you do in the city?" asked Millie, slowing for a red light and glancing at the boy. She had left the house in too much of a rush, and now, looking quickly in the rearview mirror, she attempted to smooth the front of her hair, which had fallen onto her forehead in a loose, droopy tangle. "Did you see a play? I hear there's some funny ones." Millie loved plays, but Hane didn't so much.

"No, didn't feel like buzzing the bees for a play." He said *ply*.

"Oh," said Millie. Her features sagged to a slight frown. Buzzing the bees. Ariel had used this expression once. *Money, honey, bees,* Ariel had explained impatiently. *Get it?* "Did you go down to Battery Park and see the Statue of Liberty? It's so beautiful since they cleaned it." Not that Millie had seen it herself, but it was in all the newsmagazines a while back, and the pictures had made it seem very holy and grand.

The light turned green, and she swung the car around the corner. At night this part of New Jersey could seem quiet and sweet as a real hometown.

"I just walked around and looked at the buildings," said John, glancing away from her, out the car window at the small darkened business district of Terracebrook. "I went to the top of the Empire State Building, and then I went back and went to the top again."

"You went twice."

"Twice, yeah. Twice."

"Well, good!" Millie exclaimed. And when they pulled into the driveway, she exclaimed it again. "Well, good!"

"So how was the city?" boomed Hane, rising stiff and hearty, so awkwardly wanting to make the boy feel at home that he lunged at him a bit, big and creaky in the joints from having been sitting and reading all evening.

"Fine, thank you," said John, who then went quickly to his room.

Millie gave Hane a worried look, then followed and knocked on John's door. "John, would you like some supper? I've got a can of soup and some bread and cheese for a sandwich."

"No, thank you," John called through the door. Millie thought she heard him crying – was he crying? She walked back into the living room toward Hane, who gave her a shrug, helpless, bewildered. He looked at her for some reassuring word.

Millie shrugged back and walked past him into the kitchen. Hane followed her and stood in the doorway.

"I guess I'm not the right sort of person for him," he said. "I'm not a friendly man by nature. That's what he needs." Hane took off his glasses and cleaned them on the hem of his shirt.

"You're a stack of apologies," said Millie, kissing him on the cheek. "Here. Squash this can." She bent over and put a rinsed and label-less can near his shoe. Hane lifted his foot and came down on it with a bang.

The next morning was Friday, and John Spee wanted to go into the city again. Millie drove him to catch the ten-o-two. "Have a nice time," she said to him on the platform. "I'll pick you up tonight." As the train pulled up, steamy and deafening, she reminded him again about the half-price tickets for Broadway shows.

Back at the house, Millie got out the Hoover and began vacuuming. Hane, who had no classes on Friday, sat in the living room doing a crossword puzzle. Millie vacuumed around his feet. "Lift up," she said.

In John Spee's close and cluttered room she vacuumed the sills, even vacuumed the ceiling and the air, before she had to stop. All around the floor there were matchbooks from Greek coffee shops and odd fliers handed out on the street: *Live Eddie; Crazy Girls; 20% off Dinner Specials, now until Easter.* Underwear had been tossed on the floor, and there were socks balled in one corner of the desk.

Millie flicked off the Hoover and began to tidy the desktop. This was at one time to have been her business headquarters, and now look at it. She picked up the socks and noticed a spiral notebook underneath. It looked a little like a notebook she had been using for her correspondence course, the same shade of blue, and she opened it to see.

On the first page was written, *Crazy People I Have Met in America.* Underneath there was a list.

1. *Asian man in business suit waiting on subway platform. Screaming.*
2. *Woman in park walking dog. Screaming. Tells dog to walk like a lady.*
3. *In coffee shop, woman with food spilling out of her mouth. Yells at fork.*

Millie closed the notebook quickly. She was afraid to read on, afraid of what number four might be, or number five. She put the notebook out of her mind and moved away from the desk, unplugged the Hoover, wound up the cord, then collected the odd, inside-out clumps of clothes from under the cot and thought again of her garbage business, how she had hoped to run it out of this very room, how it seemed now to have crawled back in here – her poor little business! – looking a lot like laundry. What she had wanted was garbage, and instead she got laundry. "Ha!" She laughed out loud.

"What?" called Hane. He was still doing the crossword in the living room.

"Not you," said Millie. "I'm just going to put some things in the wash for John." She went downstairs to the laundry room, with its hampers of recyclable rags, its boxes of biodegradable detergent, its cartons of bottles with the labels soaked off them, the bags of aluminum foil and tins. *This* was an office, in a way, a one-woman room: a stand against the world. Or *for* the world. She meant *for* the world.

Millie flicked on the radio she kept propped on the dryer. She waited through two commercials, and then the news came on: The garbage barge was heading back from Louisiana. "I'll bet in that garbage there's a lot of trash," she wagered aloud. This was her distinction between garbage and trash, which she had explained many times to Hane: Garbage was moist and rotting and had to be plowed under. Trash was primmer and papery and could be reused. Garbage could be burned for gas, but trash could be dressed up and reissued. Retissued! Recycled Kleenex, made from cheap, recyclable paper – that was a truly viable thing, that was something she had hoped to emphasize, but perhaps she had not highlighted it enough in her initial materials. Perhaps people thought she was talking about garbage when she was talking about trash. Or vice versa. Perhaps no one had understood. Certainly, she had neglected to stress her best idea, the one about subliminal advertising on soap operas: having characters talk about their diseases and affairs at the same time that they peeled labels off cans and bundled newspapers. She was sure you could get programs to do this.

She turned the washer dial to *Gentle* and pushed it in. Warm water rushed into the machine like a falls, like a honeymoon, recycled, the same one, over and over.

When Millie picked John up at the station, he told her about the buildings again.

"You probably didn't get a chance to see a play, then," said Millie, but he didn't seem to hear her.

"Going in tomorrow to look some more," he said. He flicked his lighter until it lit. He smoked nervously. "Great cars there, too."

"Well, wonderful," said Millie. But when she looked at him there was a grayness in his face. His life seemed to be untacking itself, lying loose about him like a blouse. A life could do that. Millie thought of people in the neighborhood she might introduce him to. There was a boy of about twenty-two who lived down the street. He worked at a lawn and seed company and seemed like the friendly sort.

"There's someone on the street I should introduce you to," she said. "He's a boy about your age. I think you'd like him."

"Really don't want to meet anyone," he said. He pronounced it *mate*. "Unless I off to."

"Oh, no," said Millie. "You don't off to." Sometimes she slipped accidentally into his accent. She hoped it made him feel more at home.

In the morning she drove him again to the station for the ten-o-two train. "I'm getting fond of this little jaunt every day," she said. She smiled and meant it. She threw her arms around the boy, and this time he kissed her back.

At midnight that same day, Ariel phoned from Europe. She was traveling through the Continent – English universities had long spring vacations, a month, and she had headed off to France and to Italy, from where she was calling.

"Venice!" exclaimed Millie. "How wonderful!"

"That's just great, honey," said Hane on the bedroom extension. He didn't like to travel much, but he didn't mind it in other people.

"Of course," said Ariel, "there's an illusion here that you are separate from the garbage. That the water and food are different from the canal sewage. It's a crucial illusion to maintain. A psychological passport."

A psychological passport! How her daughter spoke! Children just got so far away from you. "What's the food like?" asked Millie. "Are you eating a lot of manicotti?"

"Swamp food. Watercress and dark fishes."

"Oh, I so envy you," said Millie. "Imagine, Hane, being in Venice, Italy."

"How's John Spee?" asked Ariel, changing the subject. Often when she phoned her parents, they each got on separate extensions and just talked to each other. They discussed money problems and the other's faults with a ferocity they couldn't quite manage face to face.

"All right," said Millie. "John is out taking a walk right now around the neighborhood, though it's a little late for it."

"He is? What time is it?"

"It's about midnight," said Hane on the other extension. He was in his pajamas, under the covers.

"Gee, I miscalculated the time. I hope I didn't wake you guys up."

"Of course not, honey," said Millie. "You can phone anytime."

"So it's midnight and John Spee's walking around in that depressing suburban neighborhood? How frightening."

Ariel's voice was staticky but loud. The thoughtless singsong of her words sunk its way into Millie like something both rusty and honed. "Is he alone?"

"Yes," said Millie. "He probably just wanted some fresh air. He's been spending all his days in the city. He keeps going to the top of the Empire State Building, then just walks around looking at other tall buildings. And the cars. He hasn't been to any plays or anything."

There was a silence. Hane cleared his throat and said into the phone, "I suppose I'm not the best sort of person for him. He probably needs a man who is better with kids. Somebody athletic, maybe."

"Tell us more about Italy, dear," Millie broke in. She imagined Italy would be like Florida, all colors and light, but with a glorious ruin here and there, and large stone men with no clothes but with lovely pigeons on their heads. Perhaps there were plays.

"It's great," said Ariel. "It's hard to describe."

At twelve-fifteen they hung up. Hane, because he was reading the Scripture the next morning in church, went off to sleep. But Millie was restless and roamed the house, room after room, waiting for John to return. She thought about Ariel again, how much the girl's approval had come to mean to her, and wondered how one's children got so powerful that way. The week before Ariel left for England, the two of them had gone to a movie together. It was something they had not done since Ariel had been little, and so Millie had looked forward to it, like a kind of party. But during the opening credits Millie had started talking. She started to tell Ariel about someone she knew who used to be a garbage man but who was now making short industrial films for different companies. He had taken a correspondence course.

"Mom, you're talking so loudly," Ariel hissed at her in the dark of the movie theater. Ariel had pressed her index finger to her lips and said, "Shhhh!" as if Millie were a child. The movie had started, and Millie looked away, her face crumpling, her hand to her eyes so her daughter couldn't see. She tried to concentrate on the movie, the sounds and voices of it, but it all seemed underwater and far away. When afterward, in a restaurant, Ariel wanted to discuss the film, the way she said she always did – an *intellectual* discussion like a college course – Millie had just nodded and shrugged. Occasionally she had tried to smile at her daughter, saying, "Oh, I agree with you there," but the smile flickered and trembled and Ariel had looked at her, at a loss, as if her own mother were an idiot who had followed her to the movie theater, hoping only for a kind word or a dime.

Millie looked out the guest room window – John Spee's room – into the night to see whether she might spy John, circling the house or kicking a stone along the street. The moon was full, a porthole of sun, and Millie half expected to glimpse John sitting on someone's front step, not theirs, kneecaps pressed into the soft bulges of his eyes. How disappointing America must seem. To wander the streets of a city that was not yours, a city with its back turned, to be a boy from far away and step ashore here, one's imagination suddenly so concrete and mistaken, how could that not break your heart? But perhaps, she thought, John had dreamed so long and hard of this place that he had hoped it right out of existence. Probably no place in the world could withstand such an assault of human wishing.

She turned away from the window and again opened the blue notebook on the desk.

More Crazy People I Have Seen in the States (than anywhere).

11. *Woman with white worms on her legs. Flicking off worms.*
12. *Girl on library steps, the step is her home. Comb and mirror and toothbrush with something mashed in it laid out on step like a dressertop. No teeth. Screaming.*
13. *Stumbling man. Arms folded across his chest. Bumps into me hard. Bumps with hate in his eyes. I think, 'This bloke hates me, why does he hate me?' It smells. I run a little until I am away.*

The front door creaked open, and shut with a thud. Millie

closed the notebook and went out into the living room in just her nightgown. She wanted to say good night and make certain John locked the door.

He seemed surprised to see her. "Thought I'd just hit the hay," he said. This was something he'd probably heard Ariel say once. It was something she liked to say.

"Ariel phoned while you were out," said Millie. She folded her arms across her breasts to hide them, in case they showed through her thin gown.

"That so?" John's face seemed to brighten and fall at the same time. He combed a hand through his hair, and strands dropped back across his part in a zigzag of orange. "She's coming home soon, is she?" It occurred to Millie that John didn't know Ariel well at all.

"No," she said. "She's traveling on the Continent. That's how Ariel says it: *on the Continent.* But she asked about you and says hello."

John looked away, hung up his coat in the front closet, on a hook next to his baseball cap, which he hadn't worn since his first day. "Thought she might be coming home," said John. He couldn't look directly at Millie. Something was sinking in him like a stone.

"Can I make you some warm milk?" asked Millie. She looked in the direction John seemed to be looking: at the photographs of Ariel. There she was at her high school graduation, all formal innocence, lies snapped and pretty. It seemed now to Millie that Ariel was too attractive, that she was careless and hurt people.

"I'll just go to bed, thanks," said John.

"I put your clean clothes at the foot of it, folded," said Millie.

"Thank you very much," he said, and he brushed past her, then apologized. "So sorry," he said, stepping away.

"Maybe we can all go into New York together next week," she blurted. She aimed it at his spine, hoping to fetch him back. He stopped and turned. "We can go out to eat," she continued. "And maybe take a tour of the UN." She'd seen picture postcards of the flags out front, rippling like sheets, all that international laundry, though she'd never actually been.

"OK," said John. He smiled. Then he turned back and walked down the hall, trading one room for another, moving through and past, leaving Millie standing there, the way when, having decided anything, once and for all, you leave somebody behind.

In the morning there was just a note and a gift. "Thank you for lodging me. I decided early to take the bus to California. Please do not think me rude. Yours kindly, John Spee."

Millie let out a gasp of dismay. "Hane, the boy has gone!" Hane was dressing for church and came out to see. He was in a shirt and boxer shorts, and had been tying his tie. Now he stopped, as if some ghost that had once been cast from the house had just returned. The morning's Scripture was going to be taken from the third chapter of John, and parts of it were bouncing around in his head, like nonsense or a chant. *For God so loved the world* . . . John Spee was gone. Hane placed his hands on Millie's shoulders. What could he tell her? *For God so loved the world?* He didn't really believe that God loved the world, at least not in the way most people thought. *Love,* in this case, he felt, was a way of speaking. A *metaphor.* Though for what, he didn't exactly know.

"Oh, I hope he'll be OK," Millie said, and started to cry. She pulled her robe tight around her and placed one hand over her lips to hide their quivering. It was terrible to lose a boy. Girls could make their way all right, but boys went out into the world, limping with notions, and they never came back.

It was a month later when Millie and Hane heard from Ariel that John Spee had returned to England. He had taken the bus to Los Angeles, gotten out, walked around for a few hours, then had climbed back on and ridden six straight days back to Newark Airport. He had wanted to see San Francisco, but a man on the bus had told him not to go, that everyone was dying there. So John went to Los Angeles instead. For three hours. *Can you believe it?* wrote Ariel. She was back in Warwickshire, and John sometimes dropped by to see her when she was very, very busy.

The gift, when Millie unwrapped it, had turned out to be a toaster – a large one that could toast four slices at once. She had never seen John come into the house with a package, and she had no idea when or where he had gotten it.

"Four slices," she said to Hane, who never ate much bread. "What will we do with such a thing?"

Every night through that May and June, Millie curled against Hane, one of her hands on his hip, the smells of his skin all through her head. Summer tapped at the bedroom screens, nightsounds, and Millie would lie awake, not sleeping at all. "Oh!" she sometimes said aloud, though for no reason she could explain. Hane continued to talk about the Historical Jesus. Millie rubbed his shins while he spoke, her palm against the dry, whitening hair of him. Sometimes she talked about the garbage barge, which was now docked off Coney Island, a failed ride, an unamusement.

"Maybe," she said once to Hane, then stopped, her cheek against his shoulder. How familiar skin flickered in and out of strangeness; how it was yours no matter, no mere matter. "Maybe we can go someplace someday."

Hane shifted toward her, a bit plain and a bit handsome without his glasses. Through the window the streetlights shimmered a pale green, and the moon shone woolly and bitten. Hane looked at his wife. She had the round, drying face of someone who once and briefly – a long ago fall, a weekend perhaps – had been very pretty without ever even knowing it. "You are my only friend," he said, and he kissed her, hard on the brow, like a sign for her to hold close.

1989

REAL ESTATE

And yet of course these trinkets are endearing . . .
— "Glitter and Be Gay"

IT MUST BE, Ruth thought, that she was going to die in the spring. She felt such inexplicable desolation then, such sludge in the heart, felt the season's mockery, all that chartreuse humidity in her throat like a gag. How else to explain such a feeling? She could almost burst – could one burst with joylessness? What she was feeling was too strange, too contrary, too isolated for a mere emotion. It had to be a premonition – one of being finally whisked away after much boring flailing and flapping and the pained, purposeless work that constituted life. And in spring, no less: a premonition of death. A rehearsal. A secretary's call to remind of the appointment.

Of course, it had always been in the spring that she discovered her husband's affairs. But the last one was years ago, and what did she care about all that now? There had been a parade of flings – in the end, they'd made her laugh: Ha! Ha! Ha! Ha! Ha! Ha! Ha! Ha! Ha! Ha! Ha! Ha! Ha! Ha! Ha! Ha!

Ha! Ha! Ha! Ha! Ha! Ha! Ha! Ha! Ha! Ha! Ha! Ha!

Ha! Ha!

Ha! Ha!

Ha! Ha!

Holding fast to her little patch of marital ground, she'd watched as his lovers floated through like ballerinas, or dandelion down, all of them sudden and fleeting, as if they were calendar girls ripped monthly by the same mysterious calendar-ripping wind that hurried time along in old movies. Hello! Good-bye! Ha! Ha! Ha! What did Ruth care now? Those girls were over and gone. The key to marriage, she concluded, was just not to take the thing too personally.

"You *assume* they're over and gone," said her friend Carla, who, in Ruth's living room, was working on both her inner child and her inner thighs, getting rid of the child but in touch with the thighs; Ruth couldn't keep it straight. Carla sometimes came over and did her exercises in the middle of Ruth's Afghan rug. Carla liked to blurt out things and then say, "Ooops, did I say that?" Or sometimes: "You know what? Life is short. Dumpy, too, so you've got to do your best: no Empire waists." She lay on her back and did breathing exercises and encouraged Ruth to do the same. "I can't. I'll just fall asleep," said Ruth, though she suspected she wouldn't really.

Carla shrugged. "If you fall asleep, great. It's a beauty nap. If you almost do but don't actually, it's meditation."

"*That's* meditation?"

"That's meditation."

Two years ago, when Ruth was going through chemo – the oncologist in Chicago had set Ruth's five-year survival chances at fifty-fifty; how mean not to lie and say sixty-forty! – Carla had brought over lasagnas, which lasted in their various shrinking incarnations in Ruth's refrigerator for weeks. "Try not to think of roadkill when you reheat," Carla said. She also brought over sage and rosemary soaps, which looked like slabs of butter with twigs in them. She brought Ruth a book to read, a collection of stories entitled *Trust Me*, and she had, on the jacket, crossed out the author's name and written in her own: Carla McGraw. Carla was a friend. Who had many friends these days?

"I do assume," Ruth said. "I have to." Terence's last affair, two springs ago, had ended badly. He'd told Ruth he had a meeting that would go on rather late, until ten or so, but then he arrived home, damp and disheveled, at 7:30. "The meeting's been canceled," he said, and went directly upstairs, where she could hear him sobbing in the bathroom. He cried for almost an hour, and as she listened to him, her heart filled up with pity and a deep, sisterly love. At all the funerals for love, love had its neat trick of making you mourn it so much, it reappeared. Popped right up from the casket. Or, if it didn't reappear itself, it sent a relative of startling resemblance, a thin and charming twin, which you took back home with you to fatten and cradle, nuzzle and scold.

Oh, the rich torment that was life. She just didn't investigate Terence's activities anymore. No steaming open credit-card statements, no "accidentally" picking up the phone extension. As the doctor who diagnosed her now fully remissioned cancer once said to her, "The only way to know absolutely everything in life is via an autopsy."

Nuptial forensics. Ruth would let her marriage live. No mercy killing, no autopsy. She would let it live! Ha! She would settle, as a person must, for not knowing everything: ignorance as mystery; mystery as faith; faith as food; food as sex; sex as love; love as hate; hate as transcendence. Was this a religion or some weird kind of math?

Or was this, in fact, just spring?

Certain things helped: the occasional Winston (convinced, as Ruth was, despite the one lung, the lip blisters, and the keloidal track across her ribs, that at the end she would regret the cigarettes she hadn't smoked more than the ones she had; besides, she no longer coughed much at all, let alone so hard that her retinas detached); pots of lobelia ("Excuse me, gotta go," she had said more than once to a loquacious store clerk, "I've got some new lobelia sitting in a steaming hot car"); plus a long, scenic search for a new house.

"A move . . . yes. A move will be good. We've soiled the nest, in many respects," her husband had said, in the circuitous syntax and ponderous Louisiana drawl that, like so much else about him, had once made her misty with desire and now drove her nuts with scorn. "Think about it, honey," he'd said after the reconciliation, the first remission, and the initial reconnaissance through the realtors – after her feelings had gone well beyond rage into sarcasm and carcinoma. "We should probably consider leaving this home entirely behind. Depending on what you want to do – or, of course. If you have another home in mind, I'm practically certain I'd be amenable. We would want to discuss it, however, or anything else you might be thinking of. I myself – though it may be presumptuous of me, I realize – but then, hey: it wouldn't be the first time, now would it? I myself was thinking that, if you were inclined—"

"Terence!" Ruth clapped her hands twice, sharply. "Speak more quickly! I don't have long to live!" They'd been married for twenty-three years. Marriage, she felt, was a fine arrangement generally, except that one never got it generally. One got it very, very specifically. "And, please," she added, "don't be fooled by the euphemisms of realtors. This was never a home, darling. This is a *house*."

In this way – a wedding of emotionally handicapped parking spaces, an arduously tatted lace of property and irritation – they'd managed to stay married. He was not such a bad guy! – just a handsome country boy, disbelieving of his own luck, which came to him imperfectly but continually, like crackers from a cookie jar. She had counted on him to make money – was that so wrong? – and he had made some, in used-car dealerships and computer software stock. With its sweet, urgent beginnings, and grateful, hand-holding end, marriage was always its worst in the middle: it was always a muddle, a ruin, an unnavigable field. But it was not, she felt, a total wasteland. In her own marriage there was one sweet little recurrent season, one tiny nameless room, that suited and consoled her. She would lie in Terence's arms and he would be quiet and his quietness would restore her. There was music. There was peace. That was all. There were no words in it. But that tiny spot – like any season, or moon, or theater set; like a cake in a rotary display – invariably spun out of reach and view, and the quarreling would resume and she would have to wait a long time for the cake to come round again.

Of course, their daughter, Mitzy, adored Terence – the hot, lucky fire of him. In Ruth, on the other hand, Mitzy seemed to sense only the chill spirit of a woman getting by. But what was a person in Ruth's position *supposed* to do, except rebuild herself, from the ground up, as an iceberg? Ruth wanted to know! And so, in the strange, warm dissolutions that came over her these May nights silently before sleep, a pointillist's breaking up of the body and self and of the very room, a gentle fracturing to bubbles and black dotted swiss, Ruth began, again, to foresee her own death.

At first, looking at other houses on Sunday afternoons – wandering across other people's floors and carpets, opening the closets to look at other people's shoes – gave Ruth a thrill. The tacky photos on the potter's piano. The dean with no doorknobs. The orthodontist with thirty built-in cubbyholes for his thirty tennis shoes. Wallpaper peeling like birch skin. Assorted stained, scuffed floors and misaligned moldings. The Dacron carpets. The trashy magazines on the coffee table.

And those economy snacks! People had pretzel boxes the size of bookcases. And no bookcases. What would they do with a book? Just put it in the pretzel box! Ruth took an unseemly interest in the faulty angles of a staircase landing, or the contents of a room: the ceramic pinecone lamps, the wedding photo of the dogs. Was the town that boring that this was now what amused her? What was so intriguing to her about all this home owning thrown open to the marketplace? The airing of the family vault? The peek into the grave? Ruth hired a realtor. Stepping into a house, hunting out its little spaces, surveying its ceiling stains and roof rot exhilarated her. It amazed her that there was always something wrong with a house, and after awhile, her amazement became a kind of pleasure; it was pleasing that there should always be something wrong. It made the house seem more natural that way.

But soon she backed off. "I could never buy a house that had that magazine on the coffee table," she said once. A kind of fear overtook her. "I don't like that neo-Georgian thing," she said now, before the realtor, Kit, had even turned off the car, forcing Kit to back out again from the driveway. "I'm sorry, but when I look at it," Ruth added, "my eye feels disorganized, and my heart just empties right out."

"I care about you, Ruth," said Kit, who was terrified of losing clients and so worked hard to hide the fact that she had the patience of a gnat. "Our motto is 'We Care,' and that is just so true: We really, really care, Ruth. We care about you. We care about your feelings and desires. We want you to be happy. So, here we are driving along. Driving toward a thing, then driving past. You want a house, Ruth, or shall we just go to the goddamn movies?"

"You think I'm being unrealistic."

"Aw, I get enough realism as it is. Realism's overrated. I mean it about the movies."

"You do?"

"Sure!" And so that once, Ruth went to the movies with her realtor. It was a preseason matinee of *Forrest Gump*, which made her teary with weariness, hurt, and bone-thinning boredom. "Such a career-ender for poor Tom Hanks. Mark my words," Ruth whispered to her realtor, candy wrappers floating down in the dark toward her shoes. "Thank God we bought toffees. What would we do without these toffees?"

Eventually, not even a month later, in Kit's white Cabriolet, the top down, the wind whipping everyone's hair in an unsightly way, Ruth and Terence took a final tour of the suburbanized cornfields on the periphery of town and found a house. It was the original ancient four-square farmhouse in the center of a 1979 subdivision. A man-made pond had been dug into the former field that edged the side yard. A wishing well full of wildflowers stood in the front yard.

"This is it," Terence said, gesturing toward the house.

"It is?" said Ruth. She tried to study it with an open mind – its porch and dormers angled as if by a Cubist, its chimney crumbling on one side, its cedar shingles ornately leprous with old green paint. "If one of us kisses it, will it turn into a house?" The dispiriting white ranches and split-levels lined up on either side at least possessed a geometry she understood.

"It needs a lot of work," admitted Kit.

"Yes," said Ruth. Even the FOR SALE sign had sprouted a shock of dandelions at its base. "Unlike chocolates, houses are predictable: you always know you're getting rot and decay and a long, tough mortgage. Eat them or put them back in the box – you can't do either without a lawsuit or an ordinance hearing."

"I don't know what you're talking about," said Terence. He took Ruth aside.

"This is it," he hissed. "This is our dream house."

"*Dream* house?" All the dreams she'd been having were about death – its blurry pixilation, its movement through a dark, soft sleep to a hard, bright end.

"I'm surprised you can't see it," said Terence, visibly frustrated.

She squinted again toward the soffits, the Picasso porch, the roof mottled with moss and soot. She studied the geese and the goose poop, moist, mashed cigars of which littered the stony shore of the pond. "Ah, maybe," she said. "Maybe yes. I think I'm beginning to see it. Who owns it again?"

"A Canadian. He's been renting it out. It's a nice neighborhood. Near a nature conservatory and the zoo."

"The zoo?"

Ruth thought about this. They would have to hire a lot of people, of course. It would be like running a company to get this thing back in shape, bossing everybody around, monitoring the loans and payments. She sighed. Such entrepreneurial spirit did not run in her family. It was not native to her. She came from a long line of teachers and ministers – employees. Hopeless people. People with faith but no hope. There was not one successful small business anywhere in her genes. "I'm starting to see the whole thing," she said.

On the other side of town, where other people lived, a man named Noel and a woman named Nitchka were in an apartment, in the kitchen, having a discussion about music. The woman said, "So you know nothing at all? Not a single song?"

"I don't think so," said Noel. Why was this a problem for her? It wasn't a problem for him. So he didn't know any songs. He had always been willing to let her know more than he did; it didn't bother him, until it bothered her.

"Noel, what kind of upbringing did you have, anyway?" He knew she felt he had been deprived and that he should feel angry about it. But he did! He did feel angry about it! "Didn't your parents ever sing songs to you?" she asked. "Can't you even sing one single song by heart? Sing a song. Just any song."

"Like what?"

"If there was a gun to your head, what song would you sing?"

"I don't know!" he shouted, and threw a chair across the room. They hadn't had sex in two months.

"Is it that you don't even know the *name* of a song?"

At night, every night, they just lay there with their magazines and Tylenol PM and then, often with the lights still on, were whisked quickly down into their own separate worlds of sleep – his filled with lots of whirling trees and antique flying machines and bouquets of ferns. He had no idea why.

"I know the name of a song," he said.

"What song?"

"'Open the Door, Richard.'"

"What kind of song is that?"

It was a song his friend Richard's mother would sing when he was twelve and he and Richard were locked in the bedroom, flipping madly through magazines: *Breasts and the Rest*, *Tight Tushies*, and *Lollapalooza Ladies*. But it was a real song, which still existed – though you couldn't find those magazines anymore. Noel had looked.

"See? I know a song that you don't!" he exclaimed.

"Is this a song of spiritual significance to you?"

"Yup, it really is." He picked up a rubber band from the counter, stretched it between his fingers, and released it. It hit her in the chin. "Sorry. That was an accident," he said.

"Something is deeply missing in you!" Nitchka shouted, and stormed out of the apartment for a walk.

Noel sank back against the refrigerator. He could see his own reflection in the window over the sink. It was dim and translucent, and a long twisted cobweb outside, caught on the eaves, swung back and forth across his face like a noose. He looked crazy and ill – but with just a smidgen of charisma! "If there was a gun to your head," he said to the reflection, "what song would you sing?"

Ruth wondered whether she really needed a project this badly. A diversion. A resurrection. An undertaking. Their daughter, Mitzy, grown and gone – was the whole empty nest thing such a crisis that they would devote the rest of their days to this mortician's delight? Was it that horribly, echoey quiet and nothing-nothing not to have Mitzy and her struggles furnishing their lives? Was it so bad no longer to have a daughter's frustrated artistic temperament bleeding daily on the carpet of their brains? Mitzy, dear Mitzy, was a dancer. All those ballet and tap lessons as a child – she wasn't supposed to have taken them seriously! They had been intended as middle-class irony and window dressing – you weren't actually supposed to *become* a dancer. But Mitzy had. Despite that she was the fattest in the troupe every time, never belonging, rejected from every important company, until one day a young director saw how beautifully, soulfully she danced – "How beautifully the fat girl dances!" – and ushered her past the corps, set her center stage, and made her a star. Now she traveled the world over and was the darling of the critics. "Size fourteen, yet!" crowed one reviewer. "It is a miracle to see!" She had become a triumph of feet over heft, spirit over matter, matter over doesn't-matter, a figure of immortality, a big fat angel really, and she had "many, many homosexual fans," as Terence put it. As a result, she now rarely came home. Ruth sometimes got postcards, but Ruth hated postcards – so careless and cheap, especially from this new angel of dance writing to her own sick mother. But that was the way with children.

Once, over a year and a half ago, Mitzy had come home, but it was only for two weeks – during Ruth's chemotherapy. Mitzy was, as usual, in a state of crisis. "Sure they like my work," she wailed as Ruth adjusted that first itchy acrylic wig, the one that used to scare people. "But do they like *me*?" Mitzy was an only child, so it was natural that her first bout of sibling rivalry would be with her own work. When Ruth suggested as much, Mitzy gave her a withering look accompanied by a snorting noise, and after that, with a cocked eyebrow and a wince of a gaze, Mitzy began monopolizing the telephone with moving and travel plans. "You seem to be doing *extremely well*, Mom," she said, looking over her shoulder, jotting things down. Then she'd fled.

At first Terence, even more than she, seemed enlivened by the prospect of new real estate. The simplest discussion – of doorjambs or gutters – made his blood move around his face and neck like a lava lamp. Roof-shingle samples – rough, grainy squares of sepia, rose, and gray – lit his eyes up like love. He brought home doorknob catalogs and phoned a plasterer or two. After a while, however, she could see him tire and retreat, recoil even – another fling flung. "My God, Terence. Don't quit on me now. This is just like the Rollerblades!" He had last fall gone through a Rollerblade period.

"I'm way too busy," he said.

And before Ruth knew it, the entire house project – its purchase and renovation – had been turned over to her.

First Ruth had to try to sell their current house. She decided to try something called a "fosbo." FOSBO: a "For Sale by Owner." She put ads in papers, bought a sign for the front yard, and planted violet and coral impatiens in the flower beds for the horticulturally unsuspecting, those with no knowledge of perennials. Gorgeous yard! Mature plantings! She worked up a little flyer describing the moldings and light fixtures, all "original to the house." Someone came by to look and sniff. He fingered one of the ripped window shades. *"Original to the house?"* he said.

"All right, you're out of here," she said. To subsequent prospective buyers, she abandoned any sales pitch and went for candor. "I admit, this bathroom's got mildew. And look at this *stupid* little hallway. This is why we're moving! We hate this house." She soon hired back her Forrest Gump realtor, who, at the open house, played Vivaldi on the stereo and baked banana bread, selling the place in two hours.

The night after they closed on both houses, having sat silently through the two proceedings, like deaf-mutes being had, the mysterious Canadian once more absent and represented only by a purple-suited realtor named Flo, Ruth and Terence stood in their empty new house and ate take-out Chinese straight from the cartons. Their furniture was sitting in a truck, which was parked in a supermarket parking lot on the east side of town, and it all would be delivered the next day. For now, they stood at the bare front window of their large, echoey new dining room. A small lit candle on the floor cast their shadows up on the ceiling, gloomy and fat. Wind rattled the panes and the boiler in the cellar burst on in small, frightening explosions. The radiators hissed and smelled like cats, burning off dust as they heated up, vibrating the cobwebs in the ceiling corners above them. The entire frame of the house groaned and rumbled. There was scampering in the walls. The sound of footsteps – or something like footsteps – thudded softly in the attic, two floors above them.

"We've bought a haunted house," said Ruth. Terence's mouth was full of hot cabbagey egg roll. "A ghost!" she continued. "Just a little extra protein. Just a little amino-acid bonus." It was what her own father had always said when he found a small green worm in his bowl of blueberries.

"The house is settling," said Terence.

"It's had a hundred and ten years to settle; you would think it had gotten it done with by now."

"Settling goes on and on," said Terence.

"We would know," said Ruth.

He looked at her, then dug into the container of lo mein.

A scrabbling sound came from the front porch. Terence chewed, swallowed, then walked over to turn the light on, but the light didn't come on. "Was this disclosed?" he shouted.

"It's probably just the lightbulb."

"All new lightbulbs were just put in, Flo said." He opened the front door. "The light's broken, and it should have been disclosed." He was holding a flashlight with one hand and unscrewing the front light with the other. Behind the light fixture gleamed three pairs of masked eyes. Dark raccoon feces were mounded up in the crawl space between the ceiling and the roof.

"What the *hell*?" shouted Terence, backing away.

"This house is *infested*!" said Ruth. She put down her food.

"How did those creatures get up there?"

She felt a twinge in her one lung. "How does anything get anywhere – that's what I want to know." She had only ever been the lightest of smokers, never in a high-risk category, but now every pinch, prick, tick, or tock in her ribs, every glitch in the material world anywhere made her want to light up and puff.

"Oh, God, the stench."

"Shouldn't the inspector have found this?"

"Inspectors! Obviously, they're useless. What this place needed was an MRI."

"Ah, geeze. This is the worst."

Every house is a grave, thought Ruth. All that life-stealing fuss and preparation. Which made moving from a house a resurrection – or an exodus of ghouls, depending on your point of view – and made moving *to* a house (yet another house!) the darkest of follies and desires. At best, it was a restlessness come falsely to rest. But the inevitable rot and demolition, from which the soul eventually had to flee (to live in the sky or disperse itself among the trees?), would necessarily make a person stupid with unhappiness.

Oh, well!

After their furniture arrived and was positioned almost exactly the way it had been in their old house, Ruth began to call a lot of people to come measure, inspect, capture, cart away, clean, spray, bring samples, provide estimates and bids, and sometimes they did come, though once people had gotten a deposit, they often disappeared entirely. Machines began to answer instead of humans and sometimes phone numbers announced themselves disconnected altogether. "We're sorry. The number you have reached . . ."

The windows of the new house were huge – dusty, but bright because of their size – and because the shade shop had not yet delivered the shades, the entire neighborhood of spiffy middle management could peer into Ruth and Terence's bedroom. For one long, bewildering day, Ruth took to waving, and only sometimes did people wave back. More often, they just squinted and stared. The next day, Ruth taped bedsheets up to the windows with masking tape, but invariably the sheets fell off after ten minutes. When she bathed, she had to crawl naked out of the bathroom down the hall and into the bedroom and then into the closet to put her clothes on. Or sometimes she just lay there on the bathroom floor and wriggled into things. It was all so very hard.

In their new backyard, crows the size of suitcases cawed and bounced in the branches of the pear tree. Carpenter ants – like shiny pieces of a child's game – swarmed the porch steps. Ruth made even more phone calls, and finally a man with a mottled, bulbous nose and a clean white van with a cockroach painted on it came and doused the ants with poison.

"It just looks like a fire extinguisher, what you're using," said Ruth, watching.

"Ho no, ma'am. Way stronger than that." He wheezed. His nose was knobby as a pickle. He looked underneath the porch and then back up at Ruth. "There's a whole lot of dying going on in there," he said.

"There's nothing you can do about the crows?" Ruth asked.

"Not me, but you could get a gun and shoot 'em yourself," he said. "It's not legal, but if your house were one hundred yards down that way, it would be. If it were one hundred yards down that way, you could bag twenty crows a day. Since you're where you are, within the town limits, you're going to have to do it at night, with a silencer. Catch 'em live in the morning with nets and corn, then at sunset, take 'em out behind the garage and put 'em out of your misery."

"Nets?" said Ruth.

She called many people. She collected more guesstimates and advice. A guy named Noel from a lawn company advised her to forget about the crows, worry about the squirrels. She should plant her tulips deeper, and with a lot of red pepper, so that squirrels would not dig them up. "Look at all these squirrels!" he said, pointing to the garage roof and to all the weedy flower beds. "And how about some ground cover in here, by the porch, some lilies by the well, and some sunflowers in the side yard?"

"Let me think about it," said Ruth. "I would like to keep some of these violets," she said, indicating the pleasant-looking leaves throughout the irises.

"Those aren't violets. That's a weed. That's a very common, tough little weed."

"I always thought those were violets."

"Nope."

"Things can really overtake a place, can't they? This planet's just one big divisive cutthroat competition of growing. I mean, they look like violets, don't they? The leaves, I mean."

Noel shrugged. "Not to me. Not really."

How could she keep any of it straight? There was spirea and there was false spirea – she forgot which was which. "Which is the spirea again?" she asked. Noel pointed to the bridal-wreath hedge, which was joyously blooming from left to right, from sun to shade, and in two weeks would sag and brown in the same direction. "Ah, marriage," she said aloud.

"Pardon?" said Noel.

"Are you married?" she asked.

He gave her a tired little smile and said, "No. Trying to make it happen with a girlfriend, but no, not married."

"That's probably better," said Ruth.

"How about this vegetable garden?" he asked nervously.

"It's just a lot of grass with a rhubarb in it," said Ruth. "I'd like to dig the whole thing up and plant roses – unless you think it's bad luck to replace food with flowers. Vanity before the Lord, or something."

"It's up to you," he said.

She called him back that night. He personally, no machine, answered the phone. "I've been thinking about the sunflowers," she said.

"Who is this?" he said.

"Ruth. Ruth Aikins."

"Oh, say, Ruth. Ruth! Hi!"

"Hi," she said in a worried way. He sounded as if he'd been drinking.

"Now what about those sunflowers?" he asked. "I'd like

to plant those sunflowers real soon, you know that? Here's why: my girlfriend's talking again about leaving me, and I've just been diagnosed with lymphoma. So I'd like to see some sunflowers come up end of August."

"Oh, my God. Life stinks!" cried Ruth.

"Yup. So I'd like to see some sunflowers. End of summer, I'd like something to look forward to."

"What kind of girlfriend talks about leaving her beau at a time like this?"

"I don't know."

"I mean – good riddance. On the other hand, you know what you should do? You should make yourself a good cup of tea and sit down and write her a letter. You're going to need someone to care for you through all this. Don't let her call all the shots. Let her understand the implications of her behavior and her responsibilities to you. I know whereof I speak."

Ruth was about to explain further, when Noel cleared his throat hotly. "I don't think it's such a great idea for you to go get personal and advising. I mean, look. *Ruth*, is it? You see, I don't even know your name, Ruth. I know a lot of Ruths. You could be goddamned anyone. Ruth this, Ruth that, Ruth who knows. As a matter of fact, the lymphoma thing I just made up, because I thought you were a totally different Ruth." And with that, he hung up.

She put out cages for the squirrels – the squirrels who gnawed the hyacinth bulbs, giving their smooth surfaces runs like stockings, the squirrels who utterly devoured the crocuses. From the back porch, she watched each squirrel thrash around in the cage for an hour, hurling itself against the cage bars and rubbing bald spots into its head, before she finally took pity and drove each one to a faraway quarry to set it free. The quarry was a spot that Terence had recommended as "a beautiful seclusion, a rodent Eden, a hillside of oaks above a running brook." Such poetry: probably he'd gotten laid there once. Talk about your rodent Eden! In actuality, the place was a depressing little gravel gully, with a trickle of brown water running through it, a tiny crew of scrub oaks manning the nearby incline. It was the kind of place where the squirrel mafia would have dumped their offed squirrels.

She lifted the trapdoor and watched each animal scurry off toward the hillside. Did they know what they were doing? Would they join their friends, or would every last one of them find their way back to the hollow walls of her house and set up shop again?

The bats – bats! – arrived the following week, one afternoon during a loud, dark thundershower, like a horror movie. They flew back and forth in the stairwells, then hung upside down from the picture-frame molding in the dining room, where they discreetly defecated, leaving clumps of shiny black guano pasted to the wall.

Ruth phoned her husband at his office but only got his voice mail, so she then phoned Carla, who came dashing over with a tennis racket, a butterfly net, and a push broom, all with ribbons tied around their handles. "These are my housewarming presents," she said.

"They're swooping again! Look out! They're swooping!"

"Let me at those sons of bitches," Carla said.

From her fetal position on the floor, Ruth looked up at her. "What did I ever do to get such a great friend as you?"

Carla stopped. Her face was flushed with affection, her cheeks blotched with pink. "You think so?" A bat dive-bombed her hair. The old wives' tale – that bats got caught in your hair – seemed truer to Ruth than the new wives' tale – that bats getting caught in your hair was just an old wives' tale. Bats possessed curiosity and arrogance. They were little social scientists. They got close to hair – to investigate, measure, and interview. And when something got close – a moth to a flame, a woman to a house, a woman to a grave, a sick woman to a fresh, wide-open grave like a bed – it could fall in and get caught.

"You gotta stuff your dormer eaves with steel wool," said Carla.

"Hey. Ain't it the truth," said Ruth.

They buried the whacked bats in tabbouleh containers, in the side yard: everything just tabbouleh in the end.

With the crows in mind, Ruth started to go with Carla to the shooting range. The geese, Carla said, were not that big a problem. The geese could be discouraged simply by shaking up the eggs in their nests. Carla was practical. She had a heart the shape of an ax. She brought over a canoe and paddled Ruth out into the cattails to find the goose nests, and there she took each goose egg and shook it furiously. "If you just take and toss the egg," explained Carla, "the damn goose will lay another one. This way, you kill the gosling, and the goose never knows. It sits there warming the damn eggnog until the winter comes, and the goose then just leaves, heartbroken, and never comes back. With the crows, however, you just have to blow their brains out."

At the shooting range, they paid a man with a green metal money box twenty dollars for an hour of shooting. They got several cans of diet Coke, which they bought from a vending machine outside near the rest rooms, and which they set at their feet, at their heels, just behind them. They each had pistols, Ruth's from World War I, Carla's from World War II, which they had bought in an antique-gun store. "Anyone could shoot birds with a shotgun," Carla had said. "Let's be unique."

"That's never really been a big ambition of mine," said Ruth.

They were the only ones there at the range and stood fifty yards from three brown sacks of hay with red circles painted on them. They fired at the circles – one! two! three! – then turned, squatted, set their guns back down, and sipped their Cokes. The noise was astonishing, bursting through the fields around them, echoing off the small hills and back out of the sky, mocking and retaliatory. "My Lord!" Ruth exclaimed. Her gun felt hard and unaimable. "I don't think I'm doing this right," she said. She had expected a pistol to seem light and natural – a seamless extension of her angry feral self. But instead, it felt heavy and huge and so unnaturally loud, she never wanted to fire such a thing again.

But she did. Only twice did she see her hay sack buckle. Mostly, she seemed to be firing too high, into the trees behind the targets, perhaps hitting squirrels – perhaps the very squirrels she had caught in her have-a-heart cage, now set free and shot dead with her have-a-house gun. "It's all too much," said Ruth. "I can't possibly be doing this right. It's way too complicated and mean."

"You've forgotten about the damn crows," said Carla. "Don't forget them."

"That's right," said Ruth, and she picked up the gun again. "Crows." Then she lowered her gun. "But won't I just be shooting them at close range, after I catch them in nets?"

"Maybe," said Carla. "But maybe not."

When Nitchka finally left him, she first watched her favorite TV show, then turned off the television, lifted up her CD player and her now-unhooked VCR, and stopped to poise herself dramatically in the front hall. "You know, you haven't a clue what the human experience is even about," she said.

"This song and dance again," he said. "Are you taking it on the road?" She set her things down outside in the hall so she could slam the door loudly and leave him – leave him, he imagined, for some new, handsome man she had met at work. Dumped for Hunks. That was the title of his life. In heaven, just to spite her, that would be the name of his goddamn band.

He drank a lot that week, and on Friday, his boss, McCarthy, called to say Noel was fired. "You think we can run a lawn store this way?" he said.

"If there was a gun to your head," said Noel, "what song would you sing?"

"Get help," said McCarthy. "That's all I have to say." Then there was a dial tone.

Noel began to collect unemployment, getting to the office just before it closed. He began to sleep in the days and stay up late at night. He got turned around. He went out at midnight for walks, feeling insomniac and mocked by the dark snore of the neighborhood. Rage circled and built in him, like a saxophone solo. He began to venture into other parts of town. Sidewalks appeared, then disappeared again. The moon shone on one side and then on the other. Once, he brought duct tape with him and a ski mask. Another time, he brought duct tape, a ski mask, and a gun one of his stepfathers had given him when he was twenty. If you carefully taped a window from the outside, it could be broken quietly: the glass would stick to the tape and cave gently outward.

"I'm not going to hurt you," he said. He turned on the light in the bedroom. He taped the woman's mouth first, then the man's. He made them get out of bed and stand over by the dresser. "I'm going to take your TV set," said Noel. "And I'm going to take your VCR. But before I do, I want you to sing me a song. I'm a music lover, and I want you to sing me one song, any song. By heart. You first," he said to the man. He pressed the gun to his head. "One song." He pulled the duct tape gently off the man's mouth.

"Any song?" repeated the man. He tried to look into the eyeholes of Noel's ski mask, but Noel turned abruptly and stared at the olive gray glass of the TV.

"Yeah," said Noel. "Any song."

"Okay." The man began. " 'O beautiful for spacious skies, for amber waves of grain . . .' " His voice was deep and sure. " '. . . for purple mountain majesties . . .' " Noel turned back and studied the man carefully. He seemed to know it all by heart. How had he learned it all by heart? "You want *all* the verses?" the man stopped and asked, a bit too proudly, Noel thought, for someone who had a gun aimed his way.

"Nah, that's enough," Noel said irritably. "Now you," he said to the woman. He pulled the duct tape off her mouth. Her upper lip was moistly pink, raw from the adhesive. He glanced down at the tape and saw the spiky glisten of little mustache hairs. She began immediately, anxiously, to sing. " 'You are my lucky star. I'm lucky where you are /Two lovely eyes at me that were—' "

"What kind of song is this?"

She nervously ignored him, kept on: "'. . . beaming, gleaming, I was starstruck.'" She began to sway a little, move her hands up and down. She cleared her throat and modulated upward, a light, chirpy warble, though her face was stretched wide with fright, like heated wax. "'You're all my lucky charms. I'm lucky in your arms. . . .'" Here her hands fluttered up to her heart.

"All right, that's enough. I'm taking the VCR now."

"That's practically the end anyway," said the woman.

At the next house he did, he got a Christmas carol, plus "La Vie en Rose." At the third house, the week following, he got one nursery rhyme, half a school song, and "Memory" from *Cats*. He began to write down the titles and words. At home, looking over his notepad, he realized he was creating a whole new kind of songbook. Still the heart of these songs eluded him. Looking at the words the next day, a good, almost-new VCR at his feet, he could never conjure the tune. And without the tune, the words seemed stupid and half-mad.

To avoid the chaos of the house entirely, Ruth took to going to matinees. First-run movies, second-run – she didn't care. Movies were the ultimate real estate: you stepped in and looked around and almost always bought. She was especially stirred by a movie she saw about a beautiful widow who fell in love with a space alien who had assumed human form – the form of the woman's long lost husband! Eventually, however, the man had to go back to his real home, and an immense and amazing spaceship came to get him, landing in a nearby field. To Ruth, it seemed so sad and true, just like life: someone assumed the form of the great love of your life, only to reveal himself later as an alien who had to get on a spaceship and go back to his planet. Certainly it had been true for Terence. Terence had gotten on a spaceship and gone back long ago. Although, of course, in real life you seldom saw the actual spaceship. Usually, there was just a lot of drinking, mumbling, and some passing out in the family room.

* * *

Sometimes on the way back from the movies, she would drive by their old house. They had sold it to an unmemorable young couple, and now, driving past it slowly, eyeing it like a pervert, she began to want it back. It was a good house. They didn't deserve it, that couple: look how ignorant they were – pulling out all those forsythia bushes as if they were weeds.

Or maybe they *were* weeds. She never knew anymore what was good life and what was bad, what was desirable matter and what was antimatter, what was the thing itself and what was the death of the thing: one mimicked the other, and she resented the work of having to distinguish.

Which, again, was the false spirea and which was the true?

The house was hers. If it hadn't been for that damn banana bread, it still would be hers.

Perhaps she could get arrested creeping slowly past in her car like this. She didn't know. But every time she drove by, the house seemed to see her and cry out, It's you! Hello, hello! You're back! So she tried not to do it too often. She would speed up a little, give a fluttery wave, and drive off.

At home, she could not actually net the crows, though their old habitat, the former cornfield that constituted the neighborhood, continued to attract them like an ancestral land or a good life recalled over gin. They hovered in the yards, tormented the cats, and ate the still-wet day-old songbirds right out of their nests. How was she supposed to catch such fiends? She could not. She draped nets in the branches of trees, to snag them, but always a wind caused the nets to twist or drop, or pages of old newspaper blew by and got stuck inside, plastering the nets with op-ed pages and ads. From the vegetable garden now turning flower bed came the persistent oniony smell of those chives not yet smothered by the weed barrier. And the rhubarb, too, kept exploding stubbornly through, no matter how she plucked at it, though each clutch of stalks was paler and more spindly than the last.

She began generally not to feel well. Never a temple, her

body had gone from being a home, to being a house, to being a phone booth, to being a kite. Nothing about it gave her proper shelter. She no longer felt housed within it at all. When she went for a stroll or was out in the yard throwing the nets up into the oaks, other people in the neighborhood walked briskly past her. The healthy, the feeling well, when they felt that way, couldn't remember feeling any other, couldn't imagine it. They were niftily in their bodies. They were not only out of the range of sympathy; they were out of the range of mere imagining. Whereas the sick could only think of being otherwise. Their hearts, their every other thought, went out to that well person they hated a little but wanted to be. But the sick were sick. They were not in charge. They had lost their place at the top of the food chain. The feeling well were running the show; which was why the world was such a savage place. From her own porch, she could hear the PA announcements from the zoo. They were opening; they were closing; would someone move their car. She could also hear the elephant, his sad bluesy trumpet, and the Bengal tiger roaring his heartbreak: all that animal unhappiness. The zoo was a terrible place and a terrible place to live near: the pacing ocelot, the polar bear green with fungus, the zebra demented and hungry and eating the fence, the children brought there to taunt the animals with paper cups and their own clean place in the world, the vulture sobbing behind his scowl.

Ruth began staying inside, drinking tea. She felt tightenings, pain and vertigo, but then, was that so new? It seemed her body, so mysterious and apart from her, could only produce illness. Though once, of course, it had produced Mitzy. How had it done that? Mitzy was the only good thing her body had ever been able to grow. She was a real chunk of change that one, a gorgeous george. How had her body done it? How does a body ever do it? Life inhabits life. Birds inhabit trees. Bones sprout bones. Blood gathers and makes new blood.

A miracle of manufacturing.

On one particular afternoon that was too cool for spring,

when Ruth was sitting inside drinking tea so hot it skinned her tongue, she heard something. Upstairs, there was the old pacing in the attic that she had come to ignore. But now there was a knock on the door – loud, rhythmic, urgent. There were voices outside.

"Yes?" Ruth called, approaching the entryway, then opening the door.

Before her stood a girl, maybe fourteen or fifteen years old. "We heard there was a party here," said the girl. She had tar black hair and a silver ring through her upper lip. Her eyes looked meek and lost. "Me and Arianna heard down on State Street that there was a party right here at this house."

"There's not," said Ruth. "There's just not." And then she closed the door, firmly.

But looking out the window, Ruth could see more teenagers gathering in front of the house. They collected on the lawn like fruit flies on fruit. Some sat on the front steps. Some roared up on mopeds. Some hopped out of station wagons crowded with more kids just like themselves. One carload of kids poured out of the car, marched right up the front steps, and, without ringing the bell, opened the unlocked door and walked in.

Ruth put her tea down on the bookcase and walked toward the front entryway. "*Excuse* me!" she said, facing the kids in the front hall.

The kids stopped and stared at her. "May I help you?" asked Ruth.

"We're visiting someone who lives here."

"*I* live here."

"We were invited to a party by a *kid* who lives here."

"There is no kid who lives here. And there is no party."

"There's no kid who lives here?"

"No, there isn't."

A voice suddenly came from behind Ruth. A voice more proprietary, a voice from deeper within the house than even she was. "Yes, there is," it said.

Ruth turned and saw standing in the middle of her living room a fifteen-year-old boy dressed entirely in black, his head shaved spottily, his ears, nose, lips, and eyebrows pierced with multiple gold and copper rings. The rim of his left ear held three bronze clips.

"Who are you?" Ruth asked. Her heart flapped and fluttered, like something hit sloppily by a car.

"I'm Tod."

"Tod?"

"People call me Ed."

"Ed?"

"I live here."

"No, you don't. You don't! What do you mean, you live here?"

"I've been living in your attic."

"You have?" Ruth felt sweat burst forth from behind the wings of her nose. "You're our ghost? You've been pacing around upstairs?"

"Yeah, he has," said one of the kids at the door.

"But I don't understand." Ruth reached over and plucked a Kleenex from the box on the mail table, and wiped her face with it.

"I ran away from my own home months ago. I have a key to this house from the prior owner, who was a friend. So from time to time, I've been sleeping upstairs in your attic. It's not so bad up there."

"You've been what? You've been living here, going in and out? Don't your parents know where you are?" Ruth asked.

"Look, I'm sorry about this party," said Tod. "I didn't mean for it to get this out of hand. I only invited a few people. I thought you were going away. It was supposed to be a small party. I didn't mean for it to be a big party."

"No," said Ruth. "You don't seem to understand. Big party, little party: you weren't supposed to have a party here at all. You were not even supposed to be *in* this house, let alone invite others to join you."

"But I had the key. I thought, I don't know. I thought it would be all right."

"Give me the key. Right now. Give me the key."

He handed her the key, with a smirk. "I don't know if it'll

do you any good. Look." Ruth turned and all the kids at the door held up their own shiny brass keys. "I made copies," said Tod.

Ruth began to shriek. "Get out of here! Get out of here right now! All of you! Not only will I have these locks changed but if you ever set foot in this neighborhood again, I'll have the police on you so fast, you won't know what hit you."

"But we need *some*place to drink, man," said one of the departing boys.

"Go to the damn park!"

"The cops are all over the park," one girl whined.

"Then go to the railroad tracks, like we used to do, for God's sake," she yelled. "Just get the hell out of here." She was shocked by the bourgeois venom and indignation in her own voice. She had, after all, once been a hippie. She had taken a lot of windowpane and preached about the evils of private ownership from a red Orlon blanket on a street corner in Chicago.

Life: what an absurd little story it always made.

"Sorry," said Tod. He touched her arm, and, swinging a cloth satchel over his shoulder, walked toward the front door with the rest of them.

"Get the hell out of here," she said. "Ed."

The geese, the crows, the squirrels, the raccoons, the bats, the ants, the kids: Ruth now went to the firing range with Carla as often as she could. She would stand with her feet apart, both hands grasping the gun, then fire. She concentrated, tried to gather bits of strength in her, crumbs to make a loaf. She had been given way too much to cope with in life. Did God have her mixed up with someone else? Get a Job, she shouted silently to God. Get a real Job. I have never been your true and faithful servant. Then she would pull the trigger. When you told a stupid joke to God and got no response, was it that the joke was too stupid, or not quite stupid enough? She narrowed her eyes. Mostly, she just tried to squint, but then dread closed her eyes entirely. She fired again. Why did she not feel more spirited about this, the way Carla did? Ruth breathed deeply before firing, noting the Amazonian asymmetry of her breath, but in her heart she knew she was a mouse. A mouse bearing firearms, but a mouse nonetheless.

"Maybe I should have an affair," said Carla, who then fired her pistol into the gunnysacked hay. "I've been thinking: maybe you should, too."

Now Ruth fired her own gun, its great storm of sound filling her ears. An affair? The idea of taking her clothes off and being with someone who wasn't a medical specialist just seemed ridiculous. Pointless and terrifying. Why would people do it? "Having an affair is for the young," said Ruth. "It's like taking drugs or jumping off cliffs. Why would you want to jump off a cliff?"

"Oh," said Carla. "You obviously haven't seen some of the cliffs *I've* seen."

Ruth sighed. Perhaps, if she knew a man in town who was friendly and attractive, she might – what? What might she do? She felt the opposite of sexy. She felt busy, managerial, thirsty, crazy; everything, when you got right down to it, was the opposite of sexy. If she knew a man in town, she would – would go on a diet for him! But not Jenny Craig. She'd heard of someone who had died on Jenny Craig. If she had to go on a diet with a fake woman's name on it, she would go on the Betty Crocker diet, her own face ladled right in there with Betty's, in that fat red spoon. Yes, if she knew a man in town, perhaps she would let the excitement of knowing him seize the stem of her brain and energize her days. As long as it was only the stem; as long as the petals were left alone. She needed all her petals.

But she didn't know any men in town. Why didn't she know one?

In mid-June, the house he chose was an old former farmhouse in the middle of a subdivision. It was clearly being renovated – there were ladders and tarps in the yard – and in this careless presentation, it seemed an easy target. Music lovers! he thought. They go for renovation! Besides, in an old house there was always one back window that, having warped into a trapezoid, had then been sanded and resanded and could be lifted off the frame like a lid. When he worked for the lawn company, he'd worked on many houses like these. Perhaps he'd even been here before, a month ago or so – he wasn't sure. Things looked different at night, and tonight the moon was not as bright as last time, less than full, like the face beneath a low slant hat, like a head scalped at the brow.

Noel looked at the couple. They had started singing "Chattanooga Choo-Choo." Lately, to save time, inspire the singers, and amuse himself, Noel had been requesting duets. "Wait a minute," he interrupted. "I wanna write this one down. I've just started to write these things down." And, like a fool, he left them to go into the next room to get a pen and a piece of paper.

"You have a sweet voice," the woman said when he returned. She was standing in front of the nightstand. He was smoothing a creased piece of paper against his chest. "A sweet speaking voice. You must sing well, too."

"Nah, I have a terrible voice," he said. He felt his shirt pocket for a pen. "I was always asked to be quiet when the other children sang. The music teacher in grade school always asked me just to move my lips. 'Glory in eggshell seas,' she would say. 'Just mouth that.' "

"No, no. Your voice is sweet. The timbre is sweet. I can hear it." She took a small step sideways. The man, the husband, stayed where he was. He was wearing a big red sweatshirt and no underwear. His penis hung beneath the shirt hem like a long jewel yam. *Ah, marriage.* The woman, thrusting her hands into the pockets of her nightgown, took another small step. "It's sweet, but with weight."

Noel thought he could hear some people outside calling a dog by clapping their hands. "Bravo," said the owner of the dog, or so it sounded. "Bravo."

"Well, thank you," said Noel, his eyes cast downward.

"Surely your mother must have told you that," she said, but he decided not to answer that one. He turned to write down the words to "Chattanooga Choo-Choo," and with the beginning of the tune edging into his head – *pardon me, boys* – something exploded in the room. Suddenly, he thought he felt the yearning heart of civilization in him, felt at last, oh, Nitchka, what human experience on this planet was all about: its hard fiery center, a quick rudeness in its force; he could feel it catching him, a surprise, like a nail to the brain. A dark violet then light washed over him. Everything went quiet. Music, he saw now, led you steadily into silence. You followed the thread of a song into a sudden sort of sleep. The white paper leapt up in a blinding flash, hot and sharp. The dresser edge caught his cheekbone in a gash, and he seemed no longer to be standing. His shoes slid along the rug. His hands reached up, then down again, then up along the dresser knobs, then flung themselves through the air and back against the floor. His brow, enclosing, then devouring his sight, finally settled dankly against his own sleeve.

Heat drained from his head, like a stone.

A police car pulled up quietly outside, with its lights turned off. There was some distant noise from geese on the pond.

There was no echo after the explosion. It was not like at the range. There had been just a click and a vibrating snap that had flown out before her toward the mask, and then the room roared and went silent, giving back nothing at all.

Terence gasped. "Good God," he said. "I suppose this is just what you've always wanted: a dead man on your bedroom floor."

"What do you mean by that? How can you say such a heartless thing?" Shouldn't her voice have had a quaver in it? Instead, it sounded flat and dry. "Forget being a decent man, Terence. Go for castability. Could you even play a decent man in a movie?"

"Did you have to be such a good shot?" Terence asked. He began to pace.

"I've been practicing," she said. Something immunological surged in her briefly like wine. For a minute, she felt restored and safe – safer than she had in years. How dare anyone come into her bedroom! How much was she expected to take? But then it all left her, wickedly, and she could again feel only her own abandonment and disease. She turned away from Terence and started to cry. "Oh, God, let me die," she finally said. "I am just so tired." Though she could hardly see, she knelt down next to the masked man and pressed his long, strange hands to her own small ones. They were not yet cold – no colder than her own. She thought she could feel herself begin to depart with him, the two of them rising together, translucent as jellyfish, leaving through the air, floating out into a night sky of singing and release, flying until they reached a bright, bright spaceship – a set of teeth on fire in the dark – and, absorbed into the larger light, were taken aboard for home. "And what on earth was all that?" she could hear them both say merrily of their lives, as if their lives were now just odd, noisy, and distant, as in fact they were.

"What have we here?" she heard someone say.

"Look for yourself, I guess," said someone else.

She touched the man's black knit mask. It was pilled with gray, like the dotted swiss of her premonitions, but it was askew, misaligned at the eyes – the soft turkey white of a cheekbone where the eye should be – and it was drenched with water and maroon. She could peel it off to see his face, see who he was, but she didn't dare. She tried to straighten the fabric, tried to find the eyes, then pulled it tightly down and turned away, wiping her hands on her nightgown. Without looking, she patted the dead man's arm. Then she turned and started out of the room. She went down the stairs and ran from the house.

Her crying now came in a stifled and parched way, and her hair fell into her mouth. Her chest ached and all her bones filled with a sharp pulsing. She was ill. She knew. Running barefoot across the lawn, she could feel some chaos in her gut – her intestines no longer curled neat and orderly as a French horn, but heaped carelessly upon one another like a box of vacuum-cleaner parts. The cancer, dismantling as it came, had begun its way back. She felt its poison, its tentacular reach and clutch, as a puppet feels a hand.

"Mitzy, my baby," she said in the dark. "Baby, come home."

Though she would have preferred long ago to have died, fled, gotten it all over with, the body – Jesus, how the body! – took its time. It possessed its own wishes and nostalgias. You could not just turn neatly into light and slip out the window. You couldn't go like that. Within one's own departing but stubborn flesh, there was only the long, sentimental, piecemeal farewell. *Sir? A towel. Is there a towel?* The body, hauling sadnesses, pursued the soul, hobbled after. The body was like a sweet, dim dog trotting lamely toward the gate as you tried slowly to drive off, out the long driveway. *Take me, take me, too,* barked the dog. *Don't go, don't go,* it said, running along the fence, almost keeping pace but not quite, its reflection a shrinking charm in the car mirrors as you trundled past the viburnum, past the pine grove, past the property line, past every last patch of land, straight down the swallowing road, disappearing and disappearing. Until at last it was true: you had disappeared.

1997

REFERENTIAL

MANIA. FOR THE THIRD time in three years they talked in a frantic way about what would be a suitable birthday present for her deranged son. There was so little they were actually allowed to bring: almost everything could be transformed into a weapon and so most items had to be left at the front desk, and then, if requested, brought in later by a big blond aide, who would look the objects over beforehand for their wounding possibilities. Pete had bought a basket of jams, but they were in glass jars, and so not allowed. "I forgot about that," he said. They were arranged in color from brightest marmalade to cloudberry to fig, as if they contained the urine tests of an increasingly ill person, and so she thought, *Just as well they will be confiscated.* They would find something else to bring.

By the time her son was twelve, and had begun his dazed and spellbound muttering, no longer brushing his teeth, Pete had been in their lives for four years, and now it was four years after that. The love they had for Pete was long and winding, not without hidden turns, but without any real halts. They thought of him as a kind of stepfather. Perhaps all three of them had gotten old together, although it showed mostly on her, the mother, with her black shirtdresses worn for slimming and her now graying hair undyed and often pinned up with strands hanging down like Spanish moss. Once her son had been stripped and gowned and placed in the facility, she, too, removed her necklaces, earrings, scarves – all her prosthetic devices, she said to Pete, trying to amuse – and put them in a latched accordion file under her bed. She was not allowed to wear them when visiting so she would no longer wear them at all, a kind of solidarity with her child, a kind of new widowhood on top of the widowhood she already possessed. Unlike other women her age (who tried too hard with lurid lingerie and flashing jewelry), she now felt that sort of effort was ludicrous, and she went out into the world like an Amish woman, or perhaps, even worse, as when the unforgiving light of spring hit her face, an Amish man. If she were going to be old, let her be a full-fledged citizen of the old country! "To me you always look so beautiful," Pete no longer said.

Pete had lost his job in the new economic downturn. At one point he had been poised to live with her, but her child's deepening troubles had caused him to pull back – he believed he loved her but could not find the large space he needed for himself in her life or in her house (and did not blame her son, or did he?). He eyed with somewhat visible covetousness and sour remarks the front room that her son, when home, lived in with large blankets and empty ice-cream pints, an Xbox, and DVDs.

She no longer knew where Pete went, sometimes for weeks at a time. She thought it an act of vigilance and attachment that she would not ask, would try not to care. She once grew so hungry for touch she went to the Stressed Tress salon around the corner just to have her hair washed. The few times she had flown to Buffalo to see her brother and his family, at airport security she had chosen the pat-downs and the wandings rather than the scanning machine.

"Where is Pete?" her son cried out at visits she made alone, his face scarlet with acne, swollen and wide with the effects of medications that had been changed then changed again, and she said Pete was busy today, but soon, soon, maybe next week. A maternal vertigo beset her, the room circled, and the cutting scars on her son's arms sometimes seemed to spell out Pete's name in the thin lines there, the loss of fathers etched primitively in an algebra of skin. In the carousel spin of the room, the white webbed lines resembled coarse campfire writing, as when young people used to stiffly carve the words PEACE and FUCK in park picnic tables and trees, the *C* three-quarters of a square. Mutilation was a language. And vice versa. The cutting endeared her boy to the girls, who were all cutters themselves and seldom saw a boy who was one as well, and so in the group sessions he became popular, which he seemed neither to mind nor perhaps really to notice. When no one was looking he cut the bottoms of his feet with crisp paper from crafts hour. He also pretended to read the girls' soles like palms, announcing the arrival of strangers and the progress toward romance – "toemances!" he called them – and detours, sometimes glimpsing his own fate in the words they had cut there.

Now she and Pete went to see her son without the jams but with a soft deckle-edged book about Daniel Boone, which was allowed, even if her son would believe it contained messages for him, believe that although it was a story about a long-ago person it was also the story of his own sorrow and heroism in the face of every manner of wilderness and defeat and abduction and that his own life could be draped over the book, which was noble armature for the revelation of tales of *him*. There would be clues in the words on pages with numbers that added up to his age: 97, 88, 466. There were other veiled references to his existence. There always were.

They sat at the visitors' table together and her son set the book aside and did try to smile at both of them. There was still sweetness in his eyes, the sweetness he was born with, even if fury could dart in a scattershot fashion across them. Someone had cut his tawny hair – or at least had tried. Perhaps the staff person did not want the scissors near him for a prolonged period and had snipped quickly, then leaped away, then approached again, grabbed and snipped, then jumped back. At least that's what it looked like. It was wavy hair and had to be cut carefully. Now it no longer cascaded down but was close to his head, springing out at angles that seemed to matter to no one but a mother.

"So where have you been?" her son asked Pete, giving him a hard stare.

"Good question," said Pete, as if praising the thing would make it go away. How could people be mentally well in such a world?

"Do you miss us?" the boy asked.

Pete did not answer.

"Do you think of me when you look at the black capillaries of the trees at night?"

"I suppose I do." Pete stared back at him, so as not to shift in his seat. "I am always hoping you are OK and that they treat you well here."

"Do you think of my mom when staring up at the clouds and all they hold?"

Pete fell quiet again.

Her son continued, studying Pete. "Have you ever watched how sparrows can kill the offspring of others? Baby wrens, for instance? I've been watching out the windows. Did you know that sparrows can swoop into the wrens' house and pluck out the fledglings from their nests and hurl them to the ground with a force you would not think possible for a sparrow? Even a homicidal sparrow?"

"Nature can be cruel," said Pete.

"Nature can be one big horror movie! But murder is not something one would expect – from a sparrow. All things can be found in the world – but usually you have to look for them. You have to look! For instance, you have to look for us! We are sort of hidden but sort of not. We can be found. If you look in the obvious places, we can be found. We haven't disappeared, even if you want us to, we are there to—"

"That's enough," she said to her son, who turned to her with a change of expression.

"There's supposed to be cake this afternoon for someone's birthday," he said.

"That will be nice!" she said, smiling back.

"No candles, of course. Or forks. We will just have to grab the frosting and mash it into our eyes for blinding. Do you ever think about how at that moment of the candles time stands still, even as the moments carry away the smoke? It's like the fire of burning love. Do you ever wonder why so many people have things they don't deserve but how absurd all those things are to begin with? Do you really think a wish can come true if you never ever ever ever ever ever tell it to anyone?"

On the ride home she and Pete did not exchange a word, and

every time she looked at his aging hands, clasped arthritically around the steering wheel, the familiar thumbs slung low in their slightly simian way, she would understand anew the desperate place they both were in, though the desperations were separate, not joined, and her eyes would then feel the stabbing pressure of tears. The last time her son had tried to do it, his method had been, in the doctor's words, morbidly ingenious. He might have succeeded but a fellow patient, a girl from group, had stopped him at the last minute. There had been blood to be mopped. Once her son had only wanted a distracting pain, but then soon he had wanted to tear a hole in himself and flee through it. Life was full of spies and preoccupying espionage. Yet the spies sometimes would flee as well and someone might have to go after them in order, paradoxically, to escape them altogether, over the rolling fields of living dream, into the early morning mountains of dawning signification.

There was a storm in front and lightning did its quick, purposeful zigzag between and in the clouds. She did not need such stark illustration that horizons could be shattered, filled with messages, broken codes, yet there it was. A spring snow began to fall with the lightning still cracking, and Pete put the windshield wipers on so that they both could peer through the cleared semicircles at the darkening road before them. She knew that the world was not created to speak just to her, and yet, as with her son, sometimes things did. The fruit trees had bloomed early, for instance, and the orchards they passed were pink, but the early warmth precluded bees, and so there would be little fruit. Most of the dangling blossoms would fall in this very storm.

When they arrived at her house and went in, Pete glanced at himself in the hallway mirror. Perhaps he needed assurance that he was alive and not the ghost he seemed.

"Would you like a drink?" she asked, hoping he would stay. "I have some good vodka. I could make you a nice White Russian!"

"Just vodka," he said reluctantly. "Straight."

She opened the freezer to find the vodka, and when she

closed it again, she stood waiting there for a moment, looking at the photos she'd attached with magnets to the refrigerator. As a baby her son had looked happier than most babies. As a six-year-old he was still smiling and hamming it up, his arms and legs shooting out like starbursts, his perfectly gapped teeth flashing, his hair curling in honeyed coils. At ten his expression was already vaguely brooding and fearful, though there was light in his eyes, his lovely cousins beside him. There he was a plumpish teenager, his arm around Pete. And there in the corner he was an infant again, held by his dignified, handsome father, whom her son did not recall because he had died so long ago. All this had to be accepted. Living did not mean one joy piled upon another. It was merely the hope for less pain, hope played like a playing card upon another hope, a wish for kindnesses and mercies to emerge like kings and queens in an unexpected change of the game. One could hold the cards oneself or not: they would land the same regardless. Tenderness did not enter except in a damaged way and by luck.

"You don't want ice?"

"No," said Pete. "No thank you."

She placed two glasses of vodka on the kitchen table and there they sat.

"Perhaps this will help you sleep," she said.

"Don't know if anything can do that," he said, with a swig. Insomnia plagued him.

"I am going to bring him home tomorrow," she said. "He needs his home back, his house, his room. He is no danger to anyone."

Pete drank some more, sipping noisily. She could see he wanted no part of this, but she felt she had no choice but to proceed. "Perhaps you could help. He looks up to you."

"Help how?" asked Pete with a flash of anger. There was the clink of his glass on the table.

"We could each spend part of the night near him," she said.

The telephone rang. The Radio Shack wall phone brought almost nothing but bad news, and so its ringing sound, especially in the evening, always startled her. She repressed a shudder but still her shoulders hunched and curved. She stood.

"Hello?" she said, answering it on the third ring, her heart pounding. But the person on the other end hung up. She sat back down. "I guess it was a wrong number," she said, adding, "Perhaps you would like more vodka."

"Only a little. Then I should go."

She poured him more. She had said what she'd wanted to say and did not want to have to persuade him. She would wait for him to step forward with the right words. Unlike some of her meaner friends, who kept warning her, she believed there was a deep good side of him and she was always patient for it. What else could she be?

The phone rang again.

"Probably telemarketers," he said.

"I hate them," she said. "Hello?" she said more loudly into the receiver.

This time when the caller hung up she glanced at the number on the phone, in the lit panel where the caller ID was supposed to reveal it.

She sat back down and poured herself more vodka. "Someone is calling here from your apartment," she said.

He threw back the rest of his vodka. "I should go," he said and got up and headed for the door. She followed him. At the door she watched him grasp the front knob and twist it firmly. He opened the door wide, blocking the mirror.

"Good night," he said. His expression had already forwarded itself to someplace far away.

She threw her arms around him to kiss him, but he turned his head abruptly so her mouth landed on his ear. She remembered he had done this evasive move eight years ago, at the beginning, when they had first met, and he was in a condition of romantic overlap.

"Thank you for coming with me," she said.

"You're welcome," he replied, then hurried down the steps to his car, which was parked at the curb out front. She did not attempt to walk him to it. She closed the door and locked it, as the telephone began to ring again. She turned off all the lights, including the porches'.

She went into the kitchen. She had not really been able to read the caller ID without reading glasses, and had invented the part about its being Pete's number, though he had made it the truth anyway, which was the black magic of lies, good guesses, and nimble bluffs. Now she braced herself. She planted her feet. "Hello?" she said, answering on the fifth ring. The plastic panel where the number should show was clouded as if by a scrim, a page of onionskin over the onion – or rather, over a picture of an onion. One depiction on top of another.

"Good evening," she said again loudly. What would burst forth? A monkey's paw. A lady. A tiger.

But there was nothing at all.

after VN

2013

STARVING AGAIN

DENNIS'S EX-WIFE had fallen in love with a man she said was like out of a book. Dennis forgot to ask what book. He was depressed and barely dating. "I should have said to her, 'Yeah, and what book?'" Dennis was always kicking himself on the phone, not an easy thing, the tricky ouch of it. His friend Mave tended to doodle a lot when talking to him, slinky items with features, or a solitary game of tick-tack-toe. Sometimes she even interrupted him to ask what time it was. Her clock was in the other room.

"But you know," Dennis was saying, "I've got my own means of revenge: If she wants to go out with other men, I'm going to sit here and just let her."

"That's an incredibly powerful form of revenge," said Mave. She was not good on the phone. She needed the face, the pattern of eyes, nose, trembling mouth. When she was on the phone she often had to improvise Dennis's face from a window: the pug nose of the lock, the paned eyes, the lip jut of the sill. Or else she drew another slinky item with features. People talking were meant to look at a face, the disastrous cupcake of it, the hide-and-seek of the heart dashing across. With a phone, you said words, but you never watched them go in. You saw them off at the airport but never knew whether there was anyone there to greet them when they got off the plane.

They met for dinner at some sort of macrobiotic place, because Dennis had recently become obsessed. Before his wife left him, his idea of eating healthy had been to go to McDonald's and order the Filet-o-Fish, but now he had whole books about miso. And about tempeh. Mostly, however, he had books about love. He believed in studying his own heart this way. Men were like that, Mave had noticed. They liked to look in the mirror. For women, mirrors were a chore: Women looked, frowned, got out equipment, and went to work. But for men mirrors were sex: Men locked gazes with their own reflections, undressed themselves with their eyes, and stared for a shockingly long time. Mave believed that not being able to see your life clearly, to scrutinize it intelligently, meant that probably you were at the dead center of it, and that couldn't possibly be a bad thing.

This month Dennis was reading books written supposedly for women, titles like *Get Real*, *Smarting Cookie*, *Get Real* and *Why I Hate Myself*. "Those books are trouble," said Mave. "Too many well-adjusted people will endanger the arts in this country. To say nothing of the professions." She studied Dennis's flipped-over tie, the soft, torn eye of its clipped label. "You choose to be healthy, and you leave too many good people behind."

But Dennis said he identified, that the books were amazing, and he reached into the book bag he now carried with him everywhere and read passages aloud. "Here," he said to Mave, who had brought her own whiskey to the place and was pouring it into a water glass from which she had drunk all the water and left only the ice. She had had to argue with the waitress to get ice. "Oh, no – here," Dennis said. He had found another passage from *Why I Hate Myself* and started to read it, loud and with expression, when suddenly he broke into a disconsolate weep, deep and from the belly. "Oh, God, I'm sorry."

Mave shoved her whiskey glass across the table toward him. "Don't worry about it," she murmured. He took a sip, then put the book away. He dug through his book bag and found Kleenex to dab at his nose.

"I didn't get like this on my own," he said. "There are people responsible." Inside his bag Mave could see a newsmagazine with the exasperated headline: ETHIOPIA: WHY ARE THEY STARVING THIS TIME?

"Boredom is heartless," said Dennis, the tears slowing. He indicated the magazine. "When the face goes into a yawn, the blood to the chest gets constricted."

"Are you finished with my drink?"

"No." He took another gulp and winced. "I mean, yes," and he handed it back to Mave, wiped his mouth with a napkin. Mave looked at Dennis's face and was glad no one had broken up with her recently. When someone broke up with you, you became very unattractive, and it confirmed all the doubts that person had ever had about you to begin with. "Wait, just one more sip." Someone broke up with you and you yelled. You blistered, withered, and flushed. You apologized to inanimate objects and drank when you swore you wouldn't. You went around humming the theme to *Valley of the Dolls*, doing all the instruments even, lingering on the line about *gotta get off, gonna get, have to get.* . . . It wasn't good to go out on that kind of limb for love. You went out on a limb for food, but not for love. Love was not food. Love, thought Mave, was more like the rest rooms at the Ziegfeld: sinks in the stalls, big deal. Mave worked hard to forget very quickly afterward what the men she went out with even looked like. This was called sticking close to the trunk.

"All yours," said Dennis. He was smiling now. The whiskey brought the blood to his face in a nice way.

Mave looked down at her menu. "There's no spaghetti and meatballs here. I wanted to order the child's portion of the spaghetti and meatballs."

"Oh, that reminds me," said Dennis, shaking a finger for emphasis. With his books away and the whiskey in him, he seemed more confident. "Did I tell you the guy my wife's seeing is Italian? Milanese, not Brooklyn. What do you suppose that means, her falling in love with an Italian?"

"It means she's going to feel scruffy all the time. It means that he will stare at all the fuzzies on her shirt while she is telling him something painful about a childhood birthday party nobody came to. Let's face it: She's going to start to miss the fact, Dennis, that your hair zooms out all over the goddamn place."

"I'm getting it cut tomorrow."

Mave put on her reading glasses. "This is not a restaurant. Restaurants serve different things from this."

"You know, one thing about these books for women, I have to tell you. The whole emphasis on locating and accepting your homosexual side is really very powerful. It frees and expands some other sort of love in you."

Mave looked up at him and smiled. She was drawn to the insane because of their blazing minds. "So you've located and accepted?"

"Well, I've realized this. I like boys. *And* I like girls." He leaned toward her confidentially. "I just don't like *berls*." Dennis reached again for Mave's whiskey. "Of course, I am completely in the wrong town. May I?" He leaned his head back, and the ice cubes knocked against his teeth. Water beaded up on his chin. "So, Mave, who are *you* romancing these days?" Dennis was beginning to look drunk. His lips were smooth and thick and hung open like a change purse.

"These days?" There were little ways like this of stalling for time.

"These right here."

"Right here. These. I've been seeing Mitch again a little."

Dennis dropped his forehead into his palm, which had somehow flown up from the table, so that the two met midair in an unsightly smack. "Mitch! Mave, he's such a womanizer!"

"So I needed to be womanized. I was losing my sheen."

"You know what you do? You get all your boyfriends on sale. It's called Bargain Debasement. Immolation by desire."

"Look, you need to be womanized, you go to a womanizer. I don't take these things seriously anymore. I make it a point now to forget what everybody looks like. I'm being Rudolf Bing. I've lost my mind and am traipsing around the South Seas with an inappropriate lover, and I believe in it. I think everybody in a love affair is being Rudolf Bing anyway, and they're vain to believe otherwise. . . . Oh, my God, that man in the sweater is feeling his girlfriend's lymph nodes." Mave put away her reading glasses and fumbled around in her bag for the whiskey flask. That was the thing with hunger: It opened up something dangerous in you, something endless, like a universe, or a cliff. "I'm sorry. Rudolf Bing is on my mind. He's really been on my mind. I feel like we're all almost like him."

"Almost like Bing in love," said Dennis. *"What a day this has been. What a rare mood I'm in."* Mave was in a long sip. "I've been listening to that *Live at Carnegie Hall* tape too much."

"Music! Let's talk about music! Or death! Why do we always have to talk about love?"

"Because our parents were sickos, and we're starved for it."

"You know what I've decided? I don't want to be cremated. I used to, but now I think it sounds just a little too much like a blender speed. Now I've decided I want to be embalmed, and then I want a plastic surgeon to come put in silicone implants everywhere. Then I want to be laid out in the woods like Snow White, with a gravestone that reads *Gotta Dance*." The whiskey was going down sweet. That was what happened after a while, with no meal to assist – it had to do the food work on its own. "There. We talked about death."

"That's talking about death?"

"What is *kale*? I don't understand why they haven't taken our order yet. I mean, it's crowded now, but it wasn't ten minutes ago. Maybe it was the ice thing."

"You know what else my wife says about this Italian? She says he goes around singing this same song to himself. You know what it is?"

" 'Santa Lucia.' "

"No. It's the 'Addams Family' theme song: *Their house is a museum, when people come to see-um . . .*"

"Your wife tells you this?"

"We're friends."

"Don't tell me you're friends. You hate her."

"We're friends. I don't hate her."

"You think she's a user and a tart. She's with some guy with great shoes whose coif doesn't collapse into hairpin turns across his part."

"You used to be a nice person."

"I never was a nice person. I'm still a nice person."

"I don't like this year," said Dennis, his eyes welling again.

"I know," said Mave. "Eighty-eight. It's too Sergio Mendes or something."

"You know, it's OK not to be a nice person."

"I need your permission? Thank you." This was what

Dennis had been doing lately: granting everyone permission to feel the way they were going to feel regardless. It was the books. Dennis's relationship to his own feelings had become tender, curatorial. Dismantling. Entomological. Mave couldn't be like that. She treated her emotional life the way she treated her car: She let it go, let it tough it out. To friends she said things like "I know you're thinking this looks like a '79, but it's really an '87." She finally didn't care to understand all that much about her emotional life; she just went ahead and did it. The point, she thought, was to attend the meager theater of it, quietly, and not stand up in the middle and shout, "Oh, my God, you can see the crew backstage!" There was a point at which the study of something became a frightening and naive thing.

"But, Dennis, really, why do you think so much about love, of someone loving you or not loving you? That is all you read about, all you talk about."

"Put the starving people of the world together in a room, and what you get is a lot of conversation about roast beef. They should be talking about the Napoleonic Code?" At the mention of roast beef, Mave's face lit up, greenish, fluorescent. She looked past Dennis and saw the waitress coming toward their table at last; she was moving slowly, meanly, scowling. There was a large paper doily stuck to her shoe. "I mean . . ." Dennis was saying, looking pointedly at Mave, but Mave was watching the waitress approach. *Oh, life, oh, sweet, forgiven for the ice . . .* He grabbed Mave's wrist. There was always an emergency. And then there was love. And then there was another emergency. That was the sandwiching of it. Emergency. Love. Emergency. "I mean, it's not as if you've been dozing off," Dennis was saying, his voice reaching her now, high and watery. "I mean, correct me if I'm wrong," he said, "but I don't think I've been having this conversation alone." He tightened his grip. "I mean, have I?"

1989

SUBJECT TO SEARCH

TOM ARRIVED WITH his suitcase. Its John Kerry sticker did not even say "For President," so it seemed as if John Kerry might be the owner or designer of the bag. "I have to leave," Tom said, sitting down, scraping the chair along the pavement, setting the suitcase beneath the table.

"Before you eat?" she asked.

"No." He looked at his watch.

"Then order. Order quickly if you have to. Or you can have my salad, if you'd like." She indicated the watery romaine on her plate.

He scanned the menu, then put it down. "I can't even read right now. Is there couscous? Order me the lamb couscous. I'll be right back." He grabbed his cell phone. "I'm going to the gents'." His face had a grip of worry beneath the sun-beat skin; his body was lanky and his gait lopey but brisk as he wended his way inside. The suitcase stayed at the table, like a bomb.

She summoned the garçon with a gesture that was a hand flutter quickly pulled away lest the teacher actually call on you. She had no ear for languages – in that way she took after her mother, who once on her French honeymoon, seeing a "L'Ecole des Garçons," had remarked, "No wonder the restaurants are so good! The waiters all go to waiter school!"

"Pour mon ami, s'il vous plaît," she said, "le couscous d'agneau." Was that right? Did one pronounce both esses, or just one, or none, as in *cuckoo*, perhaps requesting a small musical bird from the park? When lamb was a food, was it a different word, the way pork and pig were? Perhaps she had ordered a living, breathing creature mewling in broth and fleece. The waiter nodded and did not say, "Anything more for you, madame?" but turned quickly and left. The outdoor tables were apparently all his this afternoon. It was April and the weather had changed into something oppressively lovely, with an urban breeze of garlic, diesel, and hyacinth. Where she ordinarily lived, there was not the same oniony, oily air of possibility as you walked down the street. Winter prairies choked the air clean. And spring was a brief, delicate thing quickly overtaken by tornadoes.

"Here," Tom said, when he returned, trying to lighten the mood. "I think you may have left your notebook in the loo."

He handed her a small open notebook, clearly his own, in which he had written the lyrics to Peggy Lee's "Fever." Exclamation marks and curlicues decorated all the lines. As did a small game of tic-tac-toe. At the bottom a page read, "Fish bite the least / when winds blow from the east" and "What is destiny, if you have to ask?" Also, "I love your hair the way it is, for chrissakes." That it seemed hilarious made her think, *This has always been the man for me.*

"I have to fly back to the States," he said. He put his elbows on the table and his head in his hands. She found the few people she'd known who moonlighted in the international intrigue business to be very high-energy, but there was also a price paid; Tom now seemed tired and defeated. He glanced up and added, "You know, the intelligence world: we're not James Bond. We're puny, putrid graspers and gropers, deciding things at home from our laptops, playing on a field that is far too large for us."

"Didn't Richard Burton make a speech like that in *The Spy Who Came in from the Cold*?"

"That was the speech."

"The laptop part?"

"You gotta let a guy improvise. Did you order?"

"Oui, monsieur."

"Merci." He smiled. She knew that he liked it when she said anything in French. His specialty was languages, including Urdu and Arabic, although only an hour and a half of Urdu, he declared, and then his mind turned into a blank blue screen. "And actually only four hours of Arabic," he said. "And maybe even only five of English: five hours is a long time to keep talking." Decades ago he had driven cars for a living, from Holland to Tehran, a drug runner (though he had not said this, she had surmised). Then he was recruited by American officials to teach the Shah's guards' children.

"What did you teach them?" she had once asked.

"Critical theory," he'd said, his face lit with a desire to amuse. "Movies and Marxism. Of course not *real* Marxism, nothing so practical as that. Nothing like here's how you kill people and throw them in a ditch. No, we did very abstract Marxism. Very ivory tower."

"Ha ha," she'd said.

"I taught the kids English," he mumbled in a defensive tone, "and some of their parents as well."

"Did you feel the Shah was all that bad?" she had asked and then received a long strange lecture on Chiang Kai-shek and the doubtful, simpleminded shelvings of various historical figures. She believed that in the photographs of the embassy hostages, the handsome blindfolded one, tall and bright-haired in the embassy doorway, was Tom. She herself had been a teenager at the time and had only decades later stumbled upon the photo online; the likeness took her breath away.

But he had said no, he had gotten out a month beforehand. The closed-then-open-again secrets of his work enchanted and paralyzed her, like the frog who fatally acclimates to the heating water.

He paid for everything in cash.

"Everyone looks bad now," he'd said. "Not just the Shah."

Now he held up the carafe of Côtes du Rhône, raised his eyebrows optimistically, and cocked his head. His hair was the color that strawberry blond became in middle age: bilious and bronze, as if it had been oxidized then striped with white like a ginger cat.

"No wine," she said. "It leads to cheese."

She had hoped to lose weight in time for this trip, but alas.

"You must not say anything if I tell you this." He paused, studied her, considering.

"Of course not." Did she look untrustworthy? Why did she not seem like a person of integrity, which she felt she was. It was gracefulness she was perhaps missing; people confused the two.

Tom poured some wine and drank. "In London they are reporting torture incidents involving American troops in a

Baghdad prison. Someone took pictures. It is a disaster, and I have to get back." He took another swallow.

"Are the troops OK? What do you mean?"

"The troops are kids. They don't know what they're doing. They're sheep." The waiter brought the couscous and Tom made a stab at his lamb. "It's all about to blow. The British papers are getting ready to go to press with it. It's going to be a scandal big as My Lai."

"My Lai? Well, let's not get carried away," she said, though who was she to utter such an airy thing?

His hand was trembling and he slurped his wine. "I'm serious. Believe me: the name of this prison will be a household word." And then he said the name, but it sounded like nonsense to her, and perhaps it was, though her terrible ear for languages made everything that was not English sound very, well, *mimsy*, as if plucked from "Jabberwocky": "the mome raths outgrabe."

He stabbed the air with his fork. "They are the same unit I was in when I was in the army thirty years ago. And taking their orders from military intelligence: the most notorious of oxymorons. I rue my time in Tehran and Cairo; I rue my ability to be consulted."

"You needed the money—"

"I'm sorry, but there are no more lecture slots available at this time!" he said, spreading his mouth into a smile that was like a star shining its far illusive light from long ago. "All slots have been filled by contestants who auditioned earlier!" She would never see him smile like that again. In truth probably she wasn't seeing it now. He looked through her a bit and lowered his voice. "I said to them, whatever you do, don't flush Korans down the toilet. Whatever you do don't have them be naked in front of a woman. Whatever you do don't involve them in any sexual horseplay whatsoever. Do not pantomime fellatio – which is probably good advice for everyone. I warned, don't take a Sharpie and write *Children of Akbar* on their foreheads or put women's underwear on their heads. Whatever you do don't try to reconstruct your memories of seeing Pilobolus at the civic center when you were eight. It will demoralize and degrade them."

She thought she could see what he was telling her. *Don't* code for *do*. It was what doctors sometimes did for the terminally ill who wanted to die: *whatever you do, don't take this entire prescription all at once with water.*

"Where did they get their ideas from then? The Internet?" Did he himself believe these prohibitions were not articulated this way as cover? When you fled one room of moral ambiguity, it was good to have a nice, overstuffed chair awaiting you in the next. But you then perhaps became your spook self, your ghost self, restless in a house you never knew was quite this haunted – and haunted by you.

"The Internet!" Tom said, scoffing. "The Internet just reflects what's already in the human mind. Perhaps a little less so. Cruelty comes naturally. It comes naturally to everyone. But if one is confused, and it's hot, one's bearings get even further lost. The desire to break something down so you can dominate it. Where did this idea come from? Whatever happened to simple cleverness? Instead we've got nude interrogations and sandbags soaked in pepper sauce?"

"But *you* – are MI."

"IM?"

She shifted in her seat. She couldn't recall if she had ordered any bread with her salad. "The whole planet is based on being at the right place at the right time," she said, lost herself.

"No! No!" he cried, seeing her eyes narrow into a squint. "They were supposed to de-conflict, not *gitmoize*."

"You are simply a consultant. You weren't responsible," she said, unsure. Tom, she knew, had had a close childhood friend on Mohamed Atta's plane. Sitting right up in first class with the terrorists. "Oh, my God, what a horrible shock," she had said when he had told her the tale in a coffee shop back home.

"Yeah," he'd said, hopelessly, "you don't expect things like that to happen except in coach."

Now, again, she didn't know how to console him. "You're speaking as if you were Death itself."

"Perhaps I am, little girl. Let's go for a walk and see if you return." He began to rub his temples. "I'm sorry. I'm not sure what's wrong with me, but! I have a good idea for a cure," he added, smiling slightly, as if he were afraid he had made her nervous. He turned his hand into a pistol shape and placed it at his own temple, his thumb miming a trigger.

"That might only wound," she said. "It might merely blind you, and then you'd never be able to find a gun again."

"How about this?" he said and pointed his finger into his mouth. She could see the creamy yellow of his teeth, his molars with their mercury eyes.

"It's really an extreme way to get rid of headaches, and it still might not work."

"I've got it," he said and with both hands placed each trigger finger on either side of his head. "That do it?"

Laughter in the midafternoon night. The daylilies in the Plexiglas table vase had already called it a day.

"Veterinarians really have it down," she said. "It's so much more humane than human medicine – especially the endgame. They've got the right injections. No bad morphine dreams."

"That's why I'm getting my little puppy suit ready," he said.

"Ho ho."

"If you're suicidal," he said slowly, "and you *don't actually kill yourself*, you become known as 'wry.'"

He had headaches that could be debilitating, but he had always hid in his apartment when they came on so she had never seen how crippling they were. Two years later, when he had a chip implanted in his head – a headache cure, experimental, cutting-edge, but who could not think of *The Manchurian Candidate*? – she would go visit him, bring him lunch, listen to him joke about his shaved-off hair and the battery pack implanted in his chest. Someone, it seemed, was experimenting with him, but he did not say who, precisely. He was susceptible to charming leaders and group activities despite his remarks about sheep. He was also simultaneously stoical about all. Still later, when the chip was removed, sloppily, and the trembling that had begun in that café overtook the entirety of him, leaving him frail, unsteady, leaning on a cane, filling out retirement forms – "apparently I was in the control group and the control group does not experience the experiment" – she would drive up to see him in one of the cottages in the veterans' lakeside compound in the northern part of the state. But the woman at the reception desk always said, "He's just not seeing people today." Uniformed guards would check her car at the security gate, and once when she got home she found one of the guards' cell phones in her trunk. Mostly, if allowed, she would walk the grounds and seek out his cottage – he had his own, like a high-ranking officer, so his GS number was probably substantial. Still there was no response, even though he had replied by e-mail that yes it would be good to see her. He never answered the door the four times she had gone to see him and the nine times each that she had knocked.

"By the way," he added now, "make sure I don't have one of those ostensibly green funerals where they put the unpreserved body on view on a giant heap of ice in someone's blazingly sunny backyard. I want a church. Also? I have my music picked out."

"OK."

"Just plug my iPod into some speakers in the front of the chapel."

"Positioned to Genius?" A compliment, forehanded, she thought. They were so rare in life and even less often believed.

He acknowledged it with a nod, respecting her effort. "Oh," he said, "Shuffle will do."

Her own iPod would be an embarrassment: *Forbidden Broadway*, Sting, *French for Dummies*.

She looked around at the café's brass-rimmed tables and the waxy caned chairs. Then she looked back at Tom. He was in a state of pain and worry she had never seen him in before. Back in their once-shared hometown, through the years, first when he was married, then when she was married, they had looked for each other across rooms, hovered near each other at parties, for years they had done it, taut and electrified, each stealthily seeking the other out and then standing close, wineglasses in hand, spellbound by their own eagerly mustered small talk. She would study the superficially sleepy look his face would assume, atop his still-strapping figure, the lowered lids and wavy mouth, and emanating from behind it all his laserlike concentration on her. The more a lovely secret was real the less you spoke of it. But as the secret came to evanesce, as soon as it threatened to go away on its own accord, the secret itself grew frantic and indiscreet – as a way to hang on to its own fading life.

Now they had gotten lucky at long last and neither of them was married anymore – though anything that was at long last, and that had involved such miserable commotion, was unlikely to be truly lucky. They had arranged this rendezvous in faraway France, and neither of them knew its meaning, for its meaning had not been determined out loud. "Is this a date, or independent contractors in semi-prearranged collision?" he had asked just last night, and then spring rain had poured down upon them, shining the concrete, dripping off both their eyeglasses, which they removed, and she had kissed him.

A private car now pulled up at the curb.

"Good God," he said, "the car came so fast."

"Keep eating. That comes first. Eat whatever you can. The car can wait."

She could see he had no appetite but was force-feeding, pushing the food in as if it were a job. Small bites of the lamb. "People are indeed sheep," he said now, chewing. "Stupid as sheep. Actually with sheep at least one of them is always smart and the others just turn their brains off and follow. 'What's Maurie doing now?' they ask each other. 'Where is Maurie going, let's follow!' The flock is the organism."

"Like the military," she said.

He swallowed with some difficulty and at first did not say anything. "Yeah. Occasionally. Civ-Mil has never worked properly as a unit." He pulled a bay leaf out of his couscous. "Bay leaves are bullshit," he said, flinging it down on his plate.

"What will you do with the rest of your time here?" he asked, rounding up the remaining food with his fork, pushing it into small piles, with rivulets and valleys.

"I'll find things," she said. "But it will not be the same without you."

He put his fork down and grabbed her hand, which put a knot in her chest.

"Remember: never drink alone," he said.

"I don't," she said. "I usually drink with MacNeil-Lehrer." She assumed he would call her when he got to D.C.

He withdrew his hand, fumbled with his wallet, threw cash down on the table, and grabbed his suitcase.

They got up together and walked to his car. The blue-bereted driver got out and opened the door for him. Tom tossed the bag in the back and turned to her, about to say something, then changed his mind and just got in. When the door shut, he lowered his window.

"I don't know how to say this," he said, "but, well – keep me in mind."

"How could I not?" she said.

"That's something I don't ask, ma chère." She lowered her head, and he pressed his lips to her cheek for a very long moment.

"May our paths cross again soon," she said, stepping back. And then like a deaf person she made a little gesture of a cross with the index fingers of each of her hands, but it came out like a werewolf ward-off sign. Inept even at sign language. A Freudian slip of the dumb. As the car began to roll away, she called out, "Have a good flight!" His head turned and bent toward her one last time.

"Hey, I've got all my liquids packed in my unchecked bag," he shouted, not without innuendo. She flung one palm quickly to her mouth to blow a kiss, but the car took a quick right down the Rue du Bac. A kiss blown – in all ways. But she could see him lift his left hand quickly at the window, like a karate chop that was also a salute, as the car merged and disappeared into the fanning traffic.

Years earlier, at a Christmas party of a mutual friend, their spouses both out on the wintry summer porch smoking, she had found herself next to him, in the kitchen, jiggling the open bottles of wine to see which one might not yet be empty. The day before, along with a photo of prizewinning gingerbread houses on display at the mall, he had sent her an e-mail: "I just took three Adderall and made these for you." In the next room Bob Dylan was singing "Gotta Serve Somebody."

"What is the thing you regret most in life?" he asked her, standing close. There were perhaps a dozen empty bottles, and she and Tom methodically tipped every one of them upside down, held them up to the light, sometimes peering into them from underneath. "Nothing but dead soldiers here," he murmured. "I'd like to say optimistically that they were half full, not half empty, but these are just totally empty."

"Unless you have a life of great importance," she said, "regrets are stupid, crumpled-up tickets to a circus that has already left town."

His face went bright with amusement and drink. "Then what happens to the town?" he asked.

She thought about this. "Oh, there's a lot of weather," she said, slowly. "It snows. It thunders. The sun comes out. People go to church and sit in the sanctuary and sometimes they see escaped clowns sitting in the back pews with their white gloves still on."

"Escaped clowns?" he asked.

"Escaped," she said. "Sort of escaped."

"Come in from the cold?" he inquired.

"Come in to sit next to each other."

He nodded with satisfaction. "The past is for losers, baby?"

"Kind of like that." She wasn't sure that she agreed, but she understood the power of such a thought.

His stance grew jaunty. He leaned in close to her, up against the kitchen counter's edge.

"Do you ever feel that no one knows what you're talking about, that everyone is just pretending – except for me?"

She studied him carefully. "Yes, I do," she said. "I do."

"Ah," he replied, straightening his posture. He clasped her hand: electricity burst into it then vanished as he let go. "We're all suckers for a happy ending."

2013

TERRIFIC MOTHER

ALTHOUGH SHE HAD BEEN around them her whole life, it was when she reached thirty-five that holding babies seemed to make her nervous – just at the beginning, a twinge of stage fright swinging up from the gut. "Adrienne, would you like to hold the baby? Would you mind?" Always these words from a woman her age looking kind and beseeching – a former friend, she was losing her friends to babble and beseech – and Adrienne would force herself to breathe deep. Holding a baby was no longer natural – she was no longer natural – but a test of womanliness and earthly skills. She was being observed. People looked to see how she would do it. She had entered a puritanical decade, a demographic moment – whatever it was – when the best compliment you could get was, "You would make a terrific mother." The wolf whistle of the nineties.

So when she was at the Spearsons' Labor Day picnic, and when Sally Spearson handed her the baby, Adrienne had burbled at it as she would a pet, had jostled the child gently, made clicking noises with her tongue, affectionately cooing, "Hello, punkinhead, hello, my little punkinhead," had reached to shoo a fly away and, amid the smells of old grass and the fatty crackle of the barbecue, lost her balance when the picnic bench, the dowels rotting in the joints, wobbled and began to topple her – the bench, the wobbly picnic bench, was toppling her! And when she fell backward, wrenching her spine – in the slowed quickness of this flipping world, she saw the clayey clouds, some frozen faces, one lone star like the nose of a jet – and when the baby's head hit the stone retaining wall of the Spearsons' newly terraced yard and bled fatally into the brain, Adrienne went home shortly thereafter, after the hospital and the police reports, and did not leave her attic apartment for seven months, and there were fears, deep fears for her, on the part of Martin Porter, the man she had been dating, and on the part of almost everyone, including

Sally Spearson, who phoned tearfully to say that she forgave her, that Adrienne might never come out.

Martin Porter usually visited her bringing a pepper cheese or a Casbah couscous cup; he had become her only friend. He was divorced and worked as a research economist, though he looked more like a Scottish lumberjack – graying hair, red-flecked beard, a favorite flannel shirt in green and gold. He was getting ready to take a trip abroad. "We could get married," he suggested. That way, he said, Adrienne could accompany him to northern Italy, to a villa in the Alps set up for scholars and academic conferences. She could be a spouse. They gave spouses studios to work in. Some studios had pianos. Some had desks or potter's wheels. "You can do whatever you want." He was finishing the second draft of a study of First World imperialism's impact on Third World monetary systems. "You could paint. Or not. You could not paint."

She looked at him closely, hungrily, then turned away. She still felt clumsy and big, a beefy killer in a cage, in need of the thinning prison food. "You love me, don't you," she said. She had spent the better part of seven months napping in a leotard, an electric fan blowing at her, her left ear catching the wind, capturing it there in her head, like the sad sea in a shell. She felt clammy and doomed. "Or do you just feel sorry for me?" She swatted at a small swarm of gnats that had appeared suddenly out of an abandoned can of Coke.

"I don't feel sorry for you."

"You don't?"

"I *feel for* you. I've grown to love you. We're grown-ups here. One grows to do things." He was a practical man. He often referred to the annual departmental cocktail party as "Standing Around Getting Paid."

"I don't think, Martin, that we can get married."

"Of course we can get married." He unbuttoned his cuffs as if to roll up his sleeves.

"You don't understand," she said. "Normal life is no

longer possible for me. I've stepped off all the normal paths and am living in the bushes. I'm a bushwoman now. I don't feel like I can have the normal things. Marriage is a normal thing. You need the normal courtship, the normal proposal." She couldn't think what else. Water burned her eyes. She waved a hand dismissively, and it passed through her field of vision like something murderous and huge.

"Normal courtship, normal proposal," Martin said. He took off his shirt and pants and shoes. He lay on the bed in just his socks and underwear and pressed the length of his body against her. "I'm going to marry you, whether you like it or not." He took her face into his hands and looked longingly at her mouth. "I'm going to marry you till you puke."

They were met at Malpensa by a driver who spoke little English but who held up a sign that said VILLA HIRSCHBORN, and when Adrienne and Martin approached him, he nodded and said, "Hello, *buongiorno*. Signor Porter?" The drive to the villa took two hours, uphill and down, through the countryside and several small villages, but it wasn't until the driver pulled up to the precipitous hill he called "La Madre Vertiginoso," and the villa's iron gates somehow opened automatically, then closed behind them, it wasn't until then, winding up the drive past the spectacular gardens and the sunny vineyard and the terraces of the stucco outbuildings, that it occurred to Adrienne that Martin's being invited here was a great honor. He had won this *thing*, and he got to live here for a month.

"Does this feel like a honeymoon?" she asked him.

"A what? Oh, a honeymoon. Yes." He turned and patted her thigh indifferently.

He was jet-lagged. That was it. She smoothed her skirt, which was wrinkled and damp. "Yes, I can see us growing old together," she said, squeezing his hand. "In the next few weeks, in fact." If she ever got married again, she would do it right: the awkward ceremony, the embarrassing relatives, the cumbersome, ecologically unsound gifts. She and Martin had simply gone to city hall, and then asked their family and friends not to send presents but to donate money to Greenpeace. Now, however, as they slowed before the squashed-nosed stone lions at the entrance of the villa, its perfect border of forget-me-nots and yews, its sparkling glass door, Adrienne gasped. Whales, she thought quickly. *Whales* got my crystal.

The upstairs "Principessa" room, which they were ushered into by a graceful bilingual butler named Carlo, was elegant and huge – a piano, a large bed, dressers stenciled with festooning fruits. There was maid service twice a day, said Carlo. There were sugar wafers, towels, mineral water, and mints. There was dinner at eight, breakfast until nine. When Carlo bowed and departed, Martin kicked off his shoes and sank into the ancient tapestried chaise. "I've heard these 'fake' Quattrocento paintings on the wall are fake for tax purposes only," he whispered. "If you know what I mean."

"Really," said Adrienne. She felt like one of the workers taking over the Winter Palace. Her own voice sounded booming. "You know, Mussolini was captured around here. Think about it."

Martin looked puzzled. "What do you mean?"

"That he was around here. That they captured him. I don't know. I was reading the little book on it. Leave me alone." She flopped down on the bed. Martin was changing already. He'd been better when they were just dating, with the pepper cheese. She let her face fall deep into the pillow, her mouth hanging open like a dog's, and then she slept until six, dreaming that a baby was in her arms but that it turned into a stack of plates, which she had to juggle, tossing them into the air.

A loud sound awoke her – a falling suitcase. Everyone had to dress for dinner, and Martin was yanking things out, groaning his way into a jacket and tie. Adrienne got up, bathed, and put on panty hose, which, because it had been months since she had done so, twisted around her leg like the stripe on a barber pole.

"You're walking as if you'd torn a ligament," said Martin, locking the door to their room as they were leaving.

Adrienne pulled at the knees of the hose but couldn't make them work. "Tell me you like my skirt, Martin, or I'm going to have to go back in and never come out again."

"I like your skirt. It's great. You're great. I'm great," he said, like a conjugation. He took her arm and they limped their way down the curved staircase – Was it sweeping? Yes! It was sweeping! – to the dining room, where Carlo ushered them in to find their places at the table. The seating arrangement at the tables would change nightly, Carlo said in a clipped Italian accent, "to assist the cross-pollination of ideas."

"Excuse me?" said Adrienne.

There were about thirty-five people, all of them middle-aged, with the academic's strange mixed expression of merriment and weariness. "A cross between flirtation and a fender bender," Martin had described it once. Adrienne's place was at the opposite side of the room from him, between a historian writing a book on a monk named Jaocim de Flore and a musicologist who had devoted his life to a quest for "the earnest andante." Everyone sat in elaborate wooden chairs, the backs of which were carved with gargoylish heads that poked up from behind either shoulder of the sitter, like a warning.

"De Flore," said Adrienne, at a loss, turning from her carpaccio to the monk man. "Doesn't that mean 'of the flower'?" She had recently learned that *disaster* meant "bad star," and she was looking for an opportunity to brandish and bronze this tidbit in conversation.

The monk man looked at her. "Are you one of the spouses?"

"Yes," she said. She looked down, then back up. "But then, so is my husband."

"You're not a screenwriter, are you?"

"No," she said. "I'm a painter. Actually, more of a printmaker. Actually, more of a – right now I'm in transition."

He nodded and dug back into his food. "I'm always afraid they're going to start letting *screenwriters* in here."

There was an arugula salad, and osso buco for the main course. She turned now to the musicologist. "So you usually find them insincere? The andantes?" She looked quickly out over the other heads to give Martin a fake and girlish wave.

"It's the use of the minor seventh," muttered the musicologist. "So fraudulent and replete."

"If the food wasn't so good, I'd leave now," she said to Martin. They were lying in bed, in their carpeted skating rink of a room. It could be weeks, she knew, before they'd have sex here. "'*So fraudulent and replete,*'" she said in a high nasal voice, the likes of which Martin had heard only once before, in a departmental meeting chaired by an embittered interim chair who did imitations of colleagues not in the room. "Can you even use the word *replete* like that?"

"As soon as you get settled in your studio, you'll feel better," said Martin, beginning to fade. He groped under the covers to find her hand and clasp it.

"I want a divorce," whispered Adrienne.

"I'm not giving you one," he said, bringing her hand up to his chest and placing it there, like a medallion, like a necklace of sleep, and then he began softly to snore, the quietest of radiators.

They were given bagged lunches and told to work well. Martin's studio was a modern glass cube in the middle of one of the gardens. Adrienne's was a musty stone hut twenty minutes farther up the hill and out onto the wooded headland, along a dirt path sunned on by small darting lizards. She unlocked the door with the key she had been given, went in, and immediately sat down and ate the entire bagged lunch – quickly, compulsively, though it was only 9:30 in the morning. Two apples, some cheese, and a jam sandwich. "A jelly bread," she said aloud, holding up the sandwich, scrutinizing it under the light.

She set her sketch pad on the worktable and began a morning full of killing spiders and drawing their squashed and tragic bodies. The spiders were star-shaped, hairy, and scuttling like crabs. They were fallen stars. Bad stars. They were earth's animal try at heaven. Often she had to step on them twice – they were large and ran fast. Stepping on them once usually just made them run faster.

It was the careless universe's work she was performing, death itchy and about like a cop. Her personal fund of mercy for the living was going to get used up in dinner conversation at the villa. She had no compassion to spare, only a pencil and a shoe.

"Art *trouvé*?" said Martin, toweling himself dry from his shower as they dressed for the evening cocktail hour.

"Spider *trouvé*," she said. "A delicate, aboriginal dish." Martin let out a howling laugh that alarmed her. She looked at him, then looked down at her shoes. He needed her. Tomorrow, she would have to go down into town and find a pair of sexy Italian sandals that showed the cleavage of her toes. She would have to take him dancing. They would have to hold each other and lead each other back to love or they'd go nuts here. They'd grow mocking and arch and violent. One of them would stick a foot out, and the other would trip. That sort of thing.

At dinner, she sat next to a medievalist who had just finished his sixth book on the *Canterbury Tales*.

"Sixth," repeated Adrienne.

"There's a lot there," he said defensively.

"I'm sure," she said.

"I read deep," he added. "I read hard."

"How nice for you."

He looked at her narrowly. "Of course, *you* probably think I should write a book about Cat Stevens." She nodded neutrally. "I see," he said.

For dessert, Carlo was bringing in a white chocolate torte, and she decided to spend most of the coffee and dessert time talking about it. Desserts like these are born, not made, she would say. She was already practicing, rehearsing for courses. "I mean," she said to the Swedish physicist on her left, "until today, my feeling about white chocolate was why? What was the point? You might as well have been eating goddamn *wax*." She had her elbow on the table, her hand up near her face, and she looked anxiously past the physicist to smile at Martin at the other end of the long table. She waved her fingers in the air like bug legs.

"Yes, of course," said the physicist, frowning. "You must be . . . well, are you one of the *spouses*?"

She began in the mornings to gather with some of the other spouses – they were going to have little tank tops printed up – in the music room for exercise. This way, she could avoid hearing words like *Heideggerian* and *ideological* at breakfast; it always felt too early in the morning for those words. The women pushed back the damask sofas and cleared a space on the rug where all of them could do little hip and thigh exercises, led by the wife of the Swedish physicist. Up, down, up down.

"I guess this relaxes you," said the white-haired woman next to her.

"Bourbon relaxes you," said Adrienne. "This carves you."

"Bourbon carves you," said a redhead from Brazil.

"You have to go visit this person down in the village," whispered the white-haired woman. She wore a Spalding sporting-goods T-shirt.

"What person?"

"Yes, what person?" asked the blonde.

The white-haired woman stopped and handed both of them a card from the pocket of her shorts. "She's an American masseuse. A couple of us have started going. She takes lire or dollars, doesn't matter. You have to phone a couple days ahead."

Adrienne stuck the card in her waistband. "Thanks," she said, and resumed moving her leg up and down like a tollgate.

For dinner, there was *tacchino alla scala*. "I wonder how you make this?" Adrienne said aloud.

"My dear," said the French historian on her left. "You must never ask. Only wonder." He then went on to disparage sub-altered intellectualism, dormant tropes, genealogical contingencies.

"Yes," said Adrienne, "dishes like these do have about them a kind of omnihistorical reality. At least it seems like that to me." She turned quickly.

To her right sat a cultural anthropologist who had just come back from China, where she had studied the infanticide.

"Yes," said Adrienne. "The infanticide."

"They are on the edge of something horrific there. It is the whole future, our future as well, and something terrible is going to happen to them. One feels it."

"How awful," said Adrienne. She could not do the mechanical work of eating, of knife and fork, up and down. She let her knife and fork rest against each other on the plate.

"A woman has to apply for a license to have a baby. Everything is bribes and rations. We went for hikes up into the mountains, and we didn't see a single bird, a single animal. Everything, over the years, has been eaten."

Adrienne felt a light weight on the inside of her arm vanish and return, vanish and return, like the history of something, like the story of all things. "Where are you from ordinarily?" asked Adrienne. She couldn't place the accent.

"Munich," said the woman. "Land of Oktoberfest." She dug into her food in an exasperated way, then turned back toward Adrienne to smile a little formally. "I grew up watching all these grown people in green felt throw up in the street."

Adrienne smiled back. This now was how she would learn about the world, in sentences at meals; other people's distillations amid her own vague pain, dumb with itself. This, for her, would be knowledge – a shifting to hear, an emptying of her arms, other people's experiences walking through the bare rooms of her brain, looking for a place to sit.

"Me?" she too often said, "I'm just a dropout from Sue Bennet College." And people would nod politely and ask, "Where's that?"

* * *

The next morning in her room, she sat by the phone and stared. Martin had gone to his studio; his book was going fantastically well, he said, which gave Adrienne a sick, abandoned feeling – of being unhappy and unsupportive – which made her think she was not even one of the spouses. Who was she? The opposite of a mother. The opposite of a spouse.

She was Spider Woman.

She picked up the phone, got an outside line, dialed the number of the masseuse on the card.

"*Pronto!*" said the voice on the other end.

"Yes, hello, *per favore, parla inglese*?"

"Oh, yes," said the voice. "I'm from Minnesota."

"No kidding," said Adrienne. She lay back and searched the ceiling for talk. "I once subscribed to a haunted-house newsletter published in Minnesota," she said.

"Yes," said the voice a little impatiently. "Minnesota is full of haunted-house newsletters."

"I once lived in a haunted house," said Adrienne. "In college. Me and five roommates."

The masseuse cleared her throat confidentially. "Yes. I was once called on to cast the demons from a haunted house. But how can I help you today?"

"You were?"

"Were? Oh, the house, yes. When I got there, all the place needed was to be cleaned. So I cleaned it. Washed the dishes and dusted."

"Yup," said Adrienne. "Our house was haunted that way, too."

There was a strange silence, in which Adrienne, feeling something tense and moist in the room, began to fiddle with the bagged lunch on the bed, nervously pulling open the sandwiches, sensing that if she turned, just then, the phone cradled in her neck, the child would be there, behind her, a little older now, a toddler, walked toward her in a ghostly way by her own dead parents, a Nativity scene corrupted by error and dream.

"How can I help you today?" the masseuse asked again, firmly.

Help? Adrienne wondered abstractly, and remembered how in certain countries, instead of a tooth fairy, there were such things as tooth spiders. How the tooth spider could steal your children, mix them up, bring you a changeling child, a child that was changed.

"I'd like to make an appointment for Thursday," she said. "If possible. Please."

For dinner there was *vongole in umido*, the rubbery, wine-steamed meat prompting commentary about mollusk versus crustacean anatomy. Adrienne sighed and chewed. Over cocktails, there had been a long discussion of peptides and rabbit tests.

"Now lobsters, you know, have what is called a hemipenis," said the man next to her. He was a marine biologist, an epidemiologist, or an anthropologist. She'd forgotten.

"Hemipenis." Adrienne scanned the room a little frantically.

"Yes." He grinned. "Not a term one particularly wants to hear in an intimate moment, of course."

"No," said Adrienne, smiling back. She paused. "Are you one of the spouses?"

Someone on his right grabbed his arm, and he now turned in that direction to say why yes, he did know Professor so-and-so . . . and wasn't she in Brussels last year giving a paper at the hermeneutics conference?

There came *castagne al porto* and coffee. The woman to Adrienne's left finally turned to her, placing the cup down on the saucer with a sharp clink.

"You know, the chef has AIDS," said the woman.

Adrienne froze a little in her chair. "No, I didn't know." Who was this woman?

"How does that make you feel?"

"Pardon me?"

"How does that make you feel?" She enunciated slowly, like a reading teacher.

"I'm not sure," said Adrienne, scowling at her chestnuts. "Certainly worried for us if we should lose him."

The woman smiled. "Very interesting." She reached underneath the table for her purse and said, "Actually, the chef doesn't have AIDS – at least not that I'm aware of. I'm just taking a kind of survey to test people's reactions to AIDS, homosexuality, and general notions of contagion. I'm a sociologist. It's part of my research. I just arrived this afternoon. My name is Marie-Claire."

Adrienne turned back to the hemipenis man. "Do you think the people here are mean?" she asked.

He smiled at her in a fatherly way. "Of course," he said. There was a long silence with some chewing in it. "But the place *is* pretty as a postcard."

"Yeah, well," said Adrienne, "I never send those kinds of postcards. No matter where I am, I always send the kind with the little cat jokes on them."

He placed his hand briefly on her shoulder. "We'll find you some cat jokes." He scanned the room in a bemused way and then looked at his watch.

She had bonded in a state of emergency, like an infant bird. But perhaps it would be soothing, this marriage. Perhaps it would be like a nice warm bath. A nice warm bath in a tub flying off a roof.

At night, she and Martin seemed almost like husband and wife, spooned against each other in a forgetful sort of love – a cold, still heaven through which a word or touch might explode like a moon, then disappear, unremembered. She moved her arms to place them around him and he felt so big there, huge, filling her arms.

The white-haired woman who had given her the masseuse card was named Kate Spalding, the wife of the monk man, and after breakfast she asked Adrienne to go jogging. They met by the lions, Kate once more sporting a Spalding T-shirt, and then they headed out over the gravel, toward the gardens. "It's pretty as a postcard here, isn't it?" said Kate. Out across the lake, the mountains seemed to preside over the minutiae of the terracotta villages nestled below. It was May and the Alps were losing their snowy caps, nurses letting their hair down. The air was warming. Anything could happen.

Adrienne sighed. "But do you think people have *sex* here?"

Kate smiled. "You mean casual sex? Among the guests?"

Adrienne felt annoyed. "*Casual* sex? No, I don't mean *casual* sex. I'm talking about difficult, randomly profound, Sears and Roebuck sex. I'm talking marital."

Kate laughed in a sharp, barking sort of way, which for some reason hurt Adrienne's feelings.

Adrienne tugged on her socks. "I don't believe in *casual* sex." She paused. "I believe in casual marriage."

"Don't look at me," said Kate. "I married my husband because I was deeply in love with him."

"Yeah, well," said Adrienne, "I married my husband because I thought it would be a great way to meet guys."

Kate smiled now in a real way. Her white hair was grandmotherly, but her face was youthful and tan, and her teeth shone generous and wet, the creamy incisors curved as cashews.

"I'd tried the whole single thing, but it just wasn't working," Adrienne added, running in place.

Kate stepped close and massaged Adrienne's neck. Her skin was lined and papery. "You haven't been to see Ilke from Minnesota yet, have you?"

Adrienne feigned perturbance. "Do I seem that tense, that lost, that . . ." And here she let her arms splay spastically. "I'm going tomorrow."

He was a beautiful child, didn't you think? In bed, Martin held her until he rolled away, clasped her hand and fell asleep. At least there was that: a husband sleeping next to a wife, a nice husband sleeping close. It meant something to her. She could see how through the years marriage would gather power, its socially sanctioned animal comfort, its night life a dreamy dance about love. She lay awake and remembered when her father had at last grown so senile and ill that her mother could no longer sleep in the same bed with him – the mess, the smell – and had had to move him, diapered and rank, to the guest room next door. Her mother had cried, to say this farewell to a husband. To at last lose him like this, banished and set aside like a dead man, never to sleep with him again: she had wept like a baby. His actual death, she took less hard. At the funeral, she was grim and dry and invited everyone over for a quiet, elegant tea. By the time two years had passed, and she herself was diagnosed with cancer, her sense of humor had returned a little. "The silent killer," she would say, with a wink. "The *Silent Killer.*" She got a kick out of repeating it, though no one knew what to say in response, and at the very end, she kept clutching the nurses' hems to ask, "Why is no one visiting me?" No one lived that close, explained Adrienne. No one lived that close to anyone.

Adrienne set her spoon down. "Isn't this soup *interesting*?" she said to no one in particular. "*Zup-pa mari-ta-ta*!" Marriage soup. She decided it was perhaps a little like marriage itself: a good idea that, like all ideas, lived awkwardly on earth.

"You're not a poetess, I hope," said the English geologist next to her. "We had a poetess here last month, and things got a bit dodgy here for the rest of us."

"Really." After the soup, there was risotto with squid ink.

"Yes. She kept referring to insects as 'God's typos' and then she kept us all after dinner one evening so she could read from her poems, which seemed to consist primarily of the repeating line 'the hairy kiwi of his balls.'"

"Hairy kiwi," repeated Adrienne, searching the phrase for a sincere andante. She had written a poem once herself. It had been called "Garbage Night in the Fog" and was about a long, sad walk she'd taken once on garbage night.

The geologist smirked a little at the risotto, waiting for Adrienne to say something more, but she was now watching Martin at the other table. He was sitting next to the sociologist she'd sat next to the previous night, and as Adrienne watched, she saw Martin glance, in a sickened way, from the sociologist, back to his plate, then back to the sociologist. "The *cook*?" he said loudly, then dropped his fork and pushed his chair from the table.

The sociologist was frowning. "You flunk," she said.

"I'm going to see a masseuse tomorrow." Martin was on his back on the bed, and Adrienne was straddling his hips, usually one of their favorite ways to converse. One of the Mandy Patinkin tapes she'd brought was playing on the cassette player.

"The masseuse. Yes, I've heard."

"You have?"

"Sure, they were talking about it at dinner last night."

"Who was?" She was already feeling possessive, alone.

"Oh, one of them," said Martin, smiling and waving his hand dismissively.

"Them," said Adrienne coldly. "You mean one of the spouses, don't you? Why are all the spouses here women? Why don't the women scholars have spouses?"

"Some of them do, I think. They're just not here."

"Where are they?"

"Could you move?" he said irritably. "You're sitting on my groin."

"Fine," she said, and climbed off.

The next morning, she made her way down past the conical evergreens of the terraced hill – so like the grounds of a palace, the palace of a moody princess named Sophia or Giovanna – ten minutes down the winding path to the locked gate to the village. It had rained in the night, and snails, golden and mauve, decorated the stone steps, sometimes dead center, causing Adrienne an occasional quick turn of the ankle. A dance step, she thought. Modern and bent-kneed. Very Martha Graham. *Don't kill us. We'll kill you.* At the top of the final stairs to the gate, she pressed the buzzer that opened it electronically, and then dashed down to get out in time. YOU

HAVE THIRTY SECONDS said the sign. TRENTA SECONDI USCIRE. PRESTO! One needed a key to get back in from the village, and she clutched it like a charm.

She had to follow the Via San Carlo to Corso Magenta, past a gelato shop and a bakery with wreaths of braided bread and muffins cut like birds. She pressed herself up against the buildings to let the cars pass. She looked at her card. The masseuse was above a *farmacìa*, she'd been told, and she saw it now, a little sign that said MASSAGGIO DELLA VITA. She pushed on the outer door and went up.

Upstairs, through an open doorway, she entered a room lined with books: books on vegetarianism, books on healing, books on juice. A cockatiel, white, with a red dot like a Hindu wife's, was perched atop a picture frame. The picture was of Lake Como or Garda, though when you blinked, it could also be a skull, a fissure through the center like a reef.

"Adrienne," said a smiling woman in a purple peasant dress. She had big frosted hair and a wide, happy face that contained many shades of pink. She stepped forward and shook Adrienne's hand. "I'm Ilke."

"Yes," said Adrienne.

The cockatiel suddenly flew from its perch to land on Ilke's shoulder. It pecked at her big hair, then stared at Adrienne accusingly.

Ilke's eyes moved quickly between Adrienne's own, a quick read, a radar scan. She then looked at her watch. "You can go into the back room now, and I'll be with you shortly. You can take off all your clothes, also any jewelry – watches, or rings. But if you want, you can leave your underwear on. Whatever you prefer."

"What do most people do?" Adrienne swallowed in a difficult, conspicuous way.

Ilke smiled. "Some do it one way, some the other."

"All right," Adrienne said, and clutched her pocketbook. She stared at the cockatiel. "I just wouldn't want to rock the boat."

She stepped carefully toward the back room Ilke had indicated, and pushed past the heavy curtain. Inside was a large alcove – windowless and dark, with one small bluish light coming from the corner. In the center was a table with a newly creased flannel sheet. Speakers were built into the bottom of the table, and out of them came the sound of eerie choral music, wordless oohs and oohs in minor tones, with a percussive sibilant chant beneath it that sounded to Adrienne like "Jesus is best, Jesus is best," though perhaps it was "Cheese, I suspect." Overhead hung a mobile of white stars, crescent moons, and doves. On the blue walls were more clouds and snowflakes. It was a child's room, a baby's room, everything trying hard to be harmless and sweet.

Adrienne removed all her clothes, her earrings, her watch, her rings. She had already grown used to the ring Martin had given her, and so it saddened and exhilarated her to take it off, a quick glimpse into the landscape of adultery. Her other ring was a smoky quartz, which a palm reader in Milwaukee – a man dressed like a gym teacher and set up at a card table in a German restaurant – had told her to buy and wear on her right index finger for power.

"What kind of power?" she had asked.

"The kind that's real," he said. "What you've got here," he said, waving around her left hand, pointing at the thin silver and turquoise she was wearing, "is squat."

"I like a palm reader who dresses you," she said later to Martin in the car on their way home. This was before the incident at the Spearson picnic, and things seemed not impossible then; she had wanted Martin to fall in love with her. "A guy who looks like Mike Ditka, but who picks out jewelry for you."

"A guy who tells you you're sensitive and that you will soon receive cash from someone wearing glasses. Where does he come up with this stuff?"

"You don't think I'm sensitive."

"I mean the money and glasses thing," he said. "And that gloomy bit about how they'll think you're a goner, but you're going to come through and live to see the world go through a radical physical change."

"That was gloomy," she agreed. There was a lot of silence

as they looked out at the night-lit highway lines, the fireflies hitting the windshield and smearing, all phosphorescent gold, as if the car were flying through stars. "It must be hard," she said, "for someone like you to go out on a date with someone like me."

"Why do you say that?" he'd asked.

She climbed up on the table, stripped of ornament and the power of ornament, and slipped between the flannel sheets. For a second, she felt numb and scared, naked in a strange room, more naked even than in a doctor's office, where you kept your jewelry on, like an odalisque. But it felt new to do this, to lead the body to this, the body with its dog's obedience, its dog's desire to please. She lay there waiting, watching the mobile moons turn slowly, half revolutions, while from the speakers beneath the table came a new sound, an electronic, synthesized version of Brahms's lullaby. An infant. She was to become an infant again. Perhaps she would become the Spearson boy. He had been a beautiful baby.

Ilke came in quietly, and appeared so suddenly behind Adrienne's head, it gave her a start.

"Move back toward me," whispered Ilke. *Move back toward me*, and Adrienne shifted until she could feel the crown of her head grazing Ilke's belly. The cockatiel whooshed in and perched on a nearby chair.

"Are you a little tense?" she said. She pressed both her thumbs at the center of Adrienne's forehead. Ilke's hands were strong, small, bony. Leathered claws. The harder she pressed, the better it felt to Adrienne, all of her difficult thoughts unknotting and traveling out, up into Ilke's thumbs.

"Breathe deeply," said Ilke. "You cannot breathe deeply without it relaxing you."

Adrienne pushed her stomach in and out.

"You are from the Villa Hirschborn, aren't you?" Ilke's voice was a knowing smile.

"Ehuh."

"I thought so," said Ilke. "People are very tense up there. Rigid as boards." Ilke's hands moved down off Adrienne's forehead, along her eyebrows to her cheeks, which she squeezed repeatedly, in little circles, as if to break the weaker capillaries. She took hold of Adrienne's head and pulled. There was a dull cracking sound. Then she pressed her knuckles along Adrienne's neck. "Do you know why?"

Adrienne grunted.

"It is because they are overeducated and can no longer converse with their own mothers. It makes them a little crazy. They have literally lost their mother tongue. So they come to me. I am their mother, and they don't have to speak at all."

"Of course they *pay* you."

"Of course."

Adrienne suddenly fell into a long falling – of pleasure, of surrender, of glazed-eyed dying, a piece of heat set free in a room. Ilke rubbed Adrienne's earlobes, knuckled her scalp like a hairdresser, pulled at her neck and fingers and arms, as if they were jammed things. Adrienne would become a baby, join all the babies, in heaven, where they lived.

Ilke began to massage sandalwood oil into Adrienne's arms, pressing down, polishing, ironing, looking, at a quick glimpse, like one of Degas's laundresses. Adrienne shut her eyes again and listened to the music, which had switched from synthetic lullabies to the contrapuntal sounds of a flute and a thunderstorm. With these hands upon her, she felt a little forgiven, and began to think generally of forgiveness, how much of it was required in life: to forgive everyone, yourself, the people you loved, and then wait to be forgiven by them. Where was all this forgiveness supposed to come from? Where was this great inexhaustible supply?

"Where are you?" whispered Ilke. "You are somewhere very far."

Adrienne wasn't sure. Where was she? In her own head, like a dream; in the bellows of her lungs. What was she? Perhaps a child. Perhaps a corpse. Perhaps a fern in the forest in the storm; a singing bird. The sheets were folded back. The hands were all over her now. Perhaps she was under the table with the music, or in a musty corner of her own hip. She felt Ilke rub oil into her chest, between her breasts, out along the ribs, and circularly on the abdomen. "There is something stuck here," Ilke said. "Something not working." Then she pulled the covers back up. "Are you cold?" she asked, and though Adrienne didn't answer, Ilke brought another blanket, mysteriously heated, and laid it across Adrienne. "There," said Ilke. She lifted the blanket so that only Adrienne's feet were exposed. She rubbed oil into her soles, the toes; something squeezed out of Adrienne, like an olive. She felt as if she would cry. She felt like the baby Jesus. The grown Jesus. *The poor will always be with us.* The dead Jesus. Cheese is the best. Cheese is the best.

At her desk in the outer room, Ilke wanted money. Thirty-five thousand lire. "I can give it to you for thirty thousand, if you decide to come on a regular basis. Would you like to come on a regular basis?" asked Ilke.

Adrienne was fumbling with her wallet. She sat down in the wicker rocker near the desk. "Yes," she said. "Of course."

Ilke had put on reading glasses and now opened up her appointment book to survey the upcoming weeks. She flipped a page, then flipped it back. She looked out over her glasses at Adrienne. "How often would you like to come?"

"Every day," said Adrienne.

"*Every day?*"

Ilke's hoot worried Adrienne. "Every *other* day?" Adrienne peeped hopefully. Perhaps the massage had bewitched her, ruined her. Perhaps she had fallen in love.

Ilke looked back at her book and shrugged. "Every other day," she repeated slowly, as a way of holding the conversation still while she checked her schedule. "How about at two o'clock?"

"Monday, Wednesday, and Friday?"

"Perhaps we can occasionally arrange a Saturday."

"Okay. Fine." Adrienne placed the money on the desk and stood up. Ilke walked her to the door and thrust her hand out formally. Her face had changed from its earlier pinks to a strange and shiny orange.

"Thank you," said Adrienne. She shook Ilke's hand, but

then leaned forward and kissed her cheek; she would kiss the business out of this. "Good-bye," she said. She stepped gingerly down the stairs; she had not entirely returned to her body yet. She had to go slowly. She felt a little like she had just seen God, but also a little like she had just seen a hooker. Outside, she walked carefully back toward the villa, but first stopped at the gelato shop for a small dish of hazelnut ice cream. It was smooth, toasty, buttery, like a beautiful liqueur, and she thought how different it was from America, where so much of the ice cream now looked like babies had attacked it with their cookies.

"Well, Martin, it's been nice knowing you," Adrienne said, smiling. She reached out to shake his hand with one of hers, and pat him on the back with the other. "You've been a good sport. I hope there will be no hard feelings."

"You've just come back from your massage," he said a little numbly. "How was it?"

"As you would say, 'Relaxing.' As I would say . . . well, I wouldn't say."

Martin led her to the bed. "Kiss and tell," he said.

"I'll just kiss," she said, kissing.

"I'll settle," he said. But then she stopped, and went into the bathroom to shower for dinner.

At dinner, there was *zuppa alla paesana* and then *salsiccia alla griglia con spinaci*. For the first time since they'd arrived, she was seated near Martin, who was kitty-corner to her left. He was seated next to another economist and was speaking heatedly with him about a book on labor division and economic policy. "But Wilkander ripped that theory off from Boyer!" Martin let his spoon splash violently into his *zuppa* before a waiter came and removed the bowl.

"Let us just say," said the other man calmly, "that it was a sort of homage."

"If that's 'homage,'" said Martin, fidgeting with his fork,

"I'd like to perform a little 'homage' on the Chase Manhattan Bank."

"I think it was felt that there was sufficient looseness there to warrant further explication."

"Right. And one's twin sibling is simply an explication of the text."

"Why not?" The other economist smiled. He was calm, probably a supply-sider.

Poor Martin, thought Adrienne. Poor Keynesian Martin, poor Marxist Martin, perspiring and red. *"Left of Lenin?"* she had heard him exclaiming the other day to an agriculturalist. "Left of *Lenin*? Left of the Lennon Sisters, you mean!" Poor godless, raised-an-atheist-in-Ohio Martin. "On Christmas," he'd said to her once, "we used to go down to the Science Store and worship the Bunsen burners."

She would have to find just the right blouse, just the right perfume, greet him on the chaise longue with a bare shoulder and a purring *"Hello, Mr. Man."* Take him down by the lake near the Sfondrata chapel and get him laid. Hire somebody. She turned to the scholar next to her, who had just arrived that morning.

"Did you have a good flight?" she asked. Her own small talk at dinner no longer shamed her.

"*Flight* is the word," he said. "I needed to flee my department, my bills, my ailing car. Come to a place that would take care of me."

"This is it, I guess," she said. "Though they won't fix your car. Won't even discuss it, I've found."

"I'm on a Guggenheim," he said.

"How nice!" She thought of the museum in New York, and of a pair of earrings she had bought in the gift shop there but had never worn because they always looked broken, even though that was the way they were supposed to look.

"But I neglected to ask the foundation for enough money. I didn't realize what you could ask for. I didn't ask for the same amount everyone else did, and so I received substantially less."

Adrienne was sympathetic. "So instead of a regular Guggenheim, you got a little Guggenheim."

"Yes," he said.

"A Guggenheimy," she said.

He smiled in a troubled sort of way. "Right."

"So now you have to live in Guggenheimy town."

He stopped pushing at a sausage with his fork.

"Yes. I heard there would be wit here."

She tried to make her lips curl, like his.

"Sorry," he said. "I was just kidding."

"Jet lag," she said.

"Yes."

"Jetty-laggy." She smiled at him. "Baby talk. We love it." She paused. "Last week, of course, we weren't like this. You've arrived a little late."

He was a beautiful baby. In the dark, there was thumping, like tom-toms, and a piccolo high above it. She couldn't look, because when she looked, it shocked her, another woman's hands all over her. She just kept her eyes closed, and concentrated on surrender, on the restful invalidity of it. Sometimes she concentrated on being where Ilke's hands were – at her feet, at the small of her back.

"Your parents are no longer living, are they?" Ilke said in the dark.

"No."

"Did they die young?"

"Medium. They died medium. I was a menopausal, afterthought child."

"Do you want to know what I feel in you?"

"All right."

"I feel a great and deep gentleness. But I also feel that you have been dishonored."

"Dishonored?" So Japanese. Adrienne liked the sound of it.

"Yes. You have a deeply held fear. Right here." Ilke's hand went just under Adrienne's rib cage.

Adrienne breathed deeply, in and out. "I killed a baby," she whispered.

"Yes, we have all killed a baby – there is a baby in all of us. That is why people come to me, to be reunited with it."

"No, I've killed a real one."

Ilke was very quiet and then she said, "You can do the side lying now. You can put this pillow under your head, this other one between your knees." Adrienne rolled awkwardly onto her side. Finally, Ilke said, "This country, its Pope, its church, makes murderers of women. You must not let it do that to you. Move back toward me. That's it."

That's *not* it, thought Adrienne, in this temporary dissolve, seeing death and birth, seeing the beginning and then the end, how they were the same quiet black, same nothing ever after: everyone's life appeared in the world like a movie in a room. First dark, then light, then dark again. But it was all staggered, so that somewhere there was always light.

That's not it. That's not it, she thought. But thank you.

When she left that afternoon, seeking sugar in one of the shops, she moved slowly, blinded by the angle of the afternoon light but also believing she saw Martin coming toward her in the narrow street, approaching like the lumbering logger he sometimes seemed to be. Her squinted gaze, however, failed to catch his, and he veered suddenly left into a *calle*. By the time she reached the corner, he had disappeared entirely. How strange, she thought. She had felt close to something, to him, and then suddenly not. She climbed the path back up toward the villa, and went and knocked on the door of his studio, but he wasn't there.

"You smell good," she greeted Martin. It was some time later and she had just returned to the room, to find him there. "Did you just take a bath?"

"A little while ago," he said.

She curled up to him, teasingly. "Not a shower? A bath? Did you put some scented bath salts in it?"

"I took a very masculine bath," said Martin.

She sniffed him again. "What scent did you use?"

"A manly scent," he said. "Rock. I took a rock-scented bath."

"Did you take a bubble bath?" She cocked her head to one side.

He smiled. "Yes, but I, uh, made my own bubbles."

"You did?" She squeezed his bicep.

"Yeah. I hammered the water with my fist."

She walked over to the cassette player and put a cassette in. She looked over at Martin, who looked suddenly unhappy. "This music annoys you, doesn't it?"

Martin squirmed. "It's just – why can't he sing any one song all the way through?"

She thought about this. "Because he's Mr. Medleyhead?"

"You didn't bring anything else?"

"No."

She went back and sat next to Martin, in silence, smelling the scent of him, as if it were odd.

For dinner there was *vitello alla salvia*, baby peas, and a pasta made with caviar. "Nipping it in the bud." Adrienne sighed. "An early frost." A fat elderly man, arriving late, pulled his chair out onto her foot, then sat down on it. She shrieked.

"Oh, dear, I'm sorry," said the man, lifting himself up as best he could.

"It's okay," said Adrienne. "I'm sure it's okay."

But the next morning, at exercises, Adrienne studied her foot closely during the leg lifts. The big toe was swollen and blue, and the nail had been loosened and set back at an odd and unhinged angle. "You're going to lose your toenail," said Kate.

"Great," said Adrienne.

"That happened to me once, during my first marriage. My husband dropped a dictionary on my foot. One of those subconscious things. Rage as very large book."

"You were married before?"

"Oh, yes." She sighed. "I had one of those rehearsal marriages, you know, where you're a feminist and train a guy, and then some *other* feminist comes along and *gets* the guy."

"I don't know." Adrienne scowled. "I think there's

something wrong with the words *feminist* and *gets the guy* being in the same sentence."

"Yes, well—"

"Were you upset?"

"Of course. But then, I'd been doing everything. I'd insisted on separate finances, on being totally self-supporting. I was working. I was doing the child care. I paid for the house; I cooked; I cleaned. I found myself shouting, 'This is feminism? Thank you, Gloria and Betty!'"

"But now you're with someone else."

"Pretaught. Self-cleaning. Batteries included."

"Someone else trained him, and you stole him."

Kate smiled. "Of course. What, am I crazy?"

"What happened to the toe?"

"The nail came off. And the one that grew back was wavy and dark and used to scare the children."

"Oh," said Adrienne.

"Why would someone publish six books on Chaucer?" Adrienne was watching Martin dress. She was also smoking a cigarette. One of the strange things about the villa was that the smokers had all quit smoking, and the nonsmokers had taken it up. People were getting in touch with their alternative selves. Bequeathed cigarettes abounded. Cartons were appearing outside people's doors.

"You have to understand academic publishing," said Martin. "No one reads these books. Everyone just agrees to publish everyone else's. It's one big circle jerk. It's a giant economic agreement. When you think about it, it probably violates the Sherman Act."

"A circle jerk?" she said uncertainly. The cigarette was making her dizzy.

"Yeah," said Martin, reknotting his tie.

"But six books on Chaucer? Why not, say, a Cat Stevens book?"

"Don't look at me," he said. "I'm in the circle."

She sighed. "Then I shall sing to you. Mood music." She

made up a romantic Asian-sounding tune, and danced around the room with her cigarette, in a floating, wing-limbed way. "This is my Hopi dance," she said. "So full of hope."

Then it was time to go to dinner.

The cockatiel now seemed used to Adrienne and would whistle twice, then fly into the back room, perch quickly on the picture frame, and wait with her for Ilke. Adrienne closed her eyes and breathed deeply, the flannel sheet pulled up under her arms, tightly, like a sarong.

Ilke's face appeared overhead in the dark, as if she were a mother just checking, peering into a crib. "How are you today?"

Adrienne opened her eyes, to see that Ilke was wearing a T-shirt that said SAY A PRAYER. PET A ROCK.

Say a prayer. "Good," said Adrienne. "I'm good." *Pet a rock.*

Ilke ran her fingers through Adrienne's hair, humming faintly.

"What is this music today?" Adrienne asked. Like Martin, she, too, had grown weary of the Mandy Patinkin tapes, all that unshackled exuberance.

"Crickets and elk," Ilke whispered.

"Crickets and elk."

"Crickets and elk and a little harp."

Ilke began to move around the table, pulling on Adrienne's limbs and pressing deep into her tendons. "I'm doing choreographed massage today," Ilke said. "That's why I'm wearing this dress."

Adrienne hadn't noticed the dress. Instead, with the lights now low, except for the illuminated clouds on the side wall, she felt herself sinking into the pools of death deep in her bones, the dark wells of loneliness, failure, blame. "You may turn over now," she heard Ilke say. And she struggled a little in the flannel sheets to do so, twisting in them, until Ilke helped her, as if she were a nurse and Adrienne someone old and sick – a stroke victim, that's what she was. She had become a stroke victim. Then lowering her face into the toweled cheek plates the table brace offered up to her ("the cradle," Ilke called it), Adrienne began quietly to cry, the deep touching of her body melting her down to some equation of animal sadness, shoe leather, and brine. She began to understand why people would want to live in these dusky nether zones, the meltdown brought on by sleep or drink or this. It seemed truer, more familiar to the soul than was the busy, complicated flash that was normal life. Ilke's arms leaned into her, her breasts brushing softly against Adrienne's head, which now felt connected to the rest of her only by filaments and strands. The body suddenly seemed a tumor on the brain, a mere means of conveyance, a wagon; the mind's go-cart now taken apart, laid in pieces on this table. "You have a knot here in your trapezius," Ilke said, kneading Adrienne's shoulder. "I can feel the belly of the knot right here," she added, pressing hard, bruising her shoulder a little, and then easing up. "Let go," she said. "Let go all the way, of everything."

"I might die," said Adrienne. Something surged in the music and she missed what Ilke said in reply, though it sounded a little like "Changes are good." Though perhaps it was "Chances aren't good." Ilke pulled Adrienne's toes, milking even the injured one, with its loose nail and leaky under-skin, and then she left Adrienne there in the dark, in the music, though Adrienne felt it was she who was leaving, like a person dying, like a train pulling away. She felt the rage loosened from her back, floating aimlessly around in her, the rage that did not know at what or whom to rage, though it continued to rage.

She awoke to Ilke's rocking her gently. "Adrienne, get up. I have another client soon."

"I must have fallen asleep," said Adrienne. "I'm sorry."

She got up slowly, got dressed, and went out into the outer room; the cockatiel whooshed out with her, grazing her head.

"I feel like I've just been strafed," she said, clutching her hair.

Ilke frowned.

"Your bird. I mean by your bird. In *there*" – she pointed

back toward the massage room – "*that* was great." She reached into her purse to pay. Ilke had moved the wicker chair to the other side of the room, so that there was no longer any place to sit down or linger. "You want lire or dollars?" she asked, and was a little taken aback when Ilke said rather firmly, "I'd prefer lire."

Ilke was bored with her. That was it. Adrienne was having a religious experience, but Ilke – Ilke was just being social. Adrienne held out the money and Ilke plucked it from her hand, then opened the outside door and leaned to give Adrienne the rushed bum's kiss – left, right – and then closed the door behind her.

Adrienne was in a fog, her legs noodly, her eyes unaccustomed to the light. Outside, in front of the *farmacìa*, if she wasn't careful, she was going to get hit by a car. How could Ilke just send people out into the busy street like that, all loose and dazed? Adrienne's body felt doughy, muddy. This was good, she supposed. Decomposition. She stepped slowly, carefully, her Martha Graham step, along the narrow walk between the street and the stores. And when she turned the corner to head back up toward the path to the Villa Hirschborn, there stood Martin, her husband, rounding a corner and heading her way.

"Hi!" she said, so pleased suddenly to meet him like this, away from what she now referred to as "the compound." "Are you going to the *farmacìa*?" she asked.

"Uh, yes," said Martin. He leaned to kiss her cheek.

"Want some company?"

He looked a little blank, as if he needed to be alone. Perhaps he was going to buy condoms.

"Oh, never mind," she said gaily. "I'll see you later, up at the compound, before dinner."

"Great," he said, and took her hand, took two steps away, and then let her hand go, gently, midair.

She walked away, toward a small park – il Giardino Leonardo – out past the station for the vaporetti. Near a particularly exuberant rhododendron sat a short, dark woman with a bright turquoise bandanna knotted around her neck. She had set up a table with a sign: CHIROMANTE: TAROT E FACCIA.

Adrienne sat down opposite her in the empty chair. "Americano," she said.

"I do faces, palms, or cards," the woman with the blue scarf said.

Adrienne looked at her own hands. She didn't want to have her face read. She lived like that already. It happened all the time at the villa, people trying to read your face – freezing your brain with stony looks and remarks made malicious with obscurity, so that you couldn't read *their* face, while they were busy reading yours. It all made her feel creepy, like a lonely head on a poster somewhere.

"The cards are the best," said the woman. "Ten thousand lire."

"Okay," said Adrienne. She was still looking at the netting of her open hands, the dried riverbed of life just sitting there. "The cards."

The woman swept up the cards, and dealt half of them out, every which way in a kind of swastika. Then, without glancing at them, she leaned forward boldly and said to Adrienne, "You are sexually unsatisfied. Am I right?"

"Is that what the cards say?"

"In a general way. You have to take the whole deck and interpret."

"What does this card say?" asked Adrienne, pointing to one with some naked corpses leaping from coffins.

"Any one card doesn't say anything. It's the whole feeling of them." She quickly dealt out the remainder of the deck on top of the other cards. "You are looking for a guide, some kind of guide, because the man you are with does not make you happy. Am I right?"

"Maybe," said Adrienne, who was already reaching for her purse to pay the ten thousand lire so that she could leave.

"I am right," said the woman, taking the money and handing Adrienne a small smudged business card. "Stop by tomorrow. Come to my shop. I have a powder."

Adrienne wandered back out of the park, past a group of tourists climbing out of a bus, back toward the Villa Hirschborn – through the gate, which she opened with her key, and up the long stone staircase to the top of the promontory. Instead of going back to the villa, she headed out through the woods toward her studio, toward the dead tufts of spiders she had memorialized in her grief. She decided to take a different path, not the one toward the studio, but one that led farther up the hill, a steeper grade, toward an open meadow at the top, with a small Roman ruin at its edge – a corner of the hill's original fortress still stood there. But in the middle of the meadow, something came over her – a balmy wind, or the heat from the uphill hike, and she took off all her clothes, lay down in the grass, and stared around at the dusky sky. To either side of her, the spokes of tree branches crisscrossed upward in a kind of cat's cradle. More directly overhead she studied the silver speck of a jet, the metallic head of its white stream like the tip of a thermometer. There were a hundred people inside this head of a pin, thought Adrienne. Or was it, perhaps, just the head of a pin? When was something truly small, and when was it a matter of distance? The branches of the trees seemed to encroach inward and rotate a little to the left, a little to the right, like something mechanical, and as she began to drift off, she saw the beautiful Spearson baby, cooing in a clown hat; she saw Martin furiously swimming in a pool; she saw the strewn beads of her own fertility, all the eggs within her, leap away like a box of tapioca off a cliff. It seemed to her that everything she had ever needed to know in her life she had known at one time or another, but she just hadn't known all those things at once, at the same time, at a single moment. They were scattered through and she had had to leave and forget one in order to get to another. A shadow fell across her, inside her, and she could feel herself retreat to that place in her bones where death was and you greeted it like an acquaintance in a room; you said hello and were then ready for whatever was next – which might be a guide, the guide that might be sent to you, the guide to lead you back out into your life again.

Someone was shaking her gently. She flickered slightly awake, to see the pale, ethereal face of a strange older woman peering down at her as if Adrienne were something odd in the bottom of a teacup. The woman was dressed all in white – white shorts, white cardigan, white scarf around her head. The guide.

"Are you . . . the *guide*?" whispered Adrienne.

"Yes, my dear," the woman said in a faintly English voice that sounded like the Good Witch of the North.

"You are?" Adrienne asked.

"Yes," said the woman. "And I've brought the group up here to view the old fort, but I was a little worried that you might not like all of us traipsing past here while you were, well – are you all right?"

Adrienne was more awake now and sat up, to see at the end of the meadow the group of tourists she'd previously seen below in the town, getting off the bus.

"Yes, thank you," mumbled Adrienne. She lay back down to think about this, hiding herself in the walls of grass, like a child hoping to trick the facts. "Oh my God," she finally said, and groped about to her left to find her clothes and clutch them, panicked, to her belly. She breathed deeply, then put them on, lying as flat to the ground as she could, hard to glimpse, a snake getting back inside its skin, a change, perhaps, of reptilian heart. Then she stood, zipped her pants, secured her belt buckle, and waved, squaring her shoulders and walking bravely past the bus and the tourists, who, though they tried not to stare at her, did stare.

By this time, everyone at the villa was privately doing imitations of everyone else. "Martin, you should announce who you're doing before you do it," said Adrienne, dressing for dinner. "I can't really tell."

"Cube-steak Yuppies!" Martin ranted at the ceiling. "Legends in their own mind! Rumors in their own room!"

"Yourself. You're doing yourself." She straightened his collar and tried to be wifely.

For dinner, there was *cioppino* and *insalata mista* and *pesce con pignoli*, a thin piece of fish like a leaf. From everywhere around the dining room, scraps of dialogue – rhetorical barbed wire, indignant and arcane – floated over toward her. "As an aesthetician, you can't not be interested in the sublime!" Or "Why, that's the most facile thing I've ever heard!" Or "Good grief, tell him about the Peasants' Revolt, would you?" But no one spoke to her directly. She had no subject, not really, not one she liked, except perhaps movies and movie stars. Martin was at a far table, his back toward her, listening to the monk man. At times like these, she thought, it was probably a good idea to carry a small hand puppet.

She made her fingers flap in her lap.

Finally, one of the people next to her turned and introduced himself. His face was poppy-seeded with whiskers, and he seemed to be looking down, watching his own mouth move. When she asked him how he liked it here so far, she received a fairly brief history of the Ottoman Empire. She nodded and smiled, and at the end, he rubbed his dark beard, looked at her compassionately, and said, "We are not good advertisements for this life. Are we?"

"There *are* a lot of dingdongs here," she admitted. He looked a little hurt, so she added, "But I like that about a place. I do."

When after dinner she went for an evening walk with Martin, she tried to strike up a conversation about celebrities and movie stars. "I keep thinking about Princess Caroline's husband being killed," she said.

Martin was silent.

"That poor family," said Adrienne. "There's been so much tragedy."

Martin glared at her. "Yes," he said facetiously. "That poor, cursed family. I keep thinking, What can I do to help? What can I do? And I think and I think, and I think so much, I'm helpless. I throw up my hands and end up doing nothing. I'm helpless!" He began to walk faster, ahead of her, down into the village. Adrienne began to run to keep up. She felt insane. Marriage, she thought, it's an institution all right.

Near the main piazza, under a streetlamp, the woman had set up her table again under the CHIROMANTE: TAROT E FACCIA sign. When she saw Adrienne, she called out, "Give me your birthday, signora, and your husband's birthday, and I will do your charts to tell you whether the two of you are compatible! Or—" She paused to study Martin skeptically as he rushed past. "Or I can just tell you right now."

"Have you been to this woman before?" Martin asked, slowing down. Adrienne grabbed his arm and started to lead him away.

"I needed a change of scenery."

Now he stopped. "Well," he said sympathetically, calmer after some exercise, "who could blame you." Adrienne took his hand, feeling a grateful, marital love – alone, in Italy, at night, in May. Was there any love that wasn't at bottom a grateful one? The moonlight glittered off the lake like electric fish, like a school of ice.

"What are you doing?" Adrienne asked Ilke the next afternoon. The lamps were particularly low, though there was a spotlight directed onto a picture of Ilke's mother, which she had placed on an end table, for the month, in honor of Mother's Day. The mother looked ghostly, like a sacrifice. What if Ilke were truly a witch? What if fluids and hairs and nails were being collected as offerings in memory of her mother?

"I'm fluffing your aura," she said. "It is very dark today, burned down to a shadowy rim." She was manipulating Adrienne's toes, and Adrienne suddenly had a horror-movie vision of Ilke with jars of collected toe juice in a closet for Satan, who, it would be revealed, *was* Ilke's mother. Perhaps Ilke would lean over suddenly and bite Adrienne's shoulder, drink her blood. How could Adrienne control these thoughts? She felt her aura fluff like the fur of a screeching cat. She imagined herself, for the first time, never coming here again. *Good-bye. Farewell.* It would be a brief affair, a little nothing; a chat on the porch at a party.

Fortunately, there were other things to keep Adrienne busy.

She had begun spray-painting the spiders, and the results

were interesting. She could see herself explaining to a dealer back home that the work represented the spider web of solitude – a vibration at the periphery reverberates inward (experiential, deafening) and the spider rushes out from the center to devour the gonger and the gong. Gone. She could see the dealer taking her phone number and writing it down on an extremely loose scrap of paper.

And there was the occasional after-dinner singsong, scholars and spouses gathered around the piano in various states of inebriation and forgetfulness. "Okay, that may be how you learned it, Harold, but that's *not* how it goes."

There was also the Asparagus Festival, which, at Carlo's suggestion, she and Kate Spalding, in one of her T-shirts – *all right, already with the T-shirts, Kate* – decided to attend. They took a hydrofoil across the lake and climbed a steep road up toward a church square. The road was long and tiring and Adrienne began to refer to it as the "Asparagus Death Walk."

"Maybe there isn't really a festival," she suggested, gasping for breath, but Kate kept walking, ahead of her.

"Go for the burn!" said Kate, who liked exercise too much.

Adrienne sighed. Up until last year, she had always thought people were saying "Go for the *bird*." Now off in the trees was the ratchety cheep of some, along with the competing hourly chimes of two churches, followed later by the single off-tone of the half hour. When she and Kate finally reached the Asparagus Festival, it turned out to be only a little ceremony where a few people bid very high prices for clutches of asparagus described as *"bello, bello,"* the proceeds from which went to the local church.

"I used to grow asparagus," said Kate on their walk back down. They were taking a different route this time, and the lake and its ocher villages spread out before them, peaceful and far away. Along the road, wildflowers grew in a pallet of pastels, like soaps.

"I could never grow asparagus," said Adrienne. As a child, her favorite food had been "asparagus with holiday sauce." "I did grow a carrot once, though. But it was so small, I just put it in a scrapbook."

"Are you still seeing Ilke?"

"This week, at any rate. How about you?"

"She's booked solid. I couldn't get another appointment. All the scholars, you know, are paying her regular visits."

"Really?"

"Oh, yes," said Kate very knowingly. "They're tense as dimes." Already Adrienne could smell the fumes of the Fiats and the ferries and delivery vans, the Asparagus Festival far away.

"Tense as dimes?"

Back at the villa, Adrienne waited for Martin, and when he came in, smelling of sandalwood, all the little deaths in her bones told her this: he was seeing the masseuse.

She sniffed the sweet parabola of his neck and stepped back. "I want to know how long you've been getting massages. Don't lie to me," she said slowly, her voice hard as a spike. Anxiety shrank his face: his mouth caved in, his eyes grew beady and scared.

"What makes you think I've been getting—" he started to say. "Well, just once or twice."

She leapt away from him and began pacing furiously about the room, touching the furniture, not looking at him. "How could you?" she asked. "You know what my going there has meant to me! How could you not tell me?" She picked up a book on the dressing table – *Industrial Relations Systems* – and slammed it back down. "How could you horn in on this experience? How could you be so furtive and untruthful?"

"I am terribly sorry," he said.

"Yeah, well, so am I," said Adrienne. "And when we get home, I want a divorce." She could see it now, the empty apartment, the bad eggplant parmigiana, all the Halloweens she would answer the doorbell, a boozy divorcée frightening the little children with too much enthusiasm for their costumes. "I feel so fucking *dishonored*!" Nothing around her seemed able to hold steady; nothing held.

Martin was silent and she was silent and then he began to

speak, in a beseeching way, there it was the beseech again, rumbling at the edge of her life like a truck. "We are both so lonely here," he said. "But I have only been waiting for you. That is all I have done for the last eight months. To try not to let things intrude, to let you take your time, to make sure you ate something, to buy the goddamn Spearsons a new picnic bench, to bring you to a place where anything at all might happen, where you might even leave me, but at least come back into life at last—"

"You did?"

"Did what?"

"You bought the Spearsons a new *picnic bench*?"

"Yes, I did."

She thought about this. "Didn't they think you were being hostile?"

"Oh . . . I think, yes, they probably thought it was hostile."

And the more Adrienne thought about it, about the poor bereaved Spearsons, and about Martin and all the ways he tried to show her he was on her side, whatever that meant, how it was both the hope and shame of him that he was always doing his best, the more she felt foolish, deprived of reasons. Her rage flapped awkwardly away like a duck. She felt as she had when her cold, fierce parents had at last grown sick and old, stick-boned and saggy, protected by infirmity the way cuteness protected a baby, or should, it should protect a baby, and she had been left with her rage – vestigial girlhood rage – inappropriate and intact. She would hug her parents good-bye, the gentle, emptied sacks of them, and think *Where did you go?*

Time, Adrienne thought. What a racket.

Martin had suddenly begun to cry. He sat at the bed's edge and curled inward, his soft, furry face in his great hard hands, his head falling downward into the bright plaid of his shirt.

She felt dizzy and turned away, toward the window. A fog had drifted in, and in the evening light the sky and the lake seemed a singular blue, like a Monet. "I've never seen you cry," she said.

"Well, I cry," he said. "I can even cry at the sports page

if the games are too close. Look at me, Adrienne. You never really look at me."

But she could only continue to stare out the window, touching her fingers to the shutters and frame. She felt far away, as if she were back home, walking through the neighborhood at dinnertime: when the cats sounded like babies and the babies sounded like birds, and the fathers were home from work, their children in their arms gumming the language, air shaping their flowery throats into a park of singing. Through the windows wafted the smell of cooking food.

"We are with each other now," Martin was saying. "And in the different ways it means, we must try to make a life."

Out over the Sfondrata chapel tower, where the fog had broken, she thought she saw a single star, like the distant nose of a jet; there were people in the clayey clouds. She turned, and for a moment it seemed they were all there in Martin's eyes, all the absolving dead in residence in his face, the angel of the dead baby shining like a blazing creature, and she went to him, to protect and encircle him, seeking the heart's best trick, *oh, terrific heart.* "Please, forgive me," she said.

And he whispered, "Of course. It is the only thing. Of course."

1992

THANK YOU FOR HAVING ME

THE DAY FOLLOWING Michael Jackson's death, I was constructing my own memorial for him. I played his videos on YouTube and sat in the kitchen at night, with the iPod light at the table's center the only source of illumination. I listened to "Man in the Mirror" and "Ben," my favorite, even if it was about a killer rat. I tried not to think about its being about a rat, as it was also the name of an old beau, who had e-mailed me from Istanbul upon hearing of Jackson's death. Apparently there was no one in Turkey to talk about it with. "When I heard the news of MJackson's death I thought of you," the ex-beau had written, "and that sweet, loose-limbed dance you used to do to one of his up-tempo numbers."

I tried to think positively. "Well, at least Whitney Houston didn't die," I said to someone on the phone. Every minute that ticked by in life contained very little information, until suddenly it contained too much.

"Mom, what are you doing?" asked my fifteen-year-old daughter, Nickie. "You look like a crazy lady sitting in the kitchen like this."

"I'm just listening to some music."

"But like this?"

"I didn't want to disturb you."

"You are so totally disturbing me," she said.

Nickie had lately announced a desire to have her own reality show so that the world could see what she had to put up with.

I pulled out the earbuds. "What are you wearing tomorrow?"

"Whatever. I mean, does it matter?"

"Uh, no. Not really." Nickie sauntered out of the room. Of course it did not matter what young people wore: they were already amazing looking, without really knowing it, which was also part of their beauty. I was going to be Nickie's date at the wedding of Maria, her former babysitter, and Nickie was going to be mine. The person who needed to be careful what she wore was me.

It was a wedding in the country, a half-hour drive, and we arrived on time, but somehow we seemed the last ones there. Guests milled about semipurposefully. Maria, an attractive, restless Brazilian, was marrying a local farm boy, for the second time – a second farm boy on a second farm. The previous farm boy she had married, Ian, was present as well. He had been hired to play music, and as the guests floated by with their plastic cups of wine, Ian sat there playing a slow melancholic version of "I Want You Back." Except he didn't seem to want her back. He was smiling and nodding at everyone and seemed happy to be part of this send-off. He was the entertainment. He wore a T-shirt that read, THANK YOU FOR HAVING ME. This seemed remarkably sanguine and useful as well as a little beautiful. I wondered how it was done. I myself had never done anything remotely similar. "Marriage is one long conversation," wrote Robert Louis Stevenson. Of course, he died when he was forty-four, so he had no idea how long the conversation could really get to be.

"I can't believe you wore that," Nickie whispered to me in her mauve eyelet sundress.

"I know. It probably was a mistake." I was wearing a synthetic leopard-print sheath: I admired camouflage. A leopard's markings I'd imagined existed because a leopard's habitat had once been alive with snakes, and blending in was required. Leopards were frightened of snakes and also of chimpanzees, who were in turn frightened of leopards – a standoff between predator and prey, since there was a confusion as to which was which: this was also a theme in the wilds of my closet. Perhaps I had watched too many nature documentaries.

"Maybe you could get Ian some lemonade," I said to Nickie. I had already grabbed some wine from a passing black plastic tray.

"Yes, maybe I could," she said and loped across the yard. I watched her broad tan back and her confident gait. She was a gorgeous giantess. I was in awe to have such a daughter. Also in fear – as in fearful for my life.

"It's good you and Maria have stayed friends," I said to Ian. Ian's father, who had one of those embarrassing father-in-law crushes on his son's departing wife, was not taking it so well. One could see him misty-eyed, treading the edge of the property with some iced gin, keeping his eye out for Maria, waiting for her to come out of the house, waiting for an opening, when she might be free of others, so he could rush up and embrace her.

"Yes." Ian smiled. Ian sighed. And for a fleeting moment everything felt completely fucked up.

And then everything righted itself again. It felt important spiritually to go to weddings: to give balance to the wakes and memorial services. People shouldn't have been set in motion on this planet only to grieve losses. And without weddings there were only funerals. I had seen a soccer mom become a rhododendron with a plaque, next to the soccer field parking lot, as if it had been watching all those matches that had killed her. I had seen a brilliant young student become a creative writing contest, as if it were all that writing that had been the thing to do him in. And I had seen a public defender become a justice fund, as if one paid for fairness with one's very life. I had seen a dozen people become hunks of rock with their names engraved so shockingly perfectly upon the surface it looked as if they had indeed turned to stone, been given a new life the way the moon is given it, through some lighting tricks and a face-like font. I had turned a hundred Rolodex cards around to their blank sides. So let a babysitter become a bride again. Let her marry over and over. So much urgent and lifelike love went rumbling around underground and died there, never got expressed at all, so let some errant inconvenient attraction have its way. There was so little time.

Someone very swanky and tall and in muddy high heels in the grass was now standing in front of Ian, holding a microphone, and singing "Waters of March" while Ian accompanied. My mind imitated the song by wandering: A stick. A stone. A wad of cow pie. A teary mom's eye.

"There are a bazillion Brazilians here," said Nickie, arriving with two lemonades.

"What did you expect?" I took one of the lemonades for Ian and put my arm around her.

"I don't know. I only ever met her sister. Just once. The upside is at least I'm not the only one wearing a color."

We gazed across the long yard of the farmhouse. Maria's sister and her mother were by the rosebushes, having their pictures taken without the bride.

"Maria and her sister both look like their mother." Her mother and I had met once before, and I now nodded in her direction across the yard. I couldn't tell if she could see me.

Nickie nodded with a slight smirk. "Their father died in a car crash. So yeah, they don't look like him."

I swatted her arm. "Nickie. Sheesh."

She was silent for a while. "Do you ever think of Dad?"

"Dad who?"

"Come on."

"You mean, Dad-eeeeee?"

The weekend her father left – left the house, the town, the country, everything, packing so lightly I believed he would come back – he had said, "You can raise Nickie by yourself. You'll be good at it."

And I had said, "Are you on crack?" And he had replied, continuing to fold a blue twill jacket, "Yes, a little."

"Dadder. As in *badder*," Nickie said now. She sometimes claimed to friends that her father had died, and when she was asked how, she would gaze bereavedly off into the distance and say, "A really, really serious game of Hangman." Mothers and their only children of divorce were a skewed family dynamic, if they were families at all. Perhaps they were more like cruddy buddy movies, and the dialogue between them was unrecognizable as filial or parental. It was extraterrestrial. With a streak of dog-walkers-meeting-at-the-park. It contained more sibling banter than it should have. Still, I preferred the whole thing to being a lonely old spinster, the fate I once thought I was most genetically destined for, though I'd worked hard, too hard, to defy and avoid it, when perhaps there it lay ahead of me regardless. If you were alone when you were born, alone when you were dying, *really absolutely* alone when you were dead, why "learn to be alone" in between? If you had forgotten, it would quickly come back to you. Aloneness was like riding a bike. At gunpoint. With the gun in your own hand. Aloneness was the air in your tires, the wind in your hair. You didn't have to go looking for it with open arms. With open arms, you fell off the bike: I was drinking my wine too quickly.

Maria came out of the house in her beautiful shoulderless wedding dress, which was white as could be.

"What a fantastic costume," said Nickie archly.

Nickie was both keen observer and enthusiastic participant in the sartorial disguise department, and when she was little there had been much playing of Wedding, fake bridal bouquets made of ragged plastic-handled sponges tossed up into the air and often into the garage basketball hoop, catching there. She was also into Halloween. She would trick-or-treat for UNICEF dressed in a sniper outfit or a suicide bomber outfit replete with vest. Once when she was eight, she went as a dryad, a tree nymph, and when asked at doors what she was, she kept saying, "A tree-nip." She had been a haughty trick-or-treater, alert to the failed adult guessing game of it – *you're a what? a vampire*? – so when the neighbors looked confused, she scowled and said reproachfully, "Have you *never* studied Greek mythology?" Nickie knew how to terrify. She had sometimes been more interested in answering our own door than in knocking on others, peering around the edge of it with a witch hat and a loud cackle. "I think it's time to get back to the customers," she announced to me one Halloween when she was five, grabbing my hand and racing back to our house. She was fearless: she had always chosen the peanut allergy table at school since a boy she liked sat there – the cafeteria version of *The Magic Mountain*. Nickie's childhood, like all dreams, sharpened artificially into stray vignettes when I tried to conjure it, then faded away entirely. Now tall and long-limbed and inscrutable, she seemed more than ever like a sniper. I felt paralyzed beside her, and the love I had for her was less for this new spiky Nickie than for the old spiky one, which was still inside her somewhere, though it was a matter of faith to think so. Surely that was why faith had been invented: to raise teenagers without dying. Although of course it was also why death was invented: to escape teenagers altogether. When, in the last few months, Nickie had "stood her ground" in various rooms of the house, screaming at me abusively, I would begin mutely to disrobe, slowly lifting my shirt over my head so as not to see her, and only that would send her flying out of the room in disgust. Only nakedness was silencing, but at least something was.

"I can't believe Maria's wearing white," said Nickie.

I shrugged. "What color should she wear?"

"Gray!" Nickie said immediately. "To acknowledge having a brain! A little gray matter!"

"Actually, I saw something on PBS recently that said only the outer bark of the brain – and it does look like bark – is gray. Apparently the other half of the brain has a lot of white matter. For connectivity."

Nickie snorted, as she often did when I uttered the letters *PBS*. "Then she should wear gray in acknowledgment of having half a brain."

I nodded. "I get your point," I said.

Guests were eating canapés on paper plates and having their pictures taken with the bride. Not so much with Maria's new groom, a boy named Hank, which was short not for Henry but for Johannes, and who was not wearing sunglasses like everyone else but was sort of squinting at Maria in pride and disbelief. Hank was also a musician, though he mostly repaired banjos and guitars, restrung and varnished them, and that was how he, Maria, and Ian had all met.

Now the air was filled with the old-silver-jewelry smell of oncoming rain. I edged toward Ian, who was looking for the next song, idly strumming, trying not to watch his father eye Maria.

"Whatcha got? 'I'll Be There'?" I asked cheerfully. I had always liked Ian. He had chosen Maria like a character, met her on a semester abroad and then come home already married to her – much to the marveling of his dad. Ian loved Maria, and was always loyal to her, no matter what story she was in, but Maria was a narrative girl and the story had to be spellbinding or she lost interest in the main character, who was sometimes herself and sometimes not. She was destined to marry and marry and marry. Ian smiled and began to sing "I Will Always Love You," sounding oddly like Bob Dylan but without the sneer.

I swayed. I stayed. I did not get in the way.

"You are a saint," I said when he finished. He was a sweet boy, and when Nickie was little he had often come over and played soccer in the yard with her and Maria.

"Oh no, I'm just a deposed king of corn. She bought the farm. I mean, I sold it to her, and then she flipped it and bought this one instead." He motioned toward the endless field beyond the tent, where the corn was midget and standing in mud, June not having been hot enough to evaporate the puddles. The tomatoes and marijuana would not do well this year. "Last night I had a dream that I was in *West Side Story* and had forgotten all the words to 'I like to be in America.' Doesn't take a genius to figure that one out."

"No," I said. "I guess not."

"Jesus, what is my dad *doing*?" Ian said, looking down and away.

Ian's father was still prowling the perimeter, a little drunkenly, not taking his eyes off the bride.

"The older generation," I said, shaking my head, as if it didn't include me. "They can't take any change. There's too much missingness that has already accumulated. They can't take any more."

"Geez," Ian said, glancing up and over again. "I wish my dad would just get over her."

I swallowed more wine while holding Ian's lemonade. Over by the apple tree there were three squirrels. A threesome of squirrels looked ominous, like a plague. "What other songs ya got?" I asked him. Nickie was off talking to Johannes Hank.

"I have to save a couple for the actual ceremony."

"There's going to be an actual ceremony?"

"Sort of. Maybe not *actual* actual. They have things they want to recite to each other."

"Oh yes, that," I said.

"They're going to walk up together from this canopy toward the house, say whatever, and then people get to eat." Everyone had brought food, and it was spread out on a long table between the house and the barn. I had brought two large roaster chickens, cooked accidentally on Clean while I was listening to Michael Jackson on my iPod. But the chickens had looked OK, I thought: hanging off the bone a bit but otherwise fine, even if not as fine as when they had started and had been Amish and air-chilled and a fortune. When I had bought them the day before at Whole Foods and gasped at the total on my receipt, the cashier had said, "Yes. Some people know how to shop here and some people don't."

"Thirty-three thirty-three. Perhaps that's good luck."

"Yup. It's about as lucky as two dead birds get to be," said the cashier.

"Is there a priest or anything? Will the marriage be legal?" I now asked Ian.

Ian smiled and shrugged.

"They're going to say 'You do' after the other one says 'I do.' Double indemnity."

I put his lemonade down on a nearby table and gave him a soft chuck on the shoulder. We both looked across the yard at Hank, who was wearing a tie made of small yellow pop beads that formed themselves into the shape of an ear of corn. It had ingeniousness and tackiness both, like so much else created by people.

"That's a lot of *dos*."

"I know. But I'm not making a beeline for the jokes."

"The jokes?"

"The doozy one, the do-do one. I'm not going to make any of them."

"Why would you make jokes? It's not like you're the best man."

Ian looked down and twisted his mouth a little.

"Oh, dear. You *are*?" I said. I squinted at him. When young I had practiced doing the upside-down wink of a bird.

"Don't ask," he said.

"Hey, look." I put my arm around him. "George Harrison did it. And no one thought twice. Or, well, no one thought more than twice."

Nickie approached me quickly from across the grass. "Mom. Your chickens look disgusting. It's like they were hit by a truck."

The wedding party had started to line up – except Ian, who had to play. They were going to get this ceremony over with quickly, before the storm clouds to the west drifted near and made things worse. The bridesmaids began stepping first, a short trajectory from the canopy to the rosebushes, where the *I do*s would be said. Ian played "Here Comes the Bride." The bridesmaids were in pastels: one the light peach of baby aspirin; one the seafoam green of low-dose clonazepam; the other the pale daffodil of the next lowest dose of clonazepam. What a good idea to have the look of Big Pharma at your wedding. Why hadn't I thought of that? Why hadn't I thought of that until now?

"I take thee, dear Maria . . ." They were uttering these promises themselves just as Ian said they would. Hank said, "I do," and Maria said, "You do." Then vice versa. At least Maria had taken off her sunglasses. *Young people*, I tried not to say out loud with a sigh. Time went slowly, then stood still, then became undetectable, so who knew how long all this was taking?

A loud noise like mechanized thunder was coming from the highway. Strangely, it was not a storm. A group of motorcyclists boomed up the road and, instead of roaring by us, slowed, then turned right in at the driveway, a dozen of them – all on Harleys. I didn't really know motorcycles, but I knew that every biker from Platteville to Manitowoc owned a Harley. That was just a regional fact. They switched off their engines. None of the riders wore a helmet – they wore bandannas – except for the leader, who wore a football helmet with some plush puppy ears which had been snipped from some child's stuffed animal then glued on either side. He took out a handgun and fired it three times into the air.

Several guests screamed. I could make no sound at all.

The biker with the gun and the puppy ears began to shout. "I have a firearms license and those were blanks and this is self-defense because our group here has an easement that extends just this far into this driveway. Also? We were abused as children and as adults and moreover we have been eating a hell of a lot of Twinkies. Also? We are actually very peaceful people. We just know that life can get quite startling in its switches of channels. That there is a river and sea figure of speech as well as a TV one. Which is why as life moves rudely past, you have to give it room. We understand that. An occasion like this means No More Forks in the Road. All mistakes are behind you, and that means it's no longer really possible to make one. Not a big one. You already done that. I need to speak first here to the bride." He looked around, but no one moved. He cleared his throat a bit. "The errors a person already made can step forward and announce themselves and then freeze themselves into a charming little sculpture garden that can no longer hurt you. Like a cemetery. And like a cemetery it is the kind of freedom that is the opposite of free." He looked in a puzzled way across the property toward Maria. "It's the flickering quantum zone of gun and none, got and not." He shifted uncomfortably, as if the phrase "flickering quantum zone" had taken a lot out of him. "As I said, now I need to speak to the bride. Would that be you?"

Maria shouted at him in Portuguese. Her bridesmaids joined in.

"What are they saying?" I murmured to Nickie.

"I forgot all my Portuguese," she said. "My whole childhood I only remember Maria saying 'good job' to everything I did, so I now think of that as Portuguese."

"Yes," I murmured. "So do I."

"Good job!" Nickie shouted belligerently at the biker. "Good job being an asshole and interrupting a wedding!"

"Nickie, leave this to the grown-ups," I whispered.

But the guests just stood there, paralyzed, except Ian, who, seemingly very far off on the horizon, slowly stood, placing his guitar on the ground. He then took his white collapsible chair in both hands and raised it over his head.

"Are you Caitlin?" The puppy-eared biker continued to address Maria, and she continued to curse, waving her sprigs of mint and spirea at him. *"Và embora, babaca!"* She gave him the finger, and when Hank tried to calm her, she gave Hank the finger. *"Fodase!"*

The cyclist looked around with an expression that suggested he believed he might have the wrong country wedding. He took out his cell phone, took off his helmet, pressed someone on speed dial, then turned to speak into it. "Yo! Joe. I don't think you gave me the right address . . . yeah . . . no, you don't get it. This ain't Caitlin's place. . . . What? No, listen! What I'm saying is: wrong addressee! This ain't it. No speaky zee English here—" He slammed his phone shut. He put his helmet back on. But Ian was trotting slowly toward him with the chair over his head, crying the yelping cry of anyone who was trying to be a hero at his ex-wife's wedding.

"Sorry, people," the biker said. He gave the approaching Ian only a quick unfazed double-take. He flicked one of his puppy ears at him and hurried to straddle his bike. "Wrong address, everybody!" Then his whole too-stoned-to-be-menacing gang started up their engines and rode away in a roar, kicking up dust from the driveway gravel. It was a relief to see them go. Ian continued to run down the road after them, howling, chair overhead, though the motorcycles were quickly out of sight.

"Should we follow Ian?" asked Nickie. Someone near us was phoning the police.

"Let Ian get it out of his system," I said.

"Yeah," she said and now made a beeline for Maria.

"Good job!" I could hear Nickie say to Maria. "Good job getting married!" And then Nickie threw her arms around her former caretaker and began, hunched and heaving, to weep on her shoulder. I couldn't bear to watch. There was a big black zigzag across my heart. I could hear Maria say,

"Tank you for combing, Nickie. You and your muzzer are my hairos."

Ian had not returned and no one had gone looking for him. He would be back in time for the rain. There was a rent-a-disc-jockey who started to put on some music, which blared from the speakers. Michael Jackson again. Every day there was something new to mourn and something old to celebrate: civilization had learned this long ago and continued to remind us. Was that what the biker had meant? I moved toward the buffet table.

"You know, when you're hungry, there's nothing better than food," I said to a perfect stranger. I cut a small chunk of ham. I placed a deviled egg in my mouth and resisted the temptation to position it in front of my teeth and smile scarily, the way we had as children. I chewed and swallowed and grabbed another one. Soon no doubt I would resemble a large vertical snake who had swallowed a rat. That rat Ben. Snakes would eat a sirloin steak only if it was disguised behind the head of a small rodent. There was a lesson somewhere in there and just a little more wine would reveal it.

"Oh, look at those sad chickens!" I said ambiguously and with my mouth full. There were rumors that the wedding cake was still being frosted and that it would take a while. A few people were starting to dance, before the dark clouds burst open and ruined everything. Next to the food table was a smaller one displaying a variety of insect repellents, aerosols and creams, as if it were the vanity corner of a posh ladies' room, except with discrete constellations of gnats. Guests were spraying themselves a little too close to the food, and the smells of citronella and imminent rain combined in the air.

The biker was right: you had to unfreeze your feet, take blind steps backward, risk a loss of balance, risk an endless fall, in order to give life room. Was that what he had said? Who knew? People were shaking their bodies to Michael Jackson's "Shake Your Body." I wanted this song played at my funeral. Also the Doobie Brothers' "Takin' It to the Streets." Also "Have Yourself a Merry Little Christmas" – just to fuck with people.

I put down my paper plate and plastic wineglass. I looked over at Ian's dad, who was once again brooding off by himself. "Come dance with someone your own age!" I called to him, and because he did not say, "That is so not going to happen," I approached him from across the lawn. As I got closer I could see that since the days he would sometimes come to our house to pick up Maria and drive her home himself in the silver sports car of the recently single, he had had some eye work done: a lift to remove the puff and bloat; he would rather look startled and insane than look fifty-six. I grabbed both his hands and reeled him around. "Whoa," he said with something like a smile, and he let go with one hand to raise it over his head and flutter it in a jokey jazz razzamatazz. In sign language it was the sign for applause. I needed my breath for dancing, so I tried not to laugh. Instead I fixed my face into a grin, and, ah, for a second the sun came out to light up the side of the red and spinning barn.

2013

TO FILL

THERE IS NO DIGNITY in appetites. That blanched pathetic look at salad bars, those scramblers for some endless consumption I am no exception. I was raised on Ward's catalogs god those toys and shorts sets everything, everything, wonderfully turquoise. I moaned for the large black olives of restaurants, the fancy chunky dressings. I pined like a toad at gumball machines. And now, at thirty-five, I have stolen money, for no other reason than this nameless, bullying ache. A blistery rash has crept up out of my mouth, red and slick, making my face look vaguely genital, out of control. I have a recent tic at the eye, at the outer corner, something fluttering, trying to scamper away.

My mother has convinced herself she is physically and mentally ill and has checked into St. Veronica's, although the doctors don't know what to do with her. With my stolen money I buy her things, I buy me things. In stores, in front of nuns, embarrassingly, I twitch and perspire with a sort of jazz, an improvised rhythm, unpredictable, hungry.

In the cool arterial corridors of St. Veronica's, doors swing open and shut, open and shut like valves. I am big, an overweight, natural dirt blonde with a nervous rash and think somehow this will keep nuns from harassing me I am a bit afraid of them. Out of deference, I wear a bra and no eyeshadow.

As I pass Sister Mary Marian at reception I nod and smile and then feel my face contort: the stench is worse than yesterday, an acrid medley of something like ether and old cantaloupe good god Mother how can you stand it here.

I am intent on getting her out. I have brought her a new Chinese cookbook and a wok and carry them wrapped in orange paper in a huge box in front of me. Yesterday I brought her a deep violet evening gown. You have a whole life ahead of you, I said, holding it up and dancing it around, and she stared at me acidly from her pillow, unblinking, quietly chewing gum.

Again today I head for the swinging doors. Open and shut. That's what the store detectives will say good god I must really stop this. Excuse me, I say to a brigade of wheelchairers trundling by, groggy and pale with mobile IV's. Excuse me oh god pardon me. I am awkward in the elevator. Everywhere there are nuns. I am not Catholic, but I have been to too many Baptist potlucks.

My mother sits up briskly, unsmiling. Now, what the devil is this? she asks. She has been lying on her back, clipping coupons from the *Inquirer*, a good sign, practicality.

How are you feeling today, Mother? I set the wok down by her bed. My eye begins to fidget.

What the devil is this now? she asks again. Another gift?

Ma, I just wanted you to see—

Can't keep these things here, Riva, she interrupts curtly. Can't keep all these things.

Well bring them home, Ma. Come on. You really don't need to be in this hospital anymore. The doctors all agree. It's up to you.

She looks away, then with scissors begins retrimming the coupons more closely along the dotted lines. Slivers of newsprint fall to her sheets. She says nothing.

Look, I say, if you don't want to go back to your apartment, you can come stay with Tom and me for a few weeks or so. I pause.

She stops cutting, glares up at me, and scowls: Who is this Tom guy anyway?

Tom, my husband of six years, has lately been a frequent casualty of her feigned senility. Mother, I say calmly. Tom has been my husband for six years, now you know that, and I wish you would just cut all of this out.

At this she grows especially dotty and waves her scissors at me, making little snips in the air.

You don't need to be here, I sniff, unconvinced. Besides, it smells in this place.

The scissors freeze solemnly, dramatically, in front of her face.

Riva, that's no way to talk about a good Catholic hospital. She looks away again, histrionic. I hate it, I hate it when she does this.

Whatever happened to that Phillip someone you were seeing all those years why, she sighs, we thought for sure you'd settle down and have us over for fondue on Thursdays my he was a sweet boy.

I cannot, cannot go through this again. Not today. I grab my bag and start for the door. When did my mother become such a loon?

There's a great recipe for Garlic Snow Peas in there, I say. You should take a look. A silver-toothed redhead who also shares the room, whips back her bed curtain, grins, and blows me a kiss good-bye. Gaga. They're all gaga here. My mother is shouting after me: Damn it who is this Tom guy anyway? Two nuns arrive, always, always in pairs, to calm her down.

> *I drive home. I drive the car home and think of you, Phil, faraway and invisible, even my mother speaking of you, as does this sad ache, thoughts of you, you are thoughts, springing up everywhere. The French for* plateful *also means state of mind – you wrote that on a postcard from Provence. I have it in a box somewhere. O Riva, you are a woman of whims and cravings, you said that of me, calling me expansive. You live, you said, you live from the twinges in your hips.*

I have stolen money. I have stolen money from the Leigenbaum's department store where I am manager of Scarves and Handbags. I do it with the returns. The inventory count is always clumsy, so I can take one return on a bag or scarf and double it, there are perforated receipts for both, and I can make the amount of the return and still refund the customer his money. The registers come out even, the books balance. I often stay late and alone to make sure. In a week I can make from two hundred to four hundred dollars, depending on the returns, depending on the twinges in my hips. It has been three weeks now. Ever since Mardi Gras. No one knows. I get ravenous. I buy things.

Tom is in insurance. He also likes to buy policies for himself. We have many, many policies. I have three lifes and two autos. He has four lifes, two autos, two fire and thefts, three hospital and accidents, and two mutilated limb and/or organs. One eye equals three right fingers and a thumb, says the policy. We also have something yellow with a diamond and fur clause. We sleep well at night. Unless it is raining or we've had a fight or Jeffrey is sick – then we toss like dinghies.

Why is Tom looking at me funny this evening does he suspect?

He says: How was work?

I say: Fine. How about you?

He says: Fine. Baker's coming in from Pittsburgh tomorrow to discuss the sectional meeting.

I say: Well, that will be nice. Shall I expect him for dinner?

He says: Nah, 'sgotta fly back right away. We'll grab something in Center City.

I say: Fine.

He says: What's bugging Jeffrey? Is it nursery school?

I say: I think it's his dancing class. No big deal. He's just getting behind or lost or something.

He says: Is that what his teacher told you?

I say: No, Jeffrey mentioned it. For no reason I add: He's a good honest kid.

He says: Well, what's the problem? Has he missed classes or what?

I say: Look, he's just a little frustrated trying to remember some of the steps. I really think that's all it is.

He says: Hell, why's a kid his age gotta take a goddamn pre-school dance class, anyway?

And I say: Because it's a fucking international law, why do you think?

And that's when Tom calls me hostile and says I've been snapping at him for weeks and I say, look, he's your son and if you don't encourage him early in some sort of meaningful aesthetic endeavor, he'll end up on the streets killing hubcaps and stealing prostitutes and Tom smiles slightly and says don't you have that backwards and I say Tom sometimes you really just miss the point of life sometimes you are an inexpressibly hollow, hollow man, you don't know a damn about what's important in this world and that's when he looks at me aghast and I realize I have sprung a leak somewhere and as he calls Riva please come back here I run upstairs to the bay window and hide behind my new floor-length half-silk drapes I bought just last week with the money, the money, breathing into the smooth seamless backing they smell new, new, because I really don't know myself now what it is I'm talking about, but it must be something, this jittery pang, this space, this hole must have a name I wonder what it is who is this Tom guy anyway?

A dream. A dream is like a church, cool and dark and wood and brass, the jeweled jelly-jar windows a place to scurry into from off the street in the night I dreamed of you, Phil. You stood before me and undressed, then sinking into me nuzzling with the perfect bone of your chin, the perfect O of your mouth, humming to the Bruckner or the Mahler, I didn't know, it was a name that made me think of the Bronx, and your face beneath me, close and closed and traveling briefly opened, smiling up at me, huge trembling me, and whispered: Oh the largeness.

How we loved each other with forks.

The woman in the health food store I believe is slowly losing her mind. Every time I go in there she is slumped on the wooden stool behind the register more dazed, more sad than before. She recognizes me less. Today I am the only one in there and when I say excuse me, can I get two pounds of bulgar wheat, she continues to stare at the coconut shampoos, her legs frozen and crossed, her back a curved mound beneath the same pink-gray sweater she drapes like a small cape over her shoulders. Finally she says huh but never looks up.

Bulgar wheat? I say gently. Coarse? Like last week?

Yeah. She pulls at the sweater, then goes through some sort of pelvic swivel which tilts the stool just enough to spill her down and out of it. She scuffs around the counter to the bulgar wheat, reaches for a scoop, a paper bag, and then bursts into sobs. I try to think of what to do. I quickly grab three coconut shampoos to help out her business a little and then go to her, put my arm around her, and tell her about Tom's secret affair last year in Scranton and how I visited him there as a surprise and learned of the whole thing and got drunk and stuck postage stamps all over myself and tried to mail myself home, that always cheers people up when I tell it in Scarves and Handbags. She smiles, shuffles over to the register, charges me for four not three coconut shampoos and the bulgar wheat.

I walk toward the car.

A basset hound caroms dizzily up the sidewalk ahead of me, peeing on everything.

Today I am taking Jeffrey alias Batman to visit my mother. Although he is officially too young to visit, he has won Sister Mary Marian's heart by asking her if she were his fairy godmother and she, quite enthralled with this idea, now lies incorrigibly, telling everyone that he's regulation exempt, it's fine he can go in. These are the kind of nuns I like.

Mother places the chocolate Last Supper I have paid twenty dollars for disinterestedly at the foot of the bed and reaches jubilantly for Jeffrey. Come see Gramma, she sings.

Hi Gramma, he chirps obediently and climbs up into her arms in his cape and mask, he is such a good kid. There are so many funny fairies here at your house, Gramma, he continues.

My mother shifts her feet uncomfortably beneath the covers and the Last Supper cracks onto the floor.

Well, Jeffrey dear, have you been well?

Jeffrey's head does two full expressionless bobs.

Mother tosses a look at me which for some reason seems to say: How did you and this Tom ever manage such a lovely child?

She continues: How do you like going to nursery school, Jeffrey?

Jeffrey looks at her with sudden interest, his eyes behind his mask wide as soft-boiled eggs. He pauses, then warbles: Back and forth, back and forth.

Tell Gramma, Jeffrey, what the strange clothes are that you have on today.

I'm Batman, says Jeffrey.

You're Batman?! squeals my delighted mother.

Yup, he says, and shapes his fingers into a gun and pulls the trigger, blowing off her face. Bang, he says.

She is startled. Now Jeffrey dear, you don't mean that, she coos nervously, taking his little hand and gently, quietly, returning it to his lap. It flies back up with a fierce quickness. Jeffrey looks at her face, her sour-breath face, and doesn't smile. Bang, he says again from behind the mask, the finger curling slowly, firmly. Bang.

You love once, I told you. Even when you love over and over again it is the same once, the same one. And you sent me your recipes – Ezra Pound Cake, Beef Mallarmé – and you wrote: Do you think if you eat one meal, every meal after that is the same meal, just because it too is a meal? And I said some are the same meal.

In the hospital cafeteria Jeffrey asks me if he can have a BB gun. He is eating around the crusts of his bologna sandwich, pulling out the lettuce and dropping it unsurreptitiously onto the floor.

Of course not, I say. Take your mask off while you're eating. He obeys.

Why on earth do you want a BB gun?

He shrugs his shoulders. I dunno, he says and I can hear his legs swinging beneath the table, his sneakers hitting the aluminum, vibrating his Jello-O. Dad'll let me.

No, he won't, Jeffrey, now that's the end of it.

He thinks about this for a while. Can I have some ice cream, then?

No. Finish your sandwich.

Can I . . . (now he's just thinking up any old thing) . . . take this home with me? He holds up a plastic fork.

Good god. All right.

Goody, he says.

Tuesday at work I have to yell at Amahara. She has mispriced all the Italian clutches.

Big deal, bubbleass, she mutters into her own right shoulder.

One more crack like that, Amahara, and you're through.

I didn't say nothing, she protests, wickedly wide-eyed.

Just watch it. My voice is scraping, ugly, it unnerves me. I go back out on the floor and re-mark the bags myself. It is a thankless, mechanical chore, tag after tag, one after another. The Italian clutches have brassy leering clasps and I can see myself in them, muzzy and sickeningly golden. I am suddenly embarrassed to be marking up such flimsy merchandise.

I leave early not even checking the afternoon's returns, pick up Batman from nursery school, drive home, and lying in bed later ask Tom if he thinks I have a big ass like a bubble and he says no.

When I'm working at the store, Jeffrey stays at Mr. Fernandez's nursery school on Spruce Street. He is a former aging hippie who became a panhandler outside the art museum where I met him, years ago, when I was trying to get pregnant. He thought I was Tricia Nixon and vociferously demanded a quarter. When I failed to drop one into his coffee can because I was looking at a brochure on Cézanne's *The Great Bathers*, he started hissing things at me.

Excuse me? I said, stopping on the stairs to look at him. I was disoriented after so much post-impressionism. And then he knew, glancing up at me, that he had it all wrong. Too big, he said. Too big. I'm sorry. I thought you were Tricia Nixon. And that's when he got up and walked over to me, a dusky, swaying man, and said in a slight accent: Geeze lady, I'm really sorry. He extended his right hand and I shook it, putting away the brochure, and then we talked a bit, he about the eighteenth-century Chippendale commode in the English wing, and I about him, asking what he was doing with his life, why he was here. He merely smiled sadly, I suppose the truest sort of explanation he could muster, and said what he would really like to do is raise a family and how envious he was of me, still young and newly pregnant and—

And I said: Pregnant? What makes you say that? (Sometimes I am sensitive about my size.)

And then he became even more apologetic and said, well, that it was just a way he had, a witchiness, but not a bad witchiness, and he just knew these things.

And sure enough eight months later Batman flew out, and Mr. Fernandez, newly scrubbed and reformed, the beneficiary of ten thousand dollars from a dead Ohio cousin and of manicure advice from me, threw a giant shower and gave me a yellow horse pinata never to be whacked open but simply to hang in Jeffrey's room, a lesson in hope and greed and peaceful coexistence, and it has been there ever since. And Mr. Fernandez has successfully opened a nursery school on Spruce Street called Pinata Pre-School, and only I, not even Tom, know of his museum-step past and I have promised not to divulge it, and he has hugged me gratefully on several occasions and we have become quite close friends and he is really so good, so good with children.

Amahara and I had drinks at lunch today. I guess we are on speaking terms again. We sent to La Kommissary and she told me about a guy she went out with this weekend.

He's not interested in what's inside, complains Amahara. I want a guy who wants my heart, you know? I want him to look for my heart.

You know when he's fumbling with your breasts? I flutter my eyes at Amahara. He's looking for your heart. They all do that.

What a bitter hag I have become.

Amahara grins. He's really into orange.

But what does that mean, into orange?

Like really into it. She smiles enigmatically.

The color?

Yeah. Really into it.

But what do you mean? His car? His hair? Your hair?

His life, she says dramatically. He's really into it.

Into it, I repeat dumbly, believing I am trying to understand; what is wrong with me, I thought we were on speaking terms, what are speaking terms am I on them with anyone am I from outer space, is she?

I can't believe, I say firmly, hoping it will pass, that a person could be so into it.

For damn sure, says Amahara.

I pick up the check. Amahara goes for her wallet, but I say nope, it's on me, I'm into it.

Intuit, you said, blowing out the candle. Intuition is the secret life of fat cells. And then you burrowed into me, whispering your questions.

I am becoming hugely depressed. Like last year. Just a month ago I was better, sporting a simpler, terse sort of disenchantment, a neat black vest of sadness. Elegant ironies leaped from my mouth fine as *cuisses de grenouilles*. Now the darkness sleeps and wakes in me daily like an Asian carnivore at the Philly zoo.

In my little white house I am in a slump. I look around. All these possessions, all these new things, are little teeth, death markers, my home one compact little memorial park remember when they used to be called cemeteries. Now even gravestones are called family monuments, like these things, monuments to the family. I stare at my gold faucets, my new chairs, my popcorn popper, and my outsized spice rack – thyme leaves, time leaves – and wonder how they got here, how I have arrived at this point of clutter. These things, things, things, my mind is shouting and I hurl appliances, earrings, wine glasses, into the kitchen trash and, gripped immediately by a zinging, many-knuckled panic, pick them out again, hurry, hurry, one by one, rinse them off, put them back away, behind their doors, watch TV, breathe, watch TV.

* * *

My face worsens, and my eye, yet Tom doesn't seem to notice. It seems my question about my ass, however, has made him a bit braver, and he suggests, gently, as we lie side by side in the dark, ever so delicately, that perhaps I should lose some – Christ in the foothills, Riva, why don't you lose some – weight.

He has another business trip to Scranton on Thursday, he says. Won't be back until late Saturday.

Scranton. History dangles in front of me, a terrible mobile. My arms cannot move. My forehead opens up like a garage door. You've got to be kidding, I gasp, panicked.

No, why? he murmurs. Shouldn't be too bad.

Oh come off it, Tom. These suburban, marital clichés. They've crawled into us like tapeworms. Put a sugar cube on the tongue, flash a light up the ass, and they poke out their tiny white heads to investigate, they're eating us Tom there's something eating us.

He snorts, smooths his baggy pajamas, closes his handsome eyes. He says he doesn't understand why it is always late at night that I grow so incomprehensible.

I grow so incomprehensible.

I am stealing more and more money. I keep it in my top drawer beneath my underwear, along with my diaphragm and my lipstick and my switchblade these are things a woman needs.

You are the man removing my bobby pins, my hair unfurling, the one who saunters in still, grinning then absconding with all of my pulses, over and over again, that long graceful stride toward a city, toward a bathroom, toward a door. I sleep alone this week, my husband gone, rolling into my own empty arms might they be yours, sleep on top of them as if to kill them, and in the morning they are dead as salamis until I massage the blood down into them again with my palm. Sweet, sweet Riva, you said to the blind white place behind my ear. Come live with me and be my lunch.

After I've picked up Jeffrey and the two of us have come home, we are alone in the kitchen and he teaches me what he has learned in his dance class.

Shooba plié, shooba plié, he chants, hanging on to the Formica edge of the counter, jiggling and squatting repeatedly in his corduroys. He always looks so awkward I'm sure he's doing something wrong.

What's a shooba? I inquire, silly me.

It's this, he says, doing lord knows what with his pelvis. Then you make a Driveway, he explains, indicating the newly created space between his turned-out feet, but you don't drive in it, he adds.

You mean, it's just for show? I ask, incredulous. My smile frustrates him.

Welp . . . . Mommy, listen! You just do Jellyfish fingers, hang, hang, then leapareeno! and he grand jetés, or sort of, across the linoleum, whoops loudly, slides into the potato cabinet. Then he's up again, his fallen socks now bunched at his instep, and he scoots across the floor with little brush steps, singing hoo-la, hoo-la, brock-co-lee!

How did he get this far from me? So short a time and already he is off and away, inventing his own life. I want to come up behind him, cover his head with my dirty, oniony apron, suck him back up into my body I want to know his bones again, to keep him from the world.

Mommy?

My brain feels crammed and gassy as if with cole slaw. You live, I read once, you live if you dance to the voice that ails you.

You go like this, Mom.

I stop my staring. Like this? I am no dummy. I am swiftly up on my toes, flitting past the refrigerator, my arms flapping like sick ducks. Hoo-la, hoo-la, I sing. Hoo-la-la.

Sometimes I find myself walking down the street or through Scarves and Handbags thinking about absolutely nothing, my mind worrying its own emptiness. I think: Everyone is thinking bigger thoughts than I, everyone is thinking thoughts.

Sometimes it scares me, this bone box of a head of mine, this clean, shiny ashtray.

And when after one hundred years, I am reading to Jeffrey, a prince came across Sleeping Beauty in the forest and kissed her, she awoke with a start and said, Prince! What took you so long? for she had been asleep for quite some time and all of her dreams were in reruns.

Jeffrey gulps solemnly: Like Starsky and Hutch.

And then the prince took Sleeping Beauty in his arms and said: Let us be married, fair lady, and we shall live happily ever after or until the AFC championship games, whichever comes first.

Ma-om! Jeffrey lets out a two-toned groan. That's not how it goes.

Oh, excuse me, I apologize. You're right. He says: Let us be married, fair dozing one. And I shall make you my princess. And Sleeping Beauty says: Oh, handsome prince. I love you so. But I have been asleep for a hundred years and am old enough to be your grandmother.

Jeffrey giggles.

The prince thought about this and was just about to say, Well, that being the case maybe I'll be running along now, when a magic bluebird swooped down out of the sky and made him one hundred years older as well, and then boy did Sleeping Beauty have a good laugh.

Did they live happily ever after?

Gee, honey, you know it just doesn't say. What do you think?

Yup, says Jeffrey, not smiling.

Knock, knock, says Mr. Fernandez.

Who's there? I smile, on my way home with Jeffrey. I am double-parked on Spruce Street.

Amnesia.

Amnesia who?

The moon is full is serene, wanders indolent and pale as a cow, a moon cow through my window, taking me to its breast, swaddling me in its folds of light. I leave on this moon, float out into the night on it, wash out like a wave and encircle the earth, I move with a husbandless gait, an ease about the flanks, the luminous hugeness of milk at my eyes I shift, disappear by slow degrees, travel, looking. Where did you go?

I owe. I owe the store so much money I cannot believe it. I let Amahara go home early today and then go into the back office, get the books out again, and calculate how much it has been: so much I cannot say.

At least I have done it neatly. There is something soothing in arithmetic, in little piles, little stacks of numbers that obey you.

Tuesday I stop at Wanamaker's and pick up ruby-colored satin slippers for my mother and walk out of the store without paying for them. I then head for Mr. Fernandez's to pick up Jeffrey. Together, big blonde, little blonde, we walk the sixteen blocks to St. Veronica's, no need to get home early; Tom's still in Scranton.

Sister Mary Marian is ecstatic at seeing Jeffrey again. He gives her a big juicy kiss on the cheek and she giggles and reddens. It makes me uncomfortable.

In the elevator I touch my face, touch my eyes to see if they are behaving, if they are being, if they are having, or misbehaving, miss being had. The words conflate and dizzy me, smack of the errors of my life I misbe. I mishave. Jeffrey pulls on my arm as if he wants to tell me something. We are stalled on the third floor while two orderlies wheel in a giant cart of medical supplies, glasses, and linens. I bend down so Jeffrey can whisper whatever it is he wants to say, and with both his hands he begins assiduously smoothing my hair back and out of the way. When he has the space around my ear sufficiently cleared, however, he doesn't say anything, but just presses his face close against my head.

Jeffrey, hon, what is it? The doors now shut and we resume our ascent.

Nothing, he whispers loudly.

Nothing? I ask, thinking he might be scared of something. I am still bent over.

I just wanted to look at your ear, he explains.

We walk in dully, not knowing what to expect. We leave our raincoats on.

Mother seems to be having a good day, her spirits up gliding around the white metal room greeting the world like pleasant hosts. And we are the parasites that have just trudged sixteen blocks, the pair of sights, the parricides.

Riva, dear, and Jeffrey. I was hoping you would come today. How's Tom?

But I think she's said who's Tom and I freeze, very tired, not wanting to get into that again.

Do you feel all better, Gramma? Jeffrey asks with a yawn, climbing on the metal footboard, looking as if purposefully at the meaningless clipboard there.

Gramma just has to speak to the doctor before she can leave here, she says.

I am shocked that my mother is talking about leaving. Does she no longer think of herself as mad? As Catholic? I look at her face and it is smiling, softened like ice cream.

Mother, do you mean that? Will you come home with us? I feel equivocal and liver-lipped.

We'll see, she says, has forever said, as I sometimes do now to Jeffrey. And yet it seems more hopeful, more certain. I feel, however, the slow creep of ambivalence in me: How will she behave, will she insist on refrying the pork chops, will she snore unforgivably from the den?

Ladies always say that, announces my clever son. He has now wandered over to the window and stands tiptoe, just barely able to peer out at the emergency entrance in the wing directly opposite this one. Wow, he shouts. Ampulnses. Neato.

Mother, I think it would be great for you to leave here, and as I've said before, we would love to have you. I sit at the bed squeezing her hand, having no idea what I really want her to do, astounded at my disingenuousness – would she just watch TV nice and quiet all day on the couch?

Jeffrey is still watching things out the window, saying: They take sick people for rides, right Gramma?

I haven't been able to stop eating. Amahara remarks today when I put three Lifesavers in my mouth at once: Boy, don't you know it's Lent? You haven't stopped eating for weeks. Silence. Have you?

I am reminded of a man's coat I bought once at a used clothing store, a store of dead people's clothes, and how I found an old Lifesaver in the pocket and popped it in my mouth, a dead man's candy. You'll eat anything, won't you, said Tom.

I am suddenly angry at Amahara. I march out wordlessly, straightening my spine. I stand next to Mrs. Rosenbaum our best charge customer and recommend the Korean paisleys while every cell in my body grumbles and gossips. Later I do a small operation with the Ann Klein receipts in the back. I will buy a new dishwasher.

I steal back into dreams of you, your unmade bed a huge open-faced sandwich. I lie back against you, fit the crook of your arm around my neck and into the curve at the base of my skull, bring your hand around to meet my mouth, chewing on your fingers, one by one, as a child might, listening to you tell stories.

Once upon a time I was in a strange position regarding women, you begin. I saw myself, as someone once said of Mohammed Ali, as a sort of pelvic missionary.

Ah, I murmur. The pelvic missionary position.

And your calluses press against my lips and teeth and your fingers strum my smile like a harp I am yours, yours, despite your stories I am yours.

I want to diet. I want to slink. I want to slink in a mink at the sink.

Batman is giving me dance lessons again before dinner. Glide, glide, goom-bah, he says, his lithe little body cutting

S-weaves across the floor. Mom, he sighs, feigning exasperation at my swivel-hipped attempt to do what he is doing. He is imperious, in imitation of his teacher, a frustrated bursitic Frenchman named Oleg. Move just your feet. Everything else will follow. Goom-bah!

Do I grow slinky? I think of carrot sticks and ice and follow Jeffrey's lead. I am snapping my fingers, wiggling, bumping, grinding. Mom, giggles Jeffrey. That's too kinky.

And later, alone, the night outside grows inky, like my thoughts, my thoughts.

I am dying for a Twinkie.

Tom is home tonight from Scranton. We curl up on the couch together, under a blanket, whisper I love you, I missed you, confusing tenses I think. Jeffrey comes clunking in on a small broken three-wheeled fire engine.

Dad, Mom said to ask you if I could have a BB gun.

Jeffrey, I say, flabbergasted. I told you you could *not* have a BB gun.

Your mother's right on that score, says Tom, sounding weird – on that score, what the hell is that, he sounds like some oily sportscaster.

Geeze, mutters Jeffrey, maneuvering the firetruck into a three-point turn and back down the hallway. Fuck it damn it all, he says. I am startled.

Watch the mouth, young man, shouts Tom.

During lunch hour today I stop by Mr. Fernandez's school. There are about fifteen kids there and they all seem quiet and good and engrossed in making block forts or cleaning up finger paint. Jeffrey looks up from behind some blocks, yells hi Mom, then resumes work on some precarious architectural project, which is probably also supposed to be a fort. I find a seat nearby and watch. Jeffrey suddenly stands up and looks fidgety, holding his crotch with one hand. Yikes! I gotta go! he shouts and bolts out of the room. While he is in the bathroom, I ask Mr. Fernandez about Jeffrey's language, whether he has noticed anything, any obscenities.

No, says Mr. Fernandez, looking puzzled.

Jeffrey emerges from the john, pulling up his pants.

Amahara chews an office property pen and says, aw, he's probably just reading it on bathroom walls is all.

Fuck it damn it all? He's only four-and-a-half.

Sure, she says, absently cracking plastic between her snaggle teeth. Like: Aint got no toilet paper, fuck it damn it all. Or no nukes, fuck it damn it all. Or no nukes hire the handicapped. Or nuke the handicapped. Or fuck the handicapped, damn it all.

I make a face. Amahara, I say. You're just free-associating.

Best things in life are free, she sighs.

With Amahara, clichés can take on epiphanic dimensions.

Best things in *life are free*, she repeats with emphasis, getting up, casting me a dark glance, and walking out the door, leaves me to wonder what she is driving at.

Tonight by his bed I discover a chewed crayon and a letter Jeffrey has written. It says Dear Jesus and God Hi.

Sunday. This cool cloudless afternoon I feel a pulsing at my neck and head and hips to escape. I drop Jeffrey and Tom off at the cinema for a Disney cartoon fest they both said they wanted to see, and I drive thirty miles or so out into Bucks County toward a gorge and waterfall I read about last summer in an *Inquirer* article entitled, "Nooks for Cooks – Great Spots for the Gourmet Picknicker."

All the way out I listen to the car AM radio, bad lyrics of trailer park love, gin and tonic love, strobe light love, lost and found love, lost and found and lost love, lost and lost and lost love – some people were having no luck at all. The DJ sounds quick and smooth and after-shaved, the rest of the world a mess by comparison.

I have to drive a mile on a narrow string of a dirt road, praying, as my father used to say, like a goddamned mantis that no one will come barreling toward me from the opposite direction. I then leave the car parked at the end of it – along with only one other car – and walk another quarter of a mile in. The trail is black and muddy with spring and as I slop along in old sneakers, I can hear the rush of the water already just a short distance away. Slop City, Batman would say if he were here. Slop, slop.

The trail down from the woods into the gorge is veined with large knobby roots and as I make my way down along them, strategically leaning from tree trunk to tree trunk, it occurs to me that I should be thinking I am too old for this, and yet I am not and instead am marveling, marveling. The smell of the soil is wet and silty and few of the branches of the softwoods even have buds on them yet. A raccoon, elegantly striped and masked as for a small mammalian ball, has come out of the bushes and approached the creek. I make little noises at it, noises I think might be appropriate raccoon noises: a trilling, clucking sort of chatter. The raccoon cocks its head to one side, curious. I try human language – Hey, Mr. Raccoon – and it yammers at me angrily, scurries away in a furry blur.

In the middle of the creek there are long flat slabs of slate and I can jump from rock to rock and without much difficulty land myself in the middle of the largest and sunniest of them. A few yards down, an old stone bridge spans the gorge, crumbled but stubborn, its stones chipped and spilled, its mortar cracked; it is like the weighted arc of a wise mouth, a large, tight-lipped stitch across the jagged brown banks. I turn from this, turn toward the shimmer upstream, the bright white of the water, god, the light of it, as it skis down over the rocks and ragged beginnings of mosses, all around the zig-zag of flaking shale, layered as old pastries. The light, something the article never talked about, flashing from bud and wave and ripple, everything lined and measured by it, in this sunken rip, the blinding living ice of it knocks me out, flat like a lizard on a rock I just lie here and begin to feel the sun warm my skin even through my clothes, and then I am taking them off: my jacket, my sneakers, socks, sweater, pants, underwear. The sun heats the hairs of my goose-bumps, soaks into my shoulders, the vast incontinent continent of me; sun closes my eyes, this sun, my sun. The creek roars around me, waking from winter, strong and renewed. I have the urge, lying like that, like a fat snake, to squeal or shout. I stand up and dip my right foot into the creek. No one is around and I leap from flat rock to flat rock whooping like a cowgirl. God, you devil you, moments like these I do believe are you, are gods that hold you and love you happy that's what a god should do, hold you and love you happy someone is stealing my wallet.

Behind me there is a barebacked man in denim fumbling with my jacket pocket three rocks away.

I run behind a bush.

Now he is clambering up the slope thinking I haven't seen him. I can bring myself to say nothing and he gradually disappears into the trees. I turn away, listen again to the water. I am suddenly getting cold. I go back to my rock and lie down, the earth moving, chafing beneath the blue membrane of the sky like a slow ball-bearing.

I rub my shins and get dressed.

Luckily I still have my keys. On the way back to pick up Jeffrey and Tom from the movie, the radio plays Barbra Streisand movie soundtracks. I take my time. In college there were three books I liked: *Walden*, *Agamemnon*, and *Waiting for Godot*. These were operations I understood. I hum to the radio. A Smokey the Bear commercial booms on and says that only I can prevent forest fires, I sweat with responsibility, and then the slick, mentholated DJ returns, announcing that now we return to The Way We Were. I drive slow, like an old man after a war.

Sorry I'm late, I yell out the window, parking lot gravel crunching beneath the tires. They are the only two people left at the cinema, and they are standing there like two lone cornstalks by the highway marquee, big and little in navy blue windbreakers. I reach over to unlock the door and they both climb in the front seat, Jeffrey in the middle. Tom slams the door shut.

Sorry I'm late, I say again, and Jeffrey puts one cold hand on my face to try to make me jump and Tom rubs his palms together beneath the glove compartment, saying don't you have the heater on?

I am too warm already, but I flick it to high. It responds with a roar and we are off down the road, a Maytag dryer on wheels. How was the movie?

Radishes are round, quotes my son. Radishes are red. Specially when you take them and bite off their heads.

That's what Danny the Dragon said, explains my husband.

It wasn't Danny the Dragon, argues Jeffrey. It was the duck that said that.

Tom, I chide, don't you know a duck from a dragon? A light turns yellow and I speed through it.

Tom looks out the window to his right: I'm telling you, it was the dragon.

Jeffrey looks straight ahead. There's no such thing as real dragons, right Mom?

I steal a quick look over his head at Tom, whose nostrils are flaring. We have stopped for a light at Quaker Boulevard. That's right, dear. I think, uh, they were mostly killed off in wars or something.

In the Vietnam war? he asks, so sincere, so interested.

In the War of the Roses, blurts Tom, impatiently, his hands tucked under his arms. Also heavy dragon casualties in the Glorious Revolution.

You'll confuse him, I sing through my teeth, flooring the gas as the light changes.

He's already confused! Tom suddenly shouts, angrily pounding the dashboard as Jeffrey hides his face in my sleeve. I tell you it wasn't the fucking duck!

I've been so touchy, murmurs Tom in bed as we stare at the ceiling together in the dark. I turn my head to look at him. He has been crying. Sharp triangles of hair are plastered to his forehead. Help me, Riva, he gasps, and his face cracks open again, but this time waterlessly. I feel the heaving of his rib cage. He brings his arm up over his face and hides in the angle it forms. I move toward him, on my side, press myself against him, cradle his head, pry loose his arm, and say: Tom, tell me. It's Scranton again, isn't it? He starts to shake his head no but then gives up. He nods yes and somehow it helps lessen the heaving. His eyes look at me, frantic, desperate. I place my hand gently to his cheek, but I do not kiss him.

I am sure the lady at the health food store is dying. Her eyes are puffy and her lips are dried, stuck together. If she opened her mouth, it would sound like Velcro pulling apart. The door clacks and tinkles behind me.

Hi, I say cheerily. Well, you know, guess what, Scranton's back in the picture again that tenacious dame. What can you do? No water can be thicker than water, you know what I mean?

I have no idea what I'm saying. I just want to save her life.

Tom's okay, I continue. I mean, we all have our bad habits. Me, for instance, I eat graham crackers like crazy.

Her mouth lets in air, a grinning fish. Sorry to hear that, she says.

But I don't know whether she means Scranton or the graham crackers, and so I just say yeah, well, I'm sure I need some sort of vitamin, and look woefully toward the shelf.

Amahara, can you come here please and take care of Mrs. Baker's account?

That old bag?

I grimace. Mrs. Baker is standing not six feet away. What I mean, Amahara recovers impressively, picking up a marked-down patent leather purse and smiling at Mrs. Baker, is that you really do need a new bag.

Perhaps I should do something else. Teach or something, I am saying to my mother who has relapsed into senility again but who is demanding that I confide professional and domestic secrets. She will insist she doesn't remember a thing, that I should tell her my troubles again. She already has forgotten her announced intention to leave St. Veronica's.

Has this Tom got a new mistress? she asks sternly, as if that would explain my discontent with Leigenbaum's.

No, no. That's not it, I say quickly and turn the subject to the gum she is chewing, which smells like suntan lotion.

Honey-coconut, she says. No problem with my dentures either.

There is a long silence. I look at my hands.

Good stuff, reiterates my mother. Honey-coconut. Made by Beech-Nut.

Why do you haunt me? You, like a tattoo on my tongue, like the bay leaf at the bottom of every pan. You who sprawled out beside me and sang my horoscope to a Schubert symphony, something about travel and money again, and we lay there, both of our breaths bad, both of our underwear dangling elastic, and then you turned toward me with a gaze like two matches, putting the horoscope aside, you traced my buried ribs with an index finger, lingered at my collarbone, admiring it as one might a flying buttress, murmuring: Nice clavicle. And me, too new at it and scared, not knowing what to say, whispering: You should see my ten-speed.

Jeffrey get in here, I yell out the back door. It's getting dark and dinner's ready. He is playing Murder the Leaf in the backyard with his friend Angela Dillersham. They carry large sticks.

Jeffrey do you hear me?

Yeah, he says and mumbles see ya to Angela, then shambles toward the back porch. Fuck it, damn it all, I hear him say, dragging himself up the stairs and I slap him as he comes in the door and send him crying to his room without his spaghetti or his fruit cocktail or his stick.

Where's Jeffrey? asks Tom.

He's being punished, I say, twirling spaghetti into a spoon.

But you sent him to bed without dinner two nights ago, says Tom, petulantly poking a wrinkled grape. Fuck it, damn it all, Riva, he's going to starve if you keep this up.

Go to your room, Tom, I say.

But he doesn't. He stays. He looks at me, blinking and amazed.

We are in Tom's room. My curtains and my clothes are here, but more and more it has taken on a disgruntled greenishness that is Tom's, a foggy haze like a fish tank that needs to be cleaned. We have to talk about this, he says.

What is *this*? I ask.

Scranton. Julia. You know. It's at the root of it all.

It all? I ask, a tyrant for precision.

Yes, well, this giant ravine between us, he explains.

Ah yes. Ravine. I think of my stolen wallet. There were pictures. And an eye donor's card. And then I think of the sun, the son.

I'm sure it's hard for you to believe, he continues. After all I said and promised last year and now all this . . . again . . .

All *this*? I ask, getting good at it.

Julia.

Oh, right. Scranton. I have always hated her name.

You must feel you're caught up in some vicious cycle. His voice sounds kind, sympathetic. At least I know I do, he is saying.

Cycle? I feel sarcasm flying up into my throat, shrill and inarticulate as a blue jay. Vicious cycle? I shout again. Hey. Listen. You should see my ten-speed.

I grow incomprehensible.

Easter. We try not to make too much of it. Jeffrey finds all the beans, saves me the purple ones. The air's warming, it's hard to sleep, and caterpillars sound like wind munching, denuding the spring trees. The days smell like a hamster cage, leaf bits littering the walks.

I long for you, I short for you, I wear shorts for you.

Jeffrey eats all his dinner tonight. He has been sweet all

day, brought me a potato print of what he calls the *limpbirdie* bell. Before bed I read him a story about a Mexican boy and a pinata, and Jeffrey says: Am I gonna do that, too, Mom? Smash my horse pinata? And I say that his horse pinata is different, it's a gift from Mr. Fernandez, and it's supposed to just hang there and not be broken. He yawns and stumbles off to plunk and deedle-dee, his sound words – where has he gotten this other stuff from?

Is God a giant like Hercules? asks Jeffrey just before drifting off. And I sit at the bed's edge and say God's a giant like the sun or like the sky, a huge blanket that all the planets are swimming in.

Could Hercules kill a gorilla? asks Jeffrey.

I slather heavy peach makeup over the rash by my mouth and go to see Mr. Fernandez at the lunch hour again. He insists Jeffrey is fine, although I'm still worried about his language. I sit next to Mr. Fernandez at a low, made-for-kids table, watching Jeffrey and the others play. He notices I am glum and places his hand on mine, says nothing.

Mr. Fernandez, I ask him finally. Are you happy?

He looks straight ahead for a minute.

Riva, he says, at last. You're not asking the right questions.

What's a right question?

Ah, he says mysteriously.

Ah? I ask. It sounds like tonsilitis. He nods, grins through his beard.

A little girl with short hair pale as the inside of a lemon rind runs up and places her cheek against Mr. Fernandez's knee. She has wet brown cookie remnants at the corner of her mouth. Can I have some juice now, please? she asks, running her fingers up and down the corduroy grooves of his thigh. She stops and looks up at me quizzically. A tiny cookie bit falls from her mouth. What kind of juice do you like? I ask her, solicitous, false-friendly, ridiculous.

She looks at me, knits her brows, takes Mr. Fernandez's hand, and turns away, pulling him toward the refrigerator at the far end of the room. He looks at me and shrugs and I shrug back. Not asking the right questions.

Things seem tense at work. People are wooden, scarcely polite, their eyes like fruit pits.

In bed with Tom. He holds me. I am sorry, he says. I love you. I love Jeffrey, I love that kid.

So do I, I say carefully.

There's a long moment before he says: What should we do? Do you want a divorce?

You are my husband, I say with difficulty, like a stroke victim, my tongue plugged in my throat like a scarf or a handbag.

I'm thinking of writing an herb book, says the woman in the health food store. Her hair lies in unwashed strings on the shoulders of her pink-gray sweater and against the pink-gray slope of her face.

It's good to have a project, I say, trying to sound cheerful, encouraging. Something to live with, something to always return to.

Something you love, she says, and holds up a green sprig of something, looks at me, smiles weakly.

Today I did a thousand dollars.

Things. Sometimes you just have to do them.

What do you want to be when you grow up, Jeffrey? I ask, chopping squash, squashing chops.

A car driver.

A car driver?

Yeah, you drive cars, he says and starts to zoom around the kitchen, three-point turning into cupboards.

Jeffrey, come and stir this brownie mix for me.

Okay, he says obediently, and we sit next to each other on stools at the counter. He is fidgety, restless. I push his hair back out of his face with my one clean hand. I can cradle his whole head with it, it seems.

What do *you* want me to be when I grow up? he asks, stirring, licking a fingertip.

I want you to be good.

I'm good at potato prints, he says, my earnest little potato prince.

No, I don't mean good *at* something, I mean just plain good. Being just plain good.

I'm good, he says.

You're good, I smile, mussing up his hair and smoothing it down again.

He reaches up, plays with my earring. I like it when you get dressed up, Mommy, he says.

I step out of the bathroom with nothing on.

Well, Tom, Sergeant, babydollbaby. Do I get into a prone position? A provolone position? I lumber into bed like a mammoth cheese.

Tom reaches under the covers and clasps my hand. Riva, I'm worried about you. Everything's a joke. You're always flip-flopping words, only listening to the edge of things. It's like you're always, constantly, on the edge.

Life is a pun, I say. It's something that sounds like one thing but also sounds like even means like something else.

Riva, what you just said. It's empty. It doesn't mean anything. He says this with a sort of tender reluctance, as if it were the last thing in the world he wanted to do.

It doesn't? I ask, suddenly embarrassed, confused, thinking that there is so much sanity in the insurance business. I slide down into the bed, press my face into his ribs, his strong ribs, the health food lady, I think, should have these ribs against her Velcro lips for a night, just a night, and then it occurs to me that maybe she already has.

I have brought my mother roses and a Tolkien trilogy. She smiles weakly, then lays them aside. Now, what was his name again? she asks, pouring ice water into a glass.

In the Leigenbaum's employees' ladies' room, someone

has written: I'm a virgin what is wrong with me? Beneath that, other people have written a string of feminist graffiti to reassure her, and underneath that, someone else has written in huge red letters: I don't care if I'm a fish, I still want a bicycle.

By the scarves, a woman asks me skeptically about designer names. I go into my rap about differences in French and Italian mills and also about supporting living working artists.

Do you think it really matters if you get laid in a Pucci scarf rather than one by somebody else? she asks.

I stare at her nose, tough as a root. You get laid in scarves? I finally say.

There are problems with these receipts, says the district manager, who is in for the day, on an official visit. Amahara is sitting next to him, not looking at me, her face blank as a window shade. I have just been called into the office.

I'm not sure what you mean, I say.

I think you are, he says. We could get into accusations here of gross negligence or outright criminal behavior. But the outcome would be the same. I don't know what sort of stress you've been under, but, Riva, you are fired. Without severance pay. You can pack your stuff and leave this afternoon.

Excuse me? I ask, not at all the right question, for he gets up and leaves without answering, Amahara close behind.

A smoky, hot pretzel smell in the city of blubbery love. A woman with jam on her plastic arm is attracting bees in Rittenhouse Square. Steam jostles the manhole covers, traffic resetting them, flat, flush, a regular metallic thud. The dusty burn of subway wafts up from concrete descents, and a peddler with a hint of mange at the hairline shouts fourteen carat, twenty at Bonwit's we'll give it to you for ten. Music grows loud and near, then fades and is gone, a casual invasion, hasty imprint and flight like the path of a bullet. I wander the streets frowsy and bloated, a W. C. Fields in drag, my mascara smeared like coal around my eyes, in store windows it is hard to recognize myself. I walk into places and flip through the racks, then leave, not really seeing too much, people spinning through doors, buzzing by me. They have drunk too much coffee. Caterpillars crawl the edge of the sidewalks like chromosomes. Looking for food, I roam slowly.

At Beefsteak Charley's I stop to blindly read the menu and the poster for the circus and suddenly notice Tom inside eating. He is with a thin, dark-haired woman and Jeffrey, whom he wasn't supposed to pick up from Mr. Fernandez's until six. The circus clown grins.

I pull the door open, walk in. It is fairly empty. In the center is a giant salad bar island with sneeze guards. They must have three kinds of macaroni salad here.

Tom looks up and is a bit taken aback at seeing me. Riva, he says unimaginatively. I thought you were working late tonight.

Hi Mom, chirps Jeffrey, his mouth full of corn relish and pickled beets. Look what Julia gave me. He points to the blue University of Kentucky T-shirt he is wearing.

Neat, I say.

I went to graduate school there, smiles the brunette.

Oh, introductions, says Tom, a bit frantic. Riva, this is Julia. Julia is a poet, he says hopefully. She teaches in Scranton.

Yes, I've heard, I say, my eye in third gear, hives blooming, lumps forming under my skin, near my mouth, ready to be lanced. How do you do? It sounds like the right question. I continue: I've never met a skinny poet before.

Tom looks at me oddly, vaguely yellow. Julia smiles sweet as cake.

Tom, can I talk to you for a moment? I ask, still standing, and he says sure and we walk together back toward the entrance by the unmanned cash register and a phone and extra menus and matches with "What's Your Beef?" printed on them, and I place my pocketbook in the after-dinner mints, slowly reach for a steak knife from an empty table and when he says what are you doing, what is it, I look at his murky hairline receding like a tide and I say you are my goddamned husband and jam the knife hard into his ribs.

It doesn't seem to go very far, like something thrust into

a radiator, but I let go and it sticks there for a long moment, then falls toward the carpet like a small, dumb, wingless bat. Tom's face is a horrible orgasm with eyes. He slumps toward the phone, lifts the receiver, slowly begins dialing 911, blood splotching onto his white shirt like cardinals in the snow, or sunburned nuns, I have lost my mind there is now I realize some commotion, some howling about the place, waiters in bow ties have come out from the kitchen and Julia flushed and murmuring like a very true poet holy fuck it damn it all comes stumbling over and the little University of Kentucky is frozen in his chair clutching a forkful of corn relish, his face a terrified marshmallow, oh my god, my god, I whisper into my hands.

You'll never see Jeffrey again, murmurs Tom, you can count on that, the pain on Tom's face, in his chest something enormous and sad, and then he is giving information to the operator and soon there are sirens.

I have my own room. Someone has sent me flowers. Is it you, Phil, who could it be, thinking of me?

Mr. Fernandez drops by to see me at St. Veronica's during visiting hours.

Do you realize, he says, that there's a nuclear bomb hanging over each and every one of us like a monster pinata?

I begin to understand his metaphors.

And you go off and do this, he says. Who the hell do you think you are?

I think to myself that this must be the right sort of question, the sort one is supposed to ask.

Pride cometh before the fall, I say, lost, foundering. Sometimes in May.

He leans over and kisses me. Riva, he says. I saw your husband today. He's fine but says he and Jeffrey will not come to see you.

I look out the windows, at gray, gray buildings, and say shit, and then start crying. I am crying, I can't help it.

I brought you a treat, Mr. Fernandez says, holding me

with one arm and handing me a cheese danish wrapped in cellophane.

I blow my nose, unwrap the danish, break off part and push it in my mouth. I'm bonkers, aren't I? I ask with my mouth full.

You're unhappy, says Mr. Fernandez. It can be the same thing. You are unhappy because you believe in such a thing as happy.

I stop eating. I feel sick. This danish is too sweetish to finish, I say, a little Scandinavian humor, and fillip the crumbs off the bedsheets.

I'm going to leave you now. I just stopped by for a minute.

I look at his magic Jesus beard and panic. Please don't go.

I'll stop by tomorrow, he says gently.

Thank you, I say, never more grateful for anything in my whole life.

Orderlies roll the days by me like carts.

Mr. Fernandez visits, but only him. My husband and son are off someplace, walking and trying not to cry.

Aging flowers, daisies when they die look like hopeful hags, their sunny, hatless faces, their shriveled, limp hair. Tulips wither into birdcages, six black stamens inside, each dried to a dim chirp.

The gray buildings fill my windows, my gibbering with salt: Who were you ever? An apoplexy to fill my days, to fill my insomnia with your insomnia, my bard of lard, my long ago husband, sometimes I think I made you up, but sometimes I think you live close, in this city, in my house, buried in the cellar or in paperwork and business trips, rising up at night like a past repast I can wish to death: Please die.

My mother is two floors above me. It would be humorous, but it's not humorous. We are allowed finally to meet in our bathrobes in the coffee shop downstairs.

Well, I say, quoting Humphrey Bogart in a line to Ingrid

Bergman at a table at Rick's: I guess neither one of our stories is very funny.

Riva, she says. Your father was a madman. He used to punch cars and threaten to swallow things. Maybe you inherited his genes.

I like to swallow things, I say.

Today is Friday. The nuns are friendlier, my eye flickless, my skin, body, brighter, thinner. I take an afternoon nap and dream bittersweetly that all the friends I've ever had march in here to see how I am.

When I wake up, Sister Henrietta knocks at my door and says a gentleman is here to see you, Riva.

I am disoriented from my dream, quickly straighten my hair, and say, as in the movies, Sister, you can send him in now. I turn to look out the window: the gray buildings of my life, the gray buildings.

And it is Jeffrey who appears in the doorway. He hangs there small and alone. Mom? he squeaks, then steps closer to the bed. He is wearing an oversized U. of Penn T-shirt, twisting and wringing at the bottom of it with one hand. Hi, Mom, he says.

My hips ache. My eyes burn happy sad happy. Nice shirt there, Batman, I say.

He tugs at it. Dad says this is where you went to college, he says, too far away for me to touch his arm.

How have you been doing, Jeffrey? I ask.

I broke my pinata, he says. I just broke it open, he shrugs, gulps, a small wrenching glug, looks at the ceiling. And there was nothing in it, he adds. But there's a circus coming pretty soon. There's gonna be a circus.

He stands there, away from me, afraid, holding his fingers. I am strange to him. Perhaps he thinks I have turned into Gramma.

Mom, are you my friend? he asks, barely audible, his face pale and homeless.

I nod yes.

Are you my mother?

I nod again, smiling, and he thinks about this, then approaches me, reaches and climbs up into my lap, curls into my breasts, clutching my gown, bursts into tears, his face crumpling against me. I want to go to the circus and see the horse people, he cries, wet and red, and I hold him close, warm, in my arms, in this room, and tell him we will go.

1982

TWO BOYS

FOR THE FIRST TIME in her life, Mary was seeing two boys at once. It involved extra laundry, an answering machine, and dark solo trips in taxicabs, which, in Cleveland, had to be summoned by phone, but she recommended it in postcards to friends. She bought the ones with photos of the flats, of James Garfield's grave, or an Annunciation from the art museum, one with a peacock-handsome angel holding up fingers and whispering, *One boy, two boys.* On the back she wrote, *You feel so attended to! To think we all thought just one might amuse, let alone fulfill. Unveil thyself! Unblacken those teeth and minds! Get more boys in your life!*

Her nervous collapse was subtle. It took the form of trips to a small neighborhood park, for which she dressed all in white: white blouses, white skirts, white anklets, shoes flat and white as boat sails. She read Bible poetry in the shade on the ground or else a paperback she had found about someone alone on a raft in the ocean, surviving for forty days and nights on nail parings and fish. Mary spoke to no one. She read, and tried not to worry about grass stains, though sometimes she got up and sat on a bench, particularly if there was a clump of something nearby, or a couple making out. She needed to be unsullied, if only for an afternoon. When she returned home, she clutched her books and averted her gaze from the men unloading meat in front of her building. She lived in a small room above a meat company – Alexander Hamilton Pork – and in front, daily, they wheeled in the pale, fatty carcasses, hooked and naked, uncut, unhooved. She tried not to let the refrigerated smell follow her in the door, up the stairs, the vague shame and hamburger death of it, though sometimes it did. Every day she attempted not to step in the blood that ran off the sidewalk and collected in the gutter, dark and alive. At five-thirty she approached her own building in a halting tiptoe and held her breath. The trucks out front pulled away to go home, and the Hamilton Pork butchers, in their red-stained doctors' coats and badges printed from ten-dollar bills, hosed down the sidewalk, leaving the block glistening like a canal. The squeegee kids at the corner would smile at Mary and then, low on water, rush to dip into the puddles and smear their squeegees, watery pink, across the windshields of cars stopped for the light. "Hello," they said. "Hello, hello."

"Where have you been?" asked Boy Number One on the phone in the evening. "I've been trying to reach you." He was running for a local congressional seat, and Mary was working for him. She distributed fliers and put up posters on kiosks and trees. The posters consisted of a huge, handsome photograph with the words *Number One* underneath. She usually tried to staple him through the tie, so that it looked like a clip, but when she felt tired, or when he talked too much about his wife, she stapled him right in the eyes, like a corpse. He claimed to be separating. Mary knew what *separating* meant: The head and the body no longer consult; the wife sleeps late, then goes to a shrink, a palm reader, an acupuncturist; the fat rises to the top. Number One was dismantling his life. Slowly, he said. Kindly. He had already fired his secretary, gotten a new campaign manager, gone from stocks to bonds to cash, and sold some lakefront property. He was liquidating. Soon the sleeping wife. "I just worry about the boys," he said. He had two.

"Where have I been?" echoed Mary. She searched deep in her soul. "I've been at the park, reading."

"I miss you," said Number One. "I wish I could come see you this minute." But he was stuck far away in a house with a lid and holes punched in for air; there was grass at the bottom to eat. He also had a small apartment downtown, where the doorman smiled at Mary and nodded her in. But this evening One was at the house with the boys; they were sensitive and taciturn and both in junior high.

"Hmmm," said Mary. She was getting headaches. She wondered what Number Two was doing. Perhaps he could come over and rub her back, scold the pounding and impounding out of her temples, lay on hands, warm and moist.

"How is your wife?" asked Mary. She looked at her alarm clock.

"Sleeping," said One.

"Soon you will join her cold digits," said Mary. One fell silent. "You know, what if I were sleeping with somebody else too?" she added. One plus one. "Wouldn't that be better? Wouldn't that be even?" This was her penchant for algebra. She wasn't vengeful. She didn't want to get even. She wanted to be even already.

"I mean, if I were sleeping with somebody else also, wouldn't that make everyone happy?" She thought again of Boy Number Two, whom too often she denied. When she hung up, she would phone him.

"*Happy*?" hooted Number One. "More than happy. We're talking delirious." He was the funny one. After they made love, he'd sigh, open his eyes, and say, "Was that you?" Number Two was not so hilarious. He was tall and depressed and steady as rain. Ask him, "What if we both saw other people?" and he'd stare out the window, towering and morose. He'd say nothing. Or he'd shrug and say, "Fthatz . . ."

"Excuse me?"

"Fthatz what you want." He'd kiss her, then weep into his own long arm. Mary worried about his health. Number One always ate at restaurants where the food – the squid, the liver, the carrots – was all described as "young and tender," like a Tony Bennett song. But Number Two went to coffee shops and ate things that had nitrites and dark, lacy crusts around the edges. Such food could enter you old and sticking like a bad dream. When Two ate, he nipped nothing in the bud. It could cause you to grow weary and sad, coming in at the tail end of things like that.

"You have everything," she said to Number One. "You have too much: money, power, women." It was absurd to talk about these things in a place like Cleveland. But then the world was always small, no matter what world it was, and you just had to go ahead and say things about it. "Your life is too crowded."

"It's a bit bottlenecked, I admit."

"You've got a ticket holders' line so long it's attracting mimes and jugglers." At times this was how they spoke.

"It's the portrait painters I'm worried about," said One. "They're aggressive and untalented." A click came over the line. He had another call waiting.

"It's so unfair," said Mary. "Everybody wants to sit next to you on the bus."

"I've got to get off the phone now," he said, for he was afraid of how the conversation might go. It might go and go and go.

In the park an eleven-year-old girl loped back and forth in front of her. Mary looked up. The girl was skinny, flat-chested, lipsticked. She wore a halter top that left her bare-backed, shoulder blades jutting like wings. She spat once, loud and fierce, and it landed by Mary's feet. "Message from outer space," said the girl, and then she strolled off, out of the park. Mary tried to keep reading, but it was hard after that. She grew distracted and uneasy, and she got up and went home, stepping through the blood water and ignoring the meat men, who, when they had them on, tipped their hair-netted caps. Everything came forward and back again, in a wobbly dance, and when she went upstairs she held on to the railing.

This was why she liked Boy Number Two: He was kind and quiet, like someone she'd known for a long time, like someone she'd sat next to at school. He looked down and told her he loved her, sweated all over her, and left his smell lingering around her room. Number One was not a sweater. He was compact and had no pores at all, the heat building up behind his skin. Nothing of him evaporated. He left no trail or scent, but when you were with him, the heat was there and you had to touch. You got close and lost your mind a little. You let it swim. Out into the middle of the sea on a raft. Nail parings and fish.

When he was over, Number Two liked to drink beer and

go to bed early, whimpering into her, feet dangling over the bed. He gave her long back rubs, then collapsed on top of her in a moan. He was full of sounds. Words came few and slow. They were never what he meant, he said. He had a hard time explaining.

"I know," said Mary. She had learned to trust his eyes, the light in them, sapphirine and uxorious, though on occasion something drove through them in a scary flash.

"Kiss me," he would say. And she would close her eyes and kiss.

Sometimes in her mind she concocted a third one, Boy Number Three. He was composed of the best features of each. It was Boy Number Three, she realized, she desired. Alone, Number One was rich and mean. Number Two was sighing, repetitive, tall, going on forever; you just wanted him to sit down. It was inevitable that she splice and add. One plus two. Three was clever and true. He was better than everybody. Alone, Numbers One and Two were missing parts, gouged and menacing, roaming dangerously through the emerald parks of Cleveland, shaking hands with voters, or stooped moodily over a chili dog. Number Three always presented himself in her mind after a drink or two, like an escort, bearing gifts and wearing a nice suit. "Ah, Number Three," she would say, with her eyes closed.

"I love you," Mary said to Number One. They were being concubines together in his apartment bedroom, lit by streetlights, rescued from ordinary living.

"You're very special," he replied.

"You're very special, too," said Mary. "Though I suppose you'd be even more special if you were single."

"That would make me more than special," said Number One. "That would make me rare. We're talking unicorn."

"I love you," she said to Number Two. She was romantic that way. Her heart was big and bursting. Though her brain was drying and subdividing like a cauliflower. She called both boys "honey," and it shocked her a little. How many honeys could you have? Perhaps you could open your arms and have so many honeys you achieved a higher spiritual plane, like a shelf in a health food store, or a pine tree, mystically inert, life barking at the bottom like a dog.

"I love you, too," said Two, the hot lunch of him lifting off his skin in a steam, a slight choke in the voice, collared and sputtering.

The postcards from her friends said, *Mary, what are you doing!?* Or else they said, *Sounds great to me.* One of them said, *You hog,* and then there were a lot of exclamation points.

She painted her room a resonant white. Hope White, it was called, like the heroine of a nurse novel. She began collecting white furniture, small things, for juveniles, only they were for her. She sat in them and at them and felt the edge of a childhood she'd never quite had or couldn't quite remember float back to her, cleansing and restoring. She bathed in Lysol, capfuls under the running tap. She moved her other furniture – the large red, black, and brown pieces – out onto the sidewalk and watched the city haul them away on Mondays, until her room was spare and milky as a bone.

"You've redecorated," said Number One.

"Do you really love me?" said Number Two. He never looked around. He stepped toward her, slowly, wanting to know only this.

In the park, after a Lysol bath, she sat on the paint-flaked slats of a bench and read. *Who shall ascend the hill of the Lord? . . . He who has clean hands . . .* There was much casting of lots for raiment. In the other book there was a shark that kept circling.

The same eleven-year-old girl, lips waxed a greenish peach, came by to spit on her.

"*What?*" said Mary, aghast.

"Nothin'," said the girl. "I'm not going to hurt you," she mocked, and her shoulders moved around as children's do when they play dress-up, a bad imitation of a movie star. She had a cheap shoulder bag with a long strap, and she hoisted it up over her head and arranged it in a diagonal across her chest.

Mary stood and walked away with what might have been indignation in someone else but in her was a horrified scurry. They could see! Everyone could see what she was, what she was doing! She wasn't fooling a soul. What she needed was plans. At a time like this, plans could save a person. They could organize time and space for a while, like little sculptures. At home Mary made soup and ate it, staring at the radiator. She would plan a trip! She would travel to some place far away, some place unlittered and pure.

She bought guidebooks about Canada: Nova Scotia, New Brunswick, Prince Edward Island. She stayed in her room, away from spitters, alternately flipped and perused the pages of her books, her head filling like a suitcase with the names of hotels and local monuments and exchange rates and historical episodes, a fearful excitement building in her to an exhaustion, travel moving up through her like a blood, until she felt she had already been to Canada, already been traveling there for months, and now had to fall back, alone, on her bed and rest.

Mary went to Number One's office to return some of the fliers and to tell him she was going away. It smelled of cigarettes and cigars, a public place, like a train. He closed the door.

"I'm worried about you. You seem distant. And you're always dressed in white. What's going on?"

"I'm saving myself for marriage," she said. "Not yours."

Number One looked at her. He had been about to say "Mine?" but there wasn't enough room for both of them there, like two men on a base. They were arriving at punch lines together these days. They had begun to do imitations of each other, that most violent and satisfying end to love.

"I'm sorry I haven't been in to work," said Mary. "But I've decided I have to go away for a while. I'm going to Canada. You'll be able to return to your other life."

"What other life? The one where I walk the streets at two in the morning dressed as Himmler? That one?" On his desk was a news clipping about a representative from Nebraska who'd been having affairs far away from home. The headline read: RUNNING FOR PUBLIC ORIFICE: WHO SHOULD CAST THE FIRST STONE? The dark at the edge of Mary's vision grew inward, then back out again. She grabbed the arm of a chair and sat down.

"My life is very strange," said Mary.

One looked at her steadily. She looked tired and lost. "You know," he said, "you're not the only woman who has ever been involved with a married— a man with marital entanglements." He usually called their romance a *situation.* Or sometimes, to entertain, *grownuppery.* All the words caused Mary to feel faint.

"Not the only woman?" said Mary. "And here I thought I was blazing new paths." When she was little her mother had said, "Would you jump off a cliff just because everybody else did?"

"Yes," Mary had said.

"*Would* you?" said her mother.

Mary had tried again. "No," she said. There were only two answers. Which could it be?

"Let me take you out to dinner," said Number One.

Mary was staring past him out the window. There were women who leaped through such glass. Just got a running start and did it.

"I have to go to Canada for a while," she murmured.

"Canada." One smiled. "You've always been such an adventuress. Did you get your shots?" This is what happened in love. One of you cried a lot and then both of you grew sarcastic.

She handed him his fliers. He put them in a pile near a rhinoceros paperweight, and he slid his hand down his face like a boy with a squeegee. She stood and kissed his ear, which was a delicate thing, a sea creature with the wind of her kiss trapped inside.

* * *

To Boy Number Two she said, "I must take a trip."

He held her around the waist, afraid and tight. "Marry me," he said, "or else."

"Else," she said. She always wanted the thing not proposed. The other thing.

"Maybe in two years," she mumbled, trying to step back. They might buy a car, a house at the edge of the Heights. They would grow overweight and rear sullen and lazy children. Two boys.

And a girl.

Number One would send her postcards with jokes on the back. *You hog.*

She touched Number Two's arm. He was sweet to her, in his way, though his hair split into greasy V's and the strange, occasional panic in him poured worrisomely through the veins of his arms.

"I need a break," said Mary. "I'm going to go to Canada."

He let go of her and went to the window, his knuckles hard little men on the sill.

She went to Ottawa for two weeks. It was British and empty and there were no sidewalk cafés as it was already October and who knew when the canals might freeze. She went to the National Gallery and stood before the Paul Peels and Tom Thompsons, their Mother Goose names, their naked children and fiery leaves. She took a tour of Parliament, which was richly wooden and crimson velvet and just that month scandalized by the personal lives of several of its members. "So to speak" – the guide winked, and the jaws in the group went slack.

Mary went to a restaurant that had once been a mill, and she smiled at the waiters and stared at the stone walls. At night, alone in her hotel room, she imagined the cool bridal bleach of the sheets healing her, holding her like a shroud, working their white temporarily through her skin and into the thinking blood of her. Every morning at seven someone phoned her from the desk downstairs to wake her up.

"What is there to do today?" Mary inquired.

"You want Montreal, miss. This is Ottawa."

French. She hadn't wanted anything French.

"Breakfast until ten in the Union Jack Room, miss."

She sent postcards to Boy Number One and to Boy Number Two. She wrote on them, *I will be home next Tuesday on the two o'clock bus.* She put Number One's in an envelope and mailed it to his post office box. She took another tour of Parliament, then went to a church and tried to pray for a very long time. "O father who is the father," she began, "who is the father of us all . . ." As a child she had liked to pray and had always improvised. She had closed her eyes tight as stitches and in the midst of all the colors, she was sure she saw God swimming toward her with messages and advice, a large fortune cookie in a beard and a robe, flowing, flowing. Now the chant of it made her dizzy. She opened her eyes. The church was hushed and modern, lit like a library, and full of women on their knees, as if they might never get up.

She slept fitfully on the way home, the bus rumbling beneath her, urging her to dreams and occasionally to wonder, half in and half out of them, whether anyone would be there at the station to greet her. Boy Number Two would probably not be. He was poor and carless and feeling unappreciated. Perhaps One, in a dash from the office, in a characteristically rash gesture, would take a break from campaign considerations and be waiting with flowers. It wasn't entirely a long shot.

Mary struggled off the bus with her bag. She was still groggy from sleep, and this aspect of life, getting on and off things, had always seemed difficult. Someone spoke her name. She looked to one side and heard it again. "Mary." She looked up and up, and there he was: Boy Number Two in a holey sweater and his hair in V's.

"An announcement," called the PA system. "An announcement for all passengers on . . ."

"Hi!" said Mary. The peculiar mix of gratitude and disappointment she always felt with Two settled in her joints like the beginnings of flu. They kissed on the cheek and then on the mouth, at which point he insisted on taking her bag.

They passed through the crowd uneasily, trying to talk but then not trying. The bus station was a piazza of homelessness and danger, everywhere the heartspin of greetings and departures: humid, ambivalent. Someone waved to them: a barelegged woman with green ooze and flies buzzing close. An old man with something white curled in the curl of his ear approached and asked them for a dollar. "For food!" he assured them. "Not drink! Not drink! For food!"

Two pulled a dollar from his pocket. "There you go, my man," he said. It suddenly seemed to Mary that she would have to choose, that even if you didn't know who in the world to love, it was important to choose. You chose love like a belief, a faith, a place, a box for one's heart to knock against like a spook in the house.

Two had no money for a cab but wanted to walk Mary home, one arm clamped around her back and upper arms. They made their way like this across the city. It used to be that Two would put a big, limp fish hand in the middle of her spine, but Mary would manage to escape, stopping and pointing out something – "Look, Halley's Comet! Look, a star!" – so now he clamped her tightly, pressed against his side so that her shoulders curved front and their hips bumped each other.

Mary longed to wriggle away.

At her door she thanked him. "You don't want me to come upstairs with you?" Two asked. "I haven't seen you in so long." He stepped back, away from her.

"I'm so tired," said Mary. "I'm sorry." The Hamilton Pork men stood around, waiting for another delivery and grinning. Two gave her back her suitcase and said, "See ya," a small mat of Dixie cup and gum stuck to one shoe.

Mary went upstairs to listen to the messages on her machine. There was a message from an old school friend, a wrong number, a strange girl's voice saying, "Who are you? What is your name?" and the quick, harried voice of Number One. "I've forgotten when you were coming home. Is it today?" Then another wrong number. "Who are you? What is your name?" Then Number One's voice again: "I guess it's not today, either."

She lay down to rest and didn't unpack her bag. When the phone rang, she leaped up, and the leap knocked her purse and several books off the bed.

"It's you," said Boy Number One.

"Yes," said Mary. She felt a small, short blizzard come to her eyes and then go.

"Mary, what's wrong?"

"Nothing," she said, and tried to swallow. When tenderness ended, there was a lull before the hate, and things could spill out into it. There was always so much to keep back, so much scratching behind the face. You tried to shoo things away, a broomed woman with a porch to protect.

"Did you have a good trip?"

"Fine. I was hoping you might be there to meet me."

"I lost your postcard and forgot what—"

"That's OK. My brother picked me up instead. I see what my life is: I tell my brother when I'm going to be home, and I tell you when I'm going to be home. Who's there to greet me? My brother. We're not even that close, as siblings go."

One sighed. "What happened was your brother and I flipped a coin and he lost. I thought he was a very good sport about it, though." The line fell still. "I didn't know you had a brother," said One.

Mary lay back on her bed, cradled the phone close. "How does the campaign look?" she asked.

"Money's still coming in, and the party's pleased with the radio spots. I've grown weary of it all. Maybe you could help me. What does the word *constituent* mean? They keep talking about constituents." She was supposed to laugh.

"Yes, well, Canada was a vision," said Mary. "All modern and clean and prosperous. At least it looked that way. There's something terribly wrong with Cleveland."

"Cleveland doesn't have the right people in Washington. Canada does." Number One was for the redistribution of wealth. He was for cutting defense spending. He was for the U.S. out of Latin America. He'd been to Hollywood benefits. But he'd never once given a coin to a beggar. Number Two did that.

"Charity that crude dehumanizes," said Number One.

"Get yourself a cola, my man," said Number Two.

"I have to come pick up my paycheck," said Mary.

"Sandy should have it," said One. "I may not be able to see you, Mary. That's partly why I'm calling. I'm terribly busy."

"Fund-raisers?" She wrapped the phone cord around one leg, which she had lifted into the air for exercise.

"That and the boys. My wife says they're suffering a bit, acting out the rottenness in our marriage."

"And here I thought you and she were doing that," said Mary. "Now everybody's getting into the act."

"You don't know what it's like to have two boys," he said. "You just don't know."

Mary stretched out on her stomach, alone in bed. A dismantled Number Three, huge, torn raggedly at the seams, terrorized the city. The phone rang endlessly. Mary's machine picked it up. *Hello? Hello?*

"I know you're there. Will you please pick up the phone?"

"I know you're there. Will you please pick up the phone?"

"I know you're there. I know you're there with someone." There was a slight choking sound. Later there were calls where nobody said anything at all.

In the morning he called again, and she answered. "Hello?"

"You slept with someone last night, didn't you?" said Two.

There was a long silence. "I wasn't going to," Mary said finally, "but I kept getting these creepy calls, and I got scared and didn't want to be alone."

"Oh, God," he whispered, a curse or was it love, before the phone crashed, then hummed, the last verse of something long.

In the park a young woman of about twenty was swirling about, dancing to some tape-recorded arias and Gregorian chants. A small crowd had gathered. Mary watched briefly: This was what happened to you when you were from

Youngstown and had been dreamy and unpopular in high school. You grew up and did these sorts of dances.

Mary sat down at a bench some distance away. The little girl who had twice spat on her walked by slowly, appraising. Mary looked up. "Don't spit on me," she said. Her life had come to this: pleading not to be spat on. Was it any better than some flay-limbed dance to boom box Monteverdi? It had its moments.

Not of dignity, exactly, but of something.

"I'm not going to spit on you," sneered the girl.

"Good," said Mary.

The girl sat down at the far end of the bench. Mary kept reading her book but could feel the girl's eyes, a stare scraping along the edge of her, until she finally had to turn and say, "*What?*"

"Just looking," said the girl. "Not spitting."

Mary closed her book. "Are you waiting for someone?"

"Yup," said the girl. "I'm waiting for all my boyfriends to come over and give me a kiss." She closed her eyes and smacked her lips in the air.

"Oh," said Mary, and opened her book again. The sun was beating down on the survivor. Blisters and sores. Poultices of algae paste. The water tight as glass and the wind, blue-faced, holding its breath. How did one get here? How did one's eye-patched, rot-toothed life lead one along so cruelly, like a trick, to the middle of the sea?

At home the phone rang, but Mary let the machine pick it up. It was nobody. The machine clicked and went through its business, rewound. Beneath her the hooks and pulleys across the meat store ceiling rattled and bumped. In a dream the phone rang again and she picked it up. It was somebody she knew only vaguely. A neighbor of Boy Number Two. "I have some bad news," he said in the dream.

In the park the little girl sat closer, like a small animal – a squirrel, a munk, investigating. She pointed and said, "I live that way; is that the way you live?"

"Don't you have to be in school?" asked Mary. She let her book fall to her lap, but she kept a finger in the page and her dark glasses on.

The girl sighed. "School," she said, and she flubbed her lips in a horse snort. "I told you. I'm waiting for my boyfriends."

"But you're always waiting for them," said Mary. "And they never get here."

"They're unreliable." The girl spat, but away from Mary, more in the direction of the music institute. "They're dead."

Mary stood up, closed her book, started walking. "One in the sky, one in the ground," the girl called, running after Mary. "Hey, do you live this way? I thought so." She followed behind Mary in a kind of traipse, block after block. When they got as far as the Hamilton Pork Company, Mary stopped. She clutched her stomach and turned to look at the girl, who had pulled up alongside her, perspiring slightly. It was way too warm for fall. The girl stared at the meat displayed in the windows, the phallic harangue of sausages, marbled, desiccated, strung up as for a carnival.

"Look!" said the girl, pointing at the sausages. "There they are. All our old boyfriends."

Mary took off her dark glasses. "What grade are you in?" she asked. Could there be a grade for what this girl knew in her bulleted heart? What she knew was the sort of thing that grew in you like a tree, unfurling in your brain, pushing out into your fingers against the nails.

"Grade?" mimicked the girl.

Mary put her glasses back on. "Forget it," she said. Pork blood limned their shoes. Mary held her stomach more tightly; something was fluttering there, the fruit of a worry. She fumbled for her keys.

"All right," said the girl, and she turned and loped away, the bones in her back working hard, colors spinning out, exotic as a bird rarely seen unless believed in, wretchedly, like a moonward thought.

1988

VISSI D'ARTE

HARRY LIVED NEAR Times Square, above the sex pavilion that advertised 25 CENT GIRLS. He had lived there for five years and had never gone in, a fact of which he was proud. In the land of perversities he had maintained the perversity of refusal.

"You've never even stepped in? Just once, during the day?" asked his girlfriend, Breckie. "Just to see? I mean, *I* have." Breckie was finishing up her internship at St. Luke's. She was a surgeon and worked with beating and stabbing victims brought into the emergency room. She liked getting her hands on the insides of a thing. It had to do with her childhood.

"Someday when I'm rich," said Harry. "It's not as if it's free."

Harry was a playwright, which made it, he felt, appropriate to live in the theater district. Also, the rent was cheap and he could play his Maria Callas records loud without causing a stir. The neighborhood, after all, was already in a stir. It was a living, permanent stir. He felt he felt relaxed there. He did.

He did.

And if once in a while a small rodent washed up into the toilet or dashed out from under the radiator, Breckie's cat almost always got it.

Harry had started writing plays because he liked them. He liked the idea of an audience: live guests in front of live performers. It was like company at holidays: all those real-life, blood-gorged bodies in one room, those bunches of over-dressed grapes; everyone just had to be polite. They had no choice. That, thought Harry, was civilization. Harry had had a play produced once as part of a city competition that had named him one of the three top up-and-coming under-thirty playwrights. His picture had appeared with pictures of the other two in the *New York Times*, all of them wearing the same tie. The tie had belonged to the photographer, who had made them all wear it, individually, like a jacket in a restaurant, but besides that it had been an exuberant event. The play itself was a bleak, apocalyptic comedy set in the Sheep Meadow at Central Park in the year 2050. A ranger stood stage left for the four-hour duration of the play; other characters had love affairs and conversations. It was called *For Hours See a Ranger*, and it had run for five days in a church basement in Murray Hill.

Since that time Harry had been working on what he hoped would be his masterpiece. The story of his life. *O'Neillian*, he called it.

"Sounds like *chameleon*," said Breckie. Her work took a lot out of her.

"It's about the ragtag American family and the lies we all tell ourselves."

"I know," she said. "I know."

Harry had been writing the play for years. Mostly he worked at night, tucked in out of the neighborhood's gaud and glare, letting what he called "the writing fairies" twinkle down from their night perches to commune with his pen. He was very secretive about his work. He had never shown Breckie more than a page of it, and the two or three times he had taken portions to the photocopier's it had sent him into the flush and sweat of the shy. It wasn't that he didn't have confidence in it. It was simply that the material felt so powerful to him, its arrangement so delicate, that a premature glimpse by the wrong person might curse it forever. He had drawn heavily from his life for this play. He had included the funniest family anecdotes, the most painful details of his adolescence, and the wrenching yet life-affirming death of his great-aunt Flora, Fussbudget Flora, whose dying word had been "Cripes." He had suffered poverty for this play, and would suffer more, he knew, until its completion, living off the frugally spent prize money and the occasional grant he applied for and received. When his cash was low, he had, in the past, done such things as write articles for magazines and newspapers, but he had taken the work too personally and had had too many run-ins with editors. "Don't fuck with my prose," he'd been known to say in a loud voice.

"But, Harry, we need to shorten this to fit in an illustration."

"You're asking me to eat my children so you can fit in some dumb picture?"

"If you don't want a picture, Harry, go publish in the phone book."

"I have to think about this. I have to think about whether or not I can really eat my children this way." But once he had nibbled at the limbs, he found it was not such a far cry to the vital organs, and soon Harry got good at eating his children. When his articles appeared, often there were two pictures.

And so Harry stopped writing journalism. He also turned down offers to write for "the movies, those pieces of crap" and had had to resist continually the persistent efforts of a television producer named Glen Scarp, who had telephoned him every six months for the last four years, since Harry had won the prize – "Hey, Harry, how's it goin', man?" – trying to get him to write for his television series. "TV," Scarp kept saying, "it's a lot like theater. Its roots are in theater." Harry never watched television. He had an old black-and-white set, but the reception was bad because he and Breckie lived too close to the Empire State Building, the waves shooting out over them and missing the apartment altogether. Once in a while, usually after he got a call from Glen Scarp, Harry would turn the TV on, just to see if things had changed, but it was always a blare of static and police calls from the squad cars that circled the block like birds. "We're going to have to face it," he said to Breckie. "This television is just a large, broken radio with abstract art on the front."

"I can't live like this anymore," said Breckie. "Harry, we've got to make plans. I can't stand the whores, the junkies, the cops, the bums, the porno theaters – you know what's playing at the corner? *Succulent Stewardesses* and *Meat Man*. I'm moving. I'm moving to the Upper West Side. Are you coming with me?"

"Um," said Harry. They had talked once about moving. They had talked once about marriage. They would have children, and Harry would stay home and write and take care of the children during the day. But this had troubled Harry. During the day he liked to go out. He liked to wander down the street to a coffee shop and read the paper, think about his play, order the rice pudding and eat it slowly, his brain aflame with sugar and caffeine, his thoughts heated to a usable caramel. It was a secret life, and it nourished him in a way he couldn't explain. He was most himself in a coffee shop. He imagined having a family and having to say to his children – tiny squalling children in diapers, children with construction paper and pointed scissors, small children with blunt scissors, mewling, puking children with birdhead scissors or scissors with the ears of a dog – "Now, kids, Daddy's going to a coffee shop now. Daddy'll be back in a while."

"Are you coming with me?" repeated Breckie. "I'm talking you get a job, we get an apartment in a building wired for cable, and we have a *real* life. I can wait for you only so long." She had a cat who could wait for anything: food, water, a mouse under a radiator, a twistie from a plastic bag, which, batted under the rug, might come whizzing back out again, any day now, who knew. But not Breckie. Her cat was vigilant as Madame Butterfly, but Breckie had to get on with things.

Harry tried to get angry. "Look," he said. "I'm not a possession. I may not even belong *with* you, but I certainly don't belong *to* you."

"I'm leaving," she said quietly.

"Aw, Breck," said Harry, and he sank down on the bed and put his hands to his face. Breckie could not bear to leave a man with his hands to his face until he had pulled them away. She sat down next to him, held him, and kissed him deeply, until he was asleep, until the morning, when it would be, when it was, possible to leave.

The first few weeks of living alone were difficult, but Harry got used to it in a way. "One year of living alone," said his old friend Dane in a phone call from Seattle, "and you're ruined for life. You'll be spoiled. You'll never go back." Harry worked hard, as he always had, but this time without even the illusion of company. This time there was just the voice of play and playwright in the bombed-away world of his apartment. He started not to mind it, to feel he was suited in some ways to solitude, to the near weightlessness of no one but himself holding things down. He began to prefer talking on the phone to actually getting together with someone, preferred the bodilessness of it, and started to turn down social engagements. He didn't want to actually sit across from someone in a restaurant, look at their face, and eat food. He wanted to turn away, not deal with the face, have the waitress bring them two tin cans and some string so they could just converse, in a faceless dialogue. It would be like writing a play, the cobbling in the night, the great cavity of mind that you filled with voices, like a dark piñata with fruit.

"Tell me something wonderful," he said to Dane. He would lie on his bed, the phone cradled at his cheek, and stare lonesomely at the steeple made by the shadow of the bookcase against the wall. "Tell me that we are going to die dreamfully and loved in our sleep."

"You're always writing one of your plays on the phone," said Dane.

"I said, something wonderful. Say something about springtime."

"It is sloppy and wet. It is a beast from the sea."

"Ah," said Harry.

Downstairs every morning, when he went to get the paper and head for a coffee shop, there was Deli, the hooker, always in his doorway. Her real name was Mirellen, but she had named herself Deli because when she first came to New York from Jackson, she had liked the name Delicatessen, seen it flashing all over in signs above stores, and though she hadn't known what one was, she knew the name was for her.

"Mornin', Harry." She smiled groggily. She had on a black dress, a yellow short-sleeved coat, and white boots. Scabs of translucent gray freckled her arms.

"Mornin', Deli," said Harry.

Deli started to follow him a bit up the block. "Haven't seen your Breck woman around – how things be with you-all?"

"Fine." Harry smiled, but then he had to turn and walk fast

down Forty-third Street, for Deli was smart and sly, and in the morning these qualities made him nervous.

It was the following week that the trucks started coming. Eighteen-wheelers. They came, one by one, in the middle of the night, pulled up in front of the 25 Cent Girls pavilion, and idled there. Harry began waking up at four in the morning, in a sweat. The noise was deafening as a factory, and the apartment, even with the windows closed, filled with diesel fumes. He put on his boots, over his bare feet, and threw on his overcoat, a coat over nothing but underwear and skin, and stomped downstairs.

The trucks were always monstrous, with mean bulldog faces, and eyes of glassy plaid. Their bodies stretched the length of the block, and the exhaust that billowed out of the vertical stovepipe at the front was a demonic fog, something from *Macbeth* or *Sherlock Holmes*. Harry didn't like trucks. Some people, he knew, liked them, liked seeing one, thought it was like seeing a moose, something big and wild. But not Harry.

"Hey! Get this heap out of here!" Harry shouted and pounded on the driver's door. "Or at least turn it off!" He looked up into the cabin, but nobody seemed to be there. He pounded again with his fist and then kicked once with his boot. Curtains in the back of the cabin parted, and a man poked his head out. He looked sleepy and annoyed.

"What's the problem, man?" he said, opening the door.

"Turn this thing off!" shouted Harry over the truck's oceanic roar. "Can't you see what's happening with the exhaust here? You're asphyxiating everyone in these apartments!"

"I can't turn this thing off, man," shouted the driver. He was in his underwear – boxer shorts and a neat white vest.

The curtains parted again, and a woman's head emerged. "What's happening, man?"

Harry tried to appeal to the woman. "I'm dying up there. Listen, you've got to move this truck or turn it off."

"I told you buffore," said the man. "I can't turn it off."

"What do you mean, you can't turn it off?"

"I can't turn it off. What am I gonna do, freeze? We're

trying to get some sleep in here." He turned and smiled at the woman, who smiled back. She then disappeared behind the curtain.

"I'm trying to get some sleep, too," yelled Harry. "Why don't you just move this thing somewhere else?"

"I can't be moving this thing," said the driver. "If I be moving this thing, you see that guy back there?" He pointed at his rearview mirror, and Harry looked down the street. "I move and that guy be coming to take my spot."

"Just turn this off, then!" shouted Harry.

The driver grew furious. "What are you, some kind of mental retard? I *already* told you. I can't!"

"What do you mean, you can't. That's ridiculous."

"If I turn this mother off, I can't get it started back up again."

Harry stormed back upstairs and phoned the police. "Yeah, right," said Sgt. Dan Lucey of the Eighteenth Precinct. "As if we don't have more urgent things in this neighborhood than truck fumes. What is your name?"

"Harry DeLeo. Look," said Harry. "You think some guy blowing crack in a welfare hotel isn't having one of the few moments of joy in his whole life. *I* am the one—"

"That's a pretty socially responsible thing to say. Look, mister. We'll see what we can do about the trucks, but I can't promise you anything." And then Officer Lucey hung up, as if on a crank call.

There was no way, Harry decided, that he could stay in his apartment. He would die. He would get cancer and die. Of course, all the best people – Christ, Gershwin, Schubert, theater people! – had died in their thirties, but this did not console him. He went back downstairs, outside, in nothing but his overcoat thrown over a pajama top, and a pair of army boots with the laces flapping. He roamed the streets, like the homeless people, like the junkies and hookers with their slow children and quick deals, like the guys down from Harlem with business to transact, like the women with old toasters and knives in their shopping bags, venturing out from Port Authority on those occasions when the weather thawed. With his overcoat and pajama top, he was not in the least scared, because he had become one of them, a street person, rebellion and desperation in his lungs, and they knew this when he passed. They smiled in welcome, but Harry did not smile back. He wandered the streets until he found a newsstand, bought the *Times*, and then drifted some more until he found an all-night coffee shop, where he sat in a booth – a whole big booth, though it was only him! – and spread out his *Times* and circled apartments he could never ever afford. "1500 dollars; EIK." He was shocked. He grew delirious. He made up a joke: how you could cut up the elk for meat during the winter, but in the months before you could never housebreak the thing. "Fifteen hundred dollars for a lousy apartment!" But gradually the numbers grew more and more abstract, and he started circling the ones for eighteen hundred as well.

By March, Harry found himself gassed out of his apartment, roaming the streets, several nights a week. He went to bed full of dread and trepidation, never knowing whether this particular night would be a Truck Night or not. He would phone the landlord's machine and the police and shout things about lymphoma and emphysema and about being a taxpayer, but the police would simply say, "You've called here before, haven't you." He tried sounding like a different neighbor, very polite, a family man, with children, saying, "Please, sir. The trucks are waking the baby."

"Yeah, yeah, yeah," said the police. Harry called the Health Department, the Community Board, the Phil Donahue people. He referred to Officer Lucey as Officer Lucifer and cited cancer statistics from the Science Times. Most of the time people listened and said they would see what they could do.

In the meantime, Harry quit smoking and took vitamins. Once he even called Breckie in the middle of the night at her new apartment on the Upper West Side.

"Is this an awkward time?" he asked.

"To be honest, Harry, yes."

"Oh, my God, really?"

"Look, I don't know how to tell you these things."

"Can you answer yes-or-no questions?"

"All right."

"Shit, I can't think of any." He stopped talking, and the two of them breathed into the phone. "Do you realize," he said at last, "that I have three plantar's warts from walking around barefoot in this apartment?"

"Yes," she said. "I do now."

"A barnacled sole. That's what I am."

"Harry, I can't be writing your plays with you right now."

"Do you recall any trucks hanging out in front of our building, running their engines all night? Did that happen when you were here, when we were living together, when we were together and living here so much in love?"

"Come on, Harry." There was some muffled noise, the seashell sound of hand over mouthpiece, the dim din of a man's voice and hers. Harry hung up. He put on his Maria Callas records, all in a stack on the phonograph spindle, and left the apartment to roam the streets again, to find an open newsstand, a safe coffee shop that didn't put a maraschino cherry on the rice pudding, so that even when you picked it off its mark remained, soaked in, like blood by Walt Disney.

When he trudged back to his apartment, the morning at last all fully lit, falsely wide-eyed and innocent, the trucks were always gone. There was just Deli in the doorway, smiling. "Mornin', Harry," she'd say. "Have a bad dream?"

"You're up early," said Harry. Usually that was what he said.

"Oh, is it daytime already? Well, I'm gonna get myself a real job, a daytime job. Besides, I've been listening to your records from upstairs." Harry stopped jangling his keys for a moment. The Callas arias sailed faintly out through the windowpanes. "Isn't that fag music, Harry? I mean, don't get me wrong. I like fag music. I really like that song that keeps playing about the VCR."

"What are you talking about?" He had his keys out now, pointed and ready to go. But he kept one shoulder turned slightly her way.

"*V-C-R-err,*" sang Deli. "*V-C-Dannemora.*" Deli stopped

and laughed. "Dannemora! That girl's in Sing Sing for sure."

"See you," said Harry.

On his answering machine was a message from Glen Scarp. "Hey, Harry, sorry to call you so early, but hey, it's even earlier out here. And wasn't it Ionesco who said something about genius up with the sun? Maybe it was Odets. . . ." *Odets*? thought Harry. "At any rate, I'm flying into New York in a few days, and I thought we might meet for a drink. I'll phone you when I get in."

"No," said Harry out loud. "No. No."

But it was that very morning, after a short, cold rain, just after he'd opened the windows and gotten the apartment aired out, that the bathroom started acting up. The toilet refused to swallow, gurgling if Harry ran the kitchen faucet, and the tub suddenly and terrifyingly filled with water from elsewhere in the building. Somebody else's bath: sudsy water, with rusty swirls. Harry tried flushing the toilet again, and it rose ominously toward the rim. He watched in horror, softly howling the protests – "Ahhhh! UUUaahhh!" – that seemed to help keep the thing from overflowing altogether.

He phoned the landlord, but no one answered. He phoned a plumber he found in the yellow pages, some place advertising *High Velocity Jet Flush* and *Truck Mounted Rodding Machine*. "Are you the super?" asked the plumber.

"There is no super here," said Harry, a confession that left him sad, like an admission that finally there was no God.

"Are you the landlord?"

"No," said Harry. "I'm a tenant."

"We charge two hundred dollars, automatic, if we visit," said the plumber, calmly. Plumbers were always calm. It wasn't just because they were rich. It had something to do with pipes and sticking your hands into them over and over. "Tell your landlord to give us a call."

Harry left another message on his landlord's machine and then went off to a coffee shop. It was called The Cosmic Galaxy and was full of actors and actresses talking wearily about auditions and getting work and how useless *Back Stage* was, though they bought it faithfully and spread it out over the tables anxiously to read. "What I'm trying to put together here," he overheard one actress say, "is a look like Mindy and a sound like Mork." Harry thought with compassion how any one of these people would mutilate themselves to write a TV episode for Glen Scarp, how people are driven to it, for the ten thousand dollars, for the exposure, for the trashy, shameful love of television, whatever it was, and how he had held out for his play, for his beautiful secret play, which he had been mining for years. But it would be worth it, he believed. When he came triumphantly up from the mine, emerged with his work gorgeous and completed, he would be, he knew, feted with an orchestra, greeted big by a huge brass band – trumpeted! – for there were people who knew he was down there, intelligent people, and they were waiting for him.

Of course, you could be down there too long. You could come up for air, all tired and sooty, and find only a man with a harmonica and a tin can, cymbals banging between his knees.

On Tuesday the suds were gone. Harry pulled the drain closed so that nothing else could come rushing up. Then he washed in the kitchen sink, with a rag and some dish detergent, and went off again to The Cosmic Galaxy.

But on Wednesday morning he woke once more to the sharp poison of diesel fumes in the apartment. He walked into his bathroom cautiously and discovered the tub full to the brim with a brackish broth and bits of green floating in it. Scallions. Miso soup with scallions. "What?" He checked the drain, and it was still closed. He left a message on his landlord's machine that went, "Hey, I've got vegetables in my tub," then he trudged out to a different coffee shop, a far one, on the very edge of the neighborhood, practically up by Lincoln Center, and ordered the cheeseburger deluxe, just to treat himself, just to put himself in touch with real life again. When he returned home, Deli was hovering in his doorway. "Mornin', Harry," said Deli.

"Isn't it afternoon?" asked Harry.

"Whatever," said Deli. "You know, Harry, I been thinking. What you need is to spend a little money on a girl who can treat you right." She inched seductively toward him, took his arm with one hand and with the other began rubbing his buttocks through his jeans.

Harry shook her off. "Deli, don't pull this shit on me! How long have I known you? Every morning for five years I've come out of this building and seen you here, said hello. We've been friends. Don't start your hooker shit with me now."

"Fuck you," said Deli. And she walked away, in a sinuous hobble, up to the corner to stand.

Harry went upstairs to his apartment and slowly opened the door to his bathroom. He reached for the switches to the light and fan and turned them on in a single, dramatic flick.

The tub. The miso soup was gone, but in its stead was a dark brown sludge, a foot deep, sulfurous and bubbled. "Oh, my God," said Harry. It was a plague. First suds. Then vegetables. Then darkness. He would get typhus or liver death. There would be frogs.

He left another message on his landlord's machine, then he phoned Breckie and left one on hers: "I have half the Hudson River backed up into my tub. Sea gulls are circling the building. You are a doctor. Does this mean I could get a sad and fatal ailment?" He had Maria Callas singing in the background; he always did now whenever he phoned Breckie and left messages. "Also, I want to know how seriously involved you are with this guy. Because I'm making plans, Breck. I am."

On Thursday, Glen Scarp called and Harry said yes. Yes, yes, yes.

They met that Monday for drinks at the hotel where Scarp was staying. It was on East Fifty-seventh Street and had a long vaulted entrance, dreamy and mirrored, like Versailles, or a wizard's castle. Scarp was waiting for Harry at the end of the corridor, sitting on a velveteen bench. Harry knew it was Scarp by his look of inventory and indifference for everyone who came down the passageway until he got to Harry. Then he looked bemused. Harry proceeded painfully slow, in a worn-shoed lope, toward the bench. Velveteen spread to either side of Scarp, like hips.

"Hello," said Harry.

Scarp was a short man and stood quickly, aggressively, to greet a tall. "Harry? Glen Scarp. Good to meet you at last." He was not that much older than Harry, and took Harry's hand and shook it gingerly between both of his. This was California ginger, Hollywood ginger. This was the limp of flirtation, the lightness of promise. Harry knew this, of course, but knew this only in the way everyone did, which was *knew it sort of.*

Scarp was wearing a diamond broach, a sparkly broccoli on his lapel, and Harry almost said, "Nice pin," but stopped himself. "Well, good to meet you, too," said Harry. "My whole life these days feels conducted on the phone. It's great to finally see the person behind the voice." This was not true, of course, and the lie of it trickled icily down his back.

"Let's have a drink in here, shall we?" Scarp motioned toward the cocktail lounge, which was all ficus trees and chrome and suffused in a bluish light.

"After you," said Harry, which was how he liked to do things.

"Fabulous," said Scarp, who marched confidently in ahead of Harry, so that Harry got to see the back of Scarp's hair: long, sprayed, and waved as a waterfall.

"I want to tell you again first of all how much I admire your work," said Scarp when they were seated and after they had ordered and Scarp had had a chance to push his sleeves up a bit and glance quickly down at his broach, a quick check.

"I admire yours as well," said Harry. In reality he had never seen Scarp's TV series and had actually heard negative things about it. Supposedly it was about young professionals, and there were a lot of blenders and babies. But this, here, now, was not reality. This was reality's back room. It was called dealing. The key, Harry knew, once you got done with the flattery, was to be charming and quick. That is what these people liked: a good, quick story, a snappy line, a confessional anecdote with polish and perhaps a relative in it. Then they would talk money with you. They would talk ten, fifteen thousand an episode, but that was only starters. Sometimes there was more to be had than that. But Harry was after only a single episode. In and out, like a cold bath. That was all he wanted. In and out. A single episode couldn't hurt his soul, not really. His play would have to sit for a while, but when he returned to it, like a soldier home to his wife, he would be a wealthy man. He would move. He would move somewhere with fresh air, somewhere where Breckie lived.

"Thanks," said Scarp. "So what have you been working on lately? You had the under-thirty prize thing – what was that – three years ago?"

"Three? What year is it now?"

"Eighty-eight."

"Eighty-eight," repeated Harry. "Well, the prize thing was actually then four years ago."

"Not under thirty anymore, I'll bet." Scarp smiled, studying Harry's eyes.

"Nope," said Harry, glancing away. "Not for a while."

"So what have you been doing?"

It was like talking to the playwriting police. You needed alibis. "I've been lying in my apartment," said Harry, "eating bonbons and going, 'What year is this?' "

"Right." Scarp laughed inscrutably. He picked up his drink, then put it down again without taking a sip. "As you know, I'm always looking for writers for the show. I've been doing some of the writing myself lately, and I don't mind that. But I thought you and I should get to know each other. I think you have a great handle on contemporary language and the . . . uh . . ."

"Postmodern imagination?" suggested Harry.

"Absolutely."

"Of the young deracinated American?"

"Absolutely," said Scarp.

Absolutely. It wasn't even absolutely to Harry, and he was the one who'd said it.

"So just informally, as friends, tell me what you've been up to," said Scarp. "There's no pressure here, no design. We're just getting to know each other."

"Actually I've been working on this play that I feel pretty good about, but it's long and is taking a lot out of me."

"You know, I used to want to write plays. What's this one about, or can't you talk about it?" Scarp started in on his drink, settling back into a listener's sit.

"I'm primitively secret about my work," said Harry.

"I respect that, absolutely," said Scarp. He scowled. "Your family from this country?"

Harry stared at Scarp: His eyes were lockets of distraction. What did it mean? "Yes," said Harry. He had to get Scarp back, get him interested, and so he began telling Scarp, in the most eloquent sentences he could construct, the story of the town his ancestors had founded in the Poconos, and what had become of it recently with radon gas, and the flight to Philly and Pittsburgh. It was a sad, complicated tale, jeweled with bittersweet wisdom, and he was lifting it in its entirety from the central speech of his play.

"That's amazing," said Scarp, apparently impressed, and it gave Harry confidence. He barreled on ahead, with the story of his parents' marriage, his father's alcoholism, his cousin's sex change operation, and a love affair he had once had with one of the Kennedy girls. These were fragile tales he had managed to hone carefully in the writing of his play, and as he spoke with Scarp the voices of his characters entered his mouth and uttered their lines with poignancy and conviction. One had to say words, and these were the words Harry knew best.

"Astonishing," said Scarp. He had ordered another round of drinks, at the end of which Harry was regaling him with the play's climactic scene, the story of Aunt Fussbudget Flora – funny and wrenching and life-affirming in its way.

"The lights went dim, and the moon spilled onto her pillow in pale oblongs. We were all standing there, gathered in a prayer, when she sighed and breathed her very last word on earth: 'Cripes.'"

Scarp howled in laughter. "Miraculous! What a family you have. A fascinating bunch of characters!" Harry grinned and sat back. He liked himself. He liked his life. He liked his play.

He didn't feel uneasy or cheaply spent, using his work this way, or if he did, well, he pushed that to one side.

"Harry," said Scarp, as he was signing for the check. "This has been a real pleasure, let me say."

"Yes, it has," said Harry.

"And though I've got to run right now – to have dinner with someone far less engaging, let me tell you – do I have your word that you will consider writing something for me sometime? We don't have to talk specifically now, but promise me you'll give it some thought. I'm making a troth here."

"And it shall set you free," said Harry. "Absolutely."

"I knew I would like you," said Scarp. "I knew we would hit it off. In fact, where do you live? I'll get a cab and drop you off."

"Uh, that's OK," said Harry, smiling. His heart was racing. "I could use the walk."

"If you're sure," said Scarp. "Listen, this was great. Truly great." He shook Harry's hand again, as limply as before. "Fabulous."

There is a way of walking in New York, midevening, in the big, blocky East Fifties, that causes the heart to open up and the entire city to rush in and make a small town there. The city stops its painful tantalizing then, its elusiveness and tease suspended, it takes off its clothes and nestles wakefully, generously, next to you. It is there, it is yours, no longer outwitting you. And it is not scary at all, because you love it very much.

"Ah," said Harry. He gave money to the madman who was always singing in front of Carnegie Hall, and not that badly either, but who for some reason was now on the East Side, in front of something called Carnegie Clothes. He dropped coins in the can of the ski-capped woman propped against the Fuller Building, the woman with the pet rabbit and potted plants and the sign saying, I HAVE JUST HAD BRAIN SURGERY, PLEASE HELP ME. "Thank you, dear," she said, glancing up, and Harry thought she looked, startlingly, sexy. "Have a nice day," she said, though it was night.

Harry descended into the subway, his usual lope invigorated to a skip. His play was racing through him: He had known it was good, but now he really knew. Glen Scarp had listened, amazed, and when he had laughed, Harry knew that all his instincts and choices in those lovely moments over the last four years, carefully mining and sculpting the play, had been right. His words could charm the jaded Hollywood likes of a Glen Scarp; soon those words, some lasting impression of them, might bring him a ten- or even twenty-thousand-dollar television episode to write, and after that he would never have to suffer again. It would just be him and Breckie and his play. A life that was real. They would go out and out and out to eat.

The E train rattled west, then stopped, the lights flickering. Harry looked at the *Be a Stenographer* ad across from him and felt the world was good, that despite the flickering lights, it basically, amazingly, worked. A man pushed into the car at the far end. "Can you help feed me and my hungry kids?" he shouted, holding out a paper cup, and moving slowly down Harry's side of the car. People placed quarters in the cup or else stared psychotically into the reading material on their laps and did not move or turn a page.

Suddenly a man came into the car from the opposite end. "Pay no attention to that man down there," he called to the riders. "I'm the needy one here!" Harry turned to look and saw a shabbily dressed man with a huge sombrero. He had electric Christmas tree lights strung all around the brim and just above it, like some chaotic hatband. He flicked a button and lit them up so that they flashed around his head, red, green, yellow. The train was still stopped, and the flickering overheads had died altogether, along with the sound of the engine. There was only the dull hum of the ventilating system and the light show from the sombrero. "*I* am the needy one here," he reiterated in the strangely warm dark. "My name is Lothar, and I have come from Venus to arrest Ronald Reagan. He is an intergalactic criminal and needs to be taken back to my planet and made to stand trial. I have come here to see that that is done, but my spaceship has broken down. I need your assistance so that I can get it done."

"Amen!" someone called out.

"Yahoo," shouted Harry.

"Can you help me, people, earthlings. I implore you. Anything you can spare will aid me in my goal." The Christmas tree lights zipped around his head, people started to applaud, and everyone dug into their wallets to give money. When the lights came on, and the train started to go again, even the man with the hungry kids was smiling reluctantly, though he did say to Lothar, "Man, I thought this was *my* car." When the train pulled into Forty-second Street, people got off humming, slapping high fives, low fives, though the station smelled of piss.

Harry's happiness lasted five days, Monday through Friday, like a job. On Saturday he awoke in a funk. The phone had not rung. The mail had brought him no letters. The apartment smelled faintly of truck and sewage. He went out to breakfast and ordered the rice pudding, but it came with a cherry.

"What is this?" he asked the waiter. "You didn't use to do this."

"Maraschino eyeballs." The waiter smiled. "We just started putting them on. You wanna whipped cream, too?"

When he went back home, not Deli but a homeless woman in a cloth coat and sneakers was sitting in his doorway. He reached into his pocket to give her some change, but she looked away.

"Excuse me," he said. "I just have to get by here." He took out his keys.

The woman stood up angrily, grabbing her shopping bags. "No, really, you can sit here," said Harry. "I just need to get by you to get in."

"Thanks a lot!" shouted the woman. Her teeth were gray in the grain, like old wood. "Thanks!"

"Come back!" he called. "It's perfectly OK!" But the woman staggered halfway down the block, turned, and started screaming at him. "Thanks for all you've done for me! I really appreciate it! I really appreciate everything you've done for me my whole life!"

To relax, he enrolled in a yoga class. It was held three blocks away, and the teacher, short, overweight, and knowledgeable, kept coming over to Harry to tell him he was doing things wrong.

"Stomach in! Shoulders down! Head back!" she bellowed in the darkness of the yoga room. People looked. She was not fond of tall, thin men who thought they knew what they were doing. "Head back!" she said again, and this time tugged on his hair, to get his head at the right angle.

"I can't believe you pulled my hair," said Harry.

"Pardon me?" said the instructor. She pressed her knee into the middle disks of his spine.

"I would just do better," said Harry loudly, "if you wouldn't keep touching me!"

"All right, all right," said the teacher. "I won't touch you," and she walked to the other side of the darkened room, to attend to someone else. Harry lay back for the deep breathing, spine pressed against the tough thread of the carpet. He put his hand over his eyes and stayed like that, while the rest of the class continued with headstands and cat stretches.

The next week Harry decided to try a calisthenics class instead. It was across the street from the yoga class and was full of white people in pastel Spandex. Serious acid disco blared from the corner speakers. The instructor was a thin black man, who smiled happily at the class and led them in exercises that resembled the motion of field hands picking cotton. "Pick that cotton!" he shouted gleefully, overseeing the group, walking archly among them. "Pick it fast!" He giggled, clasping his hands. "Oh, what sweet revenge!" The class lasted an hour and a half, and Harry stayed on for the next class as well, another hour and a half. It strangely encouraged and calmed him, and when he went to the grocery store afterward, he felt almost serene. He lingered at the yogurt and the freshly made pasta. He filled his cart with mineral water, feeling healthy and whole again, when a man one aisle away was caught shoplifting a can of bean-with-bacon soup.

"Hey!" shouted the store manager, and two large shelf clerks grabbed the man with the soup. "I didn't do nothing!"

yelled the man with the soup, but they dragged him by the ears across the store floor to the meat counter and the back room, where the butchers worked in the day. There they began to beat him, until he could no longer call out. Trails of red smeared the floor of the canned goods aisle, where his ears had split open like fruit and bled.

"Stop it!" cried Harry, following the men to the swinging meat doors. "There's no reason for this sort of violence!" and after two minutes, the employees finally let the shoplifter go. They shoved him, swollen and in shock, out the swinging doors toward the exit.

Harry turned to several other customers, who, also distressed, had come up behind him. "My God," said Harry. "I had two exercise classes today, and it still wasn't enough." He left his shopping cart and fled the store for the phone booth outside, where he dialed the police. "I would like to report a crime. My name is Harry DeLeo, and I am standing on the corner of Eighth and—"

"Yeah. Harry DeLeo. Trucks. Look, Harry DeLeo, we got real things," and the policeman hung up.

At night Harry slept in the other room, the "living" room, the room decorated in what Breckie called Early American Mental Institution, the room away from the windows and the trucks, on the sharp-armed sofa, damp towels pressed at the bottom of the bedroom door, so he would not die in his sleep, though that had always been his wish but just not now. He also pressed towels against the bathroom door, in case of an overflow. Safe, barricaded, sulfurous, sandwiched in damp towels like the deviled eggs his mother used to bring to picnics: When he slept he did so dreamlessly, like a bug. In the mornings he woke early and went out and claimed a booth in The Cosmic Galaxy until noon. He read the *Times* and now even the *Post* and the *News*. Sometimes he took notes in the margins for his play. *He felt shackled in nightmare, and in that constant state of daydream that nightmare gives conception to, creature within creature.* In the afternoons he went to see teen movies starring teens. For brief moments they consoled him in a way he couldn't explain. Perhaps it was that the actors were all so attractive and in high school and lived in lovely houses in California. He had never been to California, and only once in the last ten years – when he had gone home with Breck to visit her parents in Minnesota – had he been in a lovely house. The movies reminded him of Breckie, probably that was it, those poreless faces and hairless arms, those idealistic hearts knowing corruption for the first time and learning it well. Harry would leave the movie theater feeling miserable, stepping out into the daylight like a criminal, shoulders bent into coat-hanger angles, in his body the sick heat of hangover, his jacket rumpled as a sheet.

"Harry, you look like shit," said Deli in front of his building. She was passing out fliers for the 25 Cent Girls pavilion. She was wearing a patched vinyl jacket, a red dress, and black pumps with no stockings. "But hey. Nothing I can do for you – except here." She handed him a flier. *Twenty-five Cents! Cheap, Live, and Naked!* "I got myself a day job – ain't you proud of me, Harry?"

Harry *did* feel proud of her, though it surprised him. It did not feel quite appropriate to feel proud. "Deli, I think that's great," he said anyway. "I really do!" Peep show fliers were a start. Surely they were a start.

"Yeah," said Deli, smiling haughtily. "Soon you be asking me to marry you."

"Yup," said Harry, jiggling the key in the lock. Someone in the middle of the night had been jabbing at it with a knife, and the lock was scraped and bent.

"Hey, put on some of that music again, would you?" But Harry had gotten the door open, and it slammed behind him without his answering.

There was mail: a form letter from an agency interested in seeing scripts; an electric bill; a letter from the Health Department verifying his complaint call and advising him to keep after the precinct dispatcher; a postcard for Breckie from some old friend named Lisa, traveling through Italy. *What a place, gal*, it said. *Hello to Harry*. He put it on his refrigerator with a magnet. He went to his desk and from there stared over at it, then stared back at his desk. He went to the window overlooking the street. Deli was still down there, passing out fliers, but people were not taking them anymore. They were brushing by, pretending not to see, and finally she just stood there, in the middle of the sidewalk, frowning, no longer trying, not thrusting a flier out to anyone, just letting the crowds break in front of her, like a wave, until she turned and walked with them, up to the corner, to the light, and threw her fliers into the trash, the way everyone else had done.

The next day Harry got a phone call from Glen Scarp. "Harry, my man, I'm in Jersey directing a scene for a friend. I've got an hour between seven and eight to have a quick drink with you. I'm taking a chopper. Can you make it?"

"I don't know," said Harry. "I'm busy." It was important to be cagey with these guys, to be a little unavailable, to act as if you, too, had a helicopter. "Can you give me a call back later?"

"Sure, sure," said Scarp, as if he understood too clearly. "How about four-thirty. I'll give you a call then."

"Fine," said Harry. "I should know better then what my schedule's like" – he stifled a cough – "for the evening."

"Exactly," said Scarp. "Fabulous."

Harry kept his dirty clothes in a laundry bag at the bottom of his closet. He grabbed the bag up, crammed into it two other pairs of underwear, which had been floating around, and dashed across the street to the Korean laundromat with a large box of generic heavy-duty laundry detergent. He did his wash in an excited fashion, got pushy in claiming a dryer, went next door and ordered a fried egg sandwich to go, with ketchup, and ate it back at the laundromat, sitting on the window ledge, next to a pimp with a satin tie.

At four-thirty, when Scarp called, Harry said, "All's squared away. Just name the place."

This time they met at a restaurant called Zelda. Harry was wearing clean underwear and socks.

"No one ever uses apostrophes anymore, have you noticed?" said Harry. He had been here before and had, in fact, said this before. "It makes restaurants sound like hurricanes." Zelda specialized in eclectic Louisiana cooking. It served things like salmon fillets with macaroni and cheese, both with bones. Capes, ponchos, and little sundresses hung from the ceiling. It was strictly a crazed southern woman's idea of a restaurant.

Harry and Scarp sat in the bar section, near the piano, hemmed in on every side by potted plants.

Scarp was fishing for descriptions. "There's no—"

"Business like show business!" burst out Harry.

"Yes," said Scarp, a little taken aback. He was dressed in jeans and a linen shirt. Again he wore a broach, this time of peridot and garnet, fastened close to the collar. He was drinking a martini.

Harry wasn't drinking. He'd ordered seltzer water and took big handfuls of mixed nuts from the bowl in front of him. He hadn't had a cigarette since the trucks had started coming, and now he found himself needing something to put in his mouth, something to engage his hand on its journey up from the table and back down again. "So tell me about this thing you were shooting in New Jersey," Harry began amiably, but a nut skin got caught in his throat and he began to choke, his face red and crumpling, frightening as a morel. Scarp pushed the seltzer water toward Harry, then politely looked away.

"It's a project that belongs to an old buddy of mine," said Scarp. Harry nodded at him, but his eyes were tearing and he was gulping down seltzer. Scarp continued, pretending not to notice, pretending to have to collect his thoughts by studying objects elsewhere. "He's doing this film about bourgeois guilt – you know, how you can be bourgeois and an artist at the same time . . ."

"Really," croaked Harry. Water filmed his eyes.

". . . but how the guilt can harrow you and how in the end you can't let it. As Flaubert said, Be bourgeois in your life so that you may be daring in your art."

Harry cleared his throat and started to cough again. The nut skin was still down there, scratching and dry. "I don't trust translations," he rasped. He took an especially large swallow of seltzer and could feel the blood leave his face a bit. There was some silence, and then Harry added, "Did Flaubert ever write a play?"

"Don't know," said Scarp. "At any rate, I was just shooting this one scene for my friend, since he was called away by a studio head. It was a very straightforward cute meet at a pedicurist's. Have you ever had a pedicure?"

"No," said Harry.

"You really have to. It's one of the great pleasures of life. . . ."

But I have had plantar's warts. You have to put acid on them, and Band-Aids. . . .

"Do you feel all right?" asked Scarp, looking suddenly concerned.

"Fine. It's just I quit smoking. Suddenly there's all this air in my lungs. What's a cute meat?"

"Cute meet? It's Hollywood for where two lovers meet and fall in love."

"Oh," said Harry. "I think I liked myself better before I knew that."

Scarp laughed. "You writers," he said, downing his martini. "*We* writers, I should say. By the way, I have to tell you: I've ripped you off mercilessly." Scarp smiled proudly.

"Oh?" said Harry. Something lined up in him, got in order. His back straightened and his feet unhooked from the table legs.

"You know, when we met last time, I was working on an episode for the show where Elsie and John, the two principals, have to confront all sorts of family issues, including the death of an elderly relative."

"That doesn't really sound like ripping me off."

"Well, what I've done is use some of that stuff you told me about your family and the radon gas – well, you'll see – and that fabulous bit about your Aunt Flora dying while you were dating the Kennedy girl. It's due to air early next month. In fact, I'll give you a call when I find out exactly."

Harry didn't know what to say. The room revolved dizzyingly away from him, dumped him and spun, because he'd never really been part of it to begin with. "Excuse me?" he stammered. His hand started to tremble, and he moved it quickly through his hair.

"I'll give you a call. When it's on." Scarp frowned.

Harry gazed at the striated grain of the table – a tree split to show its innards. *"What?"* he said, finally, slow and muzzy. He picked up his seltzer, knocked it back fast. He set the glass down with a loud crack. "You'd do that for me? You'd really, honestly, do that for me?" He was starting to yell. The people at the table nearest the piano turned to look. "I have to go."

Scarp looked anxiously at his watch. "Yes, I've gotta run myself."

"No, you don't understand!" said Harry loudly. He stood up, huge over the table. "*I* have to go." He pushed back his chair, and it fell all the way over into a plant. He strode quickly toward the door and pushed against it hard.

The night was just beginning to come, and come warmly, the air in a sweet, garbagey thaw. Midtown was crawling with sailors. They were all youthful and ashore and excited to be this way, in their black and white-trimmed suits, exploring Manhattan and knowing it, in this particular guise, to be a movie set they had bought tickets to, knowing the park was up, *the park is up!* knowing there were girls, and places where there were girls, who would pull you against them, who knew what you knew though they seemed too bonelessly small to. Harry loped by the sailors, their boyish, boisterous clusters, then broke into a run. Old men were selling carnations on the corner, and they murmured indecipherably as he passed. The Hercules was showing *Dirty Desiree* and *Throbbin' Hood*, and sailors were going in. Off-duty taxis sped from their last fares at the theaters to the Burger King on Ninth for something to eat. Putting block after block beneath his feet would clear his heart, Harry hoped, but the sailors: There was no shaking them. They were everywhere, hatless and landlubbed with eagernesses. Up ahead on his block, he saw a woman who looked like Deli strolling off with two of them, one on each arm. And then – it *was* Deli.

He stopped, frozen midstride, then started to walk again.

"Aw, Deli," he whispered. But who was he to whisper? He had tried to be a hooker himself, had got on the old hip boots and walked, only to discover he was just – a slut.

The Battery's down, he thought. *The Battery's down*. He stood in front of the 25 Cent Girls pavilion. Golden lights winked and dashed around the marquee.

"Wanna buy, man?" hissed a guy urinating at the curb. "I got bitches, I got rods, I got crack."

Harry stepped toward the cashier in the entrance booth. He slid a dollar under the glass, and the cashier slid him back four tokens. "What do I do?" he said, looking at the tokens, but the cashier didn't hear him. Two sailors came up behind, bought four dollars' worth, and went inside, smiling.

Harry followed. The interior was lit and staircased like a discotheque, and all along the outer walls were booths with wooden doors. He passed three of them and then stumbled into the fourth. He closed the door, sat down on the bench, and, taking a deep breath, he wept, hopelessly, for Breckie and for God and for that life here that seemed always parallel to his own, never intersecting, like some opposite shore of river he could never swim across, although he kept trying. He looked at the tokens in his hand. They were leaving bluish streaks in the dampness there, melting if not used. He fumbled, placed one in the slot, and a dark screen lifted from behind the glass. Before him, lit and dancing, appeared a 25 Cent Girl, naked, thirtyish, auburn-haired and pale: *National Geographic* goes to Ireland. There was music playing, and she gyrated to it, sleepy and indifferent. But as he watched she seemed to lift her eyes, to spot him, to head toward his window, slow and smiling, until she was pressing her breast against his pane, his alone. He moaned, placed his mouth against the cold single rose of her nipple, against the hard smeared glass, though given time, in this, this wonderful town, he felt, it might warm beneath his labors, truly, like something real.

1989

WHAT IS SEIZED

MY MOTHER MARRIED a cold man. Not that he couldn't make her laugh, because he could do that: he'd pull some antic in the living room – sing nursery rhymes in an Italian accent, safety-pin an olive to his lapel, tell jokes about chickens, elephants, or morons. And because he performed with the local musical theater group every spring and fall, and usually got the funny parts, he sometimes practiced in the kitchen while she was doing stuff, making her grin in spite of herself, making her giggle into the batter bowl. My father taught clarinet and math at the high school in town. He seemed to know how to get people to like him, to do crazy stunts with furniture or time-rate problems. I would usually hear about these secondhand. People in Crasden seemed to think he was amazing somehow. Special, they said. Talented. But when he made love to my mother, he kept his eyes closed the whole time, turned his head away from her, and afterward would give her a hard, angry gaze, roll stiffly over to his side of the bed, face the wall, shake her off of him with a shudder or a flinch if she kissed his shoulder, rubbed his arm, lay a palm against his bare back. She told me this before she died. She just stared off to one side at the drapes and told me.

We lived on a lake and used to hear the water bang and slurp at the dock pilings at night. We also had a rowboat tied and afloat at the end, which would clunk against the wood when the water got rough. "Old man boat, old man boat," James would sometimes sing to be funny, instead of "Old Man River," which my mother had taught us. James and I shared the large bed in the lakeside room upstairs, in the morning often waking up staring into each other's eyes, and at night spending hours listening for the underwater world in the lake to come magically to life, when no one was looking, when it was pitch black and still except for the quietest rocking, and the good, shy fish would put on pink and orange jackets and smile and go to balls, with violins and oriental fans.

James was my foster brother – half Indian, half Pennsylvania Catholic. His parents had met in college. In 1958 his father returned for good to a small city north of Calcutta, and his mother had a nervous breakdown, came to Crasden to live, but later got sick and died. James became a public ward and came to live with us when he was five and I was four; we never talked about his past. He had smooth black hair and a wide white smile. I thought it was funny that his lips were brown and that every night he scraped his tongue with a wooden scraper. "Be kind to James," my mother said. "He is your brother now." Sometimes he would cry, but not that often.

The rooms in our house were like songs. Each had its own rhythmic spacing and clutter, which if you crossed your eyes became a sort of musical notation, a score – clusters of eighth notes, piles of triplets, and the wooden roundness of doorways, like clefs, all blending in a kind of concerto. Or sometimes, as with the bathroom, with its motif of daisies and red plastic, they created a sort of jingle, something small, likable, functional. It was the bookcase in the living room that seemed particularly symphonic, the books all friendly with one another, a huge chorus of them in a hum; they stood packed behind glass doors with loose metal knobs. My mother also kept photo albums, scrapbooks, yearbooks on the bottom shelf of the case, along with the big, heavy books like *Smith's World History* and the *Golden Treasury of Children's Stories*. In one book she had black and white pictures of herself, starting from when she was little. Gray, empty days I would take that book out and look at it. By the time I was nine, I knew all the pictures by heart. To stare at them, to know those glimpses, I felt, was to know her, to become her, to make my mother a woman with adventures, a woman in a story, a book, a movie. The photos somehow seemed powerful. Sometimes I still look at them, with a cup of coffee, with the television on.

* * *

A photo where she is six and has bangs bleached pale from the sun. She is in a white sundress, standing next to a large tricycle, squinting and frowning into the camera. Crabface. That's what my mother called it: "Oh yeah, there's me, ole crabface, pouting for soda pop."

My mother liked to sing, but she would wait until my father wasn't around because he would correct her pitch and straighten her posture and insist she use her lungs and diaphragm better. "Don't sing like a disembodied mule. You should use your whole rib cage. And sitting on the piano bench, she would poker-stare straight ahead at the sheet music and play the C above middle C over and over again with one finger, a sort of hypnosis. "Go mow the lawn, Enrico," she would say sometimes. Which was a joke, because my father's real name was Sam and because we really had no lawn, just a craggy, pine-needled slope, which galloped wildly from the road down to the lake. On the other side of the house was a slow, tiny stream, which trickled and glided gingerly over rocks, like something afraid of hurting itself.

At night with the lights out, after she had heard our prayers, my mother would sing to James and me, and we thought she was great. She'd sing "Down by the Old Mill Stream" or some Cole Porter hit she knew from college. She loved Frank Sinatra. She would stand by our bed, crooning imitations into one of the bedposts as if it were a microphone, and afterward we would clap in the dark until our hands stung. (At the end of "Pennies from Heaven," she would place a penny on each post for us to find in the morning.) "Thank you, thank you," she would whisper with a low, wonderful laugh, smiling and bending over us to wetly kiss our cheeks, her hair down, long, black, and sweeping against my chest and chin, smelling soapy and dry. And if the moon was out it lit up the lake, and the lake light shone into the room through the slats of the blinds, tentatively striping her hair and face or the arm of her sweater. And as she moved – to kiss James, to tuck in the blankets – the stripes moved up and down her. When she left she always kept the door slightly unlatched, the lamp from the hall framing the door in cracks of light interrupted only by hinges. She always called in a whisper, "Good night my sweet sparrows," that expression only later in my life seeming silly or indulgent or mad. And often James would be on his back next to me humming late into the night, invisible in the dark, singing the words to "Old Devil Moon" when he could remember them, or sometimes just whispering, "Hey, Lynnie, how does it go again?" his legs jiggling under the sheets.

A photo where she is eight and her hair is darker, wavier, and she already has the bones of her adult face beginning to grow inside, cheekbones awakening behind the skin. She is grinning in a striped shirt with her arm around Uncle Don, her blank-faced little brother, in front of a house they lived in just outside of Syracuse, a white house with a closed-in front porch and a brick chimney painted white, two large tamaracks on either side, their branches dangling curved and protective over the roof, like large mustaches. Uncle Don comes up to her chin.

My father played Liza Doolittle's father in *My Fair Lady* and the knight with the dog in *Camelot.* On Sunday afternoons my mother would bring us to watch them rehearse in the Crasden High School auditorium, but in 1956, so that it was new and strong and maroon and velvet and hadn't lost its polish. I loved the dark slope of it, and would gallop along the rows of empty flip-bottom seats as if they were my own private corridors. The director would pace out in front of the stage, a few feet beyond the orchestra pit. At early rehearsals they just used a pianist, a puffy woman named Mrs. Beales who took many trips to the ladies' room. "The entire action to the right and further downstage, downstage," the director was always shouting, waving both arms like a semaphore. He had thick, white, horse-mane hair that he combed straight back from his brow but that nevertheless flopped into his eyes from time to time. He wore white shoes and usually dressed in something of pale blue silk. My father would say things during scene cuts on stage that we couldn't hear but that made everyone laugh – a talky, theatrical, group laugh, filled with ho-ho's and oh-no's and affectionate hissing and stomping. Sometimes the director would wear sunglasses and prop them on top of his head and say, "Oh shit, let's take a break." And then the lights would go up and the actors would head for the cafeteria two long marble hallways away, and as the school was empty and lit up like a bowling alley, you could hear the echo of their steps and their loud chatter, the woman who played Liza Doolittle still screeching "Aow," adding, "Did you phone the babysitter, Ron?" and Professor Higgins, not with them but seated on the stage's edge, eating a sandwich he had brought, his legs dangling, sneakers thumping against each other, like a Little Leaguer. During these breaks, James and I would dash up onto the stage to see my father, and, if it was a dress rehearsal, we would giggle at his orange face or his wig or his fake eyebrows arched way up into his forehead. But then we would be struck by shyness when he would say, "Hi, kids," but look past us, over our heads, then turn and head busily backstage to take care of something. Standing there on the stage, we would turn and look out onto the hill of auditorium seats, spot my mother in the tenth row where we had left her reading a book, and she would wave and we would wave, then we'd race to her, like racing home, and climb hungrily all over her lap, as if looking for something. Sometimes we played with the bobby pins in her hair, which she used to hold it in a twist in the back, making antennae, making antlers, my mother allowing it all. "Your father is a talented man," my mother said, sounding like my teachers at school who said similar things to me, my mother sensing our disappointment in never getting his attention for very long. "Talented men have very busy heads. They may seem unkind sometimes." And I would think about this for a long time afterward, chewing my nails, writing letters.

A photo in which she is nine and dressed for a ballet class in a long-sleeved black leotard, in the living room in front of the fireplace. She is doing an arabesque, one arm bent slightly over her head, one arm out to the side; because it is a front view, only one leg shows, and she looks something like an amputee, the tip of her ballet shoe just visible above the outline of her shoulder, her whole body leaning into the camera as her eyes gaze off to one side of it, looking half sorrowful, half comical. "She looks like a greasehead," James said once, sitting next to me, taking note of the tight wet way her hair was pulled off her face into a bun. "You're a greasehead," I said, nurturing fantasies of becoming a ballerina myself, and I punched him in the leg. He moved farther back on the couch, a little away from me, and just chewed his gum harder. Sometimes when we had fights, I would say I'm sorry, and sometimes he would. He liked to look at the pictures, too.

"Cold men destroy women," my mother wrote me years later. "They woo them with something personable that they bring out for show, something annexed to their souls like a fake greenhouse, lead you in, and you think you see life and vitality and sun and greenness, and then when you love them, they lead you out into their real soul, a drafty, cavernous, empty ballroom, inexorably arched and vaulted and mocking you with its echoes – you hear all you have sacrificed, all you have given, landing with a loud clunk. They lock the greenhouse and you are as tiny as a figure in an architect's drawing, a faceless splotch, a blur of stick limbs abandoned in some voluminous desert of stone."

"*Dear Mom*," I wrote back. *"I am coming home on the 23rd, so should be there for the candlelight service on Sunday. Hope all is going well. Exams are merciless. See you soon."*

A photo of my mother when she is fourteen and the adult bones are at last there – stark cemented lines, startling as the curves in a mountain road, from eye to jaw, her skin lineless, and although she is not smiling there is no sadness in her face, simply an inquiring, a wide stare of scrutiny, a look of waiting, of preparedness.

My mother was the only mother I knew who wore her

hair long. Sometimes she would wear it in a single braid that hung like a dark tail, marbled with auburn sun streaks, down the middle of her back; other times she wore it in two side braids that would swing back and forth when she bent over. "You look like a featherhead Indian lady," James would tell her. He was just being made aware of the distinction between India Indian and the kind you saw on TV. "How," my mother would joke, holding up a hand. And James, not getting it, would tug impatiently at her braids and say, "Because of these, because of these."

She is fifteen and has Tonied her hair into a wild frizz that dances, dark and frenetic, way out beyond the barrettes she uses to clamp it down. She is sitting on a bench in a park somewhere, eating an ice cream cone, blue jeans rolled up mid-calf, legs spread wide and feet pigeon-toed, ankles caved outward, and she is hunched a bit forward with her cone, making a crazy face that involves sticking out her tongue and crossing her eyes.

There were nights my parents fought, woke us up with their fighting, and James would put his pillow over his face and I would lie wide-eyed, terrified and paralyzed by my father's bellowing, the doors slamming, something metal always clinking somewhere to the floor, the pounding on the walls, and my mother's "Oh god, oh god, just leave, why don't you."

One afternoon, the day after one of these night fights, I brought my friend Rachel home on the bus with me. We walked in the kitchen door and I reminded her to wipe her feet. Down the hallway that led to the bathroom I suddenly saw my mother, sitting on the toilet with the door wide open, her legs and hips bare and white, her underwear coiled at her ankles, her long hair all unbraided, a mane of unbrushed ripples floating out and downward toward her waist. She didn't move when we walked in. She just sat there in an old black shirt like some obscene statue, her head leaning frozenly on her hands, her elbows propped on her knees.

"Is that your *mother*?" whispered Rachel.

And I said maybe it was and maybe it wasn't.

My mother never saw us, but continued to stare like a drunkard at something on the floor just ahead of her.

"Come on," I said, and led Rachel upstairs to my room where James, on the bed, was reading a bird encyclopedia: cowbirds, starlings, cuckoos. "Look at this," he said. "A blue-booted boobie." And we looked and saw it was just some dumb black-faced bird. And then all three of us played "Careers" and Rachel bought a farm and lots of happiness, but I was the first man on the moon and loaded up on stars, winning everything.

Her high school graduation picture. The yearbook caption reads, "Salutatorian" and "Best All-Around." Her friends write things like, "Beautiful Anna, we will miss you off in Chicago, come back to visit." "The Windy City has a treat coming its way. Good luck." "Stay as sweet as you are. Remember the Bluebird Dance. We had fun. Good luck at U. of Chi. Love, Barbara."

That night, or was it another night, my mother came into our room late after we had already tucked ourselves in and she laid our schoolbooks on the floor next to our bed and then stood in the doorway awhile, looking wraithlike, silent, in a long white sleeveless nightgown, one bare arm dangling loosely at her side, the other bent upward, hand cupped around the back of her neck, thoughtfully, her head tilted toward the dangling arm, her dark unpinned hair obscuring one shoulder like the hood of a cape. And there was a bird outside on the lake, hooting, calling, and it was the only sound, and James murmured groggily, "That's a loon, a ruby-throated loon," and my mother turned and disappeared until morning.

"Your father wrote music, too, you know, but he never shared it with us," my mother said, a bit breathlessly, as I smoothed out her blankets. "Music ultimately left him unstirred. Like a god irritated with his own tinkerings. Despite his talent, or perhaps because of it, he heard only the machinery, the clanking and spitting. He felt nothing. No compassion." She coughed. "You would think creating something would necessarily be an act of love or compassion."

"Mother," I said, remembering the nurse's instructions. "Perhaps you should take your pill now."

She leaves behind all her friends, including Barbara. A picture of this, with streamers and cake and wine bottles. At college she falls in love with a sophomore named Jacob Fish and works toward a degree in fine arts. After four years she leaves him, inexplicably goes back home, paints and designs sets for a local Syracuse theater group. *Kismet. South Pacific.* See the scenery. She also sings in the chorus; that's her, there.

I remember overhearing a brief snatch of a fight my parents had once. Or rather my mother was crying and having difficulty explaining why to my father, as he seemed angry and distant, she said, and soon he was screaming at her that she should stop her goddamn crying and perhaps get some exercise for a change. At this my mother cried even harder and my father stormed out of the house. But the next day, and several times a week for years afterward, my mother was running along the lake in sweatclothes and old sneakers she didn't mind getting wet. Once in a while I went with her, jogging next to her, watching her breasts float up and down beneath her sweatshirt, imitating the way she breathed in and out with quick snorts. Twice we saw dead birds washed up on shore and we stopped to look at their bedraggled carcasses, their eyes already crawling with small black bugs. "What is beautiful is seized," my mother said. "My grandmother used to tell me that."

Scotch-taped to my mother's scrapbook is a thumb-sized lavender picture viewer, which, when you look through the eyehole and hold it up to a light, magnifies a tiny picture of her and Jacob Fish on New Year's Eve at a big hotel in the Catskills. On the outside of the viewer is printed in gold script, "Kiamesha Lake, N.Y.," and there is a small gold chain attached to it, so you can hang it somewhere or twirl it around your fingers. Inside of it, when you peer through, my mother is standing next to Jacob Fish, both done up like prom royalty, my mother in a strapless apricot dancing gown, her hair piled up on top of her head, fastened with pins and one pale rose, and Jacob Fish, short and tow-headed, just about her height, with a navy blue bow tie, a kindness and graciousness in his face, which, I can tell, made my mother happy, made her smile, timelessly holding his arm in the little lavender capsule.

Saturdays were motherless – she went in to Crasden to shop – and my father would sometimes make pancakes and play cards with us: "Go Fish" and "War." Sometimes he would do tricks: we would pick a card and he wouldn't know what it was and then we would put it back in the deck, which he would shuffle, cut, make piles, rows, and columns with, and eventually he would find our card. All his card tricks were variations of this. Sometimes it seemed that we were the ones to find it ourselves, as when we held the deck and he'd karate-chop it, the sole remaining card in our hand being, miraculously, the one we had chosen. "Aw, how'dya do that?" James would want to know and he would grab the cards and try to figure it out as my father put on an exaggerated, enigmatic smile, shrugged his shoulders, folded his arms. "I'll never tell, will I, Lynnie?" My dad would wink at me.

I never wanted to know. It was enough to sit in the living room in my pajamas and smell pancakes and be reassured that my father was special. To discover or expose the wheels and pulleys behind the tricks, I knew, would be to blacken Saturdays and undo my father. If his talents, his magic, his legerdemain, didn't remain inimitable, unknowable, if they weren't protected and preserved, what could he possibly be, to us, for us, what could he do?

A picture of Mom and Jacob Fish on a beach. Mom's one-piece is black like her hair and the water is gray and the sand is white. There are buckets, a small shovel, and a blanket.

Jacob Fish holds a fistful of sand over Mom's head. She laughs with her eyes closed, a momentary shutting out, the only way sometimes one can laugh.

The fall I turned ten, my father played Billy Bigelow in the Crasden Playhouse production of *Carousel.* Halfway through the show Billy Bigelow sings a song about his plans for his child to be, warbling through a lilting list of parental love promises. My mother brought us to the Sunday afternoon rehearsals (the real performance was too late for us, she said) and sat stiff and pinched through that song, staring narrowly at my father as he walked through it, following the snow-haired director's commands for the placement of his feet ("Damn it, Sam . . . you sing like a god, but you just can't dance"). Off to one side two stagehands were painting a merry-go-round red and green. "Bad colors," my mother said, shaking her head critically. A blonde woman a few seats away piped up: "Last week somebody stole all the good paint. Our budget is tight."

"What is beautiful is seized," murmured my mother, and the blonde woman looked at her oddly and said, "Yeah, I guess," and after a few minutes got up and left. Years later my mother would say to me: "That song your father sang in *Carousel.* What wonderful lies. He never spent time with you kids, never sang to you or took you places."

And when she said it, it became true. But only then, when she said it. Until then it seemed Dad was just Dad, was somehow only what he was supposed to be.

A picture of Jacob Fish standing by a river with a suitcase in one hand and a hat in another. That was the City River, opposite the train station, my mother said. The suitcase was hers. So was the hat. He was trying to look dignified and worldly and had requested props.

She cries, slumped over at her dressing table, and dreams that someone comes up behind her and bends down to hold her, to groan and weep into her neck with her, to turn her around and lift up her face, kiss her eyes, mouth on water, on cheek, on hair. But there is no one, just my father, sitting way across the room from her, in a white and rose upholstered chair (something later moved to my room at college, something I would sit in, stare at), an icy anger tucked behind his face, locked up like a store after hours, a face laced tight as a shoe. His arms are crossed behind his head like a man on vacation, but he is not relaxed. His features arrange themselves in straight, sharp lines.

"Your numbness," my mother cries softly, "is something perhaps you cannot help. It is what the world has done to you. But your coldness. That is what you do to the world."

He picks up a porcelain pill box on the lamp table, hurls and shatters it against the wall. "That's what I have to say to you," he says. "I won't do your little dances." And he walks out, slamming the door.

I only heard parts of this. She told me the rest years later when she was dying, and I spent hours brushing and brushing her hair. She liked me to do that, always managing a smile and sinking back into her pillow. "My legs, Lynnie. Can you do my legs today, dear?" she would ask. And I'd take the Norelco razor from the nightstand drawer, pull up the covers from the foot of the bed, and glide the razor up and down her calves. She liked her legs smooth and hairless, and I think she liked the metallic friction and buzz of it. That, too, made her smile.

A picture of my parents on bikes before they were married. They are at a gas station where they have stopped to fill up their tires with air. Mom smiles. Dad makes a goofy face, both hands on the handlebars. Both of them wear long, Jamaica-style shorts. An Esso sign behind them is missing the *O*. Yiddish for "eat," my mother told me once.

"They want to take things and destroy them," my mother sighed the same month she died, when we were talking of our lake house, which had been sold at first to a funeral home and then bought by the federal government, who tore it down for vaguely military purposes no one ever bothered to explain.

"They want my hair," she said another day, winking weakly at me when a nurse came in with scissors and suggested a haircut. My mother shook her head, but the nurse's air was insistent.

"I *don't* think she wants one," I said, and the nurse looked at me dumbly and padded out on the soundless rubber soles those who surround the dying always wear.

My mother coming into our room at night. My childhood sometimes simply a series of images of her swirling into the doorway, in white, over and over again, coming to hear our prayers, to sing us songs, to whisper that she loved us, to kiss me wetly on the mouth, hair dangling, making a tent in which just our faces, hers and mine, lived and breathed forever. She'd rub my nose, and James's too, and whisper, "See you tomorrow," and at the doorway, "Good night, my sparrows."

She dreams that he is trying to kill her. That he has a rifle and is calling her out of the bathroom. In the bathroom she has knives and axes. She bolts awake and he is looking at her, chilly, indifferent. "Your face," she says. "My god. It is a murderer's face."

"What the hell are you talking about?" he says.

The year after *Carousel* was *The Music Man*, and the woman who played Marian the librarian used to call our house fairly regularly, purring like older women do at babies. She would ask if my *Daddy* was home.

"My father's not here," I almost always said, even if I knew he was upstairs with lesson plans. I think of all the things I did as a child, this was the boldest.

She would ask me to tell him that Marcia called. Sometimes I would. I'd knock on the door to his study, walk in, and say: "Marcia called. She wanted you to know."

And he would turn and look at me vacantly, as if he wasn't quite sure who I was talking about, and then say, "Oh, right.

About rehearsal. Thanks." And he would turn his back to me and continue working at his desk, and I would just stand there in the doorway, staring at the back of his sweater. It seemed when he corrected papers and things that he always wore the same Norwegian sweater: green with a chain of rectangularized gold reindeer around the top, across his back and shoulders.

"Did you want anything else?" He would twist around again in his seat and lower his glasses.

And I would say, "No. I mean yes."

"What?"

"I forgot," I would say, and turn and flee.

In the wedding photos they wear white against the murky dark of trees. They are thin and elegant. They have placid smiles. The mouth of the father of the bride remains in a short, straight line. I don't know who took these pictures. I suppose they are lies of sorts, revealing by omission, by indirection, by clues such as shoes and clouds. But they tell a truth, the only way lies can. The way only lies can.

Another morning, I heard my parents up early in the bathroom, my dad shaving, getting ready to leave for school.

"Look," he sighed in a loud whisper. "I really can't say that I'll never leave you and the kids or that I'll never make love to another woman—"

"Why not?" asked my mother. "Why can't you say that?" Even her anger was gentle, ingenuous.

"Because I don't feel that way."

"But . . . can't you just say it anyway?"

At this I like to imagine that my parents met each other's gaze in the medicine cabinet mirror, suddenly grinning. But later in the hospital bed, holding my hand and touching each of my nails slowly with her index finger, my mother said to me, "Your father. He was in a dance. And he just couldn't dance." Earlier that year she had written me: "That is what is wrong with cold people. Not that they have ice in their souls – we all have a bit of that – but that they insist their every word and deed mirror that ice. They never learn the beauty or value of gesture. The emotional necessity. For them, it is all honesty before kindness, truth before art. Love is art, not truth. It's like painting scenery."

These are the things one takes from mothers. Once they die, of course, you get the strand of pearls, the blue quilt, some of the original wedding gifts – a tray shellacked with the invitation, an old rusted toaster – but the touches and the words and the moaning the night she dies, these are what you seize, save, carry around in little invisible envelopes, opening them up quickly, like a carnival huckster, giving the world a peek. They will not stay quiet. No matter how you try. No matter how you lick them. The envelopes will not stay glued.

"Dear Mom, The extra courseload makes life hectic, but I think I'm getting used to it. Spring break is the 19th. Yikes. So much to do before I can leave. See you then."

When I was thirteen, my mother left rice burning on the stove and half-tried to drown herself in the lake. At seven o'clock, my father not home yet and James late at Chess Club, I stepped out the back door and called for her. It was March and the lake was not even completely melted yet – a steely slate green with a far-off whitish center, like some monstrous wound. I walked down to the dock; sometimes she went down there "for air" just before making dinner. I found her on the shore – we really had no beach, just a stoney straggle along the waterline for jogging and rock-skipping. She was on her back, her blouse soaked and transparent, her black hair plastered in strings across her face, water lapping at her like an indifferent cat. She was clutching fistfuls of gravel and smearing them across her cheeks, down the front of her body, her legs still but her mouth opening and closing noiselessly, twisted and stretched, the first of two such expressions of hers I would witness. I couldn't move. Even years later I would see that face – in my own, in photos, in mirrors, that severely sculpted anguish moving behind mine, against mine, against my less dramatic bones and thick, squarish mouth, struggling to emerge. I cried. I didn't know what to do. I ran back to the house, burst into the kitchen, and saw my father, who had just gotten home, scraping black smoking rice angrily from the bottom of the pan. "Mom, it's Mom," I panted, and pointed toward the lake. And he shouted, "What?" and hurried out and down the path.

At eight o'clock an ambulance came and took her away. She came back, however, the next morning, looking a little pale and raccoon-eyed, trudging upstairs on my father's arm. She glanced at me, it seemed, apologetically.

My father spent that next day down on the dock, singing out at the lake, something Italian, a Puccini aria or something. He actually did this about twice a year while I was growing up, a way of releasing things inside of him, my mother said, in a way, he hoped, that would not disturb the neighbors (who were a quarter of a mile away on each side). Sometimes I would stare out the back-door window and be able to make out the outline of him, sometimes sitting, but more often pacing the dock cross-planks, his voice floating up toward the house. But not his school voice or his theater voice – this was something else, a throbbing, pained vibrato, like some creature that lived inside of him that he didn't understand, that embarrassed him, that he didn't know quite what to do with. Sometimes I would leave the house and go for a walk in the opposite direction, up past the road, through the woods, across the old train tracks. There was a boarded-up building, a small factory of some sort, and an unusable old road, bordered with ancient gaslight posts with the jets yanked from them, hollowed as skeleton eyes, and James and I both would sometimes go up there to look for berries and make up stories and dares. Dare to run to the door and back. Dare to tear off the PRIVATE PROPERTY poster. Dare to climb in the window. To touch the electric fence. To this day it remains a mystery to me what was inside the place, or what its original function was. All nailed and shuttered and papered with NO TRESPASSING signs. Sometimes we swore we heard noises inside – James would call it grumbling, but I always thought of it as being like my father on the dock, blockaded and alone, singing in its strange foreign language, a need to be exploded somehow, a need to disgorge an aria over the lake. Finally some people came from the city and did blow it up. Laced it up with dynamite and blasted out its corners, its flat roof, its broken windowpanes, its black insides laid bare and smoldering in the daylight, neighbors well beyond a quarter-mile off hearing it at breakfast, kids talking about it at school, and bits of nails and plaster we found later stuck like shrapnel in the posts of the gaslights, like a war, like there had been a war.

Another photo of my mother in her wedding dress, standing next to her mother, whose smile and hat are too big for her face; she seems vaguely eyeless, noseless. And her daughter looks not at the camera but off to one side somewhere.

I was fifteen when my father left us and my mother had her mastectomy. Both things happened suddenly, quietly, without announcement. As if some strange wind rushed in and swept things up into it, then quickly rushed out again; it simply left what it left.

When your parents divide, you, too, bifurcate. You cleave and bubble and break in two, live two lives, half of you crying every morning on the dock at sunrise, black hair fading to dusky gray, part of you traveling off to some other town where you teach school and tell jokes in an Italian accent in a bar and make people laugh.

And when your mother starts to lose her mind, so do you. You begin to be afraid of people on the street. You see shapes – old men and spiders – in the wallpaper again like when you were little and sick. The moon's reflection on the lake starts to look to you like a dead fish floating golden belly up. Ask anyone. Ask anyone whose mother is losing her mind.

When I was sixteen, I came home from school and found my mother drunk in her bathrobe, lying flat on the coffee table in the living room, spread out on top of the magazines.

She was out of control with laughter, hysterical wine-tears trickling out of the swollen slits of her eyes.

"Mom, come upstairs. Let me put you to bed," I said, setting down my books and helping her upstairs. She was leaning on me, still laughing helplessly. "My god," she said. "They lopped off my breasts, can you believe it? Lopped them right—" and she made a quick motion with her hand in the air.

I tucked her in and kissed her face and she cried into the neck of my blouse. "I'm cold. I'm thirsty. Don't leave me, honey. You're warm. If you leave I'll have to put on a sweater."

"Get some sleep," I said softly, pulling up the blue quilt, drawing the blinds, standing in the doorway, just a moment, to watch her fall asleep, the lake beating like a giant watery heart against the dock.

She takes long, silent showers, slumped against the ceramic wall, the steady jets of water bouncing off one of her shoulders, splashing against the plastic curtain, shampoo lather drizzling down into her mouth.

"Even his I love you's," she said, "were like tiny daggers, like little needles or safety pins. Beware of a man who says he loves you but who is incapable of a passionate confession, of melting into a sob."

I tuck her in. I kiss her.

A series of pictures here of mothers and daughters switching places – women switching places to take care of one another. You, the daughter, becoming the mother, the Ceres, and she the daughter, kidnapped to hell, and you roam the earth to find her, to mourn her, leaving the trees and grain to wither, having no peace, you have no peace.

"What is beautiful is seized," my mother said a final time, speaking of my father, whom she said had been destroyed by too many women, a heart picked over, scratched at, taken, lost. "It came to me in bulky bandages, seeming much larger, much more than it really was."

* * *

My mother, thin and gray in a nightgown, staring off and away, not at the camera.

"You reach a point," she wrote me once, "where you cannot cry anymore, and you look around you at people you know, at people your own age, and they're not crying either. Something has been taken. And they are emptier. And they are grateful."

When my mother died, her groaning woke the elderly woman in the bed next to hers who was supposed to have her pancreas operated on the next day. "What is happening?" cried the old woman, sleepless and distraught. Something had seized my mother in the back, arched it, stiffened her limbs, her mouth a gash across her face, revealing only her teeth, yellowed fine as old piano keys. An awful astonishment pervaded her features, her bones, as if she never really believed death would be like this, a bludgeoning by tubes and contractions, and by the time – only a minute – the nurses responded to my shouts and came running, the sweat and urine soaking into the sheets already seemed cool and old and my mother's eyes were wide as eggs and she was dead. I clutched at things – her robe, a plastic pitcher, a cup – and looking around, around the room, the window, wondered where she had gone, she must still be, had to be near, somewhere, and the lady with the pancreas, beyond the screen next to the bed, had heard it all and now wept loudly, inconsolably, and they gave her a sleeping pill although she pushed it away, saying, "Oh, please, god, no." Nothing moved. I bent over the bed. "Mom," I whispered, kissing her lips, surgical carts rackety in the hallway, a voice in the ceiling paging Dr. Davis Dr. Davis to the nurses' station, figures in white slowly gathering around me, hands on my shoulders, hard, false as angels. "Mom," I breathed.

Jacob Fish came to the funeral with a pretty brunette woman who looked like a high school French teacher. He seemed somehow like a nice man. At the end of the burial, he escorted the woman back to the car and then went off by himself, over to a tree, and ran his hands through his hair. I never really got a chance to talk with him, although I'm not certain what we would have talked about. When he was through at the tree and had thrust his hands back into his pockets, he rejoined the woman in the car and drove off.

My father did not bring anyone with him. He came up to me and hugged me tightly and for a moment the red rushed to both of our eyes. "Lynnie," he said, and I stepped to one side. I looked away from him. I looked at his shoes. I looked at the clouds. "I loved her more than you think," he said, and I listened for the needles, the safety pins. James, home from medical school and standing next to me, shook my dad's hand, then quickly embraced him. Everyone was dressed in black. "So much black, so much black," I kept repeating like some nervous mynah bird.

That night James and I left all the casseroles at my mother's apartment and went out and got drunk at a Howard Johnson's. James made me smile reminding me of the time when I was little and insisted that if you were in the woods and had to go to the bathroom really badly, all you had to do was eat a piece of bread; it would absorb everything, and you wouldn't have to go anymore.

"James," I asked him, carefully. "Do you ever think about your other mother?"

"No," he said quickly, like a doctor.

I looked at him, dismayed, confused.

"I don't know," he sighed and signaled the waiter. "I guess it's not basic to me. God, I can't get my feet all tied up in that. Why should I?"

"I'm not sure." I looked at my lap, at my shoes. I reached under the table for my purse. "Check's on me," I said.

"Dear Mom. Thanks for the cookies. I got them yesterday. Was sorry to hear about the hospital thing. Hope you're feeling better. I've got tests by the millions! Love, Lynnie."

Driving back from dropping James off at the airport, I catch a glimpse of my face in the mirror. It seems old, with too much makeup. I feel stuck, out of school, working odd jobs, like someone brooding, hat in hand in an anteroom, waiting for the future as if it were some hoop-skirted belle that must gather up its petticoats, float forward, and present itself to me. I wonder what else I could have written, those winters, looking out and seeing snow lining the elm grove like an arthritis and finding no words. I didn't lie: there were a lot of tests; I had a lot of tests.

The roads are empty and I am driving fast. I think of my father, imagine him long ago at night casually parting my mother's legs with the mechanical indifference of someone opening a cupboard. And I say to myself: I will leave every cold man, every man for whom music is some private physics and love some unsteppable dance. I will try to make them regret. To make them sad. I am driving back toward my tiny kitchen table and I will write this: forgiveness lives alone and far off down the road, but bitterness and art are close, gossipy neighbors, sharing the same clothesline, hanging out their things, getting their laundry confused.

"That's how much it costs, Miss," says the attendant at the gas station where I stop, looking rather numbly at the price on the pump.

"Oh," I say and fumble for my wallet. The oil cans stacked against an old truck tire are wordless, hard, collusive. But the triangular plastic flags strung at one end of the island flutter and ripple in the wind, flapping to get my attention, my compassion, like things that seem to want to sing but can't, things that almost tear themselves in trying to fly, like rainbow-colored birds, hung by string and their own feet.

1982

WHAT YOU WANT TO DO FINE

MACK HAS MOVED SO much in his life that every phone number he comes across seems to him to be one he's had before. "I swear this used to be *my* number," he says, putting the car into park and pointing at the guidebook: 923-7368. The built-in cadence of a phone number always hits him the same personal way: like something familiar but lost, something momentous yet insignificant – like an act of love with a girl he used to date.

"Just call," says Quilty. They are off Route 55, at the first McDonald's outside of Chicago. They are on a vacation, a road trip, a "pile stuff in and go" kind of thing. Quilty has been singing movie themes all afternoon, has gotten fixated on "To Sir with Love," and he and Mack now seemed destined to make each other crazy: Mack passing buses too quickly while fumbling for more gum (chewing the sugar out fast, stick by stick), and Quilty, hunched over the glove compartment, in some purple-faced strain of emotion brought on by the line "Those schoolgirl days of telling tales and biting nails are gone." "I would be a genius now," Quilty has said three times already, "if only I'd memorized Shakespeare instead of Lulu."

"If only," says Mack. Mack himself would be a genius now if only he had been born a completely different person. But what could you do? He'd read in a magazine once that geniuses were born only to women over thirty; his own mother had been twenty-nine. Damn! So fucking close!

"Let's just get a hotel reservation someplace and take a bath-oil bath," Quilty says now. "And don't dicker. You're always burning up time trying to get a bargain."

"That's so wrong?"

Quilty grimaces. "I don't like what comes after 'dicker.'"

"What is that?"

Quilty sighs. "*Dickest.* I mean, really: it's not a contest!" Quilty turns to feel for Guapo, his Seeing Eye dog, a chocolate Lab too often left panting in the backseat of the car while they stop for coffee. "Good dog, good dog, yes." A "bath-oil bath" is Quilty's idea of how to end a good day as well as a bad. "Tomorrow, we'll head south, along the Mississippi, then to New Orleans, and then back up to the ducks at the Peabody Hotel at the end. Does that sound okay?"

"If that's what you want to do, fine," says Mack.

They had met only two years ago at the Tapston, Indiana, Sobriety Society. Because he was new in town, recently up from some stupid quickie job painting high-voltage towers in the south of the state, and suddenly in need of a lawyer, Mack phoned Quilty the next day. "I was wondering if we could strike a deal," Mack had said. "One old drunk to another."

"Perhaps," said Quilty. He may have been blind and a recovering drinker, but with the help of his secretary, Martha, he had worked up a decent legal practice and did not give his services away for free. Good barter, however, he liked. It made life easier for a blind man. He was, after all, a practical person. Beneath all his eccentricities, he possessed a streak of pragmatism so sharp and deep that others mistook it for sanity.

"I got myself into a predicament," Mack explained. He told Quilty how difficult it was being a housepainter, new in town to boot, and how some of these damn finicky housewives could never be satisfied with what was true professional work, and how, well, he had a lawsuit on his hands. "I'm being sued for sloppy house painting, Mr. Stein. But the only way I can pay you is in more house painting. Do you have a house that needs painting?"

"Bad house painting as both the accusation and the retainer?" Quilty hooted. He loved a good hoot – it brought Guapo to his side. "That's like telling me you're wanted for counterfeiting but you can pay me in cash."

"I'm sorry," said Mack.

"It's all right," Quilty said. He took Mack's case, got him out of it as best he could – "the greatest art in the world," Quilty told the judge at the settlement hearing, "has been known to mumble at the edges" – then had Mack paint his house a clear, compensatory, cornflower blue. Or was it, suggested a neighbor, in certain streaky spots *delphinium*? At lunchtime, Quilty came home from his office up the street and stopped in the driveway, Guapo heeled at his feet, Mack above them on the ladder humming some mournful Appalachian love song, or a jazzed-up version of "Taps." Why "Taps"? "It's the town we live in," Mack would later explain, "and it's the sound of your cane."

Day is done. Gone the sun.

"How we doing there, Mack?" asked Quilty. His dark hair was long and bristly as rope, and he often pulled on it while speaking. "The neighbors tell me my bushes are all blue."

"A little dripping couldn't be avoided," Mack said unhappily. He never used tarps, the way other painters did. He didn't even own any.

"Well, doesn't offend me," said Quilty, tapping meaningfully at his sunglasses.

But afterward, painting the side dormer, Mack kept hearing Quilty inside, on the phone with a friend, snorting in a loud horselaugh: "Hey, what do *I* know? *I* have blue bushes!"

Or "I'm having the shrubs dyed blue: the nouveau riche – look out – will always be with you."

When the house was almost finished, and oak leaves began to accumulate on the ground in gold-and-ruby piles the color of pears, and the evenings settled in quickly and disappeared into that long solvent that was the beginning of a winter night, Mack began to linger and stall – over coffee and tea, into dinner, then over coffee and tea again. He liked to watch Quilty move deftly about the kitchen, refusing Mack's help, fixing simple things – pasta, peas, salads, bread and butter. Mack liked talking with him about the Sobriety Society meetings, swapping stories about those few great benders that sat in their memories like gorgeous songs and those others that had just plain wrecked their lives. He watched Quilty's face as fatigue or fondness spilled and rippled across it. Quilty had been born blind and had never acquired the guise and camouflage of the sighted; his face remained unclenched, untrained, a clean canvas, transparent as a baby's gas, clear to the bottom of him. In a face so unguarded and unguarding, one saw one's own innocent self – and one sometimes recoiled.

But Mack found he could not go away – not entirely. Not really. He helped Quilty with his long hair, brushing it back for him and gathering it in a leather tie. He brought Quilty gifts lifted from secondhand stores downtown. A geography book in Braille. A sweater with a coffee stain on the arm – was that too mean? Cork coasters for Quilty's endless cups of tea.

"I am gratefully beholden, my dear," Quilty had said each time, speaking, as he sometimes did, like a goddamn Victorian valentine and touching Mack's sleeve. "You are the kindest man I've ever had in my house."

And perhaps because what Quilty knew best were touch and words, or perhaps because Mack had gone through a pig's life of everything tearing at his feelings, or maybe because the earth had tilted into shadow and cold and the whole damned future seemed dipped in that bad ink, one night in the living room, after a kiss that took only Mack by surprise, and even then only slightly, Mack and Quilty became lovers.

Still, there were times it completely baffled Mack. How had he gotten here? What soft punch in the mouth had sent him reeling to this new place?

Uncertainty makes for shyness, and shyness, Quilty kept saying, is what keeps the world together. Or, rather, is what *used* to keep the world together, used to keep it from going mad with chaos. Now – now! – was a different story.

A different story? "I don't like stories," said Mack. "I like food. I like car keys." He paused. "I like pretzels."

"Okaaaay," said Quilty, tracing the outline of his own shoulder and then Mack's.

"You do this a lot, don't you?" asked Mack.

"Do what? Upgrade in the handyman department?"

"Bring into your bed some big straight guy you think's a little dumb."

"I never do that. Never have." He cocked his head to one side. "Before." With his flat almond-shaped fingertips, he played Mack's arm like a keyboard. "Never before. You are my big sexual experiment."

"But you see, you're *my* big sexual experiment," insisted Mack. In his life before Quilty, he could never have imagined being in bed with a skinny naked guy wearing sunglasses. "So how can that be?"

"Honey, it *bes*."

"But someone's got to be in charge. How can both of us survive on some big experimental adventure? Someone's got to be steering the ship."

"Oh, the ship be damned. We'll be fine. We are in this thing together. It's luck. It's God's will. It's synchronicity! Serendipity! Kismet! Camelot! Annie, honey, Get Your Fucking Gun!" Quilty was squealing.

"My ex-wife's name is Annie," said Mack.

"I know, I know. That's why I said it," said Quilty, trying now not to sigh. "Think of it this way: the blind leading the straight. It can work. It's not impossible."

In the mornings, the phone rang too much, and it sometimes annoyed Mack. Where were the pretzels and the car keys when you really needed them? He could see that Quilty knew the exact arm's distance to the receiver, picking it up in one swift pluck. "Are you *sans* or *avec*?" Quilty's friends would ask. They spoke loudly and theatrically – as if to a deaf person – and Mack could always hear.

"*Avec*," Quilty would say.

"Oooooh," they would coo. "And how *is* Mr. Avec today?"

"You should move your stuff in here," Quilty finally said to Mack one night.

"Is that what you want?" Mack found himself deferring in ways that were unfamiliar to him. He had never slept with a man before, that was probably it – though years ago there had been those nights when Annie'd put on so much makeup and leather, her gender seemed up for grabs: it had been oddly attractive to Mack, self-sufficient; it hadn't required him and so he'd wanted to get close, to get next to it, to learn it, make it need him, take it away, make it die. Those had been strange, bold nights, a starkness between them that was more like an ancient bone-deep brawl than a marriage. But ultimately, it all remained unreadable for him, though reading, he felt, was not a natural thing and should not be done to people. In general, people were not road maps. People were not hieroglyphs or books. They were not stories. A person was a collection of accidents. A person was an infinite pile of rocks with things growing underneath. In general, when you felt a longing for love, you took a woman and possessed her gingerly and not too hopefully until you finally let go, slept, woke up, and she eluded you once more. Then you started over. Or not.

Nothing about Quilty, however, seemed elusive.

"Is that what I want? Of course it's what I want. Aren't I a walking pamphlet for desire?" asked Quilty. "In Braille, of course, but still. Check it out. Move in. Take me."

"Okay," said Mack.

Mack had had a child with Annie, their boy, Lou, and just before the end, Mack had tried to think up words to say to Annie, to salvage things. He'd said "okay" a lot. He did not know how to raise a child, a toothless, trickless child, but he knew he had to protect it from the world a little; you could not just hand it over and let the world go at it. "There's something that with time grows between people," he said once, in an attempt to keep them together, keep Lou. If he lost Lou, he believed, it would wreck his life completely. "Something that grows whether you like it or not."

"Gunk," Annie said.

"What?"

"Gunk!" she shouted. "Gunk grows between people!"

He slammed the door, went drinking with his friends. The bar they all went to – Teem's Pub – quickly grew smoky and dull. Someone, Bob Bacon, maybe, suggested going to Visions and Sights, a strip joint out near the interstate. But Mack was already missing his wife. "Why would I want to go to a place like that," Mack said loudly to his friends, "when I've got a beautiful wife at home?"

"Well, then," Bob said, "let's go to *your* house."

"Okay," he said. "Okay."

And when they got there, Annie was already gone. She had packed fast, taken Lou, and fled.

* * *

Now it is two and a half years since Annie left, and here Mack is with Quilty, traveling: their plan is to head through Chicago and St. Louis and then south along the Mississippi. They will check into bed-and-breakfasts, tour the historic sights, like spouses. They have decided on this trip now in October in part because Mack is recuperating from a small procedure. He has had a small benign cyst razored from "an intimate place."

"The bathroom?" asked Quilty that first day after the surgery, and reached to feel Mack's thick black stitches, then sighed. "What's the unsexiest thing we can do for the next two weeks?"

"Go on a trip," Mack suggested.

Quilty hummed contentedly. He found the insides of Mack's wrists, where the veins were stiff cords, and caressed them with his thumbs. "Married men are always the best," he said. "They're so grateful and butch."

"Give me a break," said Mack.

The next day, they bought quart bottles of mineral water and packets of saltines, and drove out of town, out the speedway, with the Resurrection Park cemetery on one side and the Sunset Memories Park cemetery on the other – a route the cabbies called "the Bone Zone." When he'd first arrived in Tapston, Mack drove a cab for a week, and he'd gotten to know the layout of the town fast. "I'm in the Bone Zone," he used to have to say into the radio mouthpiece. "I'm in the Bone Zone." But he'd hated that damn phrase and hated waiting at the airport, all the lousy tips and heavy suitcases. And the names of things in Tapston – apartment buildings called Crestview Manor, treeless subdivisions called Arbor Valley, the cemeteries undisguised as Sunset Memories and Resurrection Park – all gave him the creeps. *Resurrection Park!* Jesus Christ. Every damn Hoosier twisted words right to death.

But cruising out the Bone Zone for a road trip in Quilty's car jazzed them both. They could once again escape all the unfortunateness of this town and its alarming resting places. "Farewell, you ole stiffs," Mack said.

"Good-bye, all my clients," cried Quilty when they passed the county jail. "Good-bye, good-bye!" Then he sank back blissfully in his seat as Mack sped the car toward the interstate, out into farm country, silver-topped silos gleaming like spaceships, the air grassy and thick with hog.

"I'd like to make a reservation for a double room, if possible," Mack now shouts over the noise of the interstate traffic. He looks and sees Quilty getting out of the car, leaving Guapo, feeling and tapping his way with his cane, toward the entrance to McDonald's.

"Yes, a double room," says Mack. He looks over his shoulder, keeping an eye on Quilty. "American Express? Yes." He fumbles through Quilty's wallet, reads the number out loud. He turns again and sees Quilty ordering a soda but not finding his wallet, since he'd given it to Mack for the call. Mack sees Quilty tuck his cane under his arm and pat all his pockets, finding nothing there but a red Howe Caverns handkerchief.

"You want the number on the card? Three one one two . . ."

Quilty now turns to leave, without a soda, and heads for the door. But he chooses the wrong door. He wanders into the Playland by mistake, and Mack can see him thrashing around with his cane amid the plastic cheeseburgers and the french fry swings, lit up at night for the kids. There is no exit from the Playland except back through the restaurant, but Quilty obviously doesn't know this and first taps, then bangs his cane against the forest of garish obstacles.

". . . eight one zero zero six," repeats the reservations clerk on the phone.

By the time Mack can get to him, Quilty is collapsed on a ceramic chicken breast. "Good night, Louise. I thought you'd left me," Quilty says. "I swear, from here on in, I'll do whatever you want. I've glimpsed the abyss, and, by God, it's full of big treacherous pieces of patio furniture."

"We've got a room," says Mack.

"Fantastic. Can we also get a soda?" Mack lets Quilty take his elbow and then walks Quilty back inside, where they order

Pepsis and a single apple pie the size of an eyeglass pouch – to split in the car, like children.

"Have a nice day," says the boy at the counter.

"Thanks for the advice," says Quilty.

They have brought along the game Trivial Pursuit, and at night Quilty likes to play. Though Mack complies – if that's what you want to do, fine – he thinks it's a dumb game. If you don't know the answer, you feel stupid. And if you do know the answer, you feel just as stupid. *More* stupid. What are you doing with that stupid bit of information in your brain? Mack would prefer to lie in the room and stare at the ceiling, thinking about Chicago, thinking about their day. "Name four American state capitals named after presidents," he reads sleepily from a card. He would rather try to understand the paintings he has seen that afternoon, and has almost understood: the Halloween hues of the Lautrecs; the chalky ones of Puvis de Chavannes; the sweet finger paints of the Vuillards and Bonnards, all crowded with window light and commodes. Mack had listened to the buzzing voice coming from Quilty's headphones, but he hadn't gotten his own headphones. Let a blind man be described to! Mack had his own eyes. But finally, overwhelmed by poor Quilty's inability either to see or touch the paintings, he had led Quilty downstairs to the statuary, and when no one was looking, he'd placed Quilty's hands upon the naked marble figure of a woman. "Ah," Quilty had said, feeling the nose and lips, and then he grew quiet and respectful at her shoulders, at her breasts, and hips, and when he got down past the thighs and knees to her feet, Quilty laughed out loud. Feet! These he knew best. These he liked.

Afterward, they went to a club to hear a skit called "Kuwait Until Dark."

"Lincoln, Jackson, Madison, Jefferson City," says Quilty. "Do you think we will have a war?" He seems to have grown impatient with the game. "You were in the service once. Do you think this is it? The big George Bush showdown?"

"Nah," says Mack. He had been in the army only during peacetime. He'd been stationed in Texas, then in Germany. He'd been with Annie: those were good years. Only a little crying. Only a little drinking. Later, he'd been in the reserves, but the reserves were never called up – everyone knew that. Until now. "Probably it's just a sales demo for the weapons."

"Well, they'll go off, then," says Quilty. "Won't they? If it's a demonstration, things will be demonstrated."

Mack picks another card. "In the song 'They Call the Wind Maria,' what do they call the rain?"

"It's Mar-eye-a, not Maria," says Quilty.

"It's Mar-eye-a?" asks Mack. "Really?"

"Really," says Quilty. There is something wicked and scolding that comes over Quilty's face in this game. "It's your turn." He thrusts out his hand. "Now give me the card so you don't cheat."

Mack hands him the card. "Mar-eye-a," says Mack. The song is almost coming back to him – he recalls it from somewhere. Maybe Annie used to sing it. "They call the wind Mar-eye-a. They call the rain . . . Okay. I think it's coming. . . ." He presses his fingers to his temples, squinting and thinking. "They call the wind Mar-eye-ah. They call the rain . . . Okay. Don't tell me. They call the rain . . . Pariah!"

"Pariah?" Quilty guffaws.

"Okay, then," says Mack, exasperated. "Heavy. They call the rain Heavy Rain." He reaches aggressively for his minibar juice. Next time, he's just going to look quickly at the back of the card.

"Don't you want to know the right answer?"

"No."

"Okay, I'll just go on to the next card." He picks one up, pretending to read. "It says here, 'Darling, is there life on Mars? Yes or no.' "

Mack has gone back to thinking about the paintings. "I say no," he says absently.

"Hmmm," says Quilty, putting the card down. "I think the answer is yes. Look at it this way: they're sure there are ice crystals. And where there is ice, there is water. And where there is water, there is waterfront property. And where there is waterfront property, there are Jews!" He claps his hands and sinks back onto the acrylic quilting of the bedspread. "Where are you?" he asks finally, waving his arms out in the air.

"I'm here," says Mack. "I'm right here." But he doesn't move.

"You're here? Well, good. At least you're not at my cousin Esther's Martian lake house with her appalling husband, Howard. Though sometimes I wonder how they're doing. How are they? They never come to visit. I frighten them so much." He pauses. "Can I ask you a question?"

"Okay."

"What do I look like?"

Mack hesitates. "Brown eyes, brown eyebrows, and brown hair."

"That's it?"

"Okay. Brown teeth, too."

"Really!"

"Sorry," says Mack. "I'm a little tired."

Hannibal is like all the river towns that have tried recently to spruce themselves up, make antique shops and bed-and-breakfasts from the shoreline mansions. It saddens Mack. There is still a despondent grandeur to these houses, but it radiates out, in a kind of shrug, onto a drab economy of tidbit tourism and health-care facilities. A hundred years of flight and rehab lie on the place like rain. Heavy rain! The few barges that still push this far upriver seem quaint and ridiculous. But Quilty wants to hear what all the signs say – the Mark Twain Diner, the Tom 'n Huck Motel; it amuses him. They take the tour of Sam Clemens's houses, of Mr. Clemens's office, of the little jail. They get on a tiny train Quilty calls "Too, Too Twain," which tours the area and makes the place seem even more spritely and hopeless. Quilty feels along the wide boards of the whitewashed fence. "This is modern paint," he says.

"Latex," says Mack.

"Oooh, talk to me, talk to me, baby."

"Will you stop?"

"Okay. All right."

"Pretty dog," a large woman in a violet dress says to them in the Tom Sawyer Diner. The diner is situated next to a parking lot and a mock-up of the legendary fence, and it serves BLTs in red plastic baskets with stiff wax paper and fries. Quilty has ordered his usual glass of milk.

"Thank you," says Quilty to the woman, who then stops to pet Guapo before heading for her car in the parking lot. Quilty looks suddenly annoyed. "*He* gets all the compliments, and *I* have to say thank you."

"You want a compliment?" asks Mack, disgusted. "Okay. You're pretty, too," says Mack.

"*Am* I? Well, how will I ever know, if everyone just keeps complimenting my dog!"

"I can't believe you're jealous of your goddamn dog. Here," Mack says. "I refuse to talk to someone with a milk mustache." He hands Quilty a napkin, touching the folded edge of it to his cheek.

Quilty takes it and wipes his mouth. "Just when we were getting so good at being boring together," he says. He reaches over and pats Mack's arm, then reaches up and roughly pets his head. Mack's hair is thin and swept back, and Quilty swipes at it from behind.

"Ow," says Mack.

"I keep forgetting your hair is so Irish and sensitive," he said. "We've gotta get you some good tough Jew hair."

"Great," says Mack. He is growing tired of this, tired of them. They've been on these trips too many times before. They've visited Mother Goose's grave in Boston. They've visited the battlefield at Saratoga. They've visited Arlington. "Too many cemeteries!" said Mack. "It's the goddamn Bone Zone wherever we go!" They visited the Lincoln Memorial ("I imagine it's like a big marble Oz," said Quilty. "Abraham Oz. A much better name, don't you think?"). Right next door, they visited the Vietnam War Memorial, mind-numbing in its bloodless catalog of blood, Mack preferring instead the alternative monument, the buddy statue put up by the vets, something that wanted less to be art than to be human. "It's about the guys, not just the *names of the guys*," he said. "*Guys* died there. A list didn't die there." But Quilty, who had spent an hour feeling for friends who'd died in '68 and '70, had sighed in a vaguely disgusted, condescending way.

"You're missing it totally," he said. "A list did die. An incredible heartbreaking list."

"Sorry I'm not such an intellectual," said Mack.

"You're jealous because I was feeling around for other men."

"Yeah. I'm jealous. I'm jealous I'm not up there. I'm jealous because – stupid me – I waited until peacetime to enlist."

Quilty sighed. "I almost went. But I had a high draft number. Plus, guess what? Flat feet!"

At that, they both broke, feebly, into loud, exhausted laughter, like two tense lunatics, right there by the wall, until someone in a uniform asked them to leave: other people were trying to pray.

Trying to go someplace without cemeteries, they once flew to Key West, ate a lot of conch chowder and went to Audubon's house, which wasn't Audubon's house at all, but a place where Audubon had stayed once or something, shooting the birds he then painted. "He shot them?" Mack kept asking. "He shot the damn birds?"

"Revolting," said Quilty loudly. "The poor birds. From now on, I'm going to give all my money to the *Autobahn* Society. Let's make those Mercedes go fast, fast, fast!"

To prevent Mack's drinking in despair, they later found an AA meeting and dropped in, made friends and confessed to them, though not exactly in that order. The following day, new pals in tow, they strolled through Hemingway's house in feather boas – "just to taunt Papa."

"Before he wrote about them," said Quilty, pretending to read the guidebook out loud, "Hemingway shot his characters. It was considered an unusual but not unheard-of creative method. Still, even within literary circles, it is not that widely discussed."

The next morning, at the request of a sweet old man named Chuck, they went to an AIDS memorial service. They sat next to Chuck and held his hand. Walt Whitman poems were read. Cello suites were played so exquisitely that people fell forward onto their own knees, collapsed by the beauty of grief. After the benediction, everyone got solemnly into their cars and drove slowly to the grave site. No matter how Mack and Quilty tried to avoid cemeteries, there they were again. A boneyard had its own insistent call: like rocks to sailors, or sailors to other sailors. "This is all too intense," whispered Mack in the middle of a prayer; at the grave site, Mack had positioned them farther off from the mourners than Quilty knew. "This is supposed to be our vacation. When this prayer is over, let's go to the beach and eat cupcakes." Which is what they did, letting Guapo run up and down the sand, chasing gulls, while the two of them lay there on a towel, the sea air blasting their faces.

Now, on this trip, Mack is in a hurry. He wants to leave the chipping white brick of Hannibal, the trees and huckleberries, the local cars all parked in the lot of some Tony's Lounge. He wants to get on to St. Louis, to Memphis, to New Orleans, then back. He wants to be done with touring, this mobile life they embark on too often, like old ladies testing out their new, sturdy shoes. He wants his stitches removed.

"I hope there won't be scars," he says.

"Scars?" says Quilty in that screechy mockery he sometimes puts on. "I can't believe I'm with someone who's worried about having a good-looking dick."

"Here is your question. What American playwright was imprisoned for her work?"

"*Her* work. Aha. Lillian Hellman? I doubt it. Thornton Wilder—"

"Mae West," blurts out Mack.

"Don't do that! I hadn't answered yet!"

"What does it matter?"

"It matters to me!"

There is only a week left.

* * *

"In St. Louis" – Quilty pretends again, his old shtick, to read from the guidebook as they take the bumpy ride to the top of the arch – "there is the famous gateway, or 'arch,' built by the McDonald Corporation. Holy Jesus, America, get down on your knees!"

"I am, I am."

"Actually, that's true. I heard someone talking about it downstairs. This thing was built by a company named McDonald. A golden arch of gray stone. That is the gateway to the West. At sunset very golden. Very arch."

"Whaddyaknow." Gray stone again. There's no getting away from it.

"Describe the view to me," says Quilty when they get out at the top.

Mack looks out through the windows. "Adequate," he says.

"I said describe, not *rate*."

"Midwestern. Aerial. Green and brown."

Quilty sighs. "I don't think blind men should date deaf-mutes until the how-to book has been written."

Mack is getting hungry. "Are you hungry?"

"It's too stressful!" adds Quilty. "No, I'm not hungry."

They make the mistake of going to the aquarium, instead of to an early dinner, which causes every sea creature to look delicious to Mack. Quilty makes the tour with a group led by a cute schoolteacherish guide named Judy, but Mack ventures off on his own. He feels like a dog set loose among schoolchildren: Here are his friends! The elegant nautilus, the electric eel, the stingray with its wavy cape and idiot grin, silently shrieking against the glass – or is it feeding?

When is a thing shrieking and when is it feeding – and why can't Mack tell?

It is the wrong hour of the day, the wrong hour of life, to be around sea creatures. Shrieking or feeding. Breaded or fried. There is a song Mack's aunt used to sing to him when he was little: "I am a man upon the land. I am a Silkie on the sea." And he thinks of this now, this song about a half man, half seal or bird – what was it? It was a creature who comes back to fetch his child – his child by a woman on the land. But the woman's new husband is a hunter, a good shot, and kills him when he tries to escape back to the sea with the child. Perhaps that was best, in the end. Still the song was sad. Stolen love, lost love, amphibious doom – all the transactions of Mack's own life: I am a Silkie on the sea. "My life is lucky and rich," he used to tell himself when he was painting high-voltage towers in Kentucky and the electric field on those ladders stood the hairs of his arms on end. Lucky and Rich! They sounded like springer spaniels, or two unsavory uncles. Uncle Lucky! Uncle Rich!

I am a man upon the land, he thinks. But here at sea, what am I? Shrieking or feeding?

Quilty comes up behind him, with Guapo. "Let's go to dinner," he says.

"Thank you," says Mack.

After dinner, they lie in their motel bed and kiss. "Ah, dear, yes," murmurs Quilty, his "dears" and "my dears" like sweet compresses in the heat, and then there are no more words. Mack pushes close, his cool belly warming. His heart thumps against Quilty's like a water balloon shifting and thrusting its liquid from side to side. There is something comforting, thinks Mack, in embracing someone the same size as you. Something exhilarating, even: having your chins over each other's shoulders, your feet touching, your heads pressed ear-to-ear. Plus he likes – he loves – Quilty's mouth on him. A man's full mouth. There is always something a little desperate and diligent about Quilty, poised there with his lips big and searching and his wild unshaded eyes like the creatures of the aquarium, captive yet wandering free in their enclosures. With the two of them kissing like this – *exculpatory, specificity, rubric* – words are foreign money. There is only the soft punch in the mouth, the shrieking and feeding both, which fills Mack's ears with light. This, he thinks, this is how a blind man sees. This is how a fish walks. This is how rocks sing. There is nothing at all like a man's strong kiss: apologies to the women of Kentucky.

* * *

They eat breakfast at a place called Mama's that advertises "throwed rolls."

"What are those?" asks Quilty. They turn out merely to be warm buttermilk rolls thrown at the clientele by the waiters. Mack's roll hits him squarely in the chest, where he continues to clutch it, in shock. "Don't worry," says the waiter to Quilty. "Won't throw one at you, a blind man, but just maybe at your dawg."

"Good God," says Quilty. "Let's get out of here."

On the way out, by the door, Mack stops to read the missing-child posters. He does not look at the girls. He looks at the boys: Graham, age eight; Eric, age five. So that's what five looks like, thinks Mack. Lou will be five next week.

Mack takes the slow southerly roads. He and Quilty are like birds, reclaiming the summer that left them six weeks before in the north. "I'll bet in Tapston they've all got salt spats on their boots already," says Mack. "Bet they've got ice chunks in their tires." Quilty hates winter, Mack knows. The frozen air makes things untouchable, unsmellable. When the weather warms, the world comes back. "The sun smells like fire," Quilty says, and smiles. Past the bleached doormat of old wheat fields, the land grows greener. There is cotton harvested as far north as Missouri, the fields spread out like bolts of dotted swiss, and Mack and Quilty stop on the shoulder once, get out to pick a blossom, peel back the wet bud, feel the cotton slowly dry. "See what you miss, being a Yankee," says Mack.

"Missing is all I do," says Quilty.

They come upon a caravan of Jeeps and Hummers painted beige and headed south for a ship that no doubt will take them from one gulf to another. Mack whistles. "Holy shit," he says.

"What?"

"Right now, there're about two hundred army vehicles in front of us, freshly painted desert beige."

"I can't bear it," says Quilty. "There's going to be a war."

"I could have sworn there wouldn't be. I could have sworn there was just going to be a television show."

"I'll bet there's a war." They drive to Cooter along with the Jeeps, then swing off to Heloise to look at the river. It is still the same slow mongoose brown, lacking beauty of some kind Mack can't quite name. The river seems to him like a big ticky dog that doesn't know its own filth and keeps following your car along on the side as you drive.

They get out of the car to stretch. Mack lights a cigarette, thinking of the Jeeps and the Saudi desert. "So there it is. Brown and more brown. Guess that's all there is to a river."

"You're so . . . *Peggy Lee*," says Quilty. "How about a little Jerome Kern? It don't plant taters. It don't plant cotton. It just keeps rolling along."

Mack knows the song but doesn't even look at Quilty.

"Smell the mud and humidity of it," says Quilty, breathing deeply.

"I do. Great humidity," says Mack. He feels weary. He also feels sick of trying, tired of living, and scared of dying. If Quilty wants musical comedy, there it is: musical comedy. Mack drags on his cigarette. The prospect of a war has seized his brain. It engages some old, ongoing terror in him. As a former soldier, he still believes in armies. But he believes in armies at rest, armies relaxing, armies shopping at the PX, armies eating supper in the mess hall. But armies as TV-network football teams? The quick beginning of the quick end.

"I hear the other side doesn't even have socks," says Quilty when they are back in the car, thinking of the war. "Or rather, they have *some* socks, but they don't all match."

"Probably the military's been waiting for this for years. Something to ace – at last."

"Thank God you're not still in the reserves. They're calling up all the reserves." Quilty reaches up under Mack's shirt and rubs his back. "Young people have been coming into my office all month to have their wills drawn up."

Mack was in the reserves only a year before he was thrown out for drunkenness on one of the retreats.

"The reserves used to be one big camping trip," Mack says.

"Well, now it's a camping trip gone awry. A camping trip with aspirations. A *big* hot camping trip. Kamp with a *K*. These kids coming in for wills: you should hear the shock in their voices."

Mack drives slowly, dreamy with worry. "How you doing back there, Miss Daisy?" Quilty calls over his shoulder to Guapo. Outside of Memphis, on the Arkansas side, they stop at a Denny's, next to a warehouse of dinettes, and they let Guapo out to run again.

Dinettes, thinks Mack. That's just what this world needs: a warehouse of dinettes.

"I once tried to write a book," says Quilty, seated cozily in his booth, eating an omelette.

"Oh, yeah?"

"Yeah. I had these paragraphs that were so huge, they went on for pages. Sentences that were also just enormous – two or three pages long. I had to shrink things down, I was told."

Mack smiles. "How about words? Did you use big words, too?"

"Huge words. And to top it off, I began the whole thing with a letter I razored off a billboard." He pauses. "That's a joke."

"I get it."

"There *was* a book, though. I was going to call it *Dating My Sofa: A Blind Man's Guide to Life.*"

Mack is quiet. There is always too much talking on these trips.

"Let's hit Memphis on the way back," says Quilty irritably. "For now, let's head straight to New Orleans."

"That's what you want to do? Fine." Mack has no great fondness for Memphis. Once, as a boy, he'd been chased by a bee there, down a street that was long and narrow and lined on one side with parked cars. He'd ducked into a phone booth, but the bee waited for him, and Mack ended up stepping out after twenty minutes and getting stung anyway. It wasn't true what they said about bees. They were not all that busy. They had time. They could wait. It was a myth, that stuff about busy as a bee.

"That way, coming back," adds Quilty, "we can take our time and hit the Peabody when the ducks are out. I want to do the whole duck thing."

"Sure," says Mack. "The duck thing is the thing." On the way out of Denny's, Mack pulls slightly away from Quilty to look at another missing-child poster. A boy named Seth, age five. The world – one cannot drive fast or far enough away from it – is coming at him in daggers.

"What are you looking at?"

"Nothing," says Mack, then adds absently, "a boy."

"Really?" says Quilty.

Mack drives fast down through the small towns of the Delta: Eudora, Eupora, Tallula – the poorest ones with names like Hollywood, Banks, Rich. In each of them, a Baptist church is nestled up against a bait shop or a Tina's Touch of Class Cocktails. The strawy weeds are tall as people, and the cotton puffs here are planted in soils grown sandy, near shacks and burned-out cars, a cottonseed-oil factory towering over the fields, the closest hamburger at a Hardee's four miles away. Sometimes the cotton fields look like snow. Mack notices the broken-down signs: EAT MAID-RITE EATS or CAN'T BEAT DICK'S MEAT. They are both innocent and old, that peculiar mix, like a baby that looks like a grandmother, or a grandmother that looks like a girl. He and Quilty eat lunch and dinner at places that serve hush puppies and batter-fried pickles; it reminds Mack of his aunt's cooking. The air thickens and grows warm. Sinclair brontosauruses and old-style Coke signs protrude from the road stops and gas stations, and then, closer to Baton Rouge, antique stores sell the same kinds of old Coke signs.

"Recycling," says Mack.

"Everyone's recycling," says Quilty.

"Someone told me once" – Mack is thinking of Annie now – "that we are all made from stars, that every atom in our bodies was at one time the atom of a star."

"And you believed them?" Quilty hoots.

"Fuck you," says Mack.

"I mean, in between, we were probably also some cheese at a sorority tea. Our ancestral relationship to stars!" says Quilty, now far away, making his point before some judge. "It's the biological equivalent of hearsay."

They stay in an antebellum mansion with a canopy bed. They sit beneath the canopy and play Trivial Pursuit.

Mack once again reads aloud his own questions. "Who was George Bush referring to when reminiscing: 'We've had some triumphs; we've made some mistakes; we've had some sex'?"

Mack stares. The canopy bed looks psychotic. Out the window he sees a sign across the street that says SPACE FOR LEASE AT ABSOLUTELY YOGURT. Next to it, a large white woman is hitting a small black dog with a shopping bag. What is wrong with this country? He turns the card over and looks. "Ronald Reagan," he says. He has taken to cheating like this.

"Is that your answer?" asks Quilty.

"Yes."

"Well, you're probably right," says Quilty, who often knows the answer before Mack has read it to him. Mack stares at the bed again, its canopy like the headdress the Duchess wore in *Alice in Wonderland*. His aunt would sometimes read that book to him, and it always made him feel queasy and confused.

On the nightstand, there are sachets of peach and apricot pits, the sickly sweet smell of a cancer ward. Everything here now in this room reminds him of his aunt.

"What former Pittsburgh Pirates slugger was the only player inducted into the Baseball Hall of Fame in 1988?" Mack reads. It is Quilty's turn.

"I've landed on the damn *sports* category?"

"Yup. What's your answer?"

"Linda Ronstadt. She was in *The Pirates of Penzance*. I know it went to Pittsburgh. I'm just not sure about the Hall of Fame part."

Mack is quiet.

"Am I right?"

"No."

"Well, you never used to do that – land me on those sports questions. Now you're getting difficult."

"Yup," says Mack.

The next morning, they go to a Coca-Cola museum, which the South seems to be full of. "You'd think Coca-Cola was a national treasure," Mack says.

"It's not?" says Quilty.

Individual states, Georgia and Mississippi and whichever else, are all competing for claims: first served here, first bottled there – first thirst, first burst – it is one big corporate battle of the bands. There is a strange kind of refuge from this to be found in driving through yet another cemetery, this one at Vicksburg, and so they do it, but quickly, keeping the trip moving so they will not feel, as they might have in Tapston, the irretrievable loss of each afternoon, the encroaching darkness, each improvised day over with at last – only to start up again, in the morning, oppressively identical, a checker in a game of checkers, or a joke in a book of jokes.

"They seem to have all this organized by state," says Mack, looking out over the Vicksburg grounds, the rolling green dotted as if with aspirins. He looks back at the park map, which he has spread over the steering wheel. Here he is: back in the Bone Zone.

"Well, let's go to the Indiana part," says Quilty, "and praise the Hoosier dead."

"Okay," says Mack, and when he comes upon a single small stone that says *Indiana* – not the proper section at all – he slows down and says, "Here's the section," so that Quilty can roll down the window and shout, "Praise the Hoosier dead!" There are kindnesses one can perform for a blind man more easily than for the sighted.

Guapo barks and Mack lets loose with an incongruous rebel yell.

"Whose side are you on?" scolds Quilty, rolling his window back up. "Let's get out of here. It's too hot."

They drive some distance out of the park and then stop at the Civil War Museum they saw advertised the day before.

"Is this a fifty?" Quilty whispers, thrusting a bill toward Mack as they approach the entrance cashier.

"No, it's a twenty."

"Find me a fifty. Is this a fifty?"

"Yeah, that's a fifty."

Quilty thrusts the fifty toward the cashier. "Excuse me," he says in a loud voice. "Do you have change for a great American general?"

"Do believe I do," says the cashier, who chuckles a bit, taking the fifty and lifting up the drawer to his register. "You Yankees are always liking to do that."

Inside, the place is dark and cool and lined with glass display cases and mannequins in uniforms. There are photographs of soldiers and nurses and "President and Mrs. Davis." Because almost everything is behind glass and cannot be touched, Quilty grows bored. "'The city of Vicksburg,'" Mack reads aloud, "'forced to surrender to Grant on the Fourth of July, refused to celebrate Independence Day again until 1971.'"

"When no one cared anymore," adds Quilty. "I like a place with a strong sense of grudge – which they, of course, call 'a keen acquaintance with history.'" He clears his throat. "But let's get on to New Orleans. I also like a place that doesn't give a shit."

In a restaurant overlooking the river, they eat yet more hush puppies and catfish. Guapo, unleashed, runs up and down the riverbank like a mad creature.

In the dusk, they head south, toward the Natchez Trace, through Port Gibson: "TOO BEAUTIFUL TO BURN" – ULYSSES S. GRANT, says the WELCOME sign. Quilty is dozing. It is getting dark, and the road isn't wide, but Mack passes all the slow-moving cars: an old VW bus (northern winters have eliminated these in Tapston), a red pickup piled with hay, a Plymouth Duster full of deaf people signing in a fantastic dance of hands. The light is on inside the Duster, and Mack pulls up alongside, watching. Everyone is talking at once – fingers flying, chopping, stretching the air, twining, pointing, touching. It is astonishing and beautiful. If only Quilty weren't blind, thinks Mack. If only Quilty weren't blind, he would really like being deaf.

There are, in New Orleans, all manner of oysters Rockefeller. There is the kind with the spinach chopped long and coarse like seaweed, scabs of bacon in a patch on top. Then there is the kind with the spinach moussed to a bright lime and dolloped onto the shell like algae. There is the kind with spinach leaves laid limply off the edge like socks. There is the kind with cheese. There is the kind without. There is even the kind with tofu.

"Whatever happened to clams casino?" asks Mack. "I used to get those in Kentucky. Those were great."

"Shellfish from a landlocked place? Never a great idea, my dear," says Quilty. "Stick with Nawlins. A city no longer known for its prostitutes quickly becomes known for its excellent food. Think about it. There's Paris. There's here. A city currently known for its prostitutes – Las Vegas, Amsterdam, Washington, D.C. – is seldom a good food city."

"You should write a travel book." Was Mack being sarcastic? Mack himself couldn't say.

"That's what *Dating My Sofa* was going to be. A kind of armchair travel book. For the blind."

"I thought *Dating My Sofa* was going to be a novel."

"Before it was a novel, it was going to be a travel book."

They leave behind the wrought-iron cornstalk fence of their little inn for a walk through the Quarter. Soon they are at the wharf, and with little else to do, they step aboard a glittering paddle wheeler for a Plantation River cruise. Quilty trips on a slightly raised plank on the ramp. "You know, I find this city neither big nor easy," he says. The tour is supposed to be beer and sun and a little jazz band, but there is also a stop at Chalmette, the site of the Battle of New Orleans, so that people can get off and traipse through the cemetery.

Mack takes Quilty to a seat in the sun, then sits beside him. Guapo lifts his head and smells the swampy air. "No more cemeteries," says Mack, and Quilty readily agrees, though Mack also wonders whether, when they get there, they will be able to resist. It seems hard for them, when presented with all that toothy geometry of stone and bone, not to rush right up and say hi. The two of them are ill-suited to life; no doubt that is it. In feeling peculiar, homeless, cursed, and tired, they have become way too friendly. They no longer have any standards at all.

"All the graves are on stilts here anyway," says Mack. "The sea level and all." The calliope starts up and the paddle wheel begins to revolve. Mack tips his head back to rest it against the seat and look at the sky all streaked with stringy clouds, bird blue cracked fuzzily with white. To the right, the clouds have more shape and against the blue look like the figures of a Wedgwood dish. What a fine fucking bowl beneath which they have all been caught and asked to swim out their days! "Look at it this way," people used to say to Mack. "Things could be worse" – a bumper sticker for a goldfish or a bug. And it wasn't wrong – it just wasn't the point.

He falls asleep, and by the time the boat returns to the wharf, ten thousand anesthesiologists have invaded the town. There are buses and crowds. "Uh-oh. Look out. A medical convention," says Mack to Quilty. "Watch your step." At a turquoise kiosk near the pier, he spots more missing-children posters. He half-expects to see himself and Quilty posted up there, two more lost boys in America. Instead, there is a heartbreaking nine-year-old named Charlie. There is a three-year-old named Kyle. There is also the same kid from Denny's up north: Seth, age five.

"Are they cute?" asks Quilty.

"Who?" says Mack.

"All those nice young doctors," says Quilty. "Are they good-looking?"

"Hell if I know," says Mack.

"Oh, don't give me that," says Quilty. "You forget to whom you are speaking, my dear. I can *feel* you looking around."

Mack says nothing for a while. Not until after he's led Quilty over to a café for some chicory coffee and a beignet, which he feeds pieces of to Guapo. The people at the table next to them, in some kind of morbid theatrical contest, are reading aloud obituaries from the *Times-Picayune*. "This town's wacko," says Mack. Back at the hotel, someone in the next room is playing "The Star-Spangled Banner" on the kazoo.

They speed out the next day – across the incandescent olive milk of the swamps, leafless, burned trees jutting from them like crosses. "You're going too fast," says Quilty. "You're driving like goddamn Sean Penn!" Mack, following no particular route, heads out toward the salt marshes: grebes, blackbirds, sherbet-winged flamingos fly in low over the feathery bulrushes. It is all pretty, in its bleak way. Lone cattle are loose and munching cordgrass amid the oil rigs.

"Which way are we going?"

He suddenly swings north toward Memphis. "North. Memphis." All he can think of now is getting back.

"What are you thinking of?"

"Nothing."

"What are you looking at?"

"Nothing. Scenery."

"Hot bods?"

"Yeah. Just saw a great cow," says Mack. "And a not-bad possum."

When they are finally checked into the Peabody Hotel, it is already late afternoon. Their room is a little stuffy and lit in a strange, golden way. Mack flops on the bed.

Quilty, beginning to perspire, takes his jacket off and throws it on the floor. "Y'know: what is wrong with you?" he asks.

"What do you mean, *me*? What is wrong with *you*?"

"You're so distracted and weird."

"We're traveling. I'm sight-seeing. I'm tired. Sorry if I seem distant."

"'Sight-seeing.' That's nice! How about me? Yoo-hoo!"

Mack sighs. When he goes on the attack like this, Quilty tends to head in five miserable directions at once. He has a brief nervous breakdown and shouts from every shattered corner of it, then afterward pulls himself together and apologizes. It is all a bit familiar. Mack closes his eyes, to sail away from him. He floats off and, trying not to think of Lou, briefly thinks of Annie, though the sudden blood rush that stiffens him pulls at his stitches and snaps him awake. He sits up. He kicks off his shoes and socks and looks at his pickled toes: slugs in a box.

Quilty is cross-legged on the floor, trying to do some deep-breathing exercises. He is trying to get chi to his meridians – or something like that. "You think I don't know you're attracted to half the people you see?" Quilty is saying. "You think I'm stupid or something? You don't think I feel your head turn and your gaze stop everywhere we go?"

"What?"

"You're too much," Quilty finally says to Mack.

"*I'm* too much? You are! You're so damn nervous and territorial," Mack says.

"I have a highly inflamed sense of yard," says Quilty. He has given up on the exercises. "Blind people do. I don't want you sticking your hitchhiker's thumb out over the property line. It's a betrayal and an eyesore to the community!"

"What community? What are you talking about?"

"All you sighted people are alike. You think we're Mr. Magoo! You think I'm not as aware as some guy who paints water towers and's got cysts on his dick?"

Mack shakes his head. He sits up and starts to put his shoes back on. "You really go for the juggler, don't you?" he says.

"Juggler?" Quilty howls. "*Juggler*? No, obviously, I go for the clowns."

Mack is puzzled. Quilty's head is tilted in that hyperalert way that says nothing in the room will get past him. "Juggler," Mack says. "Isn't that the word? What is the word?"

"A juggler," says Quilty, slowly for the jury, "is someone who juggles."

Mack's chest tightens around a small emptied space. He

feels his own crappy luck returning like a curse. "You don't even like me, do you?" he says.

"Like you? Is that what you're really asking?"

"I'm not sure," says Mack. He looks around the hotel room. Not this, not any room with Quilty in it would ever be his home.

"Let me tell you a story," says Quilty.

"I don't like stories," Mack says.

It now seems to have cost Mack so much to be here. In his mind – a memory or a premonition, which is it, his mind does not distinguish – he sees himself returning not just to Tapston but to Kentucky or to Illinois, wherever it is Annie lives now, and stealing back his own-blooded boy, whom he loves, and who is his, and running fast with him toward a car, putting him in and driving off. It would be the proper thing, in a way. Other men have done it.

Quilty's story goes like this: "A woman came to my office once very early on in my practice. Her case was a simple divorce that she made complicated by greed and stubbornness, and she worked up quite a bill. When she got the bill, she phoned me, shouting and saying angry things. I said, 'Look, we'll work out a payment plan. One hundred dollars a month. How does that sound?' I was reasonable. My practice was new and struggling. Still, she refused to pay a cent. I had to take out a loan to pay my secretary, and I never forgot that. So, five years later, that very same woman's doctor phones me. She's got bone cancer, the doctor says, and I'm one of the only German Jews in town and might have the same blood type for a marrow transfusion for her. Would I consider it, at least consider having a blood test? I said, 'Absolutely not,' and hung up. The doctor called back. He begged me, but I hung up again. A month later, the woman died."

"What's your point?" says Mack. Quilty's voice is flying apart now.

"That that is the truth about me," he says. "Don't you see—"

"Yes, *I* fucking see. I am the one here who does the seeing! Me and Guapo."

He pauses for a long time. "I don't forgive anybody anything. That is the point."

"Y'know what? This whole thing is such a crock," says Mack, but his voice is thin and diffident, and he finishes putting on his shoes, but without socks, and then grabs up his coat.

Downstairs, the clock says quarter to five, and a crowd is gathering to watch the ducks. A red carpet has already been rolled out from the elevator to the fountain, and this makes the ducks excited, anxious for the evening ritual, their clipped wings fluttering. Mack takes a table in the back and orders a double whiskey with ice. He drinks it fast – it freezes and burns in that great old way: it has been too long. He orders another. The pianist on the other side of the lobby is playing "Street of Dreams": "Love laughs at a king/Kings don't mean a thing" the man sings, and it seems to Mack the most beautiful song in the world. Men everywhere are about to die for reasons they don't know and wouldn't like if they did – but here is a song to do it by, so that life, in its mad spasms, might not demolish so much this time.

The ducks drink and dive in the fountain.

Probably Mack is already drunk as a horse.

Near the Union Avenue door is a young woman mime, juggling Coke bottles. People waiting for the ducks have gathered to watch. Even in her white pancake makeup, she is attractive. Her red hair is bright as a daylily and beneath her black leotards her legs are taut as an archer's bow.

Go for the juggler, thinks Mack. His head hurts, but his throat and lungs are hot and clear.

Out of the corner of his eye, he suddenly notices Quilty and Guapo, stepping slow and unsure, making their way around the far edge of the crowd. Their expressions are lonely and distraught, even Guapo's. Mack looks back at the fountain. Soon Guapo will find him – but Mack is not going to move until then, needing the ceremony of Quilty's effort. He knows Quilty will devise some conciliatory gift. He will come up and touch Mack and whisper, "Come back, don't be angry, you know this is how the two of us get."

But for now, Mack will just watch the ducks, watch them summoned by their caretaker, an old uniformed black man who blows a silver whistle and wields a long rod, signaling the ducks out of the water, out onto the carpet in a line. They haven't had a thing to say about it, these ducks, thinks Mack, haven't done a thing to deserve it, but there they are, God's lilies, year-round in a giant hotel, someone caring for them the rest of their lives. All the other birds of the world – the mange-hollowed hawks, the lordless hens, the dumb clucks – will live punishing, unblessed lives, winging it north, south, here, there, searching for a place of rest. But not these. Not these *rich, lucky* ducks! graced with rug and stairs, upstairs and down, roof to pool to penthouse, always steered, guided, welcomed toward those golden elevator doors like a heaven's mouth, and though it isn't really a heaven's mouth, it is maybe the lip of all there is.

Mack sighs. Why must he always take the measure of his own stupid suffering? Why must he always look around and compare his own against others'?

Because God wants people to.

Even if you're comparing yourself to ducks?

Especially if you're comparing yourself to ducks.

He feels his own head shrink with the hate that is love with no place to go. He will do it: he will go back and get Lou if it kills him. A million soldiers are getting ready to die for less. He will find Annie; maybe it won't be that hard. And at first, he will ask her nicely. But then he will do what a father must: a boy is a father's. Sons love their fathers like nothing else. Mack read that once in a magazine.

Yet the more he imagines finding Lou, the more greatly he suspects that the whole mad task will indeed kill him. He sees – as if again in a vision (of what he must prevent or of what he cannot prevent, who knew with visions?) – the death of himself and the sorrow of his boy. He sees the wound in his own back, his eyes turning from fish-gray jellies to the plus and minus signs of a comic-book corpse. He sees Lou scratched and crawling back toward a house, the starry sky Mack's mocking sparkled shroud.

But he will do it anyway, or what is he? Pond scum envying the ducks.

All is well. Safely rest. God is nigh.

As the birds walk up the red carpet, quacking and honking fussily, a pack of pleased Miss Americas, Mack watches them pause and look up, satisfied but quizzical, into the burst of lights from the tourists' cameras, the hollywood explosion of them along the runner. The birds weave a little, stop, then proceed again, seeming uncertain why anyone would want to take these pictures, flash a light, be there at all, why any of this should be happening, though, by God, and sometimes surely not by God, it happened every day.

Quilty, at the edge of the crowd, holds up his fingers, giving each person he passes the peace sign and saying, "Peace." He comes close to Mack.

"Peace," he says.

"People don't say that anymore," says Mack.

"Well, they should," says Quilty. His nostrils have begun to flare, in that way that always signals a sob. He sinks to the floor and grabs Mack's feet. Quilty's gestures of contrition are like comets: infrequent and brilliant, but with a lot of space garbage. "No more war!" Quilty cries. "No more devastation!"

For the moment, it is only Quilty who is devastated. People are looking. "You're upstaging the ducks," says Mack.

Quilty pulls himself up via Mack's trousers. "Have pity," he says.

This is Quilty's audition ritual: whenever he feels it is time for it, he calls upon himself to audition for love. He has no script, no reliable sense of stage, just a faceful of his heart's own greasepaint and a relentless need for applause.

"Okay, okay," says Mack, and as the elevator closes on the dozen birds and their bowing trainer, everybody in the hotel lounge claps.

"Thank you," murmurs Quilty. "You are too kind, too kind."

1997

WHICH IS MORE THAN I CAN SAY ABOUT SOME PEOPLE

IT WAS A FEAR greater than death, according to the magazines. Death was number four. After mutilation, three, and divorce, two. Number one, the real fear, the one death could not even approach, was public speaking. Abby Mallon knew this too well. Which is why she had liked her job at American Scholastic Tests: she got to work with words in a private way. The speech she made was done in the back, alone, like little shoes cobbled by an elf: spider is to web as weaver is to *blank*. That one was hers. She was proud of that.

Also, *blank is* to heartache as forest is to bench.

But then one day the supervisor and the AST district coordinator called her upstairs. She was good, they said, but perhaps she had become *too* good, too *creative*, they suggested, and gave her a promotion out of the composing room and into the high school auditoriums of America. She would have to travel and give speeches, tell high school faculty how to prepare students for the entrance exams, meet separately with the juniors and seniors and answer their questions unswervingly, with authority and grace. "You may have a vacation first," they said, and handed her a check.

"Thank you," she said doubtfully. In her life, she had been given the gift of solitude, a knack for it, but now it would be of no professional use. She would have to become a people person.

"A *peeper* person?" queried her mother on the phone from Pittsburgh.

"People," said Abby.

"Oh, those," said her mother, and she sighed the sigh of death, though she was strong as a brick.

* * *

Of all Abby's fanciful ideas for self-improvement (the inspirational video, the breathing exercises, the hypnosis class), the Blarney Stone, with its whoring barter of eloquence for love – O GIFT OF GAB, read the T-shirts – was perhaps the most extreme. Perhaps. There had been, after all, her marriage to Bob, her boyfriend of many years, after her dog, Randolph, had died of kidney failure and marriage to Bob seemed the only way to overcome her grief. Of course, she had always admired the idea of marriage, the citizenship and public speech of it, the innocence rebestowed, and Bob was big and comforting. But he didn't have a lot to say. He was not a verbal man. Rage gave him syntax – but it just wasn't enough! Soon Abby had begun to keep him as a kind of pet, while she quietly looked for distractions of depth and consequence. She looked for words. She looked for ways with words. She worked hard to befriend a lyricist from New York – a tepid, fair-haired, violet-eyed bachelor – she and most of the doctors' wives and arts administrators in town. He was newly arrived, owned no car, and wore the same tan blazer every day. "Water, water everywhere but not a drop to drink," said the bachelor lyricist once, listening wanly to the female chirp of his phone messages. In his apartment, there were no novels or bookcases. There was one chair, as well as a large television set, the phone machine, a rhyming dictionary continuously renewed from the library, and a coffee table. Women brought him meals, professional introductions, jingle commissions, and cash grants. In return, he brought them small piebald stones from the beach, or a pretty weed from the park. He would stand behind the coffee table and recite his own songs, then step back and wait fearfully to be seduced. To be lunged at and devoured by the female form was, he believed, something akin to applause. Sometimes he would produce a rented lute and say, "Here, I've just composed a melody to go with my Creation verse. Sing along with me."

And Abby would stare at him and say, "But I don't know the tune. I haven't heard it yet. You just made it up, you said."

Oh, the vexations endured by a man of poesy! He stood

paralyzed behind the coffee table, and when Abby did at last step forward, just to touch him, to take his pulse, perhaps, *to capture one of his arms in an invisible blood-pressure cuff*! he crumpled and shrank. "Please don't think I'm some kind of emotional Epstein-Barr," he said, quoting from other arguments he'd had with women. "I'm not indifferent or dispassionate. I'm calm. I'm romantic, but I'm calm. I have appetites, but I'm very calm about them."

When she went back to her husband – "Honey, you're home!" Bob exclaimed – she lasted only a week. Shouldn't it have lasted longer – the mix of loneliness and lust and habit she always felt with Bob, the mix that was surely love, for it so often felt like love, how could it not be love, surely nature intended it to be, surely nature with its hurricanes and hail was counting on this to suffice? Bob smiled at her and said nothing. And the next day, she booked a flight to Ireland.

How her mother became part of the trip, Abby still couldn't exactly recall. It had something to do with a stick shift: how Abby had never learned to drive one. "In my day and age," said her mother, "everyone learned. We all learned. Women had skills. They knew how to cook and sew. Now women have no skills."

The stick shifts were half the rental price of the automatics.

"If you're looking for a driver," hinted her mother, "I can still see the road."

"That's good," said Abby.

"And your sister Theda's spending the summer at your aunt's camp again." Theda had Down's syndrome, and the family adored her. Every time Abby visited, Theda would shout, "Look at you!" and throw her arms around her in a terrific hug. "Theda's, of course, sweet as ever," said her mother, "which is more than I can say about some people."

"That's probably true."

"I'd like to see Ireland while I can. Your father, when he was alive, never wanted to. I'm Irish, you know."

"I know. One-sixteenth."

"That's right. Of course, your father was Scottish, which is a totally different thing."

Abby sighed. "It seems to me that *Japanese* would be a totally different thing."

"*Japanese?*" hooted her mother. "Japanese is close."

And so in the middle of June, they landed at the Dublin airport together. "We're going to go all around this island, every last peninsula," said Mrs. Mallon in the airport parking lot, revving the engine of their rented Ford Fiesta, "because that's just the kind of crazy Yuppies we are."

Abby felt sick from the flight; and sitting on what should be the driver's side but without a steering wheel suddenly seemed emblematic of something.

Her mother lurched out of the parking lot and headed for the nearest roundabout, crossing into the other lane only twice. "I'll get the hang of this," she said. She pushed her glasses farther up on her nose and Abby could see for the first time that her mother's eyes were milky with age. Her steering was jerky and her foot jumped around on the floor, trying to find the clutch. Perhaps this had been a mistake.

"Go straight, Mom," said Abby, looking at her map.

They zigged and zagged to the north, up and away from Dublin, planning to return to it at the end, but now heading toward Drogheda, Abby snatching up the guidebook and then the map again and then the guidebook, and Mrs. Mallon shouting, "What?" or "Left?" or "This can't be right; let me see that thing." The Irish countryside opened up before them, its pastoral patchwork and stone walls and its chimney aroma of turf fires like some other century, its small stands of trees, abutting fields populated with wildflowers and sheep dung and cut sod and cows with ear tags, beautiful as women. Perhaps fairy folk lived in the trees! Abby saw immediately that to live amid the magic feel of this place would be necessarily to believe in magic. To live here would make you superstitious, warm-hearted with secrets, unrealistic. If you were literal, or practical, you would have to move – or you would have to drink.

They drove uncertainly past signs to places unmarked on the map. They felt lost – but not in an uncharming way. The old narrow roads with their white side markers reminded Abby of the vacations the family had taken when she was little, the cow-country car trips through New England or Virginia – in those days before there were interstates, or plastic cups, or a populace depressed by asphalt and french fries. Ireland was a trip into the past of America. It was years behind, unmarred, like a story or a dream or a clear creek. I'm a child again, Abby thought. I'm back. And just as when she was a child, she suddenly had to go to the bathroom.

"I have to go to the bathroom," she said. To their left was a sign that said ROAD WORKS AHEAD, and underneath it someone had scrawled, "No, it doesn't."

Mrs. Mallon veered the car over to the left and slammed on the brakes. There were some black-faced sheep haunch-marked in bright blue and munching grass near the road.

"Here?" asked Abby.

"I don't want to waste time stopping somewhere else and having to buy something. You can go behind that wall."

"Thanks," said Abby, groping in her pocketbook for Kleenex. She missed her own apartment. She missed her neighborhood. She missed the plentiful U-Pump-Itt's, where, she often said, at least they spelled *pump* right! She got out and hiked back down the road a little way. On one of the family road trips thirty years ago, when she and Theda had had to go to the bathroom, their father had stopped the car and told them to "go to the bathroom in the woods." They had wandered through the woods for twenty minutes, looking for the bathroom, before they came back out to tell him that they hadn't been able to find it. Her father had looked perplexed, then amused, and then angry – his usual pattern.

Now Abby struggled over a short stone wall and hid, squatting, eyeing the sheep warily. She was spacey with jet lag, and when she got back to the car, she realized she'd left the guidebook back on a stone and had to turn around and retrieve it.

"There," she said, getting back in the car.

Mrs. Mallon shifted into gear. "I always feel that if people would just be like animals and excrete here and there rather than in a single agreed-upon spot, we wouldn't have any pollution."

Abby nodded. "That's brilliant, Mom."

"Is it?"

They stopped briefly at an English manor house, to see the natural world cut up into moldings and rugs, wool and wood captive and squared, the earth stolen and embalmed and shellacked. Abby wanted to leave. "Let's leave," she whispered.

"What is it with you?" complained her mother. From there, they visited a neolithic passage grave, its floor plan like a birth in reverse, its narrow stone corridor spilling into a high, round room. They took off their sunglasses and studied the Celtic curlicues. "Older than the pyramids," announced the guide, though he failed to address its most important feature, Abby felt: its deadly maternal metaphor.

"Are you still too nervous to cross the border to Northern Ireland?" asked Mrs. Mallon.

"Uh-huh." Abby bit at her thumbnail, tearing the end of it off like a tiny twig.

"Oh, come on," said her mother. "Get a grip."

And so they crossed the border into the North, past the flak-jacketed soldiers patrolling the neighborhoods and barbed wire of Newry, young men holding automatic weapons and walking backward, block after block, their partners across the street, walking forward, on the watch. Helicopters flapped above. "This is a little scary," said Abby.

"It's all show," said Mrs. Mallon breezily.

"It's a scary show."

"If you get scared easily."

Which was quickly becoming the theme of their trip – Abby could see that already. That Abby had no courage and her mother did. And that it had forever been that way.

"You scare too easily," said her mother. "You always did. When you were a child, you wouldn't go into a house unless you were reassured there were no balloons in it."

"I didn't like balloons."

"And you were scared on the plane coming over," said her mother.

Abby grew defensive. "Only when the flight attendant said there was no coffee because the percolator was broken. Didn't you find that alarming? And then after all that slamming, they still couldn't get one of the overhead bins shut." Abby remembered this like a distant, bitter memory, though it had only been yesterday. The plane had taken off with a terrible shudder, and when it proceeded with the rattle of an old subway car, particularly over Greenland, the flight attendant had gotten on the address system to announce there was nothing to worry about, especially when you think about "how heavy air really is."

Now her mother thought she was Tarzan. "I want to go on that rope bridge I saw in the guidebook," she said.

On page 98 in the guidebook was a photograph of a rope-and-board bridge slung high between two cliffs. It was supposed to be for fishermen, but tourists were allowed, though they were cautioned about strong winds.

"Why do you want to go on the rope bridge?" asked Abby.

"Why?" replied her mother, who then seemed stuck and fell silent.

For the next two days, they drove east and to the north, skirting Belfast, along the coastline, past old windmills and sheep farms, and up out onto vertiginous cliffs that looked out toward Scotland, a pale sliver on the sea. They stayed at a tiny stucco bed-and-breakfast, one with a thatched roof like Cleopatra bangs. They slept lumpily, and in the morning in the breakfast room with its large front window, they ate their cereal and rashers and black and white pudding in an exhausted way, going through the motions of good guesthood – "Yes, the troubles," they agreed, for who could say for certain whom you were talking to? It wasn't like race-riven America, where you always knew. Abby nodded. Out the window, there was a breeze, but she couldn't hear the faintest rustle of it. She could only see it silently moving the dangling branches of the sun-sequined spruce, just slightly, like objects hanging from a rearview mirror in someone else's car.

She charged the bill to her Visa, tried to lift both bags, and then just lifted her own.

"Good-bye! Thank you!" she and her mother called to their host. Back in the car, briefly, Mrs. Mallon began to sing "Toora-loora-loora." "'Over in Killarney, many years ago,'" she warbled. Her voice was husky, vibrating, slightly flat, coming in just under each note like a saucer under a cup.

And so they drove on. The night before, a whole day could have shape and design. But when it was upon you, it could vanish tragically to air.

They came to the sign for the rope bridge.

"I want to do this," said Mrs. Mallon, and swung the car sharply right. They crunched into a gravel parking lot and parked; the bridge was a quarter-mile walk from there. In the distance, dark clouds roiled like a hemorrhage, and the wind was picking up. Rain mizzled the windshield.

"I'm going to stay here," said Abby.

"You are?"

"Yeah."

"Whatever," said her mother in a disgusted way, and she got out, scowling, and trudged down the path to the bridge, disappearing beyond a curve.

Abby waited, now feeling the true loneliness of this trip. She realized she missed Bob and his warm, quiet confusion; how he sat on the rug in front of the fireplace, where her dog, Randolph, used to sit; sat there beneath the five Christmas cards they'd received and placed on the mantel – five, including the one from the paperboy – sat there picking at his feet, or naming all the fruits in his fruit salad, remarking life's great variety! or asking what was wrong (in his own silent way), while poking endlessly at a smoldering log. She thought, too, about poor Randolph, at the vet, with his patchy fur and begging, dying eyes. And she thought about the pale bachelor lyricist, how he had once come to see her, and how he hadn't even placed enough pressure on the doorbell to make it ring, and so had stood there waiting on the porch, holding a purple cone-flower, until she just happened to walk by the front window and see him standing there. *O poetry!* When she invited him in, and he gave her the flower and sat down to decry the coded bloom and doom of all things, decry as well his own unearned deathlessness, how everything hurtles toward oblivion, except words, which assemble themselves in time like molecules in space, for God was an act – an act! – of language, it hadn't seemed silly to her, not really, at least not *that* silly.

The wind was gusting. She looked at her watch, worried now about her mother. She turned on the radio to find a weather report, though the stations all seemed to be playing strange, redone versions of American pop songs from 1970. Every so often, there was a two-minute quiz show – Who is the president of France? Is a tomato a vegetable or a fruit? – questions that the caller rarely if ever answered correctly, which made it quite embarrassing to listen to. Why did they do it? Puzzles, quizzes, game shows. Abby knew from AST that a surprising percentage of those taking the college entrance exams never actually applied to college. People just loved a test. Wasn't that true? People loved to put themselves to one.

Her mother was now knocking on the glass. She was muddy and wet. Abby unlocked the door and pushed it open. "Was it worth it?" Abby asked.

Her mother got in, big and dank and puffing. She started the car without looking at her daughter. "What a bridge," she said finally.

The next day, they made their way along the Antrim coast, through towns bannered with Union Jacks and Scottish hymns, down to Derry with its barbed wire and IRA scrawlings on the city walls – "John Major is a Zionist Jew" ("Hello," said a British officer when they stopped to stare) – and then escaping across bandit country, and once more down across the border into the south, down the Donegal coast, its fishing villages like some old, never-was Cape Cod. Staring out through the windshield, off into the horizon, Abby began to think that all the beauty and ugliness and turbulence one found scattered through nature, one could also find in people themselves, all collected there, all together in a single place. No matter what terror or loveliness the earth could produce – winds, seas – a person could produce the same, lived with the same, lived with all that mixed-up nature swirling inside, every bit. There was nothing as complex in the world – no flower or stone – as a single hello from a human being.

Once in a while, Abby and her mother broke their silences with talk of Mrs. Mallon's job as office manager at a small flashlight company – "I had to totally rearrange our insurance policies. The dental and Major Medical were eating our lunch!" – or with questions about the route signs, or the black dots signifying the auto deaths. But mostly, her mother wanted to talk about Abby's shaky marriage and what she was going to do. "Look, another ruined abbey," she took to saying every time they passed a heap of medieval stones.

"When you going back to Bob?"

"I went back," said Abby. "But then I left again. Oops."

Her mother sighed. "Women of your generation are always hoping for some other kind of romance than the one they have," said Mrs. Mallon. "Aren't they?"

"Who knows?" said Abby. She was starting to feel a little tight-lipped with her mother, crammed into this space together like astronauts. She was starting to have a highly inflamed sense of event: a single word rang and vibrated. The slightest movement could annoy, the breath, the odor. Unlike her sister, Theda, who had always remained sunny and cheerfully intimate with everyone, Abby had always been darker and left to her own devices; she and her mother had never been very close. When Abby was a child, her mother had always repelled her a bit – the oily smell of her hair, her belly button like a worm curled in a pit, the sanitary napkins in the bathroom wastebasket, horrid as a war, then later strewn along the curb by raccoons who would tear them from the trash cans at night. Once at a restaurant, when she was little, Abby had burst into an unlatched ladies' room stall, only to find her mother sitting there in a dazed and unseemly way, peering out at her from the toilet seat like a cuckoo in a clock.

There were things one should never know about another person.

Later, Abby decided that perhaps it hadn't been her mother at all.

Yet now here she and her mother were, sharing the tiniest of cars, reunited in a wheeled and metal womb, sharing small double beds in bed-and-breakfasts, waking up with mouths stale and close upon each other, or backs turned and rocking in angry-seeming humps. *The land of ire!* Talk of Abby's marriage and its possible demise trotted before them on the road like a herd of sheep, insomnia's sheep, and it made Abby want to have a gun.

"I never bothered with conventional romantic fluff," said Mrs. Mallon. "I wasn't the type. I always worked, and I was practical, put myself forward, and got things done and over with. If I liked a man, I asked him out myself. That's how I met your father. I asked him out. I even proposed the marriage."

"I know."

"And then I stayed with him until the day he died. Actually, three days after. He was a good man." She paused. "Which is more than I can say about some people."

Abby didn't say anything.

"Bob's a good man," added Mrs. Mallon.

"I didn't say he wasn't."

There was silence again between them now as the countryside once more unfolded its quilt of greens, the old roads triggering memories as if it were a land she had traveled long ago, its mix of luck and unluck like her own past; it seemed stuck in time, like a daydream or a book. Up close the mountains were craggy, scabby with rock and green, like a buck's antlers trying to lose their fuzz. But distance filled the gaps with moss. Wasn't that the truth? Abby sat quietly, glugging Ballygowan water from a plastic bottle and popping Extra

Strong Mints. Perhaps she should turn on the radio, listen to one of the call-in quizzes or to the news. But then her mother would take over, fiddle and retune. Her mother was always searching for country music, songs with the words *devil woman*. She loved those.

"Promise me one thing," said Mrs. Mallon.

"What?" said Abby.

"That you'll try with Bob."

At what price? Abby wanted to yell, but she and her mother were too old for that now.

Mrs. Mallon continued, thoughtfully, with the sort of pseudowisdom she donned now that she was sixty. "Once you're with a man, you have to sit still with him. As scary as it seems. You have to be brave and learn to reap the benefits of inertia," and here she gunned the motor to pass a tractor on a curve. LOOSE CHIPPINGS said the sign. HIDDEN DIP. But Abby's mother drove as if these were mere cocktail party chatter. A sign ahead showed six black dots.

"Yeah," said Abby, clutching the dashboard. "Dad was inert. Dad was inert, except that once every three years he jumped up and socked somebody in the mouth."

"That's not true."

"It's basically true."

In Killybegs, they followed the signs for Donegal City. "You women today," Mrs. Mallon said. "You expect too much."

"If it's Tuesday, this must be Sligo," said Abby. She had taken to making up stupid jokes. "What do you call a bus with a soccer team on it?"

"What?" They passed a family of gypsies, camped next to a mountain of car batteries they hoped to sell.

"A football coach." Sometimes Abby laughed raucously, and sometimes not at all. Sometimes she just shrugged. She was waiting for the Blarney Stone. That was all she'd come here for, so everything else she could endure.

They stopped at a bookshop to get a better map and

inquire, perhaps, as to a bathroom. Inside, there were four customers: two priests reading golf books, and a mother with her tiny son, who traipsed after her along the shelves, begging, "Please, Mummy, just a wee book, Mummy. Please just a wee book." There was no better map. There was no bathroom. "Sorry," the clerk said, and one of the priests glanced up quickly. Abby and her mother went next door to look at the Kinsale smocks and wool sweaters – tiny cardigans that young Irish children, on sweltering summer days of seventy-one degrees, wore on the beach, over their bathing suits. "So cute," said Abby, and the two of them wandered through the store, touching things. In the back by the wool caps, Abby's mother found a marionette hanging from a ceiling hook and began to play with it a little, waving its arms to the store music, which was a Beethoven concerto. Abby went to pay for a smock, ask about a bathroom or a good pub, and when she came back, her mother was still there, transfixed, conducting the concerto with the puppet. Her face was arranged in girlish joy, luminous, as Abby rarely saw it. When the concerto was over, Abby handed her a bag. "Here," she said, "I bought you a smock."

Mrs. Mallon let go of the marionette, and her face darkened. "I never had a real childhood," she said, taking the bag and looking off into the middle distance. "Being the oldest, I was always my mother's confidante. I always had to act grown-up and responsible. Which wasn't my natural nature." Abby steered her toward the door. "And then when I really was grown up, there was Theda, who needed all my time, and your father of course, with his demands. But then there was you. You I liked. You I could leave alone."

"I bought you a smock," Abby said again.

They used the bathroom at O'Hara's pub, bought a single mineral water and split it, then went on to the Drumcliff cemetery to see the dead Yeatses. Then they sped on toward Sligo City to find a room, and the next day were up and out to Knock to watch lame women, sick women, women who wanted to get pregnant ("Knocked up," said Abby) rub their rosaries on the original stones of the shrine. They drove down to Clifden, around Connemara, to Galway and Limerick – "There once were two gals from America, one named Abby and her mother named Erica. . . ." They sang, minstrel speed demons around the Ring of Kerry, its palm trees and blue and pink hydrangea like a set from an operetta. "Playgirls of the Western World!" exclaimed her mother. They came to rest, at dark, near Ballylickey, in a bed-and-breakfast, a former hunting lodge, in a glen just off the ring. They ate a late supper of toddies and a soda bread their hostess called "Curranty Dick."

"Don't I know it," said Mrs. Mallon. Which depressed Abby, like a tacky fixture in a room, and so she excused herself and went upstairs, to bed.

It was the next day, through Ballylickey, Bantry, Skibbereen, and Cork, that they entered Blarney. At the castle, the line to kiss the stone was long, hot, and frightening. It jammed the tiny winding stairs of the castle's suffocating left tower, and people pressed themselves against the dark wall to make room for others who had lost their nerve and were coming back down.

"This is ridiculous," said Abby. But by the time they'd reached the top, her annoyance had turned to anxiety. To kiss the stone, she saw, people had to lie on their backs out over a parapet, stretching their necks out to place their lips on the underside of a supporting wall where the stone was laid. A strange-looking leprechaunish man was squatting at the side of the stone, supposedly to help people arch back, but he seemed to be holding them too loosely, a careless and sadistic glint in his eyes, and some people were changing their minds and going back downstairs, fearful and inarticulate as ever.

"I don't think I can do this," said Abby hesitantly, tying her dark raincoat more tightly around her.

"Of course you can," said her mother. "You've come all this way. This is why you came." Now that they were at the top of the castle, the line seemed to be moving quickly. Abby looked back, and around, and the view was green and rich, and breathtaking, like a photo soaked in dyes.

"Next!" she heard the leprechaun shouting.

Ahead of them, a German woman was struggling to get back up from where the leprechaun had left her. She wiped her mouth and made a face. "That vuz awfhul," she grumbled.

Panic seized Abby. "You know what? I don't want to do this," she said again to her mother. There were only two people ahead of them in line. One of them was now getting down on his back, clutching the iron supports and inching his hands down, arching at the neck and waist to reach the stone, exposing his white throat. His wife stood above him, taking his picture.

"But you came all this way! Don't be a ninny!" Her mother was bullying her again. It never gave her courage; in fact, it deprived her of courage. But it gave her bitterness and impulsiveness, which could look like the same thing.

"Next," said the leprechaun nastily. He hated these people; one could see that. One could see he half-hoped they would go crashing down off the ledge into a heap of raincoats, limbs, and traveler's checks.

"Go on," said Mrs. Mallon.

"I can't," Abby whined. Her mother was nudging and the leprechaun was frowning. "I can't. You go."

"No. Come on. Think of it as a test." Her mother gave her a scowl, unhinged by something lunatic in it. "You work with tests. And in school, you always did well on them."

"For tests, you have to study."

"You studied!"

"I didn't study the right thing."

"Oh, Abby."

"I can't," Abby whispered. "I just don't think I can." She breathed deeply and moved quickly. "Oh – okay." She threw her hat down and fell to the stone floor fast, to get it over with.

"Move back, move back," droned the leprechaun, like a train conductor.

She could feel now no more space behind her back; from

her waist up, she was out over air and hanging on only by her clenched hands and the iron rails. She bent her head as far back as she could, but it wasn't far enough.

"Lower," said the leprechaun.

She slid her hands down farther, as if she were doing a trick on a jungle gym. Still, she couldn't see the stone itself, only the castle wall.

"Lower," said the leprechaun.

She slid her hands even lower, bent her head back, her chin skyward, could feel the vertebrae of her throat pressing out against the skin, and this time she could see the stone. It was about the size of a microwave oven and was covered with moisture and dirt and lipstick marks in the shape of lips – lavender, apricot, red. It seemed very unhygienic for a public event, filthy and wet, and so now instead of giving it a big smack, she blew a peck at it, then shouted, "Okay, help me up, please," and the leprechaun helped her back up.

Abby stood and brushed herself off. Her raincoat was covered with whitish mud. "Eeyuhh," she said. But she had done it! At least sort of. She put her hat back on. She tipped the leprechaun a pound. She didn't know how she felt. She felt nothing. Finally, these dares one made oneself commit didn't change a thing. They were all a construction of wish and string and distance.

"Now my turn," said her mother with a kind of reluctant determination, handing Abby her sunglasses, and as her mother got down stiffly, inching her way toward the stone, Abby suddenly saw something she'd never seen before: her mother was terrified. For all her bullying and bravado, her mother was proceeding, and proceeding badly, through a great storm of terror in her brain. As her mother tried to inch herself back toward the stone, Abby, now privy to her bare face, saw that this fierce bonfire of a woman had gone twitchy and melancholic – it was a ruse, all her formidable display. She was only trying to prove something, trying pointlessly to defy and overcome her fears – instead of just learning to live with them, since, hell, you were living with them anyway. "Mom, you okay?" Mrs. Mallon's face was in a grimace, her mouth open and bared. The former auburn of her hair had descended, Abby saw, to her teeth, which she'd let rust with years of coffee and tea.

Now the leprechaun was having to hold her more than he had the other people. "Lower, now lower."

"Oh, God, not any lower," cried Mrs. Mallon.

"You're almost there."

"I don't see it."

"There you got it?" He loosened his grip and let her slip farther.

"Yes," she said. She let out a puckering, spitting sound. But then when she struggled to come back up, she seemed to be stuck. Her legs thrashed out before her; her shoes loosened from her feet; her skirt rode up, revealing the brown tops of her panty hose. She was bent too strangely, from the hips, it seemed, and she was plump and didn't have the stomach muscles to lift herself back up. The leprechaun seemed to be having difficulty.

"Can someone here help me?"

"Oh my God," said Abby, and she and another man in line immediately squatted next to Mrs. Mallon to help her. She was heavy, stiff with fright, and when they had finally lifted her and gotten her sitting, then standing again, she seemed stricken and pale.

A guard near the staircase volunteered to escort her down.

"Would you like that, Mom?" and Mrs. Mallon simply nodded.

"You get in front of us," the guard said to Abby in the singsong accent of County Cork, "just in case she falls." And Abby got in front, her coat taking the updraft and spreading to either side as she circled slowly down into the dungeon-dark of the stairwell, into the black like a bat new to its wings.

In a square in the center of town, an evangelist was waving a Bible and shouting about "the brevity of life," how it was a thing grabbed by one hand and then gone, escaped through the fingers. "God's word is quick!" he called out.

"Let's go over there," said Abby, and she took her mother to a place called Brady's Public House for a restorative Guinness. "Are you okay?" Abby kept asking. They still had no place to stay that night, and though it remained light quite late, and the inns stayed open until ten, she imagined the two of them temporarily homeless, sleeping under the stars, snacking on slugs. Stars the size of Chicago! Dew like a pixie bath beneath them! They would lick it from their arms.

"I'm fine," she said, waving Abby's questions away. "What a stone!"

"Mom," said Abby, frowning, for she was now wondering about a few things. "When you went across that rope bridge, did you do that okay?"

Mrs. Mallon sighed. "Well, I got the idea of it," she said huffily. "But there were some gusts of wind that caused it to buck a little, and though some people thought that was fun, I had to get down and crawl back. You'll recall there was a little rain."

"You crawled back on your hands and knees?"

"Well, yes," she admitted. "There was a nice Belgian man who helped me." She felt unmasked, no doubt, before her daughter and now gulped at her Guinness.

Abby tried to take a cheerful tone, switching the subject a little, and it reminded her of Theda, Theda somehow living in her voice, her larynx suddenly a summer camp for the cheerful and slow. "Well, look at you!" said Abby. "Do you feel eloquent and confident, now that you've kissed the stone?"

"Not really." Mrs. Mallon shrugged.

Now that they had kissed it, or sort of, would they become self-conscious? What would they end up talking about?

Movies, probably. Just as they always had at home. Movies with scenery, movies with songs.

"How about you?" asked Mrs. Mallon.

"Well," said Abby, "mostly I feel like we've probably caught strep throat. And yet, and yet . . ." Here she sat up and leaned forward. No tests, or radio quizzes, or ungodly speeches, or songs brain-dead with biography, or kooky prayers, or shouts, or prolix conversations that with drink and too much time always revealed how stupid and mean even the best people were, just simply this: "A toast. I feel a toast coming on."

"You do?"

"Yes, I do." No one had toasted Abby and Bob at their little wedding, and that's what had been wrong, she believed now. No toast. There had been only thirty guests and they had simply eaten the ham canapes and gone home. How could a marriage go right? It wasn't that such ceremonies were important in and of themselves. They were nothing. They were zeros. But they were zeros as placeholders; they held numbers and equations intact. And once you underwent them, you could move on, know the empty power of their blessing, and not spend time missing them.

From here on in, she would believe in toasts. One was collecting itself now, in her head, in a kind of hesitant philately. She gazed over at her mother and took a deep breath. Perhaps her mother had never shown Abby affection, not really, but she had given her a knack for solitude, with its terrible lurches outward, and its smooth glide back to peace. Abby would toast her for that. It was really the world that was one's brutal mother, the one that nursed and neglected you, and your own mother was only your sibling in that world. Abby lifted her glass. "May the worst always be behind you. May the sun daily warm your arms. . . ." She looked down at her cocktail napkin for assistance, but there was only a cartoon of a big-chested colleen, two shamrocks over her breasts. Abby looked back up. *God's word is quick!* "May your car always start—" But perhaps God might also begin with tall, slow words; the belly bloat of a fib; the distended tale. "And may you always have a clean shirt," she continued, her voice growing gallant, public and loud, "and a holding roof, healthy children and good cabbages – and may you be with me in my heart, Mother, as you are now, in this place; always and forever – like a flaming light."

There was noise in the pub.

Blank is to childhood as journey is to lips.

"Right," said Mrs. Mallon, looking into her stout in a concentrated, bright-eyed way. She had never been courted before, not once in her entire life, and now she blushed, ears on fire, lifted her pint, and drank.

1993

WILLING

How can I live my life without committing an act
with a giant scissors?
—JOYCE CAROL OATES, "An Interior Monologue"

IN HER LAST PICTURE, the camera had lingered at the hip, the naked hip, and even though it wasn't her hip, she acquired a reputation for being willing.

"You have the body," studio heads told her over lunch at Chasen's.

She looked away. "Habeas corpus," she said, not smiling.

"Pardon me?" A hip that knew Latin. Christ.

"Nothing," she said. They smiled at her and dropped names. Scorsese, Brando. Work was all playtime to them, playtime with gel in their hair. At times, she felt bad that it *wasn't* her hip. It should have been her hip. A mediocre picture, a picture queasy with pornography: these, she knew, eroticized the unavailable. The doctored and false. The stand-in. Unwittingly, she had participated. Let a hip come between. A false, unavailable, anonymous hip. She herself was true as a goddamn dairy product; available as lunch whenever.

But she was pushing forty.

She began to linger in juice bars. Sit for entire afternoons in places called I Love Juicy or Orange-U-Sweet. She drank juice and, outside, smoked a cigarette now and then. She'd been taken seriously – once – she knew that. Projects were discussed: Nina. Portia. Mother Courage with makeup. Now her hands trembled too much, even drinking juice, *especially* drinking juice, a Vantage wobbling between her fingers like a compass dial. She was sent scripts in which she was supposed to say lines she would never say, not wear clothes she would never not wear. She began to get obscene phone calls, and postcards signed, "Oh yeah, baby." Her boyfriend, a director with a growing reputation for expensive flops, a man who twice a week glowered at her Fancy Sunburst guppy and told it to get a job, became a Catholic and went back to his wife.

"Just when we were working out the bumps and chops and rocks," she said. Then she wept.

"I know," he said. "I know."

And so she left Hollywood. Phoned her agent and apologized. Went home to Chicago, rented a room by the week at the Days Inn, drank sherry, and grew a little plump. She let her life get dull – dull, but with Hostess cakes. There were moments bristling with deadness, when she looked out at her life and went *"What?"* Or worse, feeling interrupted and tired, "Wha—?" It had taken on the shape of a terrible mistake. She hadn't been given the proper tools to make a real life with, she decided, that was it. She'd been given a can of gravy and a hairbrush and told, "There you go." She'd stood there for years, blinking and befuddled, brushing the can with the brush.

Still, she was a minor movie star, once nominated for a major award. Mail came to her indirectly. A notice. A bill. A Thanksgiving card. But there was never a party, a dinner, an opening, an iced tea. One of the problems with people in Chicago, she remembered, was that they were never lonely at the same time. Their sadnesses occurred in isolation, lurched and spazzed, sent them spinning fizzily back into empty, padded corners, disconnected and alone.

She watched cable and ordered in a lot from a pizza place. A life of obscurity and radical calm. She rented a piano and practiced scales. She invested in the stock market. She wrote down her dreams in the morning to locate clues as to what to trade. *Disney*, her dreams said once. *St. Jude's Medical*. She made a little extra money. She got obsessed. The words *cash cow* nestled in the side of her mouth like a cud. She tried to be original – not a good thing with stocks – and she began to lose. When a stock went down, she bought more of it, to catch it on the way back up. She got confused. She took to staring out the window at Lake Michigan, the rippled slate of it like a blackboard gone bad.

"Sidra, *what* are you doing there?" shrieked her friend Tommy long distance over the phone. "Where are you? You're living in some state that borders on North Dakota!"

He was a screenwriter in Santa Monica and once, a long time ago and depressed on Ecstasy, they had slept together. He was gay, but they had liked each other very much.

"Maybe I'll get married," she said. She didn't mind Chicago. She thought of it as a cross between London and Queens, with a dash of Cleveland.

"Oh, *please*," he shrieked again. "What are you *really* doing?"

"Listening to seashore and self-esteem tapes," she said. She blew air into the mouth of the phone.

"Sounds like dust on the needle," he said. "Maybe you should get the squawking crickets tape. Have you *heard* the squawking crickets tape?"

"I got a bad perm today," she said. "When I was only halfway through with the rod part, the building the salon's in had a blackout. There were men drilling out front who'd struck a cable."

"How awful for you," he said. She could hear him tap his fingers. He had made himself the make-believe author of a make-believe book of essays called *One Man's Opinion*, and when he was bored or inspired, he quoted from it. "I was once in a rock band called Bad Perm," he said instead.

"Get out." She laughed.

His voice went hushed and worried. "What *are* you *doing* there?" he asked again.

Her room was a corner room where a piano was allowed. It was L-shaped, like a life veering off suddenly to become something else. It had a couch and two maple dressers and was never as neat as she might have wanted. She always had the DO NOT DISTURB sign on when the maids came by, and so things got a little out of hand. Wispy motes of dust and hair the size of small heads bumped around in the corners. Smudge began to darken the moldings and cloud the mirrors. The bathroom faucet dripped, and, too tired to phone anyone, she tied a string around the end of it, guiding the drip quietly into the drain, so it wouldn't bother her anymore. Her only plant, facing east in the window, hung over the popcorn popper and dried to a brown crunch. On the ledge, a jack-o'-lantern she had carved for Halloween had rotted, melted, froze, and now looked like a collapsed basketball – one she might have been saving for sentimental reasons, one from the *big game*! The man who brought her room service each morning – two poached eggs and a pot of coffee – reported her to the assistant manager, and she received a written warning slid under the door.

On Fridays, she visited her parents in Elmhurst. It was still hard for her father to look her in the eyes. He was seventy now. Ten years ago, he had gone to the first movie she had ever been in, saw her remove her clothes and dive into a pool. The movie was rated PG, but he never went to another one. Her mother went to all of them and searched later for encouraging things to say. Even something small. She refused to lie. "I liked the way you said the line about leaving home, your eyes wide and your hands fussing with your dress buttons," she wrote. "That red dress was so becoming. You should wear bright colors!"

"My father takes naps a lot when I visit," she said to Tommy.

"Naps?"

"I embarrass him. He thinks I'm a whore hippie. A hippie whore."

"That's ridiculous. As I said in *One Man's Opinion*, you're the most sexually conservative person I know."

"Yeah, well."

Her mother always greeted her warmly, puddle-eyed. These days, she was reading thin paperback books by a man named Robert Valleys, a man who said that after observing all the suffering in the world – war, starvation, greed – he had discovered the cure: hugs.

Hugs, hugs, hugs, hugs, hugs.

Her mother believed him. She squeezed so long and hard that Sidra, like an infant or a lover, became lost in the feel and smell of her – her sweet, dry skin, the gray peach fuzz on her neck. "I'm so glad you left that den of iniquity," her mother said softly.

But Sidra still got calls from the den. At night, sometimes, the director phoned from a phone booth, desiring to be forgiven as well as to direct. "I think of all the things you might be thinking, and I say, 'Oh, Christ.' I mean, do you think the things I sometimes think you do?"

"Of course," said Sidra. "Of course I think those things."

"*Of course*! *Of course* is a term that has no place in this conversation!"

When Tommy phoned, she often felt a pleasure so sudden and flooding, it startled her.

"God, I'm so glad it's you!"

"You have no right to abandon American filmmaking this way!" he would say affectionately, and she would laugh loudly, for minutes without stopping. She was starting to have two speeds: Coma and Hysteria. Two meals: breakfast and popcorn. Two friends: Charlotte Peveril and Tommy. She could hear the clink of his bourbon glass. "You are too gifted a person to be living in a state that borders on North Dakota."

"Iowa."

"Holy bejesus, it's worse than I thought. I'll bet they say that there. I'll bet they say 'Bejesus.' "

"I live downtown. They don't say that here."

"Are you anywhere near Champaign-Urbana?"

"No."

"I went there once. I thought from its name that it would be a different kind of place. I kept saying to myself, 'Champagne, ur*bah* na, *champagne,* ur*bah* na! Champagne! Urbana!' " He sighed. "It was just this thing in the middle of a field. I went to a Chinese restaurant there and ordered my entire dinner with *extra* MSG."

"I'm in Chicago. It's not so bad."

"Not so bad. There are no movie people there. Sidra, what about your *acting talent*?"

"I have no acting talent."

"Hello?"

"You heard me."

"I'm not sure. For a minute there, I thought maybe you had that dizziness thing again, that inner-ear imbalance."

"Talent. I don't have *talent.* I have willingness. What *talent*?" As a kid, she had always told the raunchiest jokes. As an adult, she could rip open a bone and speak out of it. Simple, clear. There was never anything to stop her. Why was there never anything to stop her? "I can stretch out the neck of a sweater to point at a freckle on my shoulder. Anyone who didn't get enough attention in nursery school can do that. Talent is something else."

"Excuse me, okay? I'm only a screenwriter. But someone's got you thinking you went from serious actress to aging bimbo. That's ridiculous. You just have to weather things a little out here. Besides. I think willing yourself to do a thing is brave, and the very essence of talent."

Sidra looked at her hands, already chapped and honeycombed with bad weather, bad soap, bad life. She needed to listen to the crickets tape. "But I *don't* will myself," she said. "I'm just already willing."

She began to go to blues bars at night. Sometimes she called Charlotte Peveril, her one friend left from high school.

"Siddy, how are you?" In Chicago, Sidra was thought of as a hillbilly name. But in L.A., people had thought it was beautiful and assumed she'd made it up.

"I'm fine. Let's go get drunk and listen to music."

Sometimes she just went by herself.

"Don't I know you from the movies?" a man might ask at one of the breaks, smiling, leering in a twinkly way.

"Maybe," she'd say, and he would look suddenly panicked and back away.

One night, a handsome man in a poncho, a bad poncho – though was there such a thing as a good poncho? asked Charlotte – sat down next to her with an extra glass of beer. "You look like you should be in the movies," he said. Sidra nodded wearily. "But I don't go to the movies. So if you *were* in the movies, I would never have gotten to set my eyes on you."

She turned her gaze from his poncho to her sherry, then

back. Perhaps he had spent some time in Mexico or Peru. "What do you do?"

"I'm an auto mechanic." He looked at her carefully. "My name's Walter. Walt." He pushed the second beer her way. "The drinks here are okay as long as you don't ask them to mix anything. Just don't ask them to mix anything!"

She picked it up and took a sip. There was something about him she liked: something earthy beneath the act. In L.A., beneath the act you got nougat or Styrofoam. Or glass. Sidra's mouth was lined with sherry. Walt's lips shone with beer. "What's the last movie you saw?" she asked him.

"The last movie I saw. Let's see." He was thinking, but she could tell he wasn't good at it. She watched with curiosity the folded-in mouth, the tilted head: at last, a guy who didn't go to the movies. His eyes rolled back like the casters on a clerk's chair, searching. "You know what I saw?"

"No. What?" She was getting drunk.

"It was this cartoon movie." Animation. She felt relieved. At least it wasn't one of those bad art films starring what's-her-name. "A man is asleep, having a dream about a beautiful little country full of little people." Walt sat back, looked around the room, as if that were all.

"And?" She was going to have to push and pull with this guy.

" 'And?' " he repeated. He leaned forward again. "And one day the people realize that they are only creatures in this man's dream. Dream people! And if the man wakes up, they will no longer exist!"

Now she hoped he wouldn't go on. She had changed her mind a little.

"So they all get together at a town meeting and devise a plan," he continued. Perhaps the band would be back soon. "They will burst into the man's bedroom and bring him back to a padded, insulated room in the town – the town of his own dream – and there they will keep watch over him to make sure he stays asleep. And they do just that. Forever and ever, everyone guarding him carefully, but apprehensively, making sure he never wakes up." He smiled. "I forget what the name of it was."

"And he never wakes up."

"Nope." He grinned at her. She liked him. She could tell he could tell. He took a sip of his beer. He looked around the bar, then back at her. "Is this a great country or what?" he said.

She smiled at him, with longing. "Where do you live," she asked, "and how do I get there?"

"I met a man," she told Tommy on the phone. "His name is Walter."

"A forced relationship. You're in a state of stress – you're in a *syndrome*, I can tell. You're going to force this romance. What does he do?"

"Something with cars." She sighed. "I want to sleep with someone. When I'm sleeping with someone, I'm less obsessed with the mail."

"But perhaps you should just be alone, be by yourself for a while."

"Like you've ever been alone," said Sidra. "I mean, have you *ever* been alone?"

"I've been alone."

"Yeah, and for how long?"

"Hours," said Tommy. He sighed. "At least it felt like hours."

"Right," she said, "so don't go lecturing me about inner resources."

"Okay. So I sold the mineral rights to my body years ago, but, hey, at least *I* got good money for mine."

"I got some money," said Sidra. "I got some."

Walter leaned her against his parked car. His mouth was slightly lopsided, paisley-shaped, his lips anneloid and full, and he kissed her hard. There was something numb and on hold in her. There were small dark pits of annihilation she discovered in her heart, in the loosening fist of it, and she threw herself into them, falling. She went home with him, slept with him. She told him who she was. A minor movie star once nominated for a major award. She told him she lived at the Days Inn. He had been there once, to the top, for a drink. But he did not seem to know her name.

"Never thought I'd sleep with a movie star," he did say. "I suppose that's every man's dream." He laughed – lightly, nervously.

"Just don't wake up," she said. Then she pulled the covers to her chin.

"Or change the dream," he added seriously. "I mean, in the movie I saw, everything is fine until the sleeping guy begins to dream about something else. I don't think he wills it or anything; it just happens."

"You didn't tell me about that part."

"That's right," he said. "You see, the guy starts dreaming about flamingos and then all the little people turn into flamingos and fly away."

"Really?" said Sidra.

"I *think* it was flamingos. I'm not too expert with birds."

"You're *not*?" She was trying to tease him, but it came out wrong, like a lizard with a little hat on.

"To tell you the truth, I really don't think I ever saw a single movie you were in."

"Good." She was drifting, indifferent, no longer paying attention.

He hitched his arm behind his head, wrist to nape. His chest heaved up and down. "I think I may of *heard* of you, though."

Django Reinhardt was on the radio. She listened, carefully. "Astonishing sounds came from that man's hands," Sidra murmured.

Walter tried to kiss her, tried to get her attention back. He wasn't that interested in music, though at times he tried to be. " 'Astonishing sounds'?" he said. "Like this?" He cupped his palms together, making little pops and suction noises.

"Yeah," she murmured. But she was elsewhere, letting a

dry wind sweep across the plain of her to sleep. "Like that."

He began to realize, soon, that she did not respect him. A bug could sense it. A doorknob could figure it out. She never quite took him seriously. She would talk about films and film directors, then look at him and say, "Oh, never mind." She was part of some other world. A world she no longer liked.

And now she was somewhere else. Another world she no longer liked.

But she was willing. Willing to give it a whirl. Once in a while, though she tried not to, she asked him about children, about having children, about turning kith to kin. How did he feel about all that? It seemed to her that if she were ever going to have a life of children and lawn mowers and grass clippings, it would be best to have it with someone who was not demeaned or trivialized by discussions of them. Did he like those big fertilized lawns? How about a nice rock garden? How did he feel deep down about those combination storm windows with the built-in screens?

"Yeah, I like them all right," he said, and she would nod slyly and drink a little too much. She would try then not to think too strenuously about her *whole life.* She would try to live life one day at a time, like an alcoholic – drink, don't drink, drink. Perhaps she should take drugs.

"I always thought someday I would have a little girl and name her after my grandmother." Sidra sighed, peered wistfully into her sherry.

"What was your grandmother's name?"

Sidra looked at his paisley mouth. "Grandma. Her name was Grandma." Walter laughed in a honking sort of way. "Oh, thank you," murmured Sidra. "Thank you for laughing."

Walter had a subscription to *AutoWeek.* He flipped through it in bed. He also liked to read repair manuals for new cars, particularly the Toyotas. He knew a lot about control panels, light-up panels, side panels.

"You're so obviously wrong for each other," said Charlotte over tapas at a tapas bar.

"Hey, please," said Sidra. "I think my taste's a little subtler than that." The thing with tapas bars was that you just kept stuffing things into your mouth. "Obviously wrong is just the beginning. That's where *I always* begin. At obviously wrong." In theory, she liked the idea of mismatched couples, the wrangling and retangling, like a comedy by Shakespeare.

"I can't imagine you with someone like him. He's just not special." Charlotte had met him only once. But she had heard of him from a girlfriend of hers. He had slept around, she'd said. "Into the pudding" is how she phrased it, and there were some boring stories. "Just don't let him humiliate you. Don't mistake a lack of sophistication for sweetness," she added.

"I'm supposed to wait around for someone special, while every other girl in this town gets to have a life?"

"I don't know, Sidra."

It was true. Men could be with whomever they pleased. But women had to date better, kinder, richer, and bright, bright, bright, or else people got embarrassed. It suggested sexual things. "I'm a very average person," she said desperately, somehow detecting that Charlotte already knew that, knew the deep, dark, wildly obvious secret of that, and how it made Sidra slightly pathetic, unseemly – *inferior,* when you got right down to it. Charlotte studied Sidra's face, headlights caught in the stare of a deer. Guns don't kill people, thought Sidra fizzily. Deer kill people.

"Maybe it's that we all used to envy you so much," Charlotte said a little bitterly. "You were so talented. You got all the lead parts in the plays. You were everyone's dream of what *they* wanted."

Sidra poked around at the appetizer in front of her, gardening it like a patch of land. She was unequal to anyone's wistfulness. She had made too little of her life. Its loneliness shamed her like a crime. "Envy," said Sidra. "That's a lot like hate, isn't it." But Charlotte didn't say anything. Probably she wanted Sidra to change the subject. Sidra stuffed her mouth full of feta cheese and onions, and looked up. "Well, all I can say is, I'm glad to be back." A piece of feta dropped from her lips.

Charlotte looked down at it and smiled. "I know what you mean," she said. She opened her mouth wide and let all the food inside fall out onto the table.

Charlotte could be funny like that. Sidra had forgotten that about her.

Walter had found some of her old movies in the video-rental place. She had a key. She went over one night and discovered him asleep in front of *Recluse with Roommate*. It was about a woman named Rose who rarely went out, because when she did, she was afraid of people. They seemed like alien life-forms – soulless, joyless, speaking asyntactically. Rose quickly became loosened from reality. Walter had it freeze-framed at the funny part, where Rose phones the psych ward to have them come take her away, but they refuse. She lay down next to him and tried to sleep, too, but began to cry a little. He stirred. "What's wrong?" he asked.

"Nothing. You fell asleep. Watching me."

"I was tired," he said.

"I guess so."

"Let me kiss you. Let me find your panels." His eyes were closed. She could be anybody.

"Did you like the beginning part of the movie?" This need in her was new. Frightening. It made her hair curl. When had she ever needed so much?

"It was okay," he said.

"So what is this guy, a race-car driver?" asked Tommy.

"No, he's a mechanic."

"Ugh! Quit him like a music lesson!"

"Like a *music lesson*? What is this, *Similes from the Middle Class*? *One Man's Opinion*?" She was irritated.

"Sidra. This is not right! You need to go out with someone really smart for a change."

"I've been out with smart. I've been out with someone who had two Ph.D.'s. We spent all of our time in bed with the light on, proofreading his vita." She sighed. "Every little thing he'd ever done, every little, little, little. I mean, have you ever seen a vita?"

Tommy sighed, too. He had heard this story of Sidra's before. "Yes," he said. "I thought Patti LuPone was great."

"Besides," she said. "Who says he's not smart?"

The Japanese cars were the most interesting. Though the Americans were getting sexier, trying to keep up with them. *Those Japs!*

"Let's talk about my world," she said.

"What world?"

"Well, something I'm interested in. Something where there's something in it for me."

"Okay." He turned and dimmed the lights, romantically. "Got a stock tip for you," he said.

She was horrified, dispirited, interested.

He told her the name of a company somebody at work invested in. AutVis.

"What is it?"

"I don't know. But some guy at work said buy this week. They're going to make some announcement. If I had money, I'd buy."

She bought, the very next morning. A thousand shares. By the afternoon, the stock had plummeted 10 percent; by the following morning, 50. She watched the ticker tape go by on the bottom of the TV news channel. She had become the major stockholder. The major stockholder of a dying company! Soon they were going to be calling her, wearily, to ask what she wanted done with the forklift.

"You're a neater eater than I am," Walter said to her over dinner at the Palmer House.

She looked at him darkly. "What the hell were you thinking of, recommending that stock?" she asked. "How could you be such an irresponsible idiot?" She saw it now, how their life would be together. She would yell; then he would yell. He would have an affair; then she would have an affair. And then they would be gone and gone, and they would live in that gone.

"I got the name wrong," he said. "Sorry."

"You what?"

"It wasn't AutVis. It was AutDrive. I kept thinking it was vis for vision."

"'Vis for vision,'" she repeated.

"I'm not that good with names," confessed Walter. "I do better with concepts."

"'Concepts,'" she repeated as well.

The concept of anger. The concept of bills. The concept of flightless, dodo love.

Outside, there was a watery gust from the direction of the lake. "Chicago," said Walter. "The Windy City. Is this the Windy City or what?" He looked at her hopefully, which made her despise him more.

She shook her head. "I don't even know why we're together," she said. "I mean, why are we even together?"

He looked at her hard. "I can't answer that for you," he yelled. He took two steps back, away from her. "You've got to answer that for yourself!" And he hailed his own cab, got in, and rode away.

She walked back to the Days Inn alone. She played scales soundlessly, on the tops of the piano keys, her thin-jointed fingers lifting and falling quietly like the tines of a music box or the legs of a spider. When she tired, she turned on the television, moved through the channels, and discovered an old movie she'd been in, a love story–murder mystery called *Finishing Touches*. It was the kind of performance she had become, briefly, known for: a patched-together intimacy with the audience, half cartoon, half revelation; a cross between shyness and derision. She had not given a damn back then, sort of like now, only then it had been a style, a way of being, not a diagnosis or demise.

Perhaps she should have a baby.

In the morning, she went to visit her parents in Elmhurst.

For winter, they had plastic-wrapped their home – the windows, the doors – so that it looked like a piece of avant-garde art. "Saves on heating bills," they said.

They had taken to discussing her in front of her. "It was a movie, Don. It was a movie about adventure. Nudity can be art."

"That's not how I saw it! That's not how I saw it at all!" said her father, red-faced, leaving the room. Naptime.

"How are you doing?" asked her mother, with what seemed like concern but was really an opening for something else. She had made tea.

"I'm okay, really," said Sidra. Everything she said about herself now sounded like a lie. If she was bad, it sounded like a lie; if she was fine – also a lie.

Her mother fiddled with a spoon. "I was envious of you." Her mother sighed. "I was always so envious of you! My own daughter!" She was shrieking it, saying it softly at first and then shrieking. It was exactly like Sidra's childhood: just when she thought life had become simple again, her mother gave her a new portion of the world to organize.

"I have to go," said Sidra. She had only just gotten there, but she wanted to go. She didn't want to visit her parents anymore. She didn't want to look at their lives.

She went back to the Days Inn and phoned Tommy. She and Tommy understood each other. "I *get* you," he used to say. His childhood had been full of sisters. He'd spent large portions of it drawing pictures of women in bathing suits – Miss Kenya from Nairobi! – and then asking one of the sisters to pick the most beautiful. If he disagreed, he asked another sister.

The connection was bad, and suddenly she felt too tired. "Darling, are you okay?" he said faintly.

"I'm okay."

"I think I'm hard of hearing," he said.

"I think I'm hard of talking," she said. "I'll phone you tomorrow."

She phoned Walter instead. "I need to see you," she said.

"Oh, really?" he said skeptically, and then added, with a

sweetness he seemed to have plucked expertly from the air like a fly, "Is this a great country or what?"

She felt grateful to be with him again. "Let's never be apart," she whispered, rubbing his stomach. He had the physical inclinations of a dog: he liked stomach, ears, excited greetings.

"Fine by me," he said.

"Tomorrow, let's go out to dinner somewhere really expensive. My treat."

"Uh," said Walter, "tomorrow's no good."

"Oh."

"How about Sunday?"

"What's wrong with tomorrow?"

"I've got. Well, I've gotta work and I'll be tired, first of all."

"What's second of all?"

"I'm getting together with this woman I know."

"Oh?"

"It's no big deal. It's nothing. It's not a date or anything."

"Who is she?"

"Someone whose car I fixed. Loose mountings in the exhaust system. She wants to get together and talk about it some more. She wants to know about catalytic converters. You know, women are afraid of getting taken advantage of."

"Really!"

"Yeah, well, so Sunday would be better."

"Is she attractive?"

Walter scrinched up his face and made a sound of unenthusiasm. "Enh," he said, and placed his hand laterally in the air, rotating it up and down a little.

Before he left in the morning, she said, "Just don't sleep with her."

"Sidra," he said, scolding her for lack of trust or for attempted supervision – she wasn't sure which.

That night, he didn't come home. She phoned and phoned and then drank a six-pack and fell asleep. In the morning, she phoned again. Finally, at eleven o'clock, he answered.

She hung up.

At 11:30, her phone rang. "Hi," he said cheerfully. He was in a good mood.

"So where were you all night?" asked Sidra. This was what she had become. She felt shorter and squatter and badly coiffed.

There was some silence. "What do you mean?" he said cautiously.

"You know what I mean."

More silence. "Look, I didn't call this morning to get into a heavy conversation."

"Well, then," said Sidra, "you certainly called the wrong number." She slammed down the phone.

She spent the day trembling and sad. She felt like a cross between Anna Karenina and Amy Liverhaus, who used to shout from the fourth-grade cloakroom, "I just don't feel *appreciated*." She walked over to Marshall Field's to buy new makeup. "You're much more of a cream beige than an ivory," said the young woman working the cosmetics counter.

But Sidra clutched at the ivory. "People are always telling me that," she said, "and it makes me very cross."

She phoned him later that night and he was there. "We need to talk," she said.

"I want my key back," he said.

"Look. Can you just come over here so that we can talk?"

He arrived bearing flowers – white roses and irises. They seemed wilted and ironic; she leaned them against the wall in a dry glass, no water.

"All right, I admit it," he said. "I went out on a date. But I'm not saying I slept with her."

She could feel, suddenly, the promiscuity in him. It was a heat, a creature, a tenant twin. "I already know you slept with her."

"How can you know that?"

"Get a life! What am I, an idiot?" She glared at him and tried not to cry. She hadn't loved him enough and he had sensed it. She hadn't really loved him at all, not really.

But she had liked him a lot!

So it still seemed unfair. A bone in her opened up, gleaming and pale, and she held it to the light and spoke from it. "I want to know one thing." She paused, not really for effect, but it had one. "Did you have oral sex?"

He looked stunned. "What kind of question is that? I don't have to answer a question like that."

"*You don't have to answer a question like that.* You don't have any rights here!" she began to yell. She was dehydrated. "You're the one who did this. Now I want the truth. I just want to know. Yes or no!"

He threw his gloves across the room.

"Yes or no," she said.

He flung himself onto the couch, pounded the cushion with his fist, placed an arm up over his eyes.

"Yes or no," she repeated.

He breathed deeply into his shirtsleeve.

"Yes or no."

"Yes," he said.

She sat down on the piano bench. Something dark and coagulated moved through her, up from the feet. Something light and breathing fled through her head, the house of her plastic-wrapped and burned down to tar. She heard him give a moan, and some fleeing hope in her, surrounded but alive on the roof, said perhaps he would beg her forgiveness. Promise to be a new man. She might find him attractive as a new, begging man. Though at some point, he would have to stop begging. He would just have to be normal. And then she would dislike him again.

He stayed on the sofa, did not move to comfort or be comforted, and the darkness in her cleaned her out, hollowed her like acid or a wind.

"I don't know what to do," she said, something palsied in her voice. She felt cheated of all the simple things – the radical calm of obscurity, of routine, of blah domestic bliss. "I don't want to go back to L.A.," she said. She began to stroke the tops of the piano keys, pushing against one and finding it broken – thudding and pitchless, shiny and mocking like an opened bone. She hated, hated her life. Perhaps she had always hated it.

He sat up on the sofa, looked distraught and false – his face badly arranged. He should practice in a mirror, she thought. He did not know how to break up with a movie actress. It was boys' rules: don't break up with a movie actress. Not in Chicago. If *she* left *him*, he would be better able to explain it, to himself, in the future, to anyone who asked. His voice shifted into something meant to sound imploring. "I know" was what he said, in a tone approximating hope, faith, some charity or other. "I know you might not *want* to."

"For your own good," he was saying. "Might be willing . . ." he was saying. But she was already turning into something else, a bird – a flamingo, a hawk, a flamingo-hawk – and was flying up and away, toward the filmy pane of the window, then back again, circling, meanly, with a squint.

He began, suddenly, to cry – loudly at first, with lots of *ohs*, then tiredly, as if from a deep sleep, his face buried in the poncho he'd thrown over the couch arm, his body sinking into the plush of the cushions – a man held hostage by the anxious cast of his dream.

"What can I do?" he asked.

But his dream had now changed, and she was gone, gone out the window, gone, gone.

1990

WINGS

Should he find he couldn't work it there would still be time enough.
—HENRY JAMES, *The Wings of the Dove*

THE GRUMBLINGS OF their stomachs were intertwined and unassignable.

"Was that you or was that me?" she would ask in bed, and Dench would say, "I'm not sure." They lay there in the mornings, their legs moving at angles toward one another, not unlike the elms she could see through the window outside, the high branches nuzzling in the late March breeze, speaking tree to tree of the thrilling weather. Her dreams of eating meals full of meat, which caused her teeth to gnash in the night – surely a sign of spring – left the insides of her cheeks bloody and chewed, one saliva gland now swelled to the size of a raisin.

Shouldn't they be up and about already? Morning sun shot across the ceiling in a white stripe of paint. She and Dench were both too young and too old for this close, late-morning, bed-bound life, but their scuttled careers – the band, the two CDs, the newsletter (turned e-letter turned abandoned cyberlitter) on how to simplify your life (*be broke!*), the driving, the touring, the scrambling, the foraging in parks for chives and dandelions, the charging up of credit cards, the taking pictures of clothes and selling them on eBay ("Wake up!" she used to exclaim to him in the middle of the night, sitting up in bed, "wake up and listen to my *ideas*!") – had led them here, to a nine-month sublet that allowed pets. Still in their thirties, but barely, they had bought themselves a little time. So what if her investments these days were in pennies, wine corks, and sheets of self-adhesive Forever stamps? These would go up in value, unlike everything else. Beneath her bed was a shoe box of dwindling cash from their last gig, where they'd gotten only a quarter of the door. She could always cut her long, almost Asian hair again, as she had two years ago, and sell it for a thousand dollars.

Now, as she often did when contemplating wrong turns, she sometimes thought back to when it was she had first laid eyes on Dench, that Friday long ago when he had approached her at an afternoon sound check in some downtown or other, his undulating tresses not product-free, a demeanor of arrangement and premeditation that gussied up something more chaotic. Although it was winter he wore mirrored sunglasses and a thin leather jacket with the collar turned up: 150 percent jerk. Perhaps it was his strategy to improve people's opinions of him right away, to catch an upward momentum and make it sail, so when the sunglasses came off and then the jacket, and he began to play a song he had not written himself, he was on his way. He lunged onto one knee and raced through a bludgeoning bass solo. At the drums he pressed the stick into the cymbal and circled it, making a high-pitched celestial note, like a finger going round the edge of a wineglass. He smacked the tambourine against his head and against the snare, back and forth. When he then approached the piano, she stopped him. "Not the piano," she said quietly. "The piano's mine."

"OK," he said. "I just wanted to show you everything I can do." And he picked up an acoustic guitar.

Would it be impossible not to love him? Would not wisdom intervene?

Later, to the rest of the band, whose skepticism toward Dench was edged with polite dismay, she said, "I don't understand why the phrase 'like an orchestra tuning up' is considered a criticism. I love an orchestra when it is tuning up. *Especially* then."

From the beginning, however, she could not see how Dench had ever earned a living. He knew two Ryan Adams songs and played guitar fairly well. But he had never done so professionally. Or done anything professionally that she could discern. Early on he claimed to be waiting for money, and she wasn't sure, when he smiled, whether this was a joke. "From whom? Your mother?" and he only smiled. Which made her think, *Yes indeed, his mother.*

But no. His mother had died when he was a teenager. His father had disappeared years before that and thereafter for Dench there was much moving with his sisters: from Ohio to Indiana to California and back. First with his mom, then with an aunt. There was apparently in his life a lot of dropping in and out of college and unexplained years. There had been a foreshortened stint in the Peace Corps. In Swaziland. "I'd just be waiting at a village bus stop, reading a book, and women would pretend to want to borrow it to read but in truth they just wanted a few pages for toilet paper. Or the guys they had me working with? They would stick their hands in the Port-a-Potties, as soon as we got them off the trucks: they wanted the fragrant blue palms. I had to get out of there, man, I didn't really understand the commitment I had made, and so my uncle got a congressman to pull some strings." How did Dench pay his bills?

"It's one big magic trick," he said. He liked to get high before dinner and seemed never without a joint in his wallet or in a drawer. He ate his chicken – the wings and the drumsticks, the arms and the legs – clean down to the purple bones.

And so, though she could not tell an avocado plant from flax (he had both), and though she had never seen any grow lights or seeds or a framed license to grow medical marijuana from the state of Michigan, KC began to fear Dench made his living by selling pot. It seemed to be the thing he was musing about and not saying. As she had continued to see him, she suspected it more deeply. He played her more songs. Then as something caught fire between them, and love secured its footing inside her, when she awoke next to him with damp knots in the back of her hair like she'd never experienced before, the room full of the previous night's candles and the whiff of weed, his skin beside her a silky calico of cool and warm, and as they both needed to eat and eat some more together, she began to feel OK that he sold drugs. If he did. What the hell? At least there was that. At least he did something. His sleepy smiles and the occasional flash of a euro or a hundred-dollar bill in his pocket seemed to confirm it, but then his intermittent lack of cash altogether perpetuated the mystery, as did his checks, which read D. ENCHER, and she started to fear he might not sell drugs after all. When she asked him straight out, he said only, "You're funny!" And after she had paid for too many of his drinks and meals, since he said he was strapped that week and then the week after that, she began to wish, a little sheepishly, that he did sell drugs. She began to hope deeply that he did. Once she even prayed for him to do so. And soon she was close to begging. *Just a little skunk, darling. Just a little pocket rocket, some sparky bark or kick stick, just a bit of wake and bake . . .*

Instead he joined her band.

It had been called Villa and in the end it had not worked out: tours they paid for themselves with small business loans; audiences who did not like KC's own songs (too singer-songwriter, with rhymes, (*calories* and *galleries!*) that she was foolishly proud of (*dead* and *wed!*)), including one tune she refused to part with, since it had briefly been positioned to be a minor indie hit, a song about a chef in New Jersey named Jim Barber whom she'd once been in love with.

Here I am your unshaved fennel
Here I am your unshaved cheese
All I want to know? is when I'll –
feel your blade against my knees.

Its terribleness eluded her. Her lyrics weren't sly or hip or smoky and tough but the demure and simple hopes of a mouse. She'd spent a decade barking up the wrong tree – as a mouse! Audiences booed – the boys in their red-framed spectacles, the girls in their crooked little dresses. Despised especially were her hip-hop renditions of Billy Joel and Neil Young (she was once asked to please sing down by the river, and she'd thought they'd meant the song. She told this sad joke over and over). Throughout the band tours she would wake up weeping at the edge of some bed or other, not knowing where she was or what she was supposed to do that day or once or twice even *who* she was, since all her endeavor seemed separate from herself, a suit to slip into. Tears, she had once been told, were designed to eliminate toxins, and they poured down her face and slimed her neck and gathered in the recesses of her collarbones and she had to be careful never to lie back and let them get into her ears, which might cause the toxins to return and start over. Of course, the rumor of toxins turned out not to be true. Tears were quite pure. And so the reason for them, it seemed to her later, when she thought about it, was to identify the weak, so that the world could assure its strong future by beating the weak to death.

"Are we perhaps unlovable?" she asked Dench.

"It's because we're not named, like, Birth Hearse for Dog-Face."

"Why aren't we named that?"

"Because we have standards."

"Is that it?" she said.

"Yeah! And not just 'Body and Soul' as an encore, though we do that well. I mean we maintain a kind of integrity."

"Integrity! Really!" After too many stolen meals from minibars, the Pringles can carefully emptied and the foil top resealed, the container replaced as if untouched back atop the wood tray, hotel towels along with the gear all packed up in the rental truck whose rear fender bore one large bumper sticker, with Donald Rumsfeld's visage, under which read DOES THIS ASS MAKE MY TRUCK LOOK BIG?, after all that she continually found herself thinking, *If only Dench sold drugs!* On hot summer days she would find a high-end supermarket and not only eat the free samples in their tiny white cups but stand before the produce section and wait for the vegetable misters to come on, holding her arms beneath the water in relief. She was showering with the lettuces.

She and Dench had not developed their talents sufficiently nor cared for them properly – or so a booking agent told them.

Dench took offense. "You forget about the prize perplexity, the award angle – they are often looking for people like us: we could win something!" he exclaimed, with Pringles in his teeth.

The gardenia in KC's throat, the flower that was her singing voice – its brown wilt would have to be painstakingly slowed through the years – had already begun its rapid degeneration into simple crocus, then scraggly weed. She'd been given something perfect – youth! – and done imperfect things with it. The moon shone whole then partial in the sky, having its life without her. Sometimes she just chased roughly after a melody – like someone kicking a can down a road. She had not hemmed in her speaking voice, kept it tame and tended so that her singing one could fly. Her speaking voice was the same as her singing one, a roller coaster of various registers, the Myrna Loy–Billie Burke timbre of the Edwardian grandmother who had raised her, a woman who had trained at conservatory but had never had a singing career and practically sang every sentence she uttered: *Katherine? It's time for dinner* went up and down the scale. Only her dying words – *Marry well* – had been flat, the drone of chagrin, a practical warning: life-preserving but with a glimpse of a dark little bunker in a war not yet declared. *Marry well* had been uttered after she begged KC to get a teaching certificate. *Teaching makes interesting people boring, sure,* she had said. *But it also makes boring people interesting. So there's an upside. There always is an upside if you look up.*

Dench's own poor mother wasn't able to leave him – or his sisters – a dime, though he had always done what she said, even that one year they lived in motels and he obligingly wore the identical nightgown as his sisters so that they might better be mistaken for a single child, to avoid an extra room charge, in case the maid walked in. His young mother had died with breathing tubes hooked right to her wallet, he said, just sucking it all up. Dench made a big comedic *whooshing* sound when he told this part. His father's disappearance, which had come long before, had devastated and haunted her: when they were out for dinner one night his father announced that he had to see a man about a horse, and he excused himself, went to the men's room, and climbed out the window never to return. Dench made a *whooshing* sound for this part of the story as well.

"I can't decide whether that is cowardice or a weird kind of courage," Dench said.

"It's neither," KC replied. "It has nothing to do with either of those things."

Motherless children would always find each other. She had once heard that. They had the misery that wasn't misery but presumed to be so to others. They had the misery that liked company and *was* company. Only sometimes they felt the facts of their motherless lives. They were a long, long way from home. They had theme songs hatched in a spiritual tradition. There was no fondling of the gold coins of memory. The world was their orphanage.

But when they moved in together he hesitated.

"What about my belongings?" he asked.

"It's not like you have a dog who won't get along with mine," she said.

"I have plants."

"But plants are not a dog."

"Oh, I see: you're one of those people who thinks animals are better, more important than plants!"

She studied him, his eyes large with protest or with drugs or with madness. There were too many things to choose from. "Are you serious?" she asked.

"I don't know," he said and turned to unpack his things.

Now she rose to take the dog for his daily walk. She was wearing an old summer dress as a nightgown, but in the mornings it could work as a dress again, if you just tossed a cardigan over it and put on shoes. In this risky manner, she knew, insanity could encroach.

The sublet she and Dench were in now was a nice one, a fluke, a modern, flat-roofed, stone-and-redwood ranch house with a carport in a neighborhood that was not far from the hospital and was therefore full of surgeons and radiologists and their families. The hospital itself was under construction and the cranes bisected the sky. Big-jawed excavators and backhoes worked beneath lights at night. Walking the dog, she once watched as an excavator's mandibled head was released and fell to the ground; the headless neck then leaned down and began to nudge it, as if trying to find out if it might still be alive. Of course there was an operator, but after that it was hard to think of a creature like this as a machine. When a wall was knocked down, and its quiet secrets sent scattering, the lines between things seemed up for grabs.

The person who owned their house was not connected to the hospital. He was an entrepreneur named Ian who had made a bundle in the nineties on some sort of business software and who for long stretches of time lived out of state – in Ibiza, Zihuatanejo, and Portland – in order to avoid the cold. The house came furnished except, strangely, for a bed, which they bought. On their first day they found food in the refrigerator with not even mold but *dust* on it. "I don't know," said Dench. "Look at the closets. This must be what Ian was using. With hooks this strong maybe we don't need a bed. We can just hang ourselves there at night, like bats."

With Dench she knew, in an unspoken way, that she was the one who was supposed to get them to wherever it was they were going. She was supposed to be the GPS lady who, when you stopped for gas, said, "Get back on the highway." She tried to be that voice with Dench: stubborn, unflappable, keeping to the map and not saying what she knew the GPS lady really wanted to say, which was not "Recalculating" but "What in fucking hell are you thinking?"

"It all may look wrong from outer space, which is where a GPS is seeing it from," Dench would say, when proposing alternatives of any sort, large or small, "but on the ground there's a certain logic. Stick with me on this one. You can have all the others."

There were no sidewalks in this wooded part of town. The sap of the stick-bare trees was just stirring after what looked like a fierce fire of a winter. The roadside gullies that would soon warm and sprout joe-pye weed and pea were still just pebble-flecked mud, and KC's dog, Cat, sniffed his way along, feeling the winter's melt, the ground loosening its fertile odor of wakened worms. Overhead the dirt pearl sky of

March hung low as a hat brim. The houses were sidled next to marshes and sycamores, and as she walked along the roads occasionally a car would pass, and she would yank on Cat's leash to heel him close. The roads, all named after colleges out east – Dartmouth Drive, Wellesley Way, Sweet Briar Road; where was her alma mater, SUNY New Paltz Street? – were glistening with the flat glossy colors of flattened box turtles who'd made the spring crossing too slowly and were now stuck to the macadam, thin and shiny as magazine ads.

HOSPICE CARE: IT'S NEVER TOO SOON TO CALL read a billboard near the coffee shop in what constituted the neighborhood's commercial roar. Next to it a traffic sign read PASS WITH CARE. Surrealism could not be made up. It was the very electricity of the real. The largest part of the strip was occupied by an out-of-business bookstore whose plate-glass windows were already cloudy with dust. The D was missing from the sign so that it now read BOR ERS. In insolvency, truth: soon the chain would be shipping its entire stock to the latrines of Swaziland.

Cat was a good dog, part corgi, part Lab, and if KC wore her sunglasses into the coffee shop he could pass for a Seeing Eye dog, and she a blind person, so she didn't have to tie him to a parking sign out front.

The coffee shop played Tom Waits and was elegantly equipped with dimpled cup sleeves, real cream, cinnamon sticks, shakers of sugar. KC got in line. "I love this song," the man in front turned to say to her. He was holding a toddler, and was one of those new urban dads so old he looked like the kidnapper of his own child.

She didn't know what she felt about Tom Waits anymore: his voice had gotten so *industrial.* "I don't know. I just think one shouldn't have to wear goggles and a hard hat when listening to music," she said. It was not a bad song and she didn't feel that strongly about it, only sorry for her own paltry tunes, but the man's face fell, and he turned away, with his child staring gloomily at her over his shoulder.

She ordered a Venti latte, and while she was waiting, she read the top fold from the top paper in the stack below the shrink-wrapped CDs by the register. When she finished, she discreetly turned the paper over and read the bottom fold. This daily, fractured way of learning the front-page news – they had no Internet connection – she had gotten used to and even sighed about amusingly. *Be resourceful!* So their old newsletter had advised. This way of bringing Dench his morning coffee (she drank her half while walking back, burning her tongue a little) and getting the dog a walk was less resourceful than simply necessary. Sometimes she missed the greasy spoons of old, which she had still been able to find on the road when the band was touring and where a single waitress ran the register, the counter, all the tables, calling you "honey" – until you asked whether they had soy milk, at which point all endearments ceased.

Now she walked back via Princeton Place, a street she didn't usually take, but one that ran parallel to her own. Taking different routes fortified the mind, the paper had said today. This street contained a sprawling white-brick house she had seen before and had been struck by – not just its elegance and size but the magical blue sea of squill that spread across its sloped and wooded lot. She had once seen two deer there, with long tails that flicked like horses' and wagged like dogs'. And once she had seen such a deer close-up, along the road's edge on Dartmouth. It had been hit so fast it had been decapitated, and its neck lay open like a severed cable bundle.

Cat nosed along the gullies and a little up the driveways, whose cracks were often filled with clover.

She stared at the wings of the white-brick house, which were either perfectly insulated or not heated at all, since there was still unmelted snow on the roofs. Suddenly an elderly man appeared by the mailbox. "Howdy," he said. It startled her, and his stab at gregariousness belied his face, which bore a blasted-apart expression, like that of a balding, white-haired Jesus on the cross, eyes open wide and worried, his finely lined mouth the drawstring purse of the aged and fair.

"Just getting my newspaper," he said. "Nice dog."

"Hey, Catsy, get back here." She tried to pull the leash

in, but its automated spring was broken and the leash kept unspooling.

The man's face brightened. He had started to take his paper out of its plastic sleeve but stopped. "What's the dog's name? Cathy?" He did not scrunch up his face disapprovingly when he failed to hear what you said, the way deaf people often did. But he did have the recognizable waxen pee smell of an old man. It was from sweat that no longer could be liquid but accumulated like scaly air on the skin.

"Uh, Cat. It's part family name, part, um, joke." She wasn't going to get into all the Katherines in her family or her personal refrigerator magnet altar to Cat Power or the general sick sense of humor that had led this dog, like all pets, to be a canvas upon which one wrote one's warped love and dubious wit.

"I get it." He grinned eagerly. "And what's your name?"

"KC," she said. Let that suffice.

"Casey?"

"Yes," she said. A life could rhyme with a life – it could be a jostling close call that one mistook for the thing itself.

"We live the next block over. We're renting."

"Renting! Well, that explains it."

She didn't dare ask what it explained. Still, his eyes had a wet dazzle – or an amused glint – and were not disapproving. Cat started to bark loudly at a rabbit but then also turned and started barking at the man, who took a theatrical step back, raised the paper over his head, and pretended to be afraid, as if he were performing for a small child. "Don't take my crossword puzzle!"

"His bark is worse than his bite," KC said. "Get over here, Cat."

"I don't know why people always say that. No bark is worse than a bite. A bite is always worse."

"Well, they shouldn't make rabbits so cute or we wouldn't care if dogs ate them. Why are rabbits made so cute? What is nature's purpose in that one?"

He beamed. "So you're a philosopher!"

"No, not really," she murmured as if in fact she thought she might be.

"I think the rabbits are probably only accidentally cute to us. Mostly they're cute to each other. The purpose? The new urban pest made palatable: more rabbit stew for everybody."

"I see. So you're a sort of Mr. McGregor kind of guy. I was always scared of Mr. McGregor!" She smiled.

"Nothing to be scared of. But it does seem of late that there is some kind of apocalyptic plague of rabbits. Biblical bunnies! Would you like to come and finish your coffee inside?"

She didn't know what to make of this invitation. Was it creepy or friendly? Who could tell anymore? Very few people had been friendly to them since they'd moved here two months ago. The man's tea-stained teeth made a sepia smile – a dental X-ray from the nineteenth century.

"Oh, thanks, I really should be going." This time the leash caught and Cat came trotting toward her, bored and ready to move on.

"Well, good to meet you," the old man said and turned and walked back toward his house, with its portico and porch and two stone chimneys, its wings that stretched east and west and one out back smaller and south-facing, with a long double sleeping porch, she could barely see. Over here on Princeton Place things seemed bigger than they were on Wellesley Way. She hated money! though she knew it was like blood and you needed it. Still, it was also like blood in that she often couldn't stand the sight of it. This whole privileged neighborhood could use a neat little guillotine or some feed-capped crowds with pitchforks.

"Good to meet you," she said, though he hadn't given her his name.

"Here's your coffee," she said to Dench, who was still in bed.

"Yum. Tepid backwash."

"Hey, don't complain. You can go next time and bring me back half."

"I'm not complaining," he said in a sleepy stretch. "But it's like it took you longer this time."

She took a brush sharply to her scalp and began brushing. If she waited longer with her hair she might get twelve hundred. She threw it back and arched from her waist. Only in the mirror could she see her *Decatur* tattoo, put there one night in Linotype Gotharda in the crook of her neck, when they were playing in Decatur and she wanted to be reminded never to play there again. "That's a strange way to be reminded," Dench had said, and KC had said, "What better?"

"Was there a big line at the coffee shop?" Dench asked, smacking his lips.

"No. I stopped and talked to some guy. Cat is going up every driveway that ever had a squirrel or rabbit dash over it."

"Some guy?"

"Geezer."

"Hey, this backwash is good. There's something new in it. Were you wearing cherry ChapStick or something?"

"Have you noticed that there are a lot of people with money around here?"

"We should meet them. We need producers."

"You go meet them." She would look up *guillotine* on the Internet on her next trip to the library.

"You're cuter. Of course, time is of the essence in these matters."

She loved Dench. She was helpless before the whole emotional project of him. But it didn't preclude hating him and everything around him, which included herself, the sound of her own voice – and the sound of his, which was worse. The portraits of hell never ceased and sometimes were done up in raucous, gilded frames to console. Romantic hope: From where did women get it? Certainly not from men, who were walking caveat emptors. No, women got it from other women, because in the end women would rather be rid of one another than have to endure themselves on a daily basis. So they urged each other into relationships. "He loves you! You can see it in his eyes!" they lied.

* * *

"Casey!" the old man shouted the next morning. He was out in his front yard pounding together something that looked like a bird feeder on a post.

"Hi!" she said.

"You know my name?"

"Pardon me?"

"Old family joke." He still seemed to be shouting. "Actually my name is Milton Theale."

"Milton." She repeated the name, a habit people with good memories supposedly relied on. "They don't name kids Milton anymore."

"Too bad and thank God! My father's name was Hi, short for Hiram, and now that I'm old I find my head filled up with *his* jokes and stories rather than very many of my own, which apparently I've forgotten."

"Oh," she said. "Well, as long as you don't actually come to believe you are your dad, I suppose all is well."

"Well, that may be next."

"Probably that's always next. For all of us."

He squinted to study her, seemed to be admiring something about her again, but she was not sure what. No doubt something that was a complete mirage.

"Nice to see you again," he said. "And you, too," he said to the dog. "Though you are a strange-looking thing. It's like he's been assembled by Nazi veterinarians – a shepherd's head, a dachshund's body, a—"

"Yeah, I know. Sometimes he reminds me of the dog in *Invasion of the Body Snatchers*."

"Hmmm?"

"The remake."

"The remake of what?"

"Frankenstein!" she yelled. His deafness would give her a heart attack. Perhaps this was nature's plan for old people to kill each other in an efficient if irritating fashion.

She could feel the heat leaving the coffee and entering her hand. "He's like a dog made in Frankenstein's lab!" Sometimes she hated the dog. His obliviousness to the needs of others, his determined, verbally challenged conversation about his own desires – in a human this would indicate a severe personality disorder.

"Oh, he's not that bad," said Milt. "And wouldn't we like his energy. In tablet form."

"That would be fantastic."

"But you're young; you wouldn't need something like that."

"I need something." Was she whining? She had never made such an announcement to a stranger before.

"In lieu of that, come on in and have a blueberry muffin with me." Again, the line between neighborliness and flirtation was not clear to her here. She knew in this community you had to do an extroverted kind of meet and greet, but she had heard of soccer parents wandering off from their children's games and having sex in far parking lots. So the guidelines were murky and breachable. "And while you're at it you can help me with the crossword puzzle."

"Oh, I can't. I have to get home. Lot of things to tend to."

"Well, it's not ten to. It's ten past."

"To *tend* to," KC repeated. Perhaps his deafness had exhausted all the other neighbors and this accounted for his friendliness to her. On the other hand, no one seemed to walk around here. Either they jogged, their ears stuffed with music, or they drove their cars at murderous speeds. One old man could not have single-handedly caused that. Or could he have?

"Hmmm?"

"Gotta get home."

"Oh, OK," he said and waved her on.

"Maybe tomorrow," she said out of kindness.

He nodded and went back to work.

She stopped and turned. "Are you making a bird feeder?"

"No, it's a book nook! I'll put books inside and people can help themselves. Like a little library. Now that the bookstore is closed. I'm just adjusting the clasp."

"How lovely." It was a varnished pine angled to look like the ski chalet of a doll.

* * *

"Giving the old guy a thrill? Good idea."

"What's wrong with you?"

"I'm just saying," said Dench in a hushed tone. "He's probably loaded. And gonna keel soon. And . . ."

"Stop." This was the grifter in Dench, something violent in the name of freedom, like his father, who had fled through the men's room window. "Don't say another word."

"Hey – I'm not talking about murdering him! I'm just saying you could spend a little time, make him happy, and then the end result might be, well . . . we'd all be a little happier. Where's the harm?"

"You've really gone over to the dark side." He could be shameless. Perhaps shamelessness kept bitterness at bay. Not a chance Dench could ever be bitter. Never even post-bitter. Bitterness came when one had done the long good thing and then gone unrewarded. Dench would never operate that way. She, on the other hand, had been born with a sort of pre-bitterness, casting about for the good and unacknowledged deed that would explain her feelings – and not coming up with it. So instead a sourness could beset her, which she had to appease and shrink with ice cream and biographies of Billie Holiday.

"Hey, wasn't it you who wrote, 'Get your hands on some real meat'?" Now he began to sing. "'An old shoe can be made chewy like game / but it takes a raftload of herbs and it's just not the same.' You wrote that."

"That was a love song to a chef. Before I knew you."

"It's good. It's got existentialism *and* advice." His eyes avoided hers.

"You're pimping me. Is this what you call your 'talent for life'?" He had once boasted he possessed such a thing.

"It's a working view."

"You'd better be careful, Dench. I take your suggestions seriously."

He paused and looked at her, sternness in one eye and gentleness in the other. "Well, my first piece of advice is don't take my advice. And there's more where that came from."

"There's a smell in the house. Yeasty and sulfuric. Can you

smell it?" She looked at Dench with concern, but he seemed to have none.

"The zeitgeist!"

"Something rotting in the walls."

"Meat or shoe?"

"Something that died in the winter and now that it's spring is decaying in the floorboards or some crawl space or one of the walls of this room."

"Maybe my allergies are acting up. But I think I have smelled it along this side of the house, on warmer days, out there trying to get better cell phone reception. A cabbagey cheese smell: goaty with a kind of ammonia rot."

She reached for a sip of Dench's coffee.

"He probably has adult children who will inherit everything."

"Probably," said Dench, turning away and then looking back at her to study her face.

"What?" she asked.

"Nothing," he said.

Dench's sexiness, his frugal, spirited cooking (though he was no Jim Barber), his brooding gaze, his self-deprecating humor, all had lured her in. But it was like walking into a beautiful house to find the rooms all empty. In those beginning years she often saw him locking eyes with others, as if in some pact. He still had no money. She paid. At times he glanced at her with bewildering scorn. There was, in short, little romantic love. No conversation of tender feelings. Just attachment. Just the power of his voice when it spoke of things that had nothing to do with them, when it churned round and round on its loop about his childhood dogs, misdeeds, and rages at his lot. He was attractive. He was amusing. But he was not emotionally well. Intimacy was not his strong suit. "Clubs and spades," he joked. "Not diamonds, not hearts. Red cards – I just see red. They throw me out of the game every time."

"Shut up and drink your beer."

Where were the drugs?

She could see he felt sometimes that he could prey upon her insecurities and still be taken in and cared for by her. Was not the news always full of one beautiful young movie star after another thrown over for some younger and more beautiful movie star? What hope was there for ordinary women? He required a patroness but had mistakenly auditioned for her. If she possessed fewer psychic wounds than he had hoped for in a woman her age, or at least different ones, he would attempt to create some. But she was less woundable than he might think. She had not had a father who had to see a man about a horse. She in fact had a father who'd been killed by a car named after a horse. Along with her mother. A Mustang! How weird was that? Well, she had been a baby and hadn't had to deal with it.

Her grandmother had almost never mentioned her mother. Or her father. They had been scurrying across a street to get home, holding hands, which had fatally slowed them down.

Where were the drugs?

Patience was a chemical. Derived from a mineral. Derived from a star. She felt she had a bit of it. But it was not always fruitful, or fruitful with the right fruit. Once she had found a letter in Dench's coat – it was a draft in his writing with his recognizable cross-outs and it began, *It has always been hard for me to say, but your love has meant the world to me.* She did not read to the end but stuffed it back inside the coat pocket, not wanting to ruin things for him or the moving surprise of it for herself. She would let him finish his composing and choose the delivery time. But the letter never arrived or showed up for her in any manner whatsoever. She waited for months. When she finally asked about it, in a general way, he looked at her with derision and said, "I have no idea what you're talking about."

Inside the old man's house wide doorways led to shaded rooms, corridors to stairways to more corridors. Whole areas of the house were closed off with ivory quilts hung with clipped rings from fishing spears – to save on heating, she quickly surmised. There were stacks of reading material – a not uncozy clutter of magazines, some opened and abandoned, and piles of books, both new and used. On top of one was a dried-out spider plant that looked – as they used to say with blithe heartlessness of all their dying spider plants – like Bob Marley on chemo. She recognized the panic at even a moment's boredom that all these piles contained, as well as the unreasonable hopefulness regarding time. In a far room she spied a piano, an old Mason & Hamlin grand, its ebony surface matte with dust, and wondered if it was tuned. Its lid was down and stacks of newspaper sat on top.

"Don't mind the clutter, just follow me through it – the muffins are in the kitchen," he said. She followed his swaying gait into the back of the house. Beneath the wisps of white hair his skull was shiny and his scalp had the large brown spots of a giraffe – if only they weren't signs of looming death they would look appealing and whimsical and young people would probably want them – give me a liver spot! – as tattoos. Smaller versions freckled his hands. "I keep hoping this clutter is charming and not a sign of senility. I find myself not able to tell."

"It's like a bookstore or a thrift shop. That kind of clutter is always charming."

"Really?"

"Perhaps you could go all the way and put little price tags on everything." A shaming heat flushed her face.

"Ha! Well, that was partly the idea with the book nook out front. That I could put some of this to use. But feel free to add your own. All contributions welcome." The muffins were store-bought ones he had reheated in a microwave. He had not really made them at all. "I shop sparingly. You never know how long you've got. I don't even buy green bananas. That's investing with reckless hope in the future."

"Very funny."

"Is it?" He was searching her face.

"Well, I mean . . . yes, it is."

"Would you like some coffee, or do you want to just stick with your own?" He signaled with his head toward the paper cup she still held, with its white plastic top and its warted brown vest made of recycled paper bags. She looked on the counter and saw that it was instant coffee he meant, a jar of Nescafé near the stove. He turned the burner on, and gas flamed into the blue spikes of a bachelor's button beneath the kettle.

"Oh, this is fine," KC said. What did she care if Dench got no coffee today? He would prefer this mission of neighborly friendliness.

She sat down at Milt's table and he placed the muffin on a plate in front of her. Then he sat down himself. "So tell me about yourself," he said, then grinned wanly. "What brings you to this neighborhood?"

"Do I stand out that much?"

"I'm afraid you do. And not just because of those tattoos."

She only had three. She would explain them all to him later, which was what they were for: each was a story. There was "Decatur" along her neck, the vow never to return there. There was also a "Moline" one along her collarbone – a vow never to return there. The "Swanee" along her left biceps was because she liked the chord ascension in that song, a cry of homesickness the band had deconstructed and electrified into a sneer. It was sometimes their encore. When there was one. It was also a vow never to return there. She mostly forgot about all these places until she looked into a mirror after a bath.

"My music career didn't work out and I'm subletting here. I came back to this town because this is where I used to visit my grandmother in a nursing home when I was young. I liked the lake. And she was in a place that looked out onto it and when I went to see her I would go into a large room with large windows and she would race over in her wheelchair. She was the fastest one there with the chairs."

He smiled at her. "I know exactly the place you mean. It's got a hospice wing in it called Memory Station. Though no one in it can recall a thing."

KC stuffed the muffin in her mouth and flattened its moist crenellated paper into a semicircle.

"What kind of music do you play? Is it loud and angry?" he asked with a grin.

"Sometimes," she said, chewing. "But sometimes it was gentle and musing." Past tense. Her band was dead and it hadn't even taken a plane crash to do it because they hadn't been able to afford to fly except once. "I'll come by and play something for you sometime."

His face brightened. "I'll get the piano tuned," he said.

There was that smell again, thawing with the final remnants of winter, in their walls. This was the sort of neighborhood where one would scarcely smell a rancid onion in a trash can. But now this strange meaty rot, with its overtones of Roquefort.

"What do you really think that is?" KC asked Dench through the bathroom door. The change of seasons had brought new viruses and he was waterboarding himself with a neti pot.

"What?"

"The smell," she said.

"I can't smell anything right now – my nose is too congested."

She peeked into the bathroom to see him leaning sideways with the plastic pot, water running down his lips and chin. "Are you disclosing national security secrets?"

"No fucking way!" he exclaimed. "The netis will never learn a thing from me."

"You can take a book or leave it. There is a simple latch, no lock." The honey-hued planes of the hutch, angled like a bird feeder, might indeed attract birds if it didn't soon fill up with books and the clasp was not shut.

"Let's see what you have in there already." She moved in close to him. His waxy smell did not bother her.

"Oh, not much really." An old copy of *The Swiss Family Robinson* and one of *Infinite Jest*. "I'm aiming for the kids," he said. He had put up a sign that said, TAKE IT OR LEAVE IT BOOK-NOOK: HAVE A LOOK. As with a community bicycle, you could take one and never have to bring it back. Dench himself had a community bike from several communities ago. "Now that the bookstore has gone under, and with the hospital so close, I thought people might need something to read."

In addition to the elegance of the wood, there was something antique and sweet in all this – far be it from her to bring up the topic of electronic downloads.

"Probably there is a German word for the feeling of fondness one gets towards one's house the more one fixes it up for resale."

"Hausengeltenschmerz," said KC.

But he did not laugh. He was thinking. "My wife would have known," he said.

His wife had been a doctor. He told KC this now as she ate another muffin in his kitchen. It had been a second marriage for his wife and so there was a bit of sunset in it for them both: he had been stuck in his bachelor ways and hadn't married until he was sixty.

("Bachelor ways!" Dench would seize on later. "You see what he's doing?")

"She was a worldly and brilliant woman, an oncologist devoted to family medicine and public health policy," said Milt.

There was a long silence as KC watched him reminisce, his face wincing slightly as his mind sifted through the files.

"I never got on with her daughters much. But she herself, well, she was the love of my life, even if she came late to it and left early. She died two years ago. When it came it was a blessing really. I suppose. I suppose that's what one should say."

"I'm sorry."

"Thank you. But she was brilliant company. My brain's a chunk of mud next to hers." He stared at KC. "It's lonely in this neck of the woods."

She picked off a moist crumb from the front of her jacket. "But you must have friends here?" she said, and then she put the crumb quickly in her mouth.

"Well, by 'neck of the woods,' I mean old age."

"I sort of knew that, I guess," she said. "Do you have friends your age?"

"There are no humans alive my age!" He grinned his sepia teeth at her.

"Come on." Her muffin was gone and she was eyeing the others.

"I may be older than I seem. I don't know what I seem."

She would fall for the bait. "Thirty-five," she said, smiling only a little.

"Ha! Well, that's the sad thing about growing too old: there's no one at your funeral."

She always said thirty-five, even to children. No one minded being thirty-five, especially kindergartners and the elderly. No one at all. She herself would give a toe or two to be thirty-five again. She would give three toes.

He looked at her warmly. "I once studied acting and I've kept my voice from getting that quavery thing of old people."

"You'll have to teach me."

"You have a lovely voice. I take note of voices. Despite my deafness and my tinnitus. Which is a nice substitute for crickets, by the way, if you miss them in the winter. Sometimes I've got so much whistling going on in my ears I could probably fly around the room if it weren't for these heavy orthopedic shoes. Were you the singer in your band?"

"How did you know?" She slapped her hand down on the table as if this were a miracle.

"There's a way you have of wafting in and hitting the sounds of the words rather than the words themselves. I mean to clean off this piano and get you to sing."

"Oh, I don't think so. I'm very much out of tune. Probably more than the piano. As I said, my career's a little stalled right now: we need some luck, you know? Without luck the whole thing's just a thought experiment!"

"We?"

"My musical partner." She swallowed and chewed though her mouth was empty. He was a partner. He was musical.

What was wrong with her? Would she keep Dench a secret from Milt?

Dench would want it. "What can I get for you?" she had asked Dench this morning, and he had stared at her balefully from the bed.

"You have a lot of different nightgowns," Dench had replied.

"They're all the dresses I once wore onstage." And as she had gotten dressed for her walk, he'd said, "Don't forget the coffee this time. Last time you forgot the coffee."

"It's good to have a business partner," Milt said now. "But it isn't everything."

"He's sort of a genius," she lied. Did she feel the need to put Dench in competition with Milt's dead wife?

"So you've met some geniuses." He smiled. "You're having fun then. A life with geniuses in it: very good."

She lived with so much mockery this did not bother her at all. She looked deeply into his eyes and found the muck-speckled blue there, the lenses cut out from cataracts. She would see the cut edges in the light.

"Do you think our landlord, Ian, would miss a few of his books?"

"No one misses a few of their books. It's just the naked truth. Look at the sign down the road," Dench said.

The out-of-business Borders with its missing *d*: perhaps Dench had stolen it for himself, stashing it under the bed; she didn't dare look.

"Old Milt has a little book nook – I thought I'd contribute."

"I see."

"I'd only take a few. I can't donate my own since they all have the most embarrassing underlinings. In ink." Plus exclamation points that ran down the page like a fence by Christo. Perhaps it was genetic. She had once found in her grandmother's shelves her mother's own frighteningly marked-up copy of *The House of Mirth*. The word *whoa* appeared on every other page.

"Come here. Lie on top of me." Dench's face was a cross between longing and ordering lunch.

"I'll squash you. I've gained five pounds eating muffins with Milt." He grabbed her hand, but she gently pulled it away. "Give me some time. I'm going to cut out the sweets and have a few toes removed."

She had put on a necklace, of freshwater pearls so small they were like grains of arborio rice decorating the letters of *Decatur.* She combed a little rat's nest into the crown of her hair to perk it up. She dabbed on some scent: fig was the new vanilla! As she went out the door, Dench said, "Win them with your beauty, but catch them off guard with your soul." Then there was the pregnant pause, the instruments all cutting out at once – until he added, in a chilly tone, "Don't even bother with my coffee. I mean really: don't bother." After that she heard only her own footsteps.

"I brought you a couple books," she said to Milton. "For your nook."

"Well, thank you. Haven't had any takers yet but there's still room." He looked at the titles she had brought: *Collapse: How Societies Choose to Fail or Succeed* and *Lady Macbeth in the Gilded Age.* "Excellent."

They once again went inside and ate muffins. Forget coffee: this time she had not even brought the dog.

She began to do this regularly, supplying Milt with more of her landlord's books. He had taken to looking so happy to see her, his eyes brightening (blue, she had read once, was the true color of the sun) so much she could see what he must have looked like when he was young. He was probably the bachelor that all the old ladies were after. And when he had married there were probably some broken hearts. He had the look of a gentleman, but one who was used to the attention of women, even as the uriny smell of an old man had crept over him. "Here we are: two lonely fools," he said to KC once. It had the sound of a line he'd said before. Nonetheless, she found herself opening up to him, telling him of her life, and he was sympathetic, nodding, his peeled-back eyes taking on a special shine, and only once or twice did he have to lean forward disconcertingly to murmur, "Say that again?" She didn't mention Dench anymore. And the part of her that might consider this and know why was overshadowed by the unknowing part, which she knew in advance was the only source of any self-forgiveness. Ignorance ironically arranged for future self-knowledge. Life was never perfect.

When she twice stayed into the afternoon to fix Milt something to eat and once stopped by later to cook a simple dinner, Dench confronted her. "Once more I must ask: What are you doing?"

"He's a frail old man on the outs with his stepdaughters. He could use someone to help him with meals."

"You're fattening him for the kill?" They were looking into the abyss of the other, or so they both probably thought.

"What the hell are you talking about? He's alone!"

"A lone what?"

"A lone ranger for God's sake, what is wrong with you?"

"I don't understand what you're pretending."

"I'm not pretending. What I don't get is you: I thought I was doing what you wanted!"

He tilted his head quizzically the way he sometimes did when he was pretending to be a different person. Who are you doing that head-tilt thing for, she did not say.

"I don't know what I want," he said. "And I don't know what you're doing."

"You know exactly what I'm doing."

"Is that what you think? Hmmmm. Are we always such a mystery to ourselves and to others?"

"Is a disappointment the same as a mystery?"

"A disappointment is rarely a mystery."

"I'm starting to lose confidence in you, Dench." Losing confidence was more violent than losing love. Losing love was a slow dying, but losing confidence was a quick coup, a floor that opened right up and swallowed.

Now he lifted his face beatifically, as if to catch some light no one else could see. His eyes closed, and he began rubbing his hands through his hair. It was her least favorite thing that he did in the head-tilting department.

"Sorry to interrupt your self-massage," she said and turned to go and then turned back to say, "And don't give me that line about someone has to do it."

"Someone doesn't have to. But someone should." The muttered snark in their house was a kind of creature – perhaps the one in their walls.

"Yes, well, you're an expert on *should*."

It broke her heart that they had come to this: if one knew the future, all the unexpected glimpses of the beloved, one might have trouble finding the courage to go on. This was probably the reason nine-tenths of the human brain had been rendered useless: to make you stupidly intrepid. One was working with only the animal brain, the Pringle brain. The wizard-god brain, the one that could see the future and move objects without touching them, was asleep. Fucking bastard.

The books she brought this time were *Instinct for Death* and *The Fin de Millennial Lear*. She and Milt stood before the nook and placed the volumes inside.

"Now you must come in and play the piano for me. At long last I've had it tuned." Milt smiled. "You are even allowed to sing, if you so desire."

She was starting again to see how large the house was, since if they entered through a different door she had no idea where she was. There were two side doors and a back one in addition to the front two. Two front doors! Life was hard enough – having to make that kind of decision every day could wear a person out.

She sat down at the piano, with its bell-like sound and real ivory keys, chipped and grainy. As a joke she played "The Spinning Song," but he didn't laugh, only smiled, as if perhaps it were Scarlatti. Then she played and sang her love song to the chef, and then she did "Body and Soul" and then her own deconstructed version of "Down by the River," right there inside the house with no requests to leave and go down by an actual river. And then she thought that was probably enough and pulled her arms back, closed her mouth, and in imitation of Dench closed her eyes, lifted her face to the ceiling, and smoothed back her hair, prepping it for the wig maker. Then she shook her arms in the air and popped her eyes open.

Milt looked happier than she had ever seen him look. "Marvelous!" he said.

No one ever said *marvelous* anymore.

"Oh, you're nice," she said.

"I have an idea! Can you drive me downtown? I have an appointment in a half hour and I'd like you to come with me. Besides, I'm not allowed to drive."

"All right," she said. Of course she had guessed that soon she might be taking him to doctors' appointments.

Instead, she drove him in his old, scarcely used Audi, which she found stored in the garage with a dust cloth over it, to his lawyer's. "Meet my lovely new friend, Casey," he said, introducing her as they were ushered into the lawyer's gleaming office and the lawyer stared at her skeptically but shook her hand.

"Rick, I would like to change my will," Milt said.

"Yes, I know. You wanted to—"

"No, now I want to change it even more than I said before. I know we were going to leave the house to the Children's Hospital, which was Rachel's wish, but they're doing fine without us, their machinery's over there tearing things up every day on that new wing. So instead I'd like to leave everything, absolutely everything, to Casey here. And to make her executor as well."

Silence fell over the room as Milt's beaming face went back and forth between pale-feeling KC and pale-looking Rick.

"Milt, I don't think that's a good idea," KC said, clutching his arm. It was the first time she had actually touched him and it seemed to energize him further.

"Nonsense!" he said. "I want to free you from any burdens – it will keep you the angel you are."

"It hardly seems that *I'm* the angel."

"You are, you are. And I want you and your music to fly untethered."

Rick gave her a wary look as he made his way slowly behind a mahogany desk the size of a truck flatbed. He sat down in a leather chair that had ball bearings and a reclining mechanism that he illustrated by immediately beginning to bounce against it and spin slightly, his arms now folded behind his neck. Then he threw himself forward onto a leather-edged blotter and grabbed the folder he had in front of him. "Well, I can get Maryanne to change everything right now." Then Rick studied KC again, and in a voice borrowed from either his youth or his son, said to her, "Nice tats."

She did not speak of it to Dench. She did not know how. She thought of being wry – hey, Villa is back! and this time it's an actual villa – but there was no good way. She had been passive before Milt's gift – gifts required some passivity – and she would remain passive before Dench. Besides, the whole situation could change on a dime, and she half hoped it would. Like almost everything, it existed in the hypothetical – God only knew how many times Milt had changed his will – so she would try not to think of it at all. Except in this way: Milt had no one. And now he had no one but her. Which was like having no one.

Dench appeared in the bathroom doorway as she was cutting bangs into her hair with nail scissors. "I thought you were growing your hair," he said. "I thought you were going to sell it."

"It's just bangs," she said, threw down the scissors, and brushed past him.

She began to take Milt to his doctors' appointments, though she sat in the waiting room. "I've got reservations both at the hospice wing where your grandmother was and also right there," he said as they passed the Heavenly Sunset Cemetery.

"Do you have a good tree?"

"What?"

"Do you have a good space beneath a strong tree?" she said loudly.

"I do!" he exclaimed. "I'm next to my wife." He paused, brooding. "Of course she has on her gravestone ALONE AT LAST. So, I'm putting on mine NOT SO FAST."

KC laughed, which she knew was what he wanted. "It's good to have a place."

At the doctor's sometimes the nurse, and sometimes the physician's assistant, would walk him back out to her and give her hurried and worried instructions. "Here is his new medicine," they would say, "but if he has a bad response we'll put him back on the other one." Milt would shrug as if he were surrounded by a gaggle of crazy relatives.

Once, a nurse leaned in and whispered, "There's a fear it may have spread to the brain. If you have any trouble on the weekend, phone the hospital or even the hospice. Watch his balance particularly."

KC took another of Ian's books to Milt's book nook, and one day, not seeing the old man outside, she worriedly tied Cat to the book nook post, went up to the main door, and knocked. She opened it and stepped in. "Hello? Good morning? Milt?"

Out stepped a middle-aged woman with an authoritative stride. Her heels hit the floorboards and stopped. She wore black slacks and a white shirt tucked into the waistband. Her hair was cut short – thick and gray. It was the sort of hair that years ago, when it was dark, wigmakers would have paid good money for. The woman stood there staring for a long time and then said, "I know what you're up to."

"What are you talking about?"

"One of his Concertos in Be Minor. How old are you?"

"I'm thirty-eight."

"I wonder if he knows that. You look younger."

"Well, I'm not."

"Hence your needs."

"I don't know what you mean."

"No? You don't?"

"No." Denial, when one was accused, was a life force, and would trump any desire to confess. Perhaps this was the animal strength of the psychopathic brain. Or the psychopathy of the animal brain. An admission of guilt would knock the strength right out of you – making it easier for them to twist your arms behind you and put the handcuffs on. It was from Dench, perhaps, that she had learned this.

"Shall we sit?" The pewter-haired woman motioned toward one of the sofas.

"I don't think that's necessary."

"You don't."

"No, besides, I was just walking my dog, and he's still tied up outside. I was just checking on Milt."

"Well, my sister has taken him to his doctor's appointment, so he won't be needing you today."

In bed KC lay next to Dench, staring at the ceiling, and smoking a cigarette, though they were not supposed to smoke inside. Cat lay on the quilt at the foot of the bed, doing his open-eyed fake-sleep. They were all carnies at the close of Labor Day. She stared at her Hammond keyboard, which right now had laundry piled and draped over it in angles. "What illness do you suppose Milt actually has?" Dench asked.

"Something quiet but wretched."

"Early onset quelque chose?"

"Not that early. I don't think I can go on visiting him anymore. I just can't do it."

Dench squeezed her thigh then caressed it. "Sure you can," he said.

She stabbed out her cigarette in a coffee cup, then, turning, rubbed her hand down along Dench's sinewy biceps and across his tightly muscled stomach, feeling hounded back into his arms, which she had never really left, and now his arms' familiarity was her only joy. You could lose someone a little but they would still roam the earth. The end of love was one big zombie movie.

"Do you realize that if you smoke enough you will end up lowering your risk of uterine cancer?" she said.

"That's a bad one," said Dench. "The silent killer. Especially in men."

"What did you do today?"

"I worked on some songs about my slavery-oppressed ancestors. I'm blaming the white man for my troubles."

She thought of his father. "Well, in your case it's definitely a white man."

"For most people it is. That's why we need more songs."

"Life! It's a hell of a thing, isn't it."

"I wouldn't have voted for it. I wouldn't give it any stars. It's like getting a book where the sexy passages are already underlined. Who wants that?"

She wasn't sure what he meant. But she kissed him on his shoulder anyway. "Wouldn't it be lovely just to fly out of here and live far away on a cloud together?"

"To be birds and see Gawwd!"

She had given up trying to determine his facetiousness level. She suspected it was all just habit and his true intent was unknown even to himself. "Yes! We could be birds in a little birdhouse that had books and we could read them!" she exclaimed.

Dench turned his head quickly on the pillow to stare at her. "Perhaps we have that already," he said. "But darlin, we ain't seeing God."

"Because God is off in some cybercafé, so tired from all those biblical escapades that now he just wants to sit back and Google himself all day." She pulled her hand away from Dench since he had not reciprocated with his own. "If he's not completely deaf to our cries, he's certainly deaf in one ear."

"For sure. Not just the hardware of the inner ear but the hairs and jelly further in: all shot."

"You're a strange boy."

"You see? We're getting past the glaze and right down to the factory paint here."

* * *

She let a few days go by and then she resumed her stopping by at Milt's on her coffee runs. Because summer had set in she was now bringing Dench iced coffee, but invariably the ice cubes would melt and she would just drink the whole thing herself. Milt still heated up his muffins but often needed her to drive him to doctors' appointments as well as to other places, and so she ran his errands with him and watched him greet all the salespeople, the druggist, the dry-cleaning girl, all of whom he seemed to know. "I'm so glad my wife's daughters are gone," he said at one point as they were driving home. "I dread the house with them there. I'd rather just return to the cave of my own aloneness!"

"I know how you feel."

"You have no idea," he said and leaned in to kiss her on the cheek before he got out of the car. "They are as cold as they come. I mean, even the ice on Mars melts in springtime!"

Once she took the old man swimming. They went to a beach farther north on the lake, at a state park on a weekday, when there was no one there. "Don't look!" he squealed as he took off his shirt and limp-jogged into the water, where he was safer than he was on land. He was not in bad shape, merely covered with liver spots, and his stomach was only slightly rounded and his breasts about the size of her own.

"How's the water?" she called to him. A line of silver at the water's edge sparkled in the sun. The sky was the deep belligerent blue of a hyacinth.

"Expect the unexpected!" he called back. She could see he'd once been a strong swimmer. His arms moved surely, bold, precise. Of course, when you expected the unexpected, it was no longer unexpected, and so you were not really following instructions. She admired his gameness. As she approached the water she saw that the silver line along the sand was the early die-off of the alewives: washed ashore gasping and still flipping on your foot as you walked. The dead lay in a shiny line upbeach, and if one of the smelt-like fish died closer to the waves it caught the light like the foil of a gum wrapper. Another putrid perplexity of the earth. She dove out anyway – to swim among the dying. She would pretend to be an aquarium act, floating among her trained, finned minions; if she imagined it any other way it was all too disgusting. She bobbed around a bit, letting the olive waves of the lake crest up and wash over her.

They picnicked back on shore. She had brought cheese sandwiches and club soda and difficult peaches: one had to bite sharply into the thick fuzzed skin of them to get to the juice. They sat huddled in their separate towels, on a blanket, everything sprinkled with sand, their feet coated in it like brown sugar.

"Too bad about the dead fish," Milt said. "They'll be gone next week but still. So may I!" He grinned.

Should she say "Don't talk like that"? Should she in her bathing suit with her tattoos all showing feign a bourgeois squeamishness regarding conversations about death? "Please don't talk like that," she said, peach juice dripping down her chin.

"OK," he said obediently. "I'm just saying: even Nature has her wickednesses." He took out a flask she didn't know he carried and poured her a little into a paper cup. "Here, have some gin. Goes in clean and straight – like German philosophy!" He smiled and looked out at the lake. "I was once a philosopher – just not a very good one."

"Really?" The gin stung her lips.

"Terrible world. Great sky. That always seemed the gist." He paused. "I also like bourbon – the particular parts of your brain it activates. Also good for philosophy."

She thought about this. "It's true. Bourbon hits a very different place than, say, wine."

"Absolutely."

"And actually, red wine hits a different place from white." She sipped her gin. "Not that I've made an intense study of it."

"No, of course not." He smiled and rinsed gin around on his gums.

Back at his house he seemed to have caught a chill and she put a blanket around him and he grabbed her hand. "I have to go," she said.

A sadness had overtaken him. He looked at KC then looked away. "Shortly before my wife died she sat up in bed and began to shout out the names of all the sick children who had died on her watch. I'd given her a brandy and she just began reciting the names of all the children she had failed to save. 'Charlie Pepper,' she cried, 'and Lauren Cox and Barrett Bannon and Caitlin Page and Raymond Jackson and Tom DeFugio, and little Deanna Lamb.' This went on for an hour."

"I have to go – will you be OK?" He had taken his hand away and was just staring into space. "Here is my number," she said, writing on a small scrap of paper. "Phone me if you need anything."

When he did not reply she left anyway, ignoring any anguish, locking the door from the inside.

Perhaps everyone had their own way of preparing to die. Life got you ready. Life got you sad. And then blood started coming from where it didn't used to come. People revisited the deaths of others, getting ready to meet them in the beyond. KC herself imagined dying would be full of rue: like flipping through the pages of a clearance catalog, seeing the drastic markdowns on stuff you'd paid full price for and not gotten that much use from, when all was said and done. Though all was never said and done. That was the other part about death.

"I had the dog all day," complained Dench, "which was no picnic. No day at the beach."

"Well, I had Milt. He's no kiss for Christmas."

"I don't know what I'm supposed to think about all the time you spend with him."

"According to you, you never know what to think."

"It just seems to me that if things are going to take they shouldn't take so long. By the way, I've found out what that odor is."

"Really?"

The smell, even with the warm weather ostensibly drying things out, was still in the walls. There was the occasional scurrying of squirrels in the attic. It was surprising Cat didn't jump up and start barking.

"The rot of a bad conscience."

"I really doubt that."

"Well, let me show you." He opened the hatch to the crawl space that constituted the attic. He pulled down the folding ladder and motioned for her to climb it. "Take this flashlight and move it around and you'll see."

She expected to find a couple of flying squirrels, dead in each other's caped arms. But when she poked her head into the crawl space and flashed her light around, she at first saw nothing but dust and boxes. Then her eyes fell on it: a pile of furry flesh with the intertwined tails of rats. They were a single creature like a wreath and flies buzzed around them and excrement bound them at the center while their bodies were arrayed like spokes. Only one of them still had a head that moved and it opened its mouth noiselessly.

"It's a rat king," said Dench. "They were born like that, with their tails attached, and could never get away."

She scrambled down the ladder and shoved it back up. "That is the most revolting thing I've ever seen."

"They're supposed to be bad luck."

"Put the hatch door back down."

"A surprise for Ian. I did phone the pest removal place, but they charge a thousand dollars. I said, 'Where are you taking them to, Europe?' We may just have to burn the house down. It's completely haunted."

"Really."

"We could work up plausible deniability: *What kerosene can?* Or, *Many people are known to go shopping while cooking pot-au-feu.*"

She studied Dench's face as if – once again – she had no idea who he was. Now having found the rat king, he seemed to be the star of a horror film. He was trying to be funny all the time and she no longer liked it, as if he were auditioning for something. Soon he might start telling Milt's jokes: *I keep thinking of the hereafter: I walk into a room and say, What am I here after?* She only liked Dench's Jesus jokes, since in them

Jesus was kind of an asshole, which she thought was perhaps a strong possibility in real life, and so the jokes seemed true and didn't have to be funny and so she didn't have to laugh. "Don't ever show me anything like that again," she said.

Cat came up and started to hump Dench's leg. "Sheesh," said Dench, as KC turned to leave. "He's had his balls cut off and he still wants to date."

Summer warmed all the houses though most of them did not have air conditioners, Ian's and Milt's included. She took Milt one evening to a nearby café and they had to dine outside, at a wobbly metal table near the parking lot, since the air within was too slicing and cold. "I think I would have liked that cold air when I was about seventeen," he said. "Now I feel heat is good for old bones."

They ate slowly, and although the food clung to his teeth, KC did not alert him. What would be the point? At some point, good God, just let an old guy have food in his teeth! They ate squash soup with caramel corn on top – molar-wrecking.

"You know," he said, chewing and looking around. "People get fired from the barbershop, a restaurant closes, this is a slow town and still things change too fast for me. It's like those big-screen TVs: all the bars have them now. I can't watch football on those – it feels like they're running right at me."

KC smiled but said nothing. At one point he said loudly of his custard, "The banana flavor doesn't taste like real banana but more like what burped banana tastes like."

She glanced over at the next table. "I kind of know what you mean," she said quietly.

"Of course old people are the stupidest. It's the thing that keeps me from wanting to live in a whole facility full of them. Just listen to them talk: listen to me talk. It's like: I've been walking around with the dumb thought for forty years and I'm still thinking it, so now I might as well say it over and over." He then again sang the praises of his wife, her generosity and social commitment, and then turned his attention to

KC. "You are not unlike her, in a way," he said. Behind him the sun set in the striped hues of a rutabaga.

"I can't imagine," she said. Instead her mind was filled with wondering what the neighbors must think.

"Your faces are similar in a way. Especially when you smile!" He smiled at her when he said this and she returned it with a wan one of her own, her lips in a tight line.

When she walked him back to his house, the crickets had started in with their beautiful sawing. "Tinnitus!" Milt exclaimed.

But this time she didn't laugh, and so he did what he often did when he was irritated: he walked with his most deaf ear toward her so that he could stew in peace. She noticed him weaving and knew that his balance was off. At one point he began to tilt and she quickly caught him. "An old guy like me should wear a helmet all the time," he said. "Just get up in the morning and put it on."

He then turned and peered through the dusk at her. "Sometimes at home I think the ringing in my ears might be the phone and I pick it up, hoping it might be you."

She helped him into his house – he took the front stairs with greater difficulty than he used to. She turned on the lights. But he switched them off again and, grabbing her hand, sat in a chair. "Come here and sit on my lap," he said, tugging her firmly. She fell awkwardly across his thin thighs, and when she tried to find her footing to stand again, he braced and embraced her with his arms and began to nuzzle her neck, the *u* and *r* of *Decatur*. His eyes were closed, and he offered his face up to her, his lips pursed but moving a little to find hers.

KC at first let him kiss her, letting their lips meet slightly – she had to be obliging, she had to work against herself and find a way – and then his rough and pointed tongue flicked quickly in and out and she jolted, flung herself away, stood, switched the lights back on, and turned to face him. "That's it! You've gone off the deep end now!"

"What?" he asked. His eyes were barely open and his tongue only now stopped its animal darting. She swept her hair from her face. The room seemed to whirl. Life got you ready for dying. She had once caught a mouse in a mousetrap – she had heard the snap and when she looked it seemed merely to be a tea bag, a brown mushroomy thing with a tail, then it began flopping and flipping and she'd had to pick it up with a glove and put it in the freezer, trap and all, to die there.

It was time. "You're completely crazy!" she said loudly. "And there's nothing I can do at this point but call the hospice!" Words that had stayed in the wings now rushed into the crushed black box of her throat.

His face now bore the same blasted-apart look she'd seen when she first met him, except this time there was something mangled about the eyes, his mouth a gash, his body slumped in banishment. He began silently to cry. And then he spoke. "I looked him up on – what do you call it: Spacebook. His interests and his seekings."

"What are you talking about?"

"Good luck," he said. "Good luck to you and your young man – I wish you both the best."

"It's done."

She sank against the door. She had waited all night for the hospice people to come and carry Milt off the next morning, and then she had signed some forms and promised to visit, promised to come help him with the crossword puzzle, and taking the keys of the house, she had locked it, then walked hurriedly home.

Dench was putting his cell phone away. He looked at her worriedly and she returned his gaze with a hard glare. He then stepped forward, perhaps to comfort her, but she shoved him off. "KC," he said. And when he cocked his head as if puzzled and tried in forgiveness to step toward her again, she made a fist and struck him hard in the face.

Her life in the white-brick house was one of hostessing – and she poured into it all the milk of human kindness she possessed. There were five bedrooms and one suite turned entirely over to the families of children at the hospital whose new pediatric wing was now complete. She had painted the walls of every room either apricot or brown, and she kept the crown moldings white while she painted the ceilings a celestial blue. In summer she opened up the sleeping porches. Every morning she got up early and made breakfast, a ham-and-egg bake, which she served in a large casserole in the dining room, and although she made no other meals she made sure there were cookies in the front room and games for the siblings (who also played with the dog). She sometimes attempted music in the afternoons, sitting at the piano while people tried to smile at her. She wore high collars and long sleeves and necklaces of blue slag to hide her tattoos. She left magazines for people to read but not newspapers, which contained too much news. She maintained the book nook, stuffing it with mysteries. She watched the families as they went off in the morning, walking their way to the hospital to see their sick children. She never saw the sick children themselves – except at night, when they were ghosts in white nightgowns and would stand on the stairwell landings and recite their names and wave – as she roamed the house, thinking of them as "her children" and then not thinking of them at all, as she sleeplessly straightened up, but she would hear of their lives. "I missed the good parts," the mothers would say, "and now there are no more good parts." And she would give them more magazines for flipping through in the surgery lounge, in case they grew tired of watching a thriving aquarium of bright little fish.

Tears thickened her skin the way brine knitted and hardened the rind of a cheese. Her hair was still long but fuzzily linted with white, and she wore it up in a clip. There were times looking out the front windows, seeing the parents off on their dutiful, despairing visits, when she would think of Dench and again remember the day he had first auditioned raucously for their band, closing with some soft guitar, accompanied by his strong but inexpressive baritone, so the song had to carry the voice, like a river current moving a barge. She had forgotten now what song it was. But she remembered she had wondered whether it would be good to love him, and then she had gone broodingly to the window to look out at the street while he was singing and she had seen a very young woman waiting for him in his beat-up car. It had been winter with winter's sparse afternoon stars, and the girl was wearing a fleece chin-strap cap that made her look like Dante and also like a baby bird. KC herself had been dressed like Hooker Barbie. Why had she put this memory out of her mind? The young woman had clearly driven him there – would she be tossed away? bequeathed? forgotten? given a new purpose by God, whose persistent mad humor was aimless as a gnat? She was waiting for him to come back with something they could use.

2012

YOU'RE UGLY, TOO

YOU HAD TO GET OUT of them occasionally, those Illinois towns with the funny names: Paris, Oblong, Normal. Once, when the Dow Jones dipped two hundred points, the Paris paper boasted a banner headline: NORMAL MAN MARRIES OBLONG WOMAN. They knew what was important. They did! But you had to get out once in a while, even if it was just across the border to Terre Haute, for a movie.

Outside of Paris, in the middle of a large field, was a scatter of brick buildings, a small liberal arts college with the improbable name of Hilldale-Versailles. Zoë Hendricks had been teaching American History there for three years. She taught "The Revolution and Beyond" to freshmen and sophomores, and every third semester she had the Senior Seminar for Majors, and although her student evaluations had been slipping in the last year and a half – *Professor Hendricks is often late for class and usually arrives with a cup of hot chocolate, which she offers the class sips of* – generally, the department of nine men was pleased to have her. They felt she added some needed feminine touch to the corridors – that faint trace of Obsession and sweat, the light, fast clicking of heels. Plus they had had a sex-discrimination suit, and the dean had said, well, it was time.

The situation was not easy for her, they knew. Once, at the start of last semester, she had skipped into her lecture hall singing "Getting to Know You" – both verses. At the request of the dean, the chairman had called her into his office, but did not ask her for an explanation, not really. He asked her how she was and then smiled in an avuncular way. She said, "Fine," and he studied the way she said it, her front teeth catching on the inside of her lower lip. She was almost pretty, but her face showed the strain and ambition of always having been close but not quite. There was too much effort with the eyeliner, and her earrings, worn no doubt for the drama her features lacked, were a little frightening, jutting out from the side of her head like antennae.

"I'm going out of my mind," said Zoë to her younger sister, Evan, in Manhattan. *Professor Hendricks seems to know the entire sound track to* The King and I. *Is this history?* Zoë phoned her every Tuesday.

"You always say that," said Evan, "but then you go on your trips and vacations and then you settle back into things and then you're quiet for a while and then you say you're fine, you're busy, and then after a while you say you're going crazy again, and you start all over." Evan was a part-time food designer for photo shoots. She cooked vegetables in green dye. She propped up beef stew with a bed of marbles and shopped for new kinds of silicone sprays and plastic ice cubes. She thought her life was "OK." She was living with her boyfriend of many years, who was independently wealthy and had an amusing little job in book publishing. They were five years out of college, and they lived in a luxury midtown high-rise with a balcony and access to a pool. "It's not the same as having your own pool," Evan was always sighing, as if to let Zoë know that, as with Zoë, there were still things she, Evan, had to do without.

"Illinois. It makes me sarcastic to be here," said Zoë on the phone. She used to insist it was irony, something gently layered and sophisticated, something alien to the Midwest, but her students kept calling it sarcasm, something they felt qualified to recognize, and now she had to agree. It wasn't irony. *What is your perfume?* a student once asked her. *Room freshener*, she said. She smiled, but he looked at her, unnerved.

Her students were by and large good Midwesterners, spacey with estrogen from large quantities of meat and cheese. They shared their parents' suburban values; their parents had given them things, things, things. They were complacent. They had been purchased. They were armed with a healthy vagueness about anything historical or geographic. They seemed actually to know very little about anything, but they were extremely good-natured about it. "All those states in the East are so tiny and jagged and bunched up," complained one of her undergraduates the week she was lecturing on "The Turning Point of Independence: The Battle at Saratoga." "Professor

Hendricks, you're from Delaware originally, right?" the student asked her.

"Maryland," corrected Zoë.

"Aw," he said, waving his hand dismissively. "New England."

Her articles – chapters toward a book called *Hearing the One About: Uses of Humor in the American Presidency* – were generally well received, though they came slowly for her. She liked her pieces to have something from every time of day in them – she didn't trust things written in the morning only – so she reread and rewrote painstakingly. No part of a day, its moods, its light, was allowed to dominate. She hung on to a piece for over a year sometimes, revising at all hours, until the entirety of a day had registered there.

The job she'd had before the one at Hilldale-Versailles had been at a small college in New Geneva, Minnesota, Land of the Dying Shopping Mall. Everyone was so blond there that brunettes were often presumed to be from foreign countries. *Just because Professor Hendricks is from Spain doesn't give her the right to be so negative about our country.* There was a general emphasis on cheerfulness. In New Geneva you weren't supposed to be critical or complain. You weren't supposed to notice that the town had overextended and that its shopping malls were raggedy and going under. You were never to say you weren't fine thank you and yourself. You were supposed to be Heidi. You were supposed to lug goat milk up the hills and not think twice. Heidi did not complain. Heidi did not do things like stand in front of the new IBM photocopier, saying, "If this fucking Xerox machine breaks on me one more time, I'm going to slit my wrists."

But now, in her second job, in her fourth year of teaching in the Midwest, Zoë was discovering something she never suspected she had: a crusty edge, brittle and pointed. Once she had pampered her students, singing them songs, letting them call her at home, even, and ask personal questions. Now she was losing sympathy. They were beginning to seem different. They were beginning to seem demanding and spoiled.

"You act," said one of her Senior Seminar students at a

scheduled conference, "like your opinion is worth more than everybody else's in the class."

Zoë's eyes widened. "I *am* the teacher," she said. "I *do* get paid to act like that." She narrowed her gaze at the student, who was wearing a big leather bow in her hair, like a cowgirl in a TV ranch show. "I mean, otherwise *everybody* in the class would have little offices and office hours." *Sometimes Professor Hendricks will take up the class's time just talking about movies she's seen.* She stared at the student some more, then added, "I bet you'd like that."

"Maybe I sound whiny to you," said the girl, "but I simply want my history major to mean something."

"Well, there's your problem," said Zoë, and with a smile, she showed the student to the door. "I like your bow," she added.

Zoë lived for the mail, for the postman, that handsome blue jay, and when she got a real letter, with a real full-price stamp, from someplace else, she took it to bed with her and read it over and over. She also watched television until all hours and had her set in the bedroom, a bad sign. *Professor Hendricks has said critical things about Fawn Hall, the Catholic religion, and the whole state of Illinois. It is unbelievable.* At Christmastime she gave twenty-dollar tips to the mailman and to Jerry, the only cabbie in town, whom she had gotten to know from all her rides to and from the Terre Haute airport, and who, since he realized such rides were an extravagance, often gave her cut rates.

"I'm flying in to visit you this weekend," announced Zoë.

"I was hoping you would," said Evan. "Charlie and I are having a party for Halloween. It'll be fun."

"I have a costume already. It's a bonehead. It's this thing that looks like a giant bone going through your head."

"Great," said Evan.

"It is, it's great."

"Alls I have is my moon mask from last year and the year before. I'll probably end up getting married in it."

"Are you and Charlie getting *married*?" Foreboding filled her voice.

"Hmmmmmmnno, not immediately."

"Don't get married."

"Why?"

"Just not yet. You're too young."

"You're only saying that because you're five years older than I am and *you're* not married."

"*I'm* not married? Oh, my God," said Zoë. "I forgot to get married."

Zoë had been out with three men since she'd come to Hilldale-Versailles. One of them was a man in the Paris municipal bureaucracy who had fixed a parking ticket she'd brought in to protest and who then asked her to coffee. At first she thought he was amazing – at last, someone who did not want Heidi! But soon she came to realize that all men, deep down, wanted Heidi. Heidi with cleavage. Heidi with outfits. The parking ticket bureaucrat soon became tired and intermittent. One cool fall day, in his snazzy, impractical convertible, when she asked him what was wrong, he said, "You would not be ill-served by new clothes, you know." She wore a lot of gray-green corduroy. She had been under the impression that it brought out her eyes, those shy stars. She flicked an ant from her sleeve.

"Did you have to brush that off in the car?" he said, driving. He glanced down at his own pectorals, giving first the left, then the right, a quick survey. He was wearing a tight shirt.

"Excuse me?"

He slowed down at a yellow light and frowned. "Couldn't you have picked it up and thrown it outside?"

"The ant? It might have bitten me. I mean, what difference does it make?"

"It might have bitten you! Ha! How ridiculous! Now it's going to lay eggs in my car!"

The second guy was sweeter, lunkier, though not insensitive to certain paintings and songs, but too often, too, things he'd do or say would startle her. Once, in a restaurant, he stole the garnishes off her dinner plate and waited for her to notice. When she didn't, he finally thrust his fist across the table and said, "Look," and when he opened it, there was her parsley sprig and her orange slice, crumpled to a wad. Another time he described to her his recent trip to the Louvre. "And there I was in front of Géricault's *Raft of the Medusa*, and everyone else had wandered off, so I had my own private audience with it, all those painted, drowning bodies splayed in every direction, and there's this motion in that painting that starts at the bottom left, swirling and building, and building, and building, and going up to the right-hand corner, where there's this guy waving a flag, and on the horizon in the distance you could see this teeny tiny boat. . . ." He was breathless in the telling. She found this touching and smiled in encouragement. "A painting like that," he said, shaking his head. "It just makes you shit."

"I have to ask you something," said Evan. "I know every woman complains about not meeting men, but really, on my shoots, I meet a lot of men. And they're not all gay, either." She paused. "Not anymore."

"What are you asking?"

The third guy was a political science professor named Murray Peterson, who liked to go out on double dates with colleagues whose wives he was attracted to. Usually the wives would consent to flirt with him. Under the table sometimes there was footsie, and once there was even kneesie. Zoë and the husband would be left to their food, staring into their water glasses, chewing like goats. "Oh, Murray," said one wife, who had never finished her master's in physical therapy and wore great clothes. "You know, I know everything about you: your birthday, your license plate number. I have everything memorized. But then that's the kind of mind I have. Once at a dinner party I amazed the host by getting up and saying good-bye to every single person there, first *and* last names."

"I knew a dog who could do that," said Zoë, with her mouth full. Murray and the wife looked at her with vexed and rebuking expressions, but the husband seemed suddenly twinkling and amused. Zoë swallowed. "It was a Talking Lab, and after about ten minutes of listening to the dinner conversation this dog knew everyone's name. You could say, 'Bring this knife to Murray Peterson,' and it would."

"Really," said the wife, frowning, and Murray Peterson never called again.

"Are you seeing anyone?" said Evan. "I'm asking for a particular reason, I'm not just being like mom."

"I'm seeing my house. I'm tending to it when it wets, when it cries, when it throws up." Zoë had bought a mint-green ranch house near campus, though now she was thinking that maybe she shouldn't have. It was hard to live in a house. She kept wandering in and out of the rooms, wondering where she had put things. She went downstairs into the basement for no reason at all except that it amused her to own a basement. It also amused her to own a tree. The day she moved in, she had tacked to her tree a small paper sign that said *Zoë's Tree.*

Her parents, in Maryland, had been very pleased that one of their children had at last been able to afford real estate, and when she closed on the house they sent her flowers with a Congratulations card. Her mother had even UPS'd a box of old decorating magazines saved over the years, photographs of beautiful rooms her mother used to moon over, since there never had been any money to redecorate. It was like getting her mother's pornography, that box, inheriting her drooled-upon fantasies, the endless wish and tease that had been her life. But to her mother it was a rite of passage that pleased her. "Maybe you will get some ideas from these," she had written. And when Zoë looked at the photographs, at the bold and beautiful living rooms, she was filled with longing. Ideas and ideas of longing.

Right now Zoë's house was rather empty. The previous owner had wallpapered around the furniture, leaving strange gaps and silhouettes on the walls, and Zoë hadn't done much about that yet. She had bought furniture, then taken it back, furnishing and unfurnishing, preparing and shedding, like a womb. She had bought several plain pine chests to use as love seats or boot boxes, but they came to look to her more and more like children's coffins, so she returned them. And she had recently bought an Oriental rug for the living room, with

Chinese symbols on it she didn't understand. The salesgirl had kept saying she was sure they meant *Peace* and *Eternal Life*, but when Zoë got the rug home, she worried. What if they didn't mean *Peace* and *Eternal Life*? What if they meant, say, *Bruce Springsteen*. And the more she thought about it, the more she became convinced she had a rug that said *Bruce Springsteen*, and so she returned that, too.

She had also bought a little baroque mirror for the front entryway, which she had been told, by Murray Peterson, would keep away evil spirits. The mirror, however, tended to frighten *her*, startling her with an image of a woman she never recognized. Sometimes she looked puffier and plainer than she remembered. Sometimes shifty and dark. Most times she just looked vague. *You look like someone I know*, she had been told twice in the last year by strangers in restaurants in Terre Haute. In fact, sometimes she seemed not to have a look of her own, or any look whatsoever, and it began to amaze her that her students and colleagues were able to recognize her at all. How did they know? When she walked into a room, how did she look so that they knew it was her? Like this? Did she look like this? And so she returned the mirror.

"The reason I'm asking is that I know a man I think you should meet," said Evan. "He's fun. He's straight. He's single. That's all I'm going to say."

"I think I'm too old for fun," said Zoë. She had a dark bristly hair in her chin, and she could feel it now with her finger. Perhaps when you had been without the opposite sex for too long, you began to resemble them. In an act of desperate invention, you began to grow your own. "I just want to come, wear my bonehead, visit with Charlie's tropical fish, ask you about your food shoots."

She thought about all the papers on "Our Constitution: How It Affects Us" she was going to have to correct. She thought about how she was going in for ultrasound tests on Friday, because, according to her doctor and her doctor's assistant, she had a large, mysterious growth in her abdomen. Gallbladder, they kept saying. Or ovaries or colon. "You guys practice medicine?" asked Zoë, aloud, after they had left the room. Once, as a girl, she brought her dog to a vet, who had told her, "Well, either your dog has worms or cancer or else it was hit by a car."

She was looking forward to New York.

"Well, whatever. We'll just play it cool. I can't wait to see you, hon. Don't forget your bonehead," said Evan.

"A bonehead you don't forget," said Zoë.

"I suppose," said Evan.

The ultrasound Zoë was keeping a secret, even from Evan. "I feel like I'm dying," Zoë had hinted just once on the phone.

"You're not dying," said Evan. "You're just annoyed."

"Ultrasound," Zoë now said jokingly to the technician who put the cold jelly on her bare stomach. "Does that sound like a really great stereo system, or what?" She had not had anyone make this much fuss over her bare stomach since her boyfriend in graduate school, who had hovered over her whenever she felt ill, waved his arms, pressed his hands upon her navel, and drawled evangelically, "Heal! Heal for thy Baby Jesus' sake!" Zoë would laugh and they would make love, both secretly hoping she would get pregnant. Later they would worry together, and he would sink a cheek to her belly and ask whether she was late, was she late, was she sure, she might be late, and when after two years she had not gotten pregnant, they took to quarreling and drifted apart.

"OK," said the technician absently.

The monitor was in place, and Zoë's insides came on the screen in all their gray and ribbony hollowness. They were marbled in the finest gradations of black and white, like stone in an old church or a picture of the moon. "Do you suppose," she babbled at the technician, "that the rise in infertility among so many couples in this country is due to completely different species trying to reproduce?" The technician moved the scanner around and took more pictures. On one view in particular, on Zoë's right side, the technician became suddenly alert, the machine he was operating clicking away.

Zoë stared at the screen. "That must be the growth you found there," suggested Zoë.

"I can't tell you anything," said the technician rigidly. "Your doctor will get the radiologist's report this afternoon and will phone you then."

"I'll be out of town," said Zoë.

"I'm sorry," said the technician.

Driving home, Zoë looked in the rearview mirror and decided she looked – well, how would one describe it? A little wan. She thought of the joke about the guy who visits his doctor and the doctor says, "Well, I'm sorry to say you've got six weeks to live."

"I want a second opinion," says the guy. *You act like your opinion is worth more than everyone else's in the class.*

"You want a second opinion? OK," says the doctor. "You're ugly, too." She liked that joke. She thought it was terribly, terribly funny.

She took a cab to the airport, Jerry the cabbie happy to see her.

"Have fun in New York," he said, getting her bag out of the trunk. He liked her, or at least he always acted as if he did. She called him "Jare."

"Thanks, Jare."

"You know, I'll tell you a secret: I've never been to New York. I'll tell you two secrets: I've never been on a plane." And he waved at her sadly as she pushed her way in through the terminal door. "Or an escalator!" he shouted.

The trick to flying safe, Zoë always said, was never to buy a discount ticket and to tell yourself you had nothing to live for anyway, so that when the plane crashed it was no big deal. Then, when it didn't crash, when you had succeeded in keeping it aloft with your own worthlessness, all you had to do was stagger off, locate your luggage, and, by the time a cab arrived, come up with a persuasive reason to go on living.

"You're here!" shrieked Evan over the doorbell, before she even opened the door. Then she opened it wide. Zoë set her bags on the hall floor and hugged Evan hard. When she was little, Evan had always been affectionate and devoted.

Zoë had always taken care of her, advising, reassuring, until recently, when it seemed Evan had started advising and reassuring *her*. It startled Zoë. She suspected it had something to do with Zoë's being alone. It made people uncomfortable. "How are you?"

"I threw up on on the plane. Besides that, I'm OK."

"Can I get you something? Here, let me take your suitcase. Sick on the plane. Eeeyew."

"It was into one of those sickness bags," said Zoë, just in case Evan thought she'd lost it in the aisle. "I was very quiet."

The apartment was spacious and bright, with a view all the way downtown along the East Side. There was a balcony and sliding glass doors. "I keep forgetting how nice this apartment is. Twentieth floor, doorman . . ." Zoë could work her whole life and never have an apartment like this. So could Evan. It was Charlie's apartment. He and Evan lived in it like two kids in a dorm, beer cans and clothes strewn around. Evan put Zoë's bag away from the mess, over by the fish tank. "I'm so glad you're here," she said. "Now what can I get you?"

Evan made them a snack – soup from a can, and saltines.

"I don't know about Charlie," she said, after they had finished. "I feel like we've gone all sexless and middle-aged already."

"Hmmm," said Zoë. She leaned back into Evan's sofa and stared out the window at the dark tops of the buildings. It seemed a little unnatural to live up in the sky like this, like birds that out of some wrongheaded derring-do had nested too high. She nodded toward the lighted fish tanks and giggled. "I feel like a bird," she said, "with my own personal supply of fish."

Evan sighed. "He comes home and just sacks out on the sofa, watching fuzzy football. He's wearing the psychic cold cream and curlers, if you know what I mean."

Zoë sat up, readjusted the sofa cushions. "What's fuzzy football?"

"We haven't gotten cable yet. Everything comes in fuzzy. Charlie just watches it that way."

"Hmmm, yeah, that's a little depressing," Zoë said. She

looked at her hands. "Especially the part about not having cable."

"This is how he gets into bed at night." Evan stood up to demonstrate. "He whips all his clothes off, and when he gets to his underwear, he lets it drop to one ankle. Then he kicks up his leg and flips the underwear in the air and catches it. I, of course, watch from the bed. There's nothing else. There's just that."

"Maybe you should just get it over with and get married."

"Really?"

"Yeah. I mean, you guys probably think living together like this is the best of both worlds, but . . ." Zoë tried to sound like an older sister; an older sister was supposed to be the parent you could never have, the hip, cool mom. ". . . I've always found that as soon as you think you've got the best of both worlds" – she thought now of herself, alone in her house; of the toad-faced cicadas that flew around like little caped men at night, landing on her screens, staring; of the size fourteen shoes she placed at the doorstep, to scare off intruders; of the ridiculous inflatable blow-up doll someone had told her to keep propped up at the breakfast table – "it can suddenly twist and become the worst of both worlds."

"Really?" Evan was beaming. "Oh, Zoë. I have something to tell you. Charlie and I *are* getting married."

"Really." Zoë felt confused.

"I didn't know how to tell you."

"Yes, well, I guess the part about fuzzy football misled me a little."

"I was hoping you'd be my maid of honor," said Evan, waiting. "Aren't you happy for me?"

"Yes," said Zoë, and she began to tell Evan a story about an award-winning violinist at Hilldale-Versailles, how the violinist had come home from a competition in Europe and taken up with a local man, who made her go to all his summer softball games, made her cheer for him from the stands, with the wives, until she later killed herself. But when she got halfway through, to the part about cheering at the softball games, Zoë stopped.

"What?" said Evan. "So what happened?"

"Actually, nothing," said Zoë lightly. "She just really got into softball. I mean, really. You should have seen her."

Zoë decided to go to a late-afternoon movie, leaving Evan to chores she needed to do before the party – *I have to do them alone*, she'd said, a little tense after the violinist story. Zoë thought about going to an art museum, but women alone in art museums had to look good. They always did. Chic and serious, moving languidly, with a great handbag. Instead, she walked over and down through Kips Bay, past an earring boutique called Stick It in Your Ear, past a beauty salon called Dorian Gray's. That was the funny thing about *beauty*, thought Zoë. Look it up in the yellow pages, and you found a hundred entries, hostile with wit, cutesy with warning. But look up *truth* – ha! There was nothing at all.

Zoë thought about Evan getting married. Would Evan turn into Peter Pumpkin Eater's wife? Mrs. Eater? At the wedding would she make Zoë wear some flouncy lavender dress, identical with the other maids'? Zoë hated uniforms, had even, in the first grade, refused to join Elf Girls, because she didn't want to wear the same dress as everyone else. Now she might have to. But maybe she could distinguish it. Hitch it up on one side with a clothespin. Wear surgical gauze at the waist. Clip to her bodice one of those pins that said in loud letters, SHIT HAPPENS.

At the movie – *Death by Number* – she bought strands of red licorice to tug and chew. She took a seat off to one side in the theater. She felt strangely self-conscious sitting alone and hoped for the place to darken fast. When it did, and the coming attractions came on, she reached inside her purse for her glasses. They were in a Baggie. Her Kleenex was also in a Baggie. So were her pen and her aspirin and her mints. Everything was in Baggies. This was what she'd become: *a woman alone at the movies with everything in a Baggie.*

* * *

At the Halloween party, there were about two dozen people. There were people with ape heads and large hairy hands. There was someone dressed as a leprechaun. There was someone dressed as a frozen dinner. Some man had brought his two small daughters: a ballerina and a ballerina's sister, also dressed as a ballerina. There was a gaggle of sexy witches – women dressed entirely in black, beautifully made up and jeweled. "I hate those sexy witches. It's not in the spirit of Halloween," said Evan. Evan had abandoned the moon mask and dolled herself up as a hausfrau, in curlers and an apron, a decision she now regretted. Charlie, because he liked fish, because he owned fish, collected fish, had decided to go as a fish. He had fins and eyes on the side of his head. "Zoë! How are you! I'm sorry I wasn't here when you first arrived!" He spent the rest of his time chatting up the sexy witches.

"Isn't there something I can help you with here?" Zoë asked her sister. "You've been running yourself ragged." She rubbed her sister's arm, gently, as if she wished they were alone.

"Oh, God, not at all," said Evan, arranging stuffed mushrooms on a plate. The timer went off, and she pulled another sheetful out of the oven. "Actually, you know what you can do?"

"What?" Zoë put on her bonehead.

"Meet Earl. He's the guy I had in mind for you. When he gets here, just talk to him a little. He's nice. He's fun. He's going through a divorce."

"I'll try." Zoë groaned. "OK? I'll try." She looked at her watch.

When Earl arrived, he was dressed as a naked woman, steel wool glued strategically to a body stocking, and large rubber breasts protruding like hams.

"Zoë, this is Earl," said Evan.

"Good to meet you," said Earl, circling Evan to shake Zoë's hand. He stared at the top of Zoë's head. "Great bone."

Zoë nodded. "Great tits," she said. She looked past him, out the window at the city thrown glitteringly up against the sky; people were saying the usual things: how it looked like jewels, like bracelets and necklaces unstrung. You could see Grand Central station, the clock of the Con Ed building, the red-and-gold-capped Empire State, the Chrysler like a rocket ship dreamed up in a depression. Far west you could glimpse the Astor Plaza, its flying white roof like a nun's habit. "There's beer out on the balcony, Earl – can I get you one?" Zoë asked.

"Sure, uh, I'll come along. Hey, Charlie, how's it going?"

Charlie grinned and whistled. People turned to look. "Hey, Earl," someone called, from across the room. "Va-va-va-voom."

They squeezed their way past the other guests, past the apes and the sexy witches. The suction of the sliding door gave way in a whoosh, and Zoë and Earl stepped out onto the balcony, a bonehead and a naked woman, the night air roaring and smoky cool. Another couple was out here, too, murmuring privately. They were not wearing costumes. They smiled at Zoë and Earl. "Hi," said Zoë. She found the plastic-foam cooler, dug into it, and retrieved two beers.

"Thanks," said Earl. His rubber breasts folded inward, dimpled and dented, as he twisted open the bottle.

"Well," sighed Zoë anxiously. She had to learn not to be afraid of a man, the way, in your childhood, you learned not to be afraid of an earthworm or a bug. Often, when she spoke to men at parties, she rushed things in her mind. As the man politely blathered on, she would fall in love, marry, then find herself in a bitter custody battle with him for the kids and hoping for a reconciliation, so that despite all his betrayals she might no longer despise him, and in the few minutes remaining, learn, perhaps, what his last name was and what he did for a living, though probably there was already too much history between them. She would nod, blush, turn away.

"Evan tells me you're a professor. Where do you teach?"

"Just over the Indiana border into Illinois."

He looked a little shocked. "I guess Evan didn't tell me that part."

"She didn't?"

"No."

"Well, that's Evan for you. When we were kids we both had speech impediments."

"That can be tough," said Earl. One of his breasts was hidden behind his drinking arm, but the other shone low and pink, full as a strawberry moon.

"Yes, well, it wasn't a total loss. We used to go to what we called peach pearapy. For about ten years of my life I had to map out every sentence in my mind, way ahead, before I said it. That was the only way I could get a coherent sentence out."

Earl drank from his beer. "How did you do that? I mean, how did you get through?"

"I told a lot of jokes. Jokes you know the lines to already – you can just say them. I love jokes. Jokes and songs."

Earl smiled. He had on lipstick, a deep shade of red, but it was wearing off from the beer. "What's your favorite joke?"

"Uh, my favorite joke is probably . . . OK, all right. This guy goes into a doctor's office and—"

"I think I know this one," interrupted Earl, eagerly. He wanted to tell it himself. "A guy goes into a doctor's office, and the doctor tells him he's got some good news and some bad news – that one, right?"

"I'm not sure," said Zoë. "This might be a different version."

"So the guy says, 'Give me the bad news first,' and the doctor says, 'OK. You've got three weeks to live.' And the guy cries, 'Three weeks to live! Doctor, what is the good news?' And the doctor says, 'Did you see that secretary out front? I finally fucked her.' "

Zoë frowned.

"That's not the one you were thinking of?"

"No." There was accusation in her voice. "Mine was different."

"Oh," said Earl. He looked away and then back again. "You teach history, right? What kind of history do you teach?"

"I teach American, mostly – eighteenth and nineteenth century." In graduate school, at bars, the pickup line was always: "So what's your century?"

"Occasionally I teach a special theme course," she added, "say, 'Humor and Personality in the White House.' That's what my book's on." She thought of something someone once told her about bowerbirds, how they build elaborate structures before mating.

"Your book's on *humor*?"

"Yeah, and, well, when I teach a theme course like that, I do all the centuries." *So what's your century?*

"All three of them."

"Pardon?" The breeze glistened her eyes. Traffic revved beneath them. She felt high and puny, like someone lifted into heaven by mistake and then spurned.

"Three. There's only three."

"Well, four, really." She was thinking of Jamestown, and of the Pilgrims coming here with buckles and witch hats to say their prayers.

"I'm a photographer," said Earl. His face was starting to gleam, his rouge smearing in a sunset beneath his eyes.

"Do you like that?"

"Well, actually I'm starting to feel it's a little dangerous."

"Really?"

"Spending all your time in a darkroom with that red light and all those chemicals. There's links with Parkinson's, you know."

"No, I didn't."

"I suppose I should wear rubber gloves, but I don't like to. Unless I'm touching it directly, I don't think of it as real."

"Hmmm," said Zoë. Alarm buzzed through her, mildly, like a tea.

"Sometimes, when I have a cut or something, I feel the sting and think, *Shit.* I wash constantly and just hope. I don't like rubber over the skin like that."

"Really."

"I mean, the physical contact. That's what you want, or why bother?"

"I guess," said Zoë. She wished she could think of a joke, something slow and deliberate, with the end in sight. She thought of gorillas, how when they had been kept too long alone in cages, they would smack each other in the head instead of mating.

"Are you . . . in a relationship?" Earl suddenly blurted.

"Now? As we speak?"

"Well, I mean, I'm sure you have a relationship to your *work*." A smile, a weird one, nestled in his mouth like an egg. She thought of zoos in parks, how when cities were under siege, during world wars, people ate the animals. "But I mean, with a *man*."

"No, I'm not in a relationship with a *man*." She rubbed her chin with her hand and could feel the one bristly hair there. "But my last relationship was with a very sweet man," she said. She made something up. "From Switzerland. He was a botanist – a weed expert. His name was Jerry. I called him 'Jare.' He was so funny. You'd go to the movies with him and all he would notice were the plants. He would never pay attention to the plot. Once, in a jungle movie, he started rattling off all these Latin names, out loud. It was very exciting for him." She paused, caught her breath. "Eventually he went back to Europe to, uh, study the edelweiss." She looked at Earl. "Are you involved in a relationship? With a *woman*?"

Earl shifted his weight, and the creases in his body stocking changed, splintering outward like something broken. His pubic hair slid over to one hip, like a corsage on a saloon girl. "No," he said, clearing his throat. The steel wool in his underarms was inching toward his biceps. "I've just gotten out of a marriage that was full of bad dialogue, like 'You want more *space*? I'll give you more space!' *Clonk*. Your basic Three Stooges."

Zoë looked at him sympathetically. "I suppose it's hard for love to recover after that."

His eyes lit up. He wanted to talk about love. "But *I* keep thinking love should be like a tree. You look at trees and they've got bumps and scars from tumors, infestations, what have you, but they're still growing. Despite the bumps and bruises, they're . . . straight."

"Yeah, well," said Zoë, "where I'm from, they're all married or gay. Did you see that movie *Death by Number*?"

Earl looked at her, a little lost. She was getting away from him. "No," he said.

One of his breasts had slipped under his arm, tucked there like a baguette. She kept thinking of trees, of gorillas and parks, of people in wartime eating the zebras. She felt a stabbing pain in her abdomen.

"Want some hors d'oeuvres?" Evan came pushing through the sliding door. She was smiling, though her curlers were coming out, hanging bedraggled at the ends of her hair like Christmas decorations, like food put out for the birds. She thrust forward a plate of stuffed mushrooms.

"Are you asking for donations or giving them away," said Earl, wittily. He liked Evan, and he put his arm around her.

"You know, I'll be right back," said Zoë.

"Oh," said Evan, looking concerned.

"Right back. I promise."

Zoë hurried inside, across the living room, into the bedroom, to the adjoining bath. It was empty; most of the guests were using the half bath near the kitchen. She flicked on the light and closed the door. The pain had stopped and she didn't really have to go to the bathroom, but she stayed there anyway, resting. In the mirror above the sink she looked haggard beneath her bonehead, violet grays showing under the skin like a plucked and pocky bird. She leaned closer, raising her chin a little to find the bristly hair. It was there, at the end of the jaw, sharp and dark as a wire. She opened the medicine cabinet, pawed through it until she found some tweezers. She lifted her head again and poked at her face with the metal tips, grasping and pinching and missing. Outside the door she could hear two people talking low. They had come into the bedroom and were discussing something. They were sitting on the bed. One of them giggled in a false way. She stabbed again at her chin, and it started to bleed a little. She pulled the skin tight along the jawbone, gripped the tweezers hard around what she hoped was the hair, and tugged. A tiny square of skin came away with it, but the hair remained, blood bright at the root of it. Zoë clenched her teeth. "Come on," she whispered. The couple outside in the bedroom were now telling stories, softly, and laughing. There was a bounce and squeak of mattress, and the sound of a chair being moved out of the way. Zoë aimed the tweezers carefully, pinched, then pulled gently away, and this time the hair came, too, with a slight twinge of pain and then a great flood of relief. "Yeah!" breathed Zoë. She grabbed some toilet paper and dabbed at her chin. It came away spotted with blood, and so she tore off some more and pressed hard until it stopped. Then she turned off the light and opened the door, to return to the party. "Excuse me," she said to the couple in the bedroom. They were the couple from the balcony, and they looked at her, a bit surprised. They had their arms around each other, and they were eating candy bars.

Earl was still out on the balcony, alone, and Zoë rejoined him there.

"Hi," she said. He turned around and smiled. He had straightened his costume out a bit, though all the secondary sex characteristics seemed slightly doomed, destined to shift and flip and zip around again any moment.

"Are you OK?" he asked. He had opened another beer and was chugging.

"Oh, yeah. I just had to go to the bathroom." She paused. "Actually I have been going to a lot of doctors recently."

"What's wrong?" asked Earl.

"Oh, probably nothing. But they're putting me through tests." She sighed. "I've had sonograms. I've had mammograms. Next week I'm going in for a candygram." He looked at her worriedly. "I've had too many gram words," she said.

"Here, I saved you these." He held out a napkin with two stuffed mushroom caps. They were cold and leaving oil marks on the napkin.

"Thanks," said Zoë, and pushed them both in her mouth. "Watch," she said, with her mouth full. "With my luck, it'll be a gallbladder operation."

Earl made a face. "So your sister's getting married," he said, changing the subject. "Tell me, really, what you think about love."

"Love?" Hadn't they done this already? "I don't know."

She chewed thoughtfully and swallowed. "All right. I'll tell you what I think about love. Here is a love story. This friend of mine—"

"You've got something on your chin," said Earl, and he reached over to touch it.

"What?" said Zoë, stepping back. She turned her face away and grabbed at her chin. A piece of toilet paper peeled off it, like tape. "It's nothing," she said. "It's just – it's nothing."

Earl stared at her.

"At any rate," she continued, "this friend of mine was this award-winning violinist. She traveled all over Europe and won competitions; she made records, she gave concerts, she got famous. But she had no social life. So one day she threw herself at the feet of this conductor she had a terrible crush on. He picked her up, scolded her gently, and sent her back to her hotel room. After that she came home from Europe. She went back to her old hometown, stopped playing the violin, and took up with a local boy. This was in Illinois. He took her to some Big Ten bar every night to drink with his buddies from the team. He used to say things like 'Katrina here likes to play the violin,' and then he'd pinch her cheek. When she once suggested that they go home, he said, 'What, you think you're too famous for a place like this? Well, let me tell you something. You may think you're famous, but you're not *famous* famous.' Two famouses. 'No one here's ever heard of you.' Then he went up and bought a round of drinks for everyone but her. She got her coat, went home, and shot a gun through her head."

Earl was silent.

"That's the end of my love story," said Zoë.

"You're not at all like your sister," said Earl.

"Ho, really," said Zoë. The air had gotten colder, the wind singing minor and thick as a dirge.

"No." He didn't want to talk about love anymore. "You know, you should wear a lot of blue – blue and white – around your face. It would bring out your coloring." He reached an arm out to show her how the blue bracelet he was wearing might look against her skin, but she swatted it away.

"Tell me, Earl. Does the word *fag* mean anything to you?"

He stepped back, away from her. He shook his head in disbelief. "You know, I just shouldn't try to go out with career women. You're all stricken. A guy can really tell what life has done to you. I do better with women who have part-time jobs."

"Oh, yes?" said Zoë. She had once read an article entitled "Professional Women and the Demographics of Grief." Or no, it was a poem: *If there were a lake, the moonlight would dance across it in conniptions.* She remembered that line. But perhaps the title was "The Empty House: Aesthetics of Barrenness." Or maybe "Space Gypsies: Girls in Academe." She had forgotten.

Earl turned and leaned on the railing of the balcony. It was getting late. Inside, the party guests were beginning to leave. The sexy witches were already gone. "Live and learn," Earl murmured.

"Live and get dumb," replied Zoë. Beneath them on Lexington there were no cars, just the gold rush of an occasional cab. He leaned hard on his elbows, brooding.

"Look at those few people down there," he said. "They look like bugs. You know how bugs are kept under control? They're sprayed with bug hormones, female bug hormones. The male bugs get so crazy in the presence of this hormone, they're screwing everything in sight: trees, rocks – everything but female bugs. Population control. That's what's happening in this country," he said drunkenly. "Hormones sprayed around, and now men are screwing rocks. Rocks!"

In the back the Magic Marker line of his buttocks spread wide, a sketchy black on pink like a funnies page. Zoë came up, slow, from behind and gave him a shove. His arms slipped forward, off the railing, out over the street. Beer spilled out of his bottle, raining twenty stories down to the street.

"Hey, what are you doing?!" he said, whipping around. He stood straight and readied and moved away from the railing, sidestepping Zoë. "What the *hell* are you doing?"

"Just kidding," she said. "I was just kidding." But he gazed at her, appalled and frightened, his Magic Marker buttocks turned away now toward all of downtown, a naked pseudo-woman with a blue bracelet at the wrist, trapped out on a balcony with – with *what*? *"Really, I was just kidding!"* Zoë shouted. The wind lifted the hair up off her head, skyward in spines behind the bone. If there were a lake, the moonlight would dance across it in conniptions. She smiled at him, and wondered how she looked.

1989

BIBLIOGRAPHICAL NOTE

The stories "How to Be an Other Woman," "What Is Seized," "The Kid's Guide to Divorce," "How," "Go Like This," "How to Talk to Your Mother (Notes)," "Amahl and the Night Visitors: A Guide to the Tenor of Love," "How to Become a Writer," and "To Fill" were first collected in *Self-Help* and published in the United States by Alfred A. Knopf, Inc., New York, and in Canada by Random House of Canada Limited, Toronto, in 1985. Copyright © 1985 by M. L. Moore. First published in Great Britain by Faber and Faber Ltd, London, in 1985. © M. L. Moore, 1985. Some of the stories had previously appeared in *Fiction International*, *MSS Magazine*, and *Story Quarterly* in the United States. "Escape from the Invasion of the Love-Killers" from *Anagrams*, first published in the United States by Alfred A. Knopf, Inc., New York, and in Canada by Random House of Canada Limited, Toronto, in 1986. Copyright © 1986 by M. L. Moore. First published in Great Britain by Faber and Faber Ltd, London, in 1987. © M. L. Moore, 1986. The stories "Two Boys," "Vissi d'Arte," "Joy," "You're Ugly, Too," "Places to Look for Your Mind," "The Jewish Hunter," "Starving Again," and "Like Us" were first collected in *Like Life* and published in the United States by Alfred A. Knopf, Inc., New York, and in Canada by Random House of Canada Limited, Toronto, in 1990. Copyright © 1988, 1989, 1990 by Lorrie Moore. First published in Great Britain by Faber and Faber Ltd, London, in 1990. © Lorrie Moore, 1988, 1989, 1990. Most of the stories had previously appeared in somewhat different form in the following publications: GQ ("Two Boys"); *The New York Times Book Review* ("Starving Again"); *New York Woman* ("Vissi d'Arte"); *The New Yorker* ("You're Ugly, Too," "The Jewish Hunter"); *Tampa Review* ("Places to Look for Your Mind"). Grateful acknowledgment is made to the following for permission to reprint previously published material: CPP/BELWIN, INC., AND INTERNATIONAL MUSIC PUBLICATIONS: Excerpt from "Almost Like Being in Love" by Alan Jay Lerner and Frederick Loewe. Copyright 1947 (Renewed 1975) by Alan Jay Lerner and Frederick Loewe. World rights assigned to Chappell & Co., Inc. World rights assigned to and controlled by EMI U Catalog. Open market rights administered by International Music Publications. International copyright secured. Made in U.S.A. All rights reserved. Used by permission. E. P. DUTTON: Excerpt from *A Child's History of Art* by V. M. Hillyer and E. G. Huey. Copyright 1933 by Appleton-Century Co., Inc. Copyright renewed 1961 by D. Appleton-Century Co., Inc., and Mercantile Safe Deposit and Trust Co.

E L